GERMANY

Hesse

Vienna

AUSTRIA

MOROCCO

Mediterranean Sea

Menara

Abéché

SUDAN

CHAD

Banjul

Khartoum

GAMBIA

NIGERIA

N'Djamena

Lagos

Luanda

ANGOLA

© 2004 Jeffrey L. Ward

BY ORDER
OF THE
PRESIDENT

BY ORDER OF THE PRESIDENT

W.E.B. GRIFFIN

G. P. PUTNAM'S SONS
NEW YORK

P

G. P. PUTNAM'S SONS
Publishers Since 1838
Published by the Penguin Group
Penguin Group (USA) Inc., 375 Hudson Street, New York, New York 10014, USA • Penguin
Group (Canada), 10 Alcorn Avenue, Toronto, Ontario, Canada M4V 3B2 (a division of Pearson
Penguin Canada Inc.) • Penguin Books Ltd, 80 Strand, London WC2R 0RL, England • Penguin Ireland,
25 St Stephen's Green, Dublin 2, Ireland (a division of Penguin Books Ltd) • Penguin Group
(Australia), 250 Camberwell Road, Camberwell, Victoria 3124, Australia (a division of Pearson
Australia Group Pty Ltd) • Penguin Books India Pvt Ltd, 11 Community Centre, Panchsheel Park,
New Delhi—110 017, India • Penguin Group (NZ), Cnr Rosedale and Airborne Roads, Albany,
Auckland, New Zealand (a division of Pearson New Zealand Ltd) • Penguin Group (South Africa),
24 Sturdee Avenue, Rosebank, Johannesburg 2196, South Africa (Pty) Ltd

Penguin Books Ltd, Registered Offices:
80 Strand, London WC2R 0RL, England

Library of Congress Cataloging-in-Publication Data

Griffin, W.E.B.
By order of the President / W.E.B. Griffin.
p.   cm.
ISBN 0-399-15207-5
1. Government investigators—Fiction.   2. Hijacking of aircraft—Fiction.   3. Undercover
operations—Fiction.   4. Air pilots, Military—Fiction.   5. Americans—
Angola—Fiction.   6. Angola—Fiction.   I. title.
PS3557.R489137B9   2004   2004053417
813'.54—dc22

Printed in the United States of America
1   3   5   7   9   10   8   6   4   2

This book is printed on acid-free paper. ∞

This is a work of fiction. Names, characters, places, and incidents either are
the product of the author's imagination or are used fictitiously, and
any resemblance to actual persons, living or dead, businesses,
companies, events, or locales is entirely coincidental.

26 July 1777

"The necessity of procuring good intelligence is apparent and need not be further urged."

George Washington
General and Commander in Chief
The Continental Army

JOHN REITZELL
An Army officer and legend in Delta Force
who could have terminated the head terrorist of the seized cruise ship
Achille Lauro but could not get permission to do so.

RALPH PETERS
An Army intelligence officer
who has written the best analysis of our war against terrorists
and of our enemy that I have ever seen.

★

AND FOR THE NEW BREED

MARC L.
A senior intelligence officer, despite his youth,
who reminds me of Bill Colby more and more each day.

FRANK L.
A legendary Defense Intelligence Agency officer
who retired and now follows in Billy Waugh's footsteps.

OUR NATION OWES THESE PATRIOTS
A DEBT BEYOND REPAYMENT.

BY ORDER
OF THE
PRESIDENT

I
SPRING 2005

[ONE]
Quatro de Fevereiro Aeroporto Internacional
Luanda, Angola
1445 23 May 2005

As he climbed the somewhat unsteady roll-up stairs and ducked his head to get through the door of Lease-Aire LA-9021—a Boeing 727—Captain Alex MacIlhenny, who was fifty-two, ruddy-faced, had a full head of just starting to gray red hair, and was getting just a little jowly, had sort of a premonition that something was wrong—or that something bad was about to happen—but he wasn't prepared for the dark-skinned man standing inside the fuselage against the far wall. The man was holding an Uzi submachine gun in both hands, and it was aimed at MacIlhenny's stomach.

Oh, shit!

MacIlhenny stopped and held both hands up, palm outward, at shoulder level.

"Get out of the door, Captain," the man ordered, gesturing with the Uzi's muzzle that he wanted MacIlhenny to enter the flight deck.

That's not an American accent. Or Brit, either. And this guy's skin is dark, not black. What is he, Portuguese maybe?

Oh come on! Portuguese don't steal airplanes. This guy is some kind of an Arab.

The man holding the Uzi was dressed almost exactly like MacIlhenny, in dark trousers, black shoes, and an open-collared white shirt with epaulets. There were wings pinned above one breast pocket, and the epaulets held the four-gold-stripe shoulder boards of a captain. He even had, clipped to his other breast pocket, the local Transient Air Crew identification tag issued to flight crews who had passed through customs and would be around the airport for twenty-four hours or more.

MacIlhenny started to turn to go into the cockpit.

"Backwards," the man ordered. "And stand there."

MacIlhenny complied.

"We don't want anyone to see you with your hands up, do we?" the man asked, almost conversationally.

MacIlhenny nodded but didn't say anything.

Something like this, I suppose, was bound to happen. The thing to do is keep my cool, do exactly what they tell me to do and nothing stupid.

"Your aircraft has been requisitioned," the man said, "by the Jihad Legion."

What the hell is the "Jihad Legion"?

What does it matter?

Some nutcake, rag-head Arab outfit, English-speaking and clever enough to get dressed up in a pilot's uniform, is about to grab this airplane. Has grabbed this airplane. And me.

MacIlhenny nodded, didn't say anything for a moment, but then took a chance.

"I understand, but if you're a . . ."

Someone behind him grabbed his hair and pulled his head back. He started to struggle—a reflex action—but then saw out of the corner of his eye what looked like a fish-filleting knife, then felt it against his Adam's apple, and forced himself not to move.

Jesus Christ!

"You will speak only with permission, and you will seek that permission by raising your hand, as a child does in school. You understand?"

MacIlhenny tried to nod, but the way his head was being pulled back and with the knife at his throat he doubted the movement he was able to make was very visible. He thought a moment and then raised his right hand slightly higher.

"You may speak," the man with the Uzi said.

"Since you are a pilot, why do you need me?" he asked.

"The first answer should be self-evident: So that you cannot report the requisitioning of your aircraft immediately. Additionally, we would prefer that when the authorities start looking for the aircraft they first start looking for you and not us. Does that answer your question?"

MacIlhenny nodded as well as he could and said, "Yes, sir."

What the hell are they going to do with this airplane?

Are they going to fly it into the American embassy here?

With me in it?

In Angola? That doesn't make much sense. It's a small embassy, and most people have never heard of Angola much less know where it is.

What's within range?

South Africa, of course. It's about fifteen hundred miles to Johannesburg, and a little more to Capetown. Where's our embassy in South Africa?

"As you surmised, I am a pilot qualified to fly this model Boeing," the man said. "As is the officer behind you. Therefore, you are convenient for this operation but not essential. At any suspicion that you are not doing exactly as you are told, or are attempting in any way to interfere with this operation, you will be eliminated. Do you understand?"

MacIlhenny nodded again as well as he could and said, "Yes, sir."

The man said something in a foreign language that MacIlhenny did not understand. The hand grasping his hair opened and he could hold his head erect.

"You may lower your hands," the man said, and then, conversationally, added: "You seemed to be taking a long time in your preflight walk-around. What was that all about?"

MacIlhenny, despite the heat, felt a sudden chill and realized that he had been sweating profusely.

Why not? With an Uzi pointing at your stomach and a knife against your throat, what did you expect?

His mouth was dry, and he had to gather saliva and wet his lips before he tried to speak.

"I came here to make a test flight," MacIlhenny began. "This aircraft has not flown in over a year. I made what I call the 'MacIlhenny Final Test' . . ."

"Is that not the business of mechanics?"

"I am a mechanic."

"You are a mechanic?" the man asked, dubiously.

"Yes, sir. I hold both air frame and engine licenses. I supervised getting this aircraft ready to fly, signed off on the repairs, and I was making the MacIlhenny Test . . ."

"What test is that?"

"It's not required; it's just something I do. The airplane has been sitting here for more than twenty-four hours, with a full load of fuel . . . at takeoff weight, you'll understand. I take a final look around. If anything was leaking, I would have seen it, found out where it was coming from, and fixed it before I tried to fly it."

The man with the Uzi considered that and nodded.

"It is unusual for a captain to also be a mechanic, is it not?"

"Yes, sir, I suppose it is."

"And did you find anything wrong on this final test?"

"No, sir, I did not."

"And what were you going to do next if your final test found nothing wrong?"

"I've arranged for a copilot, sir. As soon as he got here, I was going to run up the engines a final time and then make a test flight."

"Your copilot is here," the man said. "You may look into the passenger compartment."

MacIlhenny didn't move.

"Look into the fuselage, Captain," the man with the Uzi said, sternly, and something hard was rammed into the small of MacIlhenny's back.

He winced with the pain.

That wasn't a knife and it certainly wasn't a hand. Maybe the other guy's got an Uzi, too. A gun, anyway.

MacIlhenny stepped past the bulkhead and looked into the passenger compartment.

All but the first three rows of seats had been removed from the passenger compartment. MacIlhenny had no idea when or why but when LA-9021 had left Philadelphia on a sixty-day, cash-up-front dry charter, it had been in a full all-economy-class passenger configuration—the way it had come from Continental Airlines—with seats for 189 people.

Lease-Aire had been told it was to be used to haul people on everything-included excursions from Scandinavia to the coast of Spain and Morocco.

MacIlhenny knew all this because he was Lease-Aire's vice president for Maintenance and Flight Operations. The title sounded more grandiose—on purpose—than the size of the corporation really justified. Lease-Aire had only two other officers. The president and chief executive officer was MacIlhenny's brother-in-law, Terry Halloran; and the secretary-treasurer was Mary-Elizabeth MacIlhenny Halloran, Terry's wife and MacIlhenny's sister.

Lease-Aire was in the used aircraft business, dealing in aircraft the major airlines wanted to get rid of for any number of reasons, most often because they were near the end of their operational life. LA-9021, for example, had hauled passengers for Continental for twenty-two years.

When Lease-Aire acquired an airplane—their fleet had never exceeded four aircraft at one time; they now owned two: this 727, and a Lockheed 10-11 they'd just bought from Northwest—they stripped off the airline paint job, reregistered it, and painted on the new registration numbers.

Then the aircraft was offered for sale. If they couldn't find someone to buy it at a decent profit, the plane was offered for charter—"wet" (with fuel and crew and Lease-Aire took care of routine maintenance) or "dry" (the lessee provided the crew and fuel and paid for routine maintenance)—until it came close to either an annual or thousand-hour inspection, both of which were very expensive. Then the airplane was parked again at Philadelphia and offered for sale at a really bargain-basement price. If they couldn't sell it, then it made a final flight to a small airfield in the Arizona desert, where it was cannibalized of salable parts.

Lease-Aire had been in business five years. LA-9021 was their twenty-first airplane. Sometimes they made a ton of money on an airplane and sometimes they took a hell of a bath.

It seemed to Vice President MacIlhenny they were going to take a hell of a bath on this one. Surf & Sun Holidays Ltd. had telephoned ten days before their sixty-day charter contract was over, asking for another thirty days, check to follow immediately.

The check didn't come. A cable did, four days later, saying LA-9021 had had to make a "precautionary landing" at Luanda, Angola, where an inspection had revealed mechanical failures beyond those which they were obliged to repair under the original contract. And, further, that inasmuch as the failures had occurred before the first contract had run its course, Surf & Sun Holidays would not of course enter into an extension of the original charter contract.

In other words, your airplane broke down in Luanda, Angola. Sorry about that but it's your problem, not ours.

When Terry, who handled the business end of Lease-Aire, had tried to call Surf & Sun Holidays Ltd. at their corporate headquarters in Glasgow, Scotland, to discuss the matter, he was told the line was no longer in service.

On his first trip to Luanda, MacIlhenny had stopped in Glasgow to deal with them personally. There had been sheets of brown butcher paper covering the plate-glass storefront windows of Surf & Sun Holidays Ltd.'s corporate headquarters, with FOR RENT lettered on them in Magic Marker.

In Luanda, he had quickly found what had failed on LA-9021: control system hydraulics. It was a "safety of flight" problem, which meant MacIlhenny could not hire a local to sit in the right seat while he made a "one-time flight" to bring it home. He had also found that most of the seats were missing. Parts—from seats to hydraulics—were often readily available on the used parts market, if you had the money. Lease-Aire was experiencing a temporary cash-flow problem.

Terry had wanted to go after the Surf & Sun bastards for stealing the seats and abandoning the aircraft, make them at least make the repairs so MacIlhenny could go get the sonofabitch and bring it home. MacIlhenny's sister had sided with her husband.

The cash-flow problem had lasted a lot longer than anyone expected, and the price of the needed parts was a lot higher than MacIlhenny anticipated, so thirteen months passed before he and four crates of parts finally managed to get back to Luanda and he could put the sonofabitch together again.

As he took the few steps from the cockpit door to the passenger compartment, MacIlhenny had an almost pleasant thought:

If these guys steal this airplane, we can probably collect on the insurance.

And then he saw the local pilot who had come on board LA-9021 expecting to pick up a quick five hundred dollars sitting in the right seat for an hour or so while MacIlhenny took the plane on a test hop. He was sitting in the third—now last—row right aisle seat. His hands were in his lap, tightly bound together with three-inch-wide yellow plastic tape. His ankles were similarly bound, and there was tape over his eyes.

"We will release him, Captain," the first man with the Uzi said, "when, presuming you have cooperated, we release you."

"I'm going to do whatever you want me to do, sir," MacIlhenny said.

"Why don't we get going?" the man with the Uzi said.

He stepped out of the aisle to permit MacIlhenny to walk past him.

MacIlhenny went into the cockpit, and, for the first time, could see the second man.

I guess there's only two of them. I didn't see anybody else back there.

The man now sitting in the copilot's seat looked very much like the first man with the Uzi, and he was also wearing an open-collared white shirt with Air Crew shoulder boards.

The right ones, too, with the three stripes of a first officer—formerly copilot.

The copilot gestured for MacIlhenny to take the pilot's seat.

As he slipped into it, MacIlhenny saw that the copilot had the checklist in his hand and that there were charts on the sort of shelf above the instrument panel. MacIlhenny couldn't see enough of them to have any idea what they were.

And I can't even make a guess where we're going.

MacIlhenny strapped himself into the seat, and then, feeling just a little foolish, raised his right hand.

"You have a question, Captain?" the man with the Uzi asked.

"Am I going to fly or is this gentleman?"

"You'll fly," the man with the Uzi said. "He will serve as copilot, and you can think of me as your 'check pilot.' "

It was obvious he thought he was being amusing.

The man with the Uzi unfolded the jump seat in the aisle into position, sat down, fastened his shoulder harness, and rested the Uzi on the back of MacIl-henny's seat, its muzzle about two inches from MacIlhenny's ear.

The man in the copilot's seat handed MacIlhenny the checklist, a plastic-covered card about four inches wide and ten inches long. MacIlhenny took it, nodded his understanding, and began to read from it.

"Gear lever and lights," MacIlhenny read.

"Down and checked," the copilot responded.

"Brakes," MacIlhenny read.

"Parked," the copilot responded.

"Circuit breakers."

"Check."

"Emergency lights."

"Armed."

There were thirty-four items on the BEFORE START checklist. MacIlhenny read each of them.

When he read number 9, "Seat Belt and No Smoking signs," the copilot chuckled before responding, "On."

When MacIlhenny read number 23, "Voice recorder," the copilot chuckled again and said, "I don't think we're going to need that."

And when MacIlhenny read number 28, "Radar and transponder," the copilot responded, "We're certainly not going to need that."

And the man with the Uzi at MacIlhenny's ear chuckled.

When MacIlhenny read number 34, "Rudder and aileron trim," the copilot responded, "Zero," and the man with the Uzi said, "Fire it up, Captain."

MacIlhenny reached for the left engine ENGINE START button and a moment later the whine and vibration of the turbine began.

"Ask ground control for permission to taxi to the maintenance area," the man with the Uzi ordered.

MacIlhenny nodded and said, "Luanda ground control, LA-9021, on the parking pad near the threshold of the main runway. Request permission to taxi to the maintenance hangar."

Luanda ground control responded twenty seconds later.

"LA-9021, you are cleared to taxi on Four South. Turn right on Four South right three. Report on arrival at the maintenance area."

"Ground control, LA-9021 understands Four South to Four South right three."

"Affirmative, 9021."

MacIlhenny looked over his shoulder at the man with the Uzi, who nodded. MacIlhenny released the brakes and reached for the throttle quadrant.

LA-9021 began to move.

"Turn onto the threshold," the man with the Uzi said thirty seconds later. "Line it up with the runway and immediately commence your takeoff roll."

"Without asking for clearance?" MacIlhenny asked.

"Without asking for clearance," the man with the Uzi said, not pleasantly, and brushed MacIlhenny's neck, below his ear, with the muzzle of the Uzi.

As MacIlhenny taxied the 727 to the threshold of the main north/south runway, he looked out the side window of the cockpit and then pointed out the window.

"There's an aircraft on final," he said. "An Ilyushin."

It was an Ilyushin Il-76, called "the Candid." It was a large, four-engine, heavy-lift military transport, roughly equivalent to the Lockheed C-130.

The man with the Uzi pressed the muzzle of the Uzi against MacIlhenny's neck as he leaned around him to look out the window at the approaching aircraft.

"Line up with the runway, Captain," he ordered, "and the moment he touches down begin your takeoff roll."

"Line up now or after he touches down?"

"Now," the man with the Uzi said and jabbed MacIlhenny with the muzzle of the Uzi.

MacIlhenny released the brakes and nudged the throttles.

"LA-9021, ground control," the radio went off. The voice sounded alarmed.

The man with the Uzi jerked MacIlhenny's headset from his head.

MacIlhenny lined up 9021 with the runway and stopped.

A moment later the Ilyushin flashed over, so close that the 727 moved. It touched down about halfway down the runway.

The Uzi muzzle prodded MacIlhenny under the ear.

He understood the message, released the brakes, and shoved the throttles forward.

My options right now are to pull the gear, which will mean I will have my brains blown all over the cockpit a full twenty seconds before the gear retracts. Or I can do what I'm told and maybe, just maybe, stay alive.

"Will you call out the airspeed, please?" MacIlhenny asked, politely.

"Eighty," the copilot said a moment later.

Unless that Ilyushin gets his tail off the runway, I'm going to clip it.

"Ninety.

"One-ten.

"One-twenty."

"Rotate," MacIlhenny said and pulled back on the yoke.

"What you will do now, Captain," the man with the Uzi said, "is level off at two-five hundred feet on this course."

"That's going to eat a lot of fuel," MacIlhenny said.

"Yes, I know. What I want to do is fall off their radar. The lower we fly, the sooner that will happen."

MacIlhenny nodded his understanding.

Five minutes later, the man with the Uzi ordered, "Maintaining this flight level, steer zero-two-zero."

"Zero-two-zero," MacIlhenny repeated and began a gentle turn to that heading.

That will take me over the ex–Belgian Congo. I wonder what that means?

Ten minutes after that, the man with the Uzi said, "Ascend to flight level two-five thousand, and turn to zero-one-five."

"Course zero-one-five," MacIlhenny repeated. "Beginning climb to flight level two-five thousand now."

"Very good, Captain," the man with the Uzi said.

Not quite two hours after they left Luanda, the man with the Uzi said, "Begin a thousand-feet-a-minute descent on our present heading, Captain."

MacIlhenny nodded his understanding, adjusted the trim, retarded the throttles, and then said, "We are in a thousand-feet-a-minute descent. May I ask where we are going?"

"We are going to take on fuel at an airfield not far from Kisangani," he said. "Once known as Stanleyville. Kisangani has a radar and I want to get under it, so level off at twenty-five hundred feet."

"Yes, sir."

MacIlhenny checked his fuel. His tanks were a little under half full.

Kisangani is in the northeast Congo, not far from the border of Sudan.

We could have made it to Khartoum—almost anywhere in Sudan—with available fuel. Sudan has a reputation for loose borders, and for not liking Americans. So why didn't we go there?

If we keep on this northeasterly flight path, we'll overfly Sudan. And on this heading, what's next is Egypt, Saudi Arabia, and Israel.

The Americans are all over Saudi Arabia and Israel with AWAC aircraft.

They're sure to see this one.

For that matter, it's surprising that there hasn't been a fighter—or three or four fighters—off my wingtip already.

You can't just steal an airplane and fly it a thousand miles without somebody finding you.

Where the hell are we going?

Lease-Aire 9021 had been flying at twenty-five hundred feet at four hundred knots for about fifteen minutes when the copilot adjusted the radio frequency to 116.5 and then called somebody.

Somebody called back. With no headset, MacIlhenny of course had no idea what anybody said. But a moment after his brief radio conversation, the copilot punched in a frequency on the radio direction finder and then pointed to the cathode display.

"Change to that heading?" MacIlhenny asked, politely.

"Correct," the man with the Uzi said. "We should be no more than 150 miles from our refuel point."

Twenty minutes later, MacIlhenny saw, almost directly ahead, a brown scar on the vast blanket of green Congolese jungle beneath him.

The copilot got on the radio again, held a brief conversation with someone, and then turned to MacIlhenny.

"The winds are negligible," he said. "If you want to, you can make a direct approach."

"How much runway do we have?"

"Fifty-eight hundred feet," the copilot said. "Don't worry. This will not be the first 727 to land here."

MacIlhenny brought the 727 in at the end of the runway. He could see some buildings, but they seemed deserted, and he didn't see any people, or vehicles, or other signs of life.

He touched down smoothly and slowed the aircraft down to taxi speed with a third of the runway still in front of him.

"Continue to the end of the runway, Captain," the man with the Uzi said.

MacIlhenny taxied as slowly as he could without arousing the suspicion of his copilot or the man with the Uzi. He saw no other signs of life or occupancy, except what could be recent truck tire marks in the mud on the side of the macadam runway.

"Turn it around, Captain, and put the brakes on. But don't shut it down until we have a look at the refueling facilities."

"Yes, sir," MacIlhenny said and complied.

"Now, here we're going to need your expert advice," the man with the Uzi said. "Will you come with me, please?"

"Yes, sir," MacIlhenny said.

He unfastened his shoulder harness, got out of his seat, and saw that the man with the Uzi had put the jump seat back in the stored position and was waiting for him to precede him out of the cockpit and into the fuselage.

"In the back, please, Captain," the man with the Uzi said, gesturing with the weapon.

MacIlhenny walked into the passenger compartment.

The local pilot was still sitting taped into one of the seats.

MacIlhenny glanced down at him as he walked past. It looked as if something had been spilled in his lap.

Spilled, hell. He pissed his pants.

At the rear of the passenger compartment, the man with the Uzi ordered, "Open the door, please, Captain."

MacIlhenny wrestled with the door.

The first thing he noticed was that warm tropical air seemed to pour into the airplane.

Then someone grabbed his hair again and pulled his head backward.

Then he felt himself being pushed out of the door and falling twenty feet to the ground. He landed hard on his shoulder, and in the last conscious moment of his life saw blood from his cut throat pumping out onto the macadam.

He was dead before the local pilot was marched—still blindfolded with yellow tape—to the door and disposed of in a similar fashion.

Then the rear door of Lease-Aire 9021 was closed and the airplane taxied to the other end of the runway, where a tanker truck appeared and began to refuel it.

[TWO]
Quatro de Fevereiro Aeroporto Internacional
Luanda, Angola
1410 23 May 2005

Quite by accident, H. Richard Miller, Jr., a thirty-six-year-old, six-foot-two, 220-pound, very black native of Philadelphia, Pennsylvania, was not only there when what he was shortly afterward to report as "the unauthorized departure of a Boeing 727 aircraft registered to the Lease-Aire Corporation of Philadelphia, Pa.," took place but he actually saw it happen.

Miller, an Army major, was diplomatically accredited to the Republic of Angola as the assistant military attaché. He was, in fact, and of course covertly, the Luanda station chief of the Central Intelligence Agency.

But, with the exception that his diplomatic carnet gave him access to the airport's duty-free shop, neither his official nor covert status had anything to do with his being present at the airport when the aircraft was stolen. He had gone out to the airport—on what he thought of as his self-granted weekly rest-and-recuperation leave—to buy a bottle of Boss cologne and have first a martini and then a late lunch in the airport's quite good restaurant. Since this was in the nature of an information-gathering mission, he would pay for the meal from his discretionary operating funds.

When he went into the restaurant, he chose a table next to one of the plate-glass windows. They offered a panoramic view of the runways and just about everything at the airport but the building he was in. He laid his digital camera on the table, so that it wouldn't be either stolen or forgotten when he left, and where he could quickly pick it up and take a shot at anything of potential interest without drawing too much—hopefully, no—attention to him.

A waiter quickly appeared and Miller ordered a gin martini.

Then he took a long look at what he could see of the airport.

Parked far across the field, on a parking pad not far from the threshold of the main north/south runway, he saw that what he thought of as "his airplane," a Boeing 727, was still parked where it had been last week, and for the past fourteen months.

He thought of it as his airplane because when he'd noticed it fourteen months ago, he'd taken snapshots of it and checked it out.

Without even making an official inquiry, he went on the Internet and learned that it was registered to the Lease-Aire Corporation of Philadelphia. From a source at the airfield—an air traffic controller who was the monthly recipient of a crisp one-hundred-dollar bill from Miller's discretionary operating funds—he had learned that the 727 had made a "discretionary landing" at Luanda while en route somewhere else.

Miller was a pilot, an Army aviator—not currently on flight status because he'd busted a flight physical, which was why he had wound up "temporarily" assigned to the CIA and sent to Luanda—and he understood that a discretionary landing was one a wise pilot made when red lights lit up on the control panel, before it became necessary to make an emergency landing.

Miller had begun to feel sorry for the airplane, as he sometimes felt sorry for himself. A grounded bird, and a grounded bird man, stuck in picturesque Luanda, Angola, by circumstances beyond their control, when they both would much rather have been in Philadelphia, where he had grown up, where his parents lived, and where one could be reasonably sure that 999 out of a thousand good-looking women did not have AIDS, which could not be said of Luanda, Angola.

Still, unofficially—although after a month he had reported to Langley, in Paragraph 15, Unrelated Data, of his weekly report, that the plane seemed to be stuck in Luanda—he had learned that Lease-Aire was a small outfit that bought old airliners at distress prices (LA-9021 came from Continental); that it then leased them "wet" or "dry"; and that LA-9021 had been dry-leased to a Scottish company called Surf & Sun Holidays Ltd. Just to play it safe, he'd asked the assistant CIA station chief in London, whom he knew, to find out what he could about Surf & Sun. In two days, he learned that it was a rinky-dink outfit that had gone belly-up shortly after leaving 153 irate Irishmen stranded in Rabat, Morocco.

That seemed to explain everything, and nothing was suspicious.

And so every time during the fourteen months that Miller took his R&R and saw the once-proud old bird sitting across the field, he had grown more convinced that it would never fly again. He was, therefore, more than a little surprised when—peering over the rim of a second martini just as good as the first—he saw LA-9021 moving.

He thought, in quick order, as he carefully set the martini glass on the table, first, that he had been mistaken, and, next, that if it was moving, it was being towed by a tug to where repair—or cannibalization—could begin.

When he looked again, he saw the airplane was indeed moving and under its own power.

How the hell did they start it up? You can't let an airplane sit on a runway for fourteen months and then just get in it and push the ENGINE START buttons.

Obviously, somebody's been working on it.

But when?

When was the last time I was here? Last Wednesday?

Well, that's a week; that's enough time.

The 727 turned off the taxiway and moved toward the threshold of the runway.

There was a Congo Air Ilyushin transport on final. Miller knew there were two daily flights between Brazzaville, Congo, and Luanda.

Miller had two unkind thoughts.

Prescription for aerial disaster: an ex–Russian Air Force fighter jockey, flying a worn-out Ilyushin maintained by Congo Air.

"Ladies and Gentlemen, this is your captain speaking. Please remain seated on the floor and try to restrain all chickens, goats, and other livestock until the aircraft has come to a complete stop at the airway. And thank you for flying Congo Air. We hope that the next time you have to go from nowhere to nowhere, you'll fly with us again."

And then he had another thought when he saw that the 727 was on the threshold, lined up with the runway:

Hey, Charley, the way you're supposed to do that is wait until the guy on final goes over you and then *you move to the threshold. Otherwise, if he lands a little short he lands on you.*

The Ilyushin passed no more than fifty feet over the tail of the 727 and then touched down.

Before the Ilyushin reached the first turnoff from the runway, the 727 began its takeoff roll.

Hey, Charley, what are you going to do if he doesn't get out of your way? What do we have here, two *ex–Russian fighter jockeys?*

The rear stabilizer of the Ilyushin had not completely cleared the runway when the 727, approaching takeoff velocity, flashed past it and then lifted off.

Well, I'm glad you're back in the air, old girl.

I wonder what kind of a nitwit was flying the 727?

Miller picked up his martini, raised it to the now nearly out of sight 727, and then turned his attention to the menu.

Thirty minutes later, after a very nicely broiled filet of what the menu called sea trout and two cups of really first-class Kenyan coffee, he paid the bill with an American Express card, collected the bags containing the newspapers, magazines, paperbacks, and the goodies he'd bought in the duty-free shop, and started walking across the terminal to get his car.

What I should do is go home, get on the ski machine to get the gin out of my system, and then spend a half hour at least on the knee.

But being an honest man, he knew that what he was probably going to do was go home, hang up the nice clothes, and take a little nap.

On impulse, however, passing a pay telephone, he stepped into the booth, fed it coins, and punched in a number that was not available to the general public.

"Torre," someone said after answering on the first ring.

Having the unlisted number of the control tower, and, if he was lucky, the right guy to answer its phone, was what the monthly dispersal of the crisp hundred-dollar bill bought.

"Antonio, por favor. É seu irmão," Miller said.

A moment later, Antonio took the phone to speak to "his brother," and, obviously excited, said, "I can't talk right now. Something has come up."

"What's come up?"

"We think someone has stolen an airplane."

"A 727?"

"How did you know?"

"Antonio, you have to take a piss."

"Please, I cannot."

Yes you can, you sonofabitch. I hand you a hundred-dollar bill each and every month. And you know what I expect of you.

"Trust me, Antonio. You have diarrhea. I'll be waiting in the men's room."

[THREE]
Office of the Ambassador
Embassy of the United States of America
Rua Houari Boumedienne 32
Luanda, Angola
1540 23 May 2005

"Thank you for seeing me, Mr. Ambassador, on such short notice," Miller said to the United States ambassador and then turned to the defense attaché, an Air Force lieutenant colonel. "And you, sir, for meeting me here so quickly."

The ambassador was a fellow African American, from Washington, D.C. Miller didn't dislike him, but he did not hold him in high regard. Miller thought the ambassador had worked his way up through the State Department to what would probably be the pinnacle of his diplomatic career by keeping his nose clean and closely following the two basic rules for success in the Foreign Service of the United States: Don't make waves; and never make a decision today that can be put off until next week, or, better, next month.

The defense attaché was Caucasian, which Miller attributed to a momentary shortage of what used to be called "black" or "Negro" officers of suitable rank when the defense attaché post came open.

According to applicable regulations, Miller was subordinate to both. To the ambassador, because he was the senior U.S. government officer in Angola; and to the defense attaché, because he was a lieutenant colonel and Miller a major, and also because the defense attaché is supposed to control the military (Army) and Naval attachés.

But in practice, it didn't work quite that way. Miller's assistant military attaché status was the cover for his being the Resident Spook and both knew it. And when he was, as he thought of it, on the job, he not only didn't have to tell the defense attaché what he was doing, but was under orders not to, unless the defense attaché had a bona fide need to know.

The ambassador was, Miller had quickly learned, more than a little afraid of him. For two reasons, one being that Miller had come out of Special Forces. Like most career diplomats, the ambassador believed that Special Forces people—especially highly decorated ones like Miller—were practitioners of the "Kill 'Em All and Let God Sort It Out" school of diplomacy, and consequently lived in fear that Miller was very likely to do something outrageous which would embarrass the embassy, the State Department, the United States government, and, of course, him.

More important than that, probably, was a photograph Miller had hung, not ostentatiously but very visibly, in the corridor of his apartment leading to the bathroom. Once a month, Miller was expected to have a cocktail party for his fellow diplomats. Anyone who needed to visit the facilities could not miss seeing the photograph.

It showed two smiling African American officers in Vietnam-era uniforms. One was a colonel, wearing a name tag identifying him as MILLER. He had his arm around a young major, from whose jacket hung an obviously just awarded Bronze Star. His name tag read POWELL.

Both officers had gone on to higher rank. Miller's father had retired as a major general. The major had retired with four stars and had been the secretary of state.

It was not unreasonable, Miller thought, to suspect the ambassador feared that Miller had influence in the highest corridors of power, and might, in fact, be sending back-channel, out-of-school reports on his performance to Secretary Powell, who was still—according to *Forbes* magazine—one of the ten most influential men in the United States.

That was nonsense, of course. Miller knew Powell well enough to know that a large ax would fall on his neck, wielded by Powell himself, if he made a habit of sending back channels to Powell or anyone in his circle. But he did nothing to assuage the ambassador's worries.

"You said this was important, Major Miller?" the ambassador said.

"No, sir. With respect, making a decision like that is not for someone of my pay grade. What I said was that I thought you and Colonel Porter might consider this important. That's why I thought I should bring this to your attention as soon as possible, sir."

"What is it, Dick?" Colonel Porter asked.

"It would seem, sir, that someone has stolen an airplane from Quatro de Fevereiro."

"Really?" the ambassador asked.

"What kind of an airplane, Dick?" Colonel Porter asked.

"A 727, sir. The one that's been sitting out there for fourteen months."

"How the hell did they do that?" Colonel Porter asked. "You can't just get in an airplane that hasn't moved for fourteen months and fire it up."

"I don't know how they did it, sir, only that they did. They just taxied from where it had been parked to the north/south, and took off without clearance, and disappeared."

"You're the expert, Colonel," the ambassador said. "Would an aircraft like that have the range to fly to the United States?"

Why am I not surprised that the World Trade towers have popped into the ambassador's head? Miller thought.

"No, sir, I don't think that it would," Colonel Porter replied, and then added: "Not without taking on fuel somewhere. And even if it did that, its tanks would be just about empty by the time it got to the U.S." He turned to Miller: "You're sure about this, Dick?"

"Yes, sir. I have a source at the airport. He told me that the plane ignored both 'Abort takeoff' and then 'Return to airfield immediately' orders after it was in the air."

"Where was it headed?"

"East, sir, when it fell off the radar."

"We don't know if terrorists are involved in this, do we?" the ambassador asked.

"No, sir," Colonel Porter said. "We don't know that for sure, certainly. But we certainly can't discount that possibility."

"It's possible, sir, that it was just stolen," Miller said.

"What would anyone do with a stolen airliner?" the ambassador asked.

"Perhaps cannibalize it for parts, sir," Colonel Porter said.

"Take parts from it?"

"Yes, sir."

"They call that 'cannibalizing'?"

Why do I think our African ambassador is uncomfortable with that word?

"Yes, sir."

"Well, Miller, you were absolutely right in bringing this up to me," the ambassador said. "We'd better start notifying people."

"Yes, sir," Colonel Porter and Major Miller said, almost in unison.

"Miller, you're obviously going to notify . . . your people?"

"I thought it would be best to check with you before I did so, Mr. Ambassador."

But not knowing where the hell you might be, or when you could find time for me in your busy schedule, and suspecting you might say, "Before we do anything, I think we should carefully consider the situation," I filed it to Langley as a FLASH satellite burst before I came here.

"I think we should immediately make this situation known to Washington," the ambassador said.

My God! An immediate decision! Will wonders never cease?

"Yes, sir," Porter and Miller said, in chorus.

"And it might be a good idea if you were both to get copies of your messages to me as soon as you can," the ambassador said. "They'll be useful to me when I prepare my report to the State Department."

Translation: "I will say nothing in my report that you didn't say in yours. That way, if there's a fuckup, I can point my finger at you." It's not really an ambassador's responsibility to develop information like this himself. He has to rely on those who have that kind of responsibility.

"Yes, sir," they said, in chorus.

Ten minutes later another FLASH satellite burst from Miller went out from the antenna on the embassy roof.

It was identical to Miller's first message, except for the last sentence, which said, "Transmitted at direction of ambassador."

When he walked out of the radio room, Miller thought that by now his message—it had been a FLASH, the highest priority—had reached the desk of his boss, the CIA's regional director for Southwest Africa, in Langley.

Miller then went to his office, plugged the high-speed cable into his personal laptop computer, and, typing rapidly, sent an e-mail message to two friends:

```
HALO101@WEB.NET
BEACHAGGIE83@AOL.COM
A BOEING 727, REGISTERED TO LEASE-AIRE, INC.,
PHILADELPHIA, PENNA., WHICH MADE A DISCRETIONARY
LANDING HERE FOURTEEN MONTHS AGO, AND HAD BEEN SITTING
HERE SINCE, WAS APPARENTLY STOLEN BY PARTIES UNKNOWN AT
1425 TODAY. MORE WHEN I HAVE IT. DICK
```

Sending such a message violated a long list of security restrictions, and Major Miller was fully aware that it did. On the other hand, whoever had grabbed the 727 knew they had grabbed it, so what was the secret?

Furthermore, the back-channel message was a heads-up—unofficial, of course—to people who would possibly, even likely, become involved in whatever the government ultimately decided to do about the stolen airplane.

This especially applied to HALO101—the screen name made reference to the number of High Altitude, Low Opening parachute jumps the addressee had made—who was a lieutenant colonel at Fort Bragg, North Carolina.

Ostensibly a member of the G-3 staff of the XVIII Airborne Corps, he was in fact the deputy commander of a unit few people had even heard about, and about which no one talked. It was officially known as the "Contingency Office" and colloquially as "Gray Fox," or "Baby D."

"D" made reference to Delta Force, about which some people actually knew something and a great many people—very few of whom knew what they were talking about—talked a great deal.

The Contingency Office—Gray Fox—was a five-officer, thirty-one-NCO unit within Delta Force that was prepared to act immediately—they trained to be wheels up in less than an hour—when ordered to do so.

BeachAggie83—the screen name made reference to the Texas Agricultural & Mechanical University, the year the addressee had graduated, and to the fact that he was now stationed in Florida—was a lieutenant colonel assigned to the Special Activities Section, J-5 (Special Operations), United States Central Command, MacDill Air Force Base, Florida.

If it was decided that Delta Force, Gray Fox—or any other special operations organization, such as the Air Commandos, the Navy SEALs, the Marines' Force Recon—were to be deployed in connection with the missing airplane, the orders would come from Central Command.

While his satburst message had reached Washington in literally a matter of seconds, it might not reach either Fort Bragg or MacDill for hours—or days—until the message had been evaluated at Langley, passed to the national security counselor, and evaluated again and a decision reached.

Major Miller's conscience did not bother him a bit for sending a heads-up that violated a long list of security restrictions. He'd done a tour with Delta and knew the sooner they got a heads-up, the better.

He unplugged the laptop and locked it in his desk drawer. Then he changed into his work clothes and caught a taxicab out to the Quatro de Fevereiro Aeroporto to see what else he could find out about what had happened to his airplane.

II

[ONE]
The Central Intelligence Agency
Langley, Virginia
1133 23 May 2005

When, at 1530 Luanda time, Major H. Richard Miller, Jr., sent his first satellite burst message announcing the apparent theft from the Luanda airport of Lease-Aire's 727, it took about three minutes in real time to reach the desk of his boss, the CIA's regional director for Southwest Africa, in Langley. There is a four-hour difference in time between Angola and Virginia. When it is half past three in Luanda, it is half past eleven in Langley.

The message was actually received by the regional director's executive administrative assistant as the regional director had not yet returned from a working lunch at the Department of State in the District.

The operative word in the job title was "executive." It meant that Mrs. Margaret Lee-Williamson was authorized to execute, in the regional director for Southwest Africa's name, certain administrative actions, among them to receive material classified top secret addressed to the regional director and to take any appropriate action the material called for.

What this meant was that when the computer terminal on Mrs. Lee-Williamson's desk pinged and the message SATBURST CONFIDENTIAL FROM

LUANDA FOR REGDIR SWAFRICA ENTER ACCESS CODE appeared on the screen, Mrs. Lee-Williamson typed in a ten-digit access code, whereupon the simple message from Miller appeared on the screen:

```
CONFIDENTIAL
SATBURST 01 LUANDA 23 MAY 1530
FOR REGDIR SWAFRICA
A BOEING 727 TRANSPORT AIRCRAFT LA-9021 REGISTERED TO
LEASE-AIRE, INC., PHILA., PENN., TOOK OFF WITHOUT
PERMISSION FROM QUATRO DE FEVEREIRO AEROPORTO
INTERNACIONAL AT 1425 LOCAL TIME 23 MAY 2005 AND
DISAPPEARED FROM RADAR SHORTLY THEREAFTER. ANGOLAN
AUTHORITIES KNOWN TO BELIEVE AIRCRAFT WAS STOLEN. MORE
TO FOLLOW. STACHIEF LUANDA
```

Mrs. Lee-Williamson read it and pressed the PRINT key.

She read the printout carefully, then decided that while the message should be forwarded it wasn't really all that important. Very few things classified confidential are ever important. Certainly not important enough for her to try to get the regional director on the phone during lunch.

Mrs. Lee-Williamson decided that she could handle this herself and tell her boss about it when the regional director returned from lunch.

She highlighted Major Miller's message with the cursor, pressed the COPY key, and then the END and WRITE keys. When a blank message form headed FROM CIA REGIONAL DIRECTOR FOR SOUTHWEST AFRICA appeared on her screen, she typed, after she thought about it a moment, DISTLIST4, and, when she pressed the ENTER key, it caused distribution list number 4 to appear in the addressee box on the message form:

```
NATIONAL SECURITY ADVISOR
SECRETARY OF DEFENSE
SECRETARY OF HOMELAND SECURITY
SECRETARY OF STATE
DIRECTOR, FBI
DIRECTOR, FAA
CHAIRMAN, JOINT CHIEFS OF STAFF
```

Then, as an afterthought, she added to the list of addressees:

```
COMMANDING GENERAL CENTRAL COMMAND
```

There had been several complaints from Central Command concerning their not being given timely notice of certain events and Angola was within CentCom's area of responsibility.

She moved her cursor to the message box and typed:

```
FOLLOWING RECEIVED 1133 23 MAY 2005 FROM LUANDA,
ANGOLA, IS FORWARDED FOR YOUR INFORMATION.
```

Then she pressed the INSERT key and Miller's message appeared on the screen.

Mrs. Lee-Williamson then pressed the SEND key and the message was on its way. Then she called up a fresh message blank and began to type.

```
STACHIEF LUANDA

REFERENCE YOUR SATBURST 01 23MAY05 RE POSSIBLY STOLEN
AIRCRAFT. WITHOUT DIVERTING SUBSTANTIAL ASSETS, ATTEMPT
TO DEVELOP FURTHER REGDIR SWAFRICA
```

When she had pressed the SEND key again, she decided it was time for a cup of coffee. She locked the printout of Miller's message in a secure filing cabinet, locked the office door, and headed for the cafeteria.

[TWO]
Office of the Commanding General
United States Central Command
MacDill Air Force Base
Tampa, Florida
1645 23 May 2005

General Allan B. Naylor routinely used two computers in his office suite. One he thought of as the "desktop" computer, although it was actually on the floor under the credenza behind Naylor's desk. The other, which he thought of as the "laptop" computer, he brought to work with him each morning and took home at night.

When he was in the office, the laptop sat either on Naylor's desk, where it could be seen by those sitting at his office conference table, which butted up against his desk, or it sat before the commanding general's chair on the larger conference table in the conference room next to his office, where it was similarly very visible to others at the table.

Quite innocently, the laptop had acquired an almost menacing aura. None of those at either table could see what was on the laptop's screen, and it is human nature to fear the unknown.

Everyone at either conference table became aware that at least once every ten minutes or so, the CG's attention was diverted from what was being discussed by the conferees to the laptop screen and he would either smile or frown, then look thoughtful, and then type something. Or return his attention to the conferees and ask a question, or issue an order obviously based on what had been on the laptop's screen.

General Naylor had learned his laptop was commonly known among the senior members of his staff as the "IBB"—for "Infernal Black Box." More junior members of his staff referred to it, privately of course, in somewhat more imaginative and scatological terms.

Having the laptop on the commanding general's desk and on the conference table had been the idea of Command Sergeant Major Wesley Suggins.

"General, if you turn that thing on and sign on to the Instant Messager, I can let you know who's on the horn. You follow, sir?"

It had taken General Naylor about ten seconds to follow Suggins's reasoning.

General Naylor often thought, and said to his inner circle, that Napoleon was right when he said, "Armies travel on their stomachs," that during World

War II someone was right to comment, "The Army moves on a road of paper," and that, he was forced to the sad conclusion, "CentCom sails very slowly through a Sargasso Sea of conferences."

The problem during these conferences was that there were always telephone calls from important people—such as Mrs. Elaine Naylor, or the secretary of defense—for the commanding general. General Naylor always took calls from these two, but some of the calls were from less important people and could wait.

Sergeant Major Suggins usually made that decision and informed the caller that General Naylor was in conference and would return the call as soon as he could. But sometimes Sergeant Major Suggins didn't feel confident in telling, for example, the assistant secretary of defense for manpower or someone calling from the White House that he was just going to have to wait to talk to the boss.

In that case, there were two options. He could enter Naylor's office, or the conference room, and go to the general and quietly tell him that he had a call from so-and-so, and did he wish to take it?

The moment the sergeant major entered the conference room, or the office, whoever had the floor at the moment in the conference would stop—often in midsentence—and politely wait for the sergeant major and the general to finish.

This wasted time, of course, and prolonged the conference.

The second option—which Naylor originally thought showed great promise—was a telephone on his desk and the conference table, which had a flashing red button instead of a bell. That had been a failure, too, as the instant the button began to flash whoever was speaking stopped talking, in the reasonable presumption that if the general's phone flashed, the call had to be more important than whatever he was saying at the moment.

From the beginning, the use of the laptop to announce calls had been a success. Naylor always caught, out of the corner of his eye, activity on the laptop's screen. He then dropped his eyes to it and read, for example:

```
MRS N??????
```

Or:

```
SEC BEIDERMAN???
```

Or:

```
GEN HARDHEAD
```

Whereupon he would put his fingers on the keyboard and type:

```
BRT
```

Which meant "Be Right There," and, further, meant that he would stand up, say, "Excuse me for a moment, gentlemen," and go into a small soundproof cubicle, which held a chair, a desk, and a secure telephone, and converse with his wife or the secretary of defense.

Or, in the case of General Hardhead, for example, he would quickly type:

```
NN. 1 HR
```

Which stood for "Not Now. Have Him Call Back in an Hour."
Or:

```
FOWDWIIP
```

Which stood for "Find Out What, and Deal With It If Possible."

General Naylor found he could get and receive messages in this manner without causing whoever had the floor to stop in midsentence and wait.

But then, starting with Mrs. Naylor, he began to get messages directly from those in his inner circle, rather than via Sergeant Major Suggins, those who were very privy to the great secret of Naylor's e-mail screen name.

There would be a muted beep, he would drop his eyes to the screen and see that Mrs. Naylor was inquiring:

```
CAN YOU PICK UP TWO DOZEN EGGS AND SOME RYE BREAD AT
THE COMMISSARY??
```

To which, without causing the conference to come to a complete stop, he could reply:

```
SURE
```

The next development—which he thought was probably inevitable—was the realization that since he was connected to the Internet, his personal e-mail was thus available.

The purpose of the conferences was to make sure everybody knew what everybody else was thinking, had done, or was planning to do. Very often General Naylor knew what most of the conferees were going to say when they stood up. Listening to something he already knew—or at least assigning his full attention to it—was a waste of time. Time that could be better spent reading what, for example, his sons thought would interest him.

Both of his sons were in the Army and in Iraq. The oldest was a lieutenant colonel who had followed his father and grandfather into Armor. The youngest was a captain who commanded a Special Forces A-Team engaged in rounding up Saddam Hussein loyalists.

Both of them—and he was very proud of the way they handled this—routinely sent him information they thought he might not otherwise get—even though everything military in Iraq was under his command—and would like to have. The information they sent met two criteria: It was not classified; and it contained not the slightest hint of criticism of any officer.

There were many periods in many conferences when Naylor felt justified in reading e-mails from his sons instead of hearing one colonel or general explain something for the fifth time to a colonel or general who just didn't seem to be able to understand what he was being told.

The conferees had no idea what the commanding general might be typing on his IBB, only that he had diverted his attention from them to it.

The little box in the lower right corner of the laptop screen flicked brightly for an instant and then reported:

```
YOU HAVE A NEW E-MAIL FROM CHARLEY@CASTILLO.COM
```

Charley Castillo had a unique relationship on several levels with Allan B. Naylor, General, U.S. Army, Commanding General of the United States Central Command, any one of which would have given him access to Naylor's private e-mail address.

One, which Naylor often thought was the most important, was that both he and Elaine considered him a third son—the middle son, so to speak—even though there was no blood connection between them. They had known him since he was twelve, when Charley had become an orphan.

He was also officially one of Naylor's officers. The manning chart of Cent-Com showed under the J-5, the Special Activities Section, and under the SAS, the Special Assignments Section, a list of names of officers and enlisted men on special assignments. One of them read CASTILLO, C.G., MAJ.

"J-5" stood for "Joint Staff Division 5, Special Operations." The Special Activities Section of J-5 had to do with things known only to a very few people, and the Special Assignments Section was sort of the holding tank—they had to appear on the manning chart somewhere.

General Naylor had had nothing to do with Major Castillo's assignment to what was colloquially known as "Jay-Five Sassas," although many people—including, he suspected, his wife and sons—suspected he did. Castillo had been assigned there routinely when he came back from Afghanistan. It was an assignment appropriate for someone of his rank and experience.

General Naylor, however, had had everything to do with Major Castillo's present Jay-Five Sassas assignment.

General Naylor was personally acquainted with Secretary of Homeland Security Matt Hall. They had met in Vietnam when Naylor had been a captain and Hall a sergeant and had stayed in touch and become close friends over the years as Naylor had risen in the Army hierarchy and Hall had become first a congressman and then governor of North Carolina and then secretary of homeland security.

Hall, over a beer in the bar of the Army-Navy Club in Washington, had asked Naylor, "Allan, you don't just happen to know of a hell of a good linguist with all the proper security clearances, do you?"

"How do you define 'good,' Matt?"

"Preferably, male and single—I need somebody around all the time and that's awkward with a female—or a married person of either gender."

Major C. G. Castillo was the next day placed on Indefinite Temporary Duty with the Office of the Secretary of Homeland Security, with the understanding between the general and the secretary being that if he wasn't what Hall needed, or they didn't get along, Castillo would be returned to MacDill.

Two weeks after Castillo had gone to Washington, Hall had telephoned Naylor about Castillo.

"How's Castillo doing?" Naylor had asked.

"Until about an hour ago, I thought he was just what the doctor ordered," Hall said.

"What happened an hour ago?"

"I found out he's living in the Mayflower. How does he afford that on a major's pay?"

"Didn't I mention that? He doesn't have to live on his major's pay."

"No, you didn't," Hall said. "Why not?"

"I didn't think it was important. Is it?"

"Yeah. Washington is an expensive place to live. Now I won't have to worry about him having to go to Household Finance to make ends meet. Can I keep him, Allan?"

"For as long as you need him."

"Would you have any objection if I put him in civilian clothing most of the time and called him my executive assistant or something like that?"

"He'll be doing more than translating?"

"Uh-huh. Any problem with that?"

"He's yours, Matt. I'm glad it's worked out."

General Naylor clicked on the READ button without thinking about it. The laptop screen filled up almost instantly.

```
WE JUST GOT THIS FROM LANGLEY
WHAT DO YOU MAKE OF IT?


FOLLOWING RECEIVED 1133 23 MAY 2005 FROM LUANDA,
ANGOLA, IS FORWARDED FOR YOUR INFORMATION.


CONFIDENTIAL
SATBURST 01 LUANDA 23 MAY 2005
FOR REGDIR SWAFRICA
A BOEING 727 TRANSPORT AIRCRAFT LA-9021 REGISTERED TO
LEASE-AIRE, INC., PHILA., PENN., TOOK OFF WITHOUT
PERMISSION FROM QUATRO DE FEVEREIRO AEROPORTO
INTERNACIONAL AT 1425 LOCAL TIME 23 MAY 2005 AND
DISAPPEARED FROM RADAR SHORTLY THEREAFTER. ANGOLAN
```

```
AUTHORITIES KNOWN TO BELIEVE AIRCRAFT WAS STOLEN. MORE
TO FOLLOW. STACHIEF LUANDA


REGARDS


CHARLEY
```

There were several things wrong with Charley's message, which caused Naylor to frown thoughtfully, and which, in turn, caused half a dozen of the people at the conference table to wonder what had come over that goddamned IBB to cause the commanding general to frown thoughtfully.

For one thing, I don't know if this is from Charley or Hall. Charley said, "We just got this message." Does "we" mean the Department of Homeland Security, or Matt and Charley, or just Charley using the regal "we"? Or what?

Was Matt standing there when the message arrived and said, "Why don't we ask Naylor?" Or words to that effect?

Or is this message a "What do you think of this, Uncle Allan?"—type message? Expressing idle curiosity? Or wanting to know what I think in case Matt asks him later?

Damn it!

The commanding general of Central Command rapped his water glass with a pencil and gained the attention of all the conferees.

"Gentlemen," he said. "For several reasons, high among them that I think we're all a little groggy after being at this so long, I hereby adjourn this conference until tomorrow morning, place and time to be announced by Sergeant Major Suggins.

"The second reason is that it has just come to my attention that an airliner has allegedly been stolen in Luanda, Angola, and I would like to know what, if anything, anyone here knows about it."

He looked at Mr. Lawrence P. Fremont as he spoke. Mr. Fremont was the liaison officer between Central Command and the Central Intelligence Agency. It was obvious that Mr. Fremont had absolutely no idea what Naylor was talking about.

Neither, to judge from the looks on their faces, did Vice-Admiral Louis J.

Warley, USN, Central Command's J-2 (Intelligence Officer); nor Lieutenant General George H. Potter, USA, the CentCom J-5; nor Mr. Brian Willis, who was the Federal Bureau of Investigation's Resident Special Agent in Charge, known as the SAC.

I didn't expect all of them to be on top of this, but none of them? Jesus H. Christ!

"I'd like Mr. Fremont, Admiral Warley, Mr. Willis, and General Potter to stay behind a moment, please. The rest of you gentlemen may go, with my thanks for your devoted attention during a long and grueling session," General Naylor said.

Everybody but the four people he had named filed out of the conference room.

Naylor looked at the four men standing by the conference table.

"If it would be convenient, gentlemen, I'd like to see you all in my office in twenty minutes, together with what you can find out about . . ." He dropped his eyes to the laptop, and read, ". . . CIA Satburst 01, Luanda, 23 May, in that time." He looked up at Potter, and added, "Larry, see if you can find out who the CIA man is in Luanda. I'd like to know who sent this message."

"I think I know, sir," General Potter said.

Naylor looked at him.

General Potter, aware that General Naylor believed that no information is better than wrong information, said, "I'm not sure, sir. I'll check."

"Yeah," General Naylor said.

He looked at the door and saw Sergeant Major Suggins.

"Suggins, would you ask General McFadden if he's free to come to my office in twenty minutes?"

General Albert McFadden, U.S. Air Force, was the CentCom deputy commander.

"Yes, sir."

General Naylor then turned his attention to the IBB, pushed the REPLY key, and typed:

WORKING ON IT. I'LL GET BACK TO YOU. REGARDS, NAYLOR.

When he looked up, he saw that General Potter was standing just inside the door.

Potter was a tall, thin, ascetic-looking man who didn't look much like what comes to mind when "Special Forces" is said. Naylor knew that he had been, in his day, one hell of a Green Beanie, a contemporary of the legendary Scotty McNab. And that he was anything but ascetic. He was a gourmet cook, especially seafood.

"You have something?" Naylor asked.

"Yes, sir. General, I know who the CIA guy is in Angola. He's one of us," Potter said.

"One of us what?"

"He's a special operator, General," Potter said, smiling again. "He took a pretty bad hit in Afghanistan with the 160th, and when he got out of the hospital on limited duty we loaned him to the agency. I thought he was going to help run their basic training program at the Farm, but apparently they sent him to Angola."

The 160th was the Special Operations Aviation Regiment.

"You have his name?"

"Miller. H. Richard Miller, Jr. Major."

"Good man," Naylor said.

"You know him?"

"Him and his father and grandfather," Naylor said. "I didn't get to meet his great-grandfather, or maybe it was his great-great-grandfather. But in the Spanish-American War, he was first sergeant of Baker Troop, 10th Cavalry, when Teddy Roosevelt led the Rough Riders through their lines and up San Juan Hill. I heard he was hit . . ." *Charley told me.* ". . . in Afghanistan. They shot down his helicopter . . . a Loach, I think."

"Yeah. It was a Loach. A piece of something got his knee."

"Have we got a back channel to him, George?"

"It's up and running, sir. We got a back channel from Miller about this missing airplane before you heard about it."

"And my notification was out of channels," Naylor said, just a little bitterly. "But I suppose, in good time, CentCom will hear about this officially. I'm really sick and tired of Langley taking their goddamned sweet time before they bring me in the loop." He heard what he had said and added: "You didn't hear that."

Potter smiled and made an "I don't know what you're talking about" gesture.

"Let me see whatever he sends," Naylor ordered.

"Yes, sir."

[THREE]

What was at first euphemistically described as "establishing some really first-rate liaison" between the CIA and the FBI and CentCom was a direct result of the events of what had universally become known as "9/11," the crashing of skyjacked airliners into the twin towers of the World Trade Center and into the Pentagon and, short of its target in the capital, into the Pennsylvania countryside.

No one said it out loud but Central Command was the most important headquarters in the Army. According to its mission statement, it was responsible "for those areas of the world not otherwise assigned."

Army forces in the continental United States were assigned to one of the five armies in the United States, except those engaged in training, which were assigned to the Training & Doctrine Command with its headquarters within the thick stone walls of Fortress Monroe, Virginia.

Southern Command, which had had its headquarters in Panama for many years, now listed its address as 3511 NW 91st Avenue, Miami, Florida 33172-1217. It was responsible for Central and South America. No one feared immediate war with, say, Uruguay, Chile, or Argentina, or even Venezuela or Colombia, although a close eye was kept on the latter two, and, of course, on Cuba.

The Far East Command had responsibility for the Pacific. There were no longer very many soldiers in the Pacific because no one expected war to break out there tomorrow afternoon. The European Command, as the name implied, had the responsibility for Europe. For nearly half a century, there had been genuine concern that the Red Army would one day crash through the Fulda Gap bent on sweeping all of Europe under the Communist rug. That threat no longer existed.

Some people wondered what sort of a role was now left for the North American Treaty Organization, whose military force was headed by an American general, now that the Soviet threat was minimal to nonexistent, and NATO was taking into its ranks many countries it had once been prepared to fight.

The Alaskan Command had the responsibility for Alaska. There was very little of a threat that the now Russian Army would launch an amphibious attack across the Bering Strait from Siberia with the intention of occupying Fairbanks or Nome.

That left Central Command with the rest of the world, and most of the wars being fought and/or expected to start tonight or tomorrow morning. Iraq is in CentCom's area of responsibility, and CentCom had already fought one war there and was presently fighting another.

But the reason General Allan Naylor believed that he commanded the most important headquarters in the Army was that it wasn't just an Army head-quarters but rather a truly unified command, which meant that Naylor more often than not had Air Force, Navy, and Marine units, as well as Army, under his command.

The operative word was "command." He had the authority to issue orders, not make requests or offer suggestions of the other services.

And for this he was grateful to one of his personal heroes, General Donn A. Starry, USA, now retired. Starry, like Naylor, was Armor. As a young colonel in Vietnam, while leading the Cambodian Incursion from the turret of the first tank, Starry had been painfully wounded in the face, had the wound bandaged, and then got back in his tank and resumed the incursion. One of his majors, who had jumped from his tank to go to the aid of his injured commander, was himself badly wounded and lost a leg.

Many people in the Army had been pleasantly surprised when Starry had been given his first star. Officers who say what they think often find this a bar to promotion, and Starry not only said what he thought but was famous for not letting tact get in the way of making his points clear. People were thus even more surprised when he was given a second star and command of Fort Knox, then a third star and command of the V Corps in Frankfurt, Germany, charged with keeping the Red Army from coming through the Fulda Gap, and then a fourth star.

The Army thought four-star General Starry would be just the man to assume command of what was then called "Readiness Command" at MacDill Air Force Base in Florida. General Starry, however, said, "No, thank you. I think I'll retire. I don't want to go out of the Army remembered as a paper tiger."

Starry's refusal to take the command came to the attention of President Reagan, who called him to the White House to explain why.

Starry told Reagan that so far as he was concerned, Readiness Command was useless as presently constituted. It was supposed to be ready to instantly respond to any threat when ordered.

But when ordered to move, Starry told the president that the way things were, the general in command had to ask the Air Force for airplanes—for which they certainly would have a better use elsewhere—and ask the Navy for ships—for which the Navy would have a better use elsewhere—and then ask, for example, the European Commander for a couple of divisions—for which EUCOM, again, would have a far better use elsewhere.

It was rumored that Starry had used the words "joke" and "dog and pony show" to describe Readiness Command to the president. No one knows for sure, for their meeting was private. What is known is that Starry walked out of the Oval Office as commanding general of Readiness Command and the word of the commander in chief that just as soon as he could sign the orders, the CG of Readiness Command would have the authority Starry said he absolutely had to have.

The president was as good as his word. Starry reorganized what was to become Central Command so that it would function when needed and then retired. When Saddam Hussein invaded Kuwait, and the first President Bush ordered CentCom to respond, its then commander, General H. Norman Schwarzkopf, went to war using the authorities Starry had demanded of Reagan and Reagan had given to CentCom.

Schwarzkopf's ground commander in the first desert war was General Fred Franks. Franks was the U.S. Army's first one-legged general since the Civil War. He'd lost his leg as a result of Vietnam wounds incurred as he rushed to help his wounded colonel, Donn Starry.

CentCom's command structure had worked in the first desert war, and it had worked in the new one. And General Allan Naylor was determined that it would remain in force. Sometimes, he thought that was just about as hard a battle to fight as were the shooting wars in Iraq and Afghanistan.

One of the ways he had done this after 9/11, when the FBI and the CIA—and some other agencies—had sent him "liaison officers," was to tell them, politely and privately, that unless they considered themselves as part of the CentCom command team, and behaved themselves accordingly, he was going to send them back where they came from as "unsatisfactory" and keep sending whoever was sent to replace them back until he was either relieved himself or CentCom had liaison officers who regarded themselves as members of the team.

That had not, of course, endeared him to the directors of the FBI and the CIA, but, in the end, he had prevailed.

"I don't have them running five miles before breakfast, honey," he told Mrs. Naylor. "Not yet. But neither do they think they were sent down here to write reports on what I'm doing wrong when they're not soaking up the sun on the beach."

There was no question in Naylor's mind that both the FBI and the CIA had dropped the ball big-time in not knowing what was going to happen on 9/11. So had the Defense Intelligence Agency and the State Department intelligence people. He didn't know the details, and made no effort to get them. But he heard things without asking that told him he was right.

He also understood that the president had been in a tight spot. He couldn't fire the heads of the CIA and the FBI in the days immediately after something like 9/11 happened no matter how justified that would have been. Legitimately frightened people need reassurance and not to hear that the heads of the country's domestic and foreign intelligence had been incompetent and had been canned.

Another direct result of 9/11 was the establishment of the Department of Homeland Security and the president's naming of Governor Matt Hall as its secretary. Naylor thought that making it a cabinet-level department was a fine idea, and not only because it meant he would have an ear at cabinet meetings.

The Department of Homeland Security did not have a "liaison officer"— at least, not a senior one; there were half a dozen or more DHS employees around MacDill. One wasn't needed. The secretary of homeland security and the commanding general of CentCom talked just about daily on a secure phone line.

And, of course, Charley's up there with Matt in Sodom on the Potomac.

General Naylor looked again at Charley's e-mail message, and, in particular, at the "we just got this from Langley" opening.

Jesus Christ, Charley! We? *You're just a lousy major!*

But he was smiling fondly, not frowning.

"General?"

Naylor looked at the door to the conference room. Sergeant Major Suggins was standing there.

"Sir, General Potter's waiting outside your office."

It was an unspoken question—"What do I do with him?"—as much as a statement.

"Be right there," General Naylor said, closed the lid of the Infernal Black Box, disconnected the ethernet cable, and then carried it into his office, set it on his desk, and connected it to the ethernet cable there.

[FOUR]

General George Potter was pouring himself and General Naylor another cup of coffee when Mr. Lawrence P. Fremont, the CIA liaison officer to CentCom, appeared in the door to General Naylor's office.

"Ears burning, Larry?" Naylor said, waving him in and then motioning to the coffee service.

"No, thank you," Fremont said, then: "I'm the subject of discussion?"

"The agency is," Naylor said. "George tells me your guy in Luanda is one of his. And we were idly wondering why they'd send a special operator to Angola."

"And your sure to be less than flattering conjecture, George?"

"Well, he's black; he probably speaks Portuguese; and he's a special operator. Langley probably decided he'd be less dangerous there."

" 'Less dangerous,' George?"

"In the sense he wouldn't have much of an opportunity to make embarrassing waves," Potter said, unrepentant. "I also said it was probably because he's black and speaks Portuguese."

"I respectfully disagree with premise one," Fremont said, smiling, "and agree with the rest. White people have trouble not standing out in crowds in Africa. But, to judge from this, your/my/our guy seems to know what he's doing."

He handed two printouts to Naylor.

"The first was on my desk," Fremont said. "That's what you had, I suppose. The second came in just now."

"Yeah," Naylor said, glancing at the first. "That's what I had."

He handed it to Potter and then read the second message and handed that to Potter.

```
SECRET


SATBURST 02 LUANDA 23 MAY 2005


FOR REGDIR SWAFRICA


(1) SOURCE AT AEROPORTO INTERNACIONAL STATES LA-9021
UNDERWENT REPAIRS DURING PAST WEEK UNDER SUPERVISION OF
CAPTAIN A.J. MACILHENNY OF LEASE-AIRE.


(2) REGISTRY OF HOTEL DEL QUATRO DE FEVEREIRO, LUANDA,
INDICATES ALEX MACILHENNY, US CITIZEN OF PHILA., PENN.,
CHECKED IN 16 MAY 2005. INSPECTION OF HIS ROOM SHOWS NO
INDICATION THAT MACILHENNY PLANNED DEPARTURE. ALL
```

CLOTHING, PERSONAL EFFECTS, ETCETERA, STILL IN PLACE. POSSIBILITY THEREFORE EXISTS THAT MACILHENNY PILOTED PROBABLY UNWILLINGLY LEASE-AIRE LA-9021.

MORE TO FOLLOW. STACHIEF LUANDA

"George, while we wait for the others can you check and see if we got this from somebody else?" Naylor ordered. "I'd like to be sure that it's up and running."

"Yes, sir," General Potter said and walked out of the office.

Naylor saw Fremont's look of curiosity.

"You don't want to know, Larry," Naylor said. "If you knew, you might feel obliged to tell someone in Langley that I think we can get things quicker than they can send them to us, and their feelings might be hurt."

Fremont raised both hands in a gesture meaning, *I didn't ask and, therefore, don't know.*

Naylor smiled at him. Fremont had just proven again he thought of himself as a member of the team.

Vice-Admiral Louis J. Warley, USN, Central Command's J-2 intelligence officer, came to the office door a moment later. He held two printouts in his hand. Naylor motioned him into the office.

"I've got the one I think you were referring to," Warley said. "And a second one just came in. Both from DIA."

He handed them to Naylor, who glanced at them and handed them back.

"That's what we're going to talk about," Naylor said.

General Albert McFadden, U.S. Air Force, CentCom's deputy commander, walked into Naylor's office without asking permission.

"Somebody's grabbed a 727?" he asked.

"Read all about it," Naylor said and motioned for Admiral Warley to give the printouts to General McFadden.

McFadden read the printouts and added: "A 727 and the crew, apparently. I wonder what the hell this is all about?"

No one answered him.

The last person to arrive was Mr. Brian Willis, of the FBI. He held a printout in his hand.

"The bureau just sent me this, General," he said. "Actually, while we were in the conference. Is that what you were talking about?"

Naylor glanced at it. It was Miller's first satburst.

"That's it, but there's already been a second," Naylor said.

"Here," General McFadden said, handing it to him.

Naylor waited until Willis had read it, then said, "Brian, can you get on the horn to the FBI in Philadelphia and see what they have on this Lease-Aire corporation, and the pilot? I think we should have that."

"So do I," Willis agreed, after a moment's thought, and then appeared to be wondering where he was to sit at Naylor's office conference table.

"How about doing that now, Brian?" Naylor asked, hoping his voice didn't reveal his annoyance. "While we're waiting for General Potter? Use the phone booth, if you'd like."

He pointed to the cubicle with the desk, chair, and secure telephone.

Willis nodded, said, "Oh. Sure. Okay," and walked into the small room.

He was still on the telephone when General Potter returned.

"Up and running, boss," he said.

"Okay. Good." Naylor looked around the room. "Everybody's here, and everybody's read the two satbursts from Angola, right?"

Everybody nodded.

"Okay," Naylor went on, "then let's get started."

He sat down, raised the lid of the laptop, and turned it on.

"Let's do two things," he began when all but Willis had taken seats. "Let's do worst-case scenario; and, in the military order, junior man first."

When it came to seniority among the liaison officers, somewhat important for some things, Naylor had used what he thought of as the George Orwell Theory of Seniority. All pigs are equal, but some pigs are more equal than others. All the liaison officers, he had decreed, were to have the assimilated rank of major general, and rank between them was to be determined by how long they had been assigned to CentCom.

That made Brian Willis of the FBI the junior man. He was the fourth FBI liaison officer. Naylor had sent back the first three as unsuitable. Fremont had had only one predecessor.

Willis slipped into a chair at the conference table.

"I talked to the SAC in Philadelphia," he began. "He got the first message from the bureau, but not the second."

"It'll probably be there in a couple of minutes," Naylor said. "Are they going to find out what they can about the pilot, and the company . . . what is it, 'Lease-Aire'?"

"They already knew something about them, General," Willis said, "and—

out of school—Jerry Lowell, the SAC, said we'd give five-to-one that Hartford is somehow going to be involved."

"I'm afraid I don't quite understand that," Naylor said.

"Insurance, General," Willis said, with a sly smile. "This Lease-Aire outfit has been stumbling along for a long time on the edge of bankruptcy. Their airplane is, quote, stolen, unquote, and they get paid."

"You did tell him that the CIA guy said there was no indication that the pilot was checking out of his hotel?" Naylor said.

"That's what they call 'setting the scene,' General," Willis explained patiently. "It *looks* as if he wasn't planning to leave. We decide he was forced to leave, to fly the plane. He turns up in South Africa, or someplace, and says, 'Yes, that's what's happened.' "

"From our standpoint," Naylor said, "if the airplane was stolen to collect the insurance . . ."

"He puts it on autopilot and aims it out over the ocean," Willis interjected, "and then goes out the back door. By now, that airplane is probably on the bottom of the sea."

"As I was saying," Naylor said, a little sharply, "from our standpoint that's a best-case scenario. The airplane will not be used in some kind of terrorist activity."

"I know I'm speaking out of turn, Allan . . ." General McFadden said.

Yeah, you are. Shut up and wait your turn. And don't call me by my first name in the presence of our subordinates.

"You have the floor, General," Naylor said.

"I had a flash Armageddon worst-case scenario as soon as I came in here," General McFadden said. "I mean, think about it. What's missing is an old airplane without the range to make a nuisance of itself anywhere important. With one exception. Think about this: What these rag-heads are really trying to do is get all the other rag-heads united against us, right? And so far they're not doing so hot, right? So what would really piss off all the world's rag-heads? An American airplane crashing into that black thing—whatever it is—in Mecca . . ."

"They call that the *'ka'ba,'* General McFadden," General Potter interrupted. "Muslims believe that it was built by Adam, then rebuilt by Ibrahim and his son Isma'il. It's a brick structure, a ten on the Holy Scale, where the Vatican is maybe a five, if you consider that at least the Catholics let others in to worship . . ."

". . . to which," General McFadden said, resuming the floor, "all the rag-heads make a pilgrimage." He paused to glower at Potter for his interruption.

Potter, undaunted, smiled at him.

"Would the rag-heads believe another rag-head had done that? Hell no, they wouldn't," McFadden went on. "Especially when the plane was traceable to us and the body of an American pilot was found in the wreckage."

"George?" Naylor asked.

"It's a little far-fetched, sir," General Potter said. "But it could be done, and I have to agree with General McFadden that it would indeed cause our Muslim brothers to think even less of us than they do now."

"All of them, Potter," McFadden said. "Every goddamned one of them!"

Out of the corner of his eye, Naylor saw activity on the laptop screen and dropped his eyes to it.

```
THIS JUST CAME BACK CHANNEL FOR GEN POTTER—SGTMAJ
SUGGINS


SECRET


SATBURST 03 LUANDA 23 MAY 2005


FOR REGDIR SWAFRICA


SOURCES AT POLICIA NACIONAL LUANDA CONFIRM THAT
SERGEI NOSTROFF (RUSSIAN NATIONAL AND KNOWN
ASSOCIATE OF VASILY RESPIN, ALLEGED ARMS DEALER) AND
PAOLO WALLI (ANGOLAN NATIONAL SUSPECTED OF VARIOUS
CRIMINAL ACTIVITIES) ARE KNOWN TO HAVE BEEN IN LUANDA
IN PAST WEEK. PRESENT WHEREABOUTS OF EITHER ARE
UNKNOWN.


UNDERSIGNED SUGGESTS POSSIBILITY THAT BOTH MAY BE
INVOLVED WITH DISAPPEARANCE OF LA-9021. RESPIN REPORTED
TO OWN AT LEAST THREE BOEING 727 AIRCRAFT. LA-9021 MAY
BE FLOWN ELSEWHERE, POSSIBLY TO SHARJAH, UNITED ARAB
EMIRATES, WHERE RESPIN CONTROLS THREE OR MORE AIRLINES
EITHER FOR USE WITH FALSE IDENTITY NUMBERS OR TO BE
STRIPPED OF USABLE PARTS FOR OTHER AIRCRAFT.
```

```
STRONGLY RECOMMEND IMMEDIATE AND WIDESPREAD USE OF
SATELLITE, AWACS, OTHER SURVEILLANCE ASSETS, AND
HUMINTEL ON ALL POSSIBLE ROUTES BETWEEN LUANDA AND
SHARJAH, AND OTHER POINTS IN MIDDLE EAST.


MORE TO FOLLOW. STACHIEF LUANDA
```

Naylor read it twice. It sounded slightly less far-fetched than General Mc-Fadden's worst-case scenario.

And anything is possible. Let's hope this is all it is.

Jesus. I hope McFadden's not even close to being right!

Naylor laid his hands on the laptop and typed:

```
COPIES FOR EVERYBODY. NOW.
```

Naylor became aware that everyone but McFadden—who was enthusiastically buttressing his "Crash It into the Ka'ba" theory—was looking at him.

"Another theory has come in," he said. "The sergeant major is making everybody copies. While we're waiting for that, would you go on, please, General McFadden?"

[FIVE]
Office of the National Security Advisor
The White House
1600 Pennsylvania Avenue NW
Washington, D.C.
2005 23 May 2005

"Natalie Cohen," the national security advisor said into her telephone. She was a small, light-skinned woman who wore her hair in a pageboy.

"It's me, Natalie," her caller said, the thick Carolina accent unmistakable.

"Yes, Mr. President?"

"I just finished reading the seven o'clock summary."

"Yes, Mr. President?"

"Natalie, as the last item, or the next-to-last item, there's an airplane missing in Angola. What's that all about?"

"We don't know much, Mr. President, but I checked with the Air Force and
they don't seem to think it poses a threat to the U.S., at least so far as making
it a flying bomb is concerned. It's too small and doesn't have enough range to
fly here. There was some concern that it might be used to crash into our embassy there, or in South Africa, but the time for that—if it was to be immediately done after it was taken—has passed. Right now, we just don't know what
happened to it."

"Don't you mean, Natalie, '*they* just don't know'?"

"Sir?"

"Our enormous and enormously expensive intelligence community," the
president said. "*We,* you and me, Natalie, are supposed to get the intelligence.
They are supposed to come up with it, and then give it to you and me. Right?"

"Yes, Mr. President, that's the way it's supposed to work."

"And they haven't been doing that very well, lately, have they?"

"Mr. President . . ."

"They haven't and we both know it," the president said.

She didn't reply.

"Sorry, I didn't mean to unload on you," the president said.

"I didn't think you did, Mr. President. I understand your frustration. I'm
often frustrated myself."

"I wish I could think of some way to shake them up," the president said.
"Any ideas?"

"I'm afraid not, Mr. President."

"Matt Hall and his wife are coming to supper. You interested?"

"I'm at your call, Mr. President, but I really have made plans."

"Well, I'll see what Matt has to say, and then you can tell me tomorrow
morning what you think."

"What's the buzzword? Buzz-*phrase*? 'Thinking out of the box'?"

"Dr. Cohen, you are absolutely right. As soon as Matt walks in, I'm going
to hand him a stiff drink and tell him to start thinking out of the box."

She chuckled.

"See you in the morning, Natalie. Have a nice night."

"Thank you, Mr. President."

"And when you come in in the morning, I hope you'll be able to tell me we
have found this missing airplane."

"I hope so, too, Mr. President."

"I just realized, Natalie, that I'm not kidding. Maybe Matt will have some ideas."

"I'm sure he will, Mr. President."

"Good night, Natalie."

"Good night, Mr. President."

She broke the connection with her finger but did not replace the handset. She pushed a button on the base that automatically connected her to another instrument on the secure network.

"Hall," a male voice said a moment later.

"A heads-up, Matt. I know where you're going tonight. He wants to discuss with you ways to shake up what he described as our 'enormous and enormously expensive intelligence community.' "

"Oh, hell. Thank you, Natalie, I owe you a big one."

"Yeah," she agreed.

"What lit his fire this time? Do you know?"

"Somebody stole an airplane in Angola. That caught his eye."

"Mine, too. Thanks again, Natalie."

"Have fun, Matt," she said with a laugh and hung up.

[ONE]
The Oval Office
The White House
1600 Pennsylvania Avenue NW
Washington, D.C.
0845 24 May 2005

"Natalie, Matt," the president of the United States said, "would you stay a minute, please?"

Dr. Natalie Cohen, the national security advisor, and the Hon. Matt Hall, secretary of homeland security, who were sitting on the same couch, and both of whom had started to get up, relaxed against the cushions. Hall then leaned forward and picked up his unfinished cup of coffee from the coffee table.

The president waited until the others in the room had filed out and then motioned to the Secret Service agent at the door to close it.

Cohen and Hall looked at the president, who seemed to be gathering his thoughts. Finally, he smiled and spoke.

"Maybe I missed something just now," the president said. "But I didn't hear from anyone that anyone knows any more about that airliner that went missing in Angola than anyone did yesterday."

Cohen and Hall exchanged glances but neither said anything.

"And I think—I may be wrong; the intelligence community is so enormous that sometimes I just can't remember every agency who's part of it—that we had in here just now just about everybody who should know what's going on with that airplane. Maybe not all of them. Maybe just a few of them, but certainly at least one of them. Wouldn't you agree?"

"Mr. President," Dr. Cohen said, "I checked with the CIA and the Air Force again this morning. They are agreed that there is virtually no possibility of that airplane being able to fly here—or, for that matter, to Europe—without being detected."

"That's reassuring, Natalie. And is that the reason, would you say, that nobody mentioned this missing airplane? Or, maybe—I realize this may sound as if I'm a little cynical—was it because they hoped I wouldn't notice that they have no idea what the hell's going on with that airplane?"

"Mr. President," Hall spoke up, "I'm sure that they—and that means the entire intelligence community, sir—are working on it."

"Come on, Matt," the president said. "We know that." He paused and then looked at Dr. Cohen.

"Remember what we talked about last night, Natalie? I told you when Matt came for supper, I was going to ask him to think out of the box—I have no idea what that really means—about this?"

"Yes, I do, Mr. President," she said and looked at Hall.

"That I wished I could think about some way to shake up the intelligence community?" the president went on.

"Yes, sir," she said and paused.

Dr. Cohen was fully aware that the man sitting at the desk across the room was the most powerful man in the world. And that she worked for him. And that meant she was supposed to do what he said, not argue with him, unless she was absolutely convinced he was dead wrong, when she saw it as her duty to argue with him.

And she wasn't absolutely sure he was right about this. Or absolutely sure he was wrong.

"Are you sure you want to shake them up, sir?" she asked. "Even more than the 9/11 commission report did?"

"If they're not doing their job," the president said, "they deserve to be shaken up."

That, Dr. Cohen thought, *is a statement of policy. And I don't think it's open for discussion.*

"And doesn't this missing 727 business give us the chance to find out whether they're doing their job or not?" the president asked. "Something real-world and real-time above and beyond what the 9/11 commission report called for?" He paused. "This could put us ahead of the curve."

"Very possibly it does, sir," she said.

"It looks to me, and Matt, like an ideal situation to run an 'internal review,'" the president went on, "without it interfering with anything important. And without anybody having to know about it unless we catch somebody with their pants down." He heard what he said. "Sorry, Natalie. That slipped out. But wouldn't you agree with Matt?"

So Matt, too, has decided arguing with him about this would be futile?

"What's your idea, Matt?" she asked.

"As I understand what the president wants," Hall said, "it's for someone—one man—to check everybody's intel files and compare them against both what he can find out, and what the others have found out, and when."

"Isn't that a lot to throw at one man?" she asked.

"That's a lot of work for one man, but I think that if we used even as few as three or four people on this, the question of who's in charge would come up; they'd probably be stumbling over each other trying to look good; and the more people involved, the greater the risk that somebody would suspect something like this was going on."

"That's the idea, Natalie," the president said. "What do you think?"

I think Matt has resigned himself to there being—what did he say? "An internal review"?—and he wants to keep it small, low-key, and, if at all possible, a secret.

"Have you got the man to do it?" she asked.

"I asked him last night to think about that," the president said.

"I think I have the man, sir," Hall said.

"Who?" the president asked.

"My executive assistant," Hall said.

"That good-looking young guy who speaks Hungarian?" Cohen asked.

Hall nodded.

"You know him, Natalie?" the president asked.

"I don't know him, but I saw him translating for Matt at a reception at the Hungarian embassy," she said.

"Why do you need a *Hungarian* translator, Matt?" the president asked with a smile.

"The Hungarian came with the package," Hall said. "He speaks seven, maybe more, languages, among them Hungarian."

"He's a linguist?" the president asked.

Hall understood the meaning of the question: *How is a linguist going to do what we need here?*

"Well, that, too, sir. But he's also a Green Beret."

"A Green Beret?" the president asked, his tone suggesting that the term had struck a sympathetic chord.

"Yes, sir," Hall replied. "He's a Special Forces major. I went to General Naylor and asked him if he could come up with somebody who had more than language skills. He sent Charley to me. He's a good man, Mr. President. He can do this."

"Makes sense to me," Cohen said. "Matt thinks he's smart, which is good enough for me. And no one is going to suspect that a Special Forces major would be given a job like this."

"I'd like to meet this guy," the president said. "Okay, what else do we need to get this started?"

"We'll need all the intelligence filings," Hall said. "I suppose Natalie will have most of them—or synopses of them, anyway."

"Mostly, all I get is the synopses," Cohen said. "I have to ask for the original filing, and raw data if I want to look at that."

The president thought that over a moment.

"We don't *know* that somebody is not going to try to fly this airplane into the White House or the Golden Gate Bridge . . ."

Hall opened his mouth to say something, but the president held up his hand in a gesture meaning he didn't want to be interrupted.

". . . so I think it could be reasonably argued that the missing 727 is something in which Homeland Security would have a natural interest."

Hall and Cohen nodded.

"So, Natalie, why don't you send a memo telling everybody to send the intelligence filings to Matt?"

"And the raw data, Mr. President?" Hall asked.

The president nodded.

"All filings and all raw data, from everybody," the president ordered.

"Yes, sir, Mr. President," Dr. Cohen said.

"Okay. We're on our way," the president said.

[TWO]
Hunter Army Airfield
Savannah, Georgia
1315 27 May 2005

The Cessna Citation X attracted little attention as it touched down smoothly just past the threshold of the runway, possibly because one of the world's most famous airplanes was moving majestically down the parallel taxiway.

The copilot of the Citation looked at the enormous airplane as they rolled past it, and turned to the pilot, as the pilot reported, "Six-Oh-One on the ground."

"Twenty-nine," the copilot said.

The pilot nodded.

"Six-Oh-One, take Four Right to the parallel," Hunter ground control ordered the smaller jet. "Be advised there is a 747 on the parallel. Turn left on the parallel. Hold at the threshold."

"Understand Four Right," the pilot replied, "then turn left to hold at the threshold. Thank you for advising about taxiway traffic. I might have not seen that airplane."

"You're welcome, Six-Oh-One," the ground traffic controller replied with a chuckle in his voice.

"And by the way, Hunter," the pilot said. "I think that's a VC-25A, not a 747."

"Thank you so much, Six-Oh-One," the controller replied. "Duly noted."

"Hunter, Air Force Two-Niner-Triple-Zero, I have that cute little airplane in sight and will endeavor not to run over it."

"Two-Niner-Triple-Zero," the pilot of the Citation said. "It's not nice to make fun of little airplanes, especially ones flown by birdmen in their dotage."

"Who is that?" the copilot of the Citation asked. "Jerry?"

"It sounds like him," the pilot said.

Both the pilot and the copilot of the Citation knew Air Force VC-25A tail number 29000 well. Both had more than a thousand hours at the controls of it, or its identical twin, tail number 28000. Flying the specially configured Boeings—whose call sign changed to Air Force One whenever the president of the United States was on board—had been their last assignment before their retirement.

Twenty-nine, both believed, was now being flown—or, actually, both strongly suspected, just taxied to the end of the runway for a precautionary engine run-up—by Colonel Jerome T. McCandlish, USAF, whom they had, after exhaustive tests and examinations, signed off on two years before as qualified to fly the commander in chief.

The proof—in addition to the sound of his voice—seemed to be that he had recognized the tail number on the Citation and felt sure he knew who was flying it.

Citation tail number NC-3055 was the aircraft provided for the secretary of the Department of Homeland Security, although there was nothing to suggest this in its appearance. It was intended to look like—and did look like—most other Citations. And with the exception of some very special avionics not available on the civilian market it was essentially just like every other Citation X in the air.

"Miss it, Jack?" the pilot inquired as 29000 fell behind them.

"Sure," the copilot said. "Don't you?"

"The question is, 'Would I go back tomorrow?,' " the pilot said, "and the answer is, 'No, I don't think so.' This is just about as much fun, and it's a hell of a lot less . . ."

"Responsibility?"

"I was going to say that, but . . . work. It's a lot less work."

"I agree."

When the time had come for them to be replaced as pilots-in-command of the presidential aircraft—six months apart—they had been offered, within reason, any assignment appropriate to full colonels and command pilots. There were problems with the word "appropriate." They were led to understand that although colonels command groups, it would not really be appropriate for them to be given command of, for example, one of the groups in the U.S. Air Force Special Operations Command.

That would be a great flying job, but the cold facts were that they had spent very little time at the controls of various C-130 aircraft, such as the Spectre and Spooky gunships best known for their fierce cannons, and actually knew very little about what Special Operations really did.

The same was true of taking command of a fighter wing or a bomber wing.

Although both had once been fighter pilots and bomber pilots, that had been early on in their careers, decades ago, and now they were almost in their fifties.

What was appropriate, it seemed, was command of one of the Flying Training Wings in the Nineteenth Air Force. They had training experience, and knowing that they were being taught how to fly by pilots who had flown the commander in chief in Air Force One would certainly inspire fledgling birdmen.

So would becoming a professor at the Air Force Academy be appropriate and for the same reasons. It would also be appropriate for them to become air attachés at a major American embassy somewhere; they certainly had plenty of experience being around senior officials, foreign and domestic. But that would not be a flying assignment and they both wanted to continue flying.

Their other option was to retire and get a civilian flying job. The problem there was the strong airline pilots' unions, which made absolutely sure every newly hired airline pilot started at the bottom of the seniority list. No matter how much time one had at the controls of a 747/VC-25A, those airline pilot positions went only to pilots who had worked their way up the seniority ladder.

In favor of retirement, however, was that the Air Force retirement pay wasn't bad, and they would get it in addition to what they would make sitting in the copilot's seat of a twin-engine turboprop of Itsy-Bitsy Airlines, and both had just about decided that's what it would be when the rag-heads flew skyjacked 767s into the World Trade Center and the Pentagon and the Pennsylvania ground.

The Department of Homeland Security had come out of that, and, with that, the secretary of homeland security. Even before Congress had passed the necessary legislation—there had been no doubt that it was going to happen—certain steps were taken, among them providing the secretary designate with suitable air transportation.

He didn't need a VC-25A, of course, or even another of the airliner-sized transports in the Air Force inventory. What he needed was a small, fast airplane to carry him on a moment's notice wherever he had to go.

The Citation X, which was capable of carrying eight passengers 3,300 miles—San Francisco, for example, to Washington—in fewer than four hours was just what was needed. There is always a financial cushion in the budget of the Secret Service to take care of unexpected expenses, and this was used to rent the Citation from Cessna.

Part of the rationale to do this was that the Secret Service was to be transferred from the Treasury Department to the Department of Homeland Security anyway.

The Secret Service had some pilots but would need four more to fly the secretary's new Citation. All the *t*s were crossed and the *i*s dotted on the appropriate Civil Service Commission Application for Employment forms, of course, and the applications examined carefully and honestly, but no one was surprised when two about-to-retire Air Force colonels who had been flying the president were adjudged to be best qualified for appointment as Pilots, Aircraft, GS-15, Step 8, to fill two of the four newly established positions.

"Citation Thirty-Fifty-Five, be advised that two Hueys are moving to the threshold," Hunter ground control announced just as the Citation X turned left onto the parallel.

"Roger that, we have them in sight," the copilot said, and then added, "Jerry, remember to lock the brakes before you start your run-up."

The Cessna pilot chuckled.

Through the windshield they could see two Army UH-1H helicopters slowly approaching the threshold of the runway about twenty feet off the ground.

The pilot touched the ANNOUNCE button.

"Mr. Secretary, we can see the choppers."

"Me, too, Frank. Thank you," Secretary Hall called back.

There were four passengers in the Citation today. Secretary Hall; Joel Isaacson, the supervisory Secret Service agent in charge of Hall's security detail; Tom McGuire, another Secret Service bodyguard; and an Army major, today in civilian clothing, whose code name for Secret Service purposes was "Don Juan."

The secretary's code name was "Big Boy," which more than likely made reference to his size and appearance.

Why the major was "Don Juan" wasn't known for sure. It could have something to do with his Spanish- or Italian-sounding name, Castillo, or, Frank and Jack had privately joked, it could have to do with what the Secret Service secretly knew about him. At thirty-six, he was a great big guy—a little bigger than the secretary—good-looking, nice thick head of hair, blue-eyed, no wedding ring, and—considering the foregoing—he probably got laid a lot.

They had no idea what his function in the department was, or, for that matter, if he was even in the department. And, of course, they didn't ask. If it was important for them to know more than his name, they would be told.

He accompanied the secretary often enough to have his own code name, and on the occasions when he did so in uniform he sported not only the usual merit badges—parachutist's wings, senior Army Aviators' wings, a Combat Infantry Badge—but also a ring signifying that he had graduated from the United States Military Academy at West Point. They found it interesting that when he took off his uniform, he also took off the West Point ring. That offered the interesting possibility that he wasn't a soldier at all but put on the uniform—and the West Point ring—as a disguise when that was required.

Their best guess, however, was that he was in fact an officer, probably a West Pointer, and more than likely some kind of liaison officer, probably between the department and the Army or the Defense Department.

The two UH-1Hs touched down on the grass just outside the threshold to the active runway as the Citation X rolled to a stop.

The Secret Service agents got out of their seats and opened the stair door and then went outside. The pilot of the closest Huey got out. She was slight and trim, with short blond hair. She tucked her flight helmet under her arm and walked toward the Citation X.

The secretary deplaned first, carrying a briefcase, and Don Juan got off last.

"Good afternoon, Mr. Secretary," the pilot said, saluting.

"Good afternoon, Colonel," the secretary said.

"Sir, I'm Lieutenant Colonel Messinger," the pilot said. "I'll be flying you to the island. I know you're familiar with the aircraft, but I'll have to ask this gentleman . . ."

"He's familiar with it, Colonel," the secretary said. "I think you're probably both graduates of the same flying school."

"You're a Huey driver, sir?"

"Yes, ma'am, I am," Don Juan said. "And you outrank me, Colonel."

"Colonel," the secretary said, visibly amused by the interchange, "this is Major Charley Castillo."

"How do you do, Major?" Lieutenant Colonel Messinger said, offering her hand and a firm handshake. "The weather's fine; it's a short hop—about thirty-five miles—I already have the clearance to penetrate the P-49 area, so there won't be Marine jets from Beaufort around, and anytime the secretary is ready we can go."

She made a gesture toward the helicopters. Joel Isaacson and Tom McGuire walked to the more distant aircraft and got in.

Major Castillo knew the drill: The Huey with the Secret Service agents in it would wait until the one carrying the secretary took off and then follow it until they reached their destination. Then the Secret Service Huey would land first to make sure there were no problems and then radio the second helicopter that it could land.

He thought it was a little silly. They were going to the Carolina White House, and, if there was something wrong there, they would certainly have heard about it.

But it's Standing Operating Procedure, which is like Holy Writ in the U.S. Army.

Colonel Messinger double-checked to see that Sergeant First Class De-Laney, her crew chief, had properly strapped in the secretary and the major in civvies, smiled at them both, and then got back in the right seat.

A moment later, the Huey went light on the skids, lifted into the air, dropped its nose, and began to move ever more rapidly across the airfield. Cooler air rushed in the big doors left open on either side of the helicopter against the Georgia heat.

Major Castillo unfastened his seat belt and started to stand.

"Sir!" Sergeant First Class DeLaney began to protest.

Major Castillo put his finger to his lips, signifying silence.

Sergeant First Class DeLaney, visibly upset, looked to the secretary for help.

The secretary signaled the sergeant that if Castillo wanted to stand, it was fine with him.

With a firm grip on a fuselage rib, Major Castillo stood in the doorway for about two minutes, looking down at what he could see of Fort Stewart.

Then he quickly resumed his seat and strapped himself in.

"I once spent a summer here, Sergeant," he said, smiling at DeLaney. "Mostly washing Georgia mud from tracks and bogie wheels. I haven't been back since."

"Yes, sir," Sergeant DeLaney said.

"Sergeant," the secretary said, smiling. "If you don't tell the colonel, we won't."

"Yes, sir."

"On the other hand, Charley," the secretary said, "I have seen people take a last dive out of one of these things when there was a sudden change of course."

"Sir," Castillo said, "I have a finely honed sense of self-preservation. Not to worry."

"So I have been reliably informed," the secretary said. "I think the colonel likes you, Charley. She spent much more time strapping you in than she did me."

"It's my cologne, sir," Castillo said. "Eau de Harley-Davidson. It gets them every time."

The secretary laughed.

Sergeant First Class DeLaney smiled somewhat uneasily.

Jesus, DeLaney thought, *what if that big bastard had taken a dive out the door?*

[THREE]
The Carolina White House
Hilton Head Island, South Carolina
1355 27 May 2005

The president of the United States was sitting in one of the upholstered wicker rocking chairs on the porch of an eight-year-old house that had been carefully designed and built so that most people thought it was bona fide antebellum and surprised that such a house had been built way back then overlooking the Atlantic Ocean.

The president, who was wearing a somewhat faded yellow polo shirt with the Brooks Brothers sheep embroidered on the chest, sharply creased but obviously not new khaki trousers, and highly polished loafers, was drinking Heineken beer from the bottle. A galvanized bucket on the floor beside his chair held a reserve buried in ice.

The president pushed himself out of his chair and set his beer bottle on the wicker table as a white GMC Yukon with heavily tinted windows pulled up.

The driver got out quickly and ran around the front of the Yukon in a vain attempt to open the driver's door before the secretary could do so himself.

"Hey, Matt!" the president greeted the secretary, his accent sounding comfortable at home in its native Carolina.

The secretary walked up on the porch and offered his hand.

"Good afternoon, Mr. President," he said.

"It's always a pleasure to see you, Matt," the president said with a smile.

Major Carlos Guillermo Castillo, Aviation, U.S. Army, stood by the Yukon waiting for some indication of what he should do.

The president looked at him and smiled and then turned his back on the Yukon.

"Don't tell me that's your Tex-Mex linguist?" the president asked.

"That's him, Mr. President," the secretary said.

"That guy's name is *Guillermo Castillo?*"

"*Carlos* Guillermo Castillo," the secretary said, smiling. "Yes, sir, Mr. President."

The president chuckled, and then with a smile and a friendly wave ordered Castillo onto the porch.

"Welcome to the island, Major," the president said, offering him his hand.

"Thank you, Mr. President."

"Where's home, Major?" the president asked.

"San Antonio, sir," Castillo said.

"I've got two questions for you, Major," the president said. "The first is, Can I offer you a beer?"

"Yes, sir. Thank you very much," Castillo said.

The president took two bottles of beer from the bucket and handed one to Castillo and the other to Secretary Hall and then produced a bottle opener.

"Every time I try to twist one of the easy-open caps off, I cut the hell out of my hand," the president announced. He waited a beat, then added with a grin: "Especially when they're not twist-off caps." He waved Hall and Castillo into wicker rockers and then sat down himself.

"My mother would tell me, Major, that a question like this is tacky, but I just have to ask it. You're really not what I expected. Where did a fair-skinned, blue-eyed guy like you get a name like Carlos Guillermo Castillo?"

"My father's family, sir, is Tex-Mex. My mother was German."

"I didn't mean to embarrass you," the president said.

"The question comes up frequently, sir," Castillo said. "Usually followed by, 'Are you adopted?,' to which I reply, sir, 'No, it's a question of genes.'"

The president chuckled, then grew serious.

"I guess the secretary has brought you up to speed on this," he said.

"Yes, sir, he has."

"What did he tell you?" the president asked.

Castillo's somewhat bushy left eyebrow rose momentarily as he visibly gathered his thoughts.

"As I understood the secretary, Mr. President," Castillo began, "a Boeing 727 which had been parked at the Luanda, Angola, airfield for fourteen months took off without clearance on 23 May and hasn't been seen since. The incident is being investigated by just about all of our intelligence agencies, none of which has come up with anything about where the aircraft is or what happened to it. The secretary, sir, led me to believe that he wants me to conduct an investigation . . ."

"*I* want you to conduct an investigation," the president interrupted.

"Yes, sir. The purpose of my investigation would be to serve as sort of a check on the investigations of the various agencies involved . . ."

"What I'd like to know," the president said, with a dry smile on his face and in his voice, "is what did they know, and when did they know it?' "

Secretary Hall chuckled.

"There is nothing to suggest," the president said, "that any of the agencies looking into the 727 gone missing have either done anything they shouldn't have or not done something they should have. Or that anyone suspects they will in the future. You should have that clear in your mind from the beginning."

"Yes, sir."

"On the other hand," the president went on, "I can't help but have in mind that a highly placed officer in the agency who was in the pay of the Russians for years was not even suspected of doing anything wrong—despite his living a lifestyle he could obviously not support on his CIA pay—until, against considerable resistance from the agency bureaucracy, an investigation was launched. You're familiar with that story?"

"Yes, sir, I am."

"And then—it came far too belatedly to light—the FBI had a highly placed officer in charge of counterintelligence who had taken a million dollars from the Russians in exchange for information that led to the deaths of people we had working for us in Moscow and elsewhere."

"Yes, sir. I know that story, too."

"That's what the agency would call the worst possible scenario," the president went on. "But there is another scenario—scenarios—that, while falling short of moles actually in the pay of a foreign intelligence service, can do just as much harm to the country as a mole can do. Are you following me, Major?"

"I hope so, sir."

"Intelligence—as you probably are well aware—is too often colored, or maybe diluted or poisoned, I learned, by three factors. I'm not sure which is worst. One of them is interagency rivalry, making their agency look good and another look bad. Another is to send up intelligence that they believe is what their superiors want to hear, or, the reverse, not sending up intelligence that they think their superiors don't want to hear. And yet another is an unwillingness to admit failure. You understand this, I'm sure. You must have seen examples yourself."

"Yes, sir, I have."

"Matt . . . Secretary Hall and I," the president said, "are agreed that in the intelligence community there is too much of a tendency to rely on what the other fellow has to say. I mean, in the absence of anything specific, the CIA will go with what the FBI tells them, or the ONI on what the DIA has developed. You're still with me?"

"Yes, sir."

"Some of that, obviously, has to do with funding. Funding is finite. One agency feels that if another agency has come up with something, there's no sense in duplicating the effort, which means spending money. That's just human nature."

"Yes, sir, I understand."

"And then Secretary Hall came up with the idea that one way to have a look at what's really going on in the field would be to have a quiet look at an active case where more than one agency—the more, the better—is involved. This gone-missing airplane is a case where not just two or three agencies but most of them are involved. I don't have to get into that with you, do I, Major? The jealously guarded turf of the various agencies?"

"No, sir. I'm familiar with the Statements of Mission."

"Okay," the president said. "In the case of this missing 727 airplane, the agency has primary responsibility. But the State Department has been told to find out what they can. And the Defense Intelligence Agency. And DHS, because one scenario is that the plane was stolen for use as a flying bomb against a target in this country. There is not much credence being placed in that story, but the fact is we just don't know. What we *do* know is that we cannot afford to allow it—or any other act of terrorism—to happen again. And certainly not as a result of interagency squabbling . . . or one agency deciding it doesn't want to spend money because it (a) would be duplication and (b) could be more profitably spent on something else.

"So that gives Secretary Hall reason to send someone to find out what he can. Because the agency and the others are involved, and he will have access— at least in theory—to what intelligence they develop, he will not be expected to send a team, just go through the motions with someone junior who can be spared. You with me, Major?"

"Yes, sir. I think I am."

"The question then became who could Secretary Hall send on this mission, and he answered that by saying he had just the man, and he thought I would like him because he was just like Vernon Walters. You know who General Walters was, of course?"

"Yes, sir, I do."

"Well, are you like Vernon Walters, Major? You do speak a number of languages fluently?"

"Yes, sir."

"Russian?"

"Yes, sir."

"Hungarian?"

"Yes, sir."

"How many in all?"

"Seven or eight, sir," Castillo said, "depending on whether Spanish and Tex-Mex are counted as one language or two."

The president chuckled. "How did you come to speak Russian?" he asked.

"When I was growing up, sir, my mother thought it would be useful if the Russians won. We lived right on the East/West German border, sir."

"And Hungarian?" the president asked.

"An elderly grandaunt who was Hungarian lived with us, sir. I got it from her."

"General Walters . . ." the president began, then paused. "I suppose protocol would dictate that I refer to him as Ambassador Walters, but I think he liked being a general far more than he ever liked being an ambassador. Anyway, he told me that languages just came to him naturally, that they hadn't been acquired by serious study. Is that the way it is with you, Major?"

"Yes, sir. Pretty much."

The president studied Castillo carefully for a moment and then asked, "You think you're up to what's being asked of you, Major?"

"Yes, sir," Major Carlos Guillermo Castillo said, confidently.

"Okay. It's settled," the president said. "I was about to say, 'Good luck, thank you for coming, and one of the Hueys will take you back to Fort Stewart to wait for Matt . . . for the secretary.'"

"There's no reason for him to stay at Fort Stewart, Mr. President," Hall said. "Actually, I promised him the long weekend off if we finished here quickly."

The president nodded, then asked Castillo: "Well, we are done. Any plans?"

"Yes, sir. I promised my grandmother a visit."

"She's where?"

"Outside San Antonio, sir."

"Would a chopper ride to Atlanta cut some travel time for you, Major?"

"Yes, sir. It would. But a ride back to Fort Stewart is all I'll need, sir."

"How's that?"

"Sir, I'm going to meet a cousin at Savannah. We're going to Texas together."

The president raised his voice. "Nathan!"

A very large, very black man appeared almost immediately from inside the house. He had an earphone in his ear and a bulge under his arm suggested the presence of either a large pistol or perhaps an Uzi. Right on his heels was one of the secretary's Secret Service bodyguards.

"Yes, Mr. President?"

"See that Major Castillo gets to a Huey and that it takes him back to Stewart," the president ordered.

"Yes, Mr. President."

The president offered Castillo his hand and put a hand on his shoulder.

"We'll see each other again," the president said. "Thank you."

"I'll do my best, Mr. President."

"I'm sure you will," the president said.

Secretary Hall shook Castillo's hand. Hall said: "See you in my office at noon on Tuesday."

A Secret Service Yukon rolled up a moment later. The president and Secretary Hall watched as Castillo got in the front seat and they waved as the SUV started off.

"A very interesting guy, Matt," the president said.

"The Secret Service dubbed him 'Don Juan,'" the secretary said. "I never asked them why."

The president chuckled.

"Where did you get him, Matt?"

"From General Naylor," the secretary said. "I got on my knees and told him I really needed him more than he did."

"That's right," the president said. "You and Naylor go back a long way, don't you?"

"To Vietnam," the secretary said. "He was a brand-new captain and I was a brand-new shake-and-bake buck sergeant."

"A what?" the president asked.

"They were so short of noncoms, Mr. President, that they had sort of an OCS to make them. I went there right out of basic training, got through it, and became what was somewhat contemptuously known as a 'shake-and-bake sergeant.'"

"Where did Naylor get him?" the president asked.

"Actually, he and Charley go a long way back, too," the secretary said.

"*Charley?*" the president parroted.

"He doesn't look much like a Carlos, does he?" the secretary said. "Yeah, I call him Charley."

"So where did Naylor get him? Where does he come from?"

"It's a long story, Mr. President," the secretary said.

The president looked at his watch.

"If you're not in a rush to get back," the president said, motioning toward the wicker rockers and the tub of iced bottles of beer, "I have a little time."

IV

WINTER 1981

[ONE]
Near Bad Hersfeld
Kreis Hersfeld-Rotenburg
Hesse, West Germany
1145 7 March 1981

"That has to be it, Netty," Mrs. Elaine Naylor, a trim, pale-faced redhead of thirty-four, said to Mrs. Natalie "Netty" Lustrous, a trim, black-haired lady of forty-four, pointing. "It's exactly three-point-three klicks from the little chapel."

"Yeah," Netty Lustrous said, slowing the nearly new black Mercedes-Benz 380SEL and then turning off the winding, narrow country road through an open gate in a ten-foot-high steel-mesh fence onto an even more narrow road.

Fifty yards down the road, a heavyset man stepped into the middle of it. He was wearing a heavy loden cloth jacket and cap and sturdy boots. A hunting rifle was slung muzzle downward from his shoulder.

Netty stopped the Mercedes and the man walked up to it.

"Guten tag," the man said.

"Is this the road to the House in the Woods?" Netty asked, in German.

"Frau Lustrous?" the man asked.

"Ja."

"Willkomen," the man said, stepped back, and somewhat grandly waved her down the road.

Netty smiled at him. *"Danke shoen,"* she replied and drove on.

"I didn't know anything was in season," Elaine said in obvious reference to the hunting rifle the man had been carrying.

"I don't think anything is," Netty chuckled. "But Jaegermeisters can carry weapons anytime in case they run into dangerous game in the woods."

"Or Americans without invitations?" Elaine asked.

"I wouldn't be surprised, from what Fred tells me, if there were three or four Jaegermeisters around here looking for things that don't belong."

The road wound upward for about a kilometer—which both women, as Army wives, had learned to call "a klick"—through an immaculate pine forest. And then the trees were gone and what had to be *das Haus im Wald* was visible.

It was large but simple. It looked, Netty thought, somehow out of place in the open country. Like a house from the city that had suddenly been transplanted to the country.

Halfway between the trees and the house was another Jaegermeister with a rifle slung from his shoulder. He didn't get into the road, but stepped to the side of it and took off his cap in respect as the Mercedes rolled past him.

The left of the double doors of *das Haus im Wald* opened and a slim woman in a black dress, her blond hair gathered in a bun at her neck, stepped out onto a small stone verandah, shrugging into a woolen shawl as she did so.

"Is that her?" Elaine asked.

"I don't know," Netty said. "I've never met her, and I don't think I've ever seen a picture of her. Fred knows her—or at least has met her. He knew her father pretty well."

Fred was Colonel Frederick J. Lustrous, Armor, United States Army, to whom Netty had been married for more than half her life.

Netty pulled the car in beside another Mercedes—which she recognized to be that of Oberburgermeister Eric Liptz of Fulda—and stopped as the blond woman in the shawl came off the verandah.

"That's the Liptzes' car, right?" Elaine asked. "Meaning Inge's here?"

"I hope so," Netty said. "But that's their car."

She unfastened her seat belt, opened the door, and got out.

"Mrs. Lustrous?" the slim blond woman asked in English.

"Netty Lustrous," Netty said.

"Welcome to the House in the Woods," the blond woman said, offering her hand. "I'm Erika Gossinger."

Her English is accentless, Netty thought. *Neither Brit nor American.*

And she didn't say "Erika von und zu *Gossinger." Interesting. On purpose?*

The von und zu *business reflected the German fascination—obsession?—with social class. It identified someone whose family had belonged to the landowning nobility.*

Was it that Erika felt that was nonsense? Or that she was trying to be democratic? Or just that she had just dropped the phrase for convenience?

"Thank you having us," Netty said.

"Thank you for coming," Erika said.

Elaine came around the front of the Mercedes.

"This is my good friend Frau Elaine Naylor, Frau Gossinger," Netty said.

The invitation, engraved in German, had said that Frau Erika von und zu Gossinger would be pleased to receive at luncheon at *das Haus im Wald* Frauoberst Natalie Lustrous (and one lady friend). A separate engraved card in the envelope had a map, showing how to reach the property, which was several klicks outside Bad Hersfeld.

The women shook hands.

"Our friend Inge is already here," Erika said. "As is Pastor Dannberg. Why don't we go in the house?"

"Thank you," Netty said.

Inge Liptz, a trim blonde in her early thirties, was in the library with a small, wizened, nearly bald old man in a clerical collar, Pastor Heinrich Dannberg, who was first among equals in the Evangalische hierarchy of the area.

Inge, who was drinking champagne, walked up to Netty and Elaine and kissed both of them on the cheek.

"I see we're all in uniform," she said.

At a social gathering a year or so before, she had smilingly observed that she and Netty and Elaine were very similarly dressed, in black dresses, with a single strand of pearls.

Netty had replied, "I don't know about you, Inge, but for Elaine and me this is the prescribed uniform of the day for an event like this."

Inge, whose husband was the Oberburgermeister of Fulda, had never heard that before and thought it was hilarious.

"You know Pastor Dannberg, of course?" Erika asked.

"Yes, of course," Netty said. "How nice to see you, Pastor Dannberg."

He took her hand in his, made a gesture of kissing it, then clicked his heels and said, "Frau Lustrous," and then repeated the process with Elaine.

A maid extended a silver tray with champagne flutes.

"Again, welcome to the House in the Woods," Erika said, raising her glass. "I don't think you have been here before, have you?"

"No, I haven't."

"Your husband has, many times, over the years," Erika said. "He and my father have taken many boar together."

"Yes, he's told me," Netty said.

"I first met your husband, Frauoberst Lustrous," Pastor Dannberg said, "when he was a lieutenant, and he and his colonel came to Saint Johan's School with a truck loaded with boar they had taken—very near here, as a matter of fact—and which they gave to us to feed our students."

"I didn't know that," Netty said.

"Oh, yes. And they did that often. It was a great service to us. The woods were overrun with boar—they had not been harvested in the last years of the war. We needed the meat, of course, and, additionally, the boar, we knew, were going to cause the badly needed corn crops severe damage. I have ever since regarded him as both a friend and a Christian gentleman."

"That's very kind of you to say so, Pastor," Netty said.

And it is. So why do I feel I'm being set up for something?

"And my father, too, thought of Colonel Lustrous as an old and good friend," Erika said.

And there it goes again.

"My husband, Frau Gossinger, was very saddened by . . ."

"My father killing himself and my brother by driving drunk at an insane speed on the autobahn?" Erika said very bitterly.

"Erika!" Pastor Dannberg said, both warningly and compassionately.

"It's the truth," Erika said. "And the truth, I believe the Bible says, 'shall make you free.' "

"It also says, 'Judge not, lest ye be judged,' " Pastor Dannberg said.

"I meant no offense," Erika said.

"And certainly none was taken," Netty said.

Erika signaled to the maid for another flute of champagne.

"I really had meant to say two things," Erika said, when she'd taken a healthy sip of the champagne. "The first was to tell you that we're having roast boar today, sort of in memory of all the boar your husband and my father and brother took together over the years."

"What a nice thought!" Netty said. And thought: *There it is again. What's her agenda?*

"And the second was to suggest that although you and Frau Naylor and I are meeting for the first time, this is really a gathering of friends. You two and Inge, I know, are very close. The pastor has been my good friend, in good times and bad, since I was a little girl. And he's told you how he feels about Oberst Lustrous, who was a good friend of my father and my brother. What I'm driving at is that I would be honored to be permitted to address you by your Christian names."

"Oh, I would really like that," Netty said.

And is this where we get the pitch?

"Welcome to my home, friend Natalie," Erika said.

"Please, my friends call me 'Netty.' "

Erika smiled. "Welcome to my home, friends Netty and Elaine," she said and kissed both of them on the cheek. And then Inge Liptz kissed all three of them on the cheek.

Why do I think Inge is on the edge of tears? What the hell is going on here?

A maid announced the luncheon was served.

The dining room was on the third floor of *das Haus im Wald*. A dumbwaiter brought the food from the kitchen on the first floor. One wall of the dining room was covered with a huge, heavy curtain.

When Erika von und zu Gossinger threw a switch and the curtains slowly opened, Netty and Elaine saw that a huge plate-glass window offered a view of farmlands.

And of the border between the People's Democratic Republic of Germany and West Germany.

Netty knew a good deal about the border. She'd spent much of her life married to a man who patrolled it. First, he'd served as a second lieutenant in a jeep or armored car, and now as the colonel of the regiment responsible for miles of it.

The border was marked with a thirteen-foot-tall steel-mesh fence topped with barbed wire. Watchtowers had been built wherever necessary so the fence and the land leading up to it could not only be kept under observation but swept with machine-gun fire, some of it automatically triggered when a detection device of one kind or another sensed someone in the forbidden zone.

The forbidden zone, several hundred yards wide, had been cleared of trees and was heavily planted with mines. There were two roads, one on either side of the fence, one for East German border guards, and the other for West

German border guards and the vehicles of the Eleventh Armored Cavalry Regiment.

"That's Gossinger land over there," Erika said. "Just about as far as you can see. You'll notice I did not say, '*Used to be* Gossinger land.' One day the family will get it back."

Netty said what came to her mind.

"That fence is an obscenity."

"Yes, it is," Erika agreed simply.

What does she do? Sit here and look at what the family's lost?

Or is this another part of the setup I now know is coming?

"Well, why don't we sit down and have our luncheon?" Erika said.

Pastor Dannberg said a brief grace, and then two maids served a course of roast boar, roast potatoes, spinach, and sauerkraut. Glasses were filled with liebfraumilch. Netty sipped hers very slowly, and held her hand, politely, over her half-full glass when one of the maids tried to fill it.

Dessert was bread pudding. Cognac was offered but declined all around, except by Frau Erika von und zu Gossinger, who held her snifter in her palm not nearly long enough to warm it before taking a hefty swallow.

"Elaine," Frau Erika von und zu Gossinger said, "I hope you won't take this to mean that Inge is a gossip but she tells me that not only are you and Netty friends but your husbands as well."

I guess that was the opening statement.

"Allan," Netty said, "Elaine's husband, saved my husband's life in Vietnam. They're very close."

"The reason I brought that up," Erika said, "is that I am about to get into a subject I would really rather share only with friends."

"I'd be happy to take a walk . . ." Elaine said.

"I'd rather you stayed," Netty said.

Frau Erika nodded.

"Netty," she said, "I'm afraid I'm going to try to impose on your friendship, and your husband's friendship, in dealing with a matter of some delicacy."

"I can't imagine you imposing," Netty said.

Oh yes I can.

"And I'm sure my husband," Netty continued, "would be honored to try to do whatever you asked of him."

"Thank you," Erika said. "A little over twelve years ago, it was on February thirteenth, a child, a boy, was born out of wedlock to an eighteen-year-old girl."

"That's always sad," Netty said.

Five-to-one Daddy's an American.

"The father was an American," Erika said. "A helicopter pilot."

No fooling? How many thousands of times has some GI knocked up a German girl and promptly said, "Auf wiedersehn!"

Pastor Dannberg slid an envelope across the table to Netty.

"That's the boy," he said. "He's a fine young man. Very bright."

Netty opened the envelope and took out a photograph of a skinny blond boy of, she guessed, about twelve.

Hell, she said, ". . . over twelve years ago."

The boy was wearing short pants, knee-high white stockings, a blue jacket with an insignia embroidered on the breast pocket, a white shirt and tie, and a cap, sort of a short-brimmed baseball cap with red-colored seams and the same insignia.

That's the uniform of Saint Johan's School, as I damn well know, for all the marks I spent sending two of mine there.

Okay. So this poor kid—not poor, unfortunate: Saint Johan's is anything but cheap—is in Saint Johan's. Which explains why Pastor Dannberg is involved.

"Handsome child," Netty said and slid the photograph to Elaine.

"Beautiful child," Elaine said.

"It has become necessary for the mother to get in contact with the boy's father," Erika said.

"A question of child support?" Netty said. "I'm sure my husband will do whatever he can . . ."

"No. Not of child support."

"The father's been supporting the boy?"

I'll be damned. A horny sonofabitch who's met his obligations.

"I don't think . . . I know . . . he doesn't know the boy exists," Erika said. "No effort was ever made to contact him."

My God, why not?

"May I ask why now?" Netty said.

"The boy's mother is very ill," Erika said. "And there is no other family."

"Oh, how sad!" Netty said.

And what will happen, if Freddy can track Daddy down, is that he will deny, swearing on a stack of Bibles, that he ever took a fraulein to bed all the time he was here and that he certainly has no intention of starting now to support somebody else's bastard.

Goddammit. Men should be castrated at birth.

But what did she say? It wasn't a question of child support?

Netty carefully considered her words, then continued: "As I'm sure you're aware . . . and you, Pastor Dannberg . . . I'm ashamed to say that this boy is not the first child to be abandoned by an American soldier. Do you have the father's name?"

"Jorge Castillo," Erika said. "He was a helicopter pilot and he was from Texas."

"May I speak bluntly?" Netty asked after a long moment's thought.

"Of course."

"I think my husband can probably find this man—that seems an unusual name—but I also think it's possible, even likely, that this man will be less than willing to acknowledge a child who, as you said, he doesn't even know he's had."

"We've thought about that, of course," Pastor Dannberg said.

"And, however remote," Erika added, "there is the possibility that he will be pleased to learn he has a son and be willing to assume his parental obligations."

There is also the possibility that pigs can be taught to whistle. In twelve years— if this guy wasn't already married—Poppa already has a wife and children and the last thing he wants his wife to know is he left a bastard in Germany who he is now expected to take into his happy home.

"Please believe me when I say I'm trying to be helpful," Netty said. "But there are certain questions I just have to ask."

"I understand."

"Does the mother have other children?"

"No. She never married."

Well, that answers my next question: What does Mamma's husband have to say about this?

"She raised the boy by herself? And never married?"

"She never married and she raised the boy by herself," Erika said.

"This is an indelicate question," Netty said. "Forgive me for asking it. But I have to. How does she know this man is the father?"

"She knows. No other possibility exists. He was her first, and only, lover. They were . . . together . . . three times. The first night, and then the next."

"I really hate to say this, but how can we know that?"

"Because I'm telling you," Erika said.

"But, Erika, how do you *know*?" Netty pursued.

"Because we are talking about my son, Netty," Erika von und zu Gossinger said.

[TWO]
Headquarters
Eleventh Armored Cavalry Regiment
Downs Barracks
Fulda, Hesse, West Germany
1545 7 March 1981

The sergeant major of the Eleventh "Blackhorse" Armored Cavalry Regiment, a stocky thirty-nine-year-old from Altoona, Pennsylvania, named Rupert Dieter, put his shaven head in the door of the colonel's office.

"You have time for the colonel's lady?" Dieter asked.

Colonel Frederick J. Lustrous, Armor, a tall, muscular forty-five-year-old, was visibly surprised at the question—Netty almost never came to the office—but rose to the occasion.

"There was some doubt in your mind, Sergeant Major?"

"She told me to ask, Colonel," Sergeant Major Dieter said.

"Inform the lady nothing would give me greater pleasure," Lustrous said.

Headquarters of the Eleventh Armored Cav was a three-story masonry building built—like most facilities occupied by the U.S. Army—in the years leading up to World War II for the German Army.

Stables built for the horses of the Wehrmacht now served as shops to maintain the tanks, armored personnel carriers, and wheeled vehicles used by the Blackhorse to patrol the border between East and West Germany.

Fulda traces its history to a monastery built in 744 A.D. It lies in the upper Fulda River valley, between the Vogelsberg and Rhoen mountain ranges.

Since the beginning of the Cold War, it had been an article of faith—with which Colonel Lustrous personally, if very privately, strongly disagreed—in the European Command that when Soviet tanks rolled into West Germany they would come through the "Fulda Gap."

The mission of the Blackhorse was to patrol the border, now marked by barbed wire, observation towers, mined fields, and whatever else the East Germans and their Soviet mentors could think of to keep East Germans from fleeing the benefits of Marxist-Leninism and seeking a better life in West Germany.

It was Colonel Lustrous's private belief—he was a student of Soviet tactics generally and of the Red Army Order of Battle in great detail—that if the Red Army did come through the Fulda Gap, they would do so in such numbers that they would cut through the Blackhorse—which was, after all, just three squadrons spread out over a very long section of the border—like a hot knife through butter.

The most the Blackhorse could do, if Soviet T-34 tanks came, would be to slow them down a little, like a speed bump on a country road. Lustrous was confident that the men of the Blackhorse would "acquit themselves well" if he was wrong and the Russians came. By that, he meant they would not run at the first sight of the Russians but fight.

Many—perhaps most—of his men would die, and the dead would be better off than those who survived and were marched off into Soviet captivity. Lustrous was a student of how the Red Army treated its prisoners, too. Lustrous knew a great deal about the Soviets and their army. He truly believed that "Know your enemy" was a military principle right up there with "Don't drink on duty." Failure to abide by either would very likely get you killed.

He was now on his third tour on the border between East and West Germany. He'd been a Just Out of West Point second lieutenant assigned to the Fourteenth Constabulary Squadron in Bad Hersfeld in 1948. The Fourteenth had been redesignated the Fourteenth Armored Cavalry Regiment when Captain Lustrous returned to the border after service in the Korean War. And when Colonel Lustrous returned from Vietnam, he found "the Regiment" was now the Eleventh "Blackhorse" Armored Cavalry, the colors of the Fourteenth having been furled for reasons he never really understood.

The desk behind which Colonel Lustrous now sat was the very same desk in the very same room of the very same building in the kaserne—now called "Downs Barracks"—before which Lieutenant Lustrous had once stood—literally on the carpet—while the then colonel had told him exactly how much of a disgrace he was to the Regiment, to Cavalry and Armor, and the United States Army in general.

Colonel Lustrous really didn't remember what he had done wrong, only that if the colonel had eaten his ass out at such length and with such enthusiasm it had probably been pretty bad, and was probably alcohol induced, as Netty, whom he had married the day after he'd graduated from the Point, had not yet joined him in Germany to keep him under control.

He had served under the colonel again in the Pentagon, when there were two stars on each of the colonel's epaulets, and he had been a light colonel, and there was no question in Lustrous's mind that he now commanded the Blackhorse because the colonel—now with four stars on each epaulet—had told somebody he thought "giving the Blackhorse to Freddy Lustrous might be a pretty good idea."

———

Lustrous, who was in well-worn but crisply starched fatigues and wearing nonauthorized tanker's boots, stood up as his wife came in the office.

He thought, as he often did, that Netty was really a good-looking woman.

She wasn't twenty as she had been when they had married, but three kids and all this time in the Army had not, in his judgment, attacked her appearance as much as would be expected.

"And to what do I owe this great, if unexpected, honor?" Lustrous said. "I devoutly hope it's not to tell me that it wasn't your fault, but that serious physical damage has happened to 'the Investment.' "

He was making reference to the Mercedes 380SEL. It was far too grand an automobile for a colonel. But Lustrous found out that if you didn't have the Army ship the battered family Buick to Germany when you were ordered there, and, instead, on arrival bought one of the larger Mercedes at the substantial discount offered by the Daimler-Benz people, you could drive the luxury car all through your tour, then have the Army ship it home for you. Then you could sell it in the States for more than you had paid in Germany. And so, to Lustrous, in that sense the family car was the Investment.

Netty was not amused.

Pissed? Or angry? Or both?

"I need to talk to you, Freddy," she said. "I'm glad you're here."

"You want some coffee?" he asked, sitting down and gesturing for her to take a seat.

"No," she said and then changed her mind. "Yes, I do. Thank you."

He spun in his chair to a table behind his desk, which held a stainless steel thermos and half a dozen white china coffee mugs bearing the regimental insignia.

He poured an inch and a half of coffee into each of them. That was the way they drank coffee: no cream, no sugar, just an inch and a half. It stayed hot that way and you tasted the coffee.

He stood up, walked to her, and handed her one of the mugs.

"How was lunch?" he asked.

"I don't think I'll ever forget it," Netty said.

The colonel took a sip of coffee and thought, *Which tells us that whatever is bothering her happened while she was at lunch.*

"Who all was there?" Lustrous asked as he walked back behind his desk.

"Well, Frauburgermeister Liptz, of course," Netty said. "And Pastor Dannberg of Saint Johan's. And Frau Erika von und zu Gossinger."

Inge Liptz, Lustrous knew, was the wife of Fulda's mayor. Pastor Dannberg was a tiny little man who ran with an iron hand not only Saint Johan's Church but the *Evangalische*—Protestant—communities of the area as well. Frau Erika von und zu Gossinger was the only daughter—*sort of the old maid aunt,* Lustrous thought privately—of the Gossinger family, who owned, among a good deal else, three of the newspapers serving the area, the Gossingerbrau Brewery, and a good deal of farmland.

Lustrous had been surprised when Netty had gotten the invitation to the House in the Woods. Although he and the Old Man had been friends before he killed himself on the autobahn, there had never been an invitation to the house for Netty. The Old Man's wife was dead, his only son had never married, and the daughter, if she entertained socially, did not, so far as Lustrous knew, ever invite Americans.

"That's surprising," Lustrous said. "What was the invitation all about?"

Netty did not reply.

"Just the five of you?" he asked.

"That was it, Fred," Netty said. "Inge, the Pastor and Frau Erika, Elaine and me."

"Well, what did you think of the House in the Woods?" he asked.

"I'm trying to frame my thoughts, Fred," Netty said, a little impatiently.

"Sorry."

"Lovely lunch," Netty said. "Roast boar. Her dining room overlooks the border. While we were eating, two of your patrols rolled by. Frau Erika showed me what used to be their property on the other side of the fence."

"I've been up there. The last time was last year, with her father, when we put the radio link in?"

"I remember," Netty said, somewhat impatiently. "Okay, here we go." She went into her purse and came out with a photograph and handed it to her husband.

"What am I looking at?" Fred Lustrous inquired.

"One of our love children," Netty said, bitterly.

"Really?" he asked.

As General George S. Patton used to say, Colonel Lustrous thought, *"A soldier who won't fuck won't fight." And that's probably true. But why can't the irresponsible sonsofbitches use a condom?*

"According to Frau Erika," Netty said, "the father is a chopper jockey who was here a dozen years ago, just long enough to sow his seed."

"How does she know that?"

"That's Karl Wilhelm von und zu Gossinger," Netty said. "Frau Erika's only child. The 'Frau' is apparently honorific."

"Let me make sure I have this right," Lustrous said. "This kid is Frau Erika's kid, and his father is an American?"

"You got it," she said. "And she wants you to find him."

"Oh, Jesus!"

"As quickly as possible," Netty said. "And, of course, as quietly and discreetly as possible."

"Why? After all this time?"

"Frau Erika doesn't have much time. She has, she said, between two and four months. Pancreatic cancer, inoperable. She's already taking medicine for the pain."

"This whole thing sounds . . . unbelievable," Lustrous said.

"That was my first reaction," Netty said. "But Pastor Dannberg has apparently been aware of the boy since . . . since she became pregnant. It's real, Fred."

"And this helicopter pilot didn't want to marry her?"

"She said she's sure he doesn't know about the child," Netty said. "This wasn't said, but it seems obvious to me: The family preferred that she bear this child . . . she was eighteen when she had him, by the way . . . out of wedlock, rather than the alternative, which was seeing the blood line corrupted by marriage."

"What do you mean, 'corrupted'? By an American, you mean?"

"Not just an American. According to her, the father of that blond boy is Jorge Alejandro Castillo. From Texas."

"Oh, boy!" Colonel Lustrous said.

"Yeah, Freddy, 'Oh, boy!' " Netty said.

"Let me see what I can do," he said. And then a thought popped into his mind and he asked it aloud, "Does the boy know?"

"I don't know," Netty said. "She'll have to tell him, if she hasn't already."

"Let me see what I can find out," Lustrous said.

Netty met his eyes, then nodded, then stood up.

"You're coming home for supper?" she asked.

He nodded.

"We're having roast boar," Netty said. "As we were getting in the investment to come back, a maid came out with an enormous platter of food wrapped in aluminum foil. The maid said Frau Erika wanted me to have it; otherwise, it would go to waste."

"I like roast boar," he said.

"I know," she said. "When you were a lieutenant, you and the colonel used to shoot them with Thompsons and give the meat to Saint Johan's."

"I've told you that story, have I?"

"I was here, dear," she said. "A still-blushing bride. And I almost left you when you walked into the house staggering under the weight of the ugliest animal carcass I had ever seen and made it clear that I was expected to turn it into dinner."

He chuckled.

"There's more than enough, if you want to ask anyone," Netty said.

"The Naylors?" he asked.

"Why not?"

She walked to him, kissed him, and said, "Do me a favor, Freddy. Don't put this on a back burner."

"I'll get right on it," he said.

He led her to the door with his arm around her shoulder.

Sergeant Major Dieter looked up from his desk.

"See if Major Naylor is available, will you, please?" Colonel Lustrous said to him.

[THREE]
Headquarters
Eleventh Armored Cavalry Regiment
Downs Barracks
Fulda, Hesse, West Germany
0740 7 March 1981

"How are we doing, Sergeant Major?" Colonel Frederick J. Lustrous greeted Sergeant Major Rupert Dieter as he walked into his office. But before Dieter could reply, Lustrous went on, "But before we get into that, you might want to put a quiet word into the ear of the mess sergeant of Baker Troop, First Squadron."

"Yes, sir?"

"I had breakfast there."

"Uh-oh."

"Uh-huh. You take my point, Sergeant Major?"

"I will have lunch there, sir."

"It was really bad, Dieter," Lustrous said. "And that's one of the things we just can't have."

"I'll take care of it, sir."

"I leave the matter in your capable hands, Sergeant Major," Lustrous said and motioned for the sergeant major to follow him into his office.

Dieter snatched one of the three stainless steel thermos bottles from the coffee machine table and followed Lustrous into his office.

"Give me a second, Colonel," Dieter said. "What I want to show you is on my desk."

Lustrous nodded, said "Sure," took off his field jacket and hung it on a coat-tree, and then went behind his desk and sat down.

Dieter came back in the office a moment later carrying an eight-inch-thick stack of paper about fourteen inches across and twenty-two inches long fastened together with enormous Ace spring metal clips. On it sat a thin book bound in maroon-colored artificial leather.

"What the hell is that?" Lustrous asked.

"The regimental newspaper, sir," Dieter said. "Specifically, for the year 1969."

"Did you find Daddy in there?"

"Yes, sir, I think I did."

Dieter laid the stack of old newspapers on Lustrous's conference table and carefully opened it in about the middle.

"Want to have a look, sir?" Dieter asked.

Lustrous heaved himself out of his chair and walked to the table.

Dieter pointed to a somewhat faded photograph of two young officers in flight suits standing by the nose of an HU-1D.

"That's a Dog model," he said, indicating the Huey helicopter.

"Uh-huh," Dieter said.

The headline over the picture read, "BLACKHORSE TO TRAIN WITH SKYCAV."

The caption under the picture read, "1st Lt. James Biden (*left*), Ithaca, N.Y., and WOJG J.A. Castillo, San Antonio, Tex., of the 322nd Aviation Company shown by their HU-1D helicopter, one of eight which will participate in a three-week-long joint training exercise with troopers of the Blackhorse."

"It's a lousy photo," Lustrous said. "But he looks like he's fifteen years old."

"I noticed that, sir," Dieter said.

"Well, you found him," Lustrous said. "Good for you."

"You better hold off on that, sir," Dieter said. "That's not all I found."

He picked up the book bound in maroon artificial leather and handed it to Lustrous.

Lustrous looked at the title.

"The Medal of Honor?" he asked, curiously.

Dieter nodded.

"I stuck a piece of paper in it, sir," he said.

Lustrous found the slip of paper and opened the book to that page.

"Jesus H. Christ!" he said when he found himself looking at another photograph of Warrant Officer Jorge Alejandro Castillo, this one, he guessed, taken when Castillo had graduated from flight school. Castillo also looked like he was fifteen years old.

"I don't think there's too many guys who flew Hueys with a name like that," Dieter said. "I think that's your guy, Colonel."

Colonel Lustrous started to read the citation: " 'On 4 and 5 April 1971, while flying HU-1D helicopters in support of Operation Lam Son 719 . . .' " He stopped and looked at Dieter. "April '71? We were out of Vietnam by then."

"Not the aviators," Dieter said. "Air Force and Army. We left a bunch of them—plus some heavy artillery—behind to support the South Vietnamese. I looked Operation Lam Son 719 up."

"And?"

"The South Vietnamese went into Laos to cut the Ho Chi Minh Trail," Dieter said. "They got clobbered. And so did our choppers. We lost more than a hundred, and five times that many were shot up."

Lustrous dropped his eyes to the book again and continued: " '. . . time and again, Warrant Officer Castillo flew his aircraft into extremely heavy fire to rescue the crews of downed American helicopters. In the process he was twice shot down himself, and suffered painful wounds, contusions and burns, for which he refused medical treatment, as a result thereof. Warrant Officer Castillo was on his fifty-second rescue mission, in the fifth helicopter he operated during this period, when his aircraft was struck by heavy antiaircraft fire and exploded . . .' "

Lustrous looked at Dieter and repeated, "*Fifty-second* rescue mission?"

"That's what it says, sir. We lost, I told you, more than a hundred choppers. They mean destroyed, by that; it doesn't count the ones that got shot down. They really kicked our ass. A lot of chopper crews had to be either picked up or the VC would have gotten them."

"Well, it says he was given the medal posthumously," Lustrous said. "So it doesn't look as if he will be able to assume his parental obligations, does it?"

"He's buried in the Fort Sam Houston National Cemetery, sir," Dieter said. "They didn't get his body back right away."

"Sonofabitch," Lustrous said. "I didn't expect this."

"We don't know for sure it's our guy, sir. For sure, I mean."

"Oh, come on, Dieter!"

"You don't think it's possible, sir, that Frau Whatsername knew about this all along?"

"No, I don't," Lustrous said automatically, but then added, "Why would she do something like that?"

"Desperate women, shit, desperate people, do desperate things, Colonel. Things that don't make a lot of sense."

"I hate to agree with you, but I do," Lustrous said. "This situation has just become something that cannot be dealt with by someone of my pay grade."

"What are you going to do, sir?"

"I'm going to try to get General Towson to find a few minutes in his schedule for me," Lustrous said. "Try to get him on the horn, Sergeant Major."

"Yes, sir," Sergeant Major Dieter said and picked up one of the telephones on Lustrous's desk—there were two: one a local, commercial telephone, and the other connected to the Army network—and dialed a number from memory.

"Hey, Tony," he said after a moment. "Rupert Dieter. How they hanging, Fat Guy?"

There was a pause.

"Tony, my boss wants to speak to your boss. Possible?"

There was another pause and then Dieter said, "Thanks, Tony," and handed the phone to Colonel Lustrous. "The V Corps Commander will be with you shortly, sir," he said.

"Thanks," Lustrous said.

He had to wait fifteen seconds before Lieutenant General Robert B. Towson, Commanding General, V United States Corps, came on the line.

"Towson."

"Good morning, General. Lustrous."

"What can I do for you, Fred?"

"Sir, I need about ten minutes of your time and some guidance. If there's a chopper available, I'd appreciate a ride. If not, I'll drive."

"Obviously, you don't want to talk about this on the phone."

"I'd rather not, sir."

"Personal matter, Fred?"

"No, sir. There's a personal element. I was just thinking: For the good of the service."

"Okay. You and I are on for lunch. A chopper will be there in thirty minutes. And you don't even have to change out of those oil-stained fatigues and illegal boots. Okay?"

"Thank you very much, General."

General Towson hung up without saying anything else.

"Okay," Lustrous said. "There will be a chopper here in thirty minutes. You, me, and Major Naylor. Locate Colonel Stevens and tell him I said I want him to come here and mind the store."

Lieutenant Colonel Charles D. Stevens was the executive officer of the Blackhorse.

"Yes, sir," Sergeant Major Dieter said.

[FOUR]
Office of the Commanding General
V Corps
The I.G. Farben Building
Frankfurt am Main, West Germany
1035 7 March 1981

"Sir, Colonel Lustrous is here," Sergeant Major Anthony J. Sanguenetti, a large, dark, almost entirely bald forty-five-year-old, said into the intercom on his desk.

"Is he alone?"

"No, sir, he has Major Naylor and a really ugly sergeant major with him."

"All of you come in, and tell Lownsdale no calls until I say so."

"Yes, sir," Sanguenetti said and looked up at Lustrous. "Sir, the Corps commander will see you, Major Naylor, and Ol' Whatsisname over there now."

Sergeant Major Dieter gave Sergeant Major Sanguenetti the finger as he walked past him to enter General Towson's office.

Lustrous, Naylor, and Dieter saluted crisply. Towson returned it with an almost casual wave of the hand.

"When Tony said 'ugly,' " he said, rising from his chair to offer his hand to Sergeant Major Dieter, "I knew it had to be you. How are you, Rupert? Too long a time no see."

"It's good to see you, too, sir."

"You look skinny," General Towson said. "He been overworking you?"

"Yes, sir. He has."

"So I guess you know what this is all about?"

"Yes, sir."

"Then you should, too, Tony," General Towson said. "Close the door."

Towson waited until the door was closed, then looked at Lustrous.

"One sentence, Fred," he said. "For the good of the service?"

"Sir, I think it's very probable that just before he went to Vietnam, where he earned a posthumous Medal of Honor, a young warrant officer impregnated a German girl to whom he was not married."

Towson looked at him for a long moment.

"That's one hell of a one-sentence summary, Fred," he said. "I was expecting to hear something like 'hanky-panky in dependent housing.' "

Lustrous didn't reply.

"You're sure of your facts?" Towson asked.

"No, sir, but I'd bet ten-to-one on what we think."

"Why did this come up now? The mother just found out the guy was a hero?"

"No, sir. The mother just found out she's dying—pancreatic cancer—and there is no other family here to take care of the boy, who is now twelve."

"Why do you think she's telling the truth?"

"I was a friend of her father's, sir. And she is not after money."

"How do you know that?"

"Because she has more than she needs. She's Frau Erika von und zu Gossinger, General. There's a brewery, three newspapers, and other properties."

"Related to the guy who wiped himself out on the autobahn?"

"That was her father, sir, and her brother."

"And how did this come to your attention?"

"She told Netty, General. Yesterday at lunch. I think she's telling the truth, sir."

"She probably is, but we can't take any chances," General Towson said. "Tony, get on the horn to Saint Louis, tell them to fax us . . . what's this fellow's name?"

"Warrant Officer Junior Grade Jorge Alejandro Castillo, sir," Sergeant Major Dieter furnished.

". . . Mr. Castillo's service record, and any other information they have about him right now, and to follow that up with Xeroxes of same sent by the most expeditious means. If they say they can't do it today, you tell them I said if they said they can't I'm going to route my request through the chief of staff. If they ask why, you don't know. Got it?"

"Yes, sir."

"Do that right now," Towson said. "Rupert can bring you up to speed about what we talk about now."

"Yes, sir," Sergeant Major Sanguenetti said and looked at Sergeant Major Dieter, who was writing Mr. Castillo's full name on a sheet of paper. When Dieter handed it to him, Sanguenetti left the office.

Towson looked at Lustrous.

"Getting records out of Saint Louis is like pulling teeth," he said. "I actually had to go to the chief of staff a couple of weeks ago. I hope they remember that." He paused thoughtfully and then went on. "Okay. Let's say you're right, Fred . . . and if Netty believes this woman, you probably are. Where do we go from here?"

Colonel Lustrous had served under General Towson twice and correctly suspected here that sentence was rhetorical and Towson did not expect an answer.

"If Mr. Castillo was married," Towson went on, "that's one situation. Death benefits and possibly a pension would have gone to his widow, benefits to which this German boy may be entitled. I'll have a talk with the judge advocate and get the details. If he wasn't married, that's another situation. Okay. We don't know enough now to make any kind of a decision. The only thing I can think of right now is to get a blood sample. A little coldheartedly, if there's a match it won't prove anything. If there's not, it would prove there was no parental relationship. So the only thing I can tell you to do, Fred, is to get a sample, a large sample, of the boy's blood, and make sure we can testify we were there when the sample was taken and that the blood never left our custody."

"Yes, sir," Lustrous said and looked at Major Naylor, who said, "Yes, sir."

"What did he do to get the Medal of Honor?" Towson asked.

"Sir, are you familiar with Operation Lam Son 719?"

Towson searched his memory, then nodded.

"Mr. Castillo was on his fifty-second rescue mission, picking up downed chopper crews, when he was hit and his Huey blew up."

"I know that story," Towson said. "He kicked his copilot and crew chief out of his bird, told them there was no sense all of them getting killed. That young man really had a large set of balls." He heard what he had said and added: "An unfortunate choice of words, right? I have an unfortunate tendency to do that."

[FIVE]
Headquarters
Eleventh Armored Cavalry Regiment
Downs Barracks
Fulda, Hesse, West Germany
1640 7 March 1981

"Sir, I have Frau von Gossinger on the line," Sergeant Major Dieter called from the outer office.

"That's 'von und zu,' Dieter," Lustrous said, gestured for Major Naylor to pick up the extension on the conference table, and then picked up the telephone on his desk.

"Fred Lustrous here, Frau Erika," Lustrous said.

"Good afternoon, Colonel."

"There have been some developments in this situation," Lustrous said. "I'd really like to discuss them with you in person rather than over the telephone. Would that be possible?"

"Of course."

"When would that be convenient for you?"

"Whenever it is for you," she said. "Now, if you'd like."

"I thought I would bring Netty with me," Lustrous said, "and Elaine Naylor, and her husband, Major Naylor, who's going to help us with this."

"Of course."

"It will take me, say, thirty minutes to go home, pick up the ladies, and change out of my work uniform, and then forty-five minutes or so to drive up there. That would make it a little after six-thirty. Would that be all right?"

"That would be fine, Colonel. And there is no necessity for you to change uniforms. And if you have the time, please take supper with us."

"That's very kind," Lustrous said. "But I don't want to impose."

"Don't be silly. It is I who is imposing on your friendship with my father. I will expect you sometime before seven. And thank you."

There was a click as the line went dead.

Lustrous looked at Naylor.

"She said 'supper with us,' Colonel," Naylor said.

"Yeah, I heard," Lustrous said. Then he raised his voice: "Rupert!"

Sergeant Major Dieter put his head in the doorway.

"I heard," he said. "You want me to drive you?"

"No, I think we'll go in the Mercedes," Lustrous said. "Will you make sure Colonel Stevens knows he's minding the store?"

"Yes, sir," Dieter said. "Sir, if you want I can give the ladies a heads-up."

"Good idea. Thank you. Lie. Tell them we're already on the way. I'll bring you up to speed first thing in the morning."

"Sir, your call. Since I couldn't make lunch with Baker Troop today, I thought I might make breakfast tomorrow."

"Do it," Lustrous ordered. "I'll see you when you get here."

[SIX]
Haus im Wald
Near Bad Hersfeld
Kreis Hersfeld-Rotenburg
Hesse, West Germany
1845 7 March 1981

The first time Major Allan B. Naylor, Armor, saw Carlos Guillermo Castillo, he was standing beside his mother on the flagstone steps of *das Haus im Wald* as they drove up in Lustrous's Mercedes. The boy was wearing a nearly black suit with a white shirt and tie and his blond hair was neatly combed.

The Naylors had two sons, a fourteen-year-old and a ten-year-old, and the first thing Allan Naylor thought was, *There's not much fun in that kid's life.*

That was closely followed by, *Shit, and now this!*

Colonel Lustrous had taken Frau Erika von und zu Gossinger at her word. He and Naylor were still wearing fatigues. Their wives were more formally dressed.

Mother and son waited on the steps for the Lustrouses and the Naylors to get out of the Mercedes and walk up to them.

"How good it is to see you again, Colonel Lustrous," Frau Erika said, offering her hand. "Welcome."

"Thank you," Lustrous said. "May I introduce my good friend, Major Allan Naylor?"

"Of course, Elaine's husband. How do you, Major?"

Netty walked up to Frau Erika and kissed her on the cheek and then Elaine did.

"And this is my son," Frau Erika said. "Karl Wilhelm."

The boy put out his hand first to Netty, then Elaine, then Lustrous, and finally Naylor, and each time said, in English, "How do you do? I am pleased to meet you."

His English, while obviously not the American variety, was accentless, neither the nasal British variety taught by English teachers at Saint Johan's—which Allan B. Naylor III had brought home and earned him the nickname "Lord Fauntleroy"—or the to be expected German-accented English of a young German boy.

"My boy goes to Saint Johan's," Elaine said. "Allan? Do you know him?"

"He is two forms before me . . . *ahead* of me," Karl Wilhelm von und zu Gossinger said. "I know who he is."

"Why don't we go in the house and have a cocktail?" Frau Erika said.

A maid in a white apron stood behind a bar set up on a table in the library. There were bottles of Gossingerbrau in dark bottles with ceramic and rubber stoppers, bottles of German and French white and red wine, French and German champagne, bourbon and scotch whiskey, gin, cognac, and an array of glasses to properly serve any of it.

Lustrous, Netty, and Allan Naylor asked for scotch; Elaine Naylor said she thought she would have a glass of Rumpoldskirchener, and Frau Erika poured a snifter heavily with cognac.

"Welcome, friends, all of you, to our home," Frau Erika said, raising her glass. "What is it you taught my father to say, Oberst Lustrous? 'Mud in your eye'? Mud in your eye!"

She took, everyone noticed, a healthy pull of her cognac.

"I don't know what that means," Karl Wilhelm von und zu Gossinger said.

"Either do I, come to think of it, Karl," Lustrous said. "Is it all right if I call you Karl?"

"Yes, sir. Of course," the boy said.

"Would you mind, Karl, if we had a private word with your mother?" Lustrous said.

"Of course not, sir."

"Frau Erika?" Lustrous said.

"Of course," she said. "Karl, would you go into Grosspappa's office for a moment?"

Karl didn't like it all, but he nodded curtly and walked to the far end of the library. Lustrous saw there was an office of some kind in an adjoining room. There was a desk, a typewriter, a leather armchair, and several tables in a small room lined with bookcases.

"When my father was very angry about something," Frau Erika said, "he used to go there to write the editorial. He said it was very difficult to stay angry in there."

"Then I have to presume most of the editorials I read were not written here," Lustrous said.

Frau Erika smiled at him.

"He also used to say losing your temper had to be a sin; it was so pleasurable," she said.

Lustrous smiled and turned to Netty.

"Can I have that, please, honey?" he asked.

Netty dug in her purse and came up with a plasticized Xerox copy of the newspaper photograph. Spec5 Sam Rowe, Sergeant Major Dieter's jack-of-all-trades, had spent several hours doing the best he could.

Netty handed it to her husband, who wordlessly handed it to Frau Erika.

She looked at it carefully and then at Lustrous.

"Yes, that's him. It must have been taken at the time. My God, he was so young! Only nineteen!"

"I'm afraid I have to tell you that he was killed in Vietnam," Lustrous said.

Erika met his eyes for a moment, then nodded.

"Somehow I knew that," she said. "He said . . . he said that I would probably not hear from him much, he wasn't much at writing letters. But that as soon as he came home from the war, he would come back. I was very young. I believed him. Even when there were no letters at all. It's easy to believe when you are young."

"For what it's worth, he died a hero," Lustrous said.

"It doesn't mean anything to me but it will to Karl," Erika said and raised her voice. *"Karl, kumst du hier, bitte!"*

She sounded almost gay. Lustrous saw the cognac snifter was just about empty and then looked at Netty and saw the pain in her eyes.

The boy came back from the small office.

"Yes, Mother?"

"Oberst Lustrous has brought a photograph, from a newspaper, of your father," Erika said.

The boy said nothing. Erika handed him the plastic-covered clipping.

He looked at it and then at his mother.

"He never came back to us, Karl, because he was killed in the war," Erika said.

"Your father was quite a hero, Karl," Lustrous said.

"Mother said he is dead," the boy said.

"He was killed while trying to rescue other helicopter pilots," Naylor said.

"So how, if I may ask, will that affect things?" the boy asked.

"Excuse me?" Lustrous said.

"If he is dead, I cannot go to him, can I?"

Naylor thought: *That means, of course, he knows about his mother. His reaction is coldblooded; to learning that his father is dead and that he now will have no family at all.*

"Karl," Netty said softly, "we've asked for his records; they will be sent here shortly. I can't promise this, but it's possible, even likely, that your father had a family . . ."

"And I would go to them? No. I will not. Pastor Dannberg says I can stay at Saint Johan's . . ."

"But if there is a family," Netty said, "they would love you . . ."

"Why would they love me? Mother says they don't know I exist."

That's true, Naylor thought. *And the boy senses, or has figured out, that it would be one hell of a transition, from das Haus im Wald to Texas, even if he doesn't understand that with a name like Castillo it's highly probable that his life in Texas would be that of a Tex-Mex, and that's not at all like that of an upper-class German.*

Naylor had developed his own theory of how nineteen-year-old Jorge Alejandro Castillo had wound up flying a Huey first in Germany and then in Vietnam.

There were two reasons seventeen- and eighteen-year-old young men had gone into the Army during the Vietnam War. It seldom had anything to do with patriotic notions of rushing to the colors, but rather with their economic situation and the draft. If there was no money to go to college, and get an educational deferment, the draft was damned near inevitable.

Jorge Alejandro Castillo had been bright enough to get into the Warrant Officer Candidate Program, which meant that he was certainly bright enough to get into college. That he had not gone suggested strongly that there hadn't been money for college. Naylor knew that Army recruiters had regularly trolled high schools for seniors about to graduate, and, specifically, for those who couldn't afford college. Their sales pitch was that if the kids enlisted now, rather than waiting for the inevitable draft, they would be "guaranteed" their choice of specialty, which almost invariably meant being trained in electronics or automobile mechanics, which also meant they wouldn't be handed a rifle and told to go kill people.

The offer was valid. The training was given as promised. The price was a three-year enlistment. Draftees had to serve two years. The Army got another year of service, during which the kid got the five to eight months of specialist training promised and he then could serve for two years in his specialty. On the kid's side, he got the training, and, if he didn't screw up in training, he didn't go to the infantry.

What happened when the kid got to the reception center was that he was given the Army General Classification Test, which was sort of a combined aptitude and intelligence test. The average GI scored between 90 and 100. Scores of 110 or better qualified the new soldier for such things as Officer Candidate School and the longer, more technical specialist courses. When a kid turned in a score of 120 or better, he came to the attention of a lot of people who needed really bright young men. Such as helicopter pilots.

Putting this all together, Naylor had reasoned that Jorge Alejandro Castillo had joined the Army to be trained as an electronics repairman, or some such, and to be kept out of the infantry. He had scored really high on the AGCT and been recruited for the Warrant Officer Candidate Program. It wasn't hard to get a kid to agree to swap his promised training as a radio fixer for training as a pilot, and the flight pay and status of a warrant officer that went with it.

Naylor remembered a sign he had seen in an Officers' Club Annex at Fort Rucker, the Army Aviation Center in Alabama. It had read:

WARRANT OFFICER PILOTS WISHING TO DRINK BEER **MUST** HAVE A PERMISSION NOTE FROM THEIR MOMMY.

That was a joke, but there had been a lot of warrant officer pilots already back from a Vietnam tour who had had to do their drinking on post because they were too young to be served alcohol off post.

Jorge Alejandro Castillo was by no means the only Huey pilot who had looked like he was fifteen.

The bottom line to this was that Major Allan B. Naylor thought it entirely likely that Karl Wilhelm von und zu Gossinger of *das Haus im Wald* was about to find himself transported to a low-income housing development in Texas, and possibly even to one in which English was a second language.

"They would love you, Karl, because they are your family," Frau Erika said.

"Mother, that's nonsense and you know it is," the boy said. "I am not going. And no one can make me."

He marched angrily out of the library.

"I will talk to him," Frau Erika said.

"This has to be tough for him," Elaine Naylor said.

"There are no other options for him," Frau Erika said.

"Erika," Colonel Lustrous said, "there's something else."

She looked at him.

"To prove that Karl is indeed Mr. Castillo's son, we're going to have to have a sample of Karl's blood."

"Really?" she replied, icily.

"And as quickly as possible," Lustrous said.

"I suppose it was naïve of me to think I would be taken at my word, even by you."

"I take you at your word," Lustrous said.

"Do you, really?"

"Yes, I do," Lustrous said, flatly.

"We all do, Erika," Netty said.

"Very well, we will bleed my son," Erika said. And then she smiled. "Shall we go into the dining room?"

Karl Wilhelm von und zu Gossinger—surprising all the Americans—was standing behind a chair at one end of the table politely waiting for the others to take their seats.

Neither he nor his mother gave any sign that he had lost his temper.

Wine was offered and poured.

Frau Erika held her hand over her wineglass and said, "I think I would like another taste of the cognac, please. Bring the bottle."

Halfway through the main course, Frau Erika said, "Karl, it will be necessary for you to have a blood sample drawn."

"The Americans won't take your word for what you have told them?" he replied.

"You will give blood," Frau Erika said. "Tomorrow, you will give blood."

"What I thought I would do, Karl," Allan Naylor said, "was come out here in the morning, drive you past the kaserne—Downs Barracks?—and, afterward, take you to Saint Johan's."

The boy studied him a moment.

"Wouldn't it make more sense, Herr Major, for Mother's driver to take me to school as he usually does and for you to meet me there? That would save you the drive all the way here."

"Yes, as a matter of fact, Karl, it would," Naylor said.

"Then it is settled. I will see you just inside the gate tomorrow morning."

"Deal," Naylor said.

The rest of the dinner was a disaster.

Erika—suddenly, Naylor thought—got very drunk, knocked over her glass, and then stood up.

"You will have to excuse me," she said. "I suddenly feel ill."

Netty and Elaine, seeing she was unsteady on her feet, jumped up and helped her out of the dining room.

"Mother's in great pain," Karl Wilhelm von und zu Gossinger said, matter-of-factly. "The cognac helps, but then she gets like that."

"We're all very sorry your mother is ill, Karl," Naylor said.

"Yes," Karl said. "It is a very unfortunate situation."

[SEVEN]
Quarters # 1
"The Pershing House"
Fort Sam Houston, Texas
0715 12 March 1981

The commanding general, Fifth United States Army, was in the breakfast room of the house named for—and once occupied by—General of the Armies John J. "Black Jack" Pershing when he was joined by Major Allan B. Naylor.

"Good morning, sir," Naylor said.

"Long time no see, Allan," General Amory T. Stevens said, offering his hand. He was a tall, very thin man with sharp features.

"Yes, sir," Naylor said. "General, I feel I'm imposing."

"Don't be silly. Could I do less for an officer who was once a darling baby boy I bounced on my knees? Sit down and have some coffee and then tell me what the hell this is all about."

"You're not eating?"

"I hate to eat alone. Marjorie's with her mother. And I didn't think you'd get up before noon. What time did you get in?"

"A little after three, sir."

"I said I don't like to eat alone. I didn't say I don't like breakfast."

"May I fry some eggs for you, sir?"

"I thought you would never ask," General Stevens said. "I will even go in the kitchen and watch."

Naylor opened the refrigerator and took out a carton of eggs and a package of bacon, and laid them on the table.

"I have what they call an 'enlisted aide' these days," General Stevens said. "Fine young man. But he's an even worse cook than I am. There's a frying pan in there." He pointed. "Sunny side up but not slimy, if you please. I know how to make toast. It's done by machine."

Naylor chuckled.

"I carry with me the compliments of Colonel Lustrous," Naylor said as he went looking for a frying pan.

"Since you won't be back over there in time to tell him and ruin the surprise, Freddy is now Brigadier General–designate Lustrous, to my—and a lot of other people's—surprise."

"Well, that's good news. He certainly deserves it. I'm not surprised."

"Freddy has always had an unfortunate tendency to tell his superiors they're wrong," Stevens said. "That usually results in getting you passed over. Your father being one of the rare exceptions."

"When did this happen?"

"Yesterday. That's where I was, in Washington, at the promotion board. Don't tell him I was on it. He'll take that as my approval of his big mouth."

"Which of course you don't?"

"There's a difference, Allan, between admiration and approval," General Stevens said. "Write that down."

"I'm going to need a spatula," Naylor said.

"One of those drawers," Stevens said, pointing. "And I know there are plates around here somewhere."

Naylor found the spatula and laid it on the stove.

"So what's this hush-hush mission for the good of the service you're on all about?" Then he had another thought: "Don't you want an apron?"

"That would be an excellent idea," Naylor said.

Stevens took an apron from the back of a door and handed it to him.

"I do know where some things are," he said. "So, what's up?"

"Twelve years ago, a young—very young—chopper pilot left a German girl in the family way before going off to Vietnam . . ."

"Oh, hell!"

". . . from which he did not return," Naylor went on. "And the mother is now terminally ill and went to Colonel Lustrous—actually, to Netty—and asked for help in finding him."

"I thought you said he didn't come back from 'Nam?"

"He didn't. What I'm doing now is making an initial reconnaissance for Colonel Lustrous to see what this guy's family is like. I have an address and after breakfast I'm going to go start looking."

"They have a thing now they call the telephone," General Stevens said. "All Freddy had to do was call me. I would have had somebody do this for you."

"General Towson 'suggested' to Colonel Lustrous that he send me over here," Naylor said.

"Bob Towson said send you?" General Stevens asked. "I must be missing something here, Allan. Why the fuss and feathers? I'm ashamed to say that a lot of our soldiers, PFCs through general officers, left German girls in the family way behind them. Thousands of them."

"Sir, I guess I left out that the father got the Medal of Honor in Vietnam."

"Yes, I guess you did," Stevens said. "That little fact does put a different color on things, doesn't it?"

"And Colonel Lustrous and the boy's grandfather—who wiped himself out on the autobahn several months ago—were good friends."

"What's Freddy concern? Personal and official?"

"I think, sir, he's worried—I know I am—that the father's family is going to be less than overjoyed to learn their son left an illegitimate child behind in Germany twelve years ago. If that's the case—they reject the idea—Colonel Lustrous wants to cushion the boy and his mother from that as much as possible."

"And Bob Towson is concerned about what would appear in the papers if the family and the mother get in a pissing match? 'GERMAN WOMAN CLAIMS MEDAL OF HONOR WINNER FATHER OF HER BASTARD CHILD'?"

"Yes, sir, I'm sure that's true."

"Well, you can't blame the mother wanting to make sure the child is fed and cared for," Stevens said. "And, on the other hand, you can't really blame the family for being suspicious of someone who claims to be the mother of a child fathered by the dead son."

"Yes, sir, that's true."

Naylor turned to the stove and flipped the bacon.

There was a knock at the kitchen door and then the door opened and a young clean-cut-looking buck sergeant came through it.

"Good morning, sir," he said.

"Pay attention to what the major is doing, Wally," General Stevens said. "One day, in a dire emergency, I may have to press you into service again."

"Yes, sir," the sergeant said with a smile.

"Major Naylor, Sergeant Wally Wallace," Stevens said.

"How are you, Sergeant?"

"How do you do, sir?"

"You had breakfast, Wally?" General Stevens asked.

"Yes, sir, I have. Thank you."

"What you hear here stays here, Wally, okay?"

"Yes, sir. Of course."

"You have a name, you said, Allan?" General Stevens asked.

"Yes, sir. The next of kin are the pilot's parents, Mr. and Mrs. Juan Fernando Castillo."

"Let me have that again?"

"The name I have for the next of kin is Castillo. Mr. and Mrs. Juan Fernando."

"This gets better and better. Or worse and worse. I shudder to think what interesting fact may next pop out of your mouth," General Stevens said.

"Sir?"

"Wally, go get Mrs. Stevens's phone book. The pink one. It's on her desk in the study."

"Yes, sir," Sergeant Wallace said.

"You know these people, sir?" Naylor asked.

"And the alleged father of this out-of-wedlock German child is Jorge Alejandro Castillo, am I right?"

"Yes, sir."

"Yeah, Allan, I know them," General Stevens said. "They own most of downtown San Antonio. Plus large chunks of the land outside the city. Plus a large ranch near Midland, under which is the Permian basin. And I don't really think Don Fernando . . ."

"*Juan* Fernando, sir," Naylor corrected him.

"I see Freddy has corrupted you, Allan. You too are too ready to correct your superiors when you make a snap judgment they're wrong. In the culture of which the Castillos are part, Mr. Juan Fernando Castillo is addressed as 'Don' Fernando as a mark of respect; much like they call upper-class Englishmen Sir John. Get it?"

"Yes, sir. Sorry."

Sergeant Wallace returned with a pink telephone book.

General Stevens sat down at the table and looked through it. Then he held up his hand. Sergeant Wallace took the handset of a wall telephone and put it in his hand. General Stevens punched in the number.

"Good morning," he said. "This is General Stevens, from Fort Sam. I apologize for calling at this hour. Would it be possible for me to speak with Don Fernando? It's a matter of some importance."

There was a reply, and then General Stevens went on.

"Perhaps Doña Alicia might be available? This is really important."

There was another reply, and then General Stevens went on again.

"Thank you very much, but no message. I'll call again. Thank you."

He broke the connection with his finger and held the telephone over his shoulder. Sergeant Wallace took it from him and hung it up.

"Don Fernando is 'out of town,' " Stevens said. "That may mean he's at their ranch, or it may mean he's in Dallas, New York, or Timbuktu. Doña Alicia is at the Alamo; she likes to get there early."

"The Alamo, sir?"

"You've heard of the Alamo, haven't you, Allan? John Wayne died there, defending it against the overwhelming forces of the Mexican General Santa Anna."

"Yes, sir."

"Being a general, Allan, as your father may have told you, is something like being an aviator. Long days and hours of utter boredom punctuated by moments of terror. I am now forced to make a decision whether to wait until I can meet with Don Fernando or to go over to the Alamo before he gets back and dump this in Doña Alicia's lap. No matter which decision I make it is likely to be the wrong one."

He paused, and then went on. "After two full seconds of thought, I have decided to go with my cowardly instincts and go to Doña Alicia. Her temper is not nearly as terrible as that of her husband."

Naylor, who didn't know what to say, said nothing.

"Wally, get on the horn and call the office and say I won't be in until I get there, and the only messages I want on the radio are from the chief of staff or an Operational Immediate saying Russian bombers are over San Antone."

"Yes, sir," Sergeant Wallace said and went to the wall telephone.

"Please tell me, Allan, that you haven't burned my bacon and eggs."

"I have not burned your bacon and eggs, sir."

[EIGHT]
Alamo Plaza
San Antonio, Texas
0835 12 March 1981

"Doña Alicia's office is in the Daughters of the Republic of Texas library," General Stevens said, pointing to the building. "And before we go in there, I think a little historical background is in order."

"Yes, sir," Major Naylor said.

"Contrary to what most people think, the Alamo is not owned by the federal government, or Texas, but is the property of the Daughters of the Republic of Texas. That organization is not unlike the Order of the Cincinnati, membership in which—I'm sure you know, since you and your father are members—is limited to direct lineal descendants of George Washington's officers. Membership in the Daughters of the Republic of Texas is limited to ladies who can claim to be direct descendants of men and women who rendered service to the Republic of Texas, before the republic struck a deal with Washington and joined the Union. It helps if your ancestor or ancestors died at the Alamo, but the battle of San Jacinto will also get you in if other ladies like you. With me so far?"

"Yes, sir."

"Doña Alicia Castillo has twice been president of this august organization, and it is reliably rumored that the Castillo family over the years has contributed a hell of a lot of money to keeping up the Alamo, and the San Jacinto Battlefield, and other historical things important to Texas. Getting the picture?"

"Yes, sir."

"I really don't know how she's going to react to the news that she has an illegitimate grandson in Germany. I suspect she's not going to be overwhelmed with joy."

"I understand, sir."

"I think the best plan of action is for me to do the talking, and for you to say no more than 'Yes, ma'am,' or 'No, ma'am.' "

"Yes, sir."

"In these circumstances, it seems to me—since Freddy and Netty Lustrous believe the mother . . ."

"Elaine and I do, too, sir," Naylor interrupted. "And we have the results of the blood test."

General Stevens gave him a frosty look and went on:

". . . that we have an obligation to see the boy gets what he's entitled to as the fruit of the loins of a fellow officer who was awarded the Medal of Honor. Among other things, the boy gets a pass into West Point, if he so desires. We cannot permit the Castillos to sweep this kid back under the rug, even if that means they are going to suffer some embarrassment."

"I understand, sir."

"So put a cork in your mouth when we get in there and let me do the talking."

"Yes, sir."

———

Doña Alicia Castillo, a trim woman who appeared to be in her late fifties, and whose jet-black hair, drawn tight in a bun, showed traces of gray, came to the door of her office when her secretary told her over the intercom that General Stevens, who did not have an appointment, was asking for a few minutes of her time.

"What an unexpected pleasure, General," she said, smiling and offering her hand. "Please, come in."

She turned and went into her office. Stevens and Naylor followed.

"Marjorie's well, I trust?" she said as she settled herself behind her desk. "I saw her last week at the United Fund luncheon."

"She's fine, Doña Alicia. She's visiting her mother."

"Please give her my regards," Doña Alicia said, and added, "Please sit down, and tell me what I can do for you."

"Doña Alicia," General Stevens said, "may I introduce my godson, Major Allan Naylor? His father and I were roommates at West Point."

"Well, I'm very pleased to meet you, Major Naylor. Welcome to the Alamo."

"Thank you, ma'am," Naylor said.

"A somewhat delicate matter has come up, Doña Alicia," General Stevens said.

"Is that so?"

"Allan, Major Naylor, has the details."

Doña Alicia smiled and looked at Naylor expectantly.

Jesus Christ, what happened to "let me do the talking" and "put a cork in your mouth"?

"The thing is, ma'am," Naylor began, hesitantly.

"Yes?"

"We have reason to believe that Mr. Castillo has a son in Germany," Naylor said.

She looked at him for a moment without a change of expression.

"Somehow, I suspect you are talking of my late son, Jorge," she said, evenly, "rather than my husband."

Jesus Christ, Naylor thought, *how fucking dumb can one major be?*

"Yes, ma'am, I am."

"And how did this come to your attention?" she asked.

"Ma'am, I'm stationed in Germany. In Fulda. The boy's mother went to my wife, and my commanding officer's wife . . ."

"Major Naylor is referring to Colonel Frederick Lustrous, Doña Alicia," General Stevens said. "I know him well. He's a very fine officer."

"I see," Doña Alicia said. "You were saying, Major?"

"Frau Gossinger . . ."

"Being the child's mother?" Doña Alicia interrupted.

"Yes, ma'am. The women are friends. And Colonel Lustrous and Frau Gossinger's late father were friends."

"And therefore you believe this . . . Frau Gossinger?"

"Yes, ma'am. And we know that the boy and Mr. Castillo . . . your late son . . . have the same blood type."

"I don't think that's conclusive proof of paternity, is it?"

"No, ma'am, it is not," Naylor admitted.

"This . . . would have had to be more than a dozen years ago?"

"Yes, ma'am. The boy is twelve."

"Do you have any idea why she brought this up now? Twelve years after the fact?"

"She is terminally ill, Mrs. Castillo," Naylor said.

"I don't suppose you would have a photograph of the child, would you?"

"Yes, ma'am, I do," Naylor said, and took several photographs from the breast pocket of his tunic.

"His name is Karl," Naylor said. "He's a really bright kid."

Doña Alicia stared at the first photograph for a long moment and then laid it down and stared at the second and then laid that down and stared at the third.

"Blond," she said. "And so fair-skinned."

"Yes, ma'am," Naylor said.

"Would you think me rude if I asked you gentlemen to wait outside for a few minutes?" Doña Alicia asked. "Grace will get you coffee. I think I should talk to my husband about this."

"Yes, of course," General Stevens and Major Naylor said, almost in unison.

They left the office and sat beside one another on a couch in the outer office. General Stevens looked at Major Naylor and raised his eyebrows.

"I don't think that went as well as it could have gone," Stevens said.

[NINE]
Room 714
The Plaza Hotel
New York City, New York
0955 12 March 1981

"Who the hell can that be?" Juan Fernando Castillo inquired almost angrily when the telephone rang, although there was no one else in the three-room suite.

He was a tall, heavyset man with a full head of dark hair. He was dressed in white Jockey shorts and a hotel-furnished terry cloth bathrobe. He had not knotted the cord, and his chest, covered with thick hair, was visible.

He laid *The Wall Street Journal* down on the room service table and tried to push back the chair he had just pulled up to it. It hung up on the carpet and fell over. In stepping over it, he bumped into the room service table, knocking over his freshly squeezed grapefruit juice, which, for some reason known only to God, the goddamned hotel served in a stemmed glass.

He walked to the telephone.

"What is it?" he snarled into it.

"Did I wake you, Fernando? It sounds as if I did."

"Actually, I was having my breakfast," he said. "Is something wrong, love of my life?"

"No, I would say quite the opposite."

"Then why did you call at this hour?"

"Because I really wanted to catch you before you left the hotel."

"What's up, Alicia?"

"I just found out we're grandparents."

"Funny, I seem to recall having five grandchildren," he said, then thought: *Four granddaughters and one grandson, out of three daughters. He has my Christian name, but his surname is Lopez. The Castillo name dies with me.*

"Now there are six. He is an absolutely beautiful boy of twelve."

"What the hell are you talking about?"

"It seems Jorge had a child, or started one, when he was in Germany."

Oh, my God!

"Start at the beginning, Alicia, please."

"You don't sound very thrilled."

"I would be thrilled if I believed it. Start at the beginning, Alicia."

"General Stevens came to the office just now," she said. "With him, he had a major who is stationed in Germany. He said that the major was his godson, that he and the major's father had been at West Point together."

What the hell has this to do with Jorge having a child?

"And?"

"The major—his name is Naylor—said that the boy's mother went to his wife and told her and some colonel's wife—they're friends—about the boy."

Oh, Sweet Jesus, please, Alicia doesn't need this!

When Jorge—their baby and their only son—had died, Juan Fernando Castillo had to seriously consider getting institutional care for his wife. It hadn't gotten that far, but she had been clinically depressed for more than a year, and she still had trouble at least twice a year, on Jorge's birthday and on the date of his death.

"Sweetheart, Jorge . . . left us . . . twelve years ago," he said.

"I know. I told you, the boy is twelve."

"What does General Stevens want us to do about this? Alicia, how does he know, how can we know, that the child is Jorge's?"

"Fernando, when I looked at the boy's picture—his name is Karl—Jorge's eyes looked back at me."

That's hardly proof of paternity.

Oh, sweetheart, I am so sorry. How could that goddamned General Stevens do this to you? What was the sonofabitch thinking?

"And what does General Stevens want us to do about this child?"

"I don't know what you mean."

"I mean, does he want us to provide support? What?"

"He didn't say anything about support. But if he's Jorge's son, our grandson, of course we'll support him. What a question!"

Oh, shit!

"Sweetheart, listen to me. If this is true . . ."

"Of course it's true!"

"We don't know that, sweetheart. Wishing it so doesn't make it so."

"He has Jorge's eyes," she said.

Screw his eyes.

"What I'm asking you to do, sweetheart, is just take it easy right now. I'll be home tomorrow and then we can talk about it. I'll have a word with General Stevens, get all the facts . . ."

"I'm telling you, Fernando, this is Jorge's child."

"If it is, no one would be happier than I would. But we don't know that, sweetheart. We have to be very careful in a situation like this."

"Now I'm becoming sorry that I called you," she said.

"Meaning what?"

"Meaning I'm sorry I called you," she said. "You're ruining this for me, Fernando. Sometimes you have a heart of ice."

"Honey, come on. I'm thinking of you. Listen to me. I can probably catch a plane later today. When I get home, we can talk about it."

She didn't reply.

"Sweetheart, will you do me a favor?"

"What?"

"Ask General Stevens if he can come to the office—or if we can go to his— first thing tomorrow morning."

The Citibank meeting will just have to wait. I simply can't let her go off the deep end again.

Why the hell didn't I bring the goddamned Lear? Because it's throwing money down the goddamned toilet to use it to carry one man in a six-passenger airplane.

I wonder if I can charter one?

Slow down, for Christ's sake. Nobody's at death's door. I'll be there later today; that's soon enough.

"If you like," she said, coldly.

"I don't know what flight I can catch, sweetheart. But I'll be on the first plane to Dallas I can catch this afternoon. And I'll have the Lear sent to Dallas to meet me. All right?"

"Do whatever you want," Alicia said.

"And in the meantime, please don't do anything, or say anything, you might regret later."

For an answer, she hung up on him.

Juan Fernando Castillo calmly put the telephone back in its cradle.

Then he looked up at the ceiling. Then he raised his spread arms above his shoulders.

"Jesus Christ, God!" he cried. "Don't do this to her! She has suffered enough."

[TEN]
Passenger Lounge, Hobie Aviation Services
Love Field
Dallas, Texas
2005 12 March 1981

"What do you mean, it's not here?" Juan Fernando Castillo demanded incredulously of the customer services agent.

For reasons known only to God, the Lear can't go into Dallas–Fort Worth International, and after I shuttle all the way over here from Dallas–Fort Worth the goddamned Lear isn't here?

"I'm sorry, Mr. Castillo. It's just not here, sir."

Don Fernando took out his cellular and punched keys several times before he realized the screen was blank and, therefore, the goddamned battery was dead.

"May I please use that telephone?"

"Yes, of course, sir."

He punched in a number from memory and a moment later heard, "Lemes Aviation."

"Who's this?"

"Ralph Porter."

"Ralph, this is Fernando Castillo."

"How can I help you, Don Fernando?"

"You can tell me where the hell my Lear is. I'm at Love and it's not here."

"Let me check a moment, sir."

Check, my ass, you sonofabitch! With all the money we spend with you, you should not only have had the goddamned Lear here when I wanted it, but you should have known without checking why it isn't and where it is.

"Don Fernando?"

"Yes?"

"It took off from Newark about an hour ago, sir. That should put it on the ground here in, say, two hours."

"You don't know what it was doing in Newark by any chance, do you?"

"Yes, sir. Doña Alicia took it there, sir. She said she had to make the six o'clock Pan American flight to Frankfurt and there was no other way she could make it except in the Lear."

"Of course. It must have slipped my mind. Thank you very much."

"Anything else I can help you with, sir?"

"No, that's it, thank you."

He put the telephone back in the cradle and then picked it up again and dialed another number from memory.

"Jacqueline, it's me," he said. "In this order, call General Stevens at Fort Sam and ask him where I'm supposed to go in Germany. He'll understand."

"Germany?" Jacqueline Sanchez, who had been his secretary for twenty years, asked.

"Germany. Then get me on the next plane out of Dallas–Fort Worth that goes wherever I have to go."

"I don't know what kind of direct flights there are from Dallas–Fort Worth to Germany," Jacqueline said. "Why don't you take the Lear and head for New York?"

"Because the goddamned Lear is on its way back from New York and won't be in San Antonio for two hours."

"Somehow, I sense that you're displeased about something," she said. "Anything I can do?"

"Just get me on the next goddamned plane to Germany, Jackie, please."

"Consider it done. Where are you?"

"I'm at Love, about to get in a goddamned taxi to go back to goddamned Dallas–Fort Worth."

"Two 'goddamned's in one sentence, you must be angry."

"Alicia is on her way to Germany to see who she thinks is Jorge's son."

"Oh my God!"

"Yeah, oh my God!"

"Call me when you get to Dallas–Fort Worth. I'll have everything set up by the time you get there."

"Thanks, Jackie."

"Jorge had a child?" she asked.

"Oh, God, Jackie, I hope this kid is really his."

"I'll say a prayer," Jackie said, and the line went dead.

[ELEVEN]
Haus im Wald
Near Bad Hersfeld
Kreis Hersfeld-Rotenburg
Hesse, West Germany
1850 13 March 1981

The Jaegermeister at the gate would not permit the Lustrous Mercedes to pass until he had authority from the house. When it finally came, and they reached the house, Karl Wilhelm von und zu Gossinger was waiting for them on the stone verandah.

"Good evening," he said.

"Hey, Karl," Major Naylor said.

"I am sorry but Mother is not receiving," the boy said.

"We really want to talk to her," Naylor said. "May we come in?"

"Of course."

He opened the door for them and then followed them into the house.

"I don't believe I know this lady," he said when they were all inside.

"Karl," Netty began, "this is your . . ."

"Karl, I'm your grandmother," Alicia Castillo said.

"Oh."

"If I had known about you, I would have been here much sooner," Alicia said. "May I give you a hug and a kiss?"

"I would rather you didn't," the boy said.

"Jesus, Karl!" Naylor said.

"It's all right," Alicia said.

"Karl," Netty said, "we would really like to see your mother for just a moment."

"Mother is not feeling well," the boy said.

"We understand, Karl," Elaine Naylor said.

"She has had a good deal to drink," the boy said.

"Karl," Alicia said, "take me to your mother."

He looked at her for a moment, and then said, "If you insist."

The room, Alicia was to remember later, reeked of cognac.

Erika von und zu Gossinger was in bed, on her side, and raised her head when the light from the corridor came into the darkened room.

"Who's that?" she challenged, in German. "Get out and leave me alone!"

"I'm sorry," Alicia said. "I don't speak German."

"Who are you?" Frau Erika asked, not pleasantly, in English.

"I am Jorge's mother, my dear," Alicia said. "And I've come to take care of you and Karl."

Frau Erika, not without effort, managed to sit up in the bed and turn the light on.

"You're Jorge's mother?"

"Yes, I am. My name is Alicia."

Frau Erika put out her hand and Doña Alicia took it.

"I am so sorry I didn't know about you and the boy," Alicia said.

Tears ran down Frau Erika's cheeks and she began to sob.

Alicia put her arms around her.

V
SPRING 2005

[ONE]
Over the Atlantic Ocean
Offshore, Savannah, Georgia
1520 29 May 2005

Five minutes out of the helipad at the Carolina White House, shortly after they had reached cruising altitude, Sergeant First Class DeLaney took a headset from a hook by the door and handed it to Major C. G. Castillo, who was now sitting down and properly strapped in.

Castillo put it on, found the mike button, and said, "Thanks, Sergeant."

"Major Castillo," a female voice said, adding jokingly, "this is your pilot speaking."

"Yes, ma'am?"

"Castillo, I was just thinking," Lieutenant Colonel Messinger said. "I'm going off-duty when we get to Hunter. I could give you a ride into Fort Stewart, if you'd like, and grease you through the process of getting into the field-grade BOQ. I live there."

Major Castillo had an unkind and perhaps less than modest thought: For female officers, keeping one's indiscretions a hundred miles from the flagpole was even more important than it was for male officers. For unmarried female officers—and if Lieutenant Colonel Messinger lived in the field-grade BOQ she was more than likely unmarried—it was even more difficult to be discreet. If they didn't opt for the chastity option, they had to be very careful. Castillo knew that every brother—and sister—officer wondered, not always privately, whom Lieutenant Colonel Messinger was banging.

Banging outside the bounds of holy matrimony was Conduct Unbecoming an Officer and Gentlelady. Banging a fellow officer, especially a married one, was bad. Banging a subordinate was even worse, a 6 or 7 on the Conduct Unbecoming Scale, and banging a *married* subordinate was a 10.

Helping a visiting fellow field-grade aviator, who was not wearing a wedding ring, through the often maddening process of getting into visiting officer quarters, after which he would naturally suggest having a drink and dinner, after which they would go to the BOQ together, was something else. No more than a 2 on the scale, or even a 1. Providing, of course, that loud cries suggesting intense carnal union were not later heard all over the BOQ.

"That's very kind of you, Colonel," Castillo said. "But someone's meeting me at Savannah International."

"Really? Then what you really need is a ride there?"

"Yes, ma'am. But I'll catch a cab or something."

"I'll take you to Savannah. Not a problem. The terminal or the private aviation side of the field?"

"The private aviation side, please."

"No problem, Major."

"I'll be coming out here again, Colonel," Castillo said. "Can I have a raincheck?"

"I'm in the book: Messinger," she said. "Call me."

"Thank you, I will."

There was no further communication between the pilot and Major Castillo while they were in the air.

But when she settled the Huey on its skids on the business aviation tarmac, Major Castillo went to the cockpit window and offered her his hand.

"Thanks for the ride, Colonel," Castillo said.

"My pleasure," she said, "and it's Anne."

"Charley," Castillo said, and when she finally let go of his hand, he waved, then turned and started walking toward a sign reading PASSENGER LOUNGE.

When he pushed open the door to the passenger lounge—a large room furnished with chrome-and-plastic armchairs and couches, a wall of Coke and snack-dispensing machines, and a table with regular and decaf coffeemakers—a man sitting in an armchair and drinking coffee from a plastic cup called out, loudly,

"Hey, Gringo!"

The man was heavyset, almost massive—it was said he took after his late maternal grandfather—dark-skinned, and dressed in a yellow polo shirt, blue jeans, and well-worn western boots.

It took Castillo a moment to locate the source of the voice, and then, smiling, he walked quickly toward the man, who, with surprising agility for someone of his bulk, came quickly out of the chair.

They embraced. Fernando Manuel Lopez effortlessly lifted Carlos Guillermo Castillo off the floor.

"How the hell are you?" he asked. "Where the hell have you been?"

"Out at the Carolina White House," Castillo said when he had finally freed himself. "The president needed my advice on foreign policy matters."

"I would say, 'Oh, bullshit,' but I never know when you're pulling my chain."

"My boss was out there," Castillo said. "I was brought along to carry his briefcase and pass the hors d'oeuvres."

"How long can you stay?" Fernando asked.

"I have to be back in Washington Monday at noon."

"Oh, Jesus, don't you ever get any time off?"

"Sure, I do. But . . ."

"I know, wiseass. 'But I prefer to spend it in the company of naked women.' Right?"

"That's cruel, Fernando," Castillo said with more than a hint of an effeminate lisp. "I can't believe you think that of me."

Fernando chuckled.

"If you need to take a leak, Gringo, take it. It's going to be a little bumpy up there and I don't want you pissing all over my new toy."

"What new toy?"

"Take your piss and then I'll show you. I may even let you steer it for a minute or two."

"Pretty," Castillo said several minutes later as he and Fernando walked around a small, sleek, glistening white jet airplane. "What is it?"

"A Learjet . . ."

"I can see that."

"A Bombardier/Learjet 45XR, to be specific."

"You said 'yours'?"

"Ours," Fernando said.

"You finally got Abuela to get rid of the old Lear?"

"Grandpa loved it," Fernando said. "She wouldn't admit that, of course. Until I finally wore her down. It was the old 'the wolf's at the door' rationale."

"What did it cost?"

"Don't ask," Fernando said. "But Grandpa's Lear belonged in a museum."

"I know," Castillo said. "But I know how she feels. It's not easy losing another connection to your past."

[TWO]
Hacienda San Jorge
Near Uvalde, Texas
1740 27 May 2005

The Bombardier/Learjet 45XR did not exactly buzz the sprawling, red-tile-roofed Spanish-style "Big House" and its outbuildings, but it did fly directly over it and wiggle its wings at maybe 1,000 feet before picking up altitude in a sweeping turn to make its approach to the paved, 3,500-foot runway a half mile from the house.

Inside the Big House, Doña Alicia Castillo, recognizing the sound for what it was, raised her eyes heavenward, made the sign of the cross, laid down the novel she had been reading, and walked quickly out of the living room onto the verandah.

She loved all of her children and grandchildren, of course, and tried to do so equally. But she knew that the airplane that had just roared overhead held the two people she really loved most in the world, her grandson Fernando—the son of her daughter Patricia—and his cousin Carlos.

She didn't like them flying at all, and she especially didn't like it when they were in the same airplane and Fernando might be tempted to show off—which, in flying so low over the Big House, he certainly was.

She got out on the porch in time to see the Lear put its landing gear down as it lined up with the runway.

If I stay out here on the verandah, it will look as if I'm desperately waiting to see them.

Which, of course, I am.

She sat down on a couch upholstered with leather pillows.

Five minutes later, they appeared in the ancient rusty jeep in which Juan Fernando, may God rest his soul, had taught them both to drive when they were about thirteen. Patricia and Francisco, her husband, had been furious when they found out, but Juan Fernando had silenced them by saying they're going to drive anyway and it was better that he teach them than have them kill themselves trying to teach themselves.

Juan Fernando had used the same argument, more or less, two years later when the boys wanted to learn how to fly. This time he said Carlos was going to fly, as his father had been a pilot even before he went in the Army, and what

Carlos did Fernando was going to do whether or not anyone liked it. Or vice versa.

They were really more like twin brothers, Doña Alicia thought, than just cousins. They didn't look at all alike—while Carlos had been a big boy, Fernando had been outsized since he was in diapers—but they were the same age, within several months, and they had been inseparable from the time she and Juan Fernando had brought Carlos home from Germany.

Doña Alicia thought both had gotten many physical genes from their grandfathers. Carlos had shown her a picture of his mother's father when his grandfather had been a lieutenant colonel in the German army at Stalingrad; Carlos looked just like him except for the eyes, which were Jorge's eyes.

Carlos got out of the jeep and walked onto the verandah.

"How's my favorite girl?" he asked, putting his arms around her and kissing her.

"Your favorite girl would be a lot happier if you hadn't flown over the house like that," she said.

Carlos pointed at Fernando.

"Not me, Abuela," Fernando said. "The Gringo was flying."

"He's lying, Abuela," Carlos said.

Doña Alicia looked at Fernando. "How many thousand times have I asked you not to call him that?"

Fernando looked thoughtful, then shrugged.

"Five maybe?" he asked, innocently.

Fernando had always called Carlos "Gringo," or "the Gringo," but anyone else who did so got punched. She and Fernando had worried, on the plane from Frankfurt, how the two twelve-year-olds were going to get along. Would Fernando resent his new cousin? Fernando was not only much larger than Carlos but had acquired his grandfather's temper as well.

The problem hadn't come up.

"You talk funny, you know that?" Fernando had challenged five minutes into their first meeting.

"So do you, if that language you're using is supposed to be English," Carlos had replied.

Fernando, who was not used to being challenged, had looked at him a long moment and then finally said, "I think I'm going to like you, even if you are a gringo. You know how to ride?"

"Of course."

"Come on, I'll show you around the place."

And they had been inseparable from then on.

"Since I didn't think you would think to," Doña Alicia said, "I called Maria and she's bringing the children out for supper."

"Abuela," Fernando demanded, "how are the Gringo and I going to get drunk if my wife and the rug rats are coming?"

"You're not going to . . . Fernando, stop! You are making me angry!"

"Yes, ma'am," he said, contritely.

"Rug rats!" Doña Alicia said. "I don't know where you got that."

"Watching television comedy, Abuela," Carlos said. "I agree with you. That's disgusting! 'Rug rats'! His own sweet and loving children!"

Doña Alicia tried and failed to keep a smile from her lips.

"Well, if you feel you must," she said, "come in the house and have a cock-tail. I may even have a glass of wine myself."

"I left my suitcase on the airplane, Abuela," Carlos said. "Have I got a change of clothes in my room?"

"Of course you do," she said. "You know that. You 'forgot your suitcase on the airplane'? How in the world could you do that?"

"Tell Abuela whose airplane it was, and where you have been, *Carlos Guillermo*," Fernando said, as they walked into the living room.

She looked at him expectantly.

"My boss's airplane. Secretary Hall. The president sent for him and I caught a ride with him," Carlos said.

"Did you get to see the president?" she asked.

"From a distance," Carlos said, not liking the lie but knowing it came with the job.

"Your grandfather knew his father," Doña Alicia said. "They did some business together in Alabama. Something, I think, to do with trees for pulp. Long-leaf pines, whatever that is."

"Really?"

That didn't come up. Didn't they make the connection? Or did they know? And did knowing that have something to do with that two-minute job interview? Until just now, I thought the president was just trusting Hall. Or maybe they knew and wanted to see if I would bring it up.

"We used to see them at the Kentucky Derby," Doña Alicia said. "The president's father, I mean. And his wife. A really lovely woman. Your grandfather really loved horses."

"Abuela," Fernando asked, from the bar. "Wine, you said?"

"Please," she said. "There's some Argentine cabernet sauvignon in one of the cabinets."

[THREE]
Baltimore-Washington International Airport
Baltimore, Maryland
0905 31 May 2005

"Lear Five-Oh-Seven-Five on the ground at five past the hour. Will you close us out, please?" Castillo, who was in the pilot's seat, said into his microphone.

"Not bad, Gringo. We'll have to report a hard landing, but not bad."

"Screw you, Fernando," Castillo said.

"BWI ground control, Lear Five-Oh-Seven-Five," Fernando said into his microphone. "Request taxi instructions to civil aviation refuel facilities."

"Correction," Castillo said after keying his mike. "Ground control, we want to go to the UPS facility."

Visibly surprised, Fernando didn't say anything until after ground control had given directions.

"UPS?" he asked.

"Yeah, UPS," Castillo said. "That's where I'm going."

"And I can't ask why, right?"

"That's right, but if you promise to keep your mouth shut . . . and I mean shut, Fernando . . . you can tag along if you'd like."

"UPS?" Fernando repeated, wonderingly.

An armed Department of Transportation security officer was waiting warily for them when they opened the Lear's cabin door.

"Can I help you, gentlemen?" he asked.

"Good morning," Castillo said and took a small leather wallet from his jacket pocket and handed it to the security guard.

The security guard carefully examined the credentials, then handed the wallet back.

"Yes, sir," he said. "Now, how can I help you?"

"You can point us toward UPS flight operations," Castillo said.

"Ground floor, second door, of that building," the guard said, pointing.

"Thank you," Castillo said. "I think you'd better come along, Lopez."

"Yes, sir," Fernando said.

Halfway to the two-story concrete-block building, Fernando asked, "What did you show him?"

"The pictures of your rug rats Maria gave me yesterday," Castillo said.

A man in an open-collared white shirt, with the four-stripe shoulder boards that are just about the universal identification of a captain of an airline, came through the second door as they walked up to it.

He smiled.

"You got past the guard, so I guess you didn't come here to blow anything up. How can I help you?"

Castillo took a regular wallet from his hip pocket and from it first one business card and then a second. He handed the first to the man in the white captain's shirt and the second to Fernando.

"You'd better have one of these, Lopez," he said.

"Thank you, sir," Fernando said, politely, and looked at it.

The card bore the insignia of the Department of Homeland Security, gave the Washington address, two telephone numbers, an e-mail address, and said that C. G. Castillo was Executive Assistant to the Secretary.

"How can I help you, Mr. Castillo?" the captain asked. He offered his hand. "I'm Jerry Witherington, the station chief here."

"I need a favor," Castillo said. "I need to talk to somebody who knows the Boeing 727, and, if there's one here, I'd really like to have a tour."

"I've got a lot of hours in one," Witherington said. "This have anything to do with the one they can't find in Africa?"

"You heard about that, did you?" Castillo said.

"I've been trying to figure it out since I heard about it," Witherington said. "How the hell can you lose a 727?"

"I don't know," Castillo said. "But I guess the CIA, the FBI, the FAA, and everybody else who is trying to get an answer will eventually come up with one."

"You're not investigating it?"

"Oh, no," Castillo said. "Were you ever in the service, Mr. Witherington?"

"Weren't we all? Air Force. Seven years."

"Okay. I was Army. So you know what an aide-de-camp is, right?"

"Sure."

"The only difference in being the secretary's special assistant and being some general's aide is that I don't get a gold rope to dangle from my shoulder."

Witherington smiled at him and chuckled.

"Among other things, like carrying his briefcase, what I try to do is get answers for the secretary before some reporter asks the question. And some reporter *is* going to ask him, 'What about the missing 727?' And since I know he knows as much about 727s as I do—almost nothing—I figured I'd better find someone who's an expert and get some facts."

"And you flew here in that Lear to do that?"

"Lopez and I were in Texas," Castillo said. "So I asked myself who would have the expert, and maybe even an airplane that I could look at and where. The answer was: UPS, and here."

"You're a pilot, right?"

"I drove mostly Hueys when I was in the Army," Castillo said. "I know nothing about big jets."

"But you were flying the Lear, right?"

"The secretary is a devout believer that idle hands are the tools of the devil," Castillo said. "So he told Lopez here, 'Instead of you watching the fuel-remaining needle drop while Castillo snores in the back, why don't you teach him how to fly the Lear? It might come in handy someday.' "

Witherington chuckled.

"He must be a good IP," he said. "I happened to be watching when you came in. You greased it in."

"They call that beginner's luck," Fernando said.

"The reason I asked the question, Mr. Castillo . . ."

"I don't suppose you could call me Charley, could you?"

"Okay, Charley," Witherington said. "I'm Jerry." He looked at Fernando.

"Most people just call me Lopez," Fernando said. "It's hard to make up a nickname if your first name is Fernando."

"Okay, Lopez it is," Witherington said as he shook his hand. "The reason I asked was to give me an idea where to start the lecture," Witherington said. "And I've been trying to guess what questions your boss will get asked."

"Well, the obvious one is, 'Do you think it was stolen by terrorists who plan to fly it into another building?' "

"That's the first thing I thought of when I heard somebody stole the 727," Witherington said.

"And what do you think?"

"I don't think so," Witherington said.

"Why not?"

"Hey, I don't want to get quoted and then have some rag-head fly this missing 727 into the White House," Witherington said.

"None of this gets written down," Castillo said. "Nobody in the office even knows I'm here. So why not?"

"It would be easier to skyjack another 767," Witherington said. "If you think about it, when they took down the Trade Center and almost the Pentagon and the White House they really thought it through. They had great big airplanes—the wingspan of a 767 is 156 feet and some inches; the 727's wingspan is 108 feet even . . ."

"A third wider, huh?" Castillo said. "I didn't realize there was that much difference."

"What the rag-heads had was airplanes with just about topped-off tanks," Witherington said. "The 767 has a range of about 6,100 nautical miles. The tanks on a 767 can hold almost 24,000 gallons of fuel."

"Jesus, that's a lot of fuel!" Castillo said.

"Yeah, it is," Witherington said. "And that's what took down the Trade Towers. When all that fuel burned, it took the temper out of the structural steel—hell, melted a lot of it—and the building came down."

"What you're saying is that it probably wouldn't have happened with a 727?"

"I really don't want to sound like a know-it-all, but . . ."

"Hey, this is just between us. I'm grateful for your expertise."

"Just don't quote me, huh?"

"You have my word," Castillo said.

"The 727's max range is no more that 2,500 miles," Witherington said. "The way most of them are configured, no more than 1,500. And that means less fuel is needed, so smaller tanks. I never heard of a 727—and I've flown a lot of them—with tanks that hold more than 9,800 gallons; most hold about 8,000."

"One-third of what a 767 carries," Castillo said.

"Right," Witherington said. "So, what I'm saying is that if I wanted to blow myself and some building up—and get a pass into heaven and the seven whores that are promised—I think I'd rather grab another 767 instead of going all the way to Africa to steal a 727, which wouldn't do nearly as much damage, and which would be damned hard to get into any place where it could do damage. They're still watching, as I guess you know, incoming aircraft pretty carefully."

"So I've heard," Castillo said.

"One of our guys was coming here from Rio in a 747," Witherington said. "He was supposed to make a stop in Caracas but didn't—there was weather, and we had another flight going in there an hour later—so he just headed for Miami. And forgot to change his flight plan. Twenty minutes after he was supposed to have landed at Caracas, he got a call from an excited controller asking him where he was and what he was doing, and he told him, and ten minutes after that—before he got to Santo Domingo—he looked out the window and saw a Navy fighter looking at him."

"So what do you think happened to the 727?" Castillo asked.

"I think they probably flew it a couple of hundred miles—maybe less—and then started to cannibalize it. There's a market for any part—engines on up—in what we call 'the developing nations'—and no questions asked."

"I hadn't thought about that," Castillo said. "That makes sense."

"Let me tell them where I'm going," Witherington said, "and get a golf cart—the one 727 we have here, as a backup for this part of the country, is too far down the line to walk."

"You're really being helpful," Castillo said. "I appreciate it."

"My pleasure. Be right back."

When Witherington was out of earshot, Castillo said, "After we get the tour—which shouldn't take long—we'll get some breakfast, and then you can head home."

"I was hoping you would say, 'Fernando, since you're staying over why don't you stay with me? We can have dinner or something.' "

"You're staying over?"

"I have to confer with our Washington attorneys."

"What about?"

"So I can truthfully tell the IRS the reason I brought the Lear to Washington was to confer with our Washington attorneys. And not using the corporate aircraft for personal business."

"What about you picking me up at Savannah?"

"That was a routine cross-country proficiency flight."

"You're a devious man, Fernando."

"Not in the same league as you, Gringo."

Castillo was about to ask him what the hell that was supposed to mean when Witherington appeared around the corner of the concrete-block building at the wheel of a white golf cart and there wasn't time.

[FOUR]
Old Executive Office Building
17th Street and Pennsylvania Avenue NW
Washington, D.C.
1155 31 May 2005

Major C. G. Castillo, wearing a dark suit and tie not unlike that of the countless civilian staffers moving in a purposeful fashion up and down the hallways of the OEOB, stopped before an unmarked heavy wooden door and put a key in its lock.

Inside there was a small antechamber with nothing in it but a somewhat ragged carpet and, mounted more or less unobtrusively high above a second door, a small television camera.

Castillo rapped at one of the panels in the door and, a moment later, there was the buzz of a solenoid and when Castillo put his hand on the door it opened.

This was the private entrance to the office that Secretary of Homeland Security Matthew Hall maintained in the old building across from the White House, which had once housed the State, War, and Navy departments—all three—of the federal government.

The secretary had seen who it was and pushed a button under his desk to unlock the door.

"I said twelve o'clock and here you are at eleven fifty-five," Hall said. "Why am I not surprised?"

"Punctuality is a virtue, sir," Castillo said. "I thought I told you that. Since it's my only one, I work hard at it."

Hall chuckled. "I've heard that chastity and temperance aren't among your virtues," he said. "What's up, Charley?"

"I went to Baltimore and got UPS to show me one of their 727s. Their guy doesn't think it will be used as a flying bomb against us here."

"I hope he's right," Hall said.

"And then I came here—about forty-five minutes ago—and have worked my way maybe one-third down the stack of stuff Dr. Cohen's memo got us."

"And?"

"After page two, and considering the urgency of our conversation with the president, I thought what I should do is go over there, and the sooner the better."

Hall considered that momentarily. After the secretary's discussions in the Oval Office with the president and Natalie Cohen, then further discussions privately between Hall and Dr. Cohen, there was no question that the president was pissed and therefore no question that Castillo now had a blank check to carry out his mission.

"Okay," he said. "Have them make the arrangements."

"I've already done that, sir. I'm on a Lufthansa flight to Rhine-Main tonight."

"You have to go through Frankfurt?"

"I want to give my boss at the *Tages Zeitung* a heads-up that he's sending me to Luanda," Charley said. "Then London to Angola on British Airways."

"You think that's necessary? Going as . . . what's your name?"

"Karl Wilhelm von und zu Gossinger," Castillo said.

"That's a mouthful. No wonder I can't remember it."

"Sir, I had the feeling that you really wanted me to be the fly on the wall on this job. That's the best way to do it, sir, I submit, as a German journalist."

"The less anyone knows what you're doing, Charley, the better. There's no sense in having it get out the president ordered this unless it has to come out."

"Yes, sir. I understand."

"Anything I can do for you before you go?" Hall asked, and then had a thought. "How are you going to get a visa for Angola on such short notice?"

"That's my next stop, sir, the Angolan embassy."

Hall stood up and put out his hand.

"If you were going as my assistant, I know the Angolan ambassador and could give him a call. But he would ask questions if asked a favor for Wilhelm Whatsisname, a German journalist."

"I don't have to go as Karl Wilhelm von und zu Gossinger, sir," Castillo said. "But I think it makes more sense."

"So do I," Hall said. "Have a nice flight, Charley. You know how to reach me; keep me in the loop—quietly. And good luck."

"Thank you, sir."

[FIVE]
Embassy of the Republic of Angola
2100–2108 16th Street NW
Washington, D.C.
1520 31 May 2005

"It was very good of you to see me, sir, on such short notice," Castillo said to the very tall, very black man in the consular section.

He was speaking in what he hoped was good enough Portuguese to be understood. His Tex-Mex and Castilian Spanish—actually, a combination thereof—had worked for him well enough in São Paulo, Brazil, but this man was from a Portuguese-speaking African country and that was something different.

The black man smiled at him and asked, in English, "How can the Angolan embassy be of service to a Spanish-speaking German journalist?"

"I was afraid my limited experience with your language would be all too transparent, sir," Castillo said.

"How may I help you?"

"My newspaper wants me to go to Luanda and write a story about the airplane no one seems to be able to find," Castillo said. "And I need a visa. I have all the documents I understand I need."

He began to lay documents on the man's desk.

They included his German passport, and three photocopies thereof; two application forms, properly filled out; a printout of an e-mail he had sent himself from Texas, ostensibly from the *Tages Zeitung*, ordering him to get to Luanda, Angola, as quickly as he could in order to write about the missing 727, as Herr Schneider is ill and cannot go; his curriculum vitae, stating he had earned a doctorate at Phillip's University, Marburg an der Lahn, and had been employed by the *Tages Zeitung* as a writer and lately foreign correspondent for the past nine years; and his White House press credentials.

And a one-hundred-dollar bill, almost hidden by all of the above.

As soon as he had spread the documents out, he found it necessary to blow his nose and politely turned away from the consular official to do so.

When he turned back, approximately twenty seconds later, the consular official was studying the documents. The one-hundred-dollar bill was nowhere in sight.

"There are some documents missing, Mr. Gossinger," the consular official said, politely. "Your proof of right of residency in the United States, for example."

"With all respect, sir," Castillo said, "I thought my White House press credentials might satisfy that requirement. They really wouldn't let me into the White House if I wasn't legally in the United States. And you'll notice, sir, I hope, that my passport bears a multiple-entry visa for the United States."

The consular officer studied the German passport.

"So it does," he agreed. "Perhaps that will satisfy that requirement. But there are some others." He paused. "Will you excuse me a moment, please?"

He walked out of the office. Castillo took another hundred-dollar bill from his pocket and put it in his passport, which concealed all but one edge of the bill. He laid the passport back on the table, mostly—but not completely—under the stack of documents. The numerals "100" were visible.

A minute later, the consular official came back into his office. Castillo felt the need to blow his nose again and did so. When he turned back to the table thirty seconds later, the passport was now on top of the stack of documents but the one-hundred-dollar bill was nowhere in sight.

"Well, you have most of the documents you'll need," the consular official said, "except of course for your return ticket, and the written statement that you understand you will have to abide by the laws of the Republic of Angola, and, of course, the Portuguese translations of your curriculum vitae, the e-mail from your newspaper, and—since I find your White House press credentials satisfactory proof that you reside legally in the United States—the Portuguese translation of those."

"It is here, sir, that I turn to you for understanding and help," Castillo said.

"And how is that?"

"I don't have my airline tickets," Castillo said. "They are electronic tickets and I will pick them up when I get to Heathrow Airport."

"And when will that be?"

"The day after tomorrow, sir."

"So soon?"

"So soon. This is an important story and they want me to get on it now."

"That's so soon."

Castillo took a small wad of currency from his pocket, three one-hundred-dollar bills, and held them in his hand.

"I realize that this is asking a good deal of you, sir, but if you could see your way to having those documents translated into Portuguese—I realize that will be expensive—and perhaps be so kind as to call British Airways yourself to verify that I have a return ticket . . ."—he laid the three one-hundred-dollar bills on the consul's desk— ". . . This should be enough, I think, for the translations."

After thirty seconds, the consul picked up the German passport, opened it to a blank page, took a rubber stamp from his desk, stamped the passport, and then scrawled his signature on the visa.

"We try to be as cooperative as possible when dealing with the press," he said, handing Castillo the passport. "The visa is for multiple entries into the Republic of Angola. Have a nice flight, Mr. Gossinger."

"I can't thank you enough for your courtesy, sir," Castillo said, offering the consul his hand.

What I have done, in addition to spending five hundred of my own money, which I will never be able to claim as a reimbursable necessary expense, is violate at least three separate provisions of the United States Code having to do with the making of, or offering to make, a bribe to an official of a foreign government.

On the other hand, I'm on my way to Luanda, Angola.

[SIX]
The Mayflower Hotel
1127 Connecticut Avenue NW
Washington, D.C.
1650 31 May 2005

Fernando Lopez was sitting at a table by a window in the bar when Castillo walked in and slipped into the other chair.

"I would offer you a pistachio," Fernando said, pointing at a bowl, "but I seem to have eaten the whole thing."

"Bored? Sorry, I got hung up."

"I am never bored when there are interesting-looking females around. Now I know why you live here."

"There's supposed to be more women in Washington than men," Castillo said. "But I'm not sure if that's true."

A waiter appeared.

"What are you drinking?" Castillo asked.

"Unless you desperately need a jolt," Fernando said, "I'd rather go to your room."

"Sure, I can wait," Castillo said, and then to the waiter added, "Check, please."

"Last of the big spenders?"

"If you pay for it, Maria will get the bill and know that you were boozing it up in the big city."

"No, she won't. My bills go to the company."

"Then Jacqueline will know."

"But she won't tell Maria," Fernando said. "Grandpa trusted her discretion completely, and I've learned I can, too."

"I wouldn't be too sure," Castillo said. "I always thought she was sweet on Grandpa. I'm not too sure how she feels about you."

"You really think Jackie had the hots for Don Fernando?" Fernando asked, smiling.

The question was never answered. The waiter appeared, Castillo scrawled his name on the check, and they walked out of the bar and into the lobby.

"What are we going to do about dinner?" Fernando asked when he came out of the bathroom, pulling up his zipper, in Castillo's suite.

"First, before I have to make an important decision like that, I'm going to have a drink. And I'll even make you one if you promise to stay sober for the next hour or so."

"Why should I do that?"

"Because I need to talk to you."

"About what? You in some kind of trouble?"

"Yeah, I guess I am. I need to talk to you, Fernando."

"You don't really talk to me, you tell me misleading half-truths."

"I thought maybe you'd noticed. What do you want to drink?"

"I've been drinking scotch, but if you're in trouble maybe we better not."

"It's not that kind of trouble. I'm still waiting to hear if a rabbit in New York died, but aside from that . . ."

"You sonofabitch!" Fernando said, chuckling.

Castillo handed him a drink and then sat down in an armchair facing Fernando's across a coffee table. They raised glasses, locked eyes for a moment, and then took swallows.

"You were telling me about this lady who seduced you in New York," Fernando said. "Or was it rape?"

"I wish it was that simple," Castillo said.

"What the fuck are you talking about?"

"I realized a while back that I was getting to the point where I didn't know who I was. Or am. I don't know how to say it. I told you, this isn't simple."

"Try. I'm not really as dumb as Maria would have you believe."

"That ID card I showed the guard at Baltimore-Washington?"

"What about it? It impressed the guard."

Castillo reached in his pocket and came out with the leather wallet and tossed it to Fernando.

Fernando failed to catch it and had to pick it up. He opened it and looked at it carefully.

"I'm impressed," he said. " 'Department of Homeland Security.' 'United States Secret Service.' 'Supervisory Special Agent.' I thought you were still in the Army."

"I am. And I'm not in the Secret Service," Castillo said. "I got that because it was the easiest way for me to carry a pistol—or anything else—onto an airplane. And that ID calls the least attention to me when I do."

"You often do that? Carry a gun?"

"I don't often carry one, but I usually have one around close. It says 'Supervisory Special Agent' instead of just 'Special Agent' in case I run into a real

Secret Service agent and his hair stands up—they're good; they can spot people who aren't what their credentials say they are. There's a double safeguard against that in there. First, they probably wouldn't want to stick their necks out and question a supervisory special agent. But if they do, there's a code on there. If they call a regional office and ask if there really is a supervisory special agent named Castillo and give the code, they're told I'm legitimate and to butt out right now. It's happened twice."

"So you're not really the . . . what did that calling card say? 'The Executive Assistant to the Director of Homeland Security'?"

"Yeah, I am."

"You just said you were still in the Army."

"And I am. Getting the picture, Fernando? When I said I was getting confused about who I really am?"

"I'm pretty confused, Gringo."

"Try living it," Castillo said. "Okay. Let's start with the Army. I'm a major, just selected for promotion—which means that I go on the bottom of a list. When some Special Forces lieutenant colonel retires, or gets dead or promoted, and there is a space for one more lieutenant colonel, the top man on the list gets promoted. Eventually, I work my way up to the top of the list and become Lieutenant Colonel Castillo."

"Are congratulations in order?"

"That may take a while. I'll let you know when it happens and you can buy me a drink."

"You just said Special Forces. I thought you were Aviation."

"I was commissioned into Aviation when I graduated from West Point . . ."

"I was there, remember? I was still an Aggie cadet, and I wanted that dollar you had to give me when I was the first one to salute you. I got it framed. It's in my office."

"I was commissioned into Aviation because of my father. Into what other branch of service could I go?"

"Makes sense."

"General Naylor wasn't so sure about that," Castillo said. "He thought I had the potential to be an armor officer."

"Hey, Gringo. Me too. I remember our first trip to Fort Knox. That's when his sales pitches started. He thinks he's your stepdaddy, and that makes me his nephew."

"Anyway, full of West Point piss and Tabasco I embarked on what I thought was going to be my career as an Army Aviator. I spent most of my graduation leave taking the ATR exams. Remember?"

"I remember. I didn't quite understand why you wanted an airline transport rating if you were going to be flying in the Army . . ."

"I wanted to be prepared. What occurred to me lately is that that's when all this bending of the rules started."

"What do you mean?"

"Brand-new second lieutenants don't go right to flight school. They spend a couple of years learning how to run a platoon in the Infantry or laying in cannon in the Artillery. Or driving tanks. I don't suspect for a second that General Naylor had anything at all to do with me being sent to Fort Knox for my initial assignment . . ."

"That's because you know he doesn't like you, right?" Fernando chuckled. "Jesus, he came to College Station and gave me a sales pitch to go in Armor that wouldn't quit. He made it clear to me that if our sacred ancestors only had a couple of tanks at the Alamo, we really would have kicked Santa Anna's ass all the way back to Mexico City."

"So you went in Armor when you finished A&M, and you learned all about the M1 Abrams, right?"

"Right. And I finished that just in time to get my ass shipped to Desert Storm."

"And I was supposed to be there, doing the same thing, but I wasn't, right?"

"They found a vacancy for you in flight school at Fort Rucker, as I recall."

"They *made* one. 'Son of Medal of Honor Recipient Enters Flight School.' Looks good in the newspapers. I had my picture taken with the post commander the day I arrived. I couldn't have flunked out of flight school if I wrecked every aircraft on Cairns Army Airfield."

"Well, so what? You could fly when you got there."

"You're supposed to forget all that and start with: 'This is a wing. Because of less pressure on its upper surface, it tends to rise in the air taking with it whatever it's attached to.' "

Fernando laughed.

" 'And this is a helicopter,' " Castillo went on. " 'It is different from an airplane because the wings go round and round.' "

Fernando chuckled and, smiling fondly, shook his head.

"I was there about three weeks, I guess, and I fell asleep in class. Basic radio procedure or something. I'd been out howling the night before. With a magnolia blossom named Betty-Sue or something. Unsuccessfully, as I remember. Betty-Sue was holding out for marriage. Anyway, the instructor, a lieutenant, stood me tall: 'Are you bored in this class, Lieutenant?' "

"Well, the answer to that was, 'Hell, yes, I'm bored,' but I couldn't say that. So I thought about what I could say.

" 'I asked you a question, Lieutenant!' he pursued.

"So I said, 'Sir, with respect, yes, sir, I am a little.'

"That was in the days when I really believed 'When all else fails, tell the truth.' I wish I still did.

"Anyway, he puffed up like a pigeon and asked why. And I told him I had an ATR and knew how to work the radios. I don't think he believed me. He kicked me out of class. Told me to go to my BOQ and stay there.

"The next morning, I was summoned before a bird colonel. I wasn't as good at reading the brass as I am now, but I could tell he was nervous. He was dealing with the son of a Medal of Honor winner, a graduate of Hudson High, who had lied.

"He said, 'Lieutenant, did you tell Lieutenant Corncob-Up-His-Ass that you hold an Airline Transport Rating?'

" 'Yes, sir, I did,' I said, and showed it and my logbook to him.

"I could tell he was relieved.

"He said, 'Eleven hundred hours? Two hundred in rotary wing? Lieutenant, why didn't you bring this to our attention?'

" 'Sir, nobody asked me.' "

Fernando chuckled and took a pull at his drink.

"So, cutting a long story short, I was sent back to the BOQ and that afternoon they took me out to Hanchey, where an IP gave me a check ride in a Huey. I blew his mind when I said I'd never flown one with only one engine before, my Huey time was in . . ."

" 'The twin-engine models used by Rig Service Aviation of Corpus Christi'?" Fernando interrupted, laughing. "Oh, Jesus, they must have loved you!"

"Shortly thereafter, I found myself wearing wings, and rated in U.S. Army UH-1F rotary wing aircraft," Castillo went on. "And enrolled in Phase IV, which was transition to the Apache. The General himself came out to Hanchey when I passed my final check ride and shook my hand while the cameras clicked . . ."

"Abuela bought twenty-five copies of the *Express-News* with your smiling face on page one and mailed one to me," Fernando said. "I was then living in a tent a hundred miles out of Kuwait City."

"I really thought I was hot shit," Castillo said. "Second lieutenants tend to do that anyway."

"Speak for yourself, Gringo. I myself was the epitome of modesty. Phrased another way, I wondered what the fuck I was doing in the desert having absolutely no idea how I was supposed to command a platoon of M1s when we went through the Iraqi berms."

"You did that well, as I recall. Silver Star."

"The way they were handing out medals all you had to do was be there and you got the Bronze Star. You got the Silver Star if you didn't squash anybody important under your tracks."

"They didn't pass out the Silver Star with the MREs, Fernando. Tell that story to somebody else," Castillo challenged, and then went on: "So there I was, at oh-two-hundred hours on seventeen January, sitting in the copilot's seat of an Apache. I couldn't understand why the CWO-4 flying it was less than thrilled to have my services. At oh-two-thirty-eight we flew over the berms you were talking about and then started taking out Iraqi radar installations."

"You were on that first strike?"

"Yeah. And we took a hit. The CWO-4 took a hit. Something came through his side window, took off his visor, and then went through my windshield and instrument panel. He had plastic and metal fragments in his eyes. He said, 'You've got it. Get us out of here and take us home.' There being no other alternative that I could think of, I did just that."

"I never heard that story before," Fernando said.

"For which I received the Distinguished Flying Cross and the Purple Heart," Castillo went on.

"I didn't hear about that, either," Fernando said. "You got hit, too?"

"I had a couple of scratches on my hands," Castillo said. "Some fragments went through my gloves. They were about as serious as a bee sting."

"You were lucky," Fernando said.

"Lucky is not like doing something that earns you a medal," Castillo said, and then went on: "Anyway, the paperwork for the new hero went to Schwarzkopf's headquarters. Naylor—by then he had his second star—was there. He was sort of the buffer between Schwarzkopf and Franks."

"Freddy Franks, the one-legged general?"

Castillo nodded. "The first since the Civil War. He commanded the ground forces. They were not too fond of one another. Anyway, when Naylor heard about the paperwork for my two medals it was the first time he'd heard I was anywhere near Arabia. He went right through the roof . . ."

WINTER 1991

[SEVEN]
Office of the Assistant Chief of Staff, J-3
United States Central Command
Ministry of Defense and Aviation Air Force Base
Riyadh, Saudi Arabia
0720 16 January 1991

Major General Allan Naylor had the giggles. And he thought he knew why: He'd had about six hours' sleep—in segments of not longer than ninety minutes—in the last forty-eight hours. And in the forty-eight hours before that, he'd had no more than eight or ten hours on his back, again for never much over an hour at a time.

There was chemical assistance available to deal with the problem, but Naylor was both afraid of taking a couple of the pink pills and philosophically opposed to the idea. He had instead consumed vast amounts of coffee, which had worked at first, but only at first.

He was exhausted. The air phase of the war against Saddam Hussein had kicked off about four hours ago. It had been decided that Iraqi radar positions had to be taken out before a massive bombing and interdiction campaign began. And it had been further decided that the Army would take them out using Boeing AH-64B attack helicopters.

The idea was that the Iraqi radar would be on the alert for Air Force and Navy bombers, fighter-bombers, and other high-flying, high-speed aircraft, and that the Apaches, flying "nap of the earth"—a few feet off the ground, "under the radar"—could sneak in and destroy the radar installations before the Iraqis knew they were there.

It was the first time—except for the invasion of Grenada, which had been a command and control disaster—that really close coordination between what really were three air forces—Air Force, Navy, and Army—would be required, and this time there could be no foul-up.

The air commander, General Chuck Horner, USAF, had the responsibility for the mission. But he would be using the Army's Apaches, so Naylor had been taking, so to speak, his operational orders from him. That had gone well. Naylor liked the former fighter pilot much more than other senior Air Force officers he had come to know, and they had worked well together.

The thirty-six hours leading up to 0238 local time had been a period of intense activity in the two-floors-below-ground command center, and Naylor, as the J-3 (*J* meaning "Joint Command," *-3* meaning "Plans and Training") had been at the center of that activity, which meant not only the final preparations but in being in close proximity to General Horner's boss, General H. Norman Schwarzkopf, USA, the overall commander.

"Stormin' Norman" had a legendary temper and it had erupted a half-dozen times. Naylor considered it among his other obligations the soothing of battered senior officer egos after they had been the target of a Schwarzkopfian tirade, and there had been three of these.

Naylor and General Horner, who was subordinate only to Schwarzkopf, had already talked—circuitously, it was true—about the absolute necessity of keeping General Freddy Franks, who would command the ground war when that started, and Schwarzkopf as far apart as possible. Freddy was a mild-mannered man who didn't even cuss, but he had a temper, too, and he would neither take—nor forgive later—the kind of abuse Stormin' Norman was liable to send his way if displeased.

And it seemed inevitable to both Chuck Horner and Allan Naylor that Freddy sooner or later would do something to displease Stormin' Norman. Yet, in the opinion of both, Desert Storm needed both Freddy Franks and Stormin' Norman Schwarzkopf.

The giggles which General Naylor was unable to shake had to deal with General Schwarzkopf and a hapless, just-arrived light colonel attached to J-2 (Intelligence). There were some classified documents in the safe to which the light colonel would need access. However, access to the documents was really restricted, and Schwarzkopf himself had to sign the authorization.

The light colonel had been told of the procedure. He was familiar with others like it, in other headquarters. And so he had sat before a computer terminal and typed up the access document for Schwarzkopf's signature and then taken his place in line of those who wanted a minute of Schwarzkopf's time.

His turn finally came. He marched into Schwarzkopf's office, saluted, identified himself, said he needed the general's signature on the access document and offered it to the general.

The general glanced at it, glowered at the light colonel, and announced, "I'm only going to tell you this once, Colonel. I'm not normal."

"Sir?"

"Goddammit, are you deaf? I said I'm not normal."

He had then tossed—possibly threw—the access document across his desk in the general direction of the light colonel, who had then, understandably confused and shaken, picked the access document from the floor and fled.

Only several minutes later, when the light colonel had reported the incident to the J-2, and the J-2 had pointed it out to him, did the lieutenant colonel realize that when he had typed the signature block for Schwarzkopf's signature he'd made a typo. What he had laid before Stormin' Norman had read, "H. Normal Schwarzkopf, General, U.S. Army, Commanding."

Naylor had been giggling uncontrollably since hearing the story, which was bad for three reasons: He was laughing at the behavior of his immediate superior. He was laughing at a mishap of a junior officer, which was worse. And it meant that he was pushing his physical envelope to the breaking point and that was worse than anything. He would need, if anything came up—and something inevitably would—not only all the brains God had given him but those brains in perfect working order.

With that it mind, he had gone to his small but comfortable office and told Master Sergeant Jack Dunham, his senior noncom, to see that he wasn't bothered unless it was really important. He closed the door and lay down on a folding cot. And giggled.

He had been in his office not quite ten minutes and was seriously debating with himself the possible merits of taking a medicinal drink when the door opened.

Colonel J. Brewster Wallace from Public Relations came into the room. As a general rule of thumb, General Naylor did not like public relations officers, and he specifically disliked Colonel J. Brewster Wallace.

"Sorry to bother you, General," Colonel Wallace began.

If you're sorry, you pasty-faced sonofabitch, why did you bull your way past my sergeant? That took some doing.

"Not a problem. What have you got, Colonel?"

"First one, General."

"First one what?"

"Recommendation for an impact award."

An impact award meant decorating a soldier immediately for something he had just done rather than running it through the bureaucratic procedure, which could take weeks or even months. The actions of the individual and the circumstances had to be such that there was no question he had done something at great personal risk above and beyond the call of duty.

"Why are you showing this to me?" Naylor asked as he reached for the computer printout.

"I thought you might want to show it to General Schwarzkopf," Colonel Wallace said. "This one's going to make all the papers. An Apache pilot, a West Pointer, whose father won the Medal of Honor in Vietnam."

Naylor read the computer printout.

```
PRIORITY


SECRET


0705 16 JANUARY 1991


FROM COMMANDING OFFICER
     403RD AVIATION BATTALION


TO COMMANDER IN CHIEF
    US CENTRAL COMMAND


ATTN: J-1


INFO: PUBLIC AFFAIRS


1. THE UNDERSIGNED STRONGLY RECOMMENDS THE IMPACT AWARD
OF THE DISTINGUISHED FLYING CROSS AND THE PURPLE HEART
MEDAL TO SECOND LIEUTENANT C. G. CASTILLO, SSN
245220136, AVIATION, 155TH ATTACK HELICOPTER COMPANY,
WITH CITATION AS FOLLOWS:


SECOND LIEUTENANT CASTILLO WAS FLYING AS COPILOT OF AN
AH-64B ATTACK HELICOPTER IN THE OPENING HOURS OF
OPERATION DESERT STORM. AFTER SUCCESSFULLY DESTROYING
SEVERAL IRAQI RADAR INSTALLATIONS AND OTHER TARGETS,
THE AIRCRAFT WAS STRUCK AND SEVERELY DAMAGED BY IRAQI
ANTI-AIRCRAFT FIRE. THE PILOT WAS BLINDED, LIEUTENANT
CASTILLO WAS WOUNDED, AND HIS WINDSCREEN WAS DESTROYED.
LIEUTENANT CASTILLO TOOK THE CONTROLS OF THE AIRCRAFT
```

```
AND DESPITE HIS PAINFUL WOUNDS AND THE LOSS OF
ESSENTIALLY ALL COMMUNICATIONS AND NAVIGATION EQUIPMENT
FLEW THE DAMAGED AIRCRAFT MORE THAN 100 MILES BACK TO
HIS BASE.

2. SUBJECT OFFICER IS A 1990 GRADUATE OF THE US
MILITARY ACADEMY. HIS NEXT OF KIN ARE HIS GRANDPARENTS,
MR. AND MRS. JUAN FERNANDO CASTILLO, BOX 19, ROUTE 7,
UVALDE, TEXAS. HIS FATHER, WOJG JORGE ALEJANDRO
CASTILLO, WAS POSTHUMOUSLY AWARDED THE MEDAL OF HONOR
AS A HELICOPTER PILOT IN VIETNAM. HIS MOTHER IS
DECEASED.

3. PHOTOGRAPHS OF SUBJECT OFFICER AND THE BATTLE
DAMAGED HELICOPTER WILL BE FORWARDED AS SOON AS
POSSIBLE.

MARTIN C. SEWARD
LT COL, AVIATION
COMMANDING
```

Major General Naylor looked at Colonel Wallace and said, "How badly was this officer wounded? Do we know?"

"He can't be too badly hurt, General, if he flew that shot-up Apache a hundred miles. I think they would have said something if he was seriously injured."

Naylor snorted.

"You see what I mean, sir?" Colonel Wallace asked. "It's a great story! The son of a Medal of Honor winner, and I think we can infer he's a Tex-Mex, with all the implications of that. This will be on the front page of every newspaper in the country tomorrow."

"No, it won't," General Naylor said.

"Sir?"

"Listen to me carefully, Colonel. I am placing an embargo on this story. It is not to be released, leaked, talked about, anything, unless and until General Schwarzkopf overrides my decision. Is that clear?"

"It's clear, sir, but I don't understand . . ."

"Good. We understand each other. That will be all, Colonel. Thank you."

The office of Major General Oswald L. Young, the J-1 (Personnel) of Central
Command, in the command bunker was almost identical to that of Major
General Naylor, and the two were old friends.

"Got a minute for me, Oz?" Naylor asked.

"Any time, Allan. I was just thinking about you—specifically, of Freddy
Lustrous—and wishing I had his ass-chewing ability. I remembered one he
gave you and me in 'Nam. I just did my best, but it wasn't in the same league."

"I'm thinking of delivering one of my own," Naylor said. "What was yours
about?"

"They had a pool out there. Twenty bucks. Winner take all. The winner was
to be the guy who picked the number closest to the actual number of casualties we'll take in the first twenty-four hours."

"Jesus!"

"Actually, there were several such pools. KIA. WIA. MIA. Plus, lost fighters, lost A-10s, lost Apaches. Goddamn, I don't understand people who could
do that. It wasn't a bunch of old sergeants, either. A couple of colonels were
happy gamblers. What's rubbed you the wrong way?"

"Aviators. Jesus Christ, they're worse than the goddamned Marines! Anything for publicity that makes them look good."

"Going down that road, I just got a recommendation for an impact DFC
for an aviator, an Apache pilot who did good."

"Who shouldn't have been anywhere near where he was. Those goddamned
sonsofbitches!"

"I thought I was the only one around here who lost his temper," a voice said
from the door. It had been opened without first knocking by General H. Norman Schwarzkopf.

Neither Major General Naylor nor Major General Young said anything but
General Young got out of his chair.

"I'm glad you're here, Allan," Schwarzkopf said. "I was coming to see you
next. After I tell you two why I'm pissed off, you can tell me what the goddamned sonsofbitches you were talking about have done. Or haven't done."

"Yes, sir," Major Generals Naylor and Young said, almost simultaneously.

"Have either of you heard about an office pool, or pools, being run around
here?"

"Sir, I have dealt with that situation," General Young said.

"You, Allan?"

"I didn't know about it until just a moment ago, sir," Naylor said. He looked at Young. "Were some of my people involved?"

Young nodded.

"Sir, I will deal with that situation immediately," Naylor said.

"Okay. So you weren't talking about that. Who has you so pissed off?"

Naylor did not immediately respond.

"Take your time, Allan," Schwarzkopf said. "I've got nothing else to do but stand here waiting for you to find your tongue."

"Sir . . . Oz, have you got the message from the 403rd?"

"Right here," General Young said, picked it up from his in-box, and handed it to Naylor who handed it to Schwarzkopf who read it.

"Something wrong with this? You don't believe it, is that what you're saying?"

"Oh, I believe he did it, sir," Naylor said. "With the trumpets of glory ringing in his ears."

"You're losing me, Allan. When I was young and a second lieutenant, I heard those trumpets. Didn't we all?"

"Sir, he graduated from the Point in June."

"I saw that. So?"

"Sir, you don't go from the plain to the cockpit of an Apache in six months."

"Uuuh," General Schwarzkopf grunted. "You know this kid, Allan?"

"Yes, sir. I talked him into going to the Point."

"You're saying he got special treatment?"

"I'm saying . . . what I said before, General, was that Aviation is worse than the Marines about getting publicity."

"Because of his father, his father's MOH, they rushed him through training and sent him over here?"

"Where he is way over his head," Naylor said.

"He seems to have done pretty well," Schwarzkopf said.

"He's over his head, sir," Naylor argued.

"You don't think he deserves the DFC?"

"Yes, sir, I think he does. And he was wounded. What I want to do is get him out of there before he kills himself trying to do something else he's not capable of doing."

"Jesus, Allan. People get killed," General Young said.

"And some sonsofbitches are willing to bet on how many," Schwarzkopf said. "I think I know what Allan's thinking. The Class of '50, right?"

"That's in my mind, sir. My brother was in the Class of '50."

"And didn't come back from Korea?" Schwarzkopf asked.

"Tom had been an officer six months when he was killed, sir."

"And your son is here, too, right, with Freddy Franks?"

"Allan's Class of '88, sir. He's had two and a half years to learn how to be a tank platoon leader."

"I take your point. I always thought it was insanity to get the Class of '50 nearly wiped out in Korea," Schwarzkopf said. "You can't eat the seeds. If you do, you don't get a crop." He paused. "Okay, Allan, I'm going to give you the benefit of the doubt on this. Handle it any way you want."

"Thank you, sir. Sir, I told Colonel Wallace to embargo this story until you gave him permission to release it."

"You think that's important?"

"Yes, sir, I do."

"Okay. It's squashed. There will be other impact awards. So far, Phase I—knock on wood—seems to be going well."

"Thank you, sir."

"I don't want to hear one more goddamned word about a how-many-casualties pool. Understood?"

"Yes, sir," Generals Naylor and Young said, almost in unison.

General Schwarzkopf momentarily locked eyes with each of them and walked out of the office.

"So what do we do with this young officer?" General Young asked.

"You're the personnel officer, Oz. You tell me."

"Okay. There aren't many options. Or at least good ones," General Young said. "If he got out of West Point six months ago, and is an Apache pilot, we can presume two things: one, that he can fly helicopters . . ."

"If my memory serves, it takes longer than six months to get qualified in an Apache, *after* you've got X many hundred hours and X many years flying Hueys."

"I think you're right. Can I go on?"

"Sorry."

"We can presume he can fly helicopters—the Huey, at least, since you have doubts that he should be flying the Apache—and is qualified in no other useful skill, like being an Infantry or Armor platoon leader."

"Okay."

"And if he stays in Aviation, and all those terrible things you think Aviation brass is doing to him are true—and I think you're probably right—and is an Apache pilot, they will continue to put him in an Apache cockpit . . ."

"Where he will get killed, and probably get a lot of people with him killed," Naylor interrupted.

"Allan, by now you should have vented your temper," General Young said. "The problem is a given. Now, let's find a solution."

"Sorry, Oz."

"Schwarzkopf has given you a blank check. At one end of that range of options is a message saying this young man is grounded, by order of H. Normal himself."

This time when Naylor heard "H. Normal" it didn't seem at all funny.

"I don't think we want to do that," General Young went on, "for a number of reasons that should be self-evident. So what's left? We have to get him out of Aviation, but where can we send him? I have a suggestion which I sort of thought you would think of first. You set it up."

"What did I set up?"

"The 2303rd Civil Government Detachment," Young said, "commanded by Colonel Bruce J. McNab. A classmate of ours. Who we can talk to. You, or me, or both of us."

"And I told you when I set it up that I didn't like it; that what it was was Green Beanie McNab playing James Bond. General Schwarzkopf was told to do it by Colin Powell personally, and he told me to do it and not to ask any more questions than I had to. But we both know that whatever Scotty McNab's involved with, it doesn't have very much to do with civil government."

"We don't *think* it has much to do with civil government," Young said. "Unless you know something I don't?"

Naylor shook his head, and then asked, "What would Castillo do there?"

"There's six, maybe eight Hueys on McNab's TO&E," Young said, referencing the Table of Organization & Equipment. "He could fly one of those."

"For all I know, Scotty is planning to fly into Baghdad in one or more of those Hueys and try to kidnap, or assassinate, Saddam Hussein."

"I frankly wouldn't be surprised. But, to repeat, you or me, or both of us, could have a word with him, and make sure he understands this young officer is not to be put in harm's way for the benefit of Army Aviation public relations."

"If McNab's doing something covert . . ." Naylor said, thoughtfully. "I said that about Hussein to be clever, but, now that I think about it, I'm not so sure it's that far off the mark—he's certainly got some cover operation up and running to hide it. A perfectly legitimate military operation, possibly even having something to do with civil governments."

"Probably," Young agreed.

"From which he can detach whatever number of people he needs to conduct whatever, almost certainly illegal, operation he wants to do without attracting much attention."

Young nodded in agreement.

"Oz, how about you transferring Castillo to the 2303rd Civil Government Detachment and I will get on the horn to Colonel Scotty McNab and tell him that whatever he does with Castillo is not to be even remotely connected with what he is doing covertly?"

"Done," Young said. "But I think I'd better talk to Scotty, not you."

"Why?"

"Because it takes you out of the loop," Young said. "Over the years, Allan, you've spoken to me of Lieutenant Castillo. Often."

"Have I?"

"Yeah. And I got the feeling you're really fond of him."

"Guilty."

"This way, I received the impact recommendation and wondered how this young officer could be flying an Apache six months out of West Point, drew the same conclusions you did, went to H. Normal, got his permission to fix it, and am doing so."

"I owe you a big one, Oz," Naylor said.

"Don't worry. I'll get it back," General Young said.

[EIGHT]
Office of the Assistant Chief of Staff, J-3
United States Central Command
Ministry of Defense and Aviation Air Force Base
Riyadh, Saudi Arabia
1530 1 March 1991

"Sir," Master Sergeant Jack Dunham said, a strange look on his face, "there's an officer out there . . ."—he gestured toward the closed door—". . . who said, and I quote, sir, 'Be a good fellow, Sergeant, present the compliments of Colonel Bruce J. McNab to the general and ask the general if I might have a few moments of his valuable time.' "

Major General Allan Naylor replied, "Why do I have the feeling, Jack, that you think Colonel McNab could not melt inconspicuously into a group of, say, a dozen other colonels?"

"I've got twenty-four years' service, General, and I never saw . . ."

Naylor chuckled and smiled.

"My compliments to Colonel McNab, Sergeant, and inform him that I would be delighted to see him at his convenience."

"Yes, sir," Dunham said, then went to the door and opened it and said, "General Naylor will see you, Colonel."

"Good show!" a voice boomed in an English accent, and through the door came a small, muscular, ruddy-faced man sporting a flowing red mustache. He was wearing aviator sunglasses. His chest, thickly coated with red hair, was visible through a mostly unbuttoned khaki jacket, the sleeves of which were rolled up. General Naylor was sure the khaki "African Hunter's Safari Jacket" had not passed through the U.S. Army Quartermaster Corps, and neither had Colonel McNab's khaki shorts, knee-length brown stockings, or hunting boots.

On McNab's head was an Arabian headdress, circled with two gold cords, which Naylor had recently learned indicated the wearer was an Arabian nobleman. The white cape of whatever the headdress was called hung to McNab's shoulders. In the center of it, barely visible between the two gold cords, was the silver eagle of a colonel. An Uzi 9mm submachine gun hung from leather straps around his neck. A spare magazine for the Uzi protruded from an upper pocket of the shooting jacket and the outlines of fragmentation grenades bulged both lower pockets.

He saluted.

"Thank you ever so much, General, for granting me your valuable time."

Naylor returned the salute.

"Close the door, please, Colonel," Naylor said.

"Yes, of course, sir. Forgive me," Colonel McNab said and went and closed the door. Then he turned and smiled at Naylor. "I was hoping that you would not be overwhelmed to see me. But for old times' sake, you may kiss me. Chastely, of course."

Despite himself, Naylor laughed and smiled.

"It's good to see you, Scotty," he said and came around his desk and offered his hand. McNab wrapped his arms around him in a bear hug.

"How the hell did you get into the building dressed like that?"

"Easily. For one, I was on the list of those summoned to the Schwarzkopf throne room. For another—perhaps as important—to whom do you think Stormin' Normal's bodyguards owe their primary allegiance?"

"I wondered where they came from," Naylor admitted.

"Nurtured to greatness by my own capable hands. You've noticed, I'm sure, that he's still walking around? Despite the many people—most of them on his staff—who would love to kill him?"

"What did General Schwarzkopf want? Did someone tell him about your uniform? Using the term loosely."

"To answer that, I have to overcome my well-known modesty," McNab said. "I got another medal, and General Schwarzkopf wanted to tell me himself that, terribly belatedly, the powers that be have recognized my potential and sent it to that collection of clowns on Capitol Hill known as the Senate, seeking their acquiescence in my becoming a brigadier general."

"It's overdue, Scotty," Naylor said.

"There are those, Allan my boy, who are going to beat their breasts and gnash their teeth while shrieking 'the injustice of it all.' Infidels are not supposed to get into heaven."

Naylor thought: *He's right. A whole hell of a lot of colonels who have spent their careers getting their tickets punched and never making waves are going to shit a brick when they hear Scotty McNab got his star.*

"When you pin the star on," Naylor said, "you'll find that it's anything but heaven."

"I told Powell I would just as soon stay where I was, thank you just the same. He talked me into it, saying it was the price I had to pay for being right again."

He means that. I am in the presence of the only colonel in the U.S. Army who would tell the chairman of the Joint Chiefs he didn't want to be a general.

"Right about what?"

"Who do you think won this war, Freddy Franks and his tanks? Chuck Horner and his airplanes?"

"I think they had a lot to do with it."

"I am a profound admirer of Generals Franks and Horner and you know it, but Special Ops won this war. We took out the Iraqi radar and communications. The only airplanes—with a couple of exceptions—Chuck Horner lost were due to pilot error or aircraft failure and he admits it. The greatest loss of life was caused by that one Scud we didn't take out and that hit the barracks in Saudi Arabia. By the time Freddy drove across the berms, the Iraqis had no communications worth mentioning and thus no command and control."

"The *one* Scud you didn't take out?"

"Or render inoperable. Or bring back with us. I understand the Air Force was really disappointed to learn how primitive those things are."

"What decoration did you get?"

McNab reached in his jacket pocket, rooted down beside the Uzi magazine, came out with a Distinguished Service Medal, and dangled it back and forth for a moment.

I can't imagine Schwarzkopf pinning the DSM on that khaki jacket, but obviously that's exactly what just happened.

"I gather the presentation ceremony was rather informal," Naylor said. Then he asked, "You do have some reason for being dressed like that?"

"Aside from I like it, you mean?"

Naylor nodded. "You want some coffee, Scotty?"

"I've got a footlocker full of booze on my dune buggy outside," McNab said. "Formerly the property of the U.S. embassy in Kuwait City. I thought you might like a drink."

"Against the rules."

"You haven't changed, have you?"

"If I drink, other people will want to and think they can."

"They don't have to know. You don't have to stand in your door and shout, 'Hey, everybody. Fuck the Arabs, I'm going to have a snort.'"

"And you haven't changed, either, I see," Naylor said.

"You wouldn't love me, Allan, if I did," McNab said.

"I wouldn't love you no matter what you did," Naylor said.

"You just want to see me cry," McNab said.

"Now, that's a thought," Naylor said.

McNab smiled at him.

"You know where you're going when you get the star?" Naylor asked.

"Bragg. Deputy commander, or some such, of the Special Warfare Center. What I'm going to be doing is writing up what we did right in this war so we can do it right when we have to do it again."

"You think we're going to have to do it again?"

"Yeah, of course we are. MacArthur was right when he said, 'There is no substitute for victory,' and so was whoever said, 'Those who don't read history are doomed to repeat it.'"

"I guess what the president was worried about was a lengthy occupation with a hell of a lot of guerrilla warfare," Naylor said.

"Freddy Franks told me (a) he could have had his tanks in Baghdad in probably less than forty-eight hours and (b) he was really worried about a lengthy occupation with a hell of a lot of guerrilla warfare. I had the feeling he was more than a little relieved he didn't have to make the decision."

"You really think we're going to have to do this again?"

"The only question is when," McNab said. "Next year. Two years from now. A decade. But we'll be here again. Saddam Hussein is a devout student of Stalin's Keep the People In Line techniques. A real sonofabitch. We're going to have to take him out sooner or later. Christ knows that if I could have found the sonofabitch, I would have taken him out myself."

"I hope you're wrong," Naylor said.

"The cross resting so heavily on my manly shoulders for all these years has been that I rarely am wrong," McNab said.

"Jesus Christ, you're impossible!" Naylor said, laughing.

" 'It is difficult to be modest when you're great,' " McNab said. "Frank Lloyd Wright said that."

"I'll try to remember," Naylor said. "Is there something I can do for you, Scotty? Or is this just a visit?"

"I thought you'd never ask," McNab said. "First, I want to thank you for sending me Second Lieutenant Castillo. Which I just did. He almost restored my respect for Hudson High."

"Let me have that again?"

"You haven't heard my speech? 'What's Wrong with West Point'?"

"I got a copy of Donn Starry's speech. The one he gave to the Association of Graduates? The one that began, 'I have many memories of my four years as an inmate of this institution, none of them favorable'?"

"Ah, yes. But General Starry has always hated to say anything that might in any way offend anyone. Mine wasn't so polite."

"I can't imagine you being anything but polite, Scotty. But that's not what I was asking. You 'just heard' that I sent you Castillo?"

"I went to Oz Young and said, mustering up my best manners, 'Thank you for sending me Castillo. And now I want to keep him.' Whereupon Oz said, 'I can't do it. See Allan Naylor. He's the one who sent you Castillo.' "

"Oz said that, did he?"

"He led me to believe that you are that splendid young officer's mentor, or sort of a de facto loving stepfather, or both."

"I've known him since he was twelve," Naylor said, "at which age he became an orphan. I've sort of kept my eye on him."

"He let me know, just now, that he has the pleasure of your acquaintance—just that, not that you have a personal thing going. He said if there was time, he would like to pay his respects."

"He's here?"

"At the moment, he's my pilot. I don't trust just anyone to haul my dune buggy around."

"You brought your dune buggy here? Slung under a helicopter?"

"Lieutenant Castillo at this very moment is seeing that it is loaded aboard the C-5 which will carry me to the Land of the Big PX later today."

"You're taking your dune buggy to the States with you?"

"I told them it was going to the museum at Bragg."

"My God!" Naylor said, and then without thinking added, "I'd love to see him."

"I told him he had until 1600. I'm sure he'll show up here to see you." McNab paused. "I want to keep him, Allan."

"What for?"

"For openers, my aide-de-camp," McNab said. "While I'm writing up what we did right here, I'll run him through Special Forces training."

"I thought you had to have five years of service to even apply for Special Forces training."

"That's right," McNab said. "And you need three years and I don't know how many hundred hours of pilot time before you can apply for the Apache program. Oz told me about that, too."

"This will probably piss you off, Scotty, but I don't like the idea of him being in Special Forces."

"Because like just about everybody else in the Army, you don't like Special Forces? We don't play by the rules? God only knows what those crazy bastards will do next?"

"I didn't say that," Naylor said.

"But that's what you meant," McNab said. "Allan, you're just going to have to get used to the idea that Special Operations is where the Army is going. Can I say something that will piss you off?"

"I'm surprised that you asked first. Shoot."

"You are, old buddy, behaving like the Cavalry types who told I. D. White that he was making a terrible mistake, pissing his assured career in Cavalry away when he left his horses at Fort Riley in 1941 and went to Fort Knox to play with tanks."

"Possibly," Naylor said, aware that he was annoyed.

"And like the paratroop types who said the same thing to Alan Burdette, Jack Tolson, and the others when they stopped jumping out of airplanes at Benning and Bragg and went to Camp Rucker in the early fifties to learn how to fly. That was supposed to have ended their chances to get a star."

"Okay."

"White wound up with four stars, Burdette and Tolson with three. They did not throw their careers away because they could see the future. I'm not asking this kid to do what I did . . ."

"What do you mean?"

"When I took the Special Forces route, Bull Simon himself told me he wanted to be sure I understood that I would be lucky to make light bird in Special Forces and that my chances of getting a star were right up there with my chances of being taken bodily into heaven."

"Point taken."

"Charley Castillo is a natural for Special Forces," McNab said.

"Because he slings your dune buggy under a Huey?"

"No. I mean he has a feel for it."

"I don't think I follow you," Naylor said. "What makes you think that?"

"I don't know how much you got to hear about the Russians we grabbed?"

"Not very much," Naylor admitted. The incident had been talked about, but not much, because it had been classified top secret, and he hadn't had any bona fide need to know.

"Okay. Quick after-action. After the air war started, when Chuck Horner had given us air superiority, that gave us more freedom of action with our choppers. The Air Force really wanted a Scud and I was asked if I thought I could get them one. I checked and there was one about eighty klicks into the desert. They were getting ready to shoot it at this place. Anyway, I staged a mission, two Apaches and four Black Hawks. Forty, forty-five minutes in, five minutes to take out the crew, fifteen minutes on the ground to figure out how to pick the sonofabitch up . . ."

"You didn't know you were going to move it?"

"We figured we would improvise," McNab said, a little sarcastically. "And forty-five minutes out. It should have gone according to schedule, but when my guys got on the ground they found that all the guys with their hands up weren't Iraqis. We had two Iraqi generals, one Russian general, one Russian colonel, and half a dozen other non-Iraqis. The generals were visiting the site; the others were there to make sure the Scud shot straight. They would really have liked to hit this place. We weren't on the ground long enough to really find out for sure, but Charley . . ."

"You're talking about Castillo? He was on this operation?"

"I tried very hard, Allan, to keep him alive. He wasn't in on the operation. We were sitting in my Huey thirty klicks from the Scud site, in the middle of nowhere. We had to get that close so we could talk to the choppers and I could relay the word that we were coming out to our air defense people. Okay?"

Naylor nodded he understood.

"So they give us a yell, tell us about the Russians and what are we supposed to do with them? Then I had to go to the site, of course. So we went to the site. It took us no more than ten minutes or so, but that added ten minutes to the operation time. The Iraqis were about to figure out that all was not well. And I had to decide what to do with the Russians, which depended on who the Russians were, and do that in a hell of a hurry.

"When I got out of the Huey, I muttered something like, 'I wish I spoke better Russian,' or words to that effect, and Charley says, 'Sir, I speak Russian.' So I took him with me. And found out he speaks Russian like a native. And German.

"So, five minutes after we touched down, thanks to Charley, I knew who was going with us and who we were leaving behind. We brought out one Iraqi general, one Russian general, one Russian colonel, and three of the technicians, who were probably ex–East Germans who moved to Russia. We weren't there long enough to find out for sure."

"And the Scud, of course," Naylor said.

"Yeah, and the Scud. One of the Black Hawks just picked it up and flew off with it."

"Well, a Black Hawk can carry a 105mm howitzer, its crew, and thirty rounds," Naylor began, then paused and added, "The story that went around here was that half a dozen Iraqi helicopters had defected."

"That happened because we came here, because of the prisoners, not where we were supposed to go, and got picked up on radar. And somebody with a big mouth here let the press know six choppers were approaching the border but were not to be shot at. We had to give some explanation."

"If you can't tell me, don't. But what happened to the prisoners?"

"We turned the Iraqi over to the Saudis and then we flew the officers and the technicians to Vienna on Royal Air Arabia and put them on an Aeroflot flight to Moscow. Still wearing the clothes they were wearing when we grabbed them. And with copies of the pictures we took of them at the site . . ." —McNab smiled—". . . including some of them with my guys' arms around their shoulders, apparently having a hell of a time."

"What was that all about? Sending them to Moscow?"

"That came from either the agency or the State Department. I don't think— at least, I never heard—that anything was ever done officially, a complaint to the UN or something, that Russians were servicing the Scuds. But they couldn't deny the whole thing. We had the pictures, and somehow they lost their identification papers and we found them."

"That's a hell of story," Naylor said.

"Which I will deny ever telling you, of course, should someone ask. The point of me telling you this war story was so I could explain why, before we got back here, I could see a hundred places where Charley would be useful with his languages, and then when we took the Russians to Vienna and I saw him working with them I decided I wanted him. Had to have him."

"What he should be doing is time with troops, now that this war is over," Naylor said. "You did it, and I did it, when we were second lieutenants, and he should, too."

"I thought it was a waste of my time when I did it," McNab said. "I knew I wasn't going to spend thirty years of my life with cannons going off in my ears. And you know as well as I do if Charley goes back to Aviation they'll pull this 'like father, like son' bullshit all over again. He'll spend his time giving speeches to Rotary Clubs and you know it. And I'm not kidding about needing him. If I had to come up with the two most important skills for an aide to a Special Forces general, they would be: fly a helicopter, and speak as many languages other than English as possible."

"And what if I say no, Scotty? What if I say, 'This young officer has done too many unusual things already in his brief career and now it's time that he had a large dose of normal.' "

"I hope you don't, Allan. I would hate to remember this so far heartwarming reunion of ours with rancor."

As if on cue, Master Sergeant Dunham put his head in the door.

"Sir, Second Lieutenant Castillo wonders if you can spare him a moment?"

Naylor made a send-him-in gesture with his hands.

Except that he wasn't wearing an Arabian headdress, Castillo was dressed very much like Colonel McNab. The buttons of his khaki African Hunter's Safari Jacket were closed, but he was wearing shorts and knee-high stockings. A CAR-16, the "carbine" version of the standard M-16 rifle, was slung from his shoulder.

Naylor didn't see any grenade outlines.

But he saw enough to realize that the young lieutenant had fallen under the spell of—as he thought of it, had been corrupted by—Scotty McNab and there was no way he would be happy doing what he really should be doing.

Castillo saluted and then saw Colonel McNab.

"I didn't expect to see you here, sir."

"You can hug that ugly old man, Charley," McNab said. "I did."

"God, it's good to see you, Charley," Naylor said and spread his arms.

"It's good to see you, sir."

They embraced.

"I just told Colonel McNab, feeling like a father selling his daughter to a brothel keeper, that if you're insane enough to want to get involved with Special Forces I will give you my very reluctant blessing."

"I really would like to go, sir."

"It's done, then," Naylor said. "Colonel McNab, why don't you kill, say, thirty minutes—go slit a few throats; blow something up—and give Charley and me a few minutes alone?"

VI
SPRING 2005

[ONE]
The Mayflower Hotel
1127 Connecticut Avenue NW
Washington, D.C.
1655 31 May 2005

"So you became this Green Beret colonel's fair-haired boy?" Fernando asked.

Castillo nodded. He asked with a raised eyebrow if Fernando wanted another drink. Fernando held out his empty glass.

" 'Fair-haired boy' does not accurately describe what I was," Castillo said. "But I went right to work for him."

"He could arrange your transfer just like that?"

"The C-5 landed us—and McNab's dune buggy—at Dover Air Force Base, in Delaware," Castillo said. "McNab told me to get the dune buggy to the Special Warfare Center at Fort Bragg and when I had I could take ten days off after which I was to report to him at Bragg. I asked him how I was supposed to get the dune buggy off the air base, much less to Fort Bragg. He said he was sure I would figure something out and left me there, right then, standing beside the dune buggy on the tarmac, in my short pants, bush jacket, and ghutra."

"Short pants? Bush jacket? And what?"

"And knee-high stockings," Castillo said. "Don't want to forget those."

Fernando's face showed he wanted an explanation.

"I got the story from guys who were with him before I got there," Castillo said. "He lined them all up, said that he had looked into previous hostilities in the area, and learned that the Brit uniform had been short pants, bush jackets, and knee-high stockings. He had therefore purchased, with his discretionary operating funds, a supply of same from a hunting outfitter in Nairobi. They made, he said, a lot more sense than what the Army was issuing to ordinary soldiers."

"And the other thing? The goot-something?"

"That came next," Castillo said, smiling. "According to the story I got, he went on to say that Lawrence of Arabia, who had been a very successful irregular warrior in the area, always wore a *ghutra an iqal,* the standard Arab headdress." He made a circular movement around the front of his head.

Fernando's nod told him he had the picture.

"Actually, there's two kinds, one with a red-and-white headcloth. That's the *shumagh,*" Castillo went on. "With a white headcloth, it's a *ghutra.* Since Lawrence had learned it was a practical item of military clothing for Arabia, that was good enough for McNab and his special operators. It obviously made more sense than a Kevlar helmet, since they were going to be out on the desert in the sun a lot. He had acquired a supply of them—one size fits all—in Riyadh."

"And you all actually wore this thing?"

"I admit, some heads turned when we showed up in Riyadh," Castillo said, chuckling.

"So how did you get the dune buggy to Fort Bragg?"

"I knew how far I would get if I went to the Air Force with my problem—especially in my Lawrence of Arabia uniform—so I went into Dover, rented a ton-and-a-half truck from U-Haul, loaded the dune buggy aboard, and drove to Bragg. Thank God for the American Express card. Then I went home, spent ten days with Abuela and Grandpa, and then went back to Bragg."

"While I sat in the goddamned desert," Fernando said, "drinking lukewarm bottled water and eating MREs."

"I admit I was really beginning to think that I was something special," Castillo said. "Which notion was promptly taken from me when I got to Bragg. By then, he was Brigadier General McNab. I expected either thanks or even congratulations for getting his damned buggy to Bragg. Instead, he chewed me out for not protecting the footlocker full of scotch and cognac . . ."

"What?"

"Before the Marines liberated Kuwait City, Special Ops guys were there. Including McNab. His first stop was the U.S. embassy, where he blew the door on the crypto room, and filled a footlocker with the booze the diplomats had locked up before getting out. I had forgotten it was still on the dune buggy.

"He said if I was going to be in Special Forces, I was going to have to understand that Special Forces people could be trusted with anything but somebody else's whiskey and I could consider myself lucky that nobody at SWC thought I could possibly have been stupid enough to leave it on the dune buggy and that it had still been there when he collected the buggy."

Fernando laughed.

"And then he said he was going to charm school . . ."

"What?"

"I didn't know what it was, either," Castillo replied. "What they do is gather all the just-promoted-to-brigadier-generals together, usually at Fort Leavenworth, the Command and General Staff School?"

"I know about Leavenworth," Fernando said.

". . . and the chief of staff and some other really senior brass tell them how to behave as general officers. McNab said the real purpose was to make sure the new generals didn't get too big for their solid striped trousers . . ."

"That's right," Fernando said. "Generals have one solid stripe down the seam of their trousers, don't they? I'd forgotten that."

". . . and with that in mind, I was on the four-forty flight from Fayetteville to Columbus, Georgia, via Atlanta, where, starting the next morning, I was to begin the course of instruction leading to being rated as a parachutist.

" 'Don't pay any attention to their bullshit, Charley,' McNab said. 'They still think what they call "airborne"—vertical envelopment, which means a thousand hanging targets floating down onto a field—is modern warfare, and getting those wings is an end in itself. Just keep your mouth shut, get through the course, and then come back here and we'll get you some useful training.'

"So less than twenty-four hours after I arrived at Bragg, a decorated, wounded hero who had been on a couple of interesting operations, and was now to be the aide-de-camp to the deputy commander of the Special Warfare Center, I found myself lying in the mud at Benning with a barrel-chested hillbilly sergeant—his name was Staff Sergeant Dudley J. Johnson, Jr.; I'll never forget that—in a T-shirt with AIRBORNE printed on it standing over me screaming— I couldn't do forty push-ups—that he couldn't understand how a fucking flaming faggot—I loved that line—like me got into the Army, much less into jump school, and I better get my act in gear or he would send me back to whatever fairy-fucking dipshit outfit I came from so fast my asshole wouldn't catch up for six months."

"I know the type of gentle, nurturing, noncommissioned officer to which you refer," Fernando said, laughing. But then he had a thought and asked:

"Didn't he know you were a lieutenant? Had been in Desert Storm? Worse, that you were a West Pointer?"

"That I was a lieutenant? Yeah, sure. But rank doesn't count in jump school. And I was still a second lieutenant. He probably thought I'd just graduated from OCS, or, more than likely, from some ROTC college. He didn't think I'd been in Desert Storm, because I was there. McNab brought me home a couple of days after the armistice. And I'd already learned what wearing a West Point ring means . . ."

"What?"

"People watch you closely to see if you're really perfect and are absolutely delighted when you fuck up. So my ring went in my toilet kit beside my wings. I was pretty stupid, but I knew better than to show up at jump school wearing pilot's wings."

"But you muddled through?" Fernando asked.

"I could even do fifty push-ups by the time I finished."

"Was there a temptation to show up at the graduation ceremony wearing your wings, ring, and DFC?"

"Yeah. But I didn't. I'd worked for McNab long enough to know that when he said I was to keep my mouth shut he meant that I was to keep my mouth shut. And Staff Sergeant Dudley J. Johnson, Jr., was really just doing his job, trying to get people through jump school alive. I did see him, come to think of it, a year, eighteen months later. He had applied for Special Forces and reported in to the SWC to go through the Q Course. It was McNab's turn to give the welcoming speech, and there behind him, in Class A uniform, wearing a green beanie, with the rope of an aide hanging from his epaulets, was this familiar-looking lieutenant, an aviator."

Fernando chuckled.

"I did check to see how he was doing," Castillo said. "He didn't make it through Camp Mackall. They busted him out as 'unsuitable.' "

"What does that mean?"

"It can mean any number of things, but it's usually because the raters, which include other trainees, conclude that he would be either a pain in the ass in an A-Team or that he couldn't carry his share of the load. Special Forces requires more brains than brawn. You can't make it on the number of push-ups you can do."

"Then how the hell did you get through if it takes brains?"

Castillo looked at him thoughtfully a moment.

"Fernando, I'm not trying to paint myself as John Wayne, but when I decided to have this little tête-à-tête with you I decided I was going to tell you everything I could."

"Okay, Gringo. I understand."

"I had already passed the real test; I'd been on operations and carried my weight. The instructors at Mackall knew that, so they knew all they had to do with me was give me skills I didn't have and polish the very few I already did. Aside from having my ass run ragged, I actually liked Mackall. The instructors knew what they were teaching and they wanted you to learn. I can't remember one of them ever shouting at me, even when I did something really stupid."

"Interesting," Fernando said.

"My weekends were free," Castillo went on. "I spent them proofreading the How to Fight in the Desert literature General McNab was preparing. And staying current as an aviator."

"How did this affect your social life?"

"If you mean how did I find time to get laid, I didn't."

"Poor Gringo."

"Anyway, I finally finished the course and went to work as his aide."

"Passing hors d'oeuvres and shining shoes?"

"At oh-dark-hundred, his driver picked me up at my BOQ and drove me to Simmons Army Airfield, where, if I was lucky, the guy given the great privilege of being the general's copilot that day had already checked the weather and had the Huey ready to go. Nine times out of ten he had not, so I did the weather, got the Huey up and running, and flew it to Smoke Bomb Hill. Then I went inside, got the coffeepot running, and checked the overnight mail. By then his driver had picked him up and delivered him to headquarters. Then the three of us took a three- or four-mile run around scenic Smoke Bomb Hill to get the juices flowing. Following which, we returned to the office where I spent part of the day taking notes at meetings of one kind or another to which the general was part, and the rest of the day flying him wherever he thought it would be advantageous for military efficiency for him to drop in unannounced. Camp Mackall, the stockade . . ."

"The stockade?"

"Delta Force is in what had been a stockade. Makes sense. It was already surrounded by large fences and barbed wire."

"You got involved with Delta Force?"

"You've just heard all I can tell you about Delta Force," Castillo said, and then went on: ". . . and other places he felt he should keep an eye on. Sometimes, we even got to eat lunch. It was a blue-ribbon day if we happened to be flying near the Fort Bragg Rod and Gun Club, out in the boonies, and the general decided he would like one of their really first-class hamburgers."

"Speaking of food . . ."

"Getting hungry?"

"All I had was two bowls of pistachios," Fernando said.

"So am I, I just realized. There's a Morton's of Chicago across the street."

"A little fancy, no?"

"They have huge lobsters. And nice steaks. I suspect I will be able to get neither where I'm going."

"And where is that?"

"Luanda, Angola."

"And where is that?"

"On the west coast of Africa."

"Looking for this missing 727?"

"Yeah. Let me check on my flight and then we'll go. I'll even buy," Castillo said. He took a notebook from his jacket, found the number he wanted, and dialed it.

"Guten abend, heir is von und zu Gossinger, Karl," he began and then inquired into the status of his business-class reservation, Dulles to Frankfurt am Main.

He hung up and looked at Fernando.

"I'm going on Lufthansa," he said. "It leaves at one-thirty in the morning."

"As Karl von und zu Gossinger?" Fernando asked.

"He's the Washington correspondent of the Fulda *Tages Zeitung,*" Castillo said. "Accredited to the White House and everything. Charming fellow. People say he has quite a way with the ladies."

He reached into his jacket again and tossed a German passport to Fernando, who looked at it.

"That's who it says you are, Gringo. You going to tell me what that's all about?"

"The passport is legitimate. Since I was born in Germany, so far as the Germans are concerned I'm a German citizen. Nobody likes journalists . . ."

"You own those newspapers and you admit to such a thing?"

Castillo chuckled.

"And every week or so, I write something for it. I generally steal it from *The American Conservative* magazine. That way, if somebody checks on Karl there's his picture, beside his latest story from Washington. And if they look closer, the masthead says it was founded by Hermann von und zu Gossinger in 1817. As I was saying, nobody likes journalists but they're expected to ask questions. When an American army officer asks questions, people tend to think he's in the intelligence business."

"Gringo, why are you suddenly telling me all this? For the last . . . Christ, I don't know . . . the last ten years, you've been like a fucking clam about what you do."

"I won't tell you anything you shouldn't know."

"Why are you telling me anything?"

"Straight answer?"

Fernando nodded.

"Because I'm sometimes not sure who I am. I used to be able to unload on General McNab, but that . . . hasn't been possible lately. And that leaves only four people I can really trust."

"Only four? That's sad, Gringo."

"Abuela, General Naylor, Otto, and you," Castillo said. "I can't tell her what I do, obviously; Otto, I'm sure, has a good idea, but I can't talk to him for different obvious reasons . . ."

"He doesn't know?" Fernando interrupted. "I wondered about that."

"I'm sure he has a damn good idea, but we've never talked about it," Castillo answered, and then went on, "General Naylor knows, but if I let him know that I sometimes get a little confused, a little shaky, he'd jerk me."

"Jerk you?"

"Send me back to the Army. 'Thank you for your services and don't let the doorknob hit you in the ass on your way out.' " He paused. "That left you. And you, thank God, know how to keep your mouth shut."

"Christ, what's wrong with going back to the Army? You said they're going to make you a light colonel."

"Because I'm very good at what I do," Castillo said. "And if I went back to the Army, what would I do?"

"Be a lieutenant colonel. Hold parades. Berate lieutenants. Fly airplanes."

"It wouldn't work. For a number of reasons."

"Come home to Texas. Make an honest woman out of the most deserving of your harem. Breed rug rats."

Castillo appeared about to respond to that but didn't.

"Let's go eat," Castillo said.

[TWO]
Washington Dulles International Airport
Sterling, Virginia
0115 1 June 2005

The stewardess, a trim redhead, led Castillo into the first-class compartment of the Boeing 767-300ER and smilingly indicated his new seat.

"Ich danke innen vielmals," he said.

"Keine Ursache, Herr von und zu Gossinger," she replied, flashed him a very cordial smile, and then went down the aisle.

Castillo had once known another redheaded stewardess, who had worked for Delta. He had blown that brief but fairly interesting dalliance because he had been unable to remember that she was a *member of the cabin crew* who *flew* for Delta. In her mind—Dorothy was her name—the distinction was very important, and anyone oblivious to it was obviously a male chauvinist not worthy of being admitted to her bed.

Occupied with memories of Dorothy mingled with thoughts of the trim Lufthansa stew who had just bumped him up to first class—and who had a very attractive tail, indeed—and with putting his laptop briefcase in the overhead bin, Castillo did not notice who was going to be his traveling companion until he actually started to sit down.

"Guten abend," he said to the good-looking, lanky blonde sitting in the window seat, and then switched to English. "Or should it be 'Good morning'?"

"I think that's up for grabs," the lanky blonde said, in English, with a smile.

"I think I should warn you I don't belong up here in the front of the bus," Castillo said. "Lufthansa took pity on me and gave me an upgrade."

"Then we're both usurpers," she said. "Me, too."

Another *member of the cabin crew*, this one a wispy male of whose masculinity Castillo had immediate doubts, came and offered a tray of short-stemmed glasses.

"Will you have some champagne, madam?" he asked, in German.

The lanky blonde replied, in not bad German, "Yes, thank you, I will."

The steward offered the tray to her and then to Castillo, who wondered, *Why is "steward" okay and "stewardess" some sort of slam?* and then said, in German, "You will go to heaven because you have just saved my life."

The lanky blonde smiled.

He raised his glass to the blonde.

"To a pleasant flight," he said.

"To a pleasant flight," she parroted and touched glasses with him.

"Why do you think Lufthansa picked you for an upgrade?" he asked.

Goddamned pity I'll be in Germany only long enough to change planes.

"I'm a journalist," she said.

Oh, shit.

"Really?"

"I work for *Forbes.* The magazine? It happens a lot if I make sure they know I work for *Forbes.*"

"I know," he said. "Same thing."

"You're a journalist? Who do you work for?"

"The Fulda *Tages Zeitung*," Castillo said. "A small newspaper in Hesse. I write mostly about American business."

"There or here? I couldn't help but notice that your English is just about perfect."

"I'm based in Washington," he said. "And I've been here a while."

"Going home on vacation?"

"I vacation whenever I can find something to write about in Florida," he said. "That way the paper pays for it. No, I'm going because they sent for me. They do that every once in a while to make sure I'm not being corrupted by you decadent Americans."

Jesus, it would be nice if just once when I met a good-looking female I could tell her the truth about who I am and what I do.

But to do that, I would have to have a job that I could talk about.

"Well, I'm a district sales manager for Whirlpool. You know, washing machines?"

"You don't look as if you would be easy to corrupt," she said.

"Oh, you're wrong," Castillo said. "I can only hope you won't take advantage of me."

She laughed at that, displaying a nice set of teeth and bright red gums.

"No promises," she said and offered her hand. "Patricia Wilson. Pat."

Her hand was warm and soft.

"My name is Karl, but I try to get people to call me Charley," he said.

"Nice to meet you, Charley."

The pilot ordered that the passenger compartment be readied for flight.

When they turned the cabin lights on the next morning, Castillo opened his eyes and saw Patricia Wilson was still asleep beside him. She had her seat all the way back—it was one of the new seats that went almost horizontal. She was straight in the seat, with the small airline pillow in the nape of her neck.

She looked good. A lot of women, he thought, did not look good first thing in the morning, especially after they had spent most of the night flying across an ocean. Some of them slept with their mouths open. And some snored, which he found amusing, if not very attractive.

He unstrapped himself and got up carefully so as not to disturb her and then took his laptop briefcase from the overhead bin and went to the toilet. He urinated and then closed the toilet seat and laid the laptop briefcase on it. He went quickly through his morning toilette, which concluded with splashing cologne on his face and examining it in the mirror as he swished Listerine around in his mouth.

That done, he opened the computer section of the briefcase and removed one of the computer-cushioning pads.

It appeared to be simply a black plastic cushion. It was not. He pried apart what looked like a heat-welded seam and then tugged on the Velcro inside until it separated. Then he arranged all the documents which identified him as Carlos Guillermo (or C. G.) Castillo—his Army AGO card, his Supervisory Special Agent Secret Service credentials, his Department of Homeland Security identification, building pass, and business cards, and his MasterCard, Visa, and American Express credit cards—inside against what looked like a random pattern of the plastic.

The lines on the pattern were actually of a special plastic that would both keep the documents from shifting around, thus making a lump in the cushion pad, and also present a faint, baffling pattern to X-ray machines.

He carefully closed the cushion pad, put it back in the briefcase, zipped everything up, and went back to his seat.

Patricia Wilson was not only awake but sitting up and sipping at a glass of tomato juice. There was another glass of tomato juice on the small flat area between their seats.

She pointed to it.

"You didn't strike me as the canned orange or grapefruit juice type," she said. "Okay?"

"You're a mind reader," he said. "Which will probably get me in trouble."

She smiled but did not respond directly.

"Let me get out and go where you have been," she said. "And then you can sit down. Take my seat, if you like."

[THREE]
Frankfurt International Airport
Frankfurt am Main, West Germany
0900 2 June 2005

When the Lufthansa 767 touched down at Frankfurt International Airport— which he always thought of as "Rhine-Main," as it was known to American military personnel—Castillo remembered, somewhat painfully, the first time he'd come there twenty-four years ago, at age twelve.

He'd said good-bye to his mother three hours before. He had understood that she was close to dying and didn't want him to see her last days. But leaving her had really been tough; they had both known it was really good-bye forever.

Otto Görner had driven him and Abuela and Grandpa down from Bad Hersfeld in his mother's Mercedes. Major Naylor and his wife and Colonel Lustrous's wife had met them in the Pan American VIP lounge. There had been a man from the American consulate there, too, to make sure things went smoothly. It had been the first proof of what his mother had said about Grandpa. That he was "a man of influence."

The Naylors and Mrs. Lustrous had told him they would see him in America. He hadn't believed them. Otto had made him promise to write, and to get on the phone if he ever needed anything, or just to talk.

Mrs. Naylor and Mrs. Lustrous had kissed him. Major Naylor had hugged his shoulders. Otto had shaken his hand. And then he and Abuela and Grandpa had gotten on the first-class-passengers-only bus, which carried them to the 747. It was not only the largest airplane he had ever seen but the first airplane he'd ever been inside of.

He had stared out the window, fighting back tears, as they taxied to the runway and then taken off. He had been surprised how little time it had taken before Germany disappeared under them.

Pat Wilson went with Castillo while he rented a car. She was on her way to Berlin, she had told him, and coming the way she had, even though it meant changing planes after a two-hour wait in Frankfurt, would get her there faster than either waiting for a direct Dulles–Berlin flight or catching one in New York would.

They had exchanged telephone numbers and promised to call whenever one of them was in the other's city—*Forbes* was published in New York City. He intended to call her the next time he had some free time in Manhattan, but the number he gave her was that of one of the answering machines in his suite in the Mayflower. He never answered the machines. The Karl von und zu Gossinger machine announced in his voice, in English and German, that Herr von und zu Gossinger was out of town but would return the call as soon as possible if the caller would leave a name and number at the beep.

He didn't want to see her in Washington. She was a journalist and there was too much in his life there that would ignite her curiosity.

Seeing her in New York was something else again. Or anywhere but Washington, for that matter. Maybe he could coincidentally find himself wherever her journalistic duties took her.

As Castillo drove away from the Hertz lot in an Opel Kapitan, he was surprised to realize he really wanted to see more of Patricia Wilson.

[FOUR]
Executive Offices
Der Fulda *Tages Zeitung*
Fulda, Hesse, West Germany
1045 2 June 2005

Castillo took the A66 Autobahn to Schultheim, where it turned into Highway 40, and continued on that until he came to the A7 Autobahn to Fulda. Once out of the Frankfurt area traffic, he made good time. He kept the speedometer needle hovering around 120 kilometers per hour, which meant he was going about 75 miles per hour, which seemed both fast enough and safe on the four-lane, gently curved superhighway.

A steady stream of cars, an occasional Audi or Porsche or Mercedes but mostly Volkswagens and other small cars, passed him as if he were standing still.

He told the burly guard—almost certainly a retired cop—at the entrance to the *Tages Zeitung* parking lot that his name was Gossinger and that he had an appointment with Herr Görner, which wasn't exactly true but got him into the parking lot.

By the time he entered the building—which had been built in the late nineteenth century, destroyed in World War II, and then rebuilt to prewar specifications afterward—and went up the wide staircase to Otto's office, Otto was standing at the head of the stairs waiting for him.

Otto Görner was a Hessian, but he looked like a postcard Bavarian. Plump, red-cheeked, and radiating *gemütlichkeit.* He was wearing a dark gray vested suit he'd probably had made in Berlin, but he would have looked just as much at home in lederhosen and a green hat with a tassel waving a liter mug of beer.

"Ach, der verlorene Sohn," Otto said. "You should have let me know you were coming. I'd have had someone meet you."

You mean, you would have been waiting for the prodigal son at Rhine-Main.

"I rented a car, no problem," Castillo said.

Otto put his arm around Castillo's shoulders when Castillo reached the head of the stairs, hugged him briefly, and then waved him into the suite of executive offices.

The two women and one man in the outer office stood up as they entered. Castillo smiled and shook hands with each of them.

They knew who he was, and thought they knew what he did. He was the owner, and was the Washington correspondent, of the Gossinger G.m.b.h newspapers. Read: Playboy/Remittance Man.

Otto followed him into his office and waved him into one of the leather armchairs facing his desk.

"I was just thinking about you, actually," Otto said.

"I'm flattered."

"I just got your monthly bill from the Mayflower," Otto said. "I've got to come see you and see what all that money is buying."

"On the other hand, you're not paying me a salary," Castillo said. "We should not forget that. Especially since you're sending me all the way to Africa."

"Is that where I'm sending you?"

"Uh-huh."

"What story is that?" Otto asked and then answered his own question. "That missing airplane? The missing 727?"

Castillo nodded.

"I've been following that yarn on Reuters," Otto said. "Actually, I think we ran sort of a wrap-up in the Sunday editions."

"Looks like a fascinating story," Castillo said.

"Dare I hope that you will send something we can use?"

"Unless I am eaten by a lion, or wind up in some cannibal's pot, I intend to file daily."

"When do you want to go?"

"I'm on British Airways Flight BA 077, departing Heathrow at seven thirty-five tomorrow night, and will arrive at Luanda at four-ten the next morning."

"And we're sending you first class, of course?"

"It's a long flight, Otto."

"You do know you'll need a visa?"

"I got one in the States. One of their assistant consul generals couldn't do enough for me."

Otto snorted.

"You can't stick around a couple of days?" he asked.

"I'd like to, Otto, but . . ."

Otto shrugged.

Not a word, not a single word, had ever been exchanged between them about what Castillo did. But that didn't mean Otto didn't know. He was a highly intelligent man and a good journalist. He knew but never asked questions.

"That's Luanda, Angola, right?" Otto asked.

Castillo nodded.

"You want me to let our embassy know you're coming?"

"That might be very helpful."

"You have a ticket to London?"

"No. And I don't have hotel reservations in Luanda, either."

Otto picked up one of the telephones on his desk and told Frau Schröder to get Herr Gossinger to Heathrow in time to make British Airways Flight BA 077 to Luanda, Angola, at seven thirty-five the next night, first class, of course; and to see what she could do for him about some place to stay; and when she had done that, to send a message to the German embassy in Luanda, Angola, saying that Herr Gossinger was coming and requesting all courtesies. And to cancel all his appointments for the rest of the day—he and Herr Gossinger were going to Bad Hersfeld and she could reach him in his car or at *das Haus im Wald*.

"We're going to Bad Hersfeld, are we?" Castillo asked when Otto hung up.

"I want you to see your godchild and the other children."

"Okay," Castillo said and smiled. "I carry the greetings of Fernando."

That wasn't true, of course. But if he had told Fernando where he was going, Fernando would have said, "Give my best to Otto."

"I am also godfather to one of Fernando's rug rats, you know. Jorge."

"One of his what?"

"His rug rats. He calls his children 'the rug rats.' "

"That's terrible," Otto said, but he laughed. "Rug rats! How is Fernando?"

"Well. I think he's still growing," Castillo said. "He's well. Working hard."

"You want something to eat before we go?" Otto asked.

"I ate a large breakfast on the plane, thank you."

"And your grandmother?"

"Very well, thank you. She spends most of her time at the hacienda, but not much gets by her. I saw her a couple of days ago."

"You will give her my best regards, Karl?"

"Of course."

As they passed through the outer office, Otto turned to Castillo and said, "Give me the keys to the rental car, Karl."

"Why?"

"So I can have someone turn it in. There's no sense paying for it if you're not going to be using it." He paused, had a thought, and added: "Unless there is some reason I can't take you to the airport?"

I'd rather you didn't. But how do I tell you no?

"It's a long ride back and forth to Frankfurt."

"Good. That will give us more time to be together."

"I left my luggage in the car," Castillo said.

"Frau Schröder, we'll leave the keys to Herr Gossinger's rental car with the guard," Otto ordered. "Have someone turn it in."

Otto's car was a black Mercedes S600, the big one, with a V-12 engine. It belonged, Castillo knew, to one of the companies. That way, it was considered essential transportation for an employee, deductible as a business expense, and not regarded as part of Otto's taxable income.

In the six days Fernando Castillo had been in Germany to meet and take his grandson home, he had seen enough of Otto Görner, who had been running the company since Hermann Wilhelm von und zu Gossinger and his son Wilhelm—Castillo's grandfather and uncle—had died on the autobahn, to make the snap judgment that he should remain in charge for the time being.

Grandpa told Carlos years later—when he'd gone home on Christmas leave during his final year at West Point and was about to turn twenty-one—that he'd, of course, had Otto investigated as quickly as he could. Grandpa said he trusted his snap character judgments only until he could get some facts to back them up.

Otto had apparently stood up under that expensive close scrutiny because he had been running everything ever since.

The estate had been complicated. Hermann von und zu Gossinger had intended to leave *das Haus im Wald* and twenty-five percent of his other assets to his daughter. The rest of his estate, less some bequests to faithful employees and Saint Johan's Church, was to go to his son.

But it was determined that Wilhelm had died first in that black Mercedes— and the implications thereof had not yet been decided by the courts when Erika von und zu Gossinger had died.

"Typical Germanic gross absurdity, Carlos," Grandpa had told him. "Everybody knew everything was going to come to you; you were everybody's only living heir. Your uncle had neither wife nor children. That meant his estate would ultimately go to his nearest living relatives, your grandfather and your mother. Her will left everything to you.

"If your grandfather had died first in that wreck, his estate would have been distributed according to the provisions of his will. But since your uncle was dead, his inheritance would have gone to your mother. But if your uncle died first, then his assets would be shared between his nearest living relatives, his father and your mother. But since his father was dead, it would go to your mother—who had already named you as her sole heir. It took fifty lawyers, five years, God only knows how many judges, and a hell of a lot of money to split those legal hairs, even though it didn't matter a damn what any of the courts decided. The bottom line was that you were going to get it all when you turned twenty-one. And that happens on February the thirteenth."

"What am I going to do with it?" Carlos had asked.

"If you're smart, you'll continue what I set up with Otto Görner. He gets a good salary, a lot of perks—including use of that house in Bad Hersfeld, a car, and an expense account our American IRS wouldn't let me or you get away with, plus a percentage of the profits. He's a hard worker, and honest, and about as smart as they come. I'll continue to keep an eye on things for you if you'd like."

And he had, so long as he had lived.

Now the family's law firm kept an eye on things in Germany, and Fernando, who had taken a law degree after Desert Storm at Grandpa's advice, kept an eye on them.

Frau Helena Görner was a blond Bavarian, but she didn't look as if she belonged in a dirndl with her hair braided into pigtails. She was a svelte blonde—which made Castillo think of Patricia Wilson—who dressed in what Castillo thought of as Neiman Marcus, or maybe Bonwit Teller, clothing.

When he went into the foyer of *das Haus im Wald,* and she kissed—or made smacking noises in close proximity to—his cheek, she smelled of expensive perfume.

He had no idea what she really thought of him, and often wondered if she was pleased, displeased, or didn't give much of a damn that he was godfather to her second son, Hermann Wilhelm, who had been named after both his grandfather and uncle.

She was ten—maybe more—years younger than Otto. They had married when Castillo had been in his junior year in high school, and Otto—ever the businessman—had combined their honeymoon trip to America with a business conference with Fernando Castillo in San Antonio.

Abuela had liked her, and been receptive to the idea that his—and, of course, Fernando's—spending their summer vacation in Germany would be a good idea.

Abuela had told him, as he and Fernando were getting on the airplane to go to Germany, that Helena had told her that Otto had told her he had several times offered marriage to Erika von und zu Gossinger but that she had refused. And that Otto had always looked on Karl as a son.

"If we knew you were coming, Karl," Helena said, "I could have prepared something. Some of your old friends from Saint Johan's or something."

Which is another reason I didn't tell Otto I was coming.

"Maybe the next time," Castillo said. "But thanks anyway, Helena."

"Karl just came to see us and our rug rats," Otto said.

"I beg your pardon?"

"That's what Fernando calls his children," Otto said, visibly pleased with himself.

"I don't understand," Helena said.

Why doesn't that surprise me?

"How is Fernando and Maria?" Helena asked, electing to get off the subject of rug rats. "And your grandmother?"

"All well, thank you, Helena. They send their best wishes."

"Well, let's go out in back—the weather is wonderful; maybe spring has finally come—and have a glass of wine before lunch," Helena said. "Or knowing you two, something stronger. The children . . ."

"The rug rats, you mean," Otto interrupted.

"The *children* normally come home about four," Helena said, not amused by either the term or her husband, "but sometimes they go off with their friends. I'll call and make sure they come home."

Shit, I didn't think to bring any of them a present. Among other things, I am a lousy godfather and sort-of uncle.

Hell, I'll give them money.

He and Otto had just touched glasses dark with scotch when one of the servants handed him a walk-around telephone.

"Frau Schröder, Herr Gossinger," his caller announced. "I have booked you on British Airways . . ."

"Hold one, please, Frau Schröder, I want to write this down."

He mimed a writing instrument to Otto, who handed him a leather-bound notebook and a gold felt-tip pen.

"A journalist without a notebook?" Otto asked.

"Go ahead, please, Frau Schröder," Castillo said.

"Herr Gossinger, I was unable to get you a first-class ticket to London . . ."

"What do you have?"

"I have a business ticket for you on British Airways Flight 907, leaving Frankfurt tomorrow afternoon at four-thirty and arriving in London at five-fifteen."

"Fine," Castillo said.

"I presume you have a ticket to Luanda?"

"Yes, I do."

"In that case, Herr Gossinger, British Airways in Frankfurt will check your luggage through to Luanda if you wish."

"Great."

"I have made reservations for you at the Le Presidente Hotel, a small suite, in Luanda. It's a Meridien Hotel. They will send a car to meet you at the airport and will bill us directly."

"Frau Schröder, you are absolutely marvelous. Thank you very much."

"It is my pleasure, Herr Gossinger. The tickets will be at the British Airways counter at Frankfurt, and, now that you have approved the itinerary, I will inform the German embassy in Luanda that you are coming."

"Thank you very much, Frau Schröder."

"It is my pleasure. Have a pleasant trip, Herr Gossinger."

[FIVE]
Heathrow Airport
London, England
1915 3 June 2005

The first-class lounge at Heathrow provided Internet access in nice little cubicles providing some privacy, but Castillo decided against sending his boss an e-mail announcing where he was and where he was going. For one thing, Secretary Hall knew where he was going and didn't expect a step-by-step report. Instead, Castillo had a drink and watched the BBC television news until an attractive British Airways passenger service representative came and collected him and an ornately costumed, tall, jet-black couple he thought were probably from Nigeria for no good reason except they were smiling and having a good time.

He also thought, perhaps unkindly, as they walked through the terminal to the boarding gate, that the Brits still had the class distinction business down pat and up and running. The passenger service rep had called him by name—including the *von* and the *zu*—in German. She had addressed the Africans, in French, as *M'Sieu et Madame Le Ministre*, which meant two things: that they were not Angolans, where the language was Portuguese, and that he was some sort of senior government official, which explained what they were doing in first class. The three of them were apparently the only first-class passengers.

The business-class passengers were lined up ahead of them in the airway, under the care of another passenger service representative, looking like so many third-graders being led into the school library. There were, he guessed, twenty or twenty-five of them; it took some time for them to pass through the final ticket check, which, of course, was waived for the upper class. The lower class had already been herded into economy, which occupied most of the rear of the Boeing 777 fuselage.

Once through the door and on the plane, three members of the cabin crew, under a steward, smilingly directed them left into the first-class compartment, which was in the nose.

He didn't intend to look to the right, into the business-class section, because he usually found himself looking at someone disappointed that he wasn't either a movie star or an oil-rich Arabian prince traveling with a high-priced, usually very blond mistress-of-the-moment.

But he did look.

And Patricia Wilson looked back at him.

Jesus H. Fucking Christ! That's the last fucking thing I need!

Was that really her?

You know goddamn well it was.

Did she recognize me?

Three to five she did. That wasn't curiosity on her charming face; it was surprise.

What the fuck do I do about this?

The cabin attendant handed him a glass of champagne. Before he was half finished with it, the pilot ordered the cabin be prepared for flight.

The seat of his pants and the sound of the engines cutting back told him that they were at cruising altitude even though the FASTEN SEAT BELTS sign remained lit.

That was explained when the door to the flight deck opened and the captain, a middle-aged man with a Royal Air Force mustache, came out and quickly disappeared into the toilet.

Well, guess who forgot Rule 13? Piss before takeoff.

Castillo unlatched his seat belt and went to the toilet door.

When the captain came out, Castillo extended his business card.

"I've got a little problem you can solve in about ten seconds, Captain."

The captain didn't like being intercepted, but you don't ignore—much less snap at—first-class passengers.

"How may I help you?" he asked.

"There's a passenger in business, a fellow journalist, a very good-looking fellow journalist, Miss Patricia Wilson, who works for *Forbes* magazine. I would like very much to make this long flight in her company. Either move me back there or her up here."

The captain looked around the first-class compartment. Only three of the eighteen seats were occupied.

He beckoned to the steward.

"The steward will take care of your little problem for you, sir," the captain said when the steward was within hearing range.

"Thank you very much, Captain, I really appreciate your courtesy."

"Not at all," the captain said. "Glad I could be of service."

"I thought that was you," Patricia Wilson said three minutes after the FASTEN SEAT BELTS sign went off. "You're going to Luanda?"

"Is that where this thing is going?"

"On the 727 story?" she asked.

He nodded.

"Me, too," she said.

You told me, you beautiful creature, that you were going to Berlin. Therefore, you were lying. Or are lying. Or both.

What the fuck is going on here?

Besides, that missing airliner is a breaking story. Forbes *comes out every other week. They don't do breaking stories.*

As if she had read his mind, Patricia Wilson said, "My editor wants an in-depth piece about sloppy air control in Africa, and I thought, Well, hell, why not start where they lost an airplane?"

Good try, Patricia, but that's bullshit.

"Good idea," Castillo said.

[SIX]
Le Presidente Hotel
Largo 4 de Fevereiro
Luanda, Angola
0605 4 June 2005

There were a dozen or more black men in business suits and chauffeur's caps holding cards with names lettered on them waiting for the passengers as they came out of customs at the airport. One of the cards read: PATRICIA WILSON.

"I guess the hotel sent a car for me, too," she said. "What do we do?"

"I suspect you'll have to pay for it anyway," Castillo said, "and I suspect both cars will be small."

"And probably French?" she asked.

"If yours breaks down—and it probably will—I'll rescue you," Castillo said. "And you can do the same for me."

"Call me later? I need the attentions of a beautician."

"Absolutely," he said.

He had put her into her car, a Citroën, and then followed his driver to a Mercedes. He wondered if that was random or whether the Meridien hotel chain had a policy: Germans get Mercedes, Americans get Citroëns.

When he didn't see her in the hotel lobby he was disappointed. He thought her driver had probably made much better time through the very early morning traffic in the small Citroën than he had in the larger Mercedes and that she was probably already in her shower. That triggered an immediate mental image.

There's no question about it. At this almost obscene hour of the morning my hormones are raging.

And you know in your bones that this one is dangerous and that you should back off.

He tried out his Portuguese on the assistant manager behind the registration desk, but the French hotelier insisted on responding in barely understandable German.

In which he said welcome to Le Presidente and that he would have to keep Castillo's passport.

Hotels did that either to make sure they got paid—not a valid excuse here because his bills were to be paid directly by the *Tages Zeitung*—or so the police could have a look at it.

The "small suite" was a sitting room, a bedroom, and an alcove with a desk and chair that wasn't large enough to be called a room. A high-speed Internet cable was neatly coiled on the desk.

The windows of both the sitting room and the bedroom looked out and fifteen stories down onto the bay. There was a basket of fruit and a bottle of wine on the coffee table and a terry cloth robe had been laid across the double bed.

Castillo wondered if the room was bugged, but that was an automatic thought. As he always assumed any gun he picked up was loaded, he always assumed hotel rooms were bugged. He knew a lot of people who really should have known better who had fired "unloaded" guns and others who had wrongly presumed "There's no way this place could be bugged."

He took his laptop from its briefcase and plugged the charger and the ethernet cable into it. The high-speed access to the Internet was up and running. There were three e-mail messages for him on tageszeitung.wash@aol.com. One was from a company promising to return the full purchase price (less shipping) if their product failed to increase the size of his male member. After a moment's thought, and pleased with himself, he forwarded that one to fernandolopez@castillo.com.

The second offered Viagra online without a prescription and the third told him now was the time to refinance his mortgage. He deleted both.

There was only one message on his MSN account, from shake.n.bake@yahoo.com:

```
UNCLE ALLAN IS WORRIED THAT YOUR CAR BROKE DOWN. SHALL
WE TELL UNCLE BILL YOU'RE COMING?
LOVE MOTHER
```

Major Castillo took a moment to consider his reply to the secretary of homeland security and then quickly typed it.

```
UNCLE ALLAN IS A WORRIER. CAR RUNNING FINE. I'LL CALL
UNCLE BILL IF I HAVE TIME TO GO THERE.
LOVE CHARLEY
```

He read the screen to make sure there were no typos and then pushed ENTER.

Going to the American embassy here would be a waste of time, and it would almost certainly draw attention to him.

Furthermore, he had already read, in Washington, the intel summaries. What the military attaché had sent to the Defense Intelligence Agency, what the CIA station chief had sent to Langley, and what the ambassador had sent to the State Department. If there had been significant developments on what happened to the missing 727 while he was on his way to Angola, the secretary would either have indicated that in the e-mail, or, at the least, ordered him to call home.

His job here wasn't to find the airplane but rather, as the president had put it, to find out who knew what and when they knew it.

The German embassy was another matter. Not only would a German journalist be expected to check in with the embassy but Otto had sent them a message saying he was coming. More important, they might know something, or have an opinion, that they almost certainly would not have shared with the Americans.

Castillo unpacked, then had a shower and a shave. He drew the blinds against the early morning sun, lay down on the bed, and went to sleep.

He intended to sleep until nine or thereabouts. When he woke, it was 9:05. He dressed, brushed his teeth, and then went down to the lobby, had a cup of coffee and a croissant in the lobby lounge, and then went out and got in a taxi.

The doorman who put him into the cab asked in Portuguese where he wanted to go and Castillo told him, in what he hoped sounded like Portuguese. The doorman seemed to understand him.

[SEVEN]

The Chief of Mission at the German embassy, whose name was Dieter Hausner, was about Castillo's age. He was thin, nearly bald, and well dressed. His office overlooked an interior garden. It was impersonal. The only picture on the walls was of the Brandenburg Gate in Berlin, and the furniture was modern, crisp, and efficient. Castillo was not surprised that the chrome-and-leather chair into which Hausner waved him was awkward to get into and would be worse getting out of.

Hausner told him the ambassador was sorry he couldn't receive Herr von und zu Gossinger personally—the press of duty—but he hoped that while Herr von und zu Gossinger was in Angola he would have the chance to offer him dinner.

"That would be very nice," Castillo said.

"You know, although I now consider myself a Berliner, I'm from Hesse myself," Hausner said. "Wetzlar."

"Oh, yes."

"And I'm an Alte Marburger."

The reference was to Phillip's University in Marburg an der Lahn, not far from either Fulda or Wetzlar. Castillo had told people he was a Marburger. He knew enough about the school to get away with it, including the fact that the university usually turned a deaf ear to inquiries about its alumni unless they came from another university. Obviously, he couldn't do that here, and get in a game of "did you know" with Hausner.

"My uncle Wilhelm—Willi—was a Marburger," Castillo said.

"But not you? Where did you go to university?"

I am being interrogated. Why? Because the ambassador wanted to check me out before he fed me dinner? Or is Dieter here really the agency spook? Or the spook or counterspook in addition to his other duties?

So far as I know, I have never done anything to arouse the curiosity of German intelligence, but that doesn't mean they don't have a dossier on Karl Wilhelm von und zu Gossinger.

Would Hausner routinely have run a security check on me when he got Otto's heads-up that I was coming? Or would he presume that if the Tages Zeitung *sent me, I was who they said I was? Or will he—if I arouse his curiosity—ask for a security check the minute I walk out of here?*

"I went right from Saint Johan's in Fulda to Georgetown, in Washington," Castillo said. "My grandfather was a believer in the total immersion system of learning a foreign language."

"And did it work?"

"I speak fluent American," Castillo said. "And passable English."

Hausner laughed.

"And you're now based in Washington?"

"It was either that or Fulda," Castillo said.

"I understand. Fulda offers about as much of the good life as Wetzlar."

"When I was a kid, I went to the school at the Leitz plant," Castillo said. Leica cameras came from the Leitz factory in Wetzlar. "I used to drink in a *gasthaus* by the bridge."

"Zum Adler," Hausner furnished. "So did I. So what brings you to Luanda?"

"The missing airplane . . ."

"Uh-huh," Hausner said.

"And the man who would ordinarily cover the story was unable to come. And I speak a little Spanish, which is a little like Portuguese."

"I understand."

"What do you think happened to that airplane?"

"How much do you know about it?"

"Only what I read in the newspapers. An airplane, a Boeing 727, which had been here for a year, suddenly took off without permission and hasn't been seen since."

"That's about all I know," Hausner said.

"Why was it here for a year? How do you hide an airplane that size? Was it stolen? What do you do with a stolen airplane?"

"You could fly it into a skyscraper in New York," Hausner said. "But I don't think that's what the thief—thieves—had in mind."

"Really?"

"It would be so much easier to steal—what's the term?—*skyjack* an airplane in the United States—or, for that matter, in London, if they wanted to fly into Buckingham Palace—than it would be to fly an airplane from here to wherever they wanted to cause mischief."

"That's true," Castillo agreed.

It probably is true, but for some reason I remain unconvinced.

"I have a theory—but, please, Herr von und zu Gossinger, I really don't want to be quoted."

"Not even as a 'high-ranking officer, speaking on condition of anonymity'?"

"Not at all."

He liked "high-ranking officer."

"All right, you have my word."

"Let me put it this way," Hausner said. "I wouldn't be at all surprised if in two or three weeks—or this afternoon—the airplane will be found not more than a couple of hundred miles from here, perhaps even closer, on a deserted field. The *empty hulk* of the airplane; everything that can be taken off of it—engines, instruments, even the wheels and tires—will have been taken off."

"For resale on the black market?"

"Uh-huh. There's a market all over Africa for aircraft parts."

"That would open the possibility that the owners of the aircraft—you don't know why it sat here for a year?"

"It may have needed parts. Do you know who owned it?"

"A small airplane dealer in Philadelphia," Castillo said, "that probably had it insured and will now place a claim. That may be enough in itself, but if they were involved in having the plane stolen and can sell the parts . . ."

"Precisely," Hausner said.

"I'd like to see where the airplane was parked all that time," Castillo said after a moment. "Is that going to be difficult?"

"There's not much to see," Hausner said. "A concrete pad in a far corner of the airfield. I've been there. But, no, it won't be a problem. I know the security man at the airfield. I'll give him a call and tell him you're coming."

Hausner opened his desk drawer and took two business cards from a box. He wrote a name on one of them and then handed both to Castillo.

"A small gift for his favorite charity might be a good idea," Hausner said, smiling.

"I think I'll go out there now," Castillo said. "Before it gets hot."

"I'll send you out there in one of our cars," Hausner said. "And then you can take a taxi to your hotel when you've finished."

"That's very kind of you," Castillo said.

"Not at all," Hausner said. He stood up and offered his hand.

[EIGHT]

Hausner was right. There was nothing much to see at the airport, although the "little gift" Castillo gave to the airport security manager for his favorite charity resulted in having that dignitary drive him to the remote parking area in his Citroën pickup truck.

There were four parking pads near the north threshold of the main runway. None were in use. The one the security manager pointed out as where the 727 had been parked was identical to the others—an oil-stained square concrete pad with grass growing through its cracks.

Controllers in the tower across the field would have seen the 727 every time they looked in the direction of the runway's northern threshold.

Taking off without permission would have been simple. All the pilot would have had to do—and almost certainly did do—was call ground control for permission to taxi to the hangar/terminal area. When that permission was granted, all the pilot had had to do was make a right turn off the taxiway onto the threshold, and then another right onto the runway and go. He would have been airborne before any but the most alert controller would have noticed he wasn't on the taxiway.

Castillo ran the numbers in his mind:

If the pilot kept the 727 close to the ground, he would have been out of sight in no more than a minute or two and disappeared from radar in not much more time. If he was making three hundred knots—and he almost certainly would have been going at least that fast—that was five miles a minute. In twenty minutes, he would have been a hundred miles from the airport. In half an hour, he would have been 150 miles from the airfield, and even if he had climbed out by then in the interest of fuel economy he would have just been an unidentifiable blip on the airfield's radar screen. He certainly would not have activated his transponder.

In the taxi—this one a Peugeot—to El Presidente Hotel, Castillo decided that he was not going to learn much more in Luanda than he already knew. The CIA and DIA and State Department intel filings would have the details of who was suspected of flying the plane off, who serviced the plane so that it would be flyable after sitting there for so long, and so on. There was no sense wasting time duplicating their efforts himself now. When he'd assembled and collated everybody's filings, he would know which of the agencies had made the same sort of decision to let another agency develop something they should have developed themselves. This is one of the things the president had said he wanted to know.

The airplane was bound to show up. When that happened, he would probably be able to determine who had done the best job of finding out what had happened, and, more important, who had not learned something that should have been learned. Plus, of course, who had made the best guess about what was going to happen.

The president had made it clear he wanted to know who had known what and when. And who had done or not done something others had done.

Castillo decided that what he would do was go to his room and write a story for the *Tages Zeitung*. He would e-mail it both to Germany and to Hall. The secretary would understand from the *Tages Zeitung* filing that he hadn't learned anything that hadn't already been reported.

Afterward, he would spend the afternoon hanging around the hotel bar. Striking up conversations with strangers often produced an amazing amount of information. If something new—or even the suggestion of something new—came up, he would run it down. If not, he'd go back to Germany, and from Germany home. Until the plane showed up, there was really nothing else he could do, and the plane might not show up for weeks. Unless, of course, he thought wryly, he went back to Washington, where the 727 would show up when he was halfway across the Atlantic.

And, as a corollary of this reasoning, Castillo decided he would stay away from Miss Patricia Wilson. For one thing, she wasn't what she announced herself to be and that made a dalliance with her, if not actually dangerous, then an awkward situation very likely to explode in his face. For another, he had the feeling she was not the sort of female who could be lured into his bed in the little time he planned to be in Luanda.

[NINE]

There was no blinking green light in the locking mechanism of Castillo's hotel room door when he slid the plastic "key" into it.

He tried reinserting it in all possible ways, simultaneously working the lever-type doorknob. He had just inserted it, as he thought of it, wrong side out and upside down, when the door was opened from the inside.

As a reflex action, he jumped away and flattened his back against the corridor wall.

There was no explosion, either per se, or of persons bursting into the corridor with weapons ready.

Instead, a chubby, smiling, very black face looked around the doorjamb into the corridor. He recognized it immediately. It belonged to Major H. Richard Miller, Jr., Aviation, U.S. Army, a USMA classmate of Castillo's. The major was wearing a not-very-well-fitting, single-breasted black suit, a frayed-collar white shirt, and a somewhat ragged black tie.

He looks like those drivers at the airport, Castillo thought. *And that's probably on purpose.*

What the hell is he doing here?

"We're going to have to stop meeting this way, Charley," Miller said, softly. "People will start to talk."

"You sonofabitch!" Castillo said. "You scared hell out of me!"

He quickly entered his room and closed the door.

The two men looked at each other for a moment.

"What the hell are you doing here?" Castillo asked.

"That's what I was about to ask you," Miller, who was fifty pounds heavier and four inches taller than Castillo, replied. "Plus, who the hell are you?"

"Oh, shit," Castillo said, and then the two embraced, in the manner of brothers. They had last seen one another, in less than pleasant circumstances, eighteen months before, in Afghanistan.

"Sorry about the door," Miller said when they broke apart.

"What the hell did you do to it?"

Miller took an unmarked black aluminum box, about the size of a cellular telephone, from his pocket.

"I give this thing ten seconds to find what it's looking for and then I hit the EMERGENCY button. That opens the lock, but sometimes it *upgefucks* the mechanism. Which, apparently, my dear Major Whatever-the-Hell-Your-Name-Is-Today, is what happened in the present instance."

Castillo shook his head.

"I suppose the lock on the minibar is similarly destroyed?"

"No. That's a mechanical lock. I opened that with a pick. All the wine is French, which of course as a patriotic American I don't drink. But there is—or was—Jack Daniel's and several kinds of scotch."

"How long have you been here?" Castillo asked as he opened the minibar.

"About an hour. Which gave me plenty of time to sweep the room. It's clean."

Castillo nodded, then held up two miniature whiskey bottles, one scotch and one Jack Daniel's. Miller pointed to the bourbon and Castillo tossed it to him.

He opened the scotch and poured it into a glass as Miller did the same with his still-half-full glass.

Castillo walked to him and they touched glasses.

"It's good to see you, Dick," Castillo said.

"Yeah, you, too, Charley," Miller said. "I never got a chance to say, 'Thanks for the ride.' "

Castillo made a deprecating gesture.

"You were pretty much out of it, Dick," he said.

"Now I know why the Mafia shoots bad mob guys in the knee," Miller said. "It smarts considerable."

"How is it?"

"That depends on who you ask," Miller said. "So far as I'm concerned, it's fine. I have so far been unable to convince even one flight surgeon of that. But hope springs eternal, or so I'm told."

"So what are you doing here?"

"You knew they sent me to the agency when I got out of the hospital?"

"I heard you were training nice young men to be spooks at the Farm."

"That didn't last long. I strongly suspect that my boss called in all favors due to have me reassigned elsewhere. Anywhere elsewhere."

"So they sent you here? To do what?"

"On paper, I'm the assistant military attaché."

"But, actually, you're the resident spook, which you can't talk about?" Miller nodded.

Jesus, I wish I had known that. It would have saved me the trip over here.

"Actually, being the resident spook is a real pain in the ass," Miller said.

"Why?"

"You met her," Miller said. "My boss."

"Excuse me?"

"Who sent me to find out who you really are. The lady suspects there is something fishy about you, my German journalist friend."

"You're talking about the blonde on the airplane?"

Miller nodded.

"Who is she?" Castillo asked.

"Her name is Wilson. *Mrs.* Patricia Davies Wilson . . ."

"She's not wearing a wedding ring," Castillo interrupted.

"Ah, so you haven't lost your legendary powers of observation," Miller said. "At the airport, I wasn't sure."

"Meaning?"

"I did everything, Charley, but blow you a kiss," Miller said.

"I didn't see you," Castillo admitted. "So who is this . . . married . . . woman?"

"The company's regional director for Southwest Africa," Miller said. "Everything from Nigeria—actually, Cameroon, not including Nigeria—to South Africa, but excluding that, too. And halfway across the continent. None of the important countries. She's spook-in-charge of what in a politically incorrect society one might think of as the African honey bucket."

Castillo smiled. In military installations, the fifty-five-gallon barrels cut in half and placed as receptacles in "field sanitary facilities"—once known as "latrines"—are known as honey buckets.

"She told me she works for *Forbes* magazine," Castillo said.

"That's what they call a cover, Charley," Miller said, dryly.

"And who is Mr. Wilson?"

"A paper pusher at Langley, middle level, maybe twenty years older than she is. One unkind rumor circulating is that he's a fag with an independent income and married the lady to keep the whispers down. Having met him, I'm prone to believe the unkind rumor."

"And what's her background?"

"She was an agricultural analyst at Langley before she was smitten by Cupid's arrow. Shortly after her marriage, she managed to get herself sent through the Farm, reclassified as a field officer, and has worked herself up to where she is now. Which she sees as a stepping-stone, which is what makes her a genuine pain in the ass, to get back to that."

"How so?"

"Her underlings make all the mistakes, and, when something is done right—that actually happens once in a while—she takes the credit. I personally know three nice young guys who quit because they couldn't take any more of her bullshit."

"And she thinks *I'm* fishy?"

"Either that or she wants to really make sure you're who you told her you are before she lets you into her pants."

"She has a reputation for that, too?"

"Charley, she's certainly not getting what she so obviously needs at home," Miller said. "There have been whispers."

"Sounds like the girl of my dreams," Castillo said.

"So how do you want me to handle this, Charley?"

"Except for letting her know we know each other, run me," Castillo said. "I'd like to know what can be turned up about Gossinger."

"Like I said, the lady is a bitch," Miller said. "What if she finds out, now or later, that we know each other?"

"I can cover that," Castillo said. "You are hereby ordered not to divulge that we are acquainted."

"You have that authority, Charley?"

"Dick, I was sent on this excursion—and you are hereby ordered not to divulge this either—by a guy who lives part-time in a *Gone With the Wind*–style mansion that overlooks the Atlantic Ocean near Savannah."

"No kidding?"

Castillo nodded.

"So what's the excursion all about? Can you say?"

"The guy I'm talking about wants to know, and I quote, 'who knew what, and when they knew it,' end quote, about this missing 727."

"I think they call that 'internal review,'" Miller said.

"I was about to send my boss an e-mail. I'll tell him I ran into you and ordered you to keep your mouth shut."

"You e-mail the president directly?"

"No. I work for Matt Hall. The secretary of homeland security?"

Miller's face showed he knew who Hall was, and was surprised that Charley had asked.

". . . who is a good guy," Castillo went on. "He was a sergeant in Vietnam. He and the president are great buddies. You're covered, Dick."

Miller made a gesture meaning he took Castillo at his word.

"So what have you learned about the airplane that went missing?" Miller asked.

"Some—maybe most—people think it's close to here, being cannibalized for parts. Only a few—very few—people think it will be flown into a skyscraper somewhere. There's also a theory that the pilot put it on autopilot and went out the back door so the owners can collect the insurance."

"And how many people, just for the hell of it, agree with my theory about what happened to it?"

"I don't understand, Dick."

"That Vasily Respin got it."

"Vasily who?"

"The Russian arms dealer. You don't know about him?"

Castillo shook his head.

"And I didn't see his name—or anything about a Russian arms dealer—on either the CIA, DIA, or State intel files, either," Castillo said. "You filed your theory?"

Miller nodded. "You're sure you saw all the files?" he asked.

"I saw everything Hall got, and I saw Cohen's memo that Hall was to get everything," Castillo said. "Which offers all sorts of interesting possibilities."

Castillo thought, but did not say: *Hey, maybe that's really what all this is about. So far as many people close to the Oval Office were concerned, there were three things wrong with Dr. Natalie Cohen, the president's national security advisor. In ascending order of importance, they were that she was a woman, brilliant, and a close personal friend of the president.*

If someone was trying to stick a knife in her back, she would (a) either sense it, or find out about it, whereupon (b) she would go to the president. The president would then logically decide that Hall was one of the guys at that level who should look into it. For a couple of reasons. Hall was also an absolutely loyal personal friend of the president, and, unlike the other cabinet officers, the secretary of homeland security did not have his own intelligence service.

Asking any of the heavy agencies to look into what was bothering Dr. Cohen would have the CIA pointing a finger at the DIA or the DIA pointing a finger at the State Department—und so viete—anywhere but at someone in their own agency.

Maybe that's what this is all about? Maybe not what it's all about, but it's an element of it certainly.

If the president—and maybe, probably, Hall too—thinks someone is screwing with Cohen, they want to know who it is and the facts about how the various agencies had handled the gone-missing 727 would point them in the right direction.

"Such as?" Miller asked.

"Dick, this may be more important than you know," Castillo said. "Let me make sure I have it right. You have a theory that some Russian arms dealer . . ."

"Vasily Respin," Miller furnished.

". . . either stole, or was responsible for the theft of, the 727?"

"I don't think he was in the cockpit, Charley, but I have a gut feeling he's at least involved in this. And I saw some of his people here."

"Tell me about him? Why do you think that?"

"You never heard of him? I'm surprised. There should be a hell of a file on him."

"Who is he? What does he do?"

"Cutting a long story short, Charley, in 1992—when Vasily was twenty-five—he bought three Antonov cargo planes from Russian military surplus. Paid 150 grand for all three, is what I heard. Anyway, the Russian black market had just begun to kick into high gear. The Russians had gold, and the Danes had things—basic things, but luxuries in Moscow—to sell and liked getting paid in gold.

"Respin made a lot of money, and quickly, and within a year he had set up an airline in Sharjah, in the United Arab Emirates. Dubai has a duty-free port. Respin—who by then had already expanded his fleet—flew everything from ballpoint pens to automobiles home to Mother Russia. He made a fortune.

"And then he got chummy with Mobutu in the Congo and that brought him to the attention of Langley, who put out the word to watch him, and, shortly afterward, the CIA in Kinshasa was sending photographs of Respin standing by an Ilyushin at a Congolese field in the middle of nowhere while Mobutu's soldiers off-loaded crates of AK-47s and more sophisticated weaponry."

"Okay," Castillo interrupted. "I know who you're talking about. But I thought his name was Aleksandr Pevsner."

"That's one name he uses," Miller said, then looked at Castillo and deadpanned: "It's really astonishing how many people you meet these days who have several names."

"From what I've heard, Pevsner—or whatever his name is—has lots of airplanes. What would he want this one for?"

"Starting with the obvious, he has—or so the story goes—several, maybe half a dozen 727s. They need parts. Okay? It's entirely possible that this one went directly to Sharjah . . ."

"It would have to refuel," Castillo interrupted.

"Probably twice," Miller quickly agreed. "No problem, with a little planning. The friendly skies over Mother Africa are pretty open, Charley. And there are probably thirty deserted airstrips in the Congo and Sudan where a 727 can sit down unseen and get itself refueled. For that matter, Respin wouldn't even have to preposition fuel on deserted fields—although my bet is that he did. Whoever was flying this 727 could land and take on fuel at Kisangani in the Congo and Kartoum in the Sudan—with no questions asked in either place—and then take off to Sharjah."

"The satellites didn't spot it—or any unidentified 727—on any airfield anywhere," Castillo argued.

"What's an 'unidentified' 727?" Miller asked. "All they had to do was land the stolen 727 somewhere close to here and do a quick paint-over of the numbers on it, using the numbers of one of Pevsner's 727s conveniently out of sight in a hangar in Sharjah. They would have had plenty of time to do that before Langley could turn the satellite cameras on."

He paused, put his hand on his hip, and, mimicking a light-on-his-feet photo analyst examining satellite downloads, lisped, "Well, that's a 727 all right, Bruce, but it's *not* the one *we're* looking for. *That* 727 belongs to Rag-Head Airways. I have *that* tail number right *here*."

"I take your point," Castillo said, chuckling.

"Maybe Pevsner'd use the airplane himself, but, more likely, if he didn't use it for parts he'd sell it to somebody . . . the Chinese, or any one of the Holy Warrior organizations . . ."

"How much of this fascinating scenario did you put in your file, Dick?" Castillo interrupted.

"I sent a satburst to Langley—the third one, I think—giving the nut of the scenario. I was in the commo room when we got the acknowledgment, so it should have been on the desk of the regional director for Southwest Africa when she went to work at Langley the next morning. Then I went to work writing what I would send when I got the 'without diverting substantial assets, attempt to develop further' response. It's SOP; I expected that would come in as soon as she read the satburst."

"Let me get this straight. You prepared more than a satburst?"

"A six-page filing," Miller said. "I even read it over very carefully to make sure I had all the big words spelled right."

"I never saw anything like that. When did you send it?"

"I never sent it," Miller said. "I never got the 'develop further' reply."

"Why didn't you send it anyway? If you had it, had done it?"

"I told you, because I never got the 'develop further' response. She wasn't interested."

"She wasn't interested? Why not? You're suggesting she just shot down your idea? Why would she do that?"

"If it was shot down by somebody at Langley, I suspect she was the shooter, but I don't know that."

"What we were supposed to get, Dick, were summaries to date, plus not yet evaluated raw data," Castillo said. "Even if Langley didn't have time to evaluate it, Hall was supposed to get it. And I read everything he got. There was no copy of your satburst, or anything from anybody about a Russian arms dealer."

Miller nodded.

"*Alleged* arms dealer," Miller said. "That may be it, Charley. You want my gut reaction, with the caveat that—as you may have suspected—I don't like the lady?"

"Yeah."

"Pevsner is smart as hell, and there's no question in my mind—if no proof— that the agency has used his services. He doesn't ask questions about what's in the boxes loaded in his airplanes; all he cares about is the cash up-front."

"Where are you going with this, Dick?" Castillo asked.

"If I strongly suspect the agency used Pevsner, Mrs. Wilson probably *knew* that the agency did. Okay. So if she passed my file upward, a couple of things could have happened. For one thing, I suspect the African section would have told her to send one of those 'without diverting substantial assets, attempt to develop further' messages to me. In her mind, if I would have looked into it further, there were only two possible results. One, I would have come up with zilch, which would have embarrassed her—one of her underlings was incompetent—or, two, I would have come up with something solid, which would have opened the Pevsner can of worms and pissed off the covert guys. Either way, it would be a speed bump on her path to promotion."

"You don't have a copy of your file, do you?" Castillo asked. "Your satburst and then what you wrote and didn't send?"

"Of course not, Charley," Miller said. "Maintaining personal copies of classified documents is a serious violation of security regulations. Anyone who does so is liable not only for immediate dismissal from CIA service but subject to criminal prosecution, either under the U.S. Code or the Uniform Code of Military Justice, whichever is applicable. You of all people should know that." Miller paused, looked impassively at Castillo, then asked: "You want to see it?"

"If I go to my boss with this, I'm going to have to have it," Castillo said.

Miller's right eyebrow rose in thought and stayed there for thirty seconds but seemed longer.

Then he took a business card from his wallet, wrote something on it, and handed it to Castillo.

"If I'm going to risk sending my brilliant career down the crapper," he said, "not to mention going to the slam, I might as well go whole hog and use e-mail. Let me have your e-mail address, Charley, and I'll go home and send it to you. It's on my laptop. It'll be encrypted. That's the key."

Castillo looked at the card. Miller had written "bullshit" on it.

"Gringo at Castillo dot-com," he said. "You want to write it down?"

Miller shook his head.

"Dick, once you do this, you might think about getting rid of your file."

Miller considered that for ten seconds before replying, "I will give that solemn thought, Charley."

He stood up and put out his hand.

"Thanks for the booze, Charley," he said. "Why don't you give me three minutes to get to the service elevator, then go outside and find there's something wrong with the lock on your door?"

Castillo nodded.

"Okay," he said, then: "Dick, I'm pretty well covered. But you're really sticking your neck out . . ."

"I know," Miller interrupted. He touched Castillo's shoulder and walked toward the door.

Castillo looked at his watch, punched the timer button, and precisely three minutes later went into the corridor, closed the door, and tried again to open it with the plastic key.

When again it wouldn't work, he walked down the corridor to the bank of elevators, where he had seen a house phone.

The concierge said that he would send someone right up.

[TEN]

It took five minutes for a bellman to show up on the fifteenth floor, and another five minutes for him to prove to himself that there was something wrong with the lock at the door to Suite 1522, whereupon he went back to the house phone by the elevator bank and reported this to someone.

Five minutes later, an assistant manager and the bell captain got off the el-

evator on the fifteenth floor. They spent another five minutes proving to themselves that there was something wrong with the lock on the door to Suite 1522.
Then the bell captain went to summon further assistance while the assistant
manager stayed behind to assure Herr Gossinger that this sort of thing almost
never happened and that it would be put right in short order.

Five minutes after that, a hotel engineer and his assistant showed up with
a device that was supposed to open door locks in situations such as this. And
after another five minutes, they managed to get the lock to function partially.
In other words, it would permit the door to be opened, but, once closed again,
the lock again refused to function with the plastic key.

The engineer and the assistant manager then held a whispered conference,
after which the assistant manager went to Herr Gossinger and said that he certainly didn't wish to alarm him but in the opinion of the engineer someone
might have tried to gain access to Herr Gossinger's room. When the engineer
opened the door again, it would probably be a good idea to see if anything was
missing.

Furthermore, the entire lock was going to have to be replaced, which would
take some time, and, if Herr Gossinger had no objections, probably the best
thing to do was move him to another suite of rooms.

Herr Gossinger had no objections.

The assistant manager went to the telephone, conferred with the front desk
about available rooms, and then told whoever he was talking to to immediately
send bellmen, plural, to Herr Gossinger's room.

"Fifteen-thirty-four is available, Herr Gossinger," he said. "It is a very nice
suite not far from here. Perhaps you would like to check your property to make
sure you have everything?"

As Castillo went through his luggage, the assistant manager paid close attention. Castillo wondered if this was simply a manifestation of his great professional interest in a guest's potential problems or whether he had other reasons.

Castillo reported that he seemed to have everything.

By that time, there were three bellmen hovering by the door. The assistant
manager snapped his fingers and pointed. The bellmen carried Castillo's possessions out of the suite and down the corridor to 1534, which was identical
to 1522, and placed everything in the new room where it had been in the old.

The assistant manager apologized once again for the inconvenience Herr
Gossinger had been caused and suggested, in almost a whisper, that if the locks
had been of German manufacture this probably wouldn't have happened.

Castillo finally got rid of him, and plugged his laptop into the high-speed
Internet connection.

There were two e-mail messages in his mailbox at castillo.com. One was from Fernando, who had obviously received the enlarge the size of your member advertisement Castillo had forwarded to him, and had replied:

```
THEY DON'T SEND ME ADVERTISEMENTS LIKE THIS, BECAUSE
THE WHOLE WORLD KNOWS I DON'T NEED SOMETHING LIKE THIS.
MAYBE YOURS WOULD GROW TO A NORMAL SIZE IF YOU DON'T
ABUSE IT SO MUCH.
```

The second message had no subject and only "herewith" as the message. It contained, however, a 203-kb download.

Castillo downloaded it, then signed off before going through the decryption process. It was simple. All he had to do was type "bullshit" and then press ENTER.

Miller's satburst appeared, and below it the analysis he had prepared and not sent.

```
SECRET


SATBURST 03 LUANDA 23 MAY 2005


FOR REGDIR SWAFRICA


SOURCES AT POLICIA NACIONAL LUANDA CONFIRM THAT SERGEI
NOSTROFF (RUSSIAN NATIONAL AND KNOWN ASSOCIATE OF
VASILY RESPIN, ALLEGED ARMS DEALER) AND PAOLO WALLI
(ANGOLAN NATIONAL SUSPECTED OF VARIOUS CRIMINAL
ACTIVITIES) ARE KNOWN TO HAVE BEEN IN LUANDA IN PAST
WEEK. PRESENT WHEREABOUTS OF EITHER ARE UNKNOWN.


UNDERSIGNED SUGGESTS POSSIBILITY THAT BOTH MAY BE
INVOLVED WITH DISAPPEARANCE OF LA-9021. RESPIN REPORTED
TO OWN AT LEAST TWO AND POSSIBLY THREE BOEING 727
AIRCRAFT. LA-9021 MAY BE FLOWN ELSEWHERE, POSSIBLY TO
SHARJAH, UNITED ARAB EMIRATES, WHERE RESPIN CONTROLS
```

```
THREE OR MORE AIRLINES EITHER FOR USE WITH FALSE
IDENTITY NUMBERS, OR TO BE STRIPPED OF USABLE PARTS
FOR OTHER AIRCRAFT.

STRONGLY RECOMMEND IMMEDIATE AND WIDESPREAD USE OF
SATELLITE, AWACS, OTHER SURVEILLANCE ASSETS, AND
HUMINTEL ON ALL POSSIBLE ROUTES BETWEEN LUANDA AND
SHARJAH, AND OTHER POINTS IN MIDDLE EAST.

MORE TO FOLLOW. STACHIEF LUANDA
```

That should have been enough, Castillo thought when he read the satburst, *of interest to anyone wondering what possibly could have happened to the missing 727.*

And it certainly should have been sent to Secretary Hall.

And then he read the six pages of what Miller had written but not sent.

I don't know if this Russian arms dealer theory holds water—there's no proof— but, goddammit, this should have been brought to the attention of everybody who could possibly check it out.

What the hell's going on here?

He read it through again and then inserted what Miller had sent to him into the middle of a lengthy article he had written—mostly paraphrased from *The American Conservative*—for the *Tages Zeitung* a week before and encrypted the whole thing. He deleted Miller's file, "shredding" it so it would not be recoverable from his laptop computer's hard drive.

Then he stood up and went to the window and looked down at the harbor and thought about what he should do next.

He went to his suitcase and took a tissue-wrapped Temple Hall cigar from a white-painted box, and by the time he had gone through the ritual of carefully unwrapping it, clipping the end, and lighting it he had made up his mind.

I told Otto Görner that I would file a story for the Tages Zeitung *about the missing 727, and I will, including in it the rumor that the Russian arms dealer variously known as Vasily Respin and Aleksandr Pevsner is somehow involved.*

I'll send a copy of the story to Hall. He'll have to have it translated from the German, but he will, and discreetly, knowing that I would not have sent to him a copy of the story unless there was a reason.

And when he gets to the part about Respin/Pevsner, he'll understand what I meant about getting something I'm surprised he didn't get.

And at that point, he'll try to find out who Dick Miller is, and, when he does, everything will make sense to him.

I hope.

He went to the laptop, opened the Word program, and began to type. It took him about thirty minutes to write about seven hundred words. He read it over a final time, then went on the Internet, entered *Tages Zeitung's* e-mail address, put Hall's private e-mail address in the BLIND COPY TO block, and sent the story.

Then he sent a second e-mail to Hall to make sure, first, that he was doing what he could to cover Dick Miller's tail, and also to make sure Hall understood what was going on.

```
I BUMPED INTO AN OLD FRIEND, DICK MILLER, WHO WORKS FOR
UNCLE CHARLEY. I TOLD HIM NOT TO MENTION TO UNCLE
CHARLEY THAT WE HAD MET OR KNEW EACH OTHER, AS I'M NOT
GOING TO HAVE TIME TO SEE UNCLE CHARLEY, AND I DON'T
WANT TO HURT HIS FEELINGS. DICK GAVE ME SOMETHING I
THINK YOU'LL BE REALLY SURPRISED YOU DON'T ALREADY
HAVE. I'M BRINGING IT HOME WITH ME. SEE YOU VERY SOON.
CHARLEY.
```

He read it over, decided *That should do it,* and clicked on the SEND button. Then he picked up the telephone and told the hotel operator to connect him with British Airways.

The British Airways representative told him their next flight to London would depart Luanda tomorrow, at 2305. If Mr. Gossinger really had to get to London and then Frankfurt am Main as soon as possible, there were of course other ways to do this, but, unfortunately, they required changing planes and airlines at least once.

The British Airways representative spent fifteen minutes detailing other travel options available. The best of these alternate routes involved catching the once-a-week Air Chad flight to N'Djamena, which was conveniently departing Luanda at ten-fifty tonight, which would arrive at N'Djamena at five tomorrow morning. After a six-hour layover—which, unless he had a Chadian visa, and he didn't, he would have to spend in the transient lounge at the airport—he could catch Egyptian Airways Flight 4044 to Cairo, where he would have his choice between three different flights to London, or, for that matter, to his ultimate destination, Frankfurt am Main. Presuming there was space on them. Making reservations in Luanda for flights departing from N'Djamena or Cairo sometimes was difficult.

"Just make sure I have a seat on your flight to London tomorrow night, please," Castillo said.

"Our pleasure, Herr Gossinger."

Castillo decided that it was beer time, no matter what time the clock said it was, and went to the minibar under the television. The key was in the lock, which surprised him until he opened the door and found the minibar empty.

I will just have to run the risk of running into Mrs. Patricia Davies Wilson in the hotel bar, in which I will take the most remote table possible. Not only am I thirsty but the rumble in my stomach just reminded me that I didn't have lunch.

[ELEVEN]

The lobby newsstand offered the international edition of the *Herald Tribune*, which was published in Paris. It was four days old. It also offered *Le Matin* and *Paris Match*, which were also published in Paris. They were two days old. He wondered if this was coincidental or whether the newsstand had two-day-old copies of the *Trib* hidden somewhere in order to promote sales of *Le Matin* and *Paris Match*.

Then he saw, partially hidden behind a stack of the local newspaper, which was in Portuguese, *Die Frankfurter Rundschau*. It was *yesterday's* paper.

What is that, another manifestation of all-around Teutonic efficiency?

He bought the *Rundschau* and took it with him into the bar, where he found a table that was not only deep inside but mostly behind a thick pillar. He could not see into the lobby and, therefore, someone in the lobby would not be able to see him.

A waiter quickly came to the table and laid a bowl of cashews and a larger bowl of what looked like homemade potato chips before him.

Castillo asked for a local beer and a menu.

The waiter said he was sorry but not only was there no food service in the bar after four o'clock—it was now four-oh-five—there was no local beer, either. There were three kinds of French beer, and two kinds each of German, Holland, and English, plus one kind of American.

"What time does the restaurant open?"

"Half past five, sir."

"I'll have a Warsteiner, please," Castillo said as he scooped a handful of cashews from the bowl.

Three Warsteiners and one bowl each of cashews and homemade potato chips later, as he was reading the *Rundschau*'s nearly vitriolic opinion of the Social Democrats' notions of fair severance pay, he sensed movement near him and lowered the *Rundschau* just in time to see Mrs. Patricia Davies Wilson slipping into the banquet seat beside him.

This is not a chance encounter, my love; you didn't just happen to see me as you walked through the lobby. You were looking for me.

"Hi," she said, showing him a mouth full of neat white teeth.

I had really forgotten how good looking you are. Watch yourself, Charley!

"Hi, yourself," he replied.

"How was your day?" she asked.

"Not bad. Yours?"

"I was out to the airport," she said.

"So was I," he said.

"You want to swap what you found out for what I found out?"

"I think you would come out on the short end of that," he said. "I didn't really learn much that hasn't already been written."

"Much, or nothing?" she asked.

He didn't have to answer. The waiter appeared with fresh bowls of cashews and homemade potato chips.

"I can't drink beer," Patricia said, indicating his nearly empty glass. "It makes me feel bloated."

That's my cue to suggest something for her to drink.

"Somehow you don't strike me as someone who drinks anything that comes with a paper parasol and a chunk of pineapple," he said.

She laughed, and there was something appealing about the laugh.

"How do you feel about martinis as a reward for a day's hard work?" she asked.

"If I knew you better, I'd tell you what my boss says about martinis."

She laughed again, softly, shaking her head the way a woman does when something naughty is intimated, telling him she knew the joke.

"Martinis, please," she told the waiter. "Beefeater's gin, if you have it." She paused and looked at him. "Okay?"

I don't think I need a martini right now. But let's see where this goes.

"Fine," he said.

She smiled at him again.

"I missed lunch," Castillo said. "And I was five minutes late to get anything to eat in the bar. The restaurant opens at five-thirty."

"I tried to get something to eat at the airport," she said, "and failed at that, too. It was supposed to be a chicken sandwich but somehow it didn't look like chicken."

"As soon as the restaurant opens, I'm going to try my luck there," he said. "Will you join me?"

"I'd hoped you'd ask. I really am hungry." She paused. "You were telling me what you'd found out."

"No, I wasn't," he said. "I belong to the get-your-own-story school of jour-nalism."

As he spoke, he thought: *That should light up her curiosity. Now she'll really want to know what I've come up with.*

What if I show her the story?

For some reason, she doesn't want the Russian connection to come out. Maybe learning that I'm bringing it out in the open will make her worry a little.

Or is it the hormones speaking? "Come up to my room, mon petit cherie, and I will show you my story."

"We're not really competitors, Karl," Patricia said. "I'm not trying to beat you into print. I work for *Forbes*, remember?"

"I bet that's what you tell all the newspaper boys, that you're not trying to beat them into print," he said, tempering it with a smile.

"And what do you tell all the newspaper girls?" she countered.

"That I'm lonely and my wife doesn't understand me," Castillo said.

"You're married?" she asked, sounding surprised.

He smiled and shook his head.

"That's so they don't immediately start thinking of marriage," he said. "A lot of women my age, unmarried women, regard an unmarried man my age as a challenge to be overcome."

"You are a bastard, aren't you?" she asked, laughing.

"Absolutely," he agreed. "And if they don't believe I'm married, I have pic-tures of my cousin's kids to show them."

She laughed and then said: "I am."

"You are what?"

"Married."

"You're not wearing a wedding ring," he challenged.

"You looked?" she asked, but it was a statement not a question.

He nodded.

"Then why did you . . . what? . . . *confess* that you're single to me?"

"Professional courtesy," he said. "That's why journalists and lawyers feel safe swimming in shark-infested waters."

She laughed again.

The waiter delivered two enormous martinis.

She touched the rim of her glass to his.

"Here's to you, even if you won't show me your story and think I'm a shark."

"I didn't say you were a shark," he said.

"That was the implication," she said.

"I meant to imply nothing of the sort," Castillo said.

"The hell you didn't," she said.

"I know that you'll find this hard to believe, but on more than one occasion I've had a story stolen from me by women nearly as good-looking as you. I've learned that when a woman—a good-looking woman—bats her eyes as me, I'm putty in her hands."

"You're outrageous!" she laughed. "I can't believe that any woman has ever taken advantage of you, Karl."

"I expected you would say something like that," he said. "While you were batting your eyes."

"I was not," she protested.

"If you weren't, then I can only hope you won't," he said. "I'm not sure I could resist."

She shook her head.

"So what do you think happened to the 727?" she asked.

"It was stolen by parties unknown for unknown purposes," he said. "It is alleged."

"You're not going to tell me what you found out, are you?"

He shook his head.

"Tell me about Mr. Wilson," he said, changing the subject. "Where is he now, home with the kiddies?"

"No kiddies," she said. "Do I look like the motherly type?"

"Let me think about that," he said.

"I'm not," she said.

"And Mr. Wilson's not the fatherly type, either?"

"No, he's not," she said. "He's somewhat older than I am. It was too late for us when we got married."

"Somewhat older? How much older is 'somewhat'?"

"That's none of your business!"

"What does he do? Doesn't he have a hard time with you rushing off to the four corners—in this case, to darkest Africa—in hot pursuit of a story?"

"None at all," she said. "He has his professional life and I have mine, and mine requires from time to time that I travel. He's very understanding."

"Sounds like a nice arrangement," Castillo said.

"What's that supposed to mean?"

"Just what I said. It sounds like a nice arrangement."

"Somehow, it didn't come across that way. It sounded sarcastic."

"I think you'll know when I'm being sarcastic," he said, then added, "All I'm doing is trying to keep you off the subject of you wanting a look at my story."

"Really?"

"Really."

"That didn't work, either. All you're doing is making me really curious," she said.

"Tell you what I'll do," he said. "As an olive branch. I think we're in the same time zone here as Germany . . ."

"We are," she furnished.

"The *Tages Zeitung* goes to bed at one in the morning. If we're still up then, I'll show you my story. If not, I'll show it to you at breakfast."

"You seem pretty sure I'll want to have breakfast with you."

"I don't know what you're thinking but what I had in mind was that we might still be here in the bar—not drinking martinis, of course, which would be likely to get either or both of us in trouble; but maybe coffee—at one A.M.—or that we could meet in the restaurant at, say, half past nine tomorrow morning."

"No, you weren't," she said.

He looked at her a moment.

"Okay, no, I wasn't," he said. "Ye shall know the truth, and the truth shall make you free. Or, in your case, probably angry. What happens now? You storm out of the bar? With or without throwing what's left of your martini in my face?"

She met his eyes for a long moment.

"You understood me before when I said my husband was very understanding, didn't you?"

"I don't know if I did or not."

"He's twenty-three years older than I am," she said.

"And very understanding."

"Yes, very understanding."

"Yes, I think I understood you," he said. "Would you like another martini?"

"Yes, I would," she said. "Do you think we could get one from room service?"

"I'm sure we could, but why would we want to do that?"

"Because we're going to have to go to your room sooner or later so that you can show me your story, so why not go now?"

"I told you, not until after the *Tages Zeitung* goes to bed," he said.

"I'll split the difference with you, Karl," she said. "How about after we do?"

"You drive a hard bargain," Castillo said. "But, what the hell, business has been slow."

VII

[ONE]
Office of the Director
The Central Intelligence Agency
Langley, Virginia
1725 6 June 2005

"Secretary Hall is on Secure 2 for you, boss."

The director of Central Intelligence's private reaction to the announcement was somewhat less than unrestrained joy. He had a headache, for one thing, and for another he had promised his wife that he would *really* try to get home for once on time, if not early. They were having dinner at the White House.

But he smiled his thanks at his executive assistant, picked up his phone, and pushed the second of four red buttons on his telephone.

"And a very good afternoon to you, Mr. Secretary," he said. "And how may the Central Intelligence Agency be of service?"

"I'm glad I caught you, John."

"I was, literally, about to stand up and walk out the door. What's on your mind?"

"We have what might be a problem," the secretary of homeland security said.

"You sound serious, Matt."

"Unfortunately, I am."

"You're on a secure line?"

"Yeah."

"So tell me."

"Are you going to the White House tonight?"

"I don't think you're just idly curious, Matt. Yeah. Aren't you?"

"I think we should talk this through before we go there and are asked about it."

"Talk what through? You want to come over here? I'll wait for you."

"What I'd really like for you to do is come to the Mayflower. Suite 404."

"You mean right now?"

"Right now, John. I wouldn't ask if I didn't think it was important."

The director didn't reply for a moment. Then he said, "Matt, I don't want to have to come all the way into the District only to have to go back across the bridge to get dressed and then go back across that damned bridge again. At rush hour. Will this wait until I go home and put on a black tie? That way I can bring Eleanor with me and we'll be right around the corner from the White House."

"How would Eleanor feel about having a drink in the Mayflower bar with one of your bodyguards while we talk?"

"She won't like it but she'll do it."

"Okay, John, thank you. I'll be expecting you."

"I'll be there as soon as I can, Matt. Four-oh-four, you said?"

"Four-oh-four," Hall said.

"Okay," the DCI said and hung up.

Then he telephoned his wife, told her that he was just now leaving the office for the house, but as soon as he got there he would have to take a quick shower, put on a dinner jacket, and leave immediately. He told her she had her choice of going with him right now and having a drink in the bar of the Mayflower while he talked to someone or going into the District later alone and meeting him outside the Mayflower or at the White House, whichever she preferred.

Eleanor said that what she really would prefer was that he come home as he said he would really try to do and that they go to the White House together, but since that was obviously out of the question, again, she would do whatever was best for him.

"Let me think about it on the way home," he said.

"Do that, John," she said. "Think about it."

Then she hung up.

[TWO]
The Mayflower Hotel
1127 Connecticut Avenue NW
Washington, D.C.
1925 6 June 2005

The director of Central Intelligence had been driven alone—his choice—from his home to the Mayflower hotel in a dark blue GMC Yukon. The Yukon was armored and the windows were deeply tinted. There were three shortwave antennae on the roof.

But the vehicle, the director believed, would not attract very much attention. There were probably three hundred nearly identical vehicles moving around the district and by no means did all of them belong to the government. He suspected that maybe half of them belonged to, say, middle-level bureaucrats in, say, the Department of Agriculture, who had bought them to impress the neighbors, as a, say, middle-level bank manager in St. Louis, Missouri, would have bought a Jaguar or a Cadillac he really couldn't afford for the same purpose.

In Washington, prestige came with power rather than money. In Washington, and environs, the way to impress the neighbors was to look as if you were important enough to move around in an armored, window-darkened Yukon with antennae on the roof.

The DCI's Yukon and the DCI himself attracted little attention when he rolled up in front of the Mayflower, quickly got out, and marched across the lobby to the bank of elevators, even though he was preceded and trailed by security men.

They ascended to the fourth floor. One of the security men got off the elevator first, looked up and down the corridor, and then indicated the direction of Suite 404 with a nod of his head.

The security man waited until the DCI started off the elevator, then led the way down the corridor to 404, where he knocked three times on the door.

It was opened by a young man in a dinner jacket. The security man quickly scrutinized the guy. He was not of the beady-eyed political lackey sort that the security man was accustomed to encountering in this town. He showed confidence and control.

"Who are you?" the security man asked, not very politely.

The young man glanced down the corridor, saw the DCI approaching, and evenly replied, "If you're looking for Secretary Hall, this is it." He opened the door wider.

The DCI appeared in the doorway.

"Come on in, John," the secretary of homeland security called.

The DCI entered the suite.

The living room looked like someone lived there, he thought, rather than as if it were just one more "executive suite" occupied by some businessman— not government employee; a government per diem allowance wouldn't come close to paying for this place—in Washington for a few days.

The young man in the dinner jacket started to close the door in the face of the security guard, who held it open with his foot and hand and looked to the DCI for guidance.

"It's okay," the DCI said, and the security man removed his foot and hand and the door closed in his face.

"John, this is my executive assistant, Charley Castillo," the secretary said.

The DCI smiled and put out his hand but didn't say anything.

"How do you do, sir?" Castillo said politely, shaking the hand.

"Eleanor downstairs?" the secretary asked.

"No. She's coming in later. I told her to call my cellular when she got close," the DCI said.

"Well, maybe we can wrap this up before she gets here," the secretary said. "Can we get you a drink, John?"

"Thank you, no. What's this all about, Matt?"

The secretary picked up a folder from the coffee table—the DCI noticed that it bore no security stamps of any kind—and handed it to him.

The document inside, six single-spaced pages, also was barren of security stamps of any kind. But two sentences into it, the DCI was aware he was reading an intel filing.

This one suggested the strong possibility that the Boeing 727 that had gone missing from Luanda, Angola, had been stolen by or for a Russian arms dealer by the name of Vasily Respin either for parts to be used by one of his enterprises or to be sold to others.

"This sounds more credible than some of the other theories I've heard," the DCI said. "Where did this come from? And is this why you asked me to come here?"

"I asked you to come here because I thought we could handle something that's come up between us," Hall said. "I'd rather, if possible, that we kept this out of school, John."

The DCI nodded and waited for Hall to go on.

"John, did you see Natalie Cohen's memo that I was to get everything, including raw data, from everybody about the 727?" Hall asked.

"I saw it, wondered about it, and ordered that it be carried out," the DCI said.

"Would you say that that file met the criteria for material I was to get?"

"Obviously."

"I didn't get it, John. That's the problem," the secretary said.

"You obviously got it from somebody, Matt. I don't understand."

"The problem is that I should have gotten it from you and I didn't. The satburst was filed to Langley by your station chief in Luanda," Hall said, nodding at the file the DCI was still holding in his hand.

"And the filing?"

"The satburst was either spiked or lost, or something, in Langley. I never got it from you."

"And the filing?" the DCI repeated, somewhat impatiently.

"That was never sent, because there was no response to the satburst."

"I can't believe that," the DCI said.

"Well, that's what happened, John," Hall said.

"Then where did you get it? The satburst *and* the filing?"

"Charley brought them to me just before I called you," the secretary said, and then added, "When he came back from Luanda."

The DCI glanced at Castillo. *I thought he said this guy was his executive assistant. So what was he doing in Luanda? And with his nose obviously into something that's none of the Department of Homeland Security's business? How did he come into possession of this file? How did he know this file was sent to Langley? That it was either spiked there or that something else happened to it?*

"You are going to tell me what's going on here, right, Matt?"

"I am, and I'm afraid you're not going to like it."

"We won't know that until you tell me, will we? How about starting with what Mr. Castillo was doing in Luanda and how he came into possession of this?" The DCI held up the file.

"He was in Luanda because the president ordered him to find out what everybody knows about the missing 727 and when they learned it," Hall said.

"Everybody meaning who?"

"The CIA, the DIA, the FBI, the State Department, the Office of Naval Intelligence . . . everybody," Hall said.

"I wasn't told," the DCI said, a little coldly.

"Nobody was," Hall said.

"Except you," Powell said, more coldly.

"That's the way the president wanted it, John."

"Is Natalie involved in this?"

"She knows about it," Hall replied. "The president told her why he wanted everybody to send me everything . . . why she was to send the memo."

"I will be goddamned!" Powell said, white-faced.

"Charley thought, after he'd gone through all the material Natalie's memo produced, that the obvious place for him to start was in Luanda. I agreed, and that's where he went."

"You're telling me, unless I'm getting this wrong, that the president authorized you to sniff around on my lawn," the DCI said.

"He did. Yours and everybody else's," Hall said.

"I wonder whose idea this was?" the DCI asked, almost of himself.

"It doesn't really matter, does it? The president ordered that it be done."

The DCI turned to Castillo.

"Castillo, isn't it?"

"Yes, sir."

"How did you come into possession of this?" the DCI asked. "How do you know that it was sent to Langley?"

Castillo looked at Hall, who nodded.

"The officer who wrote it gave it to me," Castillo said.

"And who is this officer?"

Castillo looked at Hall again and Hall nodded again.

"H. Richard Miller, sir."

"And he is?"

"He's the CIA station chief in Luanda, sir," Castillo said. "His cover is assistant military attaché at the embassy."

"And why would he do any of the foregoing?" the DCI asked, icily.

"Easy, John," the secretary said.

". . . Reveal his CIA connection?" the DCI went on, angrily. "His cover? Give you access to classified CIA files?"

Castillo didn't reply.

"Answer the question, Mr. Castillo," the DCI said, not pleasantly.

"That sounded like an order, John," the secretary said. "I think you should keep in mind that Charley doesn't work for you . . ."

The DCI glared at the secretary.

". . . And that the only superior authority either one of us can appeal to is the president," the secretary went on. "Given that, I think we should really make an effort to deal with this between us."

The DCI looked at the secretary for a moment but didn't speak.

"Answer the director's question, Charley, please," the secretary said. "Tell him what you told me."

"Yes, sir," Castillo said. "Sir, I informed Miller that what I was doing was at the direct order of the president," Castillo said. "I can only presume that he felt that orders from the commander in chief carried greater weight than any others to which he was subject."

"Disclosure of classified material to unauthorized persons is a felony under the U.S. Code," the DCI said. "As is the receipt by unauthorized persons of classified material."

"The operative word there, John, is 'unauthorized,' " the secretary said. "Charley was authorized to see the file first because of Cohen's memo, and, second . . . or maybe first . . . because he was acting at the orders of the president. There has been no disclosure of classified material to unauthorized persons. Let's get at least that straight between us. I don't want Miller to get in trouble over this."

"Miller doesn't work for you, Matt," the DCI said. "I decide what is acceptable—for that matter, criminal—behavior on his part and what's not."

Hall looked at him for a long moment and then said, "That being the case, I don't think we have anything more to talk about, do you, John?"

The telephone on the side table by the couch rang.

Castillo looked at the secretary for guidance.

"Answer it, Charley," Hall ordered.

Castillo went to the telephone and picked it up.

He said "Hello" and then immediately switched to German. The conversation lasted not much more than a minute and then he hung up.

"That was very interesting, sir," he said to Hall.

"Well, as soon as the director leaves, you can tell me what it was all about," the secretary said. "You are about to leave, Mr. Director, aren't you?"

It was a moment before the DCI answered. "I don't want to leave on this kind of a sour note, Matt. Exactly what is it you want of me?"

"My hope, which, now that I think about it, was probably naïve, was that you would accept this situation as a problem for both of us. Instead . . ." He paused, obviously searching for the right words.

"Go on, Matt."

"Instead, you're acting like a typical bureaucrat protecting his turf."

"That's what you think, eh?"

"Frankly, John, you seem far more concerned that somebody has found out the CIA has egg on its face—and that the president's going to hear about it—than you do about fixing what's wrong."

"Is that so?"

"What I had hoped our friendly chat would accomplish was that I could truthfully tell the president that we had uncovered a stoppage in the flow of information at Langley, that I had told you about it and had your assurance you would personally look into it and get back to me."

The DCI looked at him.

"The president's going to know about that filing tonight, John, and hear how I came by it," Hall went on. "And I'm going to relay Charley's concern that Miller is probably—how do I put this?—in some jeopardy because he decided his first duty was to obey the orders of the commander in chief and acted accordingly."

The DCI looked as if he was going to say something, then changed his mind.

"And now if you'll excuse me, John," Hall said, "I have to go home and put on my tux."

"And if I gave you my assurance that I will personally look into this—what did you call it? 'stoppage in the flow of information'—and get back to you?"

"Then that's what the president will hear," Hall replied. "I would also like to tell him I had your assurance that you're not going to make a sacrificial lamb of Miller."

"Frankly, I haven't made up my mind about Mr. Miller."

"I suggest you do, John. The president's going to hear one thing or the other."

Powell did not respond directly.

"You said you're going to give the president that filing?" he asked.

"The satburst and tell him about the unfiled filing. I don't think he'll want to take the time to read the filing, but if he asks for it I'll of course give it to him. I'll tell him what's in it, and I'll also make sure that Charley is available to personally answer any questions the president might have."

"Okay. Deal," the DCI said. "I'll take your word that Castillo here is authorized to be made privy to material like this. Since that's the case, Miller did nothing to violate the law. So he gets a pass on this."

Powell walked to Hall, handed him the file, and put out his hand.

Hall shook Powell's hand and said, "It was never my intention, John—and, damn it, you should know it—to go to the president with the intention of embarrassing you or the CIA."

"I know that, Matt," the DCI said, not very convincingly.

The DCI looked at Castillo—closely, as if trying to figure him out—then nodded at him, but neither spoke nor offered his hand. Then he crossed the room to the door, opened it, and walked out.

The automatic closing mechanism didn't quite work and Castillo went to the door and pushed it closed.

"Your lady friend called at what I think they call a propitious moment, Charley," the secretary said. "I really didn't want Powell to walk out of here marshaling his troops for a turf war."

"It wasn't my lady friend, sir," Castillo said. "It was my boss."

"Excuse me?"

"My editor, Otto Görner," Castillo corrected himself.

Hall's eyebrows showed interest. "What did he want? You said it was interesting."

"Very interesting," Castillo said. "He said that he'd heard from Respin/ Pevsner or whatever the hell his real name is—the Russian?"

"He heard from him?" Hall asked, sounding as if he was either confused or disbelieving.

"From some guy who said he was speaking for him," Castillo said. "Otto said he's made several requests for an interview of Respin/Pevsner and this was the first time there's been any kind of a response."

"What was the response?"

"That he will give me—Karl Gossinger—an interview in Vienna."

"You specifically?"

"Yes, sir. Otto asked me what I wanted him to do."

"How much does your editor—what's his name?"

"Otto Görner."

"How much does Görner know about what you do?"

"That's a tough question, sir. He's a highly skilled journalist and very intelligent. That specific question has never come up between us, but that doesn't mean he doesn't have a very good idea of what I do."

"And he won't talk because why? You own those newspapers?"

"That's part of it, sure. But Otto is like an uncle to me. He was very close to my mother."

"The kind of relationship you have with Allan and Elaine Naylor?"

"Just about, sir. I've known Otto all of my life. Even before I met the Naylors."

"What about your real family?" Hall asked. "What do they think you do for a living?"

"My cousin, Fernando—he's a Texas Aggie; he won a Silver Star as a tank platoon commander in the first Iraqi war—has got a pretty good idea. Nothing specific, but he knows where I work, for example; that I was at the Carolina White House. He knows how to keep his mouth shut. I'm not close to any of my other relatives in Texas and none of them has any idea. Or, for that matter, is interested."

Hall thought that over a minute and nodded.

"Why do you suppose this Russian arms dealer suddenly changed his mind about talking to the press?" he asked.

"It probably had something to do with the story I wrote for the *Tages Zeitung*, sir. Otto gave me a byline."

Hall grunted and then said: "Until just now, I guess I didn't understand that that story would be printed. I thought it was just a means to give me a heads-up about what you'd found over there."

"It was printed in the *Tages Zeitung* on 5 June, sir," Castillo said. "Before I even left Luanda. A number of the German papers picked it up, and so did the Associated Press. It's logical to presume Respin/Pevsner saw it. Hell, he might even have a clipping service. His man called Otto just before Otto called here. The timeline works."

"What do you think I should do with that interesting bit of information? Turn it over to the DCI and see what the CIA can find out from—or about—this guy?"

"I was hoping you'd tell me to get on a plane to Vienna."

"My God, Charley, those people are dangerous! Somebody—the police commissioner in Philadelphia, as a matter of fact—told me the Russian immigrant gang there makes the Italian Mafia look like choirboys, and from everything I've read—not only your pal Miller's filing—Respin, or whatever else he calls himself—"

"Respin *and* Pevsner and there are probably other names," Charley furnished and chuckled and then asked, "Hereafter Pevsner, sir?"

It was a reference to the rules laid down for writing intelligence reports, which permitted, for example, references to the Arabic scholar Sheikh Ibn Taghri Birdi, to be shortened after the first use of his name in a filing by adding the phase "hereafter Birdi."

Hall smiled at Charley. "Hereafter Pevsner," he said. "Hereafter Pevsner is the head thug. If he didn't like seeing his name in the newspaper, he's entirely capable of having you assassinated. Both for writing the story and to discourage others."

"I don't think he would telegraph his moves, sir. He would simply have sent somebody to eliminate me in Fulda. I think we ought to see what he wants."

"What could he want?"

"I don't know, but I don't think he's really going to give an interview as the first step to getting on *Larry King Live*. He wants something."

Hall smiled again.

"But what could he want, Charley?"

"We'll never know, sir, unless you tell me to get on the next plane to Vienna."

"I don't know," Hall said, doubtfully.

"Sir, I also respectfully suggest that having me out of town for the next few days might be a good idea."

"Because of our encounter with the DCI just now?" Hall asked.

Castillo nodded, then said, "I had the feeling he thinks killing the messenger is probably a very good way to handle something like this."

"I don't think he'd go that far, Charley, but he didn't seem to be taken very much with your charm and good looks, did he?"

"No, sir. I didn't think so."

Hall looked at Castillo thoughtfully for fifteen seconds and then said, "Okay, Charley. Bring me a Sacher torte. And I mean *bring* me. I don't want it shipped here with your body."

"Yes, sir. White or dark chocolate, sir?"

Hall shook his head, touched Castillo affectionately on the shoulder, and walked out of the apartment.

[THREE]
The Mayflower Hotel
1127 Connecticut Avenue NW
Washington, D.C.
1925 6 June 2005

The leading security officer accompanying the DCI—the trailing security officer was following the DCI—glanced through the plate-glass door leading from the Mayflower lobby, saw the Yukon was where he expected it to be and that there was nothing suspicious on the street, and pushed the door open.

Then he turned and found the DCI was nowhere in sight.

Jesus Christ!

He hurried back into the lobby.

The trailing security officer was standing, his hands folded in front of him, near the front desk. He made a small gesture indicating what looked like the entrance to a hallway near the end of the front desk and smiled at his colleague.

The sonofabitch thinks it's funny!

The leading security officer started into what he thought was a corridor.

It was instead an alcove, holding four house telephones and two pay telephones. The DCI was using one of the pay phones.

The leading security officer sort of backed out of the alcove and took up a position facing the trailing security officer, who smiled at him and said, "Vigilance, Pete. Constant vigilance!"

The leading security officer mouthed, *Fuck you!*

The DCI was on the pay phone for almost twenty minutes. In that time he had spoken with the CIA's regional director for Africa and the deputy director for Personnel, both of whom were in their homes.

The regional director for Africa told him that he had not seen either a satburst or a filing suggesting that a Russian arms dealer had stolen the Boeing 727 missing in Angola.

"Get on the horn, and right now, to whoever is directly responsible for Angola . . ."

"That would be the regional director for Southwest Africa, Mr. Director."

"Whatever. And find out what he knows about this. I'll call you back in ten minutes. Have a number where I can reach him."

"It's a her, Mr. Director. Mrs. Patricia Davies Wilson."

"All right, when I call you back have a number where I can reach *her.*"

"She's over there, Mr. Director."

"In Luanda?"

"Yes, sir. Actually, sir, she's on her way back. By now, I think she'd probably be in either London or Paris."

"Find out," the DCI said. "If there's time to make contact with her in London or Paris, get word to her that she is to come directly to my office from the airplane and is to speak to no one but you or me about anything."

"Has something come up, Mr. Director?"

"That's pretty obvious, wouldn't you say? And if you can't contact her before her plane takes off, have someone—you, if that's possible—meet her plane when it lands and bring her directly to my office."

"I don't have an ETA on her plane, Mr. Director."

"Well, get one!"

"If I have to contact you, Mr. Director, will you be at home?"

"I'll be at the White House. I don't want you calling me there about this. I'll get back to you later."

"Whatever you wish, Mr. Director."

———

The deputy director for Personnel, when asked "Who is this man Miller we have in Luanda?" didn't know off the top of his head, but he called his duty officer in Langley, who got the information.

The station chief in Luanda was an H. Richard Miller, Jr. His cover was assignment as the assistant military attaché.

"Where did he come from? How long has he been with us? What do we know about him?"

It took another ten minutes to get the answers: H. Richard Miller, Jr., had come to the agency from the Army, that he was a major in the Army, that he had been on temporary duty with the agency for seventeen months, five months as an instructor at the Farm, and since then in Luanda. Since he had been in Luanda, he had received two letters of official reprimand from the regional director for Southwest Africa, one for exceeding his authority and the other for exceeding the limits of his discretionary operating funds.

"He's relieved, as of now," the DCI said. "His security clearances are suspended as of now. I want him out of Angola in twenty-four hours or less. I want somebody—somebody good; somebody we wouldn't ordinarily send someplace like Angola—on his way there within four hours to replace him."

"Gregory Leese is in Johannesburg, Mr. Director."

"I don't think I know him."

"Good man, sir. He was in Caracas until recently. Did a fine job there."

"Okay, if you say so. Send him. Tell him I ordered it and I'll be in touch with him."

"Yes, sir. May I ask what this is all about?"

"Not right now."

"Should I have this man Miller report to Langley, Mr. Director? If so, to whom? If he asks why he's being relieved, what may I tell him?"

"You don't know, to answer that first. No. I don't want him in Langley until I have a chance to chat with this Mrs. Wilson."

"Yes, sir?"

"If he's on temporary duty to us, that must be from someplace. Where do military people like that come from?"

"Usually either from the Pentagon, Mr. Director, or from Central Command. In this case—I'll have to check—I should think it would be Central Command. Major Miller is Special Forces."

Why am I not surprised to hear that?

"Well, find out and send him back where he came from. Say that he's under investigation."

"Yes, sir. Investigation concerning what?"

"Don't say."

"Yes, sir. Anything else, Mr. Director?"

"Secretary Hall of Homeland Security has an assistant named Castillo. I want to know about him. If we don't have anything, make inquiry—very discreet inquiry—of the Civil Service Commission. They should have the results of his background investigation. If that doesn't work, ask somebody we know we can trust in the FBI."

"You have a first name on this fellow, Mr. Director?"

Hall called him "Charley."

"It's probably 'Charles.'"

"I'll get right on it, Mr. Director."

"Thank you," the DCI said and hung up.

Then he pulled his head out of the translucent shell over the pay phone and looked down the alcove to the lobby.

The security guys were waiting for him.

The DCI made a gesture toward the Connecticut Avenue entrance and the lead security man started to move in that direction.

[FOUR]
Apartment 6-B
Rua Madre Dios 128
Luanda, Angola
0515 7 June 2005

The peculiar tinkle of the telephone that came with the apartment woke Major H. Richard Miller, Jr., quickly more as a strange sound than as a telephone. He rarely used the French-manufactured dial instrument. The cellular phone system was far more efficient.

He picked up the handset, which placed a brass conelike microphone before his mouth as well as the speaker against his ear.

Ten-to-one, it's a wrong number.

"Hello," he said.

"Major Miller?" an American male voice inquired.

"Speaking."

"Major, this is Colonel Porter."

What the hell does he want at oh-dark-hundred?

"Yes, sir?"

"I am five minutes from your apartment, Major," Lieutenant Colonel James R. Porter, Artillery, the defense attaché of the United States embassy in Luanda, said, somewhat stiffly. "Please be prepared to admit me."

"You're coming here?" Miller asked, really surprised. He belatedly added, "Sir?"

"I am coming there. Please be prepared to admit me."

"Yes, sir," Miller said.

There was a click as the connection was broken.

Miller found the light switch in the dark, put the old telephone handset in its cradle, and then swung his legs out of bed, wincing at the pain in his knee.

"Fuck!" he said aloud and then walked to the bathroom, where a terry cloth robe hung on the back of the door.

If Porter's going to be here in five minutes, I'm not going to have time for a shower and to get dressed.

He pulled the robe around him and then decided he'd better add undershorts. Then he went back in the bathroom and swirled Scope around in his mouth.

What the hell does he want?

The lobby buzzer went off three minutes later. Miller went into the kitchen and pushed the intercom's SPEAK button.

"Yes?"

"This is Colonel Porter, Major Miller," Porter's voice came metallically over the wire.

"Pushing the solenoid now, sir," Miller said.

Miller had the door to his apartment open by the time the elevator came up. Colonel Porter, in uniform, walked off the elevator, followed by one of the embassy's Marine guards.

The Gunny, Miller thought as he recognized the noncommissioned officer in charge of the guard detachment. Miller knew the large and muscular shaven-headed man a lot better than he was supposed to. Majors and E-7s are not supposed to socialize. But Miller and the gunny had in common both being black and not quite being fully recovered from the hits they had taken from the ragheads in Afghanistan. This was not the gunny's first visit to Miller's apartment.

But this time Gunnery Sergeant Roscoe Fortenaux, USMC, was obviously on duty. He had a Smith & Wesson .357 in a holster on his hip.

Roscoe had told him that the State Department insisted the Marine guards be armed with the S&W revolver, rather than with the standard-issue Beretta 9mm semiautomatic. Neither of them had been able to understand the logic of that. Even the cops had gone to semiautomatic pistols.

"Good morning, sir," Miller said to Lieutenant Colonel Porter. "How are you, Gunny?"

"Good morning, sir," Gunny Fortenaux said.

"After you, sir," Miller said, motioning Porter into the apartment.

Porter took six steps into the corridor of Miller's apartment, then turned as if to make sure Miller had followed him inside.

Miller gestured for him to go farther into the apartment.

Porter turned and walked into the living room, then turned again to wait for Miller.

"Major Miller," Lieutenant Colonel Porter said, formally, "you stand relieved, sir. And you will consider yourself under arrest to quarters."

Oh, shit! Charley couldn't cover me!

"Yes, sir," Miller said. "Sir, relieved of what?"

"Of your duties with the CIA, and, of course, as assistant military attaché. Your security clearances have been suspended, pending an investigation."

"An investigation of what, sir?"

"You will be informed in due time," Porter said.

"Sir, with all possible respect, I don't believe you have the authority to relieve me of my CIA duties," Miller said.

"A message from Washington, from the CIA in Washington, has ordered your relief. The ambassador has ordered me to implement your relief."

"May I see the message, sir?"

"Don't make this any more difficult than it already is, Miller," Porter said.

"Sir . . ."

Porter cut him off.

"I am also to take possession of any and all classified materials in your possession."

"Sir, I am not in possession of any classified material of any kind."

Porter looked at him closely, almost visibly deciding whether or not to believe him.

"You will remain under arrest to quarters until such time as transportation can be arranged for you to leave Angola. That will occur within the next few hours."

"Yes, sir. Sir, two questions?"

After a moment, Porter nodded his head.

"Sir, transportation to where?"

Porter started to reply but stopped and took a small notebook from his shirt pocket. He flipped through the pages, then said, "You will report to the Special Activities Section, J-5, U.S. Central Command, MacDill Air Force Base, Tampa, Florida."

"Yes, sir. Thank you, sir. And with all respect, sir, I again ask the nature of the charges against me."

"You will be informed in due time."

"Yes, sir. With respect, sir, in that circumstance, I will not consider myself under arrest to quarters until such time as I am advised of any charges against me."

Porter lost his temper. "You're under arrest to quarters because I say you are! Is that clear enough for you, Major?"

"Sir, if the colonel will consult the Uniform Code of Military Justice, 1948—I have a copy, sir—I think you will find that prior to being placed in confinement, including arrest to quarters, the accused will be notified of the nature of charges being considered against him."

"You're a guardhouse lawyer, too, are you, Miller?"

"Sir, I am simply informing you of my position in this matter."

Porter inhaled and then exhaled slowly.

"Very well, Major Miller. I am informing you that in the very near future you will be advised of your travel plans. With that in mind, I am ordering you to remain in your quarters until that happens. Does that satisfy you?"

"Yes, sir. So long as we are agreed that I am not in arrest to quarters."

"I suggest that you start packing, Major Miller."

"Yes, sir."

"Sergeant Fortenaux, you will station yourself outside Major Miller's door and report to me immediately by telephone if the major leaves his apartment."

"Yes, sir."

"May I suggest, sir," Miller said, "that the sergeant could keep a closer eye on me if he was inside my apartment. I also suggest, sir, that if my neighbors see an armed Marine standing outside my door there would be talk."

Porter glowered at him.

"Very well," he said finally, then started for the door. He turned. "I'll be in touch shortly, Major Miller, just as soon as your transportation has been arranged."

"Yes, sir."

Porter went down the corridor to the door. After a moment, they heard it close.

Miller went to the corridor to see if Porter was really gone, then turned to look at Gunnery Sergeant Fortenaux.

"Relax, Roscoe," Miller said. "I read the sign. I understand your problem."

"What sign is that, sir?"

"The one behind Station One at the embassy: A MARINE ON GUARD HAS NO FRIENDS."

"That's boot camp bullshit," Fortenaux said. "What the fuck did you do?"

"I'm going to make coffee. You want some?"

Fortenaux nodded.

They went into the kitchen.

Miller took coffee from a cupboard and then pointed at the coffee machine.

"If you think you can work that thing, I'll take a shower."

"Go on," Fortenaux said.

Fortenaux, carrying two mugs of coffee, came into Miller's bedroom as Miller was getting dressed. Miller took one and nodded his thanks.

"Like I said, what the fuck did you do?" Fortenaux asked.

"You don't want to know."

"Something to do with that honky bitch from the CIA?"

"Hey, Roscoe! How can we get pissed when they call us niggers if we call them honkies?"

"Point taken," Fortenaux said. "Something to do with that white lady bitch from the CIA?"

Miller nodded. "But you really don't want to know more than that."

"You in the really deep shit?"

"I've got a pal who said he's got me covered," Miller said. "Until I learn for sure otherwise, I'm going to believe that."

"Your pal has the clout?"

Miller nodded again.

"And you trust him?"

"He's gotten me out of the deep shit before," Miller said. "When I got shot down in Afghanistan, I knew I was *really* in the *deep* shit. I was bleeding like a stuck pig and I couldn't walk fifty feet. And the weather was way below minimums, so I knew the candy asses wouldn't launch a medevac chopper. And then all of a sudden a Black Hawk appears, right on the fucking deck. Charley's flying it, wearing his rag-head suit and beard. He stole the Black Hawk to come and save my ass."

"You told me that war story. But not about your pal dressed up like a rag-head. He's a spook, too?"

"Yeah. And a Green Beanie. And we go all the way back to West Point. I trust him."

"Okay, then. You going to pack? Porter wasn't kidding about getting you out of here quick. They were breaking their asses at the embassy getting you on the next plane out."

"I guess I better," Miller said.

"I'll make sure they don't rob you blind when the shippers pack you up," Fortenaux said.

"Thanks," Miller said and went into a closet and started taking out suitcases.

[FIVE]
Room 426
Hotel Bristol
Kaerntner Ring 1
Vienna, Austria
0840 7 June 2005

Castillo pushed open the heavy draperies over the window beside the bed and looked out. He could see the rear of the Vienna State Opera and the red awnings over the sidewalk café of the Hotel Sacher on Philharmonikerstrasse.

He had suspected as the bellman had led him down the corridor that he might have such a view but hadn't been sure.

He put his head against the glass and looked to see how much of the front of the opera and the Opernring—"The Ring"—he could see.

Not much. It didn't matter. He was simply curious.

Once, when he'd stayed at the Bristol as a kid—Grosspappa Gossinger loved the opera and they'd come at least once a year—his grandfather had pulled aside the drapes in their suite and motioned him over.

He pointed down at the Opernring in front of the opera.

"You see that, Karlchen?" he'd asked. "That's Austria."

"Excuse me?"

"You see those three men, resetting a cobblestone?"

"Yes, sir."

"In Hesse, when a cobblestone needs resetting they send one man to replace it. That's all it takes. In Austria, they send three men. One does the work. The second drinks a beer and eats a wurst. And the third supervises the other two."

"Poppa!" his mother had complained, which had only served to fuel his grandfather's desire that his grandson should understand the Austrians.

"Behind all this *gemütlichkeit*, Karlchen, they're really a savage people."

"Poppa! Stop!"

"You know they had an empire here, Karlchen?"

"Yes, sir."

"And an imperial family?"

"Yes, sir."

"Let me tell you what they did when a member of the imperial family died, Karlchen. They cut open the body and took out the heart and the guts. Then they buried the heart in one place, the guts in another, and the gutted corpse in Saint Stefan's Cathedral. If that isn't savage, what is?"

"Why did they do that?" Karl had asked.

"To make sure he was dead, I suppose," his grandfather had said. "And I'll tell you something else, Karlchen."

"Enough, Poppa!" his mother had said.

"You know what the SS was, Karlchen? The worst of the Nazis?"

"Yes, sir."

"Most of their officers, the bastards, were Austrians, not Germans."

At that point, his mother had dragged him out of the room and taken him to a pastry shop called Demel's. Over a cup of hot chocolate almost hidden by a mountain of whipped cream, she had told him that Grosspappa had had bad experiences in the Army with the SS and Austrians.

"What kind of bad experiences?"

"In Russia, he saw all the terrible things the SS did, and he had an SS officer on his staff who reported everything your grandfather did. But, *meine hartz*, all the Austrians aren't like that, and you shouldn't pay too much attention to Grosspappa."

The story about eviscerated imperial bodies had of course stuck in the mind of a ten-year-old boy, and, a decade later, Sergeant Carlos G. Castillo of the United States Corps of Cadets had found in the library of the United States Military Academy at West Point confirmation of both that interesting custom and of what his grandfather had told him about the officer corps of the Schutzstaffel: somewhere between seventy and eighty percent had been Austrian.

He'd asked one of his professors about it. Colonel Schneider had told him it was probably something like the joke about people converting to Roman Catholicism trying to be more catholic than the pope.

"After the anschluss, Castillo, one way to keep from being treated as a second-class German because you hadn't been born in Germany before the anschluss was to become a true believer in National Socialism and Adolf Hitler, and, if you could, join the SS and put on the death's-head insignia."

Castillo let the drape fall back into place and unpacked. Then he took a shower, put his dirty linen in a plastic bag to have it washed—he had no idea how long he would be in Vienna—and then left his small suite and walked down to the lobby.

He stopped before entering the lobby and mentally filed away pictures of people sitting there who could see people getting off one of the elevators. That done, he started across the lobby and at the last moment stopped himself from picking up a copy of the international edition of the *Herald Tribune* that the hotel had stacked on a table for the convenience of its guests.

Americans—and some English—read the *Herald Tribune*. A reporter from the *Tages Zeitung* probably would not.

He went through the revolving door, declined the offer of a taxi, and went and stood on the corner for a moment, taking in the sights, and making mental notes of other people standing around where they could see who entered and left the Hotel Bristol.

Then he walked down Kaertnerstrasse to Philharmonikerstrasse and turned left, walking past the sidewalk café of the Hotel Sacher, again making mental note of the people sitting at its tables.

The bar inside the Sacher—just barely visible from the street—was where he was supposed to go every afternoon at five until Pevsner made contact.

That done, he made his way to Demel's and made breakfast of white chocolate–covered croissants and hot chocolate topped with whipped cream.

He thought of his mother.

And he thought: *If I were Michael Caine or Gene Hackman or Whatsisname, the latest 007, and doing what I'm doing, I would have a gun. Several guns. With which, shooting from the hip, I could hit a bad guy at fifty yards and drop him permanently.*

But that's not the case here.

I'm about to meet with a really bad guy and I don't have so much as a fingernail file with which to defend myself. I could have, of course, packed a fingernail file in my suitcase, thus eluding the attentions of my coworkers in the Department of Homeland Security at the airport.

And a knife. But not a gun. The only way I could legally get my hands on a gun here is from the CIA and they wouldn't give me one without authorization, which would be hard to get, inasmuch as they don't know why I'm here and Hall is not about to tell Powell.

Tonight, I can probably buy one. That will mean first finding a hooker and, through her, her pimp, and through him a retail dealer in firearms—as opposed to Mr. Pevsner, who is in the wholesale weapons business—who will get me a pistol of some sort for an exorbitant price, not a dime of which can I expect to get back from the government.

But I can't do that until late tonight, and it's possible, but improbable, that when I go to the Sacher bar Pevsner will send someone to fetch me to the rendezvous. To which I would be very foolish to go without a weapon of some sort.

To which I would be foolish to go armed with all the weapons in the combined arsenals of Mssrs. Caine, Hackman, and Whatsisname, 007.

The answer is a knife. Knives.

Despite the best efforts of professionals in the knife-fighting profession to teach me how to use a blade, the archbishop of Canterbury is probably a better knife fighter than I am.

But as it's said, desperate times call for desperate measures.

In a sporting goods store on Singerstrasse, not far from Saint Stefan's Cathedral, Castillo bought two knives, telling the salesman he wanted something suitable to gut a boar, which he intended to hunt in Hungary.

"I thought there were boar in Hesse," the salesman said, more to make it known that he had cleverly picked up on Castillo's Hessian accent—which Viennese believed was harsh and coarse—than anything else.

"They're a lot cheaper to hunt in Hungary," Castillo replied, which happened to be true.

He bought a horn-handled hunting knife with an eight-inch blade, a folding knife with a six-inch blade, and whetstone and oil and took it all back with him to the Bristol.

None of the faces of people standing around on the sidewalk or sitting where they could see who got onto the elevators looked familiar. Which meant that either Pevsner hadn't sent someone to keep an eye on him or that whoever had been sent had been relieved and replaced.

He went to his room, ordered a large pot of coffee, and, when it had been delivered, placed a towel on a small desk and began to sharpen the blades of both knives. When he'd finished, he worked on the mechanism of the folding knife until he was able to bring it to the open position with a flick of his wrist.

Then he lay down on the bed, turned the television on, found the pay-per-view movie selection, and chose a film called *The Package*, starring Gene Hackman.

VIII

[ONE]
Abéché, Chad
1325 7 June 2005

There are no hangars at the Abéché airport, only an open-sided shack that serves as the terminal building for the one "scheduled flight" from N'Djamena each week—which is more often canceled than flown.

There is not much call for transportation to Abéché, a town of some forty thousand inhabitants 470 miles east of N'Djamena, the capital of Chad. Most travelers catch rides on trucks—a three-day journey—if they have reason to go to what is actually a picturesque small city of narrow streets, falling-down build-ings, markets—and mosques.

But there is an airfield on which a Boeing 727 aircraft can land—except in the rainy season—and if it is the intention of those controlling the aircraft to strip the aircraft of its paint and registration numbers, then repaint it, and do so without attracting any attention whatever, Abéché is ideal.

For one thing, the available labor pool is large and grateful for any kind of work and the wage scale is minimal. A job involving sandpapering paint off an aircraft under a "sun shield" patched together from tents is better than no job at all.

And a patched-together sun shield on an airfield categorized in most offi-cial aviation publications as "dirt strip, no radio or navigation aids" is unlikely to attract the attention of those scrutinizing satellite photography looking for a missing Boeing 727.

It took three days, with workers swarming around the wings and fuselage like so many ants feasting on a candy bar, to remove the markings of Lease-Aire LA-9021 from the wings, fuselage, and tail.

It was taking considerably longer to repaint the aircraft in the paint scheme and appropriate registration numbers of Air Suriname. The generator providing power to the air compressor for the spray guns, which those in charge of the aircraft had thoughtfully shipped ahead of them by truck, had failed and there was no way of making repairs to it in Abéché.

It was thus necessary to apply the paint—including a primer coat; they didn't want the new paint scheme and markings to come off thirty thousand feet in the air—by hand, and the two men in charge of the aircraft were agreed that a genuine-looking—that is to say, neat—paint scheme was essential to their plans.

They were also agreed, when examining the progress of the work, that another three—perhaps four—days would pass before the job was finished.

They had hoped to be finished long before then but it couldn't be helped.

It was the will of Allah.

[TWO]
Hotel Bristol
Kaerntner Ring 1
Vienna, Austria
1650 7 June 2005

When Karl W. Gossinger, of the Fulda *Tages Zeitung*, got off the elevator, he glanced around the lobby looking for a familiar face. There was none.

He went onto The Ring through the revolving door and turned right, again looking for someone familiar. Then he started walking down Kaertnerstrasse toward Saint Stefan's Cathedral.

Walking was easier than he thought it would be. After experimenting, Castillo had decided the best way to carry the bone-handled hunting knife was to strap the sheath to the inside of his left calf with adhesive tape. It wouldn't be easy to get at it there, but it would probably go unnoticed. The flip-open knife was in his shirt pocket even though that meant he had to keep his jacket buttoned.

He was aware of the weight of the hunting knife, but he didn't think it made him walk funny. The only problem was the flip-open: He would have to remember not to bend over.

He turned left onto Philharmonikerstrasse and walked past the Hotel Sacher to the corner before turning and walking back and going into the bar.

There were six people in the bar, four men and two women, none of whom looked as if they were likely to be connected with a big-time Russian arms dealer like Aleksandr Pevsner.

Castillo took a seat at the bar and after studying the array of beer bottles lined up under the mirror behind the bar ordered a Czech beer, a Dzbán.

It came with a bowl of pretzels, a bowl of peanuts, and a bowl of potato chips, which he thought was a nice custom until the barman laid the bill on the bar and Castillo turned it over to see that the beer was going to cost about eleven dollars, American.

As discreetly as he could, Castillo studied his fellow drinkers in the none-too-reflective mirror. And turned his ears up. The couple at the end of the bar was speaking American English, which permitted him to devote his attention to the others.

They were all speaking Viennese German. The second couple was probably married, for they had the rings and he heard the woman say, "You've never liked my mother and you know it."

The remaining two men were alone, and, aside from ordering drinks, said nothing.

And no one showed more than a slight and quickly passing interest in him.

He had had three Dzbán lagers between five and quarter to six when he decided that if Aleksandr Pevsner was going to send someone to meet him—he thought it highly unlikely that Pevsner would come himself—it wasn't going to be tonight.

He paid the bill with an American Express card that had both Karl Gossinger's name and *Der Tages Zeitung* on it and left the bar. On the way back to the Bristol, he didn't see anyone on Philharmonikerstrasse or Kaertnerstrasse or The Ring who either looked familiar or who showed any interest in him.

He had another beer, this time an Ottakringer Gold Fassl, as the Bristol didn't stock Dzbán. The Gold Fassl came with a bowl of potato chips.

The bar was crowded. No one showed any interest in him. He signed the tab, noticing the Gold Fassl was as expensive as the Dzbán, and then walked across the lobby to the restaurant. No one in the lobby showed any interest in him.

He ordered—*What the hell, I'm in Vienna*—a Wiener schnitzel and was happy that he did. The pounded very thin, breaded veal cutlet covered a very large plate and was delicious.

He had—*What the hell, I'm in Vienna*—an *Apfelstrudel* for dessert and then went to his room.

He undressed to his undershorts and removed the knife taped to his thigh, wincing as the adhesive pulled hair. Next, he hooked up his laptop and sent Otto, with a copy to Hall, a short e-mail message:

```
NO SHOW, BUT I JUST HAD THREE GREAT BEERS AND A
MARVELOUS WIENER SCHNITZEL. REGARDS, KARL
```

Then he went to bed and watched another movie, an old one, black-and-white, called *The Third Man*, starring Joseph Cotten, Trevor Howard, and Orson Welles. It was laid in Vienna, right after World War II, and there was a long sequence on the enormous Ferris wheel in Vienna's amusement park, the Prater, down by the not-really-blue Blue Danube. Orson Welles was the villain, dealing in black market penicillin.

Castillo decided that he'd kill time tomorrow by taking a cab out there. He remembered his first ride on the wheel: Grosspappa had taken him when he was about six or seven.

What I'll do is take a ride on the Ferris wheel and then have one of those great würstchen *on a crusty roll, with that sinus-clearing mustard, and maybe some roasted chestnuts and a beer for lunch. What the hell, I'm in Vienna.*

With that pleasant prospect in mind, Castillo turned off the lights and punched the pillow under his head.

Then lewd and lascivious mental images of the two hours he had spent with Mrs. Patricia Davies Wilson in his room in the Le Presidente Hotel popped into his mind.

Well, if that turns out to be Ol' Charley's last piece of tail in this world, no complaints.

[THREE]
Office of the Director
The Central Intelligence Agency
Langley, Virginia
0915 8 June 2005

"Good morning, Mr. Director," Mrs. Patricia Davies Wilson said as she was shown into DCI Powell's office.

Powell stood up courteously.

"I understand you came directly from Dulles," Powell said. "Would a cup of coffee be in order?"

"Oh, yes. Thank you very much."

He gestured for her to take one of the two upholstered chairs facing his desk as he picked up his telephone to order coffee.

"How was the flight?" Powell asked. "More to the point, how are things in Angola?"

"Under control, Mr. Director," she said. "I hope."

It was clear that she meant *Unless there's something I don't know about* and Powell smiled his understanding.

"Something has come up, actually," he said and interrupted himself as a secretary came in with a tray holding a coffee service.

They were silent until after the coffee was poured and handed to them and the secretary had left.

"Thank you *so* much," Patricia Wilson said. "Frankly, for the last hour of the flight I was looking forward to a long bath and a *gallon* of coffee."

Powell smiled at her.

"As I was saying, something has come up," he said. "And I wanted to talk to you about it as soon as possible."

"I understand, Mr. Director."

"Are you aware, Mrs. Wilson, of a filing from Luanda suggesting that a Russian arms dealer by the name of Aleksandr Pevsner has had something to do with the airplane, the 727, that's gone missing over there?"

"Mr. Director, there was a satburst from Miller—the station chief . . . ?"

Powell nodded to tell her he knew whom she meant.

". . . suggesting that something like that was possible."

"And?"

"I didn't think it was credible, Mr. Director," she said. "Everything that's come to me suggests that the most likely scenario is—what's the phrase?—'an insurance scam.' And everything I was able to develop myself when I was in Angola supports that."

"When you got the satburst, what did you do?"

"Nothing, Mr. Director. I dismissed it as a wild hair."

"You didn't send a 'develop further'?"

"No, sir. I did not. But I looked into it when I was in Luanda, as I said a moment ago."

"You, so to speak, just dismissed the satburst out of hand?"

"Yes, sir, I did. Perhaps if it had come from someone else . . ."

Powell made a "Go on" gesture with his fingers.

"May I speak frankly, Mr. Director?" she asked.

"So far as I know, this office is not wired for sound," he said with a smile.

"Mr. Director, the thing is . . . After I had my bath and gallon of coffee, the third thing I was going to do was come here and ask—almost demand—that Miller be relieved and replaced."

"You have found him wanting?"

"Yes, sir. I'm sorry to say I have. Mr. Director, I never had the chance to sign off on Miller's assignment. If I had been asked, I would not have concurred in the assignment."

"Why not?"

"Let me say, Mr. Director, that I understand the human resources problem personnel had to deal with to fill that vacancy. A qualified individual simply wasn't available. There simply aren't enough African American officers to go around. And even fewer who speak Portuguese. And we—the agency—needed someone over there desperately. The slot had been vacant for months. They had to scrape the bottom of the barrel—and they did—and they came up with Miller, who really was just not qualified to hold down the job."

"Interesting," Powell said.

"I should have asked that he be relieved a long time ago . . ."

"And why didn't you?"

"Because Luanda is not one of the more important postings. Until this airplane was stolen, sir, nothing much has really happened there in a year, eighteen months. Aware of the human resources problem, I decided I would just let it slide and hope for the best. I realize now that was an error in judgment."

Powell grunted.

"Does the name Charles Castillo mean anything to you, Mrs. Wilson?"

She searched her memory before replying.

"No, Mr. Director. I can't say that it does. May I ask who he is?"

"At the moment, I don't know much about him myself," Powell admitted. He paused, then he went on: "You said that you were going to come here first thing and ask that Miller be relieved. Why now?"

"Well, I was frankly annoyed, or disappointed, or both, that the best theory Miller came up with was the absurd idea that a Russian arms dealer stole this old airplane and . . ."

He waited fifteen seconds for her to go on, and, when she did not, asked, "And?"

"I'm reluctant to go into this, Mr. Director."

"Go into it."

"Miller . . . you know he's Army and not really one of us?"

Powell nodded.

"He may have a drinking problem, sir."

"Oh?"

"We had dinner, sir," she said, modestly averting her eyes. "And after two martinis and a bottle of wine, Miller made it plain to me that he would . . . like to enter a personal relationship with me."

"He made a pass at you?" Powell asked.

"Yes, Mr. Director, he did," Patricia Wilson said. "Sir, I'm perfectly capable of dealing with situations like that. But if that's indicative of his behavior . . ."

"I take your point, Mrs. Wilson," Powell said.

"We can't afford to have people who lose control, sir."

"No, we can't. And you're right about this man Miller being out of control."

"Sir?"

"Apparently, in anticipation of a 'develop further' from you Miller did a five- or six-page filing."

"Really?"

"And then when it became obvious to him that he wasn't going to get a 'develop further' from you, instead of shredding the filing he apparently gave it to this Mr. Charles Castillo, who works for the secretary of homeland security."

"That violates . . ."

". . . just about every regulation concerning filings," Powell furnished.

"Yes, it does," Patricia Wilson said, righteously indignant. "Mr. Director, that sort of behavior simply cannot be tolerated!"

"It hasn't been," Powell said. "It won't be necessary for you to request Miller's relief, Mrs. Wilson. I have already relieved him."

She met his eyes.

"What will happen to him?" she asked.

"He goes back to the Army, of course. They'll have to decide what to do with him."

"I see," she said.

"My first reaction was to see that he was disciplined for his breach of security, but, on reflection, I think that an Army service record indicating his relief for cause from a sensitive position and the revocation of his security clearances will be enough punishment."

"I probably shouldn't say this, Mr. Director, but I always feel badly when something like this is necessary."

"I do too," Powell said.

He thought: *Especially when I'm going to have to explain this goddamned mess to the president.*

[FOUR]
Special Activities Section, J-5
United States Central Command
MacDill Air Force Base
Tampa, Florida
1110 8 June 2005

Master Sergeant Omar Perez, Special Forces, U.S. Army, who was the non-commissioned officer in charge of the Special Activities Section, J-5, looked at the officer standing in front of his desk and rose to his feet as a gesture of respect. Perez—who hated his present behind-desk assignment but had philosophically decided that it was a dirty job that somebody had to do and he had been selected by the fickle finger of fate to do it—didn't always do this, but this guy was obviously no candy ass.

This guy had two Silver Stars, three Bronze Stars, and two Purple Hearts to go with his I-Wuz-There ribbons, plus Master Parachutist's and Senior Aviator's wings. And, of course, he had a green beret in his hand.

"Good morning, sir," Perez said. "How may I help you, sir?"

"Oh, Sergeant," Major H. Richard Miller, Jr., said, smiling. "Would that you could, but I think I better see an officer—a light colonel, at least, and more senior if you have one around. My name is Miller."

"I gather the major does not wish to discuss with me what he wishes to discuss with the most-senior officer I have on tap?"

"The major does not," Miller said. "Who is the most-senior officer you have on tap?"

"Colonel Peter J. Grasher, sir."

"And does the sergeant have any idea what sort of a mood 'Grasher the Gnasher' is in?"

"I would say, sir, that the colonel is in his usual charming mood."

"I was afraid of that," Miller said. "Nevertheless . . ."

"I'll see if Colonel Grasher is available, sir," Perez said.

Perez went through a door and closed it. Twenty seconds later, it opened. Colonel Peter J. Grasher, a stocky, nearly bald forty-year-old, was standing in it.

"I knew goddamn well something bad was going to happen today," he said. "Get your ass in here, Dick."

"Good morning, sir."

As Miller walked past Colonel Grasher, Grasher draped an arm around his shoulders.

"I was hoping you'd get et by cannibals," he said. "What brings you back here?"

"I have been relieved, sir."

Grasher met his eyes.

Miller is scared, humiliated, or both. What the hell?

"Jesus Christ," Grasher said. He pointed. "Coffee, chair," he said.

"Thank you, sir."

"Half a cup, half of one of those envelopes of phony sugar," Grasher ordered. "Thank you very much."

Miller poured the coffee, handed a cup to Colonel Grasher, and then sat down.

"Some candy ass in the State Department found out about you sending back-channel stuff?" Grasher asked.

"No, sir. I think I got away with that," Miller said.

"Then what didn't you get away with?"

"There have been no specific charges, sir," Miller said. "I asked the mil-attaché, and he said I would be advised 'in due course.' "

I really don't like where this is going.

"What job were you relieved from? The attaché job or the agency?"

"Both, sir. And my security clearances have been revoked. He said he had been ordered to 'implement my relief' by the ambassador, who also apparently told him to get me out of the country as quick as possible. Which he did. I was on a South African Airways turboprop three hours after Colonel Porter came to my apartment and relieved me."

"A South African Airways turboprop?"

Miller nodded.

"Yes, sir. It was the first plane out. Luanda to Kinshasa in the Congo on the turboprop, then Brussels on Air France—which bothered me: I'm boycotting all things French and I hated to see them getting my tax dollars—then London on another puddle jumper, and then Orlando on a Virgin Airlines 747 full of Disney World–bound tourists. I rented a car in Orlando, drove here, found a motel, took a shower and had a shave, put on my uniform, and came here."

He's being witty. But as much to convince himself he's tough and in charge than to amuse me.

But, Jesus! They must have really wanted him out of there right then! There's all kinds of explaining to do when you have to move an American on a foreign carrier.

Or maybe that's something else the goddamned CIA routinely gets away with. What the hell did Miller do?

Colonel Grasher held up his hand, palm out, as a signal for Miller to say nothing else for the moment. Then he picked up one of the telephones on his desk.

"Omar, have we had a heads-up on Major Miller? For that matter, have we had anything on Major Miller?"

He listened to the reply and then said, "If anything comes in, get it to me right away."

He replaced the telephone in its cradle.

"Be imaginative, Miller," he said. "Come up with some reason why you might have incurred the displeasure of the CIA, the State Department, and the Defense Intelligence Agency."

"Sir, you have not advised me of my rights to have legal counsel, right? What I tell you will not appear on a charge sheet?"

If he didn't think he was really in the deep doo-doo, he wouldn't have said that.

"Jesus, that bad, huh? Okay. What you say here is forgotten as soon as you say it."

"When that airplane . . . the . . . 727?"

Grasher nodded.

". . . went missing, I sent a satburst suggesting a Russian arms dealer named Aleksandr Pevsner may have had something to do with it . . ."

"I saw that. The boss showed it to me," Grasher said. "The satburst and, before that, your back channel."

"Sir, I expected I would get a follow-up message, what the agency calls a 'develop further,' so as soon as I had time I did a filing. The 'develop further' never came."

"And?"

"So I suppose what I should have done was shred my filing. But I didn't."

You suppose you should have done? You know goddamn well it should have been shredded.

"Why not?"

"Sir, I thought I was right and I thought that maybe the 'develop further' would come late but that it would come."

And they found the filing that should have been shredded on his computer? And shit a brick? Is that what this is all about?

"What about the filing? Did someone find out it hadn't been shredded?"

Whatever comes next is important. He's trying to figure out the best way to say it.

"Sir, I gave my filing to Major Castillo."

Jesus H. Christ!

He doesn't mean "gave"; he means "sent." The last I heard Castillo was passing hors d'oeuvres in Washington.

"Charley Castillo?"

"Yes, sir."

"You mean you sent it to him?"

"He was in Luanda, sir. Undercover. As a German journalist."

I knew goddamn well Castillo was doing something besides passing hors d'oeuvres in Sodom on the Potomac.

"He went to you?"

"No, sir. He came on the same plane as Mrs. Wilson . . ."

"Who is?"

"Sir, Mrs. Patricia D. Wilson is the company's regional director for Southwest Africa. My immediate supervisor in the CIA."

"Okay."

"Sir, she smelled something wrong about Castillo—that he wasn't really who he said he was, Karl Gossinger or something like that—and she told me to check him out. So I did, I went to the hotel, and found out he was Charley . . . Major Castillo."

"And you gave Major Castillo your filing?"

"Yes, sir."

"Because you believed you had valuable intel that was being ignored and that you should get it into the right hands even if doing so violated security regulations?"

Noble thought; dumb fucking thing to do. Good God, Miller, you're a West Pointer and a field-grade officer. You know better than to do something like that.

"Yes, sir, that too," Miller said.

What the hell does that mean? "That too"?

" 'That too,' Miller?"

"Sir, Major Castillo told me he was—sir, what he actually said was that he had been sent by . . . 'by a guy who lives part-time in a *Gone With the Wind* mansion on Hilton Head island.' "

Two hundred and six guys live part-time in mansions on Hilton Head!

"Which you understood to mean he meant the president?"

"Yes, sir," Miller said. "And, sir, he ordered me not to divulge that."

"Did Major Castillo tell you what he was doing for the president in Angola?"

"Yes, sir. He said that he had been sent to look into the missing 727 aircraft."

Jesus Christ, this is unreal. Every intelligence agency under the moon is look-

ing for that aircraft and Miller is telling me the president personally sent a major to find it?

It is so unreal that I'm starting to believe it.

Colonel Grasher pressed the button on his intercom.

"Omar, would you see if General Potter can give me five minutes?"

"Yes, sir. Right away, sir. Colonel, I have . . . uh . . . a message about Major Miller."

"Bring it in," Grasher ordered.

"Yes, sir."

Master Sergeant Perez appeared almost immediately, walked to Colonel Grasher's desk, and laid a sheet of radioteletype paper on it. Master Sergeant Perez avoided looking at Major Miller as he walked out of the office.

Colonel Grasher picked up the message and read it.

```
SECRET


PRIORITY


1005 8 JUNE 2005


FROM COMMANDING GENERAL DEFENSE INTELLIGENCE AGENCY
     WASH DC


TO COMMANDING GENERAL US CENTRAL COMMAND
     MACDILL AF BASE FLA


ATTN: SPECIAL ACTIVITIES SECTION, J-5


SUBJECT MILLER, H RICHARD, JR, MAJ, SPF, RELIEF OF


1. THE DIRECTOR CENTRAL INTELLIGENCE AGENCY HAS
SUMMARILY RELIEVED SUBJECT OFFICER FOR CAUSE, REVOKED
SUBJECT OFFICER'S SECURITY CLEARANCES, AND ORDERED THAT
HE BE RETURNED TO US ARMY CONTROL.
```

2. IN VIEW OF THE FOREGOING, COMMANDING GENERAL, DIA,
HAS RELIEVED SUBJECT OFFICER AS ASSISTANT MILITARY
ATTACHÉ US EMBASSY, LUANDA, ANGOLA, REVOKED ANY
SECURITY CLEARANCES SUBJECT OFFICER MAY HAVE BEEN
GRANTED BY DIA AND ORDERED THAT SUBJECT OFFICER BE
RETURNED TO HIS UNIT OF ORIGIN, SPECIAL ACTIVITIES
SECTION, J-5, US CENTRAL COMMAND. SUBJECT OFFICER'S
TRAVEL ROUTING AND ETA WILL BE FURNISHED WHEN
AVAILABLE.

3. IT IS THE UNDERSTANDING OF THIS HQ THAT THE
ALLEGATIONS MADE AGAINST SUBJECT OFFICER INVOLVE A
SECURITY BREACH OF THE MOST SERIOUS NATURE;
INSUBORDINATION; EXCEEDING HIS LAWFUL AUTHORITY; AND
CONDUCT UNBECOMING AN OFFICER AND GENTLEMAN. THE REPORT
OF AN INVESTIGATION WHICH WILL COMMENCE IMMEDIATELY
WILL BE MADE AVAILABLE TO YOU WHEN AVAILABLE.

FOR THE COMMANDING GENERAL, DIA

ROBERT B. STAMMLE
COL, MI
CHIEF, DEFENSE ATTACHÉ SYSTEM
DIRECTORATE FOR HUMAN INTELLIGENCE
DEFENSE INTELLIGENCE AGENCY

SECRET

Grasher laid the message on his desk and looked at Miller.

"They don't think much of you in Angola, do they?" he asked.

"Sir," Master Sergeant Perez's voice came over the intercom. "General Potter is in conference with General Naylor. It's going to take at least another forty-five minutes. Shall I set it up for then?"

"No. Call General Naylor's office, Omar, and tell Sergeant Whatsisname that I have to see General Naylor and General Potter right now and that Major Miller and I are on our way over there. Got it?"

"Yes, sir."

[FIVE]

"Hey, Allan. What's up?" the secretary of homeland security asked, over the secure telephone in his office, the commanding general, U.S. Central Command, who was sitting at his secure telephone in the small room off the conference room of his headquarters.

"One question, Matt."

"Shoot."

"Did the president send Charley to Luanda, Angola?"

"Damn," Hall said, and then asked, "Where'd you hear that?"

"From Major H. Richard Miller, Jr., formerly the CIA station chief in Luanda."

"*Formerly* the CIA station chief?"

"He was relieved for cause and sent back here."

"He's in Tampa?"

"He's in Tampa. He got here just now, and, just before, we got a TWX from DIA saying he had been relieved for cause. 'Cause' apparently meaning everything from a serious breach of security to conduct unbecoming."

"That sonofabitch!" Hall said.

"You're not referring to Major Miller?" Naylor said, testily.

"No, I am not," Hall said. "Major Miller is one of the good guys, Allan."

"I'm really happy to hear that," Naylor said. "You going to tell me what's going on?"

"Not right now," Hall said after a moment's hesitation. "Did DIA tell you what you're supposed to do with him?"

"DIA can't tell me what—or what not—to do. But their TWX said that I would be furnished with the results of an investigation which will begin immediately. I had the feeling they will be disappointed if I don't nail him to a cross," Naylor said.

"Nothing like that is going to happen," Hall said, firmly. "What I'd like you to do, Allan, is send him up here. Is there any reason you can't do that?"

"Not that it matters, but officially or unofficially?"

"Whichever is easiest for you."

"Where do I tell him to go?"

"Can you get him a cell phone? Or does he have one?"

"If he doesn't, I'll see that he gets one."

"Get the number to me. And give him my personal number, to be used only if he thinks he has to."

"Okay."

"And tell him the key to Charley's apartment will be waiting for him at the Mayflower's front desk. Tell him to hang around the apartment as much as possible; that I'll contact him if—when—I need him."

"Okay."

"That probably won't be until Charley gets back."

"Back from where?"

"I told him to bring me a Sacher torte," Hall said.

It took Naylor a moment to take the meaning of that.

"What's Charley doing in Vienna?"

"Meeting with a Russian arms dealer by the name of Aleksandr Pevsner," Hall said.

"Jesus Christ!"

"Allan, I think it would be better if Miller wore civvies. But make sure he has a uniform with him."

"Done."

"As soon as I can, I'll explain all this to you, Allan."

"I'd like that, Matt. I hate to stumble along in the dark."

"As soon as I can, Allan."

"Good enough," Naylor said. "And thanks, Matt."

"We'll be in touch," Hall said and broke the connection.

[SIX]
Hotel Sacher Wein
Philharmonikerstrasse 4
Vienna, Austria
1650 8 June 2005

There had been no familiar faces in the lobby of the Bristol, nor on the sidewalk outside, nor on Kaertnerstrasse as Castillo walked to Philharmonikerstrasse and the Sacher.

And there was no one in the bar when he went inside.

The barman remembered him from last night.

"Ein anderes Dzbán, meine herr?" he asked.

"Ja. Bitte," Castillo said.

He had finished about half of the beer when the American couple he had seen last night came. The man remembered him, too, apparently. He nodded and gave Castillo a brief smile as he walked past him to sit where they had sat last night.

Castillo had just signaled the barman for another Dzbán when two men came in. He could not remember having seen them before. They were in their forties, and, from the cuts of their suits, Castillo decided they were from somewhere east. Czechoslovakia or Hungary. Or maybe Poland.

That aroused his interest.

But neither man paid any interest to Castillo at all. One of them took some stapled-together papers from a ratty-looking briefcase and both men studied them with care. They spoke very softly—almost whispered—as if afraid that someone would eavesdrop on their conversation. Castillo could not make out what they were saying.

When he finished—slowly—the second bottle of Dzbán, Castillo signaled for another and then went to the men's room.

He had just begun to relieve himself when he heard the door whoosh open and turned from the urinal, aware that his heart had jumped.

It was the American from the bar.

The American smiled. "Beer goes right through me," he announced.

Castillo nodded and returned his attention to the urinal, more than a little embarrassed at his jumping heart.

And then . . . *Oh, shit!*

Someone had pulled his jacket down, effectively immobilizing his arms.

"Careful," the American said, "you don't really want to piss all over the silk brocade wall."

The American patted him down, finding both knives.

He took the folding knife and flipped it open with a flick of the wrist.

"Nice," he said. "I suppose a journalist does need something like this to sharpen his pencils, doesn't he?"

Then he closed the knife and put it back in Castillo's shirt pocket.

"What I was looking for was a wire," the American said, and then, in Russian, said, "Adjust Mr. Gossinger's jacket, Sergei."

Whoever was behind him pulled the jacket back in place.

Castillo had trouble maintaining the direction of the flow of his urine into the urinal but did well under the circumstances.

The American went to the adjacent urinal and pulled down his zipper.

He looked over at Castillo.

"Beer really does go right through me," he said.

Castillo said nothing.

When his bladder finally emptied he pulled up his zipper and wondered what he was going to do next.

He saw that the men's room wall was indeed upholstered in red silk brocade.

If they were going to hurt—kill—me, they certainly had the opportunity. What the hell is going on?

The American completed his business with a satisfied sigh and Castillo heard him pull up his zipper.

The American went to a washbasin and started to wash his hands.

Over his shoulder, he said, "When you finish, Mr. Gossinger, Mr. Pevsner hopes that you will join him on the Cobenzl."

"May I turn around?" Castillo asked.

"Of course."

Castillo turned.

One of the Eastern Europeans—the larger one—was standing three feet from him with his hands crossed at his crotch. The American was still washing his hands.

As much to have something to do as for reasons of hygiene, Castillo took the half steps to the small row of washbasins and started to wash his hands.

The American carefully dried his hands.

"Well?" he asked.

"Well, what?"

"Are you going to join Mr. Pevsner on the Cobenzl?"

"Do I have a choice?"

"Of course you do."

"Why the Cobenzl?"

"You know the Cobenzl?"

Castillo nodded. It was on top of a hill at what Castillo thought of as the beginning of the Vienna Woods. The street leading up it—he remembered the name: Cobenzlgasse—was lined with *Heuriger, Gasthausen* that sold new wine, which, Castillo also remembered, had a hell of a kick and produced memorable hangovers.

"Mr. Pevsner likes to watch the sun set over Vienna at this time of the year," the American said. "He thought you might enjoy it yourself."

"I'll go," Castillo said.

"Mr. Pevsner will be pleased," the American said.

This guy thinks I'm an asshole and wants me to know he does.
Unfortunately, he's right.

I was taken just now like a bumbling idiot. Like Peter Seller's Inspector Clouseau.

Castillo dried his hands.

"The car's outside," the American said. "I took care of your tab."

"Thank you," Castillo said, adding mentally, *the asshole said politely.*

The car at the curb was a Mercedes, a new 220, with deeply tinted windows and Prague license plates. The other East European stood on the curb holding the rear door open. The large East European got in the front seat and the American motioned for Castillo to get in the back.

"It'll be a little crowded in here, I'm afraid. Say hello to Ingrid."

The woman Castillo had thought was the American's wife was already in the car. She smiled at him.

"Guten abend, Herr Gossinger," Ingrid said offering her hand.

"Guten abend," Castillo replied.

She was, he saw now, a trim woman with luxuriant dark red hair.

She's much better looking than I remembered. I just didn't pay attention to her before.

Does terror kill my sex drive, or is it that that area of my brain is completely filled with lewd images of Patricia Wilson?

The American got in the backseat—and it was a little crowded; he could feel Inge's hip against his—and the door was closed.

"Inge works in our Prague office," the American said. "Among other things, she brought the cars from Prague for us to use."

What the hell is he doing? Telling me that Inge is available? Or even, presuming I'm a good boy, that Inge is the prize?

Or just making polite conversation?

"Do you know Prague, Herr Gossinger?" Inge asked as the car started to move.

"Yes, I do," Castillo said, politely.

[SEVEN]

The other car was another black Mercedes, another new one, but the big one, like Otto Görner's, the 600 with the V-12 engine. Its windows were similarly deeply tinted, and it, too, carried a Prague license tag.

It was parked sideway, across three pull-in spaces, at the observation point on the Cobenzl, which was nothing more than a flat area paved with gravel, and with a steel, waist-high fence to keep people from falling down the hill. There were no other cars, although there was space for seven or eight.

A tall man, dark-haired, well-dressed, was leaning on the metal guardrail puffing on a long light brown cigar. Another hefty East European type was resting his rear end on the front left fender of the Mercedes.

There was a small folding table beside him, something like a card table but smaller. On it was a bottle of cognac, two snifters, and a small wooden box.

The tall man, who appeared to be in his late thirties, turned and looked at the smaller Mercedes.

The American got out of the 220 and Castillo followed his lead. The American got back in the car.

"Herr Gossinger?" the tall man asked in German.

Castillo walked toward him and put out his hand.

"I'm Gossinger," he said. "And you're Herr Pevsner?"

"Why not? What's a name, after all?" Pevsner said with a warm smile. Pevsner's German was fluent and he sounded like a Berliner.

The next thing that Castillo noticed was Pevsner's eyes. They were large and blue and extraordinarily bright.

I wonder if he's on something?

Pevsner's grip was firm without being aggressive. Castillo noticed that his teeth were not only healthy looking but clean. That was not always the case with Russians.

Well, I guess if you've made multiple fortunes in the arms business you can afford a good dentist.

"Tell me, Herr Gossinger," Pevsner asked, "are you by chance a cigar smoker?"

"Yes, I am."

Pevsner picked up the wooden box, a small cigar humidor, and extended it to Castillo.

"Try one of these. These are the *good* Upmanns," he said.

"Excuse me?" Castillo asked as he took one.

"From the Canary Islands factory," Pevsner said. "I don't think there's any question that they're much better than the ones Castro is making in Cuba, in the plant he took away from the Upmann people in the name of the people."

"I've heard that," Castillo said. "Thank you."

And an arms merchant can afford really good cigars. And big black Mercedeses.

Pevsner handed him a silver guillotine and Castillo trimmed the cigar.

"I've always wondered if those things were patterned after the head chopper or the other way around," Pevsner said.

"I think the . . . big one is named after a French doctor named Guillotin, without the *e*," Castillo said.

"Well, I'm glad to know that," Pevsner said. "And not surprised that you knew. I suppose journalists have to have brains stuffed with odd facts, don't they?"

"I've heard that, too," Castillo said.

Pevsner handed him a gold Dunhill butane lighter and Castillo carefully lit the cigar, took a couple of good puffs, then said, "Very nice indeed. Thank you, Herr Pevsner."

And gold Dunhill butane lighters.

"My pleasure, Herr Gossinger," Pevsner said. "Now, another question. Do you like French cognac?"

"Yes, I do."

Pevsner picked up the bottle and poured three-quarters of an inch into one of the snifters, and then added more to his glass.

That's a big snifter; there's a lot of booze in that glass.

Castillo picked up the snifter and began to warm the bowl in his palm.

"We are now equipped to watch darkness fall over Vienna," Pevsner said. "But, as aviators know, darkness doesn't fall, it rises. Isn't that so?"

"That's what I'm told," Castillo said.

"Tell me what you think of the cognac," Pevsner said.

Castillo held up a finger, indicating he wanted a moment, and then swirled the cognac around in the snifter for another twenty seconds. Then he took a sip.

"Very good," he pronounced.

And very good cognac. Who said crime doesn't pay?

"I'm pleased," Pevsner said and smiled at him. "You seem like such a nice fellow," Pevsner went on. "I am really pleased that it was not necessary to give you an Indian beauty mark."

"Excuse me?"

With a sudden movement—so quick Castillo didn't have time to jerk his head out of the way—Pevsner touched Castillo in the center of his forehead with his index finger.

What the hell is that all about?

Indian beauty mark?

Jesus Christ! He's talking about a bullet hole in the center of my forehead!

Pevsner picked up his cognac snifter and carried it to the guard fence. He very carefully balanced the glass on the top railing of the fence, relit his Upmann with the Dunhill, and then leaned on the fence with his hands supporting him.

After a moment, Pevsner looked over his shoulder, then waved with his left hand for Castillo to join him.

Castillo walked to the fence.

Pevsner gestured at Vienna.

"There it is," he said, "laid out before us. As it was for Emperor Franz Josef, and, before him, Napoleon. And you're right on time. We will shortly begin to see darkness—as you well know—*rise* and gradually mask Vienna."

"I suppose we will," Charley said.

"So here we are. We are drinking rather decent cognac and smoking what I think are really good cigars, and when darkness has finished *rising* from the ground, and all we will be able to see is a sea of lights under us, I hope you will be my guest at dinner."

"That's very kind of you," Castillo said.

Two inane responses in a row. Attaboy, Charley! Dazzle this guy with your quick mind and verbal agility.

"Under those circumstances, wouldn't it be nice if we could be honest with one another? As we begin what could be—and, I hope, will be—a long and mutually profitable association?"

What's he going to do? Offer to put me on his payroll not to mention his name in print?

"That would be very nice, Herr Pevsner," Castillo said.

That's three in a row, Charley.

"I really hope you mean that, Major Castillo," Pevsner said, in English.

Jesus H. Fucking Christ!

"Please don't act as if you have no idea what I mean," Pevsner said.

"How the hell did you find out?" Castillo asked after a long moment.

"It doesn't really matter, does it? But I understand your curiosity." Pevsner inclined his head toward the smaller Mercedes. "Before he became associated with me, Howard spent twenty years with the FBI."

"Is that his first name or his last?"

"Howard Kennedy," Pevsner said. "Over the years, our relationship has changed from employer-employee to being friends. I call him by his Christian name."

It took a surprisingly short time for darkness to rise, until all that could be seen of Vienna was a sea of lights.

Pevsner had said nothing more. He had sipped his cognac and puffed on his cigar. It went out once and he relit it with the gold Dunhill and then politely offered the lighter to Castillo.

"Mine's still going, thank you," Castillo had said.

Finally, Pevsner said, "Well, that's all there is to see. Unless we want to stay here until the sun rises. Shall we go?"

"Fine," Castillo said.

Pevsner started toward the 600. There was just enough light for Castillo to see the East European hurry to open the rear door for them.

Pevsner waved Castillo into the backseat ahead of him. When he was inside, he saw that Howard Kennedy was in the front seat.

I guess Inge doesn't get to ride with the boss.

Kennedy turned and extended his hand over the seat back.

"It's a pleasure to meet you, Castillo. In certain circles, you have quite a reputation."

Castillo shook the hand but said nothing.

"I'm sorry about that business in the men's room," Kennedy went on. "But Mr. Pevsner, for obvious reasons, doesn't like his conversations recorded."

Castillo nodded.

Out the window, he saw the East European first move the cognac snifters, the bottle, and the small humidor to the trunk of the smaller Mercedes, and then fold the table and put that in the trunk. Then he got behind the wheel and they started off.

They followed the 220 down Cobenzlgasse into Vienna, and then through the early evening traffic back to the center of the city, finally turning off The Ring onto Kaertnerstrasse.

"Do you know the Drei Hussaren, Major Castillo?"

"Yes, I do."

"What do you prefer to be called? 'Carlos'? Or 'Charley'? Or perhaps 'Karl'?"

" 'Charley' is what my friends call me."

"That's what Howard thought," Pevsner said. "You're really amazing, Howard."

"Thank you," Howard chuckled.

Pevsner touched Castillo's arm.

"In that case, since I really hope we are to become friends may I call you Charley?"

"Of course."

"My Christian name is Aleksandr," Pevsner said. "Howard calls me 'Alex.' Would you be comfortable calling me Alex, Charley?"

At the last split second, Castillo stopped himself from saying, "Yes, sir."

"Yes, I would. Thank you."

That's a lie. I am not comfortable calling you Alex. I am not comfortable, period. I can't remember the last time I felt so helpless, so much at the mercy of a situation I don't understand and over which I have absolutely no control.

"And the Drei Hussaren is all right with you for dinner? If you have another . . . ?"

"The Drei Hussaren is fine with me," Castillo said, as the Mercedes pulled up in front of the entrance to the restaurant.

And what would have happened if I had said, "Come to think of it, I know a very nice place just off Gumpendorferstrasse"?

The doorman of the Drei Hussaren pulled the doors open. Kennedy and Pevsner got out, and Castillo slid across the seat and joined them.

The headwaiter was standing inside the entrance, greeted them effusively, and led them down the stairs into the dining room, and then across it and into a private dining room. There were three places set at a table that could hold eight.

I guess Inge doesn't get to eat with the boss, either.

Glasses were produced and a waiter poured a white liquor into them.

In German, Pevsner said, "Since you have been here before, Karl, you know about the slivovitz. The management has learned the more slivovitz they can give away, the less likely their customers are to complain about the service, the size of the portions, the quality, and, most important, the size of the bill."

Castillo knew about the plum brandy—the best came from Moldavia—and suspected that what Pevsner said was absolutely true.

He chuckled.

"Herr Barstein," the headwaiter said, "that's a terrible thing to say about us!"

Castillo picked up on the Barstein.

"But it's truth. And the truth is important, isn't it, Karl?"

"Very important," Castillo said, picked up the glass, tipped it toward the headwaiter, said, *"Prosit,"* and tossed it down.

Pevsner laughed.

"Karl, one of the few things they do half decently around here is the sauerbraten. They make it with deer—venison. May I suggest that?"

"That sounds fine," Castillo said.

"For all of us," Pevsner ordered. "And aware I'm taking an awful chance, a dry red wine of your choice. You can leave the slivovitz."

"Jawohl, Herr Barstein," the headwaiter said.

After he left, Kennedy went to the door and made sure it was closed.

"Howard," Pevsner said. "Charley is curious about how we learned he is not all the time Herr Karl Wilhelm von und zu Gossinger."

Kennedy chuckled, helped himself to some more slivovitz, poured some in Castillo's and Pevsner's glasses, and said, "I know I really shouldn't drink this stuff but I like it."

Pevsner and Charley chuckled.

Kennedy looked at Castillo.

"Well, when the story came out, and Mr. Pevsner decided we should have a talk with you, we sent some people to Fulda . . ."

To give me an Indian beauty mark on my forehead?

". . . and when they reported that Gossinger was in Washington, Mr. Pevsner asked me to personally take over. I put a lot of time in D.C. when I was with the bureau."

Did taking over mean that you were going to personally apply the Indian beauty mark?

"Anyway, it wasn't hard to find out that Gossinger was sharing Suite 404 in the Mayflower with a fellow named Carlos Castillo. For a bit, we thought that Castillo might be Gossinger's playmate—a handsome Cuban or Tex-Mex might explain why Gossinger wasn't married. And that might have been useful . . ."

He took a sip of water, then continued.

". . . but then we found out, lo and behold, that Gossinger and Castillo were one and the same. And then we started asking about Señor Castillo. The first thing I thought then was that you were probably with the agency, but then I found out first that you're an Army officer—a West Pointer, a Green Beret, an aviator—and then that you are Matt Hall's special assistant. At that point, Mr. Pevsner decided we should have a talk with you . . ."

A talk-talk, as opposed to a beauty spot chat?

". . . so we had someone call Herr Görner and tell him that Mr. Pevsner was willing to give Herr Gossinger an interview and here you are."

"My original purpose in all this, Charley," Pevsner said, "was—for that matter, still is—to keep the U.S. government off my back. And, of course, to keep my name out of the newspapers. I had nothing to do with stealing that old airplane in Angola. Where did you get that, anyway?"

"You had nothing to do with stealing the 727?"

"Absolutely nothing. For one thing, I have airplanes. Just last week, I bought another one—a nearly new 767 from an airline that went under in Argentina—and I don't need an old 727. Particularly, I don't need to steal one, which would attract the sort of attention I really don't want from the U.S. government and a lot of other people."

I'll be damned. I believe him. Or is that because I had two beers in the Sacher, two hefty snifters of cognac on the Cobenzl, and two slivovitz here?

"Where did you get the idea I had anything to do with it?" Pevsner asked.

"Two of your people were seen in Luanda just before the airplane was stolen," Castillo said.

"You don't happen to remember their names, do you?" Kennedy asked, casually.

If I did, I wouldn't give them to you.

"No," Castillo said, simply. "I don't."

"Howard?" Pevsner said.

"I'll look into it," Kennedy said.

Jesus Christ, what did I just do? Cause two people I never met, never saw, to take a bullet in the forehead?

The conversation was interrupted by two waiters, who delivered a rich-looking meat-and-vegetable soup and two bottles of red wine.

"This one, Herr Barstein," the waiter said as he poured a sip into Pevsner's glass, "is Hungarian. The other is from the north of Italy. Definitely not a Chianti. Whichever is your pleasure will be a small gift from Drei Hussaren."

As Pevsner raised the glass to his nose, he signaled with his finger for the waiter to give Castillo and Kennedy a taste. The waiter poured wine into their glasses.

Pevsner took a sip and nodded his approval.

"Very nice," he said. "Now, let's try the other one."

The ritual was repeated for everyone, which required other glasses to be produced from a cabinet against the wall.

"Decisions, decisions," Pevsner said. "What do you think, Karl?"

"I like the Hungarian," Castillo said.

"So do I," Pevsner said.

"I like the Italian," Kennedy said. "The Hungarian's a little too sweet for me."

Well, Kennedy doesn't apparently feel compelled to agree with the boss about everything.

"In that case," Pevsner said, "we accept the Drei Hussaren's kind gift of both. Thank you very much."

"Our great pleasure, Herr Barstein."

The waiters filled glasses and then left.

The vegetable soup was as good as it looked.

As he reached for his wineglass, Castillo thought, *Easy on the sauce, Charley. You're already half-crocked.*

He took a very small sip, and, when he put the glass down, sensed Pevsner's eyes on him.

"If you didn't steal the 727, who do you think did?" Castillo asked.

"I'm not absolutely sure about this but right now I think it was stolen by an obscure group of Somalian lunatics . . ."

"Somalian?" Castillo interjected, surprised.

". . . who call themselves the Holy Legion of Muhammad," Pevsner went on. He paused and then added: "Who plan to crash it into the Liberty Bell in Philadelphia, Pennsylvania."

"That's crazy," Charley blurted.

"Sounds that way, doesn't it?" Kennedy agreed. "But that's what we've got so far."

"I used the word *lunatics*," Pevsner said. "Crazy people tend to do irrational things. That's what makes them so very dangerous."

"The Liberty Bell?" Castillo argued. "Not the Statue of Liberty? The White House? The Golden Gate Bridge? Why would they want to hit the Liberty Bell?"

"We think two reasons," Kennedy said. "Maybe three. For one thing, since 9/11 the White House, Statue of Liberty, most important bridges, etcetera, have been pretty well covered. Nobody gives much of a damn about Philadelphia, so they stand a better chance of carrying it off. Second, these holy warriors probably—hell, almost certainly—think the Liberty Bell is more of a symbol than it is."

"It's a third-rate tourist attraction, that's all," Castillo thought aloud.

"I'm surprised at that comment, from someone like you," Pevsner said. "That's what they call 'mirror thinking': looking in the mirror and working on the premise that other people think like what you see in the mirror. They don't, and that's especially true of people who call themselves something like the Holy Legion of Muhammad."

Goddammit, he's right. The booze is clouding my thinking.

"You're right," Castillo said. "I am supposed to know better."

"And, third—here I admit I don't know what I'm talking about," Kennedy said. "I have a feeling there's a Philadelphia connection."

"A Philadelphia connection?" Castillo asked.

"If these holy warriors intend to take out the Liberty Bell, somebody gave them the idea. They never would have come up with it themselves. And that suggests somebody in Philadelphia did just that."

"Who?"

"Some converts to Islam. Idn bin Rag-on-His-Head, born John James Smith."

Castillo grunted.

"Did you ever give any serious thought to why so many American blacks converted to Islam?" Kennedy asked.

"No," Castillo admitted.

"Maybe you should," Kennedy said.

"You tell me."

"Because they hate Whitey as much as the rag-heads hate all infidels," Kennedy said. "And for exactly the same reason: They got left behind and they don't like it."

"That's what this war is all about, Charley," Pevsner said. "The Muslim world getting left behind. Think about it."

He paused and took a spoonful of the soup.

"Take away their oil reserves and what do they have?" Pevsner went on. "They once dominated the known world. Now, with the exception of their oil, they are completely unimportant—more to the point, powerless—in the modern world. They simply don't have the skills and the culture to compete in it. They gave the world mathematics, and some of the most wonderful architecture—so long as the architecture is based on one stone laid on top of another.

"All the skyscrapers in the Arab world were designed and built by the infidels. And their airplanes were designed and built by infidels and their telephone systems . . . even their sewers. And they need infidels to keep everything running.

"This isn't the way Muhammad told them it was going to be. He promised them, in the Koran, that they would control the world. And they all know this because higher education in the Arab world consists mostly of men—only men—memorizing the Koran. And since nothing is their fault, it has to be someone else's—the infidels'."

"That seems pretty simplistic," Castillo said, and immediately thought: *Careful, Charley, you don't want to piss Pevsner off.*

"Because an answer is simple doesn't mean it's not the answer," Pevsner said.

He took another sip of the soup and then a healthy swallow of the Hungarian wine.

"The Muslim world is four hundred—maybe five hundred—years behind the Western world," Pevsner went on. "And adding to that problem is their religious hierarchy who likes it that way. People in power are never in favor of a system change that will see their power diminished. That's also true in the Western world, of course. The Roman Catholic and my own Orthodox hierarchies—who also go around in medieval clothing—are as guilty of this as the mullahs. The difference is that as the influence of the Christian hierarchies on their societies has diminished over time, the Muslim hierarchies' influence has grown.

"They have—as we see examples of just about every day—thousands, tens of thousands, perhaps many hundreds of thousands of faithful who are perfectly willing to sacrifice their lives because their mullahs tell them it will please God. And also send them directly to heaven, where they will receive the attentions of grateful whores. This, I think you will have to agree, makes for a very dangerous situation for Western society."

He stopped and took another healthy sip of the Hungarian red.

"Excuse me," Pevsner said. "I really didn't mean to deliver a lecture."

"You make some interesting points," Castillo said.

"We were talking about the Holy Legion of Muhammad's intention of crashing into the Liberty Bell, I believe?"

"We were."

"Howard?" Pevsner said.

"We found out the 727 was flown to Chad," Kennedy said. "But we don't know where in Chad and Chad is a big country. Lots of remote places where you could hide a 727. And we don't know if it's still there. They may have finished."

"Painting new registration numbers on it, you mean?"

"I think they're going to do more than that. The only way they can hope to get close to the U.S.—Philadelphia—is to disguise the airplane so it looks like somebody else's. The question there is, whose?"

"When we have more information, we'll get it to you," Pevsner said.

"Why are you giving me this information?" Castillo asked.

"Because the U.S. government is better able to deal with the Holy Legion of Muhammad than I am," Pevsner said. "If I could deal with these people myself, I would. I don't want these lunatics to get away with this."

"Why should you care?" Castillo asked.

For the first time, he sensed anger in Pevsner. His head snapped toward Charley and his eyes were cold.

"Because I am on the same side in this war as you are," Pevsner said. "I hoped I had made that clear."

And if we find the airplane, the pressure is off you?

I can't say that. He's already angry.

People sometimes say things when they're angry they shouldn't.

"And also because if we find the 727, the pressure is off you?" Castillo asked, meeting Pevsner's eyes.

Pevsner didn't reply for a moment. Then, evenly, he asked, "Are you married, Charley?"

Castillo shook his head.

"And you prefer women to men?"

"Yes, I do," Castillo said, and blurted, "Jesus Christ!"

"Howard told me that you have a certain reputation in that area," Pevsner said. "But I wanted to see your reaction to a question like that."

Well, fuck you, Alex!

"There has been some speculation about my own—what's the word they use now?—*orientation,*" Pevsner said. "Probably because very little is known about my personal life. The truth is . . ."

Jesus Christ, is he going to tell me he's a fag?

". . . that I have a wife, whom I adore, and we have three lovely children. Two boys and a girl."

Pevsner reached into his jacket pocket, came out with an alligator-skin wallet the size of a passport, and took from it a color photograph and handed it to Castillo.

"My family, Charley," he said.

The photo showed Pevsner and a blond, svelte woman seated on chairs. Charley thought she looked something like Otto's Helena. A slim blond girl of about thirteen stood to their left, a blond boy of maybe ten stood to their right, and a six-year-old boy, dressed in white, was on his knees in front of his father, smiling mischievously at the camera.

"Very nice," Castillo said as he handed the picture back and thinking that it could have easily been a fabricated photo, one showing a family that did not exist except for an arms dealer's convenience. Castillo wondered how hard it would be to check it out. There had been nothing in the dossier on Pevsner that he'd read that mentioned a family.

"Yes," Pevsner agreed. "They are very important to me, Charley. I don't want them blown up, or poisoned, or machine-gunned by some lunatic from a culture five hundred years behind ours who believes that he's pleasing God."

Charley nodded understandingly.

"As I said before," Pevsner said. "I am on the same side in this war as you are. There are other reasons, but the only reason I need is my family. Do you understand?"

"Of course."

"I believe I can make a contribution to this war," Pevsner said. "I have what I think is a pretty good intelligence apparatus and I have many contacts."

"I'm sure you do," Castillo thought aloud.

"What I want to do is get the information I sometimes have to someone in the U.S. government who is in a position to do something about it." He paused to let that sink in and then continued. "Right now, the CIA—and, to a lesser extent, other intelligence agencies—are of two minds about me, neither of them very flattering. One opinion held is that I am an arms dealer and the sooner I can be put out of business—preferably, imprisoned—the sooner the world will be a safer, better place. The second opinion is that I am a useful asset for the movement of things, and people, when the Operations Division needs to have things and people moved covertly. They 'handle' me; I have a 'handler.'"

He makes "handler" *sound like an obscenity.*

"And the ops division, Charley," Kennedy said, "is not about to tell the FBI—or anyone else—that Mr. Pevsner does contract shipping for them; or that when they feel the need to provide weapons to some group of people, they often turn to Mr. Pevsner, who often knows where they can buy such weapons very quietly."

The door opened again and two waiters began to clear the soup bowls away, replace the silver, and lay a steaming tray of *Hirschbraten* in a thick reddish brown sauce, *Kartoffelknodel,* and sauerkraut on the table. They also brought two more bottles of wine.

When a waiter started to fill Castillo's glass, he put his hand over it and said, "I've had enough, thank you."

Pevsner did the same thing.

"Like you, Charley," Pevsner said, "wine loosens my tongue. I tend to say things I shouldn't."

Was that some sort of a reprimand or simply an observation?

"I tend to do things I shouldn't," Castillo heard himself say.

"But then, Charley, you're a bachelor. You have that freedom," Pevsner said. "God, that smells good!"

He waved the waiters out of the room and served the venison.

"And just about everything that needed to be said has been said," Pevsner said. "Wouldn't you say?"

"I'm not sure I know what you mean," Castillo said.

"Mr. Pevsner hopes that you will go to Matt Hall and tell him . . ."

"That I had nothing to do with the theft of the 727 airplane in Luanda," Pevsner interrupted.

". . . and that we are going to do whatever we can to help you stop the Holy Legion of Muhammad from attacking the Liberty Bell," Kennedy picked up without missing a beat.

"And make other contributions, as we can, to help in the war between the modern Western world and Islam," Pevsner interrupted again.

"In exchange for which Mr. Pevsner hopes that Hall will do what he can . . ."

"And I expect him to do something concrete," Pevsner interrupted again.

". . . with regard to keeping Mr. Pevsner from undue attention," Kennedy finished.

"You understand that, Charley? 'Undue attention'?" Pevsner asked and then added: "And both what I intend to do and why I am doing it?"

"You have to understand that I just work for Hall," Castillo said. "I take orders, run errands, that's all."

"That's not what I hear," Kennedy said.

"Well, then, you hear wrong."

"But you will, Charley, won't you, talk to Secretary Hall?" Pevsner asked.

And just in time again Castillo stopped himself from replying "Yes, sir."

"Yes, I will. Of course I will."

"All right, then, let's enjoy our meal," Pevsner said.

No one had room for dessert, but there was, of course, cognac, and a cigar to go with the coffee.

Castillo knew that he shouldn't take the cognac but decided there was no way he could refuse.

When Kennedy slid the cognac bottle across the table to Pevsner, who had gone through his cognac quickly, Pevsner held up his hand.

"We have to go, Howard," he said and stood up.

He put out his hand to Castillo, who took it and somewhat ungracefully stood up himself.

"It's been a pleasure, Charley. I look forward to seeing you again. And I'll be in touch."

"I have no idea how Matt . . . Secretary Hall will react to this," Castillo said.

"Nothing ventured, nothing gained. Isn't that what they say?" Pevsner said. "The other car will take you back to the Bristol. Good night, Charley."

"Good night, Alex," Castillo said.

"Watch your back, Charley," Kennedy said. "You don't want to piss on the red silk brocade, do you?"

He touched Castillo's shoulder and then followed Pevsner out of the room.

"Jesus Christ!" Castillo said aloud when they had gone.

The Mercedes 220 was at the curb when he left the restaurant. Pevsner's car was nowhere in sight.

He half expected to find Inge in the backseat. But she wasn't there.

He went to his room in the Bristol and decided the first thing he needed was a cold shower and some coffee. Lots of black coffee. He called room service and ordered coffee and then stood under the shower, as cold as he could stand it, for as long as he could stand it, and tried to think.

He finally reached the conclusion that he was in no condition to make any but the most basic decisions.

As he, shivering, dried himself and pulled on the terry cloth bathrobe hanging on the back of the bathroom door, he made three of these:

First, that he was not going to see Pevsner again in Vienna. Pevsner had said all he intended to say. He had probably gone from the Drei Hussaren to the airport, where, almost certainly, a private jet was waiting for him.

Second, that he would not try to put anything down on the computer and/or send any kind of a message. Maybe in the morning but not now.

And, third, that he had to get to Washington as quickly as possible.

He called the concierge and told him that something had come up and he really needed to get to Washington as soon as he could, even if that meant getting there by a circuitous route. The concierge said he would do what he could and call him.

There was a knock at the door while he was still on the phone with the concierge. It was the floor waiter with his coffee.

When the floor waiter had gone, Charley realized the coffee posed another problem: *What's smarter? Take the coffee and see if it clears my thinking? Or just go to bed and sleep it off?*

And then, not two minutes later, there was another knock at the door.

What did I do? Forget to sign the bill?

When he opened the door, Inge was standing there. She ducked past him and entered the room. He saw that she held a bottle of cognac.

"Hello, Charley," Inge said. "I thought you might like some company."

"You thought, or Alex Pevsner thought?"

She laughed in her throat and walked close to him.

"Does it matter?" she asked.

And then he felt her hand on him under the terry cloth robe.

And, a moment later, she laughed again deep in her throat.

"And Howard was afraid you were a poofter," she said.

What the hell, why not? Maybe it'll get Patricia Wilson out of my mind.

[ONE]
Baltimore-Washington International Airport
Baltimore, Maryland
1440 8 June 2005

The beagle headed for Major Carlos G. Castillo's suitcase with a delighted yelp, dragging his master, a hefty, middle-aged, red-haired woman in too-tight trousers, and who wore both a cell phone and a Smith & Wesson .357 revolver on her belt, after him.

The other passengers who had traveled from Munich aboard Lufthansa 5255 and were waiting for their luggage to appear on the carousel were fascinated.

"Excuse me, sir," the woman said to Castillo. "What do you have in that bag?"

"Just personal possessions," Castillo said. "A couple of gifts."

"You don't happen to have any fresh bakery products in there, do you?"

"I think it would be a good idea if you called your supervisor," Castillo said.

"First, I'd like to have a look at what you have in that suitcase, sir," the redhead said.

She snatched the cell phone from her belt, spoke into it, and in a very short time another uniformed, armed, female officer, this one a wiry black whose hands didn't look large enough to handle her .357, appeared. She was pushing a small cart.

"Sir, if you will put your luggage on the cart and come with me, please?" the wiry woman said.

"I have one more bag," Castillo said. "What about that?"

Castillo's second bag had somehow become lost deep in the Airbus's baggage compartment and it was ten minutes before it finally appeared on the carousel and he could load it on the cart.

"Right this way, sir," the wiry female said, pointing to a door with an AUTHORIZED PERSONNEL ONLY sign hanging above it.

Castillo resisted the temptation to wave good-bye to his fellow passengers. There was a low counter in the room.

"Place your bag on the counter, please, sir," the wiry woman said.

"May I ask that you call your supervisor?"

"Sir, it is a violation of federal law to bring fresh bakery products, meat, fruit, or vegetables into the United States. If you have any such products in your luggage and declare them now, they will be confiscated. If you do not make such a declaration and I am forced to search your luggage . . ."

"Please call your supervisor," Castillo said.

The wiry woman snatched her telephone from her uniform belt and ninety seconds later a very large, uniformed, armed black man with captain's bars on his collar points appeared.

"Probably bakery products," the wiry woman said.

"Sir," the captain said, "would you please open your luggage?"

"That one," the wiry woman said, pointing.

"That one," the captain parroted.

Castillo worked the combination and opened the suitcase.

It was almost concealed beneath Hotel Bristol toweling, but there it was, a box nine inches deep and about a foot square. It was wrapped in white paper, sealed with silver tape, with a gold label reading DEMEL stuck in the middle.

"What's that, sir?" the captain said.

"It's a cake. What they call a Sacher torte," Castillo said. "My boss asked me to bring him one from Vienna."

"Your boss should have known better," the captain said, not unkindly. "And what you should have not done was bring it onto the airplane in the first place. And then you should have declared it. We'd have confiscated it and you would be out the cost of the cake and that would have been the end of this. But now . . ."

"I understand," Castillo said.

"May I see your passport, sir?"

Castillo handed him instead his Secret Service credentials. In the leather folder was the business card identifying him as the executive assistant to the secretary of homeland security.

The captain handed both back to Castillo, looked at him without expression, and said nothing.

"Either way, I will tell him—and he always asks—that the security procedures at BW seemed to be working just fine," Castillo said. "Your call, Captain."

The captain looked at Castillo for a long moment.

"I've heard tell he's a pretty good guy," the captain said, finally.

"What did he show you?" the wiry woman asked.

The captain held up a massive hand to tell her to shut up.

"He's a really good guy," Castillo said.

"I'll take this from here," the captain said. "You can go back on the floor."

When the wiry woman hesitated, the captain pointed somewhat impatiently at the door.

When she went through it, the captain said, "Close your suitcase, sir."

"Thanks," Castillo said.

"I heard he was a sergeant in Vietnam," the captain said.

"He was," Castillo said and closed his suitcase.

The captain picked up one of the suitcases and led Castillo out a back door and then into the arrival lobby.

"Tell him another 'Nam sergeant hopes he likes the cake," the captain said.

"I will," Castillo said and then started dragging his suitcases toward the buses and taxis door.

[TWO]
The Mayflower Hotel
1127 Connecticut Avenue NW
Washington, D.C.
1625 8 June 2005

A bellman pushing an ornate baggage cart followed Castillo into his apartment.

"Just put them in the bedroom, please," Castillo said as he handed him his tip.

"I keep telling you, Charley, we have to stop meeting in hotel rooms like this," Major H. Richard Miller, Jr., said from behind him. "People are going to talk."

Charley startled, looked around the living room.

Miller was sprawled low in an armchair. He was wearing a suit. His shirt collar was open and his tie pulled down. A bottle of Heineken beer sat on the table beside him.

"What the hell are you doing here?" Charley asked.

"An old pal told me not to worry, he could cover for me. Turns out he couldn't. You are looking at a disgraced you-know-what relieved for cause."

"Oh, shit," Castillo said. "Relieved for cause?"

"They did everything but cut off my uniform buttons and march me through the gate at the Luanda airport while a band played 'The Rogue's March.' "

"How did you know where to find me?"

"General Naylor knew where you were, or at least about this apartment. He told me a key would be waiting for me and I was to make myself as invisible as possible until whatever is going to happen happens."

"I'll be damned," Charley said.

"Nice place, Charley. You must be on a different per diem scale than I am."

"It's close to where I work," Charley said. "My boss likes to have me available."

"Yeah," Miller said, disbelievingly, then added, "I have a cell phone with the number of your boss, to be used only if necessary."

"What does that mean?"

Miller shrugged. "General Naylor gave it to me. I guess if somebody shows up here with a cross to nail me to, your boss wants to know."

"Well, let me see what's going on," Charley said and took out his cellular telephone.

"Where the hell have you been?" Miller asked.

Castillo put up his hand to tell him to wait.

"Sir, this is your personal FedEx international courier," he began. "I have your Sacher torte for you—

"Yes, sir. I just walked into my apartment—

"Yes, sir. He's here. If I can have twenty minutes for a shower and a shave, I'll be right over—

"Sir, I can come over there—

"Yes, sir. I'll be waiting for you."

He hung up and turned to Miller.

"Get your ass off the chair and try to look respectable, my boss is on his way over here. And before he gets here, I need a shower."

"You want me here?" Miller asked.

"I think he wants to see you, too," Charley said after a just barely perceptible hesitation.

Castillo, freshly shaved and wearing crisp trousers and a dress shirt, opened the door to Secretary Hall.

"Good afternoon, sir."

"I tried to call you in Vienna," Hall said. "I had all kinds of second thoughts

about you and Pevsner. And all the Bristol would tell me was that you had
checked out early this morning. I was really getting worried, Charley."

Hall saw Miller.

"I'm Matt Hall, Major Miller," he said, putting out his hand.

"How do you do, sir?"

"Now that our friend is back, in one piece, I'm feeling a lot better than I was
a half hour ago. Did he tell you where's he's been, what he was trying to do?"

"No, sir," Miller said. "I picked up on 'Vienna.' "

Charley walked into the bedroom and came back with the Sacher torte
from Demel's.

"Here you go, sir," he said. "One cake of fourteen raspberry layers."

"I was kidding, Charley!"

"You sounded serious to me, sir. And it's fresh. I picked it up on the way to
the airport this morning."

Hall took the box and shook his head.

"How'd you get it into the country?"

"A customs service captain at BW is one of your admirers. He said to tell
you, one Vietnam sergeant to another, that he hopes you enjoy it."

"You told him you worked for me?"

"It was either that or go to jail. I was in custody. Two armed females and a
beagle. The beagle sniffed the cake."

Hall shook his head but chuckled.

"My God, Charley!" he said. "But thank you. What do I owe you?"

"My pleasure, sir. I was happy to do it."

"We'll argue about that later," Hall said. "Right now all I want to say is that
I'm glad you had second thoughts about trying to meet with Pevsner, too."

"Sir?"

"He's really a dangerous character, Charley. I asked Joel Isaacson if he knew
anything about him and got a five-minute lecture. All frightening."

"He's a frightening man," Charley agreed.

"The FBI is sending me his dossier," Hall went on, and then he thought
aloud: "Which I should have had by now. Anyway, I'm glad you missed him."

"I met with Pevsner, sir."

"You met with him?"

"Yes, sir. I've got a long story you're going to have a hard time believing. I'm
not sure I believe it myself."

"Well, let's hear it, Charley."

"Sir," Miller asked, "would you like me to make myself scarce?"

Hall looked at him.

"No," he said after a moment. "It was your filing, after all, that started this whole thing." He paused. "And I have the feeling that what one of you knows, so does the other. So, no, Major Miller, don't make yourself scarce."

He looked at Charley.

"The bottom line," Castillo began, "is that he said he didn't steal the 727 . . ."

"Which is precisely what one would expect him to say," Hall said.

". . . and that he's going to help us find it," Charley said. "In exchange for which he wants you to use your influence to get the government to . . . reduce the attention it's paying to him."

The telephone rang. Castillo looked at Hall for guidance.

"Answer it," Hall said.

Charley walked to the telephone and picked it up and said, "Hello."

He was silent a moment, then replied, "Yes, it is—

"The Drei Hussaren—

"No. Wait."

He patted his chest, and finding no pen, gestured to Miller to give him something to write with. Hall beat Miller to it.

"Okay," Charley said. "Now I need some paper."

Miller picked up *The Washington Post* from the couch and handed it to Castillo.

"Okay," Castillo said into the receiver. "Shoot."

He made notes on the newsprint, then said, "Let me make sure I have that right. I spell Able-Baker-Echo-Charley-Hotel-Echo. Right? Hello? *Hello?* Shit."

He put the phone back in the cradle.

"He hung up."

"Come on, Charley," Hall said, gesturing for details.

"It was a man. American accent. He asked if I was Major Castillo. I said I was. He said he had a message from Alex, if I would tell him where I had dinner last night. I told him. He said that as of 1700 last night, the 727 was on the ground in Abéché, Chad."

"Alex being Pevsner?" Hall asked.

"Yes, sir."

"Why would he refer to you as Major Castillo?"

"He knew who I was before he called Otto Görner," Charley said. "That's why he agreed to the interview. Before he knew I'm me, he was going to take out Gossinger."

"He told you that?" Hall asked.

"The way he put it was that Gossinger was going to get an Indian beauty mark," Charley said. "That's a small red circle in the middle of the forehead."

"Jesus!" Hall said. "And he was serious, right?"

"I believed him," Charley said.

"I never should have let you go over there. At least not alone."

"If I hadn't been alone, I don't think he would have met with me."

"Permission to speak, sir?" Miller asked.

Hall gave him a strange look but said, "Permission granted."

"Two things," Miller said. "I don't think it was a coincidence that phone call came fifteen minutes after Charley walked in here. That's the first time it's rung since I've been here. Which means they have somebody here, are paying a bellman or someone."

"Yeah," Castillo grunted his agreement.

"Two," Miller went on, "Pevsner would know where the 727 is because he put it there."

"I don't think he stole it," Charley said. "He told me he has airplanes. That he just bought a nearly new 767 from an Argentine airline that went belly-up."

"Charley, I think you should take it from the top," Hall said.

"Yes, sir."

"And you, Miller, if you have any questions while he's telling us ask them."

"Yes, sir," Miller said.

"Sir, I sent an e-mail saying he didn't show at the Sacher the first night," Charley began. "So I went back the next night—that's last night—and . . ."

"So how did you handle the woman who went to your room?" Hall asked with a smile. "You left it that she showed up at your door with a bottle of cognac and then drove you to the airport in the morning."

"I was hoping you wouldn't ask, sir," Charley said.

"You dumb sonofabitch, Charley!" Miller said.

"Agreed," Charley said. "And that brings up the equally embarrassing fact that I was at least half drunk, which should be factored into this."

"You think Pevsner purposefully got you drunk?" Hall asked.

"We all had a lot to drink," Charley said. "But do I think there was a conscious effort to get me drunk? No. He was drinking cognac when I met him on the Cobenzl, offered me some, which I didn't think I should refuse, and I kept up with him. He had as much to drink—for that matter, so did Kennedy—as I did."

"And how reliable do you think this information is—that the 727 is or was last night in Chad?"

"I think Pevsner thinks it is," Charley said. "I don't think he would take a chance, at the beginning of the 'long and mutually profitable association' he says he wants, by giving me anything that was doubtful—and certainly he wouldn't give me anything false."

"Okay. That means we're going to have to tell Powell," Hall said.

He took his cellular telephone from his jacket pocket and pressed one of the autodial numbers.

"Matt Hall for the DCI, please," he said.

"John, I'm on my cellular, but I wanted to get this to you as soon as possible. The thing we're looking for was, according to information I consider reliable enough to pass on to you, at a place called Abéché—Able-Baker-Echo-Charley-Hotel-Echo—Chad last night at five o'clock—

"No, not over a cellular I'm not. I'll tell you more in the situation room tonight. What I'm doing is giving you information I consider reliable enough for you to really look into—

"Okay. Again. Able-Baker-Echo-Charley-Hotel-Echo. Got it?—

"I'll see you shortly."

He put the cellular in the palm of his hand and pressed another autodial key.

"Matt Hall for Director Schmidt, please—

"I'm fine, Mark. Thank you. Yourself?—

"Mark, I never got the FBI's dossier on Aleksandr Pevsner I asked for. Is something holding it up?—

"Well, if it's on your desk, I can't read it, can I?—

"What do you mean, you weren't sure I still wanted it?"

The tone of Hall's voice changed and both Miller and Castillo looked at him. His face showed that he didn't like what he was hearing.

"Well, Mark, first the DCI has not found time in his busy schedule to tell me he doesn't think there's much to 'this Pevsner nonsense scenario from that loose cannon Special Forces guy in Luanda,' but that doesn't really have anything to do with this, does it?—

"Yes, of course, I still want it—

"As soon as I can have it. Send it over by messenger right now—

"Yes, of course, I realize it's classified—

"Then I'll send one of my Secret Service agents to get it—

"I sound like I'm angry? I can't imagine why—

"Actually, I'm not in my office. I'm in Room 404 at the Mayflower. But if that's going to cause any problems, I can have a Secret Service agent in your office in five minutes—

"Okay. Fine. I'll be looking for him. And while I've got you on the line, Mark, there's something else I need as soon as I can have it. I want the dossier on one of your special agents, maybe an ex–special agent. A man named Howard Kennedy—

"That's right. Howard Kennedy—

"Well, if you have probably a half-dozen agents named Howard Kennedy I guess you'll have to send me the dossiers on all of them—

"I don't mean to sound confrontational, Mark, and I'm sorry you feel that way. I don't suspect for a moment that you and the DCI are deciding together what to send me in response to Dr. Cohen's memo, because that would probably make me confrontational, but I am getting more than a little curious why this is turning into a problem—

"What would you call it, Mark?—

"How long is it going to take you to assemble the dossiers on how ever many Howard Kennedys are, or were, FBI special agents?—

"Frankly, I don't think I should have to wait that long. If there's some reason I can't have the Kennedy dossiers by nine tomorrow morning, why don't you send me a memo for record that I can show Dr. Cohen?—

"Yes, I think you're right. We do seem to be having a communications problem. I'll be waiting for the Pevsner dossier. Nice to talk to you, Mark."

He pushed the END CALL button and put the phone in his pocket.

"The turf war has begun," he announced. "I was afraid of that." He turned to Major Miller and said, "I hope you'll understand I have to ask this."

"Sir?"

"Did you make a pass or anything that could be construed as a pass at Mrs. Wilson?"

"No, sir, I did not."

"When you had dinner with her, how much did you have to drink?"

"I have never had dinner with Mrs. Wilson, sir."

"Did you have drinks with her?"

"No, sir."

"I did," Charley said.

"*You* did?" Hall asked, and, when Charley nodded, asked, "And did you make a pass at her?"

"It was more that she made a pass at me," Charley said.

"And?"

"I was in a receptive mood, sir," Charley said.

"Jesus Christ!" Miller said. "I told you she was dangerous!"

"You also told me she wasn't getting what she needed at home. And she is a very attractive female. At the time, I was supposed to believe her story that she was a reporter for *Forbes* and she thought I was a fellow journalist named Gossinger."

"But you knew who she was?" Hall pursued.

"Yes, sir. Dick told me who she was."

"And that 'she wasn't getting what she needed at home.' Just what did you mean by that, Miller?"

"Sir, the fact is that Mrs. Wilson is twenty years or so younger than her husband. The rumors going around have it he likes young men and married the lady as a beard."

Hall looked at him for a long moment but didn't respond. Instead, he turned to Castillo.

"Tell me, Charley. And the truth, please. The cow is out of the barn, so to speak. Why did you take Mrs. Wilson to bed?"

"In hindsight, sir, it was irresponsible. What happened was that she wanted to look at my story . . ."

"Why?"

"Probably to see if I really had a story; was, in fact, a journalist. She smelled something; she sent Dick to check me out. And then, presuming I had a story, she wanted to know what I had found out and was reporting about the missing 727."

"What's that got to do with taking her to bed?"

"I told her she could have the story just as soon as the *Tages Zeitung* went to bed. She replied, 'Why not as soon as we do?' "

"Whereupon you shut off your brain and turned on your dick," Miller blurted, almost in disbelief.

"You could put it in those terms, I suppose," Charley said.

"That strikes me as a succinct summing-up, Charley," Hall said, shaking his head. "A little crude but right on the money. I hope she was worth it. That—little dalliance—is likely to turn out to be costly."

Hall looked at his wristwatch.

"I don't know how soon the FBI will show up, but I don't think I can risk going back to the office. I very much doubt if they'd give the Pevsner dossier to you. Could we get coffee and something to munch on, do you think?"

"Coffee and a large hors d'oeuvres coming up, sir," Charley said, heading for the telephone.

"Sir, am I allowed to make a suggestion?" Miller asked.

Hall considered that before replying, "Sure, why not?"

"What Pevsner said—or the ex–FBI agent, one of them—about there being a Philadelphia connection?"

Hall nodded his understanding.

"Sir, I might be useful in running that down."

"How?"

"My father and the police commissioner are friends, sir. Commissioner Kellogg?"

"Miller, I'm going to pass on to the FBI what Charley heard in Vienna. They'll certainly look into it, including asking the police what they might have."

"Sir, sometimes the cooperation between the FBI and the police isn't all that it should be."

"Meaning?"

"I'm sure the cops will answer any specific questions put to them by the FBI. But probably not very quickly. And I'm also sure they're not going to volunteer anything that might give up their snitches, or if they have somebody undercover with the Muslims, his identity. Or . . ."

"And you think they'd confide in you?"

"More than they would in the FBI," Miller said. "Particularly if Commissioner Kellogg knew I was asking the questions for you."

Hall exhaled and shook his head.

"Charley, did you hear this?" he asked.

"Yes, sir."

"That wasn't really the question, Charley, and you know it. What do you think?"

"I was thinking, sir, that if the president . . . may I talk about that?"

Hall studied Miller a moment, then turned to Castillo. "He knows you're working by order of the president, doesn't he?"

"I think he's figured that out, sir."

"Since the cow is out of the barn . . ." Hall said, gesturing for Castillo to continue.

"Sir, if the president wants to know who knew what and when, and the cops in Philadelphia know something, isn't he going to want to know when the FBI found out about it?"

Hall looked at him a long moment.

Charley thought, *He's thinking, but not about Miller going to Philadelphia.*

"I just had a Washington bureaucrat's thought that I'm a little ashamed of," Hall confessed. "I was thinking, *My God, if we find the 727 before anyone else does a lot of people are going to have egg on their face and really be annoyed with us. We can count on payback.*"

"So Miller doesn't go to Philadelphia?" Charley asked.

"That depends," Hall said. He took his cellular telephone from his pocket again and pressed an autodial key.

"Matt Hall for General Naylor—

"Well, I have to talk to him, and now."

He turned to Castillo and Miller.

"The commander in chief of Central Command is out jogging on the beach," he announced with a smile.

The commanding general of Central Command is never out of touch; it took fewer than ninety seconds to get a telephone to Naylor.

"You sound a little winded, Allan," Hall said. "And what about sunburn? At your age . . ."

The commanding general was apparently not amused. Hall smiled.

"Temper, temper, Allan. And, no, this couldn't wait. It's important, but we're both on cellulars, okay? So you're just going to have to trust me. That last fellow you just sent to me? I would like to use him the same way I'm using the first one. Would that be okay with you? More important, if it will get him in any trouble, say so—

"Of course he volunteered."

Hall handed Miller the telephone.

"Yes, sir?—

"Yes, sir, I understand. Thank you, sir. Yes, sir."

He handed the phone to Castillo.

"Yes, sir?—

"Yes, sir, I'm fine—

"Yes, sir. I will."

Castillo handed the cellular to Hall.

"Thank you, Allan. I'll be in touch when we can talk. Have a nice jog."

Hall put the cellular back in his pocket.

"What did he say to you, Miller?"

"Sir, he said that, VOCG, I am to place myself at your orders. CentCom orders will be published tomorrow."

"VOCG?" Hall asked.

" 'Verbal Orders of the Commanding General,' sir," Miller furnished.

"Okay. I'd forgotten that phrase. If I ever knew it. I never saw a general up close when I was in the Army."

"It's SOP, sir," Charley said, "when there is no time to get a set of orders published."

Hall nodded.

"I understand your security clearances have been revoked," he said to Miller. "So I'm unrevoking them as of right now. Charley, call the office and dictate a memorandum for the record."

"Yes, sir. What are you going to give him?"

"Everything he had before they were pulled," Hall said. "In addition, I authorize you to tell him anything you think he needs to know about your orders from the president."

"Yes, sir."

"Put that in the memo for record, too," Hall ordered.

"Yes, sir," Castillo said and punched an autodial key on his cellular.

"While he's doing that," Hall ordered, "see if you can get Commissioner Kellogg on the phone."

"Yes, sir," Miller said.

"Thank you, Commissioner," Hall said. "When you get to the office at eight, Major Miller and my executive assistant, a man named Castillo, will be waiting for you. This is important and I'm grateful for your understanding."

He saw Castillo's eyes on him as he pushed the phone's CALL END button.

"Yeah, you're going. For several reasons. We obviously don't have time to get Miller any identification, for one. For another, I want you both out of town for a while."

"Yes, sir. What if there's another message from Pevsner?"

"I thought, if it's all right with you, that I'd have Joel Isaacson put a man in here, in the apartment. He would know only what he has to know. That if there is a call for you, you're out of town but can be reached on your cellular and give the caller your number."

"That'll work, sir, so far as Pevsner is concerned. But if you put Secret Service people in here, they'll know I live here. Isn't that going to cause problems?"

"They already know where you live. And a lot more about you than you probably think. Why do you think your code name is Don Juan?"

"Really?" Miller chuckled.

"And you didn't think Isaacson and McGuire let me walk over here by myself, did you?"

"I wondered about that, sir. But once they get in here . . ."

"You're talking about the improbability of your being able to pay the rent on this place on your Army pay?"

"That's the sort of thing that causes gossip, sir."

"Why should it? If I know about it, my approval is implied."

"Yes, sir."

"I don't think I'd have to tell Joel to remind them to keep their mouths shut but I will."

"When do you want us to go, sir?"

"I'd like you to see what the FBI has on your friend Pevsner, but that can wait until you get back. I'd like to have you out of town before I go to the White House."

Castillo looked at his watch.

"We just missed the Metroliner," he said. "There's another in an hour?"

"That'd do it," Hall ordered.

Castillo went to the telephone.

"Who're you calling?" Miller asked.

"The concierge," Castillo answered and then spoke to the phone: "This is Mr. Castillo. I'll need two first-class tickets on the next Metroliner to New York, charge them to my room, and have a cab waiting in thirty minutes to take me to Union Station."

"You said 'two tickets to New York,' you know," Miller said when Castillo had hung up.

"Yeah, I know. I think you were right about the timing of that call from Pevsner's man. I was thinking that if I wanted information about somebody in a hotel, I would lay lots of long green on the concierge. I think he's probably the villain. I'm pretty sure that's how Kennedy found out that Carlos Castillo was not Karl Gossinger's boyfriend. And I wouldn't . . ."

"He thought that?" Miller asked, highly amused.

"Yeah, he did. And I wouldn't be surprised if someone from the CIA asked him about the guy in 404, either. DCI Powell seemed very curious about me."

"You really think he would order something like that?" Hall asked.

Castillo nodded. "And either promised money or appealed to his patriotism to have him keep an eye on me. Maybe I'm wrong—I'd like to be wrong—but if I'm right, I sort of like the idea of two pairs of spooks—Powell's and Pevsner's—frantically searching through the people getting off the train in Penn Station in New York looking for me and whoever's with me."

"What have you got against the DCI?" Hall asked.

"I don't like the way he handled Dick," Castillo replied. "He told you he wouldn't do anything to him and then he had him relieved for cause. Once that happens to an Army officer, he might as well resign and he knew it."

"I'm dealing with that," Hall said. "I'm . . ."

The door knocker rapped.

It was a bellman with a large tray of hors d'oeuvres and two pots of coffee.

Fifteen minutes later, there was another rapping of the door knocker.

Castillo opened it. There were two men in business suits. One of them carried a briefcase. When Charley glanced down the corridor, he saw Joel Isaacson coming toward the door from one direction and Tom McGuire coming from the other.

There must be something about these two people they think is fishy.

"Yes?" Castillo said.

"We're looking for Secretary Hall," the elder of the two men at the door said.

"Who are you?"

The man who had spoken took a leather folder from his pocket and held it up.

"Oh, my, the FBI!" Castillo said, more loudly than was necessary.

He got a smile from Isaacson before Isaacson stopped at a nearby door, and appeared to be slipping a plastic card into its lock.

"Come in, please," Castillo said. "The secretary expects you."

"Good afternoon, Mr. Secretary," the man from the FBI said. "I'm Inspector Doherty from Director Schmidt's office."

Hall smiled at him and put out his hand.

"Mr. Secretary, we have a dossier for you," Inspector Doherty said, "but it's from the director's personal files and he'd like it back—if possible, he'd like us to take it back now, after you've had a chance to read it."

He handed Hall an expanding cardboard folder. Hall looked at the folder and then at Doherty. The look on his face showed he didn't like at all hearing that Schmidt wanted his dossier back right away.

"Director Schmidt will have everything xeroxed for you, sir," Doherty offered.

"In that case, Charley," Hall said, handing the folder to Castillo, "I think you and Miller had better have a quick look at the dossier before you go."

The look on Doherty's face showed he didn't like that announcement at all.

"With all respect, sir, do these gentlemen have the proper security clearances?"

Hall didn't reply. The look on his face was answer enough.

"You understand, sir, I had to ask."

Inside the expanding folder was the dossier, a thick stack of paper held together with a large aluminum clip.

"There's coffee, Mr. Doherty," the secretary said.

"Thank you but no thank you, sir."

Castillo walked to the couch, laid the dossier on the coffee table, and started flipping through it. After a minute, Miller sat down beside him.

"I hope you, Mr. Secretary—and these gentlemen—understand that some of the material in these files has not been confirmed," Doherty said.

Castillo closed his dossier.

"Sir, I'll need more time than Miller and I have," he said.

"Okay," Hall said. "Then you better leave. You and Miller can read the Xeroxes when you get back."

Castillo took the dossier and started to put it back in the expanding file.

"Just leave it there, please," Hall said. "I'll read as much as I can before I have to go to the White House."

"Yes, sir," Castillo said.

He and Miller went into the bedroom. In five minutes—Castillo now wearing a necktie and suit jacket—they came out carrying suitcases.

Hall looked up from the dossier on the coffee table.

"Keep in touch," he ordered.

[THREE]
The White House
1600 Pennsylvania Avenue NW
Washington, D.C.
1725 8 June 2005

Secretary Hall had heard—and it had not displeased him—that the passengers of only three vehicles were ever exempted from careful scrutiny before being passed onto the White House grounds: the presidential limousine, the vice-presidential limousine, and the blue GMC Yukon XL that he ordinarily rode in.

He thought of that as his Yukon approached the gates and was pleased to realize he enjoyed that little perk and John Powell and Mark Schmidt did not. Right now, he was not very fond of the DCI or the director of the FBI.

And he was therefore surprised, and a little disappointed, when the uniformed Secret Service officer waved the Yukon to stop.

Joel Isaacson rolled down the driver's window.

"Good evening, Mr. Secretary," the guard said. "Sir, the president requests you to go to the quarters before you go to the situation room."

Natalie Cohen was sitting with her legs tucked under her skirt on a couch in the sitting room of the president's apartment. She raised her hand in a casual greeting when Hall walked in.

The president was sitting slumped in an armchair, holding a crystal tumbler of what was almost certainly his usual bourbon, Maker's Mark, on the rocks.

"You want one of these, Matt?" he asked, raising the glass. "To give you courage to grovel before Powell?"

"I'm not going to grovel before Powell," Hall blurted, then remembered to add, "Mr. President, am I?"

"Let me tell you where our little fishing expedition has crashed on the rocks," the president said.

He pointed at an array of bottles on a sideboard. Hall walked to it, told himself he was in trouble, would need all his wits not a drink, and then poured two inches of the bourbon into a glass and took a sip.

Then he leaned against the sideboard and looked at the president.

"The FBI has learned that Lease-Aire, Inc., has filed a claim for the loss of its airplane, which is now with a seventy percent probability at the bottom of the Atlantic Ocean."

"Sir, isn't that to be expected?"

The president held up his hand as a signal for him not to interrupt.

"The DCI has reported that he found it necessary to relieve the station chief in Luanda for, one, turning over to your major the linguist-classified material that had already been evaluated and found useless by Langley because your major told him he was working for me—this was to be a secret operation, remember?—and, two, incidentally getting shit-faced at dinner—sorry, Nat—"

Dr. Cohen raised her hand in exactly the same way she had raised it when Hall had walked into the room.

". . . and making a pass at his boss."

The president took a sip of his drink and then looked at Hall, waiting for his reaction.

The secretary of homeland security, after three seconds of thought, made a profound philosophical decision that he learned in Vietnam, when lives also were at stake: *Pick men you trust, and trust the men you pick.*

"In my judgment, Mr. President," Hall said, "there is an almost one hundred percent probability that the missing airplane is not at the bottom of the Atlantic."

"*That's* interesting," Dr. Cohen said.

"You don't happen to know where it *is*, do you, Matt?" the president asked very softly.

"Mr. President, there is an almost eighty percent possibility that as of five o'clock yesterday afternoon it was at a remote airfield in Chad, a place called Abéché. I have so informed the DCI."

"And the source of your information, Matt?" Dr. Cohen asked, very softly.

"A Russian arms dealer by the name of Aleksandr Pevsner."

"And what did the DCI say when you told him you had learned from Mr. Pevsner that the airplane was in Chad?" the president asked, and then, without giving Hall time to reply, asked, "And did Mr. Pevsner happen to tell you what the 727 is doing in Chad?"

"In a short answer, sir, the airplane is being prepared to be flown into the Liberty Bell in Philadelphia by a Somalian group which calls itself the Holy Legion of Muhammad."

"You told this to Powell?" the president asked.

"No, sir. Only that I had reliable information that the aircraft was at Abéché."

"He didn't ask for your source?"

"Yes, sir, he did. But I told him I was on a non-secure telephone."

"This guy Pevsner has come up before," the president said. "According to Powell, he's a Russian gangster, the head of the Russian Mafia. Are you aware of that?"

"Did the DCI also tell you, sir, that the agency uses Pevsner's fleet of airplanes to move things covertly for them? And as a source for weapons of all kinds?"

"No," the president said, thoughtfully. "He didn't happen to mention that."

"What was your contact with Pevsner?" Dr. Cohen asked. "How did that happen?"

"My contact was through Major Castillo," Hall said. "You want all the details?"

"Every one of them, Mr. Secretary," the president said. "Every goddamned last-minute detail!"

It took about ten minutes.

"Okay, Dr. Cohen," the president said. "You've heard this fascinating yarn; you're my security advisor—advise me."

"Have I got everything, Matt?" Dr. Cohen said.

"There's one or two more things, but nothing bearing on the location of the airplane or what the terrorists intend to do with it."

"Goddammit, I said I wanted every detail, Matt!"

"Yes, sir. Major Miller did not make a pass at Mrs. Wilson."

"So he would say, right?"

"Mrs. Wilson made a pass at Major Castillo when she thought he was the German journalist. And he caught it."

"Interesting," Dr. Cohen said.

"And . . ."

"I'd like to hear that from Major Castillo," the president said. "I'd like to hear the whole goddamned wild, incredible story again from him."

"Sir, at the moment he's on the Metroliner to Philadelphia. I can call him and have him return, but that would take several hours . . ."

"He's checking into the possible Muslim connection in Philadelphia?" Dr. Cohen asked, and, when Hall nodded, went on: "Mr. President, you're not going to have time to check Castillo's story out yourself. You're going to have to make a decision and right now."

"I know that I have to make a decision, Natalie," the president said. He sounded tired rather than sarcastic. "What I want from you is advice on what that decision should be."

She did not immediately reply.

"Come on, Natalie. This is why you make the big bucks," the president said.

"Sir, my advice—your wife's in Chicago, right?"

The president nodded.

"Sir, what I think you should do is call the Marines and chopper out to Camp David, taking Matt with you. No explanation to anybody."

"What do I do with Powell?"

"I will go to the situation room and tell him—and Schmidt—that just before you left for Camp David you told me to tell him you really want to know whether or not the missing airplane is—or was—at this place in Chad . . ."

"Abéché," Hall furnished.

"Thank you," she said. "And that he is to let me know immediately what he finds out."

"Why should I go—Matt and I go—to Camp David?" the president asked.

"Because if you were going to ask for Matt's resignation, that's where you'd take him to ask for it," Dr. Cohen said.

"They should know whether that airplane is where Matt thinks it is by morning," the president thought aloud.

"May I suggest, Mr. President, that you come back here about this time tomorrow?" Dr. Cohen said.

"Okay," the president said after a moment's thought. "Let's do it."

Dr. Cohen picked up the handset of a multibuttoned telephone on the coffee table and pushed one of the buttons.

"This is Dr. Cohen," she said. "The president will require Marine One for a flight to Camp David immediately. No prior or post-takeoff announcement. Refer all inquiries you can't handle to me."

She put the handset back in the cradle.

"Thank you, Natalie," the president said. And then he looked at Matt Hall. "Jesus H. Christ, Matt! They really want to crash that airplane into the Liberty Bell?"

[FOUR]
Aboard Marine One
The White House
1600 Pennsylvania Avenue NW
Washington, D.C.
1810 8 June 2005

The pilot of the helicopter said, "Marine One lifting off," and the Sikorsky VH-3D "Sea King" of HMX-1, the Marine Corps' Presidential Helicopter Squadron, did just that, rising quickly and smoothly from the White House lawn and then making a smooth, climbing turn which would put it on course for Camp David.

The president of the United States said, "I feel like Nixon fleeing from the angry crowds at the White House with a very insincere smile on my face."

"Mr. President," Secretary of Homeland Security Matthew Hall began and then stopped.

"What, Matt?"

"I was about to say I'm sorry—and I am because of the trouble that's developed—but what I really want to say is thank you for trusting me on this."

The president waved his right hand, meaning "unnecessary," and said, "I know you believe what you told me. And it seems pretty obvious that I can't take a chance and ignore—however incredible it may sound—the possibility that these lunatics actually intend crashing this airplane into downtown Philadelphia and may have the means to carry it off."

Hall didn't reply.

"And we're about to see how efficient all the technology really is, aren't we? Just about now, Natalie is telling Powell that I want to know what's on, or what has been on, the field in Chad, and very soon satellite sensors will be having a look."

"Mr. President, fully aware that I'm taking another walk on DCI Powell's lawn, there's something else that might be done."

"What?"

"Sir, I've not brought any of this up to General Naylor."

"Naylor? Why should you have?"

"He may have some means to find out what's going on at Abéché, and possibly before the CIA—and whoever else the DCI enlists to help him—can."

"You don't think Powell will do that anyway? Jesus, you really don't like him, do you?"

"That's two questions, sir. No, I don't really like him. And, no, I don't think he'll seek assistance from General Naylor until his back is against the wall and he has to. Right now what he wants to do is make the agency look good."

"That's a pretty serious accusation, Matt."

"Yes, sir, I realize that. But my responsibility is homeland security and I'm willing to admit I need all the help I can get."

"Two more questions. One, what do you think Naylor could do to help? And, two, what's really caused this trouble between you and Powell? Until yesterday, I thought the two of you got along pretty well."

"He lied to me," Hall said. "He gave me his word that he would take no punitive action against Major Miller and then did just that."

"What did he do?"

"He relieved him for cause—I won't even get into that business of accusing him of making a pass at Mrs. Wilson—fully aware that when an officer is relieved for cause his career is down the toilet."

"He chose to believe Mrs. Wilson. I think they call that 'loyalty downward,'" the president said. "And from where I sit, you are showing the same thing to Major Castillo . . . and to Major Miller, who doesn't even belong to you."

"He does now, sir. General Naylor put him on temporary duty with me. And, sir, I don't know what General Naylor can do. But he may have something—even if only an idea—and I think we should ask for whatever he has."

"Let me think," the president said.

As the president stood in the doorway to exit Marine One and get in one of the golf carts lined up to carry people to the cabins of Camp David, he turned and met Hall's eyes.

"It looks to me as if Major Miller is an innocent bystander caught in the line of fire. I don't like that. What can I do to help him?"

The question took Hall by surprise. He had never even considered the possibility that the president would offer to help Miller.

"Sir, I think if you wrote Miller a letter of commendation for his service—unspecified, but under very difficult conditions for someone of his rank and experience—and sent it to him via the Defense Intelligence Agency—they're the ones who want to crucify him . . ."

"You write it and I'll sign it," the president interrupted him. "But call General Naylor first, and, without getting into your problems with the DCI, tell him if he has any means of finding out whether or not the airplane is, or was, in Chad, to use them."

"Yes, sir. Thank you, Mr. President."

[FIVE]
The Warwick Hotel
1701 Locust Street
Philadelphia, Pennsylvania
2030 8 June 2005

"I really wish you'd come out to the house with me, Charley," Major H. Richard Miller, Jr., said as the taxi stopped in front of the hotel.

"I'm sure you can eventually make your father understand what happened, but in the time between when you tell him that you were relieved because of something I asked you to do and the time he understands—thirty seconds or thirty minutes—I'd just as soon rather not be around General Miller, thank you just the same."

"Coward," Miller said, chuckling, and left it there. "I'll pick you up in the morning at half past seven," he said. "Be standing on the sidewalk shaved and sober and full of energy because you gave your pecker the night off."

Castillo gave him the finger and got out of the taxi.

His initial impression of the Warwick Hotel was that it was a nice one. Nice lobby, with a really impressive floral display—real flowers; as he walked by, he checked—on a beautiful table. To the right was the entrance to the restaurant—he could see enough of that to make the judgment it, too, looked first-rate—and a bar.

There was a young woman sitting alone at the bar. She didn't look like a hooker, but sometimes it was hard to tell. He decided to give the brunette and the hotel the benefit of the doubt. The Warwick didn't look like the kind of a place where ladies of the evening were either encouraged or permitted to practice their profession. And the brunette really didn't look like a hooker.

He was pleased, too, with the room. It was large, high-ceilinged, with a king-sized bed, and the bathroom shelf was loaded with small bottles of high-quality shampoo and mouthwash and crisp packages of expensive soap of the type he liked to put in his toilet kit at checkout time against the inevitability that the next hotel would not much care if their guests bathed or washed out their mouths.

Not that I need either a bath or a mouth rinse.

What I need is a drink, maybe two—no more than two—and then something to eat, and then some sleep. Dick said to be on the sidewalk outside at half past seven.

Jesus, the last time I went to bed was in Vienna. That—and Cobenzl and the Drei Hussaren and Pevsner and Inge—was last night?

One *drink and then something to eat and then to bed.*

But not in the restaurant. I don't want a full meal, and I hate to eat alone at a restaurant table.

Maybe I can get a sandwich at the bar.

That is based solely upon my desire to have something simple to eat, not on the brunette.

It really is, and, anyway, by the time I get back down there she'll more than likely be gone. Nice girls—and we have decided that's what she is—do not sit around hotels where young men with out-of-control gonads might think they're available.

Major Carlos G. Castillo had been in his room no more than ten minutes before he left it, got back on the elevator, and rode it down to the lobby.

The brunette was still sitting alone at the bar.

At that point, Major Castillo told himself, he would have headed right for the restaurant had he not also seen there were four men sitting at a table in the bar eating some kind of good-looking sandwiches on crusty bread.

He entered the bar, taking care not to look at the brunette but taking a stool separated from hers by only one stool.

His cellular went off as the bartender approached him.

"Is there a local beer on draft?" Castillo asked. The waiter gave him a name he'd never heard before.

"One of those, please," Castillo said. "And a menu."

As the phone rang a third time, he pushed its ANSWER button. "Hello?—

"Yes, sir?—

"I just checked into a hotel, sir. The Warwick. I'm about to have dinner—

"Well, that was certainly nice of the . . . him, sir. And thank you for telling me. I'll past the word to Dick, sir—

"He's going to pick me up here at oh-seven-thirty, sir—

"Thank you again, sir. Good night, sir."

He put the cellular back in his pocket as the bartender approached with a glass of beer and a menu.

"What are those gentlemen eating?" Castillo asked, nodding his head slightly toward the four men sitting at the corner table.

"Two cheesesteaks, one meatball and one sausage-and-peppers," the bartender said.

"Italian sausage and peppers?" Castillo asked. The bartender nodded. "Get me one, will you please?"

"Are you some kind of a serviceman?" the brunette asked and moved to the stool next to him.

Wrong again, Charley, you master of analysis you.

"What gave you an idea like that?"

"Yes, sir . . . No, sir . . . Thank you, sir . . . Oh-seven-thirty, sir," the brunette said.

"I'm a Texan; we talk that way."

"You sounded as if whoever you were speaking to was a general or something."

"Actually, he's a member of the president's cabinet and he was calling to tell me the president just did something very nice for a friend of mine who was in a little trouble."

She chuckled, almost laughed.

Nice smile.

"What do you do, actually?"

I'll be damned. She really doesn't look like a hooker.

"Actually, I work for a company called Rig Service, Incorporated, of Corpus Christi, and what we do is service rigs."

"What's a 'rig'?"

"An enormous oil well drilling platform, sitting in the Gulf of Mexico."

"And how do you service them?"

"My end of it is the catering," Castillo said. "You know, the food. And also the laundry. 'Personal needs,' they call it."

"May I ask you something?"

Am I looking for a little action? Am I married? Am I a fag?

"Why not?"

"Could you keep talking to me for a little while?"

"Sure. I'd be happy to."

"I have a little problem," the brunette said.

My sainted, crippled mother desperately needs brain surgery. I don't have the money and I'm willing to do anything—anything—to come up with it.

"My boyfriend was supposed to meet me here a half hour, no, forty-five minutes ago," the brunette said.

"And he's stood you up, you think?"

"No," she said, firmly. "He'll be here. And I'm not trying to get you to buy me a drink or anything like that. But I've been sitting here alone and—you see those men at the table?"

Castillo nodded.

"They keep looking at me. Like I'm a . . . hooker."

"Well, you certainly don't look like a hooker to me."

"Thank you. Well, will you?"

"Will I what?"

"What Frankie does, all the time, is forget to charge his cell phone," the brunette said. "So the battery goes dead and he can't call me. He's somewhere on I-95 right now, I know—he's driving up from Washington, D.C., and it's hard to find a pay phone anywhere anymore, much less on the interstate . . ."

"I would be happy to talk with you until Frankie either gets his batteries charged or shows up, whichever comes first, and would be even happier if you would permit me to buy you a beverage of your choice."

"I couldn't let you do that," the brunette ordered. "But let me treat you!"

She waved at the bartender.

"Give this gentleman another beer," she said. "My treat."

"Sir?" the bartender said.

Jesus, he thinks she's a hooker, too.

Goddammit, I don't think she is.

"We'll have another round, but put it on my tab."

"No, I insist," the brunette said, firmly.

Charley looked at the bartender, who shrugged.

"Okay. Thank you."

Fifteen minutes later, as Castillo was finishing his Italian sausage-and-peppers sandwich, a large young man wearing a zippered jacket and a look of gross annoyance marched into the bar and up to them.

Once Betty explained to Frankie what had happened and how nice Mr. Castle here had been to her while she was waiting for him without a telephone call, much—but by no means all—of the look of annoyance left his face.

Betty and Frankie left. Betty said maybe they'd bump into each other sometime, which did not seem to please Frankie very much.

But when Charley asked for the bill, the barman said, "The broad's boyfriend took care of it."

Charley tipped the bartender anyway and went to his room, and, after leaving a call for quarter to seven, got in bed and went to sleep wondering what it would be like to really work in the catering end of Rig Service, Inc., a wholly owned subsidiary of Castillo Petroleum, Inc., and maybe meet a nice girl—and Betty was a nice girl—by accident in a bar somewhere and seeing what would develop.

[ONE]
Office of the Commanding General
United States Central Command
MacDill Air Force Base
Tampa, Florida
2105 8 June 2005

When General Albert McFadden, USAF, CentCom's deputy commander, appeared in General Naylor's office in response to Naylor's "Right now, please" summons, Lieutenant General George H. Potter, USA, CentCom J-5, was already there.

"I had just bought another bucket of balls," McFadden announced. "What's up, Allan?"

General McFadden was wearing a lemon yellow golf shirt and powder blue slacks. General Potter was wearing a translucent Filipino-style shirt-jacket over white shorts. General Naylor was wearing khaki slacks and a gray USMA sweatshirt. Only Command Sergeant Major Wesley Suggins was in uniform.

"Close the door, please, Wes," General Naylor ordered. "No interruptions."

"Yes, sir," Suggins said.

"I just had a telephone call from the secretary of homeland security," Naylor announced. "In the middle of the call, the president came on the line, primarily, I think, to make it clear that Hall was acting at the president's orders."

Naylor let that sink in for a couple of seconds and then went on.

"There is some reason to believe that the missing 727 is, or was, at a remote airfield in Chad. A place called Abéché."

He pointed to a map laid on the conference table. McFadden and Potter got out of their chairs and examined the map.

"They could make it from there to Mecca easily," General McFadden said.

"Secretary Hall has information suggesting that the airplane was taken by a Somalian terrorist group calling itself the Holy Legion of Muhammad and that it is their intention to crash the plane into the Liberty Bell in Philadelphia," Naylor said.

"Jesus Christ!" General McFadden said. "Where did he get that?"

General Potter rolled his eyes but said nothing.

"The credibility of Secretary Hall's intel depends in large measure on whether or not the 727 is, or was, at Abéché. In other words, if it is there, or was there, the rest of the scenario—that it was seized by the Holy Legion of Muhammad and that they intend to crash it in Philadelphia—becomes more credible . . ."

"The *Liberty Bell*? In *Philadelphia*? Why the hell would they want to do that?" General McFadden asked, incredulously.

". . . And if it is not at Abéché, or was not at Abéché," Naylor went on, a suggestion of impatience in his tone, "then the scenario is probably unlikely. But in the absence of any other intel regarding the missing airplane, the secretary—and/or the president—has obviously decided to go with what he has. CentCom has been ordered to find out as quickly as possible . . ."

"What's the CIA got to say about this?" General McFadden interrupted.

"Let me finish, please, General," Naylor said, icily.

"Sorry, sir," McFadden said, not sounding very apologetic.

"But to get that question out of the way," Naylor said, "while I am sure the CIA is already working on this problem—satellites and human intel, if they have anyone in the region—we have been ordered to find out as quickly as possible—without sharing our intentions with the CIA—whether or not the missing 727 is, or has been, at Abéché or not."

"The CIA's not in the loop?" General Potter asked.

"The CIA is not in the loop," Naylor confirmed. "Suggestions?"

"Off the top of my head," General McFadden said, "I don't know where the nearest Air Commando Pave Low* is. But I can find out in a couple of minutes. We could send one in under the radar—I don't imagine there's much of that in Chad."

Goddammit, Naylor thought, *there you go again. Doesn't the Air Force teach its officers to let—make—the junior officer speak first, so he says what he thinks, rather than what he thinks his seniors want, or don't want, to hear?*

"That would probably take longer than the time we have," Naylor said. "I think the president wants an answer as soon as he can get it. We're talking about hours."

"Delta, sir," General Potter said. "Maybe . . . probably . . . Gray Fox."

Delta Force was Special Forces' elite unit. It was famous; there had even been movies—almost hilariously inaccurate—about it. There had been no movies about Gray Fox, which was an elite unit within Delta, because very few people had even heard rumors about it.

That's the answer I knew I was going to get. And knew I wouldn't like.

"Let's see what General McNab has to say, what he can contribute," Naylor said. "Get him on the horn, please, Wes."

"Yes, sir," Command Sergeant Major Suggins said and went into the "phone booth."

Fifteen seconds later, Suggins called from the phone booth: "Sir, General McNab will be on the line momentarily."

"Bring it in here, Wes, and put it on speakerphone."

Sergeant Major Suggins came into the office carrying the secure telephone, and its thick connecting cable, and placed the instrument on a table between Naylor, Potter, and McFadden. Then he pushed the SPEAKERPHONE button.

Why do I know telling him to do that was a mistake?

The answer came immediately.

"Good evening, sir," the voice of the commanding general of XVIII Airborne Corps, Lieutenant General Bruce J. McNab, boomed over the speaker. "My delay in getting to the telephone was caused by an irresistible summons of nature. My apologies, sir."

---

*The MH-53J "Pave Low III" heavy-lift helicopter is the most technologically advanced helicopter in the world. Its terrain-following, terrain-avoidance radar and forward-looking infrared sensor, along with a projected map display, enable it to perform low-level, long-range, undetected penetration into denied areas, day or night, in adverse weather, for infiltration, exfiltration, and resupply of special operations forces. The helicopter is equipped with armor plating, and a combination of three 7.62mm miniguns or .50 caliber machine guns. It can transport 38 troops or 14 litters and has an external cargo hook with a 20,000-pound (9,000-kilogram) capacity.

"Thank you for sharing that with me, General," Naylor said, his annoyance audible in his voice.

"You're most welcome, sir," McNab said, brightly.

"Goddammit, Scotty, do you always have to be such a wiseass?" Naylor flared.

Naylor was immediately sorry and embarrassed.

"If the general has in any way offended the general, sir," McNab said, sounding very much like a West Point plebe answering the wrath of an upperclassman, "the general is sorry. Sir."

When Naylor glanced at the others, Sergeant Major Suggins was studying the ceiling, General McFadden the floor, and General Potter his wristwatch.

Sonofabitch!

"Scotty, do you know where Abéché, Chad, is?" Naylor asked.

"One moment, sir," McNab said.

Everyone heard what sounded like fingers snapping.

Ten seconds later, General McNab went on.

"Sir, Abéché, Chad, is in a remote section of the country. The coordinates are 13.50.49 north latitude . . ."

"I know where it is, Scotty," Naylor interrupted. "The question was, 'Do you know?' A simple 'Yes, sir' would have sufficed."

"Yes, sir."

"There is a possibility that the 727 stolen from Luanda, Angola, is, or was, there."

"There's a 9,200-foot runway; more than enough for a 727. What's your source?"

Naylor did not answer the question. Instead, he asked, "How soon could you get someone in there to find out for sure, Scotty?"

"Sir, black or out in the open?"

"Under the circumstances, General, I don't believe we'll have time to enter into any diplomatic negotiations with anyone," Naylor said.

Everyone heard, faintly but clearly, General McNab issue an order. "Tommy, sound boots and saddles for Gray Fox."

Then, more clearly, they heard General McNab say, "I understand, sir. Sir, how much support may I expect?"

"What do you need, Scotty?"

"I'd like something available to back up the C-22."

C-22 is the USAF designation for the Boeing 727-100. Ostensibly, all of them are assigned to the Air National Guard. One, however—with a number of modifications—is kept in a closely guarded hangar at Pope Air Force Base, which adjoins Fort Bragg.

"You intend to fly into Abéché?" Naylor blurted.

"No, sir. What I have in mind is Royal Air Maroc flying over Abéché at 35,000 feet," McNab said, his tone suggesting he was talking to a backward child. "Royal Air Maroc, you know, has permission to overfly all those un-friendly countries between Morocco and Saudi Arabia."

What he did not say, but which everyone at the table understood, was that McNab intended to parachute people from his 727 onto the Abéché airfield.

"You think that'll do it, Scotty?"

"Yes, sir. That'll do it. What am I supposed to do with the airplane if it's there?"

"Right now, just find out if it's there or if it was there."

"Yes, sir."

"Will communications be a problem?"

"No, sir."

"I mean to communicate between there and here?"

"We'll have communications between here and there; linking to you is not a problem."

"Why do you want backup for your airplane?"

"I'd sort of like to get my people back, sir. And the communications equipment. Some of that stuff costs a lot of money."

"How quietly can you do this, Scotty?"

"I doubt if anyone will even suspect we're there, sir. Unless, of course, the airplane is there and you tell me to take it out. A blown-up airplane would tend to make people suspect that something was not going quite the way they wanted it to."

"Worst-case scenario, Scotty. Something goes wrong and they find out you're there?"

"That's why I want a little backup. A C-17 III would be nice."

The Boeing C-17 III was a cargo aircraft, capable of using unimproved landing fields. Its four 40,400-thrust-pound engines could drive it at three-quarters the speed of sound to a service ceiling of 45,000 feet with nearly 600,000 pounds of cargo. With in-air refueling, it was capable of flying any-where on the globe.

Naylor looked at McFadden, who nodded, meaning there was a C-17 im-mediately available.

And probably more than one; McFadden's nod had been immediate.

"How do you plan to use it?"

"I'm an optimist. They don't find out we're there. Abéché is not what you can call a bustling airport. Tommy just handed me a data sheet saying there's a once-a-week flight from N'Djamena and that's irregular. I'm going to put maybe four or five people on the ground. They find out about the 727. I am not ordered to take it out. They hide out somewhere near the end of the runway. The C-17—en route somewhere; I haven't figured that out yet—makes a discretionary landing at Abéché. It goes to the end of the runway, opens the door, my guys jump in, and the C-17 takes off. More or less the same scenario if I'm ordered to blow the 727, except that my guys hide out in the boonies near the nearest flat area a C-17 can use. Worst scenario, my guys are on the run from indignant Chad authorities. I'll have some heavy firepower on the C-17 and twenty people. They jump onto the flat area and hold it long enough for the C-17 to touch down and get everybody on board."

"I don't want you to start World War III, Scotty," Naylor thought aloud.

"Funny, I thought we were already fighting World War III," McNab replied.

"I think you take my point, General," Naylor said, coldly.

"I take your point, sir."

"Where do you want the C-17?" Naylor asked.

"Here, as soon as I can have it. It can follow us to Menara."

"Menara?" General McFadden asked.

"Menara, Morocco," McNab replied. "Who was that?"

"General McFadden," Naylor said.

"Good evening, sir," McNab said.

"Good evening, General McNab," McFadden said. "Have you considered a Pave Low?"

"Yes, sir. Time- and distance-wise, it wouldn't work here."

"How are you, Scotty?" Potter said.

"I recognize that unpleasant nasal voice. How are you, George? More important, how many other people are eavesdropping on this fascinating conversation?"

"That's it, Scotty," Naylor replied. "Generals McFadden and Potter, Wes Suggins, and me."

"Good. I'm a devout believer in the theory that the more people who know a secret, the sooner the secret is compromised."

"On that subject, General," Naylor said, "the CIA is not privy to this operation and are not to be made privy to it."

"Jesus, I must have done something right! Thank you for sharing that with me, General."

General Naylor glanced at Command Sergeant Major Suggins and Lieutenant General Potter, both of whom were trying and failing to suppress smiles.

"How soon can you get started on this, Scotty?" Naylor asked.

"We shoot for wheels up in sixty minutes and generally shave a chunk off that."

"Okay," Naylor said. "Get the operation going, General McNab."

"Yes, sir."

[TWO]
Royal Air Force Base
Menara, Morocco
0930 9 June 2005

Among other modifications made to USAF C-22 tail number 6404 was provision for removable fuel bladders. When installed, they gave the aircraft transoceanic range. When 6404 landed—after a six-hour ten-minute flight from Pope Air Force Base—at Menara, which is 120 miles south of Casablanca, it had 2.4 hours of fuel remaining in its main tanks.

Enough, for example, so that it could have diverted to any number of U.S. airbases in Europe, from Spain to Germany, had that been necessary. Diversion was not necessary. At 0805 local time—an hour off the Moroccan coast—the Casablanca control operator cleared U.S. Air Force 6404 to make a refueling stop at Menara.

It touched down smoothly at 0925 and, five minutes later, it had been tugged into a hangar, whereupon the hangar doors had closed.

Royal Moroccan Air Force technicians quickly plugged in power and air-conditioning ducts. The rear door of the aircraft—under the tail—extended from the fuselage, and two men came quickly down the stairs, both wearing khaki pants and white T-shirts.

A slight man in a light brown flight suit stood at the foot of the stairs. A leather patch on the chest of the flight suit identified him as a colonel—and pilot—of the Royal Moroccan Air Force. Behind him stood another pilot colonel in a flight suit. He was older, much stockier, and had a thick, British-style mustache.

Both Moroccan officers saluted and both Americans returned them.

"Good morning, General," the slight man said in only faintly accented English.

"Good morning, Your Royal Highness," Lieutenant General Bruce J.

McNab, USA, replied as he returned the salute. "I am deeply honored that Your Royal Highness has found time in his busy schedule for me."

"I always have time for you, General," the colonel said. "And not only because I'm fond of you."

"Let me guess," McNab said, "a member of your family has questions."

" 'I need a favor' covers a lot of ground, General, even between friends."

"You remember Colonel Thomas, don't you, Your Royal Highness?"

"Of course," the colonel said. "It's good to see you again, Tommy."

"Always a pleasure, sir," Lieutenant Colonel H. Alexander Thomas said.

"And how are you, Colonel?" McNab asked.

"Very well, General," the man with the mustache said.

The slim man made a gesture with his hand and McNab followed him until they stood beside the landing gear.

"An American 727 was stolen a couple of weeks ago from Luanda," McNab said.

"I saw that."

"There is some reason to believe it's either on the ground, or was, at Abéché, Chad. I'm supposed to find out if that's so."

"And retake it? Or destroy it?"

"My orders right now are just to see if it is, or was, there," McNab said.

"Orders subject to change, of course."

"I don't think they will be. If retaking it was on the agenda, I would have been told, I think, to send a crew with my people. If they wanted to take it out, sending in an unmanned aerial vehicle would be a lot cheaper and less riskier than this." He pointed to the C-22.

The slim man didn't say anything for a long, thoughtful moment.

"That's it, General?"

"That's all I have, Your Royal Highness."

"And the basic plan?"

"Drop five people on Abéché. From a Royal Air Maroc transport overflying Chad en route to Jiddah. Have them find out what they can."

"How are you going to get them out?"

"A C-17's about two hours behind me. I'm going to use that."

"So all you want to do is fly to Jiddah?"

"And back here."

Again, the slim man thought over what he had heard.

"Is that somehow disturbing to you?" McNab asked.

"Why was the airplane stolen? Do you know, can you tell me?"

"I can tell you that we think it was stolen by a Somalian group who call themselves the 'Holy Legion of Muhammad.' "

"Never heard of them," the slender man said. *"Somalian?"*

"Neither had we, Your Royal Highness," McNab said. "There are two possible scenarios, neither with much to support them. The first is that they intend to crash it into the *ka'ba* in Mecca . . ."

"That's absurd!"

"It sounds absurd, Your Royal Highness, but, on the other hand, the airplane—if it is in Abéché—is within range of Mecca."

"The Holy Legion of Muhammad?" the slim man repeated and then raised his voice and called, "Satu!"

The bearded colonel walked quickly to them.

"Your Highness?"

"One moment," the slim man said. "And the other scenario, General?"

"That they intend to crash it into the Liberty Bell in Philadelphia," McNab said.

"I don't know what that means."

"In Philadelphia, where our Founding Fathers signed our Declaration of Independence, is Constitution Hall . . ."

"I know about Constitution Hall," the slim man said. "I've actually been there, as a matter of fact. But what's that got to do with a bell?"

"Immediately adjacent to it, Your Royal Highness, is the Liberty Bell. It has a certain emotional, historical significance to Americans. Much like Constitution Hall itself."

"I wonder why the Holy Legion of Muhammad would be interested," the slim man said. "For that matter, I wonder how they even heard of it. What do we know about these people, Satu?"

"What people, Your Highness?"

"The Holy Legion of Muhammad," the slim man said, impatiently. "They're Somalis."

"I never heard of them, Your Highness."

"To answer your question, General," the slim man said, "yes, I find this disturbing. I will have to ask a certain member of my family how to proceed. But in the meantime, I think you should ask Tommy to begin the chameleon process."

"Thank you, sir."

"You and I will go to the officers' mess for breakfast," the slim man said. "Colonel Ben-Satu will stay here long enough to ensure that Tommy has whatever he needs. Then he finds out what he can about the Holy Legion of Muhammad and brings that information to the mess."

"Yes, Your Highness."

"Tommy!" the slim man raised his voice.

"Coming, sir!" Lieutenant Colonel Thomas said as he started at a trot toward them.

"Yes, sir?"

"How many men do you have with you?"

"Counting the Air Force, Your Highness . . ."

"Yes, by all means, let's count the Air Force," the slim man said.

"Fifteen, sir. That includes the general and me."

"Good. Let's count you two as well," the slim man said. "I will have the mess send breakfast for thirteen here. When you believe your chameleon operation is sufficiently under way, you might wish to join General McNab and me at the mess. I'll leave a car for you."

"Yes, sir. Thank you, sir."

"Tommy, please make sure that none of your men leave the hangar for any purpose."

"Yes, sir."

"Colonel Ben-Satu will ensure that you have whatever you need."

"Thank you, Your Highness."

"Shall we go, Scotty?" the slim man said.

There were three identical black Mercedes 320L sedans outside the hangar. One of them took the slim man and McNab to the officers' mess, a long, sand-colored building near the flight line.

The twenty-odd officers in the dining room rose as one man when someone spotted the slim man, who immediately waved them back into their chairs.

He led McNab to a table in the corner of the room.

"Order fried eggs, potatoes, toast, and coffee for me, please," the slim man said. "I have a couple of calls to make."

Then he walked out of the room.

Ten minutes later, he came back into the dining room. All of the officers—now including McNab and Thomas—rose to their feet and were immediately waved back into them by the slim man.

"That was quick, Tommy," the slim man said as he sat down.

"They don't need me to help with the plane, sir," Thomas said. "I'm just in the way."

A waiter delivered three plates of fried eggs, potatoes, and toast.

"That fellow we were talking about earlier, Scotty?" the slim man said.

"Yes, sir?"

"He doesn't believe either of your scenarios, either, but he thinks that looking into it is a very good idea."

"Thank you, Your Royal Highness."

"And, of course, he is pleased to be of some small service to an old friend," the slim man said. "He asked me tell you that."

"I'm honored that he thinks of me as an old friend," McNab said.

"I'm sure he does, but I believe he was talking of our countries," the slim man said. "Did you know, Tommy, that Morocco was the first nation to recognize the U.S.? Even before it was the U.S. In 1777?"

"No, Your Highness. I didn't know that," Lieutenant Colonel Thomas confessed.

"My own history is a little fuzzy. But I think your seat of government was then in Philadelphia."

"I believe it was," McNab said.

"And was this bell—the 'Liberty Bell,' you said? Was that in Philadelphia at the time? And, if so, what is the connection?"

"Your Highness, I am more than a little ashamed to say I have no idea," General McNab confessed. "It probably was but I just don't know."

The slim man waved a finger at General McNab.

"That is terrible," he said.

[THREE]
Royal Air Force Base
Menara, Morocco
1220 9 June 2005

A red-and-yellow tug pulled what three hours earlier had been U.S. Air Force C-22 tail number 6404 from the hangar.

What the slim man had called "the chameleon process" had been completed twenty minutes before.

Plastic decalcomania had been applied to the fuselage with just enough adhesive to hold them in place for a short time. There were now green and red stripes running from the nose to the tail down both sides of the 727's fuselage. The words ROYAL AIR MAROC now appeared from just aft of the flight compartment windows rearward. There was now a red shooting star on both sides of the vertical stabilizer. Beneath it, in the largest letters of all, were the initials R A M in red.

Once everything had been stuck in place, the decalcomania had been sprayed with a very expensive clear, quick-drying paint. It was by no means permanent, but tests had shown it would stand up to fifty hours of high-speed flight at altitude, thirty-six hours in the sun at 120 degrees Fahrenheit, and forty-eight hours at −20 degrees Fahrenheit.

It was not believed the paint was going to have to last anywhere near that long. Within thirty-six hours, at the most, it was hoped that Royal Air Maroc 905, now named *Rabat*, would be back in the hangar at Menara, where it would be sprayed with a solvent even more expensive than the paint. The solvent would in a matter of minutes chemically attack the paint and permit both the paint and the decalcomania to be removed in a very short time.

The engines were started and *Rabat* taxied to the threshold of the runway, and—having been cleared to do so—turned onto the runway without stopping and lifted off.

The Royal Air Force controller in the tower informed Casablanca Area Control that RAM 905 was off the ground at two-five past the hour, destination Jiddah, Saudi Arabia.

At that precise moment, Major Carlos G. Castillo pushed his way through the circular door of the Warwick Hotel in Philadelphia and took the few steps down to Locust Street.

[FOUR]
The Warwick Hotel
1701 Locust Street
Philadelphia, Pennsylvania
0725 9 June 2005

Castillo looked up and down Locust Street, his eyes falling on a life-sized statue of a man with an umbrella erected almost directly across the street. Then he heard two beeps of a horn and when he looked for the sound saw Miller's arm waving from the front seat of a dark blue Buick sedan parked fifty feet from the hotel entrance.

He walked quickly toward it, and, as he approached, Miller opened the rear door from the inside.

The driver was a small, wiry, light-skinned man with a precisely manicured mustache.

"Good morning, General," Castillo said, courteously.

Major General H. Richard Miller, Sr., USA, Retired, turned on the seat and pointed a finger at Castillo.

"The first time I saw you, Castillo—you were a plebe at the time—I knew you were going to be trouble."

"Sir, if the general is referring to Dick's . . . return . . . from Africa. That situation has been taken care of, sir."

" 'Taken care of'? What the hell does that mean? Good God, a Miller relieved for cause!"

"How, Charley?" Major H. Richard Miller, Jr., asked.

"The president is sending you a letter of commendation, via the Defense Intelligence Agency CG," Castillo said. "Secretary Hall called last night to tell me."

"What that will do," General Miller said, not at all mollified, "is cause Dick's records to be flagged 'political influence.' That's almost as bad as the comment 'relieved for cause.' "

General Miller moved his icy glare from Castillo long enough to look for a break in the traffic, found one, and pulled away from the curb.

Major Miller turned on the seat, and with a combination of facial expressions, shrugged shoulders, and other body language managed to convey to Castillo that he was sorry his father had attacked Castillo, but, on the other hand, that Charley knew the general and thus what to expect.

Charley used a combination of gestures to signal that he understood the situation and that he didn't mind.

Castillo thought: *Jesus Christ, thank God I didn't go home with Dick last night! If I had, I would have had nonstop General Miller in an outrage. This will be over as soon as we get to Police Headquarters, and, no thank you, Dick, I will not go home with you later to at least say hi to your mother.*

Their route to Police Headquarters took them around City Hall and toward the Delaware River. Castillo thought he remembered that Constitution Hall and the Liberty Bell were somewhere in the area but he wasn't sure.

Jesus, here I am, trying to keep a bunch of lunatic terrorists from crashing an airplane into it and I don't even know where it is!

Police Headquarters turned out to be a curved building a couple of blocks off Market Street. The parking lot into which General Miller drove the Buick had a sign reading POLICE VEHICLES ONLY. General Miller pulled the car into a parking slot with a sign reading CHIEF INSPECTORS ONLY, turned off the ignition, and opened the door.

Then he put his head back in the door and announced, "Let's go, Castillo! We don't want to keep the commissioner waiting, do we?"

My God, he's going with us!

"Sir, are you going with us?"

General Miller's response was a shake of the head, indicating his disgust with a stupid question, followed by an impatient hand gesture meaning, "Let's go, let's go!"

There is absolutely nothing I can do about this.

What the hell is he up to?

A policeman walked up to them.

"Sir, you can't park there, that's reserved for chief inspectors."

"I'm General Miller, here to see the commissioner," the general replied. "He advised me to park there. I'm surprised you weren't so notified. If there is a problem, I suggest you call him."

The policeman looked at General Miller carefully and then nodded and walked away.

Inside the building, through a glass door, there were four waist-high columns through which police and civilian employees passed swiping identity cards. To the right of the columns was a desk for visitors manned by a uniformed officer.

"General Miller and two others to see Commissioner Kellogg," General Miller announced.

"Sir, I was led to believe that the commissioner expects us at eight," Castillo said. "It's only seven-forty."

"Then your information is incorrect," General Miller said.

They were obviously expected, for the policeman immediately produced three visitor badges and pushed the button which released the barrier in the visitor turnstile.

They boarded an elevator, which was, like the rest of the building, curved, and rode up.

When the elevator door opened, a detective, or a plainclothes policeman, was waiting for them.

"Good morning, General," he said. "The commissioner expects you."

General Miller's response was a curt nod of the head.

They followed the police officer—Castillo couldn't see any kind of a badge, but there was a Glock 9mm semiautomatic pistol in a skeleton holster on his belt—down the corridor, to another desk, manned by another plainclothes officer, where they signed the visitors' register and were allowed to pass first through an outer office and then into what was apparently the commissioner's office.

A very large black man in a well-fitting dark blue suit rose from behind his desk and smiled.

"Good morning, Richard," he said, offering his hand and then offering it to Major Miller. "It's good to see you, Dick. It's been a while."

"Good morning, sir."

"And this is?"

"That, Commissioner," General Miller said, "is Major Carlos G. Castillo, and I am here to tell you something about him."

"I was expecting the special assistant to the secretary of homeland security," Commissioner Kellogg said. "But how do you do, Major?"

"How do you do, sir?" Charley said.

"Will what you have to tell me about Major Castillo wait until we have some coffee?" the commissioner asked as he waved them into chairs.

"I'll pass on the coffee, thank you," General Miller said. "I realize your time is valuable and this won't take long."

The commissioner sat in his chair and made a go-ahead signal with both hands.

"I have known Major Castillo since he and Dick were plebes at West Point," General Miller began. "They were then, and are now, like a container of gasoline and a match. One or the other lights the match and the other blows up."

"Really?" the commissioner said with a smile.

"Furthermore, Major Castillo, rather than adhering to the West Point code of Duty, Honor, and Country at all times, has frequently chosen to follow the Jesuit philosophy that the end justifies the means."

"There is a point, right, Richard, to this character assassination?" the commissioner asked. He was smiling, but it was strained.

"On one such occasion," General Miller went on, "three very senior officers reluctantly concluded that the weather, the time of day, and enemy ground-to-air missile and automatic weapons capability absolutely precluded the dispatch of a medical evacuation—"dust off"—helicopter to attempt to rescue the crew of a shot-down helicopter in mountainous terrain in Afghanistan.

"When they presented their recommendation to the general officer in overall command, they told him they had reached their conclusion despite their painful awareness that a no-fly decision would almost certainly result in the death of two of its crew members, who were seriously wounded, and the death or capture of the other personnel on the helicopter, a total of five officers and three enlisted men.

"The bottom line, as they say, was that sending a rescue helicopter, which would almost certainly either be itself shot down or crash because of the weather conditions, could not be justified.

"The commanding general, with a reluctance, I submit, that only another senior commander who has been forced to make such decisions can possibly understand, accepted the recommendation of his staff and gave the no-fly order.

"Major Castillo, who was serving in what I shall euphemistically describe as a 'liaison capacity' to that headquarters, was privy to the final discussion of the situation and the commanding general's decision.

"On hearing that decision, he went to the flight line and, in direct disobedience to the general's order, took over —stole—a Black Hawk helicopter and flying it alone—it has a two-pilot crew—went to the crash site and rescued everyone there."

"Jesus!" the commissioner said, looking at Castillo.

"One of the two seriously wounded officers Major Castillo rescued was Dick," General Miller said.

"With all respect, sir," Castillo blurted. "They were wrong. I knew I could do it. It wasn't anywhere near as foolhardy as you make it sound."

"Major, you are a West Pointer," General Miller said evenly, measuring each word. "You knew full well the meaning of the oath you took to obey the orders of the officers appointed over you. It did not mean obedience to only such orders as you happen to agree with; it meant cheerful and willing obedience to any and all orders."

Castillo said nothing.

"On the other hand," General Miller went on, trying but not quite keeping his voice from quavering, "it is equally clear to me that I am deeply indebted to you for saving my son's life. Since I have not previously had the opportunity, permit me to thank you now. My wife and I, and Dick's brother and sisters, are deeply in your debt, Major Castillo."

General Miller stood. "Thank you, Commissioner, for allowing me this opportunity in your office, in your presence, before an old friend."

"Sir," Castillo said, softly, "Dick would have done the same thing for me."

"Yes, I daresay he would. That brings us back to what I said about you two being a gasoline can and a match."

He started for the door, then turned.

"Mrs. Miller would be pleased if your schedule would permit you to take dinner with us," he said and then went through the doorway.

The commissioner shook his head.

"Your dad does have a way of capturing your attention, doesn't he?"

"Sir, I had no idea he was going to come up here with us," Miller said.

"I suspected that," the commissioner said. "May I ask you a question, Major Miller?"

"Certainly, sir."

"What did he mean when he said 'euphemistically describe as a "liaison capacity" '?"

Castillo hesitated.

"Sorry I asked," the commissioner said.

I can't let him think that I'm not telling him everything, Castillo thought, then said slowly, "Sir, I was with a Delta Force detachment. We were looking for Usama bin Laden."

"You were commanding the Delta Force detachment, Charley," Miller corrected him. "There's a difference."

The commissioner shook his head in amazement, or disbelief, and then smiled.

"Funny, you don't look like Sylvester Stallone," he said. "Okay, let's get to it. What can the Philadelphia Police Department do for the Department of Homeland Security?"

"Sir," Castillo began, "on May twenty-third, a 727 aircraft belonging to Lease-Aire, Inc., of Philadelphia, was stolen from the airport in Luanda, Angola . . ."

"Apparently, Secretary Hall thinks this incredible story is credible enough to send you here to warn me about this," the commissioner said. "I presume the governor and the mayor have been notified?"

"Sir, that's not why I was sent here," Castillo said. "What Dick and I are to do is find out what we can—if there is anything to find out—about a possible connection between somebody in Philadelphia and the people we think stole the airplane."

"You're telling me the mayor and the governor have not been notified?" the commissioner asked, incredulously.

"Sir, we don't *know* that the airplane was stolen by terrorists, and, even if that is the case, that they intend to use it as a flying bomb here. What we're doing is trying to find out what happened to it. Every agency of the federal government with any interest in this at all is trying very hard, using all their assets, to find out what happened to that airplane."

"But you think, don't you, that it was stolen by terrorists of some sort, Somalians or somebody else?"

"Yes, sir, but that's my personal opinion. No more."

"And you think it's possible, at least, that these people intend to fly the airplane into the Liberty Bell?"

"Yes, sir, I do. But again, that's just my personal opinion. I have nothing to go on except what Pevsner told me in Vienna. And we won't know whether or not the airplane is, or was, in Chad for some time."

"Going off at a tangent, how are you going to find out one way or the other if it's where this Russian said it is? Or was."

"I haven't been told that, sir. I'm sure the satellites will really give that airport some close study. I don't know what humint sources the CIA or anyone else . . ."

"Humint, meaning 'human intelligence'? CIA agents? That sort of thing?" the commissioner interrupted.

"Yes, sir. And it's possible—even likely, if we don't have people in the area—that they'll send in an Air Force Special Ops Pave Low helicopter. They'll find out just as soon as they can. Maybe within an hour, maybe not for twenty-four hours. And until they do, all we have is speculation."

"I wonder if you understand my problem, Major Castillo."

"I'm not sure I follow you, sir."

"There are two people responsible for the safety of people in Philadelphia. One is the mayor, and the other one is me. Don't misunderstand this. The mayor is probably the best one we've had since Frank Rizzo. But he doesn't know how to direct traffic, much less handle the nuts-and-bolts problems that would result from a plane crash in downtown Philadelphia."

The commissioner saw the look on Castillo's face.

"You can see where I'm going, right?" he asked. "And none of this occurred to you before?"

"No, sir," Castillo confessed.

"If there is even a slight chance that this incredible scenario is going to come to pass, then it would seem we should have whatever precautionary measures we can, right? Warn the citizens, etcetera, etcetera."

"Yes, sir."

"There are problems with that," the commissioner said. "Starting with panic. And there is also the problem of crying wolf. If the mayor puts these measures into play and nothing happens, not only is he going to look like a fool but the next time this happens people would not pay attention. Most people are already starting to think of the World Trade towers going down as something they saw in a movie starring Charlton Heston and Paul Newman." He paused. "Still with me?"

"Yes, sir. I believe I am."

"The mayor, as I say, is about as fine a leader as they come. Unfortunately, he is also a politician. I have absolute confidence in my deputy commissioners. I have virtually none in the mayor's staff. I am very much afraid that if I pass this situation on to the mayor—and it is clearly my duty to do so—he will pass it on to certain members of his staff and they will either panic and let the story out or they will do so consciously, seeing the mayor on television defending the city from terrorist attack as a very good way to ensure his reelection.

"If there is a flurry of activity against this potential attack and nothing happens, I think it might well cost him reelection and I would hate to see that happen."

"Jesus H. Christ!" Miller said, softly.

"Your father just now alluded to making unpleasant choices when it is clearly your duty to do so," the commissioner said. "I am about to do something like that. I am going to both fail to do what I know I am duty bound to do and I'm going to lie, and so are you."

"Sir?"

"When you and Dick came in here, Major, you told me nothing of this crash of an aircraft into the Liberty Bell scenario. Your visit to my office was in the nature of a courtesy call. Secretary Hall wanted my assistance in your investigation of Lease-Aire, Incorporated. I of course told you I would be happy to cooperate."

"Yes, sir," Castillo said.

"You said a moment ago, Major, that you believe there will be information regarding the location of this missing airplane within twenty-four hours?"

"Yes, sir. Perhaps a little less time than that."

The commissioner looked at his watch.

"It is now eight-thirty," he said. "In thirty-two hours, it will be four-thirteen tomorrow afternoon. At that time, I'm going to the mayor with this. He will like that because it will give him time to make the six o'clock news. You understand me? I don't want any misunderstandings about this, and it goes without saying that I expect you to immediately bring me up to speed on any further developments."

"I understand, sir," Castillo said.

"And, Dick," the commissioner went on, "I don't want you to tell your dad about this under any circumstances. I love him like a brother, but he has, as he says and has shown, that West Point Duty, Honor, Country philosophy, and I don't want him doing something he feels duty and honor require him to do. What this situation requires is someone with the philosophy your dad says the major has: that the end—protecting Philadelphia—justifies the means."

"I understand, sir," Miller said.

The commissioner rose from behind his desk.

"We're now going to the Counterterrorism Bureau. I will ask the commanding officer of the Organized Crime and Intelligence Unit—they're in the same building—to meet us there," he said. "I don't know what they have on any connection between our local African American terrorists—who so far have limited their efforts to bring Philadelphia to its knees by taking potshots at passing patrol cars—and any other terrorists, but if anyone has that information they will. I will tell Chief Inspector Kramer and Captain O'Brien that they are to give you anything and everything they have or can develop. I will tell Chief Inspector Kramer that twice because he has an unfortunate tendency to obey only those orders he considers wise and reasonable."

"Thank you very much, Commissioner," Castillo said.

"Be warned that neither of these officers is going to be willing to share any more than he feels he absolutely has to with either an Army officer or the special assistant to the secretary of homeland security. But if either of them really gets his back up, get back to me—right away—and I'll have another chat with him."

"Sir, how does—Chief Inspector Kramer and Captain O'Brien, you said?—feel about the Secret Service?"

"The Secret Service? I don't know. I know Kramer hates the FBI with a fine Pennsylvania Dutchman's passion. And I don't think O'Brien thinks very highly about the FBI, either. The Secret Service? I don't know. Why do you ask?"

"Sir, I have credentials identifying me as a supervisory special agent of the Secret Service," Castillo said.

The commissioner looked at him for a long moment, shaking his head.

"What do we say about Dick? Or does he have a Secret Service shield, too?"

"I think we can probably get by by showing my credentials," Castillo said.

"Okay. That'll work."

The commissioner waved them through his office door ahead of him.

He stopped at a desk manned by a uniformed sergeant.

"Put out the arm for Chief Inspector Kramer and Captain O'Brien," he ordered. "Have them meet me right now in Kramer's office at the arsenal."

"Yes, sir."

"Have an unmarked car, a good one with all communications, delivered out there right away. If one isn't available, take one away from somebody else."

"Yes, sir."

"We are cooperating with the Secret Service, that's all you know."

"Yes, sir."

"Come on, Jack," the commissioner said to the plainclothes policeman who had been waiting for them at the elevator. "We're going for a ride."

"Yes, sir."

"Jack, this is Supervisory Special Agent Castillo of the Secret Service and Special Agent Miller. Gentlemen, this is my executive officer, Captain Jack Hanrahan."

The men shook hands as they walked to the elevator.

[FIVE]
Frankford Industrial Complex
Philadelphia, Pennsylvania
0825 9 June 2005

"Déjà vu, all over again," Major H. Richard Miller, Jr., said, shortly after Captain Jack Hanrahan had turned the commissioner's unmarked Ford Crown Victoria off Tacony Street in Northeast Philadelphia into what looked like an old industrial complex of brick warehouses. "I have been here before. What is this place?"

The commissioner chuckled.

"It used to be the Frankford Arsenal," he said.

"Yeah," Miller said, remembering. "We used to come to the commissary here when I was a little kid."

"When they closed the arsenal, the city tried to turn it into an industrial park," the commissioner said. "That didn't work, so they let unimportant parts of the city government—the police, for instance—use the buildings."

Hanrahan pulled up before a small, century-old, two-story brick building, into a slot marked CHIEF INSPECTOR KRAMER, picked a microphone from the seat, and said, "C-One at CT."

Castillo looked for a sign on the redbrick building but couldn't see one.

Everybody got out of the car, and the commissioner walked purposefully into the building, visibly startling two uniformed police officers on their way out who obviously did not expect to run into the commissioner. The others followed him.

Just inside the small lobby, to the right, was an unmarked door. There was a door buzzer button set into the wall beside it. The commissioner pressed it.

A not very charming voice came over a small loudspeaker: "Yeah?"

"Open the door," the commissioner ordered.

"Who is it?"

"It's the commissioner."

"Bullshit!"

"What do I have to do, take the damned door?"

There was the sound of a solenoid, and, when the commissioner pushed on the door, it now opened.

Beyond the door was a stairway. The commissioner went up the stairs two at a time. At the head of the stairs was an embarrassed-looking black man wearing a shoulder holster.

"Commissioner, I'm sorry. I didn't . . ."

The commissioner waved a hand, meaning, "No problem."

"Chief Inspector Kramer?" the commissioner asked.

"I just don't know, sir. I'll put the arm out for him. Captain O'Brien's waiting for him, too."

He nodded across the room toward a glass-walled office.

"The arm's already supposed to be out," the commissioner said.

"I'll find out what's happened, sir," the man—Castillo and Miller both assumed he was a detective—said.

The commissioner walked across the crowded room to the glass-walled office, signaling the others to follow him. As they got close, a uniformed captain got out of a chair.

The commissioner shook his hand but made no introductions, instead saying, "We'll wait for Fritz."

He sat down at a desk that had a small nameplate on it reading CHIEF INSPECTOR F.W. KRAMER, took out his wallet, and looked inside.

"Anybody got two bucks?" he asked. "Kramer is very sensitive about his coffee kitty."

Castillo was first to come up with the money. Captain Hanrahan took it from his hand and left the office.

Miller nudged Castillo and indicated with a nod of his head at what first appeared to be a poster for *The Green Berets* movie in 1968 starring John Wayne, but when Castillo took a second look he saw that Wayne's face had been painted over. The face was now that of a smiling young man and the blaze on the beret was now that of the 10th Special Forces Group.

The detective put his head in the door.

"Two minutes, Commissioner," he announced.

"Thank you," the commissioner said.

Captain Hanrahan returned with a tray holding mugs of coffee thirty seconds before a very tall, trim, very tough-looking man with a full head of curly gray hair walked into the office. He was wearing a shirt, tie, and tweed jacket that had left a clothing store a long time ago. The butt of a Colt .45 ACP semi-automatic pistol rose above his belt.

"To what do I owe the honor?" he demanded, then, "Hanrahan, you better have fed the kitty."

"The kitty's been fed, Inspector," Captain Hanrahan said.

"Gentlemen, this is Chief Inspector Kramer, who commands the Counterterrorism Bureau," the commissioner said. "We go back a long way. About the time of Noah's ark, we were sergeants in Major Crimes. And this is Captain O'Brien, who heads the Organized Crime and Intelligence Unit. This is Supervisory Agent Castillo of the Secret Service and Special Agent Miller."

Kramer examined Castillo and Miller carefully but didn't so much as nod his head. O'Brien offered his hand to both.

"Listen carefully, both of you," the commissioner said. "You are to give them not only whatever they ask for but whatever else—anything—you even suspect they might have use for."

Captain O'Brien said, "Yes, sir."

Chief Inspector Kramer said nothing.

"You heard me, Fritz?" the commissioner said. "You understand me?"

Kramer didn't reply directly.

"You going to tell me what this is all about?" he asked.

"Mr. Castillo will tell you what you have to know. Which will not be all you'd like to know. Understood?"

Kramer nodded, just perceptibly.

"And the fewer people around here who even know they're here, the better. Understood?"

Kramer nodded again.

"I want you to assign somebody—somebody who knows what's going on around here—full-time, until this is over. I ordered an unmarked car sent here."

"I get another car? This must be important," Kramer said.

"It is, Fritz, believe me. And I don't want to hear from Mr. Castillo that either one of you is not giving him anything he wants. And I've told him to call me the minute he suspects that."

"Okay. I heard you," Kramer said.

"We'll be in touch," the commissioner said to Castillo and Miller, and then, waving to Hanrahan to follow him, walked out of Kramer's office.

Chief Inspector Kramer went behind his desk, sat down, leaned back in the chair, and put both hands behind his head.

"Okay, Mr. Castillo, ask away. What does the Secret Service want to know?"

"What I'd like to know," Miller said, nodding at the John Wayne movie poster, "is who's the ugly character wearing the blaze of the Tenth Group."

Kramer's glower would have cowed a lesser man. Captain O'Brien's face showed clearly that he understood it was not wise to comment on the poster, or say anything that could possibly be construed as criticism of U.S. Army Special Forces in Kramer's hearing.

"What do you know about the Tenth Special Forces Group?" Kramer asked, icily.

"He was in the Tenth," Castillo said. "Then they found out he could read and write and wasn't queer and sent him to flight school."

"Two wiseasses?" Kramer asked, but there was the hint of a smile on his thin lips.

"Charley spent too much time in the stockade at Bragg," Miller said. "His brain got curdled."

"Delta Force? No shit?" Captain O'Brien asked.

"Delta Force? What's Delta Force?" Castillo replied.

"The name Reitzell mean anything to you, Mr. Castillo?"

"If your Reitzell is Johnny, and has a wife named Glenda, yeah, I know him."

"And if I called the colonel up and asked about you, what would he say?"

"He'd probably tell you he never heard of Delta and to mind your own business," Castillo said.

"Yeah, that's probably exactly what Colonel Johnny would do," Kramer said.

He got out of his chair and offered his hand first to Miller and then to Castillo.

"As I was saying, Mr. Castillo, what does the Secret Service want to know?"

"You've heard about the 727 that's gone missing from Angola?"

Kramer and O'Brien both nodded.

"Not for dissemination, anywhere; there's a scenario that it was stolen by Somalian terrorists who intend to crash it into the Liberty Bell."

O'Brien's face showed incredulity at that announcement. Kramer's face didn't change, but he took a moment to consider it.

"You wouldn't come in here with a yarn like that unless you and some other people who can actually find their asses with one hand in the dark believed there was something to it," Kramer said, finally.

"It's not even close to being for sure, but it's all we've got at the moment. The same source who told us the airplane was grabbed by Somalians and is probably in Chad—or was in Chad; they're running that down—said there may be a Philadelphia connection. That's what we need."

"Maybe," Kramer said. "We have some AALs—that stands for 'African American Lunatics'—in town who would love to see something like that. Right now, all they're doing is throwing Molotov cocktails at patrol cars, sniping at—correction, *shooting at* patrol cars; they're not snipers, as we understand the term—but they're ambitious. I'll see what I can turn up."

"Inspector . . ."

"Call me 'Dutch,' " Kramer interrupted. "That's what they called me in Special Forces."

"I'm Charley," Castillo said.

"Dick," Miller said.

"Dutch, we need what you have yesterday," Castillo said.

"I've got some people inside," Kramer said. "And so does Captain O'Brien—sometimes intelligence and counterterrorism overlaps. There's four major groups of AALs, and, between us, we've got one, two, or three people in each bunch, but they're in deep, you follow me? We can't get on the phone and say, 'Jack, I need what you have on a Somalian connection.' It'll take us several hours, at least, to get in touch with any one of them. And anywhere from an hour or more after that to set up a meet."

"You're talking about cops or informants?" Castillo asked.

"Cops," Kramer said. "Good cops who have their balls on the chopping block twenty-four hours a day. We don't want to blow their cover, and we don't want them killed. Understand?"

Castillo nodded.

Kramer said, "Nothing has come across my desk . . ."

"Mine, either," O'Brien interrupted.

". . . which could mean there is nothing," Kramer went on, "or it could mean they're afraid to say something because it sounds like something that would come from a coke-fried brain."

"I understand," Castillo said.

"The fing FBI was in here a couple of days ago . . ."

"The what?" Miller asked.

"A couple of fing assholes from the fing FBI, wanting to know what, if anything, I had on Lease-Aire, Inc."

"Fing?" Miller pursued.

"That's not nearly as offensive in mixed company as 'fucking,' is it?" Kramer asked, innocently.

"And what did you tell the fing FBI?" Castillo asked, smiling.

"The fing truth. I didn't have a fing thing on Lease-Aire, Inc."

The four men were now smiling at one another.

"But maybe you should go out and have a talk with them. I'll send one of my people with you," Kramer said.

"Makes sense," Miller said. "Thank you."

"Who's that young woman?" Castillo asked.

O'Brien and Miller followed the nod of his head.

A good-looking young woman in a skirt and sweater, which almost, but not entirely, concealed the Glock semiautomatic she wore in the small of her back, was bent over the second drawer of a filing cabinet.

"Why do you want to know?" Kramer inquired.

"I think I met her last night," Castillo said.

He saw the look on Miller's face, which said, *Jesus Christ, Charley. We lucked out and got to play the Special Forces card with this guy and now you and your constant hard-on are going to fuck it up big-time!*

"It's not what you think, Dick," Castillo said, the response to which was another facial distortion that meant, *Oh, bullshit!*

"Schneider!" Kramer boomed. "Get in here, please!"

The brunette walked to the office door, her face registering mild surprise at seeing Castillo, and stopped.

"Inside, Sergeant," Kramer ordered, "and close the door."

"Yes, sir," she said and complied.

"I understand you've seen this guy before," Kramer said. "But somehow I don't think you've been properly introduced. Sergeant Betty Schneider, this is Supervisory Special Agent Castillo, of the Secret Service. Sergeant Schneider works for Captain O'Brien."

"He told me he was in the food-catering business for oil well rigs, or whatever they call them."

"And what did you tell him?"

"That I was waiting for my boyfriend," she said.

"Tell him what you were really doing. He has the commissioner's personal blessing, and, more important, mine."

"Tony Frisco and Cats Cazzaro were having a sandwich at the Warwick bar with two characters from the Coney Island Mafia . . ."

"That's the Russian mob, Mr. Castillo. Really nice folks," O'Brien explained.

"The table was wired. They were giving me the eye, so I made a play for . . . this gentleman."

"Get anything?" O'Brien asked.

She shook her head.

"You think they made you?" he asked.

She shook her head again.

"But they were antsy enough about you to worry you?"

"Yes, sir."

"Which means O'Brien can't use you again for a while there," Kramer said. "Right, Frank?"

O'Brien nodded. "Which makes her available to Mr. Castillo . . ."

"He said his name was Castle," she blurted.

"That okay with you, Frank?" Kramer asked.

"Done. Schneider, until further orders you will sit on these two gentlemen."

"Yes, sir," she said.

"There's supposed to be an unmarked car here. If it's not here already, it will be soon. Take Mr. Castillo and Special Agent Miller out to Lease-Aire at the airport and wherever else they think, or you think, they should go. Do whatever they want you to do. And don't tell anybody what you're doing."

"Can I ask what this is all about?"

"Mr. Castillo will tell you what you have to know, Sergeant," Kramer said, then asked, "This okay with you, Charley?"

"It's fine, Dutch. Thank you very much."

"And while you're out at the airport, I'll put the arm out for those other people we were talking about."

"The sooner, the better," Castillo said.

"I know," Kramer said.

"Anytime, gentlemen," Sergeant Schneider said.

Castillo and Miller followed her out of the office.

"Let me see about the car," she said and walked across the room.

When she was out of earshot, Miller said, "Put a fing padlock on your dick, Charley, please."

Captain O'Brien looked at Castillo intently but did not comment directly.

"If you can think of anything I could be doing?"

"All scraps of information gratefully received," Miller said.

XI

The unmarked car Commissioner Kellogg had ordered delivered to the Counterterrorism Bureau—so far as Castillo could tell, it was identical to the commissioner's car—was moving at ten miles per hour over the speed limit as they drove I-95 along the Delaware River.

Castillo was in the backseat. Miller had elbowed him out of the way to claim the front seat.

"I really hope you can keep your mouth shut, Sergeant Schneider," Castillo said.

"You can call me Betty, if you like," she said. "And, yes, I know how to keep my mouth shut."

"I'd like that," Castillo said. "How about the boyfriend last night?"

"Jesus Christ, Charley!" Miller said.

"I want to make the point that I don't want you confiding in your boyfriend, either," Castillo said.

"I'll tell him I can't talk about this," she said. "He'll be pi . . . He won't like it but he'll understand. He's a cop."

"Good."

"He's a lieutenant in Highway Patrol. And he's not my boyfriend, he's my brother," Betty said.

"He was a very convincing jealous boyfriend last night," Castillo said.

"I hope the international Mafia thought so," Betty said, and then asked, "Are you now going to tell me what this is all about?"

"You'll pick up more than you have to know from listening to me on the phone," Castillo said.

"You're going to call him on your cell?" Miller asked.

"Unless you happen to know where we can find a convenient secure phone," Castillo said as he put his phone to his ear.

A moment later, he said, "I need to talk to him right now, Mrs. Kellenhamp—

"Where is he?—

"What's he doing at Camp David?—

"How do I call Camp David? Maybe it would be better if you called him there and asked him to call me on my cellular—

"You're right. It'd be better to go through the White House—

"If he calls, please ask him if he's talked to me, and, if he hasn't, to please call me right away. This is important."

He took the cellular phone from his ear and punched another autodial number.

"My name is Castillo. I'm Secretary Hall's executive assistant. You can verify my identity by calling Mrs. Kellenhamp at Secretary Hall's office. You have the number. He's at Camp David. Patch me through to him, please."

He took the cellular from his ear.

"They'll check," he announced. "I wonder what's going on at Camp David?"

He put the phone back to his ear and mumbled, "Guess they didn't check," then said louder, "Yes, sir. Sir, I wouldn't normally call you there but another problem has come up—

"Sir, the commissioner is being more than helpful, but at four-fifteen tomorrow afternoon he's going to tell the mayor what we think may happen to the Liberty Bell—

"Sir, he doesn't want to cause panic and he doesn't want to cry wolf. He's afraid if the mayor—the mayor's staff—hears anything at all about this, it will get leaked to the press. But he can't stall indefinitely—

"Yes, sir. I should have thought about this. I don't know why the hell I didn't—

"Yes, sir. Four-fifteen tomorrow afternoon—

"We're on our way to talk to the people who own Lease-Aire, sir. They gave us a sergeant and a car. And Chief Inspector Kramer, who runs their Counterterrorism Bureau, is trying to make contact with somebody—maybe more than one person—he has inside the black groups who may have heard something relative to what Pevsner was talking about—

"I don't know how long that will take, sir—

"Yes, sir, the minute I hear anything—

"Yes, sir. Sir, I'm sorry to be the bearer of bad news—

"Thank you, sir. When are we going to have word about Abéché?—

"I understand, sir."

He took the telephone from his ear and exhaled audibly.

"He says he's going to have to tell the president about the commissioner's 1615 deadline," Castillo said.

"Jesus!" Miller said.

"What is the commissioner going to tell the mayor at four-fifteen tomorrow?" Sergeant Schneider asked.

Castillo looked toward the front of the car and saw that Sergeant Schneider had adjusted the rearview mirror so that she could look at him.

He met her eyes in the mirror and thought she had eyes that were at once attractive and intelligent.

"That we think there is a possibility—operative word *possibility*—that a group of Somalian terrorists who call themselves the Holy Legion of Muhammad, and who may—operative word *may*—have stolen a Boeing 727 in Luanda may—repeat, may—try to crash it into the Liberty Bell."

"My God! You're serious!"

"I'm afraid so."

"I knew this was important when the commissioner gave you a new unmarked car," she said. "But nothing like that. The Liberty Bell? Why would they want to do that?"

"Two theories," Miller said. "One is that they think it's an important symbol to America, much more so than most of us think it is. And the second— sort of tied in with the first—is that somebody in Philadelphia told these people they should hit the Liberty Bell."

"What we're trying to find out is if there is some link between Lease-Aire and the terrorists or between anybody else in Philadelphia and the terrorists," Castillo continued. "If we can do that, then maybe we can find out exactly what they're planning and when. That's why we're going to the airport, to talk to the Lease-Aire people."

The Ford suddenly accelerated.

Miller glanced over at the speedometer.

"We don't want to get pinched for speeding, Sergeant," he said.

"There's blue flashers under the grille," she said. "If there's a Highway Patrol car out here, he'll see them."

"Or die young in a fiery crash," Miller said. "You're going almost ninety." She laughed.

"Relax," she said. "And you can call me Betty, too. I thought I told you."

Castillo saw her eyes on him in the rearview mirror.

"Chief Kramer said you were a Secret Service supervisory agent," she said.

"I am."

"You told the White House operator—I assume that was the White House operator . . . ?"

"It was."

". . . that you were Secretary Hall's executive assistant."

"I am."

"Curiouser and curiouser," she said and returned her attention to the road.

The corporate headquarters of Lease-Aire, Inc., was on the second floor of an unimpressive two-story, concrete-block building attached to the end of an old and somewhat run-down hangar on a remote corner of Philadelphia International Airport.

There was a sign—it looked as if it had been printed on a computer's ink-jet printer—on the steel door announcing, CLOSED DUE TO ILLNESS IN THE FAMILY.

"Now what?" Miller asked.

Sergeant Schneider took a cellular phone from her purse and pushed an autodial button.

"Jack, Betty," she said a moment later. "I need a favor. Look in the lower drawer of my filing cabinet. There's a folder called 'Lease-Aire.' I need the home address of a guy named Terry Halloran. And a phone number, if there is one."

"Who's he?" Castillo asked.

"President of Lease-Aire, right?" Miller asked.

Betty nodded.

"How'd you happen to have that information?" Castillo asked Sergeant Schneider.

"The FBI came to us asking what we had on them," she said. "We'd never heard of them. But Captain O'Brien told me to have a look at them in case there was something we should know."

"And what did you find out?" Castillo asked.

She held up her hand in a signal for him to wait and then repeated the address and telephone number that Jack Whoever on the other end of the line gave her.

"Thanks, Jack," she concluded and turned the phone off.

"Aren't you going to write that down?" Miller asked.

She returned her cellular to her purse and came out with a voice recorder.

"It's a bugger," she said. "It bugs my cellular. I turn it on whenever I make a call like that."

She pushed buttons on the digital recorder and from its memory chip it played back her voice reciting the address and phone number.

"I'm impressed," Castillo said.

"Me, too," Miller said.

"Well, we're not the Secret Service, but we're getting fairly civilized. There's even a rumor that we're going to get inside plumbing in Building 110 next year."

Castillo and Schneider smiled at each other. Miller's smile was strained.

"Hey, no offense," she said. "The problems I have with Feds are with the FBI."

"He's worried that I'm going to make a pass at you," Castillo said.

"Jesus, Charley!" Miller said.

Betty asked Castillo, evenly, "Are you?"

"From what I've seen so far, I would be afraid to," Castillo said.

"Good. Let's keep it that way."

"You were telling me what you found out when you had a look at Lease-Aire?" Castillo said.

"Shoestring operation, family owned. The president's—Terry Halloran's—wife is secretary-treasurer. Her brother, name of Alex MacIlhenny, is vice president and chief and only pilot. Also chief mechanic. He learned how to fly in the Air Force, got out, went to work for the airlines—several of them—kept getting placed on unpaid furlough when business wasn't good, got sick of that and went in business with his brother-in-law buying and reselling worn-out airliners. Nothing on any of them except the pilot's wife had him arrested one time on a domestic violence rap that didn't hold up. They're divorced. Until you told me about this terrorist business, I was almost willing to go along with the FBI theory that they were trying to collect the insurance."

"You did your homework," Castillo said, admiringly.

"The sister and husband seem okay. They checked out; no prior record, etcetera. He's a muckety-muck in the Knights of Columbus. I never met the pilot, but I can't imagine the sister or her husband getting involved with terrorists no matter how much they needed money."

"I think that 'illness in the family' business is not the reason they're closed," Castillo said, nodding at the sign. "I want to talk to them."

She took her cellular from her purse again.

"I'll give them a call and see if they're home," she said and punched in the number from memory, which also impressed Castillo.

"If there's an answer, hang up," he ordered.

She raised her eyebrows momentarily and then nodded.

"There's no answer," she said, finally.

"I still think we should go to their home," Castillo said.

"It's off Roosevelt Boulevard," Betty said. "The other side of town."

"Which means another blood-chilling ride down the interstate?" Miller asked.

"Only if you're a coward," Castillo said.

"Or you can ride in the backseat," Betty said. "Statistics say it's safer there."

Castillo thought: *I don't think there is anything more in that comment than what she said.*

When they got to the unmarked car, he got in the backseat.

But when she turned on the seat to back the car away from the building, their eyes met again.

[TWO]
2205 Tyson Avenue
Philadelphia, Pennsylvania
1040 9 June 2005

Two-two-zero-five Tyson Avenue was a neat brick three-story house just about in the middle of the block. The other houses, built wall to wall, were apparently identical, differing only in the color of the paint trim and the style of awnings and screen doors.

There was no answer to the doorbell, which played chimes. The third time Sergeant Schneider pressed the button, Castillo noticed that one of the chime notes was missing.

"No answer," Miller said, quite unnecessarily. "What do we do now?"

"I don't know how the Secret Service does it," Betty Schneider said, "but we simple cops listen for sounds of life. I heard either a radio or a television."

I didn't, Castillo thought, *because I wasn't listening. She's good!*

"Well, they don't want to answer the doorbell," Miller pursued. "What do we do? Keeping punching the bell until they do?"

"No," she said. "Yahoo."

"What?" Castillo asked.

"You know," she said. "Yahoo on the Internet? It stands for 'You Always Have Other Options.'"

She went down the steps, waving for Castillo and Miller to follow her, and got behind the wheel. This time Castillo got in the front seat. Her eyebrow rose when she saw him there and their eyes met momentarily but she didn't say anything.

Miller rested his elbows on the back of the front seat.

"Where are we going?" Miller said. "Can I ask?"

"Harrisburg," she said.

"Harrisburg?"

"Harrisburg," she repeated. "If I step on it, we can probably make it in a little under three hours."

Castillo, who sensed she was pulling Miller's chain, said nothing. Miller shook his head, and then sat back on the seat and buckled his seat belt with a sure click.

She drove to the end of the block, made a left turn, and then almost immediately made another into a narrow alley splitting the block.

"It was the fifth house from the far end of the block," she said, and Castillo saw her pointing and counting. She stopped the car.

"And there they are, Mr. Terrence Halloran and his charming wife, Mary-Elizabeth," she said, indicating the Hallorans' backyard.

Each of the row houses had a small backyard, with a fence separating it from its neighbors. The Halloran backyard had a small flower garden and a paved-with-gravel area with a gas charcoal grill, a round metal table, matching chairs, and a two-seater swing.

A stocky man in his fifties with unruly white hair was sitting on the swing with his feet up on one of the chairs. He was holding a can of beer and there was a cooler beside him. A plump woman with startlingly red hair sat at the table with what looked like a glass of iced tea.

Sergeant Schneider stopped the car and got out, and Castillo and Miller followed her.

There was a waist-high, chain-link fence separating the yard from the alley.

"Good afternoon," Betty Schneider called from the gate in the fence. She took her identification folder from her purse and held it up. "I'm Sergeant Schneider."

"What the hell do the cops want now?" Mary-Elizabeth Halloran said, unpleasantly.

"We'd like to talk to you, please," Betty said.

"Go the hell away," Mrs. Halloran said.

Well, Castillo thought, *that explains that sarcastic "charming wife." She's dealt with this woman before.*

Terrence Halloran got off the swing and walked to the fence, carrying his beer. He pulled the gate inward and motioned for them to enter.

"What now?" he asked.

"These gentlemen would like to ask a few questions, Mr. Halloran," Betty said.

He took a closer look at them.

"You're not cops, are you?"

"No, sir, we're not," Castillo said.

"I already talked too much to the goddamned FBI," he said.

"We're not the FBI," Castillo said. "We're from the Department of Homeland Security."

He gave Halloran a calling card, taking long enough to read it to confirm Castillo's first impression that Halloran was well into a second six-pack of Budweiser. Then Halloran made a "follow me" gesture and walked to the table, where he handed the card to his wife.

"Homeland Security, he says."

"Talk to them if you haven't learned your lesson," she said. "I won't."

"Okay," Halloran said. "Make it quick. I have a busy schedule."

He sat down on the swing.

"Sir," Miller said. "I don't think Captain MacIlhenny voluntarily disappeared with the missing aircraft."

"The goddamned FBI thinks he put it on autopilot on a course that would take it out to sea and then jumped out the rear door," Halloran said. "Jesus, Mary, and Joseph!"

"I don't think that's the case, sir," Miller said,

"Well, that's what they think, and that's what they told the goddamned insurance company!"

"Who told us they were not going to pay up until 'the matter is settled,' " Mrs. Halloran said. "And then gave us thirty days to find—what was that line, Terry?"

" 'Another carrier,' " Halloran said. "They canceled us, in other words."

"I'm sorry to hear that," Castillo said.

"Why should you be sorry?" Mrs. Halloran asked, unpleasantly.

"Because it's unfair," Castillo said.

"Well, what the hell are you going to do?" Halloran said. "They're the goddamned FBI and I'm a small-time used airplane dealer. Who's the insurance company going to believe?"

"You said," Mrs. Halloran said, pointing a finger six inches from Miller's nose. "What the hell did you say? That you didn't think Alex voluntarily did something or other?"

"I think you're going to have to consider the unpleasant possibility that Captain MacIlhenny was forced to fly that airplane off Quatro de Fevereiro," Miller said.

"Off where?" Mrs. Halloran demanded.

"That's the airport in Luanda," Halloran said and then turned to Miller. "How did you know that?"

"The full name, Mrs. Halloran," Miller said, "is Quatro de Fevereiro Aeroporto Internacional. It means 'the Fourth of February,' the day Luanda got its independence from Portugal."

"So, what the hell?" she replied.

"I was there, ma'am, when the airplane took off," Miller said.

"You were there?" she challenged.

"Yes, ma'am," he said and handed her his Army identification card. "I'm an Army officer. I was the assistant military attaché in Luanda."

"I thought you said you was from the Homeland Security?"

"Jesus, Mary-Elizabeth, put a lid on it!" Halloran snapped. He snatched the card from his wife's hand, examined it, and handed it back to Miller.

"Major, huh? You said you was there when it took off?"

"I happened to be at the airport," Miller said. "I saw it take off. And then, when we—the embassy, I mean—learned it had refused orders to return to the field, I was sent to the hotel to see what I could find out about Captain MacIlhenny. The manager let me into Captain MacIlhenny's room. And it was clear that he hadn't taken his luggage with him. Or even packed it . . ."

"Leading you to believe what?" Halloran interrupted.

"I think somebody made him fly that airplane off," Miller said.

"Like who?"

"Like someone who wanted to use it for parts, maybe," Miller said.

"Yeah," Halloran said. "So what are you doing here, Major?"

"I've been temporarily assigned to Homeland Security to see if I can find out what really happened to that airplane. And Captain MacIlhenny."

"So what's *your* theory, Mr. Assistant Attaché, or whatever you said you are, about what happened to my brother?"

"I just don't know, ma'am," Miller said.

"They got him to fly the airplane where they wanted it and then they killed him," Halloran said.

"How can you even think such a thing?" Mrs. Halloran challenged.

"I'm facing facts, is what I'm doing," Halloran said.

"We just don't know," Miller said.

"What we're wondering is if there's a Philadelphia connection," Castillo said.

"Meaning what?" Mrs. Halloran demanded from behind the handkerchief into which she was sniffing.

"Meaning the airplane was there for over a year," Miller said. "Maybe somebody here—somebody who works for Lease-Aire—knew it was getting ready to fly . . ."

"Bullshit," Mrs. Halloran said. "You see what he's doing, Terry, I hope? He's trying to get us to say we let somebody know the airplane was there available to get stolen. They stole it and we collect the insurance."

"That's just not true, Mrs. Halloran," Castillo said.

Mrs. Halloran snorted.

"We don't have many employees," Halloran said. "We contract out just about everything. But that's possible, I suppose."

"All it would take would be someone who could overhear something, maybe Captain MacIlhenny saying he was going to Africa, saying when he expected to be back, something like that," Castillo said.

"About the time he was packing up to go over there, we had an MD-10 in the hangar," Halloran said. "Got it from Delta. We were cleaning it up. I mean, we had ACSInc.—that means 'Aviation Cleaning Services, Inc.'—in the hangar. But what they send us is a bunch of North Philadelphia blacks. You know, minimum wage. It doesn't take a rocket scientist to wash an airplane. I can't believe any of them would be smart enough to get into something like that. No offense, Major."

"None taken," Miller said. "But maybe if the thieves—let's go with the idea there are thieves—maybe they told the airplane cleaners what to look for."

"Yeah," Halloran said, thoughtfully.

"Have you got the payroll records of these people?" Betty asked.

"No," he replied. "ASCInc. does all that. We pay by the body/hour. And ASCInc. handles the security, you know, to get them onto the airport. But they'd have a list of the names."

"Where are they?" Castillo asked.

"Out at the airport," Halloran said. "Two hangars down from ours." He looked at Castillo. "Would you like me to go out there with you?"

"We'd appreciate that very much, Mr. Halloran," Betty said.

"Well, let me change clothes and get a quick shave," he said. "Could I interest you in a beer while you wait?"

"You certainly could," Castillo said.

"I sure hope you know what you're doing, Terry," Mrs. Halloran said.

"I'm doing the best I can," he said as he bent over the cooler. He came out with three cans of Budweiser and passed them around. "At least these people don't think we're trying to rip off the insurance company."

The next step, Castillo thought, *once they had the names of the work crew, was to see if there was a match with any names the cops had. There were several problems with that. For one thing, if there was a terrorist connection they would probably use a phony name. Or if they used the name they were born with the cops might not have it. They would know John James Smith as Abdullah bin Rag-head, his Muslim name. Or if security was anywhere near as tight as it was supposed to be, airport passes would not be given to anyone on the cops' suspicious list. That didn't rule out a bad guy, who couldn't get a pass because the cops were watching him, getting his brother or girlfriend, who had not come to the attention of the cops, a pass to look for what he wanted to know.*

Or a bad guy who couldn't get an airfield pass knew somebody who had a pass and borrowed it to get on the field. It was unlikely that anyone took a close look at a work gang coming onto the airfield. If they had a pass hanging around their neck, that would be good enough.

They would have to do a check on friends and relatives of everybody who had worked in the Lease-Aire hangar when MacIlhenny had been getting ready to go to Luanda. That was going to take time—a lot of time.

This was likely to be a wild-goose chase.

If anything was going to pop up, it probably would come from the undercover cops Chief Inspector Kramer had inside the AAL—African American Lunatic—groups.

But you never knew. Wild-goose chase or not, it had to be done.

"It won't take me long," Halloran said and headed for his house.

Castillo held open the front door of the unmarked car.

"Why don't you ride up in front with Sergeant Schneider, Mr. Halloran?" Halloran considered that.

"No," he said. "I'll get in the back with the major. That'll really give my goddamned neighbors something to talk about. 'You saw the cops hauling Halloran off?' "

"They won't think that," Castillo said.

"You don't know my goddamned neighbors," Halloran said and got in the backseat.

Castillo got in beside Sergeant Schneider.

"Lucky you," she said, softly.

"No good deed goes unpunished," Castillo said.

She smiled at him and their eyes met momentarily again as she started the car.

Castillo wondered if Chief Inspector Kramer had managed to make contact with one or more of his undercover cops.

And he wondered how long it was going to take for somebody—probably a spook using a CIA-controlled satellite—to find out whether the 727 was, or had been, in Abéché. All Secretary Hall had said was that they hoped to have confirmation, one way or the other, soon.

Castillo looked at his watch.

It was five minutes after eleven. He thought that made it five after five in the afternoon in Abéché. He wondered what time sunset was there. Not long after that, certainly. If the CIA had not managed to get satellites over Abéché by now—or, say, in the next hour—daylight would be gone and they'd have to rely on heat-sensing techniques, which were not nearly as good.

[THREE]
Aboard Royal Air Maroc 905
Flight level 35,000 feet
19.55 degrees North Latitude
22.47 degrees East Longitude
1705 9 June 2005

"About seven minutes, Colonel," the pilot's voice came over the cabin loud-speaker. "Starting to slow it down now. I'll depressurize in about five minutes. I'll give you a heads-up."

Lieutenant Colonel Thomas J. Davenport, Special Forces, U.S. Army, a tall, lithe thirty-nine-year-old, glanced at his team of paratroopers prepping for the High Altitude, Low Opening (Halo) jump and nodded. He touched a small microphone button on his chest. "Understand seven minutes," he said. "How do you read?"

"Loud and clear, five by five," the pilot replied.

Colonel Davenport's mouth and nose were hidden by a black rubber oxygen mask. The rest of his face and neck were just about covered with a brownish black grease. He was wearing what looked like black nylon tights.

Davenport looked at his watch. It told him that he—and everybody else in the rear cabin—had been taking oxygen for the past hour and eleven minutes. On one wall of the cabin was a rack of oxygen bottles and a distribution system to which everybody was connected by a rubber umbilical cord, which also carried current to the jump suits.

What looked like black tights were actually state-of-the-art cold weather gear. Several thin layers of insulating material were laced with wire—like a toaster—providing heat. The heating wire current would be activated just before depressurization of the rear cabin began. Timing here was critical. The heating system was very efficient. If the heating wire was turned on too soon—when the cabin temperature was not double digits below zero—the jumpers would be quickly sweat soaked and suffering the effects of too much heat.

In theory, the heat generated was thermostatically controlled. And that usually worked. Usually.

Presuming it did and the jumpers exited the aircraft neither sweat soaked nor frozen, when the umbilical severed, a battery strapped to the right leg would continue to power the heating wires. Similarly, at the cutoff of the umbilical, oxygen would be fed to the jumper's mask from an oxygen flask strapped to him.

In theory, an hour of the oxygen—which everyone called "Oh-Two" because of its chemical symbol—was sufficient to drive the nitrogen from the blood of the jumpers, so they would not suffer the very-high-altitude version of the bends when the cabin was depressurized and then when they were falling through the sky. Flight level 35,000 is in the troposphere.

The theory presumed that every jumper had breathed nothing but pure oxygen for an hour and that he had not taken off his mask long enough to have taken even one breath of the "normal" air in the pressurized cabin. Taking even one breath of normal air set the one hour on Oh-Two timer back to zero.

The cabin was pressurized to protect the jumpers against the temperatures of the troposphere. The temperature outside an aircraft at 35,000 feet above the earth is about forty degrees below zero—on both the Fahrenheit and the Celsius scales, interestingly.

Colonel Davenport moved a lever which changed his microphone's function from PRESS-TO-TALK to VOICE ACTUATED.

"Okay. In six-fifteen, we will start to depressurize. Balaclavas and helmets now. Carefully. Carefully."

The balaclava mask came from the ski slopes. It was knitted of wool and covered the entire head except for the eyes. The ones used by Gray Fox were black. They were protection against cold, of course, but they also effectively concealed facial features.

Holding their breath, the jumpers removed their oxygen masks, quickly pulled the balaclavas over their heads, replaced the oxygen masks, and then quickly put their helmets on. The helmets had plastic face shields.

"Everybody manage to do that the way it's supposed to be done?" Colonel Davenport inquired, almost conversationally.

Three "Yes, sir"s and two "Check"s came over the earphones.

Captain Roger F. Stevenson, Special Forces, U.S. Army, who was also lithe and a head taller than Colonel Davenport but whose skin did not require what he thought of as makeup to hopefully give the appearance that he was of the Negroid race, walked up to Colonel Davenport.

"Permission to speak freely, sir?"

"Right now, anything your little heart desires, Roger. What's on your mind?"

"With all respect, sir, you don't look like one of us. When you take off the balaclava, you'll look like Al Jolson."

"Oh, and I tried *so* hard," Colonel Davenport said with a feminine lisp as he put his hand on his hip. "You've just ruined my *whole* day, Roger."

Stevenson smiled but went on.

"One look at you, Colonel, and the sure to be unfriendly natives are going to say, 'Who dat skinny white man wit all dat black grease on his face?' Or words to that effect."

"I think you're trying to tell me something, Roger."

"Sir, I respectfully suggest (a) that we're prepared to do this job by ourselves and (b) your presence is therefore not necessary and (c) if anybody sees you . . ."

"That has been considered by General McNab," Davenport said. "Who has ordered me to go. It doesn't mean that either General McNab or I think you couldn't handle what has to be done. You should know better than that by now."

"Did the general, sir, share his thinking with you? Can you share it with me?"

"He used the phrase 'If there's a change in the orders, I want you there.' I think he thinks we may be ordered to take out the airplane. If it's there."

"I know how to do that, sir."

"I know you do. What I think he was really saying was that if the circumstances look like it's the thing to do, we should take the airplane out without orders. And he wants me to make that decision. You shouldn't be put in a spot like that. If there's a flap, all they can do is retire me; I've got my twenty years. You don't. And Gray Fox needs you, Roger. I'm actually getting a little too old for this sort of thing."

"I'll take my chances with a flap, sir."

"You just proved, Captain, the wisdom of General McNab's reasoning," Davenport said, and now there was an edge in his voice. "Think that over as we float silently through the African sky. Now, go see to your men."

For a moment, it looked as if Stevenson was going to say something else but all that came over the earphones was, "Yes, sir."

Stevenson walked toward the rear of the aircraft where four other men in black tights were checking—again, for the fourth or fifth time—their gear. With their balaclavas and helmets in place, it was hard to tell by looking but two of them were African American, one was a dark-skinned Latin, and the fourth Caucasian.

When the latter two took off their masks, as they almost certainly would do sometime during the reconnaissance phase of this operation, they would also look like Al Jolson about to sing "Mammy" in the world's first talking movie, Captain Stevenson thought.

One of the modifications to the aircraft had been the installation of an airtight interior door about halfway down the passenger compartment. This permitted the rear section of the fuselage to be depressurized at altitude while leaving the forward section pressurized.

The seats had been removed from the rear section. The walls held racks for weapons, radios, parachutes, and other equipment, as well as an array of large bottles of oxygen.

The rear stair door had been extensively—and expensively—modified. It had come from the factory with fixed steps, for the on- and off-loading of passengers. They had been designed to be opened when the aircraft was on the ground and not moving.

Metal workers had spent long hours modifying the steps and their opening mechanisms. Three-quarters of the stairs—the part that had been designed to come into contact with the ground—had been rehinged near the foot and fitted with a opening mechanism that, when activated, allowed the steps to be raised *into* the fuselage.

The original opening/closing mechanism had been modified to handle what was now a four-step doorstep. The lowering mechanism now had enough power to force open the door into the air flowing past the fuselage at 170 or more miles per hour. It had also been necessary to reinforce the door itself to stand up against the force of the slipstream, and everything on the step that could possibly snag equipment had been faired over.

The parachutes the jumpers would use were essentially modified sports parachutes. That is, when deployed they looked more like the wings of an ultralight aircraft than an umbrella. And they could be "flown." Instead of falling more or less straight downward as a parachutist using a conventional canopy does, the "wing chutes" could, by manipulation, exchange downward velocity for forward movement. They could travel as much as thirty miles horizontally after exiting the aircraft.

The parachutes—the wings—were larger than civilian sports parachutes because they had to carry more weight. The jumpers would take with them a large assortment of equipment, including weapons, radios, rations, water, and what they all hoped would turn out to be authentic-looking clothing as worn by native Chadians.

Each jumper would carry with him a Global Positioning System satellite receiver connected to him by a strong nylon cord. The coordinates of the field at Abéché were known within feet. A position one hundred yards off the north end of the runway had been fed to the device. The GPS device had two modes. Mode I showed a map of the area and the present position of the GPS receiver—the jumper—with regard to the selected destination. Mode II showed, with an arrow, the direction to the selected position and the distance in kilometers and meters. In Mode II, the GPS device also combined GPS position, GPS altitude, and topographical mapping to give the jumpers a remarkably clear picture of the terrain onto which they were dropping.

All of this data would be shown on the face mask of their helmets in a "heads-up" display very similar to that which is provided to pilots of high-performance fighter aircraft and advanced helicopters.

Although each man on the team had been allowed to select his own weaponry for the mission—Colonel Davenport didn't think he should superimpose his notions of ideal weaponry on men who were almost as highly skilled and experienced in keeping themselves and their teammates alive as he was—when he had inspected the weaponry just before takeoff he saw that they had all chosen just about the same gear.

Everyone had a 5.56mm M-4 carbine, which was a cut-down and otherwise modified version of the standard M16A2 Army rifle. These carbines had had another modification: Special Warfare Center armorers had installed "suppressors." They didn't actually silence the sound of firing but the sound was substantially reduced, as was the muzzle flash.

Each man had elected to carry from eight to a dozen spare thirty-round magazines. Everybody, too, had chosen to take eight to a dozen minigrenades. They weren't anywhere near as lethal as the standard grenades because of their small size. But they were lethal up close, and they were noisy. They came in handy to encourage a pursuer to pursue slowly and to confuse him about the direction you were taking.

A relatively new, very small and light—about two pounds—antipersonnel mine also served as a fine tool to discourage pursuers. When activated, the mines threw out a very fine, very hard to see wire in five directions. Detonation came as a great surprise to anyone who stepped on any of the wires.

Colonel Davenport's inspection had turned up twenty-four of the miniature mines among the team's weaponry—in addition to the four he would jump with himself. He was also carrying a silenced (as opposed to suppressed) .22 caliber pistol in case it was necessary to take someone out silently. Davenport knew that Captain Stevenson was similarly armed, and, although he hadn't seen any during the inspection at Pope AFB, he supposed that there were two— or more—silenced .22s in the team's gear.

There was also a variety of knives strapped to boots, harnesses, or in pockets. Colonel Davenport personally was not much of a fan of the knife as a lethal weapon. He had been known to comment that if you were close enough to cut someone's throat with a knife, you were also close enough to put a .22 bullet in his ear, and that was a lot less messy.

On this mission, it was devoutly hoped they could accomplish what they had been ordered to do without unsheathing a knife, much less using any of their other weaponry.

"Colonel," the pilot's voice came over the speaker. "I'm going to open it up in sixty seconds."

"Go," Colonel Davenport said.

"Sixty, fifty-nine, fifty-eight . . ." the pilot began to count.

Davenport and the others, moving with speed that had come only after long practice, checked the functioning of all their Halo equipment—the oxygen masks and the flask that would jump with them; the functioning of the headsets for their man-to-man radios; the GPS receivers; and the umbilical they would leave behind on the aircraft. This was best done with the fingers. Only after everything had been checked and found functioning did anyone begin pulling on their electrically heated gloves.

". . . Five, four, three, two, one. Depressurizing now," the pilot's voice said.

"Radio check," Colonel Davenport ordered.

One by one, everybody checked in.

"Compartment altitude fifteen kay," the pilot reported.

"Everybody's magic compass working?" Colonel Davenport inquired.

He got a thumbs-up from everyone.

"Compartment altitude twenty kay," the pilot reported. "Airspeed four-two-five."

"Check everybody," Davenport ordered Stevenson, who nodded.

"Compartment altitude twenty-five kay," the pilot reported.

Davenport walked to the rear of the compartment, where he got into his parachute harness and then helped Stevenson get into his.

"Compartment altitude thirty kay," the pilot reported. "Airspeed three-zero-zero."

"Okay, that's it. We're decompressed," the pilot said. "As soon as I can slow it down a little more, I'll start opening the door. Airspeed now two-six-zero."

"Okay, here goes the door. *Slowly.* Indicating two-two-zero."

There was a whine of hydraulics, followed by a first blast of cold air, as the door pushed into the slipstream, and then a steady, powerful rush of extremely cold air.

The door acted as sort of an air brake, slowing the aircraft now more quickly.

"One-ninety, one-eighty-five, one-eighty, one-seventy-five. One-seventy. Holding at one-seven-zero," the pilot reported.

The door step was now open.

Davenport went to it and waited until Stevenson hoisted his parachute and then connected it to him. Then he sat down on the floor and, reaching beside him, placed a bag connected to his harness on the stairs in front of him.

One by one, the others took their places behind him. The next-to-last man connected Stevenson's parachute to his harness and then got in line. Finally, Stevenson got in the line of jumpers.

"Everybody ready?" Colonel Davenport asked.

Everybody checked in.

"Pilot?" Davenport inquired.

"About two minutes, Colonel."

"Two minutes," Davenport responded.

"You ready, Colonel?" the pilot inquired.

"Ready."

"Fifteen seconds, thirteen, eleven, nine, seven, five, four, three, two, one."

Colonel Davenport walked awkwardly down the steps and then pushed himself off and into the air. The slipstream caught his body and hurled him away from the airplane.

It would take him five seconds, maybe a little more, until he could gain control of his fall and assume the position—facedown, legs and arms spread—that he would keep until he popped his parachute.

The object was to get out of the deadly cold troposphere before the toaster battery ran out of juice and the Oh-Two flask was empty. Otherwise, you died.

As quickly as they could, the others waddled under the weight of their equipment to the steps and went down them and into the night.

"Everything go all right?" the pilot radioed.

When there was no answer, he repeated the question.

When there was no answer again, he said to the copilot, "Michael, get on the horn and give them, 'Mail in the box at seventeen-twenty-two.'"

Then he reached for the control that would retract the stairs and door into place. When the green lights came on, he tripped the lever that would pressurize the rear cabin.

[FOUR]
Philadelphia International Airport
Philadelphia, Pennsylvania
1345 9 June 2005

"That's him," Mr. Terrence Halloran said, indicating with a nod of his head a guy in a white Jaguar XJ-8 pulling up to the hangar.

"Finally," Major H. Richard Miller, Jr., said, softly and bitterly. They had been waiting for him since quarter to twelve.

A very large African American in his late thirties got out of the car. Not without difficulty. He was as tall as Miller but at least fifty pounds heavier. Castillo had the unkind thought that this guy didn't get in the Jaguar; he put it on. He was wearing a green polo shirt, powder blue slacks, alligator loafers, a gold Rolex, and had gold chains around his neck and both wrists.

"What the hell is so important, Halloran?" he greeted them.

"These people need to talk to you, Ed," Halloran said. "Mr. Castillo, this is Ed Thorne, who owns Aviation Cleaning Services, Inc."

"I'm with the Secret Service, Mr. Thorne," Castillo said and held his Secret Service identification folder out to Thorne.

Thorne examined it and then pointed at Miller and Sergeant Schneider.

"And these two?" he asked.

"I'm Sergeant Schneider of the Philadelphia PD," Betty said.

"My name is Miller, Mr. Thorne. I work for Mr. Castillo."

"So what's this all about?"

"We need to look at some of your personnel records, Mr. Thorne," Castillo said. "Specifically, we need the names and addresses, etcetera, of the people who you sent to work at Lease-Aire from May first through the fifteenth."

"No fucking way," Thorne said.

"Excuse me?" Castillo said.

"I said, 'No fucking way,' " Thorne said.

"Mr. Thorne, perhaps you don't understand," Castillo said. "I'm with the Secret Service. We're asking for your cooperation in an investigation we're conducting . . ."

"What kind of an investigation? Investigating what?"

"The disappearance of the Lease-Aire 727 in Africa," Castillo said.

"Yeah, that's what I figured. What are you trying to do, tie me to that?"

"No, sir, we are not. But we'd like to check out the people, your people, who worked for Lease-Aire in the . . ."

"You didn't think I was really going to hand over my personnel records to you just like that," Mr. Thorne said and snapped his fingers. "What are you try-ing to do, get me fucking sued?"

"Mr. Thorne . . ." Castillo began.

"You got some kind of a search warrant?"

"We hoped that wouldn't be necessary," Castillo said. "We were hoping for your cooperation."

"You get a search warrant and run it past my attorney."

"That would take time we just don't have, Mr. Thorne," Castillo said.

"You don't look stupid," Thorne said. "What part of 'No fucking way' don't you understand?"

"Mr. Thorne," Miller said, courteously. "Can I have a private word with you?"

Thorne looked at him with contempt.

"Please?" Miller asked.

Thorne shrugged his massive shoulders.

"Thank you," Miller said, courteously. "Over there, maybe?" he asked, in-dicating the space between two of the hangars.

Thorne shrugged his shoulders again.

"Make this quick," he said. "I have business to attend to."

"I'll try," Miller said with a smile.

Thorne walked a few steps into the space between the two hangars and turned.

"Okay, brother," he said. "Like I said, make it quick."

Two seconds later, he found his face scraping painfully against the concrete-block wall of the hangar. His arm was twisted painfully upward on his back.

"What the fuck?" he protested and then yelped with pain.

"Didn't your mother, back in the kennel, try to teach you not to use that word in the presence of ladies?" Miller asked, almost conversationally.

"Let me the fuck go!" Thorne yelped. Then yelped again in pain.

"You're apparently retarded, blubber belly, so I'll speak slowly," Miller said. "To begin, I'm not your brother. I'm an officer of the federal government, conducting an investigation. And you are not cooperating. That annoys me. When I'm annoyed, I tend to hurt whoever is annoying me. You understand that?"

Thorne yelped again in pain.

"Good," Miller said.

"You'll go to fucking jail for this," Thorne said.

He yelped again in pain.

"There's that naughty word again," Miller said. "You really are a slow learner, aren't you?"

Thorne groaned as his arm was pushed farther upward.

"Say, 'Yes, sir,' " Miller said.

There was no response until after Thorne again yelped—this time almost pathetically—after which he said, "Yes, sir. Jesus Christ, man!"

"Let's talk about jail," Miller said. "I'm not going to jail. You are. You will be charged with assault upon a federal officer, which is a felony calling for five years' imprisonment. During the assault your shoulder was dislocated. If you say 'fuck' one more time, both shoulders. That smarts."

Thorne groaned again as Miller demonstrated the pain which accompanies a shoulder about to be dislocated.

"That white man out there is a supervisory special agent of the Secret Service. Who do you think a judge is going to believe, him or a fat slob wearing gold chains and a Rolex who got rich exploiting his African American brothers and sisters by paying them minimum wage to clean dirty airplanes?"

"Jesus Christ, man!"

"Yahoo," Miller said. "You know what that means, blubber belly?"

Thorne shook his head and moaned.

"You Always Have Other Options," Miller said. "You understand? Say, 'Yes, sir.' "

Thorne audibly drew a painful breath, then said, "Yes, sir."

"Would you like to know what your other option is? Say, 'Yes, sir.' "

"Yes, sir," Thorne said, nodding.

"We go back out there and I tell Mr. Castillo that after talking it over you decided that you were wrong and now realize it is your duty as a citizen to co-operate with the investigation and that just as soon as we can get to your office you'll give us whatever records we want. You understand your other option? Say, 'Yes, sir.' "

"Okay, okay. Jesus!"

He yelped in pain, then said, "Yes, sir."

"And which option do you choose, blubber belly? You cooperate? Or you go to the slam with both arms hanging loosely from your shoulders?"

"Okay, I'll cooperate. I'll cooperate."

"Good."

"Are you going to let me go now?"

"One more thing. If you say 'fuck' one more time in the presence of that lady, I will rip your arm off and shove it up your fat ass. Understand? Say, 'Yes, sir.' "

"Yes, sir," Thorne said.

"I had the feeling you and I could work this out amicably between us," Miller said and let him go.

[FIVE]
Philadelphia Police Department
Counterterrorism Bureau
Frankford Industrial Complex
Building 110
Philadelphia, Pennsylvania
1505 9 June 2005

"It's going to take some time to check out all these people," Chief Inspector Kramer said, tapping his fingers on the stack of Daily Employment Records Mr. Ed Thorne of Aviation Cleaning Services, Inc., had somewhat less than graciously provided to them, and then went on to explain, "I want to run them past as many people as I can, not just the undercover guys."

"I understand," Castillo said. "Have you been able to contact any of your undercover people?"

"All of them," Kramer said. "But all that means is they know we *want* a meet. The problem is setting up the meets. That has to be done very carefully. And that won't happen in the daytime."

He paused and then raised his eyes to Castillo. "Is there anything else you'd like to look into, like to see?"

Castillo smiled. "You mean that not only wouldn't we be useful around here but in the way?"

"You said it, I didn't," Kramer said.

"Dick, when was the last time you saw the Liberty Bell?" Castillo asked.

"Aside from driving past it, I guess I was in the eighth grade," Miller replied.

"I think maybe you should have a fresh look at it," Castillo said.

"Good idea," Kramer said, smiling. "If anything opens up, I'll give you a call."

"I'm sure you noticed the NO PARKING sign," Miller said to Betty Schneider as she slowed the Crown Victoria, stopped, turned on the seat, and started to back up to the Market Street curb.

He was in the front passenger seat beside her.

"Not only can I read but I can tie my own shoes," she said. "We're on official police business."

She saw Castillo smiling and smiled back.

"Tell him, Sarge," Castillo said.

"That's a National Park Service sign," Miller argued, pointing. "Does that 'official police business' business work on the feds? On federal property?"

"Market Street belongs to Philadelphia," she said. "Federal property begins just past the sidewalk." She pointed down the open area to the structure erected over the Liberty Bell and to Constitution Hall behind it. "Sometimes, there's a jurisdictional problem."

"Really? How so?" Castillo asked.

She was getting out of the car and didn't reply.

When he was standing on the sidewalk, Castillo saw a Philadelphia police officer walking quickly down the sidewalk toward them. Then the policeman took a close look at the car, nodded, half smiled, and started walking back up Market Street, toward City Hall.

He sensed that Betty had seen him watching the policeman.

"How did he know you were a cop?" Castillo asked. "And on official business?"

"Masculine intuition, is what I think they call it," she said.

"Touché," Castillo chuckled.

"I don't think I've been here since eighth grade, either," Betty said as they started to walk down the plaza toward the Liberty Bell and Constitution Hall.

"I don't remember that," Miller said, pointing at the words cast into the bell.

"I thought everyone knew that 'Proclaim LIBERTY throughout all the Land unto all the Inhabitants thereof' was cast into the bell," Castillo said, piously. "How many times did you say they kept you behind in the eighth grade?"

Betty smiled and shook her head. Concealing the fingers of his right hand from Betty with the palm of his left hand, Miller gave Castillo the finger.

"I meant that they misspelled Pennsylvania, wiseass," Miller said. "Only one *n*."

Castillo looked.

"So they did," he said. "I guess they had trouble with eighth grade, too."

"It also says the 'Province' of Pennsylvania," Betty said. "I never saw that before. I always thought it was called a 'commonwealth.' "

Miller walked around the bell. Castillo looked down the plaza toward Market Street.

"What are you thinking?" Betty asked.

"It's a beautiful day."

"It is, but that's not what you're thinking," she said.

"No," he admitted. "I was thinking that on the tenth of September there were probably fewer than fifty people who considered suicidal lunatics crashing airliners into the World Trade Center was even a remote possibility."

"And you think an attack here is likely, right?"

"I wish I didn't," he said. "And I feel a little guilty doing nothing about it but playing tourist."

"Until Chief Inspector Kramer runs those names past everybody, including the undercover people, what else can you do?"

He shrugged. "That's what I've been telling myself."

Miller came walking quickly back to them.

"Think of something?" Castillo asked.

"My mother," Miller said. "I promised to call her when I knew if we could come to supper. I've got to tell her one way or the other. She really wants to see you, Charley."

Castillo looked at Betty.

"Do your radios work as far as Bala Cynwyd?"

"Sure," she replied, "and then we have this cellular phone gadget."

"Dick, call your mommy and tell her the cops are bringing you home again," Castillo said.

Betty chuckled and smiled at Castillo.

"Can we?" Miller asked. "What about Kramer?"

"He calls, we go," Castillo said. "We're not doing anything useful here."

"She really wants to see you, Charley," Miller repeated.

Castillo gestured in the direction of Market Street and they started to walk toward the car.

Castillo looked at his watch. It was ten minutes to four.

1550 here is 2150 in Abéché. Which means it's dark. I don't know what the CIA had to do to get satellites over Abéché but they probably couldn't do it before nightfall, which means they're having to use infrared and other exotic technology, which obviously hasn't worked. Secretary Hall would have called to tell me what the CIA reported, one way or the other. Which means we don't know if that goddamned airplane is—or was—there. And won't know until daylight, when the satellites can work their photo magic. Which doesn't always work.

Jesus, getting a call from Hall means my phone has to be working.

When was the last time I checked the battery?

He took his cellular out and looked at it.

There was still some battery charge left but not much.

He saw Betty's eyes on him.

"I'm going to have to charge this soon," he said.

"I've got a plug-it-in-the-lighter charger in my purse," Betty said, inspecting the fitting on Castillo's phone. "It'll probably fit your phone."

When they reached Market Street and the unmarked car, Castillo got in the passenger seat beside Betty. She fished in her purse and came out with a phone charger and handed it to him.

XII
SPRING 1991

[ONE]
Office of the Deputy Commander
U.S. Army Special Warfare Center
Fort Bragg, North Carolina
0930 6 June 1991

Second Lieutenant C. G. Castillo, who was the aide-de-camp to Brigadier General Bruce J. McNab, the deputy commander, USASWC, answered the phone in the prescribed manner:

"Office of the deputy commander, Lieutenant Castillo speaking, sir."

"What's his name?" the caller inquired.

"What's whose name?" Castillo responded, so surprised by the question, and the manner in which it was asked, that he almost forgot to append: "Sir?"

"The deputy commander's name?" the caller said.

"Brigadier General McNab is the deputy commander, sir."

"Senator Frankenheimer would like to speak to *General McNab*. Can you get him on the phone or is he, too, 'not available at the moment'?"

"May I ask what this is about, sir?"

"No, you may not. If he's there, Lieutenant, get him on the phone."

"One moment, please, sir," Castillo said.

He went quickly from his desk to General McNab's office door, rapped his knuckles on the jamb, and waited for General McNab to acknowledge his presence, which he did thirty seconds later by glancing up at Castillo from the sea of paper on his desk with a look of exasperation.

"They just nuked Washington, right?" General McNab inquired, not kindly.

General McNab, who disliked being interrupted when he was thinking, had on going into his office instructed Lieutenant Castillo that only if one thing happened was he to be disturbed.

"Sir, I think you should take this one."

General McNab considered this for at least two seconds and then pointed to one of several telephones on his desk. This was an order to Castillo to pick it up so that he would be party to the conversation. When Castillo had done so, McNab picked up another telephone.

"General McNab," he announced.

"You are, I understand, the deputy commander of the Special Warfare Center?"

"I am."

"I am led to believe the commander is not available at the moment?"

"If you were told that, it's probably the truth as we know it."

"Hold one, please, for Senator Frankenheimer," the caller said.

Senator George J. Frankenheimer (Republican-Nevada) was chairman of the Senate Armed Forces Committee.

General McNab and Lieutenant Castillo heard their caller—faintly, as if he had his hand over the telephone microphone—say, "All I could get was the deputy commander, Senator."

Another voice faintly said, "Shit," and then a moment later, more audibly, said: "Good morning, General. This is Senator Frankenheimer. I'm afraid I didn't get your name."

"McNab, Senator."

"How are you this morning, General?"

"Very well, thank you."

"General McNab, are you familiar with the AFC Corporation?"

"I know the name, Senator."

"They are, as they like to say, the cutting edge of data transfer technology."

McNab didn't reply.

"AFC stands for 'Aloysius Francis Casey,'" Senator Frankenheimer announced. "The founder, who also serves as chairman of its board of directors."

Again, McNab said nothing.

"Can you hear me all right, General?"

"I hear you fine, Senator."

"AFC has facilities all over the country—primarily in Massachusetts, where they are close to MIT, and in Silicone Valley in California—and they have chosen to establish their primary research and development laboratory in Las Vegas, where Mr. Casey maintains his primary residence. He's a constituent of mine, in other words, and has been very generous in contributing to my election funds and to those of the Republican party."

McNab said nothing.

"Mr. Casey wants to come to the Special Warfare Center, General McNab, and asked me to sort of smooth his path, which I am, of course, delighted to do."

"What does he want to do here?" McNab asked.

"He didn't share that with me, General."

"When would he like to come?" McNab asked.

"He will arrive at Pope Air Force Base about eleven o'clock."

"In a military aircraft?"

"In his own airplane."

"Senator, are you aware that Pope is closed to civilian aircraft?"

"Mr. Casey is apparently aware of this, as another thing he asked me to do—and I was happy to do—was ask the secretary of the Air Force to make an exception for him. He will land, as I said, at Pope around eleven. May I suggest, General, that it would be in all our interests if Mr. Casey was made to feel he was welcome?"

"I take your point, General," McNab said.

"Roll out and brush off the red carpet, so to speak."

"Right."

"Good talking to you, General," Senator Frankenheimer said and hung up.

General McNab took the telephone from his ear, held it in his hand, glared at it, and said, "Sonofabitch!"

Then he looked at Lieutenant Castillo.

"Charley, this Irish sonofabitch with political connections is yours. I don't know whether he's just curious, or wants to sell us something, but I'll bet it's sell us something."

"Sir, what am I supposed to do with him?"

"I'll buy the bastard lunch, but that's all. Set that up at the club for one o'clock. Get him into the VIP quarters, in case he wants to spend the night. But keep him, as much as humanly possible, as far from me as you can. Take him on a walking tour of Smoke Bomb Hill. Take him to the museum. Take him for a chopper ride over scenic Fort Bragg. Anything. Just keep the sonofabitch away from me. Clear?"

"Yes, sir."

Two vehicles were in attendance to the deputy commander of the Special Warfare Center outside the headquarters building. One was a glistening olive drab Chevrolet staff car, the other a Bell HU-1F helicopter, the paint of which was designed to be nonreflective.

The regular driver of the staff car, Sergeant Tom Fenny, was conversing with that day's copilot of the Huey, a chief warrant officer whose name—Kilian, Robert—Castillo remembered only at the last second as he walked up to them.

Sergeant Fenny saluted as Castillo approached. Chief Warrant Officer Kilian, who was ten years older than Castillo, did not, which neither surprised nor offended Castillo.

"We've got to go pick up a VIP at Pope," Castillo announced.

"You want me to bring the car over there?" Fenny asked.

Until that moment, Castillo had intended to meet Mr. Aloysius Francis Casey with the staff car.

I don't think the general's going to want the Huey.

If he does, with me at Pope, Kilian can't—or, at least, shouldn't—fly it alone.

I've got to occupy Mr. Aloysius Francis Casey until lunch; that's almost two hours.

The general said, "Take him for a chopper ride."

Maybe he won't like that suggestion.

Should I ask the general if I should use the chopper?

"Goddammit, Castillo. Tattoo NEVER LET ANYTHING GET IN THE WAY OF YOUR MISSION! *on your forehead!*

"I already told you once, don't disturb me unless you get a flash they just nuked Washington!"

"Yeah, Tommy, bring the car over there," Lieutenant Castillo ordered and then looked at Kilian. "Are the rubber bands all wound up, Mr. Kilian?"

"Is this VIP a civilian?"

"Yeah."

"You need written authority, Lieutenant, to haul civilians."

"There is an exception to every rule."

Parking on the tarmac directly in front of the base operations building at Pope Air Force Base is reserved for colonels and up and Pope ground control was unhappy when Castillo requested permission to park the Huey there.

"You have a Code Six aboard, right?"

"I will be picking up a VIP."

"Pope Ground clears Army Six-Two-Two to the Base Operations VIP area."

At two minutes past eleven, a Learjet taxied into a space beside the Huey.

As Castillo got out of the Huey to walk toward the Lear, an Air Force colonel and an Air Force lieutenant colonel—the latter wearing the brassard of the Air Officer of the Day—came out of the base operations building obviously headed for the Lear.

Both gave Lieutenant Castillo a "What the hell do you want?" look as he saluted.

The door of the Learjet unfolded and a very small, pale-faced man in a baggy black suit got out.

The Air Force colonel put on a smile and put out his hand.

"Mr. Casey? Welcome to Pope Air Force Base."

Casey nodded and took the hand.

"We don't know why you're visiting us but we're honored to have you here."

"I'm here to see Special Forces," Casey interrupted. He pointed at Castillo. "Is that you?"

"Yes, sir," Castillo said. "I'm General McNab's aide. The general is sorry that he couldn't be here . . ."

"Is McNab a little Scot?" Casey interrupted again. "About this high?" He held his hand up, estimating. "Mean little bastard?"

"General McNab is about that tall, sir," Castillo said.

"When do I get to see him? He was supposed to be told I'm coming."

"Sir, the general hopes you'll have lunch with him . . ."

Casey checked his watch. "It's a couple of minutes after eleven. When's lunch?"

"At thirteen hundred, sir. One. At the officers' club."

"That's two hours. What does he think I'm supposed to do in the meantime?"

"Sir, the general thought you might like a tour . . ."

"In that?" Casey asked, pointing at the Huey.

"Yes, sir. Are you familiar with the Huey, sir?"

"I've got a couple of them," Casey said and started walking toward the helicopter.

Castillo made a "wind it up" gesture to Kilian, saluted the Air Force officers, and trotted after Mr. Aloysius Francis Casey.

By the time he got to it, Casey was inside, fastening his seat belt.

Castillo took a headset from a hook and extended it to the wiry Irishman.

"If you'd like to put this on, sir, I could give you a briefing as we fly."

"Like a tour bus guide, right? 'And on our left . . .' You're going to fly?"

"Yes, sir."

"How much time do you have in one of these?"

"A little over six hundred hours, sir."

"You're a second lieutenant," Casey said. It was an accusation.

"Yes, sir, I am."

Casey examined him intently for a moment, shrugged, and took the headset and examined it with visible disdain.

"Okay," Casey said, "Smoke Bomb Hill first and then Mackall. Okay?"

"Whatever you'd like, sir."

Casey put the headset on.

"Okay, let's go. Maybe Fayetteville, too. The train station, the bus station, and the airport."

At five minutes to one, after an aerial tour of Fort Bragg, Camp Mackall, and the Fayetteville rail and bus stations and the airport, Castillo set the Huey down on the helipad by the Main Officers' Club.

Casey was already out of the helicopter by the time Castillo could make it to the fuselage door.

"I guess we cheated death again, right?" Casey inquired.

"Yes, sir, I guess we did."

"Where's Colon . . . *General* McNab?"

"I'm sure he's waiting for you inside, sir."

Casey marched toward the main door of the Officers' Open Mess, with Castillo trotting after him. Once inside the lobby, Casey turned and looked at Castillo with an "Okay, where now?" expression on his face.

"I believe the general will be in the main dining room, sir," Castillo said, pointing.

Brigadier General Bruce J. McNab rose when he saw the wiry Irishman in the baggy suit headed toward his table, with Castillo on his heels.

"Mr. Casey?" he said, offering his hand. "My name is McNab."

"I know who you are, General," Casey said.

"May I offer you a cocktail, sir?"

"You drinking?"

"It's duty hours, Mr. Casey. I generally . . ."

"I'll have a Schlitz, please," Casey said. "There was everything on the airplane but beer."

McNab signaled to a waitress and ordered a bottle of Schlitz and then changed his mind.

"Make that three," he said. "I think a beer is a very good idea."

"I'll wait for you outside, sir," Castillo said.

"You stay," Casey ordered.

McNab looked at him but said nothing.

"Lieutenant Castillo—what is that, Italian?"

"Tex-Mex, sir."

"You don't look Tex-Mex," Casey said. "Lieutenant Castillo just gave me an aerial tour of the main post, Mackall, and Fayetteville," Casey said.

"I'm glad you enjoyed it."

"Auld lang syne," Casey said. "Can I ask you a question about him?"

"Certainly."

"Where'd he get that CIB he's wearing?"

"In Iraq."

"I've been on patrols longer than that war," Casey said. "You think he deserves it?"

"I gave it to him, Mr. Casey," McNab said, bristling a little. "He earned it."

"He's a pilot, right?"

"And he earned the CIB on the ground, Mr. Casey," McNab said, measuring his words to control what he feared was his building temper.

"I thought, on the chopper just now," Casey began, then hesitated, and then went on, "I remembered a guy, an aviator, a Signal Corps captain named Walker. He was trying to exfiltrate us up in Laos . . ."

"Do I understand that you were in SOG, or something like that, in Vietnam?"

"I was a Green Beanie in Vietnam, General," Casey said. "Let me finish my story. Anyway, his Huey took some automatic weapons fire from Charley on his way in and he bent the bird pretty badly getting it on the ground. He wasn't hurt, but the chopper wasn't going to be able to fly out of there.

"The exec—the old man had taken a couple of hits and was in pretty bad shape—ran up to this Walker character and said, 'Not to worry, we're Green Beanies and we'll get you out of here. We can probably make it back in a week or ten days.'

"Walker looked at our exec—he was a lieutenant; looked a lot like this one—and decided while he might be a nice guy and would try real hard, he was no John Wayne.

" 'Lieutenant,' he says, 'let me tell you something about the structure of the U.S. Army. The Signal Corps is both a technical service and a combat arm. As the senior combat arm officer present, I hereby assume command.'

"Then he looked around at the rest of us. 'Anyone got any problems with that?'

"He was a great big, mean-looking sonofabitch with scars on his face he didn't get shaving. There was a couple of grenades in his pockets, he had a .45 shoved into his waist, and he was carrying a shotgun—a Remington Model 1100 with the stock cut off at the pistol grip. Nobody had any problems.

" 'Okay,' he goes on, 'first we torch my machine and then we get the hell out of here. Anybody got a thermite grenade?'

"It took us fifteen days to walk out of there—we couldn't make very good time bringing Captain Haye along with us—longer than your, quote, war, unquote, in Iraq—and when the colonel heard what Walker had done he pinned the CIB on him. I heard he was the only Signal Corps aviator with the CIB."

"I've heard that story before," General McNab said as the waitress approached carrying a tray with three bottles of Schlitz and three frosted glass mugs. "Welcome home, Mr. Casey."

The men watched quietly as the waitress distributed the drinks before each, then said, "I'll be back shortly for your order," and turned and left.

"Yeah," Casey said when she was gone. "I never volunteered for Special Forces, General. I mean, yeah, I signed the papers, but the guy who recruited me was a lying sonofabitch, but I was eighteen years old and too dumb to know it.

"I was a ham—a radio amateur—when I was a kid, and, before I got drafted, I took the exam and got an FCC first-class radio telephone license. They sent me right from basic training to Fort Monmouth and put me to work as an instructor. Everybody but me was a sergeant, so I spent more time on KP than instructing.

"So this guy shows up and says if I volunteer for Special Forces, where they really need radio guys, I get to be a sergeant. So I signed up.

"What that bastard didn't tell me was that I got to be a sergeant *after* I got through jump school at Benning and the Q Course at Mackall."

"Does that sound familiar, Lieutenant Castillo?" General McNab asked, and then explained, "Lieutenant Castillo is himself a very recent graduate of the parachute school at Fort Benning and the Q Course."

Casey looked at Castillo but didn't respond to McNab's statement.

"So I finished the Q Course," he went on, "and they made me a buck sergeant, gave me a five-day leave and shipped my just-turned-nineteen-year-old ass to 'Nam, which turned out to be one of the less pleasant experiences of my life. I did all of my time in 'Nam on an A-Team, mostly in Laos.

"But I managed not to get blown away and they sent me home. A long-haired sonofabitch and his girlfriend—who wasn't wearing a bra; I still remember her tits—spit on me in the airport and called me a 'baby killer.'

"I got the same sort of shit in the Atlanta airport; this time, the spitter looked like my grandmother. And then I got here and went through separation processing. I figured it was good-bye, fuck you, and don't let the doorknob hit you on the ass on your way out. There was a final ceremony. The only reason I went was because I figured the bastards were entirely capable of court-martialing me for AWOL.

"So this sergeant major lines us all up, calls us to attention, and out marches this feisty little Green Beanie light colonel.

" 'Take your handkerchiefs out, girls,' he said. He meant it. So in a minute or so we're all standing there holding our handkerchiefs. 'All right, girls,' this bastard said. 'Blow your noses.'

"We wondered what the fuck was going on, but he was the sort of officer you did what he said so we all blew our noses.

" 'Okay,' he said. 'Put them away. Crying time is over. I know you all feel you've been crapped on by everybody from God on down in the chain of command. But the truth is, you've been given a gift. For one thing, you're part of a brotherhood of warriors. You'll never lose that. And you better understand that what you've been through has turned you into something special. You can do anything, *anything* you put your mind to doing. You're ten steps ahead of everybody else. You can be anyone you want to be. I don't feel sorry for you. I'm proud to have served with you. I salute you.'

"And he saluted, said, 'Dismiss the formation, Sergeant Major,' and marched off."

Casey and McNab locked eyes. There was no question in Castillo's mind that General McNab had been that lieutenant colonel.

"So I went back to Boston and tried to drink all the beer in the VFW post," Casey went on, "and then my father said I had to start thinking of my future and that maybe I should take advantage of my veteran's preference and get on with the city as a fireman, or a cop, or maybe at the post office.

"I didn't want to deliver the mail or be a cop or a fireman and I began to wonder how much of that light colonel's spiel was the real thing and how much was bullshit. Maybe I could do what I wanted to do.

"It took me a couple of days to get my shit together, but one day I went out to Cambridge, to MIT, asked to see a professor of electrical engineering and told him I had flunked out of high school but had learned in 'Nam that I knew more, understood more, about signal radiation than most people and that I wanted to learn more. There aren't very many poor Irish kids with lousy high school records in MIT, but that fall I was one of them. The first year, I went to MIT in the daytime and to adult education at night and got a high school diploma.

"I graduated with a B.S.—summa cum laude—two years after that and got my master's and Ph.D. in three more years. I was still at MIT when I started up AFC."

"I gave that same thanks-and-so-long talk fifty, a hundred times," McNab said.

"But you meant it, right?"

McNab nodded.

"So, at the risk of repeating myself, welcome home, Sergeant Casey," McNab said. He raised one of the beer bottles in salute.

"Thank you," Casey said, raising a bottle to meet McNab's and, now following suit, Castillo's.

"So what can we do for you?" McNab asked.

"It's payback time," Casey said.

"Excuse me?"

"Me to you," Casey said. "Unless I'm very wrong—which doesn't happen often—your communications gear is five, ten years behind state of the art."

McNab took a moment before replying.

"You've got equipment you think the Army should buy, is that it?"

"I've already got some equipment I think—I know—Special Forces should have," Casey said. "But I have no intention of getting involved with the Army procurement system or Fort Monmouth."

"I'm not sure I follow you," McNab said.

"No charge. I'll show you what's available. Take what you want. I'll charge it off to research and development," Casey said. "And, down the road, you give me your wish list and I'll see if AFC can make it work."

"You're talking about a lot of equipment," McNab said. "You must know that."

"I know. I'm a rich—very fucking rich—Irishman, which I know I wouldn't be if I hadn't taken the chance that you meant your speech and got my shit together and went out to MIT."

"Jesus Christ!" McNab said.

"No strings, General," Casey said. "When I heard what you guys were doing over there in Iraq, I decided it was high time I got back together with my brothers. So here I am."

"Before you change your mind, how do we start this?" McNab asked.

"Why don't you send the boy wonder here back to Nevada with me in the Lear?" Casey said. "Let him do some preliminary reconnoitering?"

"You mean now?" McNab asked.

"I think I'd like another beer and maybe something to eat first."

"Pack, Charley," General McNab ordered.

Castillo started to stand.

"Shortly," Casey said, motioning with his beer for Charley to stay seated. He looked at McNab. "If you don't mind, General. It's been too long since I last broke bread with my brothers."

SPRING 2005

[TWO]
303 Concord Circle
Bala Cynwyd, Pennsylvania
1655 9 June 2005

Charley Castillo's cellular phone tinkled as Betty Schneider turned the car into the drive of a brick colonial house sitting behind half an acre of immaculately manicured lawn.

"Hello?"

There was no reply, but there was the faint hiss of a connection suggesting there was someone on the line.

"Hello?"

There was still no reply.

After a moment, the hiss stopped. Castillo pushed the CALL END key.

Castillo looked out the window and saw they were close to the three-car garage. There was an apartment over the garage; he had stayed in it when, in his last year at West Point, the Army-Navy game had been played in Philadelphia.

He also saw Major General H. Richard Miller, Sr., USA, Retired, who was walking purposefully across the lawn toward a flagpole. When he reached it, he stopped and looked at the Ford Crown Victoria.

Betty stopped the car and they all got out.

"I could use a little help here," General Miller called. It was clearly an order.

Major H. Richard Miller, Jr., trotted toward his father and the flagpole. Betty looked at Charley and saw that he was sort of standing at attention. When Major Miller reached the flagpole, he, too, came to attention. General Miller began to slowly lower the national colors. Major Miller put his hand over his heart. When Betty looked at Castillo, she saw he had his hand over his heart and put her hand on her breast.

Major Miller caught the end of the flag as it approached the lawn and he and his father then folded it in the prescribed manner, ending up with a tightly folded triangle, which he then tucked under his arm.

"Okay," Castillo said and started to walk toward the Millers.

"Yes, sir," Betty said and followed him.

"Good afternoon, sir," Castillo said.

"The colors have been lowered; it's evening," General Miller corrected him. He looked at Betty Schneider.

"General, this is Sergeant Betty Schneider of the Philadelphia Police Department," Castillo said.

"How do you do, Sergeant? Welcome to our home."

"Thank you, sir," Betty replied.

A trim, gray-haired, light brown–skinned woman ran across the lawn to them, cried "Charley!," grabbed both of Castillo's arms, rose on her toes, kissed him, and said, "Thank you, Charley! God bless you!," and then hugged him tightly.

"Helene," General Miller said, "this young woman is Sergeant Schneider of the Philadelphia Police Department."

"We finally got Dick released into our company, Mrs. M.," Charley said. "But I had to promise you'd keep him chained in the backyard."

Mrs. Miller shook her head, then put out her hand to Betty.

"I'm very pleased to meet you. Welcome!"

"Thank you," Betty said.

Castillo's cellular tinkled again.

"Hello?"

"Hiya, Charley! How are things in Bala Cynwyd, P.A.?"

Charley recognized the voice of Howard Kennedy, Aleksandr Pevsner's former FBI agent personal spook.

"How nice of you to call, Mr. Kennedy," Castillo said.

Major Miller's eyes lit up.

"Aren't you going to ask how I know where you are?"

"You have friends from the old days, right?"

Castillo noticed curiosity on Betty's face and disapproval on General Miller's.

"I don't know about 'friends,' " Kennedy said. "But you've heard, I'm sure, that money talks?"

If he knows I'm here in Bala Cynwyd—nobody knew we were coming here— he's got somebody in the cellular phone business. They can trace a call to the nearest cell antenna. That's what the first no-answer call was all about. He wanted to locate me before he talked to me.

"So I'm told."

"You want to tell me who's answering your phone in the Mayflower?"

What the hell! Don't lie unless you have to.

"One of Secretary Hall's Secret Service guys. His personal detail. My boss thought you might call and he didn't want me to miss it."

"Not somebody from the Fumbling Bureau of Investigation, Charley? Please don't lie to me, Charley."

"No. As a matter of fact, right now Secretary Hall's relationship with the FBI is rather strained."

"I would really hate to think that you were trying to set up some sort of a rendezvous between me and my former colleagues, Charley. That would distress me almost as much as it would distress Alex."

"Neither you nor he have to worry about that, Howard."

"Good. When Alex is distressed, he can get very unpleasant. For the moment, I'll give you the benefit of the doubt."

"Thank you."

"I like you, Charley. Respect you. I checked you out. There's more to you than your West Point poster boy image suggests. I think we could become pals."

Does he mean that? Or is he schmoozing me?

"What did you want to tell me when you called the Mayflower?"

"Alex wanted me to tell you that that airplane's no longer where we told you it would be," Kennedy said.

"No longer, or never was?"

"No longer. Since last night."

"How do you know?"

"And something else. In addition to changing the registration numbers, they took all the seats out and put in fuel bladders."

"How do you know that?"

"Well, I know somebody who talked to somebody who talked to the truck drivers who took the bladders to Abéché."

"And how did somebody who talked to somebody know of your interest?"

"Just between us, Charley, a mutual friend of ours in the air cargo business flew them from Mogadishu—you know that's in Somalia, right?"

"I even passed Basic Geography 101 at West Point," Castillo said.

"Do they grade on the alphabetic or numerical scale at West Point? I always wondered."

"Numeric. You were saying these bladders were flown to where?"

"N'Djamena. That's in Chad, I suppose you know."

"Is it really? When did our friend do this?"

"About three weeks ago. And knowing our friend would be a little curious about why anyone would want fuel bladders in Chad, I asked the pilots to snoop around a little. They found out they were to be trucked to Abéché."

"I wonder why our friend's customer didn't want them flown directly to Abéché?"

"Putting all the little dots together, are you? I wondered, too."

"And putting your little dots together, what did you conclude?"

"I'll bet I concluded the same thing you have," Kennedy said. "I hope you understand, Charley, that if our friend had any idea about Abéché he would have declined the charter. As I hope we've made clear, our friend really wants to avoid the spotlight of public attention."

"So that's how you know—actually, think—that the airplane was in Abéché?"

"No. I have what the FBI would call 'eye witnesses' to that."

"I don't suppose you know where the airplane is now? Or have the new registration numbers?"

"New registration numbers and a new airline paint job. No, I don't."

"Wonderful!"

"But I'll bet it isn't in Somalia . . ."

"Why fly the bladders from there if the airplane was going there, right?"

"Great minds travel similar paths."

"Got a guess where it might be?"

"Not a clue. But I'm working on that, and the new identification, even as we speak. If I find out something, you'll be the first to know."

"Thank you."

"I don't suppose you have anything you'd like to share with me?"

"Not now. Maybe tonight."

There was a pause before Kennedy went on.

"Charley, I really don't want to accidentally bump into anyone working for my former employer."

"I understand."

"I really hope you do. I'll be in touch, Charley."

The line went dead.

I wonder where he is? Probably New York, because it's easier to be less visible in a big city than a small one. But maybe Washington. Hell, he could be anywhere.

And even if the agency or the FBI somehow latched on to that call and traced it, it was almost certainly made over a cellular he bought at a newsstand and dumped in a trash can the moment he hung up on me.

I wonder what the hell he did that he's so afraid the FBI will find him?

Castillo became aware that General and Mrs. Miller, Dick, and Betty were all looking at him.

Mrs. Miller broke the silence first. "Come in the house, Charley," she said. "Everybody's here to say thank you."

"I've got to make a call," Charley said. "I really do. It's important."

"Then we'll give you a minute," General Miller said.

"Why don't you come with us, Betty," Mrs. Miller offered, "and meet the rest of the family? Perhaps you'd like to freshen up."

"Thank you."

Castillo waited until they disappeared into the house and then looked at Dick Miller.

"Kennedy," he said.

"I heard."

"The plane is not there. It was. They tossed the seats out and loaded fuel bladders . . ."

"Loaded? Or installed? Hooked up?"

"He didn't say. One of Pevsner's airlines hauled the bladders from Mogadishu to N'Djamena. Then they were trucked overland to Abéché."

"You believe him?"

Castillo nodded.

"He has no idea where the airplane is now and is really worried that I'm going to flip him to the FBI."

"Is there a warrant out for him?"

Castillo shrugged.

"Go in the house, Dick. This won't take me more than a minute."

Miller looked at the house. His older brother and his aunt Belle were in the door about to come on the lawn.

"Keep me in the loop, right?" Miller said and then moved to intercept Kenneth Miller and their aunt Belle.

Castillo punched the autodial button that would connect him with the White House switchboard.

[THREE]
Camp David
Catoctin Mountains, Maryland
1700 9 June 2005

The president of the United States, who had been resting his hand on the king with which, when the telephone light flashed, he had been about to checkmate the secretary of homeland security, finally took his hand away and leaned back in the pillow-upholstered armchair and tried to make sense of the one side of Hall's telephone conversation he could hear.

After a moment, he gave up on that, too, and pushed a small button under the table beside his chair. A moment later, a white-jacketed steward appeared.

"Yes, Mr. President?"

"Booze time," the President said. "A little Maker's Mark for me . . ."

He stopped, said, "Matt?," and, when Hall looked at him, mimed drinking a shot.

"Scotch, please," the secretary of homeland security said.

"And scotch. Cheap scotch. The secretary of homeland security is not looked favorably upon by his president at this time."

The steward, a dignified, gray-haired black man, smiled.

"One good bourbon and one cheap scotch. Yes, sir. Something to munch on, Mr. President?"

"In lieu of the hearty meal customarily offered to the condemned, why not?"

The steward smiled again and left.

"Okay, Charley," Matt Hall said to the telephone. "Keep at it. Let me know if anything comes of it."

He thoughtfully put the telephone back in its cradle, leaned back in his chair, and raised his eyes to the president.

"First things first," the president said, pointing to the chessboard on the low table between them. "Checkmate."

The secretary examined the board.

"Shit."

"I always beat you," the president said. "Why are you surprised?"

"I was hoping your mind might be on other things," Hall said. "That was Major Castillo."

"Our no-longer-so-secret secret agent," the president said. "I picked up on that much."

"He just had another call from Howard Kennedy, the ex–FBI man who now works for the Russian arms dealer."

"And?"

"Kennedy told him the 727 was in Abéché but has left. With new—un-known—identification numbers, and painted in the color scheme of an airline. Which airline, no one knows. Nor did Mr. Kennedy have any idea where the airplane might be now."

"God!"

"Charley—Castillo—said something else. Kennedy knew where Castillo was—made a point of letting him know he knew. Charley said the only way he can think of that Kennedy could know that was he has a contact with the cellular telephone people, who can trace a call to the nearest antenna."

"In other words, this Kennedy character can do what the FBI can't do without getting a warrant from a federal judge?"

Hall nodded.

"Castillo also said Kennedy seemed very worried that we were going to tip off the FBI about him. Castillo said he has no idea where Kennedy is—was—and Kennedy knows that. So Kennedy's worries are a little unusual."

"Is there a warrant out for this fellow?"

"I don't know. I told you, the FBI . . . Mark Schmidt himself was . . . Schmidt gave me a hard time about getting Kennedy's dossier. I had to really lean on him to get him to promise to get it to me by nine o'clock this morning." He paused. "And, I'm embarrassed to say, I haven't checked to see if he actually came up with it this morning."

"Okay. Try this on. Mark Schmidt, the FBI, knows this Kennedy is a really bad apple. He's an embarrassment to them. They don't want you or anybody to know how high this bad apple rose in the bureau or how much trouble he caused."

"Okay."

"Okay, so maybe that doesn't justify Schmidt's ignoring Natalie Cohen's memo that you were to get whatever you asked for. That's a separate issue and I'll deal with that."

"Yes, sir."

"But why should I be expected to believe anything this guy says? Your man . . ."

"Charley Castillo? He's now my man, is that the way it is?"

"No. Sorry. Bad choice of phrase. *I* set this up. Castillo is *my* responsibility. *My* Major Castillo tells *us* that the reason Kennedy is being so helpful is that he wants us to stop watching him closely. He sure sounds helpful when he tells us where the 727 is, but, before we can do anything about it, lo and behold he tells us the airplane isn't in Chad anymore. Why should we believe that it ever was there?"

"All I have, Mr. President, is what Castillo tells me. He believes him, and Charley is very good at separating the truth from the bullshit."

The president snorted.

"And what is *our* secret agent doing right now? Where is he?"

"He's at Miller's father's house outside Philadelphia. Miller's father is a retired two-star general. The counterterrorism people in the Philadelphia police department are going to set up a meeting between Castillo and Miller and some police working undercover with Muslim groups—two kinds, Arab-type Muslims, and converts to Islam, mostly African Americans—to see if they can come up with a Somalian connection."

The steward came into the room carrying a tray with two large glasses dark with whiskey, together with a bowl of ice and a pitcher of water.

"One very good bourbon for the president," he said. "And one really cheap scotch for the secretary."

"Thank you very much," Hall said, smiling.

"The reason we got it cheap, Mr. Secretary, is that nobody wanted to buy it. Can you believe that stuff sat in a barrel in Scotland for twenty-four years before they could sell it?"

"Now that we know where you stand, Jerry," the president said, "that means that I am not the only friend Matt Hall has in the whole world."

The steward left.

"What now, Mr. President?" Hall asked.

"Natalie said I should go back to Washington about now. Maybe with your resignation in my pocket. So what I'm going to do is wait until we hear from General Naylor that the 727 is not in Chad and never has been."

"Mr. President, I serve at your pleasure," Hall said. "Would you like me to prepare my resignation?"

"No. I may have to ask for it eventually, but I don't like throwing people to the wolves because of my mistakes, especially when they've done nothing but their very best to do what I told them to do."

[FOUR]
Abéché, Chad
2305 9 June 2005

Two men dressed in the loose cotton robes worn by inhabitants of the Chadian desert sat in a small, light tan–colored tent three hundred yards off the end of the runway of the Abéché airfield.

One was Sergeant First Class Frederick Douglass Lewis, a very tall, very thin twenty-six-year-old from Baltimore, in whose home was hung a framed photograph of himself in full uniform. He was shown with his arm around an African—a very tall, very thin Watusi—in a sort of a robe, standing on one leg, sort of supporting himself on a long spear. Both men were smiling broadly at the camera. On closer examination, one might notice both men had the same face. Lewis, who was pretty good at screwing around with digital photographs, had superimposed his face on that of the African tribesman.

He had also superimposed the face of his wife on a photograph of Janet Jackson in a very revealing costume. Mrs. Lewis, whose father was pastor of Baltimore's Second African Methodist Episcopal Church and still carried a lot of that around with her, had not been amused.

Sergeant Lewis was the Gray Fox team communicator. He sat down with a communications device between his legs, making minor adjustments trying, as he thought of it, to make all the lights go green.

It was taking a little longer than it usually did, but finally all the LEDs were green.

"We're up, Colonel," Sergeant Lewis said.

Lieutenant Colonel Thomas J. Davenport, who commanded Gray Fox and who was unusually in personal command of this team operation, gave Sergeant Lewis a thumbs-up signal but did not raise his eyes from the communications device on the ground between his legs. It looked, more than anything else, like a small laptop computer.

He read what he had typed:

```
1. ALL WELL.

2. (PROB-NINER) BIRD WAS HERE UNTIL DUSK YESTERDAY.

3. RECON PRODUCED:

   A. COVERT INTERROGATION OF FIFTEEN NATIVES INDICATES
      (RELIABILITY EIGHT).

        I. A "BIG AIRLINER HERE."

       II. AIRLINER MARKERS WERE STRIPPED AND NEW
           MARKERS PAINTED; NO DETAILS ON NEW MARKERS
           AVAILABLE YET.

      III. ALL AIRLINER SEATS REMOVED.

       IV. LARGE "RUBBER TENTS" PLACED ABOARD;
           DESCRIPTION OF SAME FITS (PROB-FIVE) FUEL
           BLADDERS.

        V. AIRLINER WAS NOT REPEAT NOT FUELED.

       VI. WITH EXCEPTION OF AIRCRAFT CREW (TWO-MAN)
           WHO WERE IN "PILOT'S UNIFORMS" AND NEGROID
           IN APPEARANCE, NO WHITE MEN OR "OTHER
           WESTERNERS" WERE SEEN.
```

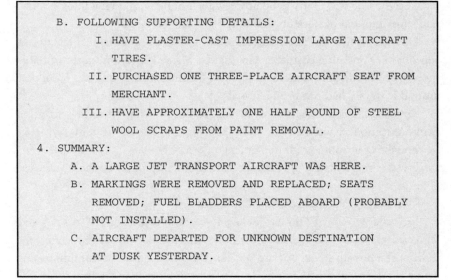

```
   B. FOLLOWING SUPPORTING DETAILS:
        I. HAVE PLASTER-CAST IMPRESSION LARGE AIRCRAFT
           TIRES.
       II. PURCHASED ONE THREE-PLACE AIRCRAFT SEAT FROM
           MERCHANT.
      III. HAVE APPROXIMATELY ONE HALF POUND OF STEEL
           WOOL SCRAPS FROM PAINT REMOVAL.
4. SUMMARY:
   A. A LARGE JET TRANSPORT AIRCRAFT WAS HERE.
   B. MARKINGS WERE REMOVED AND REPLACED; SEATS
      REMOVED; FUEL BLADDERS PLACED ABOARD (PROBABLY
      NOT INSTALLED).
   C. AIRCRAFT DEPARTED FOR UNKNOWN DESTINATION
      AT DUSK YESTERDAY.
```

The first paragraph—"All well"—covered a lot of ground: Six men, and all their equipment, had successfully made a Halo parachute descent from a jet transport at 35,000 feet and landed with all their equipment (and themselves) intact and functioning precisely where they had intended to land. They had carried out their reconnaissance mission without being detected, which of course also meant that no one had been killed, injured, or lost.

The second paragraph reported—with a probability factor of nine on a one-to-ten scale—what Colonel Davenport believed to be the facts. The rest of the message gave his reasons and his best guesses.

There was no address and no signature. The way the system was set up at the moment, the message was going to Lieutenant General Bruce J. McNab only and he knew that only one person could have sent it.

When Colonel Davenport pushed the SEND key, the message would be first encrypted and then sent to a satellite circling the earth at an altitude of 27,000 miles. The satellite—having been programmed to do so—then would relay the message to a device which another Gray Fox communicator had set for General McNab in the VIP Guest Quarters assigned to him at the Royal Air Force Base at Medina, Morocco. There, when General McNab typed in the seven-digit access code, the message would be decrypted and displayed on the screen of what without the secret communications technology would be an ordinary laptop computer.

The entire process would take from three to ten seconds, depending mostly on how quickly General McNab typed in the access code.

Colonel Davenport looked at Sergeant Lewis, who checked to make sure all the LEDs were still green and then gave Colonel Davenport a thumbs-up.

Colonel Davenport pushed the SEND key and then straightened up and flexed his shoulders.

For some reason, whenever he was involved in something like this Colonel Davenport always thought of the signaling device that had fascinated him when—then a young lieutenant—he had first seen it in the museum at the Army Intelligence Center at Fort Huachuca, Arizona.

Like the signaling device he was using now, the purpose was to communicate between a scouting unit and a headquarters.

The device at Huachuca—which Davenport guessed had lain in a warehouse at the old Indian fighting post in the desert for maybe a century before someone had stumbled across it and decided it belonged in the museum—had never been issued. It had looked as if had come from the factory in Waltham, Massachusetts, last week.

It was mounted on a varnished wooden tripod, the legs of which were adjustable both for height and for uneven terrain. On top—where a camera would go—was a collection of simple mirrors, a lever, and a sighting device.

Cavalry patrols scouting for hostile Indians carried the signaling device with them, and, while looking for the Indians, also kept an eye open for high ground from which they could see their command post and on which the device could quickly be set up.

The transmission of data was simplicity itself: The rays of the sun were reflected by mirrors toward the command post. Operating the lever blocked the reflected sunlight. Momentarily removing the blocking bar sent a Morse code "dot." Holding the lever down a little longer sent a "dash."

Sending data in this manner had been, of course, a lengthy process, but it had been infinitely faster than sending a trooper galloping across the plains to report the hostiles had been located.

If the minutemen had had something like the cavalry signaling device, Colonel Davenport thought, it would have been unnecessary for Paul Revere to gallop out of Boston crying, "One if by land, two if by sea!"

He also theorized that the cavalry had probably used two, three, or an infinite number of the signaling devices in series. That is, when the scouting party's device was out of line of sight with its headquarters, devices were set up on hills in between so that sun flashes could be relayed from one signaling device to another. That would require, of course, that the data sent would have to be recorded at an intermediate station and then retransmitted.

That would take a good deal of time, of course, but it was still a hell of a lot faster than having a trooper gallop back carrying the message. And, of course, the flashing of sunlight was far faster than the Indian's means of long-range communication, holding a blanket or deer skin over a smoky fire and sending smoke in bursts into the air.

For his part, Sergeant Lewis was not surprised that all the green LEDs were up when he looked nor, twelve seconds later, when two amber LEDs flashed, telling him the message had been delivered to the designated addressee and that decryption of same had been successful.

This was pretty good goddamned gear. State of the art. Lewis knew for a fact that the Army didn't have anything like it; that Special Forces gear, while good, wasn't as good as this stuff, which only went to Delta and Gray Fox.

This stuff came right from the R&D labs of AFC, Inc., in Nevada. There was a story that the guy who ran AFC, and who got this stuff to Delta and Gray Fox, had once been the commo sergeant on an A-Team in Vietnam. That sounded like bullshit—God knows, half the stories you heard about stuff like this were bullshit—but it was sort of nice to think it might be true.

Thirty seconds after the amber LEDs flashed, a yellow LED began to flash. Sergeant Lewis pushed the RECEIVE VOICE button and, three seconds later, a blue LED flashed a few times and then remained illuminated.

"Stand by for voice, Colonel," Sergeant Lewis said as he put a small earphone in his ear.

Lieutenant Colonel Davenport put a similar earphone in place, then moved a small microphone in front of his lips.

"You reading me, One-Oh-One?" the voice of Lieutenant General Bruce J. McNab asked.

"Five-by-five, sir."

There was a delay of about seven seconds, during which time Colonel Davenport's words were digitalized, encrypted, transmitted into space, retransmitted from space, decrypted, and played in General McNab's ear, and then General McNab's reply went through the same process.

"Good show, One-Oh-One," McNab's voice said in Davenport's ear. "Pass the word. I'm working on getting you picked up at first light. So . . ."

The voice shut off abruptly.

Encrypting and transmitting voice communication was somewhat more difficult than doing so with data and the communications equipment had certain limits.

Seven seconds later, the message resumed.

". . . get Sergeant Lewis sober and out of the whorehouse by then. Bring the souvenirs. More follows in one hour. Acknowledge. Scotty out."

Sergeant Lewis was known as Gray Fox's designated driver and his devotion to his wife was regarded with something close to awe by his peers.

"Acknowledged," Colonel Davenport said into his microphone. "One-Oh-*Two*, I say again, One-Oh-*Two* out."

Sergeant Lewis looked at Colonel Davenport.

"Sir, the general knows that I don't use that stuff anymore and . . ."

"If I were you, Sergeant, I would take the general's comments as a compliment."

"Yeah," Sergeant Lewis said after a moment, and then he asked, "This was your one hundred and second Halo?"

"After the first one hundred, they get a little easier to do," Colonel Davenport said.

[FIVE]
Office of the Secretary of Defense
The Pentagon
Arlington, Virginia
1710 9 June 2005

Mrs. Teresa Slater, who was forty-two, naturally blond, pleasantly buxom, stylishly dressed, and who had worked for the Honorable Frederick K. Beiderman, the United States secretary of defense, for half of her life—Beiderman had brought her with him from the Ford Motor Company and, quietly, and perhaps illegally, personally made up the substantial difference between what he had made Ford pay her and what the government paid her now—put her head in his office door.

"General Withers is here, sir," she announced.

"How nice! Would you ask the general to come in, please?" he replied, loud enough for whoever was in the outer office to hear.

"Yes, sir."

She smiled at him. She was aware that the secretary of defense regarded the commanding general of the Defense Intelligence as a PB who was UN because he was VFG at what he did.

They had brought the acronyms with them from Detroit, too, where they had been used between them to describe a vast number of Ford executives. They stood, respectively, for "Pompous Bastard," "Unfortunately Necessary," and "Very Fucking Good."

Lieutenant General William W. Withers, USA, carrying a small leather briefcase, marched into the secretary's office a moment later, trailed by a lieutenant colonel and a first lieutenant. Both wore the insignia of aides-de-camp and each carried a heavy leather briefcase.

On his part, General Withers regarded Secretary Beiderman as someone who suffered from a severe superiority complex and who had proven again and again that he could be a ruthless sonofabitch. But, on the other hand, Withers had learned that Beiderman said what he was thinking, never said anything he didn't mean, and whose word was as good as gold—all attributes General Withers had seldom found in other civilian officials of government and certainly not in political appointees.

"Good afternoon, Mr. Secretary," General Withers said.

"Good afternoon, gentlemen," Beiderman said, gesturing for everybody to sit down in the chairs arrayed in a semicircle before his desk.

"Before we get into the briefing," Beiderman began as he opened the cigar humidor on his desk and removed an eight-inch-long, very black Dominican Lonsdale. "Personal curiosity. Did they ever find that 727 that was stolen?"

Smoking was forbidden in the Pentagon. General Withers had heard a story—which he believed—that when someone had brought this to Beiderman's attention, the secretary's response was that so far as he was concerned the vice of smoking was henceforth to be considered within the Defense Department in the same light as carnal relations between members of the same sex; that is, "Don't ask, don't tell."

General Withers waited until Secretary Beiderman had gone through the ritual of cutting off the end of the cigar with a silver cutter and then had lit it with a gold butane lighter before replying.

"Mr. Secretary, actually, that's at the head of my list."

That caught Beiderman's attention.

"Uh-oh. What's happening?"

General Withers made a waving gesture with his left hand. The lieutenant and the lieutenant colonel immediately stood up and walked out of the office.

"What the hell is going on, Withers?" Beiderman demanded. "Your people don't have the need to know?"

"This is a matter of some delicacy, Mr. Secretary," General Withers said.

"For Christ's sake, out with it."

"I regret that I don't have the complete picture, Mr. Secretary," General Withers said.

"Jesus Christ! Let's have what you do have!"

"Mr. Secretary, are you aware of a Gray Fox operation currently in progress?"

"No, I am not."

"I have information that there is such a Gray Fox operation."

"Authorized by whom? To do what?"

"I have information that the initial foreign shores destination was the Royal Moroccan Air Force Base at Menara."

"My questions were, 'Who authorized it?' and 'To do what?' "

"I don't know, sir."

"Did you ask?"

"I have been unable to make contact with General McNab, Mr. Secretary. He's the Eighteenth Airborne Corps . . ."

"I know who he is. What about his deputy?"

"His deputy referred me to Central Command, sir."

"And?"

"General Naylor—I had some difficulty getting him on the phone, sir— finally told me that I didn't have the need to know."

"He said there was an operation and you didn't have the need to know? Or that you didn't have the need to know about Gray Fox operations generally?"

"General Naylor's comments could be interpreted either way, sir."

Secretary Beiderman picked up one of the telephones on his desk and said, "Teresa, get Naylor on a secure line for me and don't let them stall you."

General Withers unzipped a compartment of his briefcase and came out with a single sheet of paper.

"And there's this, Mr. Secretary."

Beiderman snatched it from him.

"What the hell is this?" he asked. "A goddamned letter of commendation?"

"Yes, sir. It was delivered first thing this morning by helicopter, sir."

"The president sent this to you by helicopter?" Beiderman asked, incredulously, and then without giving Withers a chance to reply went on: "Who the hell is Major H. Richard Miller, Jr.? And what the hell did he do of a 'covert nature' in Luanda, Angola? 'Demonstrating wisdom normally expected only of officers of far senior grade and experience'? And how the hell did the president . . ."

He broke off in midsentence when a light on his telephone began to flash. He snatched the telephone from its cradle.

"Is that you, Naylor?—

"I've got General Withers in here and he tells me when he asked you about a Gray Fox operation supposedly now under way you told him he didn't have the need to know. Is that right?—

"For Christ's sake, he's the commanding general of the Defense Intelligence Agency and he doesn't have the goddamned need to know?—

"More to the point, General, what is this Gray Fox operation? And how come this is the first I've heard of it?—

"Those were your orders? Orders from who?—

"The president personally? Or someone who said he was speaking for the president?—

"And this was when?—

"And the president specifically said I was not to be informed?—

"No one was to be informed? And you assumed that included the secretary of defense?—

"Those were your orders, huh? Jesus Christ, Naylor!"

He slammed the handset into the cradle and then immediately picked it up again.

"Teresa, see if you can get the president on the line," he ordered and slammed the handset down again.

He looked at Withers.

"That airplane was stolen from Luanda, right? There's a connection between that and this major?"

"Apparently, sir."

"Which is?"

"I don't know, sir."

"You don't know?" Beiderman snapped. "This little chat is becoming surreal, General!"

"Mr. Secretary, Major Miller was the assistant military attaché in Luanda when the aircraft was stolen. He was assigned to DIA, sir."

"So?"

"He was also the CIA station chief there," Withers said. "From which post he was relieved for cause by the DCI. When I was so informed, I relieved him of his attaché assignment and ordered him returned to Central Command."

"I thought you said he worked for you in DIA?"

"It's an administrative thing, sir."

"Relieved for cause? What cause?"

Withers took another sheet of paper from his briefcase and read from it.

" 'A security breach of the most serious nature; insubordination; exceeding his lawful authority; and conduct unbecoming an officer and gentleman.' I don't know the specific details, Mr. Secretary. That's what I got from the DCI . . ."

"The DCI himself? Or one of his 'senior subordinates'?"

"The message was signed by the DCI himself, sir."

"What the hell is the conduct unbecoming charge all about?"

"I believe Major Miller behaved inappropriately toward his immediate superior in a social situation, sir."

"You mean he's a fag?"

"His immediate superior is a female, sir."

"And he was fucking her or just *trying* to fuck her? Which?"

General Withers looked uncomfortably toward the office door. Beiderman followed his gaze. Mrs. Teresa Slater was standing in, a half smile on her face, one eyebrow raised.

"Am I interrupting one of those man-to-man chats?" she asked.

Beiderman smiled at her.

"Answer the question, General," he said.

"I believe the latter, Mr. Secretary," General Withers said.

"The DCI is trying to hang this horny major of yours and the president sends him a letter of commendation—special delivery by helicopter—for 'demonstrating wisdom normally expected only of officers of far senior grade and experience'? I'd love to know what the hell that's all about."

"I had ordered an investigation into Major Miller's behavior, sir. Before I received the president's letter, I . . . ."

"I think I'd hold off on that for a while, General," Beiderman interrupted and then looked at Mrs. Salter. "Teresa?"

"Dr. Cohen is on the line, boss," she said. "When I insisted on speaking to the president, they switched me to her."

Beiderman snatched a telephone from its cradle.

"Natalie," he began abruptly, "what the hell is going on?"

Secretary Beiderman was a great admirer of the national security advisor and he thought the feeling was at least partially reciprocated.

"The president's not available at the moment," Dr. Cohen said.

"That brings us right back to question one," Beiderman said.

"Will this wait until, say, six, seven tonight?"

"Never answer a question with a question. Didn't your mother teach you that's not nice?"

"My mother never thought I would have a job like this."

"You don't happen to know of a Gray Fox operation that's currently running, do you?"

"No, I don't."

"That's funny. I thought the Memo of Understanding said that both you and I would always be advised of a Gray Fox operation."

"Are you sure there is one?"

"According to General Withers there is. Are you stalling me, Natalie? In the public interest?"

"No," she said, simply, and he immediately decided she was telling him the truth.

"Where's the president?"

There was a brief but perceptible pause before she answered.

"He's at Camp David with Matt Hall."

"What's that all about?"

"I can't tell you. Or anyone else. I'm not even supposed to tell you where he is."

"Or whether Matt is in trouble?"

"Or whether Matt is or is not in trouble. Will this wait until six or seven?"

"No. It won't."

"Your call, Fred. I'll have the switchboard patch you through to Camp David."

"Thank you, no. But you might call out there and tell them I'm on my way out there."

"You can't go to Camp David without permission, Fred."

"What are they going to do? Shoot down my helicopter? Unless there's something else nobody's telling me, I'm still the secretary of defense. Thanks, Natalie."

He put the handset in the cradle.

"Call the helipad, Teresa, and then take General Wither's briefing. If there's anything important, call me on the chopper." He looked at General Withers. "Don't tell me you didn't even suspect that Teresa always listens to everything said in this office?"

"Yes, sir," General Withers said.

Secretary Beiderman didn't reply. He was already through his office door.

[SIX]
Camp David
Catoctin Mountains, Maryland
1720 9 June 2005

"Well, that's interesting, Matt," the president of the United States said, looking across the low table at Secretary of Homeland Security Hall. "The secretary of defense is on his way here."

"In connection with this?" Hall asked.

The president nodded.

"He tried to call me at the White House. Natalie's taking calls like that. He asked her if she was familiar with a Gray Fox operation under way. She was not and said so. Whereupon Beiderman told her he had General Withers in his office and Withers said he knew there was one, with some connection to a Moroccan airfield."

"Oh, shit!"

"Natalie and the secretary of defense are always supposed to be kept in the loop about a Gray Fox operation."

"And I didn't tell either of them," Hall said.

"A simple oversight, Matt? Or on purpose?"

"I just didn't do it, Mr. President," Hall said. "I suppose subconsciously I didn't want Beiderman to . . . I don't know. And I guess I didn't tell Natalie— didn't want to tell Natalie because I didn't want to hear her clear arguments that running a Gray Fox was ill advised."

"The result of which is that I now have Natalie and Beiderman with severely ruffled feathers. Justifiably ruffled feathers, Matt, and I will have to atone for that."

"With all respect, sir, you're wrong," Hall said. He stood up. "Natalie and Beiderman know we're old friends. They will understand why you brought me out here to explain why I have to go. They will have no reason to be angry with you. I screwed this up and I'll take the rap."

The president met his eyes but didn't say anything.

"If you'll excuse me, Mr. President, I'll go find a typewriter and prepare my resignation. With your permission, sir, I think that it would be best if I'm gone by the time Secretary Beiderman gets here."

After a long moment, the president said, softly, "I'm really sorry, old pal."

"Not half as sorry as I am, Mr. President," Hall said.

He was halfway across the room when the light on the telephone flashed.

The president picked it up and said, "Hello?—

"Who is this? Who's calling?—

"This is the president, General Naylor. I picked up Secretary Hall's line. He's not here at the moment. May I give him a message?"

Hall stopped and asked with his eyes if he should, or perhaps could, stay.

The president signaled him to come back and sit down.

"Well, let's have it, please, General Naylor."

Thirty seconds later, the president said, "General, you probably won't understand this but this is one of those times when bad news is also good news. Please relay my deepest appreciation and admiration to General McNab and all his men—

"Oh, here's Secretary Hall, General. Perhaps you'd like to tell him what you just told me?"

He handed the telephone to Hall.

In the phone booth in Tampa, General Naylor faintly heard the president of the United States say, "Jesus Christ, Matt, talk about getting saved by the fucking bell!"

XIII

[ONE]
Camp David
Catoctin Mountains, Maryland
1730 9 June 2005

There was a discreet knock at the door of the president's living room and then the door was slowly swung open. The president, who was sitting slumped back in a pillow-upholstered armchair across a low table from Secretary of Homeland Security Hall—who was talking on the telephone—waved Secretary of Defense Frederick K. Beiderman into the room and then onto a couch facing the table.

The president raised an index finger in a signal that could mean "Wait" or "Quiet while Hall's on the phone."

Beiderman sat down, more than a little tensely, on the edge of the couch.

The president gestured toward the steward and asked with a raised eyebrow if Beiderman wanted anything. Beiderman shook his head. The president signaled to the steward that he should refill his and Hall's glasses.

Beiderman looked between the president and Hall. The president touched his ear, which Beiderman understood to mean that he was supposed to listen to Hall's end of the conversation.

He didn't hear much.

"The secretary of defense just came in," Hall was saying. "I'll have to get back to you, Charley."

He looked at Beiderman as he replaced the handset in its cradle.

The president smiled at Beiderman.

"What an unexpected pleasure, Mr. Secretary," he said. "Actually, Matt and I were just talking about you."

Secretary Beiderman was visibly not amused.

"All your righteous indignation should be directed at me," the president said. "Everything that's been done—or should have been done and wasn't—was at my orders."

Beiderman didn't say anything.

"No comment?" the president asked.

"Mr. President, are you going to tell me what's going on?"

"Two things of importance," the president said. "The first, and this comes from a source which so far has been right on the money, is that a group of Somalian terrorists stole the 727 in Angola to crash it into the Liberty Bell. The plane made a stop in Abéché, Chad, to change its markings and install fuel bladders and now—right now—is apparently en route from there to someplace unknown on its way to Philadelphia."

"May I ask why I have not been informed, Mr. President?" Beiderman asked, coldly.

"The second thing," the president went on, ignoring the question, "is that the police commissioner of Philadelphia—who had to be told of the possibility—intends to inform the mayor of Philadelphia at four-fifteen tomorrow afternoon. The ramifications of that are obvious: It will be received by the public with a yawn as just another elevation of the terror threat color code—or with mass hysteria. Matt and I have been waiting for you so that we can set up a conference call between here and Natalie Cohen, so that we may chew the situation over between us and decide what we should do."

"How reliable is your source?" Beiderman said. "*The Liberty Bell?* Jesus Christ, why the Liberty Bell?"

"That's everyone's reaction, frankly. We really don't know why it's a target. Matt was just on the telephone with Major Castillo, who is in Philadelphia, and who hopes to have an answer to that later tonight."

"Who the hell is Major Castillo?" Beiderman blurted.

"The man I charged with finding out who among the intelligence community knew what about the missing airplane and when they knew it," the president said. "He's Matt's executive assistant."

"I don't understand, Mr. President."

"I know, and it's my fault you don't," the president said. "I'm sure you may have a question or two . . ."

He chuckled.

"Am I missing something?" Beiderman snapped. "Is there something funny here that I'm missing?"

"It's not funny at all," the president said. "Levity, flippancy, is often the outward reaction of people who are terrified." He paused. "And I am, Fred."

Beiderman looked at him intently for a moment.

"How reliable is your source, Mr. President? That someone intends to crash that airplane into the Liberty Bell?"

"On one hand, he apparently is not the kind of source in which the CIA, the FBI, the DIA, etcetera, etcetera, would place much credence, as they have chosen either (a) not to tap him for information or (b) to ignore him. He's a Russian arms dealer. Perhaps the most infamous of that breed. A fellow named Aleksandr Pevsner . . ."

"I know that name," Beiderman interrupted.

"So far, as I've said, what he's given us has been right on the money."

"Given you how?"

"Through Major Castillo."

"I'm having a hard time understanding this, Mr. President," Beiderman said. "What's in it for Pevsner? Why should we trust a man like that?"

"I think we'd better take it from the top," the president said.

Beiderman nodded.

"Have a drink, Fred," Hall said. "You're probably going to need one, and, when you write your memoirs, I'd rather you didn't recall that we were drinking and you weren't."

Beiderman looked at Hall and then at the president, who was holding his Maker's Mark, then shrugged.

"Why not?"

The president pressed the button that would summon the steward and then looked at Beiderman.

"When I became annoyed that no one in the entire intelligence community—*no one*, mind you—seemed to be able to locate the airplane stolen in Angola," the president began, "I called in Natalie and Matt and . . ."

[TWO]
303 Concord Circle
Bala Cynwyd, Pennsylvania
1731 9 June 2005

The "Yes, sir" that Major C. G. Castillo said to his cellular telephone was more a reflex action than a reply to Secretary of Homeland Security Matthew Hall. Castillo had heard the click of the breaking connection a split second after Hall had said, "I'll have to get back to you, Charley."

As he slipped the telephone into his shirt pocket, he saw that Major General H. Richard Miller, Sr., had come into the corridor where Charley had gone to take the call after leaving the living room.

"I was not trying to overhear your call, Major," the general said. "But I would like a word with you in private."

"Major"? What is he up to now?

"Yes, sir. Of course."

General Miller opened a door and motioned Charley ahead of him. Inside was a small, book-lined, very neat study. There were a dozen framed photographs on the bookcase shelves. One was of the general—then a major—and Colonel Colin Powell, obviously taken in Vietnam. There were three photographs of Dick Miller. One was of him in dress uniform standing with his father at West Point taken—Castillo knew; he had taken the picture—just before the final retreat parade. A second showed Miller getting his captain's bars from General Miller and the third showed General Miller, now retired and in civilian clothing, pinning on Dick's major's leaves.

"This will do," General Miller said, closing the door. "Please feel free to use my office for any further calls."

"Thank you, sir."

"You'll understand, Major, that I am not asking for information that may be classified."

"Yes, sir?"

"You are obviously in command here and I would like to offer to help with whatever it is you're doing."

"That's very kind of you, General, but I can't think of a thing."

"I understand," General Miller said. "Thank you for your time, Major Castillo."

He turned and started to open the door.

Fuck it! If you can't trust a West Point two-star whose grandfather was at San Juan Hill with the 10th Cavalry . . .

"General, now give me a minute, please," Castillo said.

General Miller turned around.

"What I'm about to tell you, sir, may not be shared with anyone without my express permission," Castillo said. "Mine or Dick's."

"Then perhaps it would be best if you told me nothing," General Miller said. "Sentiment has no place in matters of security or intelligence."

A lecture. I should have known that was coming.

He still thinks of me as a cadet who almost got himself—and Dick—booted out of West Point and then not only became a Special Forces cowboy promoted before his time but who dragged Dick from the holy family cavalry tradition into the Green Beanies with him.

On the whole, were I Major General Miller I wouldn't like Major Castillo much, either.

"That was Secretary Hall just now, General . . ."

"Is that who you work for?"

"Yes, sir. But on indefinite TDY. I am still a serving officer. May I go on, sir?"

"Of course. Excuse me."

"Secretary Hall called to tell me that a Gray Fox team which made a Halo insertion to the airfield in Abéché, Chad, has confirmed that the 727 stolen from Luanda has been in Abéché, where it was given new registration numbers and loaded with several fuel bladders."

"May I ask why he thought you should be made privy to that information?"

Lowly majors—especially ones promoted before their time—should not even know what Gray Fox is, right? Much less be "privy" to operational details?

"Because I gave him the initial intel, sir, that the airplane was probably there."

General Miller looked at Castillo for a long moment, almost visibly deciding whether to believe him or not.

Not that he's wondering if I'm lying. He really believes that West Pointers do not lie, cheat, or steal nor tolerate those who do. It's just that, as a general, based on his own experience, he knows that I simply can't have the experience to really know what I'm talking about.

"What is the connection between that missing aircraft and Philadelphia?" General Miller asked, finally. "Can you tell me that?"

"My best intel is that a group of Somalians calling themselves the Holy Legion of Muhammad intends to crash it into the Liberty Bell complex here."

"May I ask where that came from? The Liberty Bell does not seem, symbolism aside, to be a worthwhile target."

"That I can't tell you, General, because we just don't know. But the Gray Fox team confirmed what my source gave me—first, that the airplane was in Chad, that the registration numbers had been changed and fuel bladders placed aboard, and, second, that it had left."

"To what end, Major? Where is the aircraft now?"

"We don't know, sir."

"With the fuel bladders would it have the range to fly here?"

"That's possible, sir. But I think the purpose of the bladders is to have a large amount of fuel—either JP-4 or gasoline—aboard as explosive material. They're trying to duplicate the effectiveness of the big birds the terrorists turned into bombs on 9/11 with the smaller 727 that, being old and common, is effectively off everyone's radar."

"And you believe this aircraft is headed for Philadelphia?"

"Yes, sir."

"And that's why you're here?"

"Our source believes there is probably a connection between the Holy Legion of Muhammad and someone here in Philadelphia. Commissioner Kellogg's trying to help us find it, if there is one."

"Does Kellogg know about the airplane? Your belief that it will be used as a flying bomb?"

"Yes, sir. And after 1615 tomorrow, he's going to tell the mayor."

"The mayor doesn't know?" General Miller asked, surprised.

"Not yet, sir."

"He's the mayor!"

In other words, the commanding general, right?

"The decision not to tell the mayor was Commissioner Kellogg's, sir."

"The mayor should be informed," General Miller said.

Jesus Christ, is that an announcement that he's going to tell him?

"I really believe that's Commissioner Kellogg's decision to make, sir."

General Miller thought that over and finally nodded.

"Yes, it is," he said. "And Dick's role in all this? Can you tell me about that?"

"CentCom—General Naylor—put him on TDY to Secretary Hall, sir. We're working together on this."

"Why was he relieved for cause in Angola?"

"For doing his duty, sir. And that unjustified relief is being dealt with. There will be nothing on his record about Angola except that he received a letter of commendation from the president."

General Miller considered that for a moment and then asked, "Is there something I can do to be helpful?"

"Not that I can think of, sir," Castillo said. "Except . . . you may tell Commissioner Kellogg that I have told you what I have. I don't know the nature of your relationship with him . . ."

"We have been friends for a very long time."

"Perhaps you might be helpful to him."

"Yes," General Miller said, thoughtfully.

He was about to say something else when there was a knock on the door.

"Hello? Major Castillo?" Sergeant Betty Schneider called, softly.

General Miller opened the door.

"Ah, Sergeant Schneider," he said.

She ignored him.

"We've had a call. We're going to meet those people we talked about in forty-five minutes."

"Where?" General Miller asked.

Betty Schneider looked at Castillo for guidance.

"I've been bringing General Miller up to speed on what's happening," Castillo said.

"A couple of blocks from the North Philadelphia station," she said. "But we're going to have to change cars."

"Change cars? Why?" Castillo asked.

"Because on West Seltzer Street—where we'll do the meet—a new Ford is either a fool from the Main Line trying to score dope or an unmarked car," Betty said. "We're trying *not* to attract attention, Major."

"I thought you agreed to call me Charley," Castillo said.

"Now we're working, okay? And this is my turf."

"Oddly enough, Sergeant," General Miller said, "I really didn't think you were from the Visitors' Bureau."

The presence of Sergeant Betty Schneider of the Philadelphia Police Department had been explained with a rather convincing fabrication, loosely based on the facts but not touching in any way on the possibility that the Liberty Bell was about to be the target of a terrorist attack.

Castillo had told Mrs. Miller, and the rest of the family, that the Department of Homeland Security, to which he had been assigned for some time as a liaison officer between the department and Central Command, and to which Major Miller had just been assigned, wanted to establish a closer relationship with the Philadelphia Police Department, in particular the Counterterrorism Bureau and the Organized Crime and Intelligence Unit. Commissioner Kellogg, more as a courtesy to Secretary Hall than to Castillo or Miller, had arranged for the Visitors' Bureau—which dealt with visiting movie stars and the like—to provide them with a car and a driver, Sergeant Schneider, to escort them around and answer what questions she could.

Castillo smiled at Betty Schneider.

"You may tell him, Sergeant," he said.

"I'm with the Organized Crime and Intelligence Unit, General," she said.

"And we got lucky with the commanding officer of the Counterterrorism Bureau, General," Castillo explained. "He served with Special Forces. He 'asked' the commanding officer of Organized Crime and Intelligence if he could spare Sergeant Schneider to help us."

"There's one more thing, Major," Betty said. "Chief Inspector Kramer strongly suggests that Major Miller do the meet, not you. And that he dress appropriately."

"Because of where you're going?" General Miller asked.

She nodded and said, "White men, like new Ford sedans, on West Seltzer Street, after dark . . ."

"Dress appropriately?" General Miller asked.

"Work clothes, preferably dirty and torn," Betty said.

"I think we have what you need in the garage," General Miller said.

"You said change cars," Castillo said. "Where do we do that?"

"Internal Affairs has been told to give us whatever we want," she said. "They have a garage full of them, mostly drug bust forfeitures. Dungan Road. Downtown. Not far from where we're going."

"Is there a weapon Dick can have, General?" Castillo asked.

"Is he going to need one?" General Miller asked, looking at Betty Schneider.

"You never need a gun unless you really need one, General," she said.

General Miller opened the center drawer of his desk and took out what looked like a cut-down Model 1911A1 .45 ACP semiautomatic pistol. He ejected the clip, racked the action back to ensure the weapon was not loaded, and then handed it to Betty.

"They used to make these at the Frankford Arsenal," he said, "cutting down a standard Model 1911A1. Shorter slide, five- rather than seven-shot magazine, etcetera. They were issued to general officers; the American version, so to speak, of the general officer's baton—swagger stick—in other armies."

She examined it carefully.

"Very nice," she said, then raised her eyes to his. "I can put this in my purse and give it to him later," she said.

"Why don't you do that?" General Miller replied, handing her the clip he had ejected and a second one, also loaded with five rounds, he pulled from the drawer. "And when you do, please tell him that if at all possible I'd like it back in the same condition it is now."

"Yes, sir," she said, but she was obviously confused by the remark.

"That is, never fired in anger," General Miller said.

[THREE]
Camp David
Catoctin Mountains, Maryland
1755 9 June 2005

"May I speak freely, Mr. President?" Beiderman asked several minutes later.

The president held up both hands, palms upward, yielding the floor.

"Until about thirty seconds ago," the secretary began, "I wasn't buying your argument that you were justified, or fair, in not bringing me in on this from the git-go. I am the secretary of defense. I have the right to know what's going on."

"And what happened thirty seconds ago?" the president asked, softly.

"I realized that I was letting my delicate ego get in the way of reality," Beiderman said. "The two pertinent facts—maybe it's only one fact—here are that you're the president and the commander in chief of the Armed Forces of the United States. The Constitution lays the defense of the nation on your shoulders. You have all the authority you need to do any goddamned thing you want to do that.

"Once I got past that, what I had decided was the dumbest idea you've had in a long time, sending a goddamned major—a major, for Christ's sake—to check on how all the generals and the top-level civilians are doing their jobs, didn't seem so dumb after all.

"It made a hell of a lot more sense than setting up one more blue-ribbon panel—particularly after the 9/11 commission's report—which would have taken three months to determine that what wasn't working the way it should—what was wrong—was the other guy's fault.

"And, knowing you as well as I do, I knew that what you had against using a commission or panel or something of the ilk to find out what's wrong had nothing to do with the other—perhaps the most significant—thing that panels are good for, giving your political enemies ammunition to use against you."

"The truth, Fred," the president said, "is that forming a blue-ribbon panel never entered my mind. All I wanted to do was quietly find out who knew what and when they knew it. I thought this would put us ahead of the curve. Using Major Castillo to that end seemed to be the way to do that very quietly. No one was going to pay attention to a major. It just got out of hand, is all."

"Out of hand, Mr. President?" Beiderman said. "I don't follow that."

"I've stirred up a hornet's nest. If you've learned about this Gray Fox operation—and you were, you admit, furious when you did—wait until the DCI and the director of the FBI find out."

"Excuse me, Mr. President. And with all respect, so what? You found out—this Major Whatsisname found out . . ."

"Castillo," Secretary Hall interrupted. "Major Carlos G. Castillo."

". . . among other things," Beiderman went on, "that the DCI was prepared to hang another major out to dry for doing his job in Angola and was far more interested in covering his ass about his connections with this Russian arms dealer than getting the intelligence that was apparently there for the asking."

The president looked at him with a raised eyebrow but said nothing.

"And without Charley, Mr. President," Hall interjected, "we would never have found out about Kennedy. Schmidt damned sure wasn't going to volunteer that information."

"About Kennedy?" Beiderman asked. "Who's he?"

"A former FBI agent who now works for Pevsner," the president said. "We don't know how important he was in the FBI before he left but, to judge from Mark Schmidt's reluctance to come up with his dossier when Matt asked for it, I don't think he was a minor functionary."

"If I were paranoid," Hall said, "and, God knows, I'm starting to feel that way, I'd say there's a conspiracy on the part of Schmidt and the DCI to tell us—the president—only what they want him to hear."

"That's a pretty strong accusation, Matt," the president said.

"What other interpretation can we put on it, Mr. President?" Hall responded.

"Mr. President," Beiderman said, "wouldn't giving Matt anything and everything he asked for as soon as he asked for it come under that memo Natalie Cohen sent around?"

The president looked at him for a moment.

"Point taken, Fred," he said.

"More important," Beiderman went on, "Major Whatsis . . . *Castillo* has come closer to finding this airplane than anybody else. And isn't that the priority? Neutralizing the goddamned airplane before these lunatics fly it into the Liberty Bell or do something else insane with it?"

"Are you suggesting, Fred, that we don't rein Major Castillo in?" the president said.

"Exactly. I was about to suggest sending him to Fort Bragg to bring Delta and Gray Fox—which, I submit, we're really going to have to use to take this airplane out—up to speed on this, but . . ."

"But what?"

"Do you know General McNab?" Beiderman asked. "I mean, personally? Feisty little bastard. He's not going to listen to a major. Maybe I better go down there myself, or at least get on the horn to McNab."

"Charley Castillo flew McNab's helicopter around Iraq in the first desert war," Hall said. "And after 9/11, Charley commanded one of McNab's Delta Force operations in Afghanistan. McNab will listen to him."

"Especially," the president said, "after we tell General McNab that I personally ordered him to Fort Bragg."

[FOUR]
The Oval Office
The White House
1600 Pennsylvania Avenue NW
Washington, D.C.
1910 9 June 2005

Fifteen minutes after Natalie Cohen, the national security advisor, had telephoned John Powell, the director of the Central Intelligence Agency, to tell him "the president would like you to come to the White House as soon as you can," the director's Yukon XL was passed onto the White House grounds by the Secret Service.

As he got out of the vehicle at the side door of the White House, he heard the familiar sound of Marine One, the President's Sikorsky VH-3D "Sea King" helicopter, on its final approach to the South Lawn.

He reached the outer office of the Oval Office before the president did. Natalie Cohen was there.

"Natalie," Powell said, nodding at her, and then he asked, "Where's he been?"

"At Camp David," she said.

"What's going on?"

"I think we're both about to find out, John," she said.

The president came into the outer office just over a minute later.

"John," he said. "Good. You're here."

"Good evening, Mr. President."

Beiderman, Hall, and Powell nodded at each other but didn't speak.

"I'd like a moment with the DCI before we start this," the president said. "And I just remembered: Natalie, did you call Fort Bragg?"

"No, sir. I thought you were going to."

"How about doing that right now?" the president ordered.

The president waved Powell ahead of him into the Oval Office, closed the door, and waved him into one of the chairs before his desk. The president remained standing, looking out the window onto the meticulously manicured lawn, as he composed his thoughts.

"Yes, Mr. President?" DCI Powell asked.

After a moment, the president turned and spoke. "I was hoping you'd be prepared to tell me whether the missing 727 is in Chad or not. Or, if it's not, where it might be."

"There will be satellites over Abéché at first light, Mr. President. Actually, there are—have been—satellites over that site for some time, but the heat-seeking, metallic-mass-seeking sensors haven't come up with anything we can rely on. With daylight . . ."

"In other words, you don't know?" the president interrupted.

"I'm afraid I don't, Mr. President."

"I don't know where it is," the president said, "but I know it's not in Abéché, Chad."

"Then Matt Hall's information was not reliable, Mr. President?"

"Matt Hall's information was right on the money," he replied, meeting Powell's eyes. "We have confirmation that the airplane was there, that the seats have been removed, fuel bladders loaded aboard, and that after new registration numbers were painted on it, that it took off for an unknown destination."

Powell shifted uncomfortably in his chair and after a moment said, "I have to ask, Mr. President, why you think that information is credible?"

"Because I authorized a Gray Fox insertion and that's what they reported." The president let that sink in and then went on: "Our problem now is to find where the airplane is now, something more precise than on its way to Philadelphia."

Powell raised his eyebrows but didn't respond.

"I wasn't sure whether I should get into this with you now, John, but I think I will. If nothing else, it will clear the air between us before the others come in here."

"Yes, Mr. President?"

"You took action based on faulty intelligence someone gave you, action that I had to correct."

"I don't think I follow you, Mr. President. What action did I take?"

"You relieved for cause your station chief in Luanda, the causes including a serious breach of security, exceeding his authority, and . . . Jesus Christ . . . conduct unbecoming an officer and a gentleman. What the hell was that? Making sure the spikes held him to the cross?"

"Obviously, sir, you're making reference to Major Miller."

"Yes, I am."

"My information came from his immediate supervisor, sir."

"Well, giving any kind of classified information to my personal representative doesn't constitute a breach of security of any kind," the president said.

"No, sir. Of course not. I was apparently misled."

"Yeah, you were. Miller didn't make a pass at that woman; she made a pass at my man."

"If those are the facts, sir, I will . . ."

"Those *are* the facts," the president interrupted.

". . . take immediate steps to rectify the situation."

"So far as Major Miller is concerned, that won't be necessary," the president said. "I've done that myself. And as far as *rectifying* the rest of it, I've always found it useful to be able to trust the people who work for me."

The president locked eyes with Powell for a moment.

"Would you ask the others to come in now, please?" he said.

[FIVE]
West Seltzer and West Somerset Streets
Philadelphia, Pennsylvania
1925 9 June 2005

Castillo could see much better out of the deeply tinted windows of the five-year-old, battered and rusty BMW sedan Betty Schneider had selected from the cars lined up in the Internal Affairs Division garage than he thought he would be able to.

"Nice neighborhood," he said, looking at litter-strewn streets and sidewalks and the run-down brick row houses, many of them with concrete blocks filling their windows.

Betty had told him she had used the car before but didn't think anyone had made it.

"It was a forfeiture," Betty said. "But from a customer, not a dealer. It looks like something a less than successful dealer would drive, but no dealer is going to make it. Or, so far, none has."

"What's the drill?" Dick Miller asked.

He was in the backseat, now dressed in a torn and soiled light blue jumpsuit, a light zipper jacket, and a well-worn pair of white Adidas shoes. He had the general officer's model pistol in the side pocket of the jacket; he would have to keep his hand in the pocket to conceal the outline of the pistol, but there was no other place to put it. His cellular telephone was in the chest pocket of the coveralls.

"We'll loop through here again," Betty said. "This time, when we're at the corner I'll stop and you get out. Quickly, and don't slam the door. The turn-the-interior-lights-on thingamajib in the door has been disabled. When you're out, walk quickly away in the opposite direction. Go to the corner, stop, look around, then walk slowly back toward the corner and either lean against one of the buildings or sit on one of the stoops. Our guy is supposed to be in one of the buildings. He'll wait to see if you attract any attention."

"Has he got a name?"

"He knows your name is Miller and he has a description. Let him make the approach. You don't talk to anybody. Okay?"

"Got it. Then what happens?"

"You go where he takes you; more than likely, into one of the bricked-up buildings. You tell him what you want and he may or may not be able to help you. When you're finished, you call. He'll show you how to get back on West Seltzer and then go on his way. You go back to the stoop, or leaning on the wall, and when I come by you get in. Got it?"

"Got it."

"If something goes wrong, there's an unmarked Counterterrorism car somewhere around here and a Highway supervisor—actually, my brother—in the area, probably parked near the North Philadelphia Station. Either or both can be here in a minute or so. But the real name of the exercise is not blowing the cover of our guy. Understood?"

"Understood."

"Then when we finish here, there's another meet set up, we hope, for half past nine at North Twenty-fifth and Huntington streets, about twenty blocks from the station. And maybe one more after that."

"Watch your back, Dick," Castillo said as Betty slowed the BMW and approached the intersection of West Seltzer and West Somerset streets again.

"You behave, Casanova," Miller said.

Betty stopped the car. Miller got out, pushed—rather than slammed—the door closed, and walked away. Betty made a left turn on West Seltzer, then a right turn on North Broad Street.

"There's my brother," she said as they passed the station. "And another Highway car."

"They won't attract attention?"

"Highway is all over the city, all the time. Not that it would bother him. He takes very good care of his baby sister."

"I saw that in the bar at the Warwick. I really thought he was your boyfriend."

"And he asked me if you had hit on me," she said.

"You will recall I had not."

"I also recall that you told me you were the catering manager for some oil company. And I believed you. You're a very good liar. You could have been a con man."

"I'll take that as a compliment."

"Take that as a statement of fact," Betty said. "I also suspect that your not hitting on me in the hotel was the exception to your normal behavior."

"Why would you think that?"

"Dick keeps warning me about you, and telling you to behave."

"Trust me, Sergeant," Charley said. "Your virtue is not about to be attacked."

"I'll bet you say that to all the girls," Betty said.

"Would you feel better if I got in the backseat?"

"Unnecessary. I can take care of myself."

"Changing the subject, where are we going now?"

"I'm going to turn off Broad in a couple of blocks and make our way back to the general area where we dropped Dick off."

She had just made the turn when Castillo's cellular rang.

"Hello—

"Yes, sir—

"We just dropped Dick off to meet with one of the undercover cops—

"Sergeant Betty Schneider of the Intelligence Unit."

"Organized Crime and Intelligence Unit," Betty corrected him.

"*Organized Crime and* Intelligence Unit, I have just been corrected—

"When he calls, we'll go pick him up. There's at least one more meet tonight—

"Probably late into the night, sir. This is difficult to do—

"No. Chief Inspector Kramer made it pretty clear that Dick would do much better at this than me. Dick's black.

"No, sir. I'm not really needed for this—

"Fort Bragg? What for?—

"Yes, sir. I don't know how long it will take me to get there. Probably Philly-Atlanta-Fayetteville. I'll call you—

"What time will it get to Philly, sir?—

"It'll take me that long to pack and get out to the airport, sir—

"Yes, sir. Mr. Secretary, could I stay here until Dick finishes doing what he's doing? Maybe he'll come up with something—

"Yes, there is the telephone, sir. But it's not secure. And I really hate to just leave Dick—

"Yes, sir. I understand. Secretary Beiderman's now in the loop, is he?—

"Yes, sir. I'll call you when I get there. If Dick comes up with something while I'm in the air—

"Yes, sir. I understand."

As Castillo put his cellular into his pocket, he realized that Betty Schneider had pulled the Crown Victoria to the curb and stopped.

She was looking at him.

"The secretary of defense now knows what's going on," Castillo said, "and thinks I should go to Fort Bragg to meet with General McNab. So I'm going to Fort Bragg. Right now. My boss has sent his plane here to pick me up."

"Dick will be all right, Charley," Betty said. "We have him pretty well covered. The risk is really to the undercover cops."

"Yeah," he said.

"You really are worried about him, aren't you? I would have thought . . ."

"What?"

"Oh, I don't know. Macho stuff. Green Berets can do anything. But you really care."

"Dick and I go back a long way. And he doesn't have any experience with anything like this."

"And you've always taken care of him, right?"

"Meaning what?"

"His mother told me what you did in Afghanistan. No wonder she hugged you the way she did."

Castillo met her eyes for a moment.

"Can you take me someplace where I can catch a cab?"

"I can do better than that," she said and took out her cellular and punched an autodial key.

"Tom, I need to transport our guest first to the Warwick and then to the airport. And right now."

She looked at Castillo.

"My big brother," she said.

"I figured."

"Okay," Betty said to the telephone. "On the south side, in five minutes. Thanks, Tom."

She broke the connection, dropped the cellular into her purse, and pulled away from the curb.

"Tom's sending a Highway car to North Philadelphia Station. They'll take you to the Warwick and out to the airport."

"Thank you."

There was nothing that looked like a Highway Patrol car near the North Philadelphia Station when they got there.

Betty drove the BMW to an unlit area, stopped, and turned the headlights off.

A moment later, two cars pulled into the area beside the station.

"There's your Highway car," Betty said. "And, more than likely, Tom."

Betty flashed the headlights once.

"Do I go there or will they come here?"

"You start walking, and when they see you . . ."

"You've been great, Betty. Thank you very much."

"And I'll take care of Dick," she said. "Don't worry."

And then their faces were close.

And then she moved her face even closer and he felt her lips—warm and soft—on his.

Not chaste, Castillo thought. *And certainly not passionate. Something in between.* Tender.

"Jesus!" he said.

"Yeah, Jesus," Betty said, softly. "I really didn't mean for that to happen."

Castillo touched her cheek with the pads of his fingers but made no attempt to kiss her again.

"Go, Charley," Betty said.

He moved his head quickly and kissed her again. She responded for a moment, then averted her head.

"Go, Charley," she said. "Please."

He got out of the car and walked toward the railroad station.

One of the Highway cars started toward him. He stopped walking and waited. The car drove right past him. The second car moved toward him and stopped next to him.

Castillo got in and pulled the door shut.

There was a barrier between the front and rear seats. The upholstery in the back was of heavy plastic material.

A very large, very black police officer wearing a brimmed cap that seemed several sizes too small for him turned in the seat as the car started to move.

"The Warwick and then the airport, right?" he asked.

"Yes, please."

"Sit back and enjoy the ride," the Highway Patrol officer said as the car started down North Broad Street.

[SIX]

The very large Highway Patrol officer—Castillo saw for the first time he was a sergeant—was leaning against the car when Charley came out of the Warwick with his luggage.

He took the suitcase from Charley, opened the rear door, tossed the suitcase in the trunk, waited for Charley to get in, then closed the door.

The Warwick's doorman was obviously wondering what was going on.

They were five or six blocks down South Broad Street, stopped at a light, when the officer's cellular telephone rang.

"Hold on, Lieutenant," the sergeant said and turned on the seat. "It's for you, but the phone won't go through the barrier."

The car pulled to the curb, the sergeant got out, opened the rear door, and handed the phone to Castillo.

"Hello?"

"This is Tom Schneider."

"I think we've met before," Charley said. "I really appreciate the . . ."

"Yeah. So what are you, DEA or something?"

"Or something."

"Well, listen good, Mr. DEA hotshot. I saw what you was doing with my sister in her car."

"I don't really know how to respond to that," Charley said. "It was . . ."

"Don't respond. Just listen. You fuck around with my sister again, I'll break both of your legs. You understand me?"

"I hear you loud and clear, Lieutenant."

"See if you can not come back to Philadelphia," Lieutenant Schneider said and broke the connection.

Charley handed the cellular back to the sergeant, who had apparently been able to hear the conversation because he said, "He means it. You better pay attention."

Then he closed the door, got back in the front seat, and the car moved into the traffic flowing down South Broad Street.

"Which airline?" the Highway Patrol sergeant said as they approached Philadelphia International Airport.

That subject had not previously been considered by Major C. G. Castillo, whose mind had, all the way down South Broad Street, been occupied with the memory of Betty Schneider's eyes—and then her lips—on his, and the multiple ramifications thereunto pertaining.

"Not an airline," he said. "They sent a plane for me."

"Who 'they'?"

"The Department of Homeland Security," Charley said. "It's a Secret Service airplane."

"No shit?"

"Is there a general aviation terminal?" Charley asked. "Or something like that?"

"Beats the shit out of me," the Highway sergeant confessed. "Let me see if I can find one of the airport guys. They got sort of a district out here."

Halfway down the line of departing passenger gates of the various airlines, the Highway officer driving the car spotted a policeman wearing a white-brimmed cap, and blew his horn to attract his attention. When that didn't work, he made the siren growl for a moment, which produced the desired effect. The airport detail officer trotted over to the car, to the fascination of thirty or more departing passengers.

"Your name Castingo?" the officer inquired after having been asked where a Secret Service airplane would be parked.

"Castillo," Charley said.

"Whatever. Close enough. The arm is out for a guy who would probably ask about a Secret Service airplane," the officer said. Then he looked at the sergeant. "They want him over at the unit."

The unit turned out to be a small building at the end of one of the parking lots. The sergeant opened the rear door of the patrol car for Charley, and, after Charley grabbed his gear from the trunk, led him into the building.

It was, Charley saw, a small police station. There was a "desk"—an elevated platform—manned by a sergeant and a corporal, and, on one side of the room, there were two holding cells. The "bars" were made of chain-link fence, but since the cells were in sight of the desk sergeant it was unlikely that a prisoner could get through them unnoticed.

Joel Isaacson, the supervisory Secret Service agent in charge of Secretary Hall's security detail, was leaning against the makeshift desk.

Charley walked toward him with the Highway sergeant on his heels. When Isaacson saw Charley, he smiled, then bent his head slightly toward the voice-activated microphone under his lapel.

"Tom," he said. "Don Juan just walked in here."

Castillo wondered how unlikely it was that the Highway sergeant, when reporting the successful delivery of the passenger to the airport, would fail to mention that he had been met by some kind of a federal agent, probably Secret Service, who referred to him as "Don Juan."

"Hey, Charley," Isaacson said. "Good timing. I don't think I've been here five minutes. Your flying chariot awaits."

"I didn't expect to see you, Joel," Castillo said as they shook hands.

"The FBI came through with that dossier the boss asked for," Isaacson said. "On your new friend?"

Castillo nodded.

"The boss wants you to read it on our way to where we're going. I'm to bring it back."

"Okay."

"And you're in luck. The suitcase you left on the airplane the last time you were on it?"

Charley searched his memory.

Christ! I left my go-right-now bag on the secretary's airplane the day I met the president and he gave me this job. The day Fernando picked me up in his new Lear and flew me to Texas to see Abuela.

Jesus, I'd forgotten all about it. How long ago was that? It seems like last year, but it was really only a couple of weeks ago. Less than two weeks: thirteen days.

"It's still on the plane," Joel said. "I tagged it inspected."

"Thanks."

"It could have been a bomb, Charley," Isaacson said. "You're lucky somebody didn't take it to the end of the runway at Andrews and blow it up."

"I forgot to tell anyone I left it on board," Charley said.

"I'm not sore at you, Don Juan . . ."

Thanks a lot, Joel. The sergeant here might have missed "Don Juan" the first time.

". . . egg is on my face. Don't tell the boss."

"Of course not."

"You about ready to go?"

"Anytime," Charley said. He turned to the Highway Patrol sergeant. "Thanks for the ride. I appreciate it."

"No problem," the sergeant said and then looked at Isaacson. "Why do you call him that? 'Don Juan'? Can I ask?"

Isaacson smiled, then made an exaggerated search of the room with his eyes.

"I don't see any members of the gentle sex who might take offense, so why not? Take a look at him, Sergeant. Nice-looking guy. Young. Not married. Lives very well. Meets a lot of interesting women. Would you suspect that he gets laid a lot?"

The Highway Patrol sergeant chuckled.

"I thought it was probably something like that," he said.

[SEVEN]
On board Cessna Citation X NC 601
Flight level 31,000 feet
Near Raleigh, North Carolina
2135 9 June 2005

"Did you read this?" Charley Castillo asked, raising his eyes from the personnel file of Kennedy, Howard C., each page of which was stamped SECRET in red.

Joel Isaacson and Tom McGuire were in the rear of the cabin, both lying nearly horizontally in fully reclined seats and both holding a bottle of beer. And both nodded.

"I decided I had the need to know," McGuire said, mock serious.

Isaacson smiled.

"Something's missing," Castillo said. "Or I'm missing something."

Isaacson raised his right eyebrow but again said nothing.

"The FBI's been leaning on me—or the boss—to tell them where he is. And he's really worried that I will."

"Uh-huh," Isaacson agreed.

"There's nothing in here that explains that," Charley said. "And there's nothing in here about a warrant or an indictment, anything like that. What's going on? Why's it classified secret? It's just a personnel record. Confidential, maybe, but secret?"

"There's a story going around that the FBI internal phone book is classified secret," Tom McGuire said. "They're big on keeping things to themselves."

"What does it say he did for the FBI?" Isaacson asked.

Castillo dropped his eyes to the file again.

"He was 'assistant special agent in charge of the professional standards unit,'" Castillo read. "What the hell is that?"

"It's what the cops call 'internal affairs,'" McGuire said. "Think about it, Charley."

"You mean he was involved with dirty FBI agents?"

"There is no such thing as a dirty FBI agent," Isaacson said. "I'm surprised you, a supervisory special agent of the Secret Service, don't know that."

McGuire laughed. Castillo didn't think they resented his having Secret Service identification, but sometimes they needled him. Castillo gave Isaacson the finger.

"What about their counterintelligence guy who was on the Russian's payroll?"

"They couldn't deny that one," McGuire said. "The CIA bagged him. Think of him as the exception that proves the rule."

"I never said, with Tom as my witness, what I'm about to say," Isaacson said. "Okay?"

"Okay," Castillo said.

"I, of course, don't know what I'm talking about. But let me throw this scenario at you," Isaacson said. "It probably goes all the way back to J. Edgar Hoover, but the basic philosophy of the FBI is protect the FBI, closely followed by make the FBI look good and never do or admit anything that could in any way make the FBI look bad. *¿Está claro, mi amigo?*"

Castillo nodded, smiling.

"With that in mind, they don't call their internal affairs unit 'Internal Affairs.' To have an internal affairs unit would be an admission that there was a possibility, however remote, that there might be, from time to time, one or two—maybe even three—FBI agents who are not absolutely one hundred percent squeaky clean and perfect in every way. On the other hand, it has to be faced that there are, from time to time, some agents whose behavior might not meet in every detail the professional standards expected of everyone in the FBI. Hence, the 'Professional Standards Unit,' to root these miscreants out, and do so very quietly."

"You don't like the FBI much, do you, Joel?"

"Like every other right-thinking, patriotic American, I hold the FBI in the highest possible regard. I am simply unable to accept any suggestion that any FBI agent would ever do anything wrong."

Tom McGuire chuckled.

"Okay, so what are you thinking, Joel?"

"Read the file, Charley. The FBI put your pal Kennedy on the fast track from the time he left Quantico. He was always assigned some place important— he was never in someplace like the Cornhole, Kansas, field office; he was in New York, LA, Dallas, with frequent tours in Washington. He was good. I could tell that on the phone."

"Excuse me?"

"In your apartment, when he called. I answered the telephone, 'Hello?' he asked, 'Charley?' I said, 'Who's calling, please?,' and he hung up. He smelled a cop—maybe an FBI agent—answering your phone. He called back five minutes later—time enough to leave wherever he was calling from and to get on a cellular that would be hard to trace."

"Okay," Charley said.

"So, again, I don't know what I'm talking about, but here's a possibility. Your pal Kennedy was assigned—as a very bright, absolutely trustworthy member of the FBI Palace Guard—to Professional Standards, where he got to know where all the bodies are buried. Not all of the miscreants Professional Standards catches with their hands in the petty cash drawer—or in the drawers of somebody else's wife—get prosecuted, or even canned."

"Why not?"

"The higher they are on the FBI pyramid, the more embarrassing it is for the FBI to haul them before the bar of justice. May I go on?"

"Certainly. I'm not sure how much of this I believe, but it's interesting."

"Well, then, fuck you, Charley. My lips are now sealed."

"You can't leave me hanging like this, Joel."

Isaacson made him wait long enough for Charley to think, *I'll be damned, he is going to stop,* before he went on.

"With whatever they did hanging over their heads, the powers that be can trust them to behave. That works fine as long as the guy—guys—who know what they did are in the FBI. But your pal is no longer with the bureau, is he?

He now works for a Russian bad guy. But he can still use the same lever to . . . how do I put this? . . . *gain the cooperation* of a lot of people in the bureau for his ends, which are not necessarily in the best interests of the FBI."

"Okay, so what?" Charley asked. "Why is Kennedy so worried that they'll be able to locate him?"

McGuire made a pistol with his hand and said, "Bang!"

"Oh, come on, Tom!" Charley said.

"Accidents happen," Isaacson said. "People get run over by hit-and-run drivers, fall off balconies, etcetera."

Jesus Christ, they mean it!

"Watch your ears back there," the pilot's voice came over the cabin speaker. "I finally got cleared to make an approach to Pope. It's going to be steep."

The nose of the airplane immediately dipped.

In his mind, Charley saw the altimeter unwinding and the digital airspeed indicator on the glass panel beginning to flash red as they approached maximum safe speed.

[EIGHT]
Pope Air Force Base, North Carolina
2155 9 June 2005

The copilot of the Citation came out of the cockpit as soon as the aircraft was safely on the ground and stood by the door prepared to open it the moment the aircraft stopped. The pilot obviously wanted to get airborne again as quickly as possible. So long as the Citation was transporting Charley, it wasn't available to Secretary Hall.

When the Citation stopped on the tarmac in front of base operations, the copilot immediately opened the door.

Charley went down the steps carrying his laptop computer briefcase and the suitcase he'd brought from Philadelphia, and Joel Isaacson followed him off the airplane with the go-right-now bag, handed it to Charley, affectionately punched him on the shoulder, and got back on the airplane.

Charley hung the laptop's strap around his neck, picked up the two suit-cases, and with the laptop bumping him uncomfortably with each step walked toward the double glass doors of base operations. Before he got there, the Citation was just visible as it approached the threshold of the active runway, and, as Charley pushed through the doors with his back, he saw the Citation turn onto the runway without stopping and begin its takeoff roll.

Charley wondered again why it was so important that he come to Fort Bragg *right now* that Hall had sent the plane for him. The only thing he could think of was that otherwise it would have taken him forever to get here on an airline.

There was an Air Force sergeant on duty behind the base operations counter.

"I'm going to need a ride over to the Special Warfare Center," Charley announced.

"You just get off that Citation?"

"Yes, I did."

"You military?"

Good question. Who am I? The special assistant to the secretary of homeland security? A supervisory special agent of the Secret Service? Major C. G. Castillo of the U.S. Army? Or maybe a Drug Enforcement Agency agent? Which is what I told Betty's brother just before he offered to break both my legs.

"Yes, I am," Charley told the sergeant.

"I'll need to see some identification, sir," the sergeant said. "And your orders."

Where the hell is my Army identification?

In the lid of the laptop briefcase, where I put it when I went to Germany. And I am not going to take it out now and give the sergeant something interesting to tell the boys.

"Not possible, Sergeant, sorry," Charley said. "Would you call the duty officer at SWC and tell him that Major Castillo needs a ride over there? They expect me."

"I really have to see some identification, sir."

"That wasn't a suggestion, Sergeant. Call the SWC."

"Sir, this is Sergeant Lefler at Pope base ops. I have a gentleman here who doesn't have any identification but says he's a Major Castillo and that you expect him."

Fifteen seconds later, after repeating Castillo's name, the sergeant almost triumphantly turned to Castillo and said, "They never heard of you, sir."

"Let me talk to him, please," Charley said.

The sergeant didn't reply, instead dialing a number from memory.

"Sir, I hate to bother you," he said a moment later, "but I think you better come down here. We may have an attempted breach of security."

A moment later, he added, "No, sir. Not to worry," and then hung up.

"Sir, would you please have a seat over there?" he said to Charley, pointing to a row of chrome-and-plastic chairs.

"What's going on, Sergeant?"

"Sir, the Airdrome Officer of the Day is on his way here. He will answer any questions you might have. Please take a seat, sir."

The sergeant rested his hand on the holster hanging from his pistol belt.

What the hell is going on here?

They don't expect me?

Charley walked to the row of chairs and sat down.

Fuck it, I'll give him something to talk about.

"Sergeant, could I walk over there and get into my briefcase, please?"

"You just sit right there, please, sir," the sergeant replied. "You can talk about your briefcase to the major when he gets here, sir."

The telephone on the desk rang. Without taking his eyes from Castillo, the sergeant answered it.

"Pope base operations, Sergeant Lefler speaking, sir—

"Sir, the AOD is not here at the moment—

"He should be here in a couple of minutes, sir. Would you like to call back?—

"Sir, there already has been a civilian Citation in here. It just left—

"Yes, sir. A man did get off. He doesn't have any identification, sir, but he says he's a major—

"I don't think I'd better do that, sir, until the AOD gets here. He may let you talk to him—

"No, sir, I don't know who I'm talking to. You didn't give me your name."

The sergeant looked stricken at the response he was given.

An Air Force major, a pilot, wearing the brassard of an Airdrome Officer of the Day, came into the area.

Charley suspected the Airdrome Officer of the Day had been catching a few winks on a cot somewhere near.

"What's going on, Sergeant?" he asked.

"Sir, I think you better take this," the sergeant said, extending the telephone to him. "It's the deputy commander of Eighteenth Airborne Corps."

The major took the telephone.

"This is Major Treward, sir. The AOD. How may I help you, sir?"

The major looked at Castillo.

"Excuse me, sir, are you the special assistant to the secretary of homeland security?"

Castillo nodded.

"Yes, sir, he's right here," the major said and extended the telephone to Castillo.

"Sir," Sergeant Lefler said, "he told me he was an Army major."

"This is Major Castillo, sir," Charley said into the telephone.

"See, he just did it again, sir," Sergeant Lefler told the AOD.

"That's me, too, sir," Charley said into the phone. "I'm assigned to Homeland Security—

"Yes, sir. I just arrived here on the secretary's plane. My orders are to report to General McNab."

"He wouldn't show me any orders, either, Major," Sergeant Lefler said. "I asked."

"Yes, sir. I'll be here," Charley said into the telephone. "Thank you, sir."

He handed the telephone to the Air Force major. "The general is coming to pick me up."

"Sir, the Security SOP says nobody leaves the building without proper identification," Sergeant Lefler announced.

The major looked at him but didn't respond.

"What I'd like to know is how a civilian aircraft landed here without special permission and why I wasn't told it had," he said to the desk sergeant.

"The pilot filed his flight plan as Secret Service One," Charley offered. "That gets him clearance to land just about any place he wants to."

"Are you in the Secret Service?" the major asked.

Actually, I'm a supervisory agent of the Secret Service. Wanna see my badge?

Charley chuckled. It was almost a giggle.

"I say something funny?"

"No. All I am, Major, is another major."

Major General H. V. Gonzalez, who was about five-foot-five, olive-skinned, weighed no more than 130 pounds, and looked meaner than hell, marched purposefully into base operations ten minutes later, trailed by his aide and a full colonel, both of whom were well over six feet tall. They were all wearing desert camouflage battle dress uniforms (BDUs).

The deputy commander of XVIII Airborne Corps glanced around the room and then marched to where Castillo was sitting. Charley got up quickly as he approached.

"You're Castillo?"

"Yes, sir."

General Gonzalez switched to Spanish.

"The name Elaine Naylor mean anything to you?"

"*Sí, señor.*"

"And what's her husband's first name?"

"Allan, señor."

"But we are not privileged to call him by his first name, are we?"

"I'm not, sir."

"General Naylor tells me you're a Tex-Mex from San Antone who speaks pretty good Spanish and works for the secretary of homeland security and that he doesn't have a clue why Dr. Natalie Cohen called me up to tell me the president was sending you here. That about sum things up?"

"*Sí, señor.*"

"Harry," the general said, switching to English to speak to his aide. "Help Major Castillo with his bags."

There was a powder blue Plymouth Caravan parked outside the base operations building.

"You ride up front with me," General Gonzalez ordered, in Spanish, as he got behind the wheel.

"*Sí, señor,*" Charley replied.

"What was that Chinese fire drill back there all about?" Gonzalez asked.

"My fault, sir. I asked the sergeant to call SWC to get me a ride. They'd never heard of me. And then I couldn't come up with my Army ID."

"Why did you call the SWC? Didn't they tell you General McNab is the Eighteenth Airborne Corps commander?"

"Unless stupidity is an excuse, sir, no excuse. When General McNab was deputy commander of SWC, I was his aide. I called there. Not bright."

"Oh, so you know General McNab?"

"Yes, sir. Sir, where is he?"

"I don't think you have the need to know that."

"Sir, knowing General McNab as I do, I'm guessing he's as close to the Gray Fox operation at Abéché as he can get."

"I'd love to know how you heard about Abéché," General Gonzalez said. "Most of the people at Bragg who know about it are in the backseat."

"Sir, the operation was to confirm intel I developed."

"And?"

"If you're asking, sir, was it confirmed? Yes, sir, it was. The missing airplane was there but has gone."

"Okay. If you know that much, you're in the loop. General McNab is in Menara, Morocco, with some more Gray Fox people standing by with a C-17 in case anything goes wrong with the extraction, which is scheduled for first light. As soon as he hears it's wheels-up, he and the backup team will return here in their C-17. It's about a five-hour flight."

"Thank you, sir."

"The problem I have right now is, what to do with you."

"Sir?"

"Until I talked to General Naylor twenty minutes ago, I expected some civilian VIP. The lights in the windows of the VIP guesthouse are burning for you, Major Castillo."

"How about dropping me at a Smoke Bomb Hill BOQ, sir?"

"No. The last thing we need is another Chinese fire drill when you can't produce an ID card. We'll take you to the VIP guesthouse. Just don't tell anyone you're a major."

"Yes, sir."

The general drove through Fort Bragg for several minutes before saying anything else; then he said:

"There are a lot of lousy jobs in the Army, but right at the head of the list has to be aide-de-camp to Scotty McNab. That's probably even worse than being his deputy commander."

"I tried to think of it as an educational experience, sir."

General Gonzalez laughed.

"Harry, did you hear that?"

"Yes, sir."

"Write it down."

"Yes, sir."

"Harry, I want you to stay with Major Castillo. Give him a drink and then send him to bed. He looks worn-out and I suspect tomorrow is going to be very 'educational.' "

"Yes, sir."

XIV

The VIP suite into which Castillo was installed had a bedroom, a sitting room with a small dining room table at one side, a small office, and a kitchenette. It was about two-thirds the size of his apartment in the Mayflower.

It also came with a young sergeant in a crisply pressed desert camouflage battle dress uniform.

"Can I have the sergeant fix you something to drink, sir?" General Gonzalez's aide-de-camp asked.

He was a captain. His name tag said BREWSTER. He had a CIB and senior parachutist's wings sewn above his pocket. And there was a Ranger tab sewn to his sleeve above the XVIII Airborne Corps shoulder insignia. But his beret was black—as General Gonzalez's beret had been, Castillo remembered—so neither Captain Brewster nor General Gonzalez was Special Forces. Green Beanies wore green berets, of which they were justifiably proud.

What color beret does General McNab wear these days? Black or green?

Whatever color pleases him, obviously.

"No," Castillo said. "What you can do is point me in the direction of the booze and send the sergeant home."

"Yes, sir," the aide said, not quite able to conceal his surprise at Castillo's abruptness.

Castillo picked up on it.

Jesus Christ, what's the matter with me?

"Sergeant, I've had a bad day," Castillo said. "What I'm going to do is have one drink and then get in bed. There's no sense in you sticking around for that."

"Yes, sir," the sergeant asked. "Sir, what are your breakfast plans?"

"Nothing beyond a cup of coffee. Is there a coffee machine in the kitchen?"

"Yes, sir. But I'd be happy . . ."

"Is there someplace I can call you if I need you?"

"The number of the protocol office is taped to the telephones, sir, if you need anything."

"Thank you, Sergeant," Castillo said and smiled at him.

When the sergeant had gone, Castillo looked at Captain Brewster.

"I didn't mean to snap at the sergeant," Castillo said.

"I'm sure there's no problem, sir," Captain Brewster said.

"I can fix myself a drink and get in bed by myself, Captain," Castillo said. "There's no reason for you to stick around, either."

"I can stick around outside the suite if that would make you more comfortable, sir, but . . ."

"But General Gonzalez said stay with him, right?"

"Yes, sir."

Castillo walked into the small kitchen, where he had seen a line of bottles on a counter under the closets.

"I know how that is. I been dere, done dat, got duh T-shirt," Castillo said.

Captain Brewster smiled.

"You want one of these?" Castillo asked, holding up a bottle of scotch.

"I better not."

"As one dog robber to another, I won't tell your general."

" 'Dog robber'?"

"General McNab told me, when I was wearing the rope," Castillo said, touching his shoulder where the aiguillette of aides-de-camp hung from the epaulets of dress uniforms, "that when he had worn the rope as a young officer aides-de-camp were known as 'dog robbers' because they were expected to do whatever was required, including robbing from dogs, to make their general happy."

"I never heard that," Brewster said, smiling. Then he nodded at the bottle Castillo was holding. "Okay. Why not? Thank you."

Castillo poured whiskey in a glass and handed it to him.

"How long were you General McNab's aide?" Brewster asked.

"Too long," Charley said. "Twenty-two months. Long enough to know that when he finds out I spent the night in the VIP quarters, he will have something unpleasant to say."

Brewster chuckled.

"How about you?"

"It's supposed to be for a year," Brewster said. "Another two months."

"And then?" Castillo said, handing him a glass of whiskey. "I suppose there's ice and water, but I drink mine neat."

"Neat's fine," Brewster said, then added: "I put in for Special Forces. Maybe I'll get lucky and make the cut."

Castillo's cellular phone rang.

"Hello?"

There was a buzz and then a click.

Castillo put the telephone back in his shirt pocket.

"Bad connection?" Captain Brewster asked.

No, that was probably from a renegade FBI agent who works for a Russian arms dealer who wants (a) to know where I am and (b) that I be impressed with his ability to find that out.

Castillo nodded and said, "I'll bet it rings again in a minute."

He pressed the TIMER button on his watch and then tipped glasses with Brewster.

Then he took the telephone out again and pressed an autodial button.

Screw Kennedy. When he calls back, my voice mail can answer—and I bet he won't leave a message, even to let me know he knows where I am.

"Yes?" the woman's voice answered.

"Is this my favorite female law enforcement officer?"

"Not now. Call back in ten minutes," Sergeant Betty Schneider replied, curtly.

"Is something wrong?" Castillo asked. Even as he spoke the words, he knew she had broken the connection and he was speaking to a dead telephone.

What the hell! Has something gone wrong with Dick?

"Favorite female *law enforcement officer*?" Captain Harry Brewster asked with a knowing smile.

The look Captain Brewster got from Major Castillo told him he had crossed a dangerous line.

Castillo took a sip of his drink.

The last thing I need is liquor. My brain is already slipping gears. Jesus, I called the SWC instead of XVIII Airborne Corps!

On the other hand, as keyed up as I am I'll never get to sleep tonight without a little sauce to slow me down.

And even if Dick is at this moment being roasted over a slow fire by the African American Lunatics in Philadelphia, there is not a goddamned thing I can do about it in Fort Bragg.

He took another sip and had just taken the glass from his lips when the telephone rang again.

He snatched it almost angrily from his pocket.

"Yeah?"

"Your phone has been out of service," Howard Kennedy said.

"Aren't you going to tell me where I am?"

"That tells me you are probably no longer in Philadelphia."

"Where are you?"

"Somewhere over North Carolina, I would guess. Using one of those back-of-the-seat, ten-dollars-a-minute telephones. You're not going to tell me where you are?"

"What are you doing somewhere over North Carolina? Going somewhere?"

"Cancún, actually," Kennedy said. "Okay. Now it's your turn."

Since I don't know that he's actually in an airplane en route to Mexico, and may have been in touch with his friends in the wireless telephone business, and is entirely capable of—entirely likely to—see if I'm lying to him, it's truth time.

"Would you believe the VIP guest quarters at Fort Bragg, North Carolina, Howard?"

"Of course. Since we have agreed to be entirely truthful with one another. What the hell are you doing in Fort Bragg? Do you have something you want to share with me?"

He seems genuinely surprised. Or is it that he's almost as skilled a liar as I am?

"The answer to question one is that I'm here because my boss sent me here. He has not seen fit to explain his reasons. And, no, I don't have anything much to share with you. Miller's still in Philadelphia meeting with undercover cops. I don't know what—if anything—he's come up with, but I should hear something soon. If I do, how do I pass it on to you? I never tried to call anybody on an airliner before."

"Neither have I," Kennedy said. "But to demonstrate my faith in your veracity—taking a hell of a big chance, in other words, which I really hate to do—I'm on Mexicana 455, Newark to Mexico City. If you hear anything, give it a try, Charley. This is the age of miraculous communication. If that doesn't work—and I'm not met in Mexico City by representatives of my former employer—I'll call you from the airport."

"If anybody meets you, I didn't send them."

"Boy Scouts' honor?"

"Were you a Boy Scout?"

"Certainly. Weren't you?"

"I am now holding my pinky with my thumb, the other fingers extended vertically, my arm raised to shoulder level," Castillo said as he did so.

Captain Brewster, who could not hear the conversation but, as an Eagle Scout himself, knew the gesture, looked curiously at him.

"As one Boy Scout to another, I accept your word of honor," Kennedy said.

"Does that mean you're also going to tell me why you're going to Cancún?"

"I thought you'd never ask," Kennedy said. "Do you know where Khartoum is, Charley?"

"There's a K-town in Sudan."

"You're halfway to your World Geography merit badge. How about Murtala Muhammad International Airport?"

"You've got me there," Charley confessed after a moment.

"Lagos, Nigeria. Write that down."

"Is there a point to this quiz?"

"A 727 bearing the paint scheme of Air Suriname—you don't happen to know where Suriname is, do you, Charley?"

"Upper right corner of South America?"

"Not quite the upper-right corner; a little down the coast from the upper-right corner. But you got the continent right."

"You were saying?"

"An Air Suriname 727 landed at N'Djamena, Chad, after a flight from Khartoum, took on fuel—lots of fuel—filed a flight plan to Murtala Muhammad International Airport, which you now know is the airport serving Lagos, Nigeria, and took off." He paused to let that register, then added, "It never got to Murtala Muhammad International—"

"Okay. I follow. But—"

Kennedy ignored the interruption and continued: "Even more fascinating than that is the friendly folks in Khartoum tell us they have no record of Air Suriname 1101 having visited their airfield in the last six months."

Charley gestured almost frantically to Captain Brewster, miming writing. Brewster quickly took a small notebook and a ballpoint pen from a shoulder pocket of his BDU and handed it to him.

"So you think it's the one we're looking for?" Charley said as he hurriedly scribbled "Air Suriname" and the flight number in the notebook.

"I think it probably merits further investigation," Kennedy said, sarcastically. "Wouldn't you agree?"

"Absolutely. You don't happen to have the registration number?"

"P-Papa, Z-Zero, 5059. Fiver-Zero-Fiver-Niner."

Castillo scribbled PZ5059 in the notebook.

"I'll pass this right on," he said. "Thanks."

"You will tell them where it came from, won't you?"

"What if you're wrong?"

"I'll take that chance, Charley."

He's serious about that. He must believe what he's telling me. Or wants me to believe he's serious.

"Any idea where it really went?"

"There's any number of airfields on the west coast of Africa, some of them even sophisticated enough to have paved runways and navigation aids. If I had to guess, I'd say Yundum International."

"Yumdum?" Castillo blurted.

"Yundum, Why You *En* Dum. No Bee After Dum."

"Where the hell is that?"

"Outside Banjul. You know that charming metropolis, I'm sure."

"Come on, Howard!"

"How about Gambia? You do know where Gambia is, don't you?"

"West coast of Africa?"

"Next to Senegal," Kennedy said. "Banjul is maybe a hundred miles down the coast from Dakar."

"Why there?"

"It's a pretty good jumping-off place if you want to fly across the ocean."

"Cross it to where?" Castillo asked.

There was no response. Castillo thought he detected a change in the background hiss.

"Cross it to where?" he asked again, then added, "You still there, Howard?"

There was nothing but the hiss.

"Damn!" Charley said and pushed the hang-up key.

He sensed Captain Brewster's eyes on him.

"Cut off," Castillo explained and then pushed the autodial key for Betty Schneider again.

"Yeah?" Her voice came matter-of-factly over the cellular.

"Is everything all right?" Charley asked.

There was no reply for a moment and then Dick Miller came on the line.

"There's a connection," Miller said.

"You all right?"

"I've decided I don't want to be an undercover cop, but otherwise I'm fine."

"You're sure?"

"I'm fine, Charley."

"What kind of a connection?"

"Right now, I just know that. They're going to bring the undercover cop in. I don't really know what that means, but it's apparently damned hard to do. But if I get something concrete, I don't want to tell you over a cellular. I think you better get up here, Charley."

"Betty tell you where I am?"

"Yeah."

"I was *ordered* here, Dick," Castillo said. "I'm not sure I can come back up there. Not tonight, anyway. Jesus, I don't know how I'd get there. I'll get back to you. If it's really important, call Secretary Hall."

"It'll wait until you know for sure you can't get up here," Miller said.

"I'll get back to you, Dick," Castillo said and ended the call.

He pushed the autodial key for Secretary Hall, then changed his mind, broke off the call, and turned to Captain Brewster.

"What's General McNab's ETA here?"

Brewster obviously didn't want to answer the question and when he said, "I really don't know, sir," it was equally obvious that he was lying. "In the van on the way over here," Charley snapped, "General Whatsisname said something about everybody in the van being in on the Abéché Gray Fox operation, meaning you are. I really don't have the time to fuck with you, Brewster. Now, give me McNab's ETA or get General Whatsisname on the horn for me."

Brewster met his eyes for a moment, then shrugged. "It's General Gonzalez, Major. General McNab—and the backup force—will be airborne over Morocco in the Globemaster at midnight Bragg time. That's 0600 Abéché time. The extraction from Abéché is scheduled for daybreak—0612 Abéché time; twelve after midnight here. If the general gets a successful wheels-up report, he plans to head directly back here. If something goes wrong in Abéché . . ."

"If nothing goes wrong?"

"Then he should be on the ground here at about 0615."

"Thank you," Charley said and pressed the autodial key for Secretary Hall again.

"Charley, sir. I'm sorry I'm calling so late."

"I heard you were at Bragg. Any word about General McNab?"

"He'll probably be back here about six in the morning, sir."

"See what he has to say and call me as soon as you can."

"Yes, sir. There have been two developments, sir."

"Let's have them."

"I heard from my friend Kennedy. He believes the 727 is headed for someplace in South America, if it's not already there. It was in N'Djamena, Chad, took on a load of fuel, and filed a flight plan to Murtala Muhammad International Airport—Lagos, Nigeria—and took off. It never landed there . . ."

"Does it have the range to make it across the Atlantic from N'Djamena?" Secretary Hall interrupted.

"It might if those fuel bladders were installed," Charley said. "I just don't know. Kennedy thinks it probably went to Yundum International, in Gambia."

"Where?"

"On the west coast of Africa, about a hundred miles south of Dakar, Senegal."

"He say why there?"

"Kennedy said it's a convenient jumping-off place to cross the Atlantic to South America, which I suspect means he knows—probably from experience—that they don't ask too many questions of transient aircraft."

"He doesn't know or wouldn't tell you where the airplane is headed?"

"I think if he knew, he would have told me. He did tell me that it's been painted with the color scheme of Air Suriname, so it may be going there, operative word *may*. I have the new registration numbers."

"Let me have them. Wait 'til I get something to write with."

Charley covered the microphone with the heel of his hand and turned to Captain Brewster.

"When you report this conversation to General Gonzalez—and that had better be on your agenda—I'm talking to my boss, Matthew Hall, the secretary of Homeland Security. How much have you been able to overhear?"

Brewster looked uncomfortable but said, "Most of it."

"Okay, Charley," Hall's voice came faintly but clearly over the cellular, "let's have the numbers. You said Air Suriname, right?"

"Yes, sir. The numbers are *P* as in Papa, *Z* as in Zero, 5059. Fiver-Zero-Fiver-Niner."

"Pee-Zee-fifty-fifty-nine?"

"Yes, sir."

"I'll get this to the CIA right away. Maybe, now that we have the registration numbers, their satellites may have a location on the plane."

"Sir, I just talked to Miller. He said he's come up with connections, plural, in Philadelphia."

"He say what they were?"

"We don't have secure phones, sir. He thinks I ought to hear what he's got in person. I'd like to go back up there."

"We need to know for sure what General McNab found out."

"Sir, what I was thinking was talk to General McNab, then go to Philadelphia."

"It would take you all day to go up there and back, Charley. And I agree with the secretary of defense that you should be at Bragg. Whatever happens, it will involve Gray Fox. Maybe all of Delta. You should be there, if for no other purpose than staying in the loop—and keeping me in it."

"Yes, sir. I agree. And I agree going commercial wouldn't work; it would take too long, and we're running out of time, but . . ."

"Yes, we are," Hall interrupted. "At four tomorrow afternoon, the police commissioner's going to tell the mayor what he knows. I don't even like to think what's going to happen when he does."

"Yes, sir. But if I had a plane, I could get up to Philadelphia and be back in a matter of hours."

"I need my plane here," Hall said, evenly, answering the question he expected next. "That's why it barely did more than a touch-and-go when it dropped you at Bragg."

"I can get a plane—I'm almost sure I can—but what I need is permission for it to land at Pope."

"What are you talking about, renting a plane yourself?"

"No, sir. My family has an airplane. I can—presuming it's not down for maintenance or something—just borrow it."

"You think it's important?"

"Yes, sir. I do. I also may need it to meet with Kennedy."

"Where is he?"

"I don't know, sir," Charley replied, comfortable in the fact that he did not know for certain if Kennedy was telling the truth about being en route to Mexico City and that it was always better to pass only information that had been confirmed. "But I expect another call at any time."

"I'm going to have to give the FBI this latest bulletin, and, when I do, they're going to ask where Kennedy is."

"I'm glad I really don't know, sir."

"Okay, Charley, I'll call Secretary Beiderman and have him get landing clearance for you."

"Thank you."

"Wait a minute, Charley. I just thought there's probably one—or more—of those Army Beechcraft King Airs . . ."

"C-12s," Charley furnished.

". . . at Fort Bragg. I can have Beiderman arrange for you to use one. For that matter, I can probably just as easily have Beiderman get you a small Air Force jet."

"Sir, that would cause problems, starting with talk. And I'd really rather have what the cops would call an unmarked airplane."

"But is your family's airplane fast enough? The clock is ticking."

"Yes, sir. It's a Learjet 45XR."

Castillo heard Hall exhale.

"You're going to borrow your family's *Learjet 45XR*? Every time I think there's nothing else you could tell me that could possibly surprise me, you do. Okay, Charley. Do it your way. You better give me the registration numbers."

"Jesus, I don't know," Charley said and then corrected himself immediately. "Yeah, I do. I flew it into Baltimore just before I went to Angola. Five-Oh-Seven-Five."

"Learjet 45XR. Five-Oh-Seven-Five," Hall repeated. "Anything else, Charley?"

"I'm going to see if I can't borrow some Gray Fox radios," Charley said. "The secure kind."

"I can have Beiderman arrange that, too, if you want."

"I think the Gray Fox people who have them—or I hope do have them— would probably stall even him until McNab okayed it," Charley said. "Let me see how far I get by myself."

"Your call. Are you running into any kind of hassle with anyone down there? I thought I picked up . . ."

"No, sir. General Gonzalez even loaned me his aide to see that I get whatever I think I need."

He looked at Captain Brewster as he spoke.

"Okay. Keep me in the loop, Charley."

"Yes, sir, of course."

He broke that connection and pushed another autodial number.

"Maria," he said a moment later, in Spanish, "this is Carlos. I realize it's late, and I hope I didn't wake you up, but I really have to talk to Fernando."

He saw the surprise on Captain Brewster's face at the Spanish and wondered how much Spanish Gonzalez's aide knew.

He probably speaks it. Or at least has been trying hard to learn it. A wise move, considering his general is named Gonzalez and he likes to speak Spanish.

"What's up, Gringo?" Fernando Lopez, sounding sleepy, asked.

"Fernando, I need the Lear," Castillo said.

There was a just perceptible hesitation before Fernando replied, "As long as *you* deal with the lawyers and the IRS, Gringo, you're welcome to it. You know that."

"I mean, I need it right now. Tonight."

The hesitation was more evident this time.

"You want to tell me why?" Fernando asked.

"How soon can you find a pilot to fly it here?"

"Where's here? The last I heard from you, you were on your way to Africa."

"I'm at Fort Bragg."

"Welcome home, Gringo. How was the Dark Continent?"

"Hey! I'm not fooling around. I need you to find a pilot and have it brought up here."

"Jesus Christ, do you know what time it is?"

"Yeah, I do. This is important."

"But you're not going to tell me why?"

"And leave your Jeppesen case in it. I'm presuming you've got approach charts for Mexico?"

"Yeah, I've got them. Until the lawyers screamed, I was going to take the family to Cozumel and call it a proficiency flight. What the hell are you going to be doing in Mexico?"

"Just do what I ask. For the third or fourth fucking time, Fernando, this is important."

"Okay, okay. If you don't hear from me in an hour—your cellular is up and running?"

Charley replied by giving him the number.

"I have that number," Fernando said. "If you don't hear from me in an hour, you can presume the Lear is wheels-up for Fort Bragg. Which, I just realized, is a restricted zone. And I don't think they allow civilian airplanes to land at Pope Air Force Base. What to do about that?"

"The plane'll be cleared for the restricted area and to land at Pope. Have the pilot give them his ETA and I'll meet him and get him a ride into Fayetteville. You better give him some money, too. I haven't had a chance to cash a check lately."

"Jesus Christ, Gringo, this better be important. I think you've just destroyed my happy marriage."

"I'm sorry, Fernando."

"But it's important, right?" The line went dead in Fernando's ear.

Charley turned to Captain Brewster.

"We're going to need wheels," he said.

"I can probably get the staff duty officer's van," Brewster replied. "Where do you want to go?"

"Out to the stockade."

"Now, sir?"

"Now. And I think it would be better if I—we—had our own wheels."

"Major, I just don't know . . ."

"Call the motor pool, identify yourself as General Gonzalez's aide, and tell them to send a car, or a pickup, a van—something—here right now. And call

Delta Force and have them have the senior officer present meet me at the stockade in twenty minutes."

"Major . . ."

"Alternatively, Captain, get General Gonzalez on the phone. I told you before, I just don't have time to fuck with you."

Without waiting for an answer, Castillo picked up his laptop briefcase and the go-right-now bag and carried them into the bedroom.

He was not going to try to talk the Delta/Gray Fox communications officer out of Mr. Aloysius Francis Casey's latest communication jewels while he was dressed in his Washington middle-level bureaucrat's gray-black suit.

As he unzipped the go-right-now bag, he heard Captain Brewster on the telephone:

"This is Captain Brewster, General Gonzalez's aide. I need a van and driver right now at the VIP guesthouse."

Among other things, the go-right-now bag held a very carefully folded Class A uniform. He hated it. It—and the shirt that went with the tunic and trousers—were sewn from miracle fabrics that didn't pick up unwanted creases. But the by-product of that convenience was that he itched wherever the material touched his skin. If he had the damn thing on for more than six hours, he could count on having a rash around his neck and on his calves and thighs. And the miracle fabrics did not absorb perspiration as cotton and wool did; after wearing it a couple of hours, he smelled as if he hadn't had a shower for a couple of days.

That thought, as he held up the uniform to confirm that it indeed did look amazing crisp, triggered the thought that a lot had happened since he had taken a shower in the Warwick hotel early that morning.

He took fresh linen and the go-right-now toilet kit from the go-right-now bag, stripped off the clothing he was wearing, and marched naked into the bathroom.

Five minutes later, freshly showered and shaved—he had shaved under the shower, a time-saving trick he'd learned at West Point—he replaced the razor in the toilet kit and saw the ring that testified to his graduation from Hudson High with the Class of 1990.

He slipped it on.

Ninety seconds after that, he was sitting on the bed lacing up his highly polished jump boots. And ninety seconds after that, after having walked back into the bath in the unfamiliarly heavy boots, he was examining himself in the full-length mirror on the back of the door.

Something was missing, and, after a moment, he understood what. He went back to the go-right-now bag and took out his green beret. Then he took one more check in the mirror.

He thought: *Okay. Major Carlos G. Castillo, highly decorated Special Forces officer, all decked out in his incredibly natty Class A uniform, is prepared to try to talk the Delta/Gray Fox commo officer out of his best radios.*

Then he had a second thought.

Shit, my ID card is still in the lid of the laptop briefcase and I'm going to have to have it. Otherwise, I'm likely to get myself arrested for impersonating an officer.

He had the lid open and was extracting his ID card when Captain Brewster knocked on the jamb of the open door.

"Sir, a van is on the way, and Lieutenant Colonel Fortinot will be at the Delta compound when we get there."

"Good," Castillo said and smiled at him.

"That was a quick change," Brewster said.

"I also do card tricks," Castillo said.

[TWO]
Police Administration Building
8th and Race Streets
Philadelphia, Pennsylvania
2305 9 June 2005

Two detectives, one a very slim, tall white man, the other a very large African American, came out of the Roundhouse and walked purposefully to an unmarked Crown Victoria, which had just pulled up to the entrance.

The slim white man opened the rear door and got in beside the African American in the backseat.

"Face the other door and put your hands behind you," he ordered matter-of-factly as he produced a set of handcuffs.

"Is this necessary?" Major H. Richard Miller, Jr., asked as he complied.

"No. I just do it for laughs," the detective said as the cuffs clicked closed.

Then he put his hand on Miller's wrists and half-pulled, half-helped him back out of the rear seat.

As soon as Miller was on his feet, the slim detective put his hand firmly on Miller's left arm while the large detective put his hand even more firmly on Miller's right arm and they marched him into the Roundhouse.

Miller expected that he would be led into the entrance foyer of the Round-house and then to the elevator bank, as he, his father, and Charley Castillo had entered the building when they'd gone to see Commissioner Kellogg. Instead, he was marched to the right, through a procession of corridors, through a room lined with holding cells, and finally down another corridor to an elevator door guarded by a uniformed police officer.

"You just shut the fuck up!" the larger detective snarled and pushed Miller's arm, although Miller hadn't said a word.

The cop at the elevator shook his head in understanding and put a key in the elevator control panel. The door opened and Miller was almost pushed inside. The door closed.

"Keep to yourself whatever you want to say until we get to Homicide," the larger detective said, conversationally. "You never know who's liable to get on the elevator."

The elevator stopped, the door opened, and a black woman pushed a mop bucket onto elevator, looked without expression at everyone, then pushed the button for the fourth floor.

When the door opened again, Miller was half-pushed off and then down a curved corridor to a door marked HOMICIDE BUREAU, and then pushed through that. Inside, there was a railing. The slim detective reached over it, pushed what was apparently a solenoid release, and then pushed the gate in the railing open.

Inside a door just past the railing was a large, desk-cluttered room. Against the interior wall were a half-dozen doors, three of them with INTERVIEW ROOM signs on them. Miller was pushed into the center of these.

Sergeant Betty Schneider and a black man wearing a dark blue robe, san-dals, and with his hair braided with beads were sitting on a table. The last time Miller had seen the man, who was an undercover Counterterrorism Bureau de-tective, was three hours before in a room in a bricked-up row house in North Philadelphia. There hadn't been much light, but there had been enough for Miller to decide the undercover cop was a mean-looking sonofabitch.

Seeing him in the brightly lit interview room confirmed his first assess-ment. The man with the bead-braided hair examined Miller carefully.

What the hell, why not? He didn't get a good look at me, either.

There was a steel captain's chair firmly bolted to the floor. It had a pair of handcuffs clipped to it, one half open and waiting to attach an interviewee to the chair.

Miller felt his handcuffs being unlocked and then removed.

"Thanks, John," Sergeant Schneider said to the black detective. "Anybody see him?"

"Everybody in detention, plus a cleaning woman who rolled her bucket onto the elevator. She may even have really been on her way to mop up the fourth floor."

The detective left the room and closed the door.

"If you promise to behave," the man with the beaded braids said, "we won't cuff you to the chair."

There was a faint hint of a smile on his face. Miller smiled back at him but didn't say anything.

The Homicide detectives left the interview room.

"Schneider tells me you're an Army officer, a major," the detective with the bead-braided hair said.

"That's right."

"Jack Britton," the man with the braided hair said, extending his hand. "Aka Ali Abd Ar-Raziq."

"What do I call you?"

"Suit yourself. Where are you from, Miller?" Ali Abd Ar-Raziq asked.

"Here."

"Philly?"

Miller nodded.

"You don't sound like it. You sound like a Reading nigger."

I'll be a sonofabitch!

"I have family in Reading," Miller said, coldly. "On my mother's side. Neither they or me like that term."

"I don't even know what it means," Betty said.

"Sergeant Schneider, I'm disappointed," Ali Abd Ar-Raziq said. "Word is that you know everything about everything." He paused, smiled, and went on. "To make you conversant with a little Afro-American history not usually found in history books, Reading was one of the termini of the Underground Railroad of fame and legend. A number of the slaves who made it out of the South stayed there and became truly integrated. They even picked up Pennsylvania Dutch accents, started eating scrapple, etcetera. They went to school, college, started businesses, joined the Army, etcetera, etcetera. And soon, having made it, began to look down their noses at other African Americans."

"Hey!" Miller protested.

The man with the braided hair raised his palm to shut him off and went on: "The reason I know all this is my father's family are Reading niggers. I'll bet the major and I have acquaintances in common. You don't happen to be kin to a General Miller, do you?"

"He's my father," Miller said.

"See?" Britton said. "Your father and my father are friends."

"I'll be damned," Betty Schneider said.

"If you're not nice, Sergeant, the major and I will start speaking Dutch and leave you in the dark. You do speak Dutch, don't you, Major?"

"Only what I learned listening to my mother when we went to the Reading Terminal Market to buy stuff from the Amish," Miller said.

"Where'd you go to school?" the man with the braided hair asked in the German patois known as Pennsylvania Dutch. "Where'd you get your commission?"

"West Point," Miller said.

"Yeah, sure," the man with the braided hair said, switching back to English. "Of course. Your father's a West Pointer."

Miller nodded.

"So what did you learn about Islam when you were at West Point?"

"What is this, a quiz?"

That was opening your mouth before engaging your brain. Watch it, Richard, you can't afford to piss off Ali Abd Ar-Raziq, aka Detective Jack Britton.

"Before I start to tell you about the lunatics, it would help to know how much you know about Islam. Save us both time."

"I learned zilch at the military academy," Miller said. "But after 9/11, I started to read."

"Give me three minutes of what you learned," the man with the braided hair said.

"You're serious, right?"

The man with the braided hair nodded.

"Where was Muhammad born, for example? When?"

"In 570, into the Quraysh tribe, in Mecca."

"And the Qur'an? Where did that come from?"

"The Angel Gabriel gave it to him—the first part of it—in a cave on Mount Hira in 610. Then he started playing prophet."

"Something like Joseph Smith, the Angel Moroni, and the Mormons, right?" Britton asked, smiling.

"I thought about that," Miller said, smiling back.

"What's the definition of 'Islam'?"

" 'Submission to God,' " Miller said. "A Muslim is someone who's done that."

"Like a born-again Baptist, right? You a born-again Christian, Miller?"

"I'm Presbyterian."

"Pity. If you were a born-again Christian, it might help you understand something about how some guy raised in North Philadelphia, in a house like the one where we met, who converted to Muslim from, say, the Holy Ghost First Church of Christ, African, feels about Islam."

Miller didn't reply.

"What's the first and great commandment for a Muslim?" Britton asked.

" 'There is no god but God . . . Allah . . . and Muhammad is His Prophet.' "

"And the 'Pillars of Faith'?"

"There's five," Miller said. "One is reciting the creed—'There is no god but God, etcetera.' The second is daily prayers—formal prayers, with the forehead touching the ground. Third is fasting during Ramadan . . ."

"What's Ramadan?" Britton interrupted.

"The ninth month of the Muslim calendar. Last year—2004—it started in October. The fifth of October, I think."

Britton made a "Give me more" gesture.

"It lasts a lunar month," Miller went on. "No eating, drinking, smoking, or sex during the day. It starts when you can tell a white thread from a black thread by daylight and ends at nightfall with a prayer and a meal called *iftar*, and then starts up again the next morning."

Britton nodded at him. "And the Fourth Pillar?" he asked.

"Almsgiving. The Fifth is making a pilgrimage to Mecca."

Britton nodded again. "Tell me about jihad," he said.

"Holy war," Miller said. "To take over territories, countries, which are ruled by non-Muslims."

"This is new, right, something dreamed up recently by belligerent rag-heads? And having really nothing to do with the gentle teachings of the Prophet himself?"

"No. It goes all the way back to Muhammad. By the time he died, in 632, jihad saw the Muslims in control of the Arabian Peninsula. In the next hundred years, jihad had taken Islam all over the Middle East, from Afghanistan to Spain."

"Okay," Britton said. "The pop quiz is over. You're not exactly an Islamic scholar, but neither are you wholly ignorant of who you're dealing with like most people I've met in your line of work."

"My line of work? The Army, you mean?"

"No. Intelligence, counterterrorism. You may be a soldier, but you're not here to line your troops up and march down Broad Street."

"I'm here—as I told you in that house off Broad Street—because we have reason to believe that a group of Somalian terrorists have stolen a 727 with the intention of crashing it into the Liberty Bell, and, further, we have reason to believe that there may be a connection with some—how do I say this?—*native Philadelphian Muslims.* Can we get to that? You said you knew something."

"You see the movie *Black Hawk Down*? Read the book? Mogadishu?"

Miller nodded.

Both were right on the money. Do I tell Britton that the Black Hawk belonged to the 160th Special Forces Aviation Regiment and that First Lieutenant Richard H. Miller, Jr., was flying Black Hawks in Somalia for the 160th at the time?

"A guy on *The Philadelphia Inquirer* wrote the book," Britton said.

"So I understand. He did a good job."

"When that happened, when they dragged the bodies of the American soldiers through the streets, the reaction of some of the lunatics here was that it was the will of Allah, about time, right on, brother. That shock you?"

Miller shook his head.

"And, right away, some of the local lunatic mullahs—who have no more idea where they come from in Africa than you or I do—started claiming they were from Somalia. Pure bullshit, of course, to impress the brothers. And then, because that seemed to work, they embellished the story. They had contacts with Somalia, they said, and we—meaning, the mullahs—have to go over there.

"We had a series of fund-raisers, some of them your standard church chicken supper, all proceeds to the cause, and some your standard knock over the local grocery store, your friendly neighborhood drug dealer and hooker, etcetera. And they came up with the money for the plane tickets, got passports, and went."

"You tell anybody about this?"

"I turned in a report. A couple of weeks later, the FBI wanted to talk to me. So I got myself arrested—did this routine—and two guys from the FBI talked to me—in this interview room, come to think of it—and I told them what was going down, and they laughed, and said, one, the AALs couldn't get into Somalia and, two, even if they could the Somalians would not only not talk to the wannabes but would probably cut their throats and steal whatever they were carrying."

"So what happened?"

"Off the AALs went, they said to Somalia."

"You sound as if you don't believe they actually went."

"What the FBI said made sense to me. None of these wannabes speak Arabic, much less Somali. I figured they wouldn't get any further than Kenya, or Ethiopia, where they would find out what Somalia was really like and decide it was the Will of Allah to whoop it up with the local hookers instead of actually going there. Who would know they hadn't gone? Or they would actually try to go there and get knocked over by some really professional bad guys."

"So what actually happened?"

"I don't know," Britton said. "Right about that time, my wife was about to have our first son, so I did almost a year in the Pennsylvania Correctional Facility in Camp Hill."

"Excuse me?"

"I was picked up on an armed robbery charge, plea-bargained it down to four years, and was sent to the state slam at Camp Hill, near Harrisburg. When I was a bad boy, which was often, they put me in solitary, from which I was surreptitiously removed and sneaked out of the joint in the warden's trunk. That way, I got two weeks with my wife—a couple of times, three—we had a nice apartment in Harrisburg—before they sneaked me back in. The department shrink said I had suffered severe mental stress on the job, so technically I was on medical leave."

"Jesus Christ!" Miller said.

"Anyway, like I said, it was about a year before I got back to the mosque."

"I don't understand," Miller confessed.

"The mosque hired a pretty good lawyer to appeal my conviction. The sonofabitch used to come to Camp Hill—which meant I had to sneak back into the prison to meet with him and then sneak back out—every other month to tell me how he was doing. After about a year, like I said, the Supreme Court ordered a retrial, the district attorney declined to prosecute, and I was sprung."

"You volunteered to go back?" Miller asked, incredulously.

Britton met his eyes for a moment before replying.

"I'm in pretty deep with the mullahs," he said. "It would have been hard to get anybody else into the mosque who would have learned much."

"You couldn't pay me enough to do what you're doing," Miller said.

"Yeah, but, like I was saying, when I got back to the mosque the mullahs were, quote, back from Somalia, end quote, they were watching me pretty closely . . ."

"They were suspicious?"

"I wasn't the only guy from the mosque, by a long shot, in Camp Hill," Britton said. "And they hadn't seen much of me while I was in there. Yeah, they were suspicious. They're very suspicious people. Anyway, I didn't want to ask too many questions, and they weren't talking much about Somalia—which I figured was because they really hadn't been to Somalia—so I let it rest.

"And then, about six months ago, two mullahs showed up. They said they were from Somalia. I don't know if they were or weren't. But they certainly were from someplace other than here. Spoke English like Englishmen. And what they were up to, I don't know. They kept me out of their meetings."

"You tell the FBI about them?"

"I told Chief Kramer. He told the FBI, and the FBI told him they had nothing on the names I'd given him. So the chief staked the mosque out, got pictures of them, and gave the pictures to the FBI. The chief got word to me that the FBI had run them. They were pilots for an Arab airline—Yemen Airways, I think—and were in the country legally. Going to some flight school in Tulsa, Oklahoma. All approved by the U.S. Government."

"And?"

"And that was the end of it until a couple of weeks ago—about the time your airplane went missing in . . . where?"

"Luanda, Angola," Miller finished.

". . . when the lunatics began talking more than a little smugly about what was going to happen when the Liberty Bell was no more."

"You report that? To Chief Kramer? The FBI?"

"These people come up with some nutty idea once a week. They're going to blow up City Hall or the Walt Whitman Bridge or the Benjamin Franklin Bridge or one of the sports arenas. Poison the water. Assassinate the archbishop. It's just talk. I don't report much—or any—of it until I have more than hot air to go on. You heard about the kid who kept crying 'Wolf'?"

Miller nodded.

"And then you showed up," Britton went on.

"And asked you if you had heard anything about the Liberty Bell," Miller said.

Britton nodded.

"You have to admit that flying an airplane into the Liberty Bell sounds bizarre," Britton said.

"Bizarre or not, we think that's what they intend to do," Miller said. "You have the names of the two Somalians?"

"They'd be in my report. Schneider?"

"I can get that," Sergeant Betty Schneider said. "But you said the FBI said they had nothing on those names. What about the names the FBI put on the stakeout photos?"

"The chief never gave them to me," Britton said. "I suppose he has them."

"He went out for coffee," Betty said. "Maybe he's back."

She left the interview room and a minute later returned with Chief Inspector Kramer.

"They never gave me names," he announced. "Just said the two were on the

up-and-up. I can call there, but it's late and all I'm going to get is the duty officer, who'll probably stall me until he can clear it with the Special Agent in
Charge."

"Chief," Miller said. "I'd like to suggest we wait until I can tell Castillo about
this." He turned to Britton. "How long can you stay?"

Chief Kramer answered for him: "We picked him up on suspicion of murder. We can probably keep him until breakfast—say, eight o'clock—without
making the AALs more than usually suspicious."

"Castillo said he'd get back to me as soon as he could. Why don't we wait
for that?"

"Okay with me," Chief Inspector Kramer said. "Okay with you, Britton?"

Detective Jack Britton said, with no enthusiasm whatever, "Why not?"

[THREE]
Delta Force Compound
Fort Bragg, North Carolina
2310 9 June 2005

Around the time the first Delta Force was organized, the Army had about finished implementing a new personnel policy regarding offenders of the Uniform
Code of Military Justice.

Someone had pointed out—many soldiers, officers, and enlisted thought
very late in the game—that only a very few soldiers committed what in civilian life would be called "serious felonies," that is to say, rape, murder, armed
robbery, and the like. The vast majority of prisoners in Army stockades all over
the world had been found guilty of offenses against the Army system and most
of the offenses had to do with being absent without leave, mild insubordination, drunk on duty, and the like.

Those sentenced by court-martial to six months or less were normally con-
fined to prisons, called "stockades" on the larger military bases—forts like
Bragg, Knox, and Benning—where they spent their days walking around the
base, guarded by shotgun-armed "prisoner chasers," picking up cigarette butts
and trash.

Someone had pointed out that not only did this punishment not contribute
much to the Army but that the prisoner chasers—usually, one for every two prisoners, sometimes one for each prisoner—had to be taken off their regular duties to perform that guard duty, which was not an effective use of manpower.

Furthermore, if a soldier disliked the Army so much that he went "over the hill" or told his sergeant to take a flying fuck at a rolling doughnut when chastised, for example, for having a dirty weapon, or needing a shave, he probably wasn't making much of a contribution to the Army when he wasn't in the stockade.

The ideal was "cheerful, willing obedience to a lawful order," and, if a soldier wasn't willing to offer that, what was he doing in the Army?

If a first sentence to the stockade didn't serve to make someone see the wisdom of straightening up and flying right, then hand him a Bad Conduct discharge and send him home.

That would do away with having to have large, heavily guarded stockades, with barbed wire, chain-link fences, guard towers, and everything else that went with them all over the Army, and having to take a hundred or so men on each post away from their normal duties on any given day to serve as prisoner chasers.

It might also result in an Army where most soldiers believed that cheerful, willing obedience to a lawful order was really not such a bad idea.

The new personnel policy was implemented. Post stockade populations dropped precipitously all over the Army, including Fort Bragg, at just about the time the new, supersecret Delta Force was formed.

It was decided that Delta Force should have a very secure base, isolated from the rest of sprawling Fort Bragg, protected by a double line of chain-link fences topped with razor wire, with floodlights, guard towers, and the like, and that inside the fence there should be barracks, a mess hall, supply buildings, and so on.

Someone then pointed out that a system designed to keep people in, like the Fort Bragg stockade, would probably, with minor modifications, be entirely suitable to keep people out.

Delta Force moved into the old stockade.

Most of the Delta Force people, who were of course the cream of Special Forces, thought moving into the stockade was not only hilarious but also had the additional benefit of keeping Fort Bragg's complement of candy-ass officers from snooping around to see where they could apply chickenshit.

No one was allowed in the Delta Force compound without specific authorization and only a few senior officers had the authority to issue that authorization, and, as a rule of thumb, they checked with Delta Force officers before granting it.

From his seat in the motor pool van, Major C. G. Castillo, who had done his time in the Fort Bragg stockade, was not at all surprised to see a tall, muscular lieutenant colonel wearing a green beret and a shoulder holster standing inside the outer fence of the Delta Force compound, or that the gate in the twelve-foot, razor wire–topped fence was closed.

Floodlights pushed back the deep darkness of the North Carolina night to provide enough illumination to make the signs hanging from the chain-link fence every twenty feet clearly legible.

They read:

DO NOT APPROACH FENCE
RESTRICTED AREA
ABSOLUTELY NO ADMISSION
GUARDS WILL FIRE WITHOUT WARNING

Castillo got out of the back of the van, marched up to the outer fence, and saluted crisply. The tall officer returned the salute casually.

"Colonel Fortinot?" Castillo asked.

The tall officer nodded, just perceptibly.

"Sir, my name is Castillo . . ."

"Stop right there, Major," Lieutenant Colonel Fortinot said. "This is a restricted area. You need written authorization to enter this area. Do you have such authority?"

"No, sir. I do not."

Lieutenant Colonel Fortinot pointed at Captain Brewster.

"Are you the officer who called the duty officer here, asking that I come here?"

"Yes, sir."

"You're General Gonzalez's aide?"

"Yes, sir."

"Then you should know better than bringing any unauthorized personnel out here. I think you can count on General Gonzalez getting a memo for record reporting this incident. Good night, gentlemen."

He turned, marched toward the inner gate, and made an "open it up" gesture.

"Colonel," Castillo called out. "Before you go through that gate, I respectfully suggest you hear me out."

Colonel Fortinot continued walking.

"Sir," Castillo called, "I'm privy to the Gray Fox op in progress."

Colonel Fortinot stopped, turned, and walked back to the fence. He looked intently at Castillo for a moment. "Major, I don't have any idea what you're talking about. Gray Fox? Never heard of it."

Then he turned and made another "open it up" gesture toward the compound.

The gate began to swing inward.

A barrel-chested, very short, totally bald civilian—in a red polo shirt and khaki trousers and carrying a CAR-4 in his hand—came out.

"Goddamn, I thought that was you!" CWO-5 Victor D'Alessandro, USA, Retired, called. "How the hell are you, Charley?"

"Hello, Vic," Castillo called.

Saved by the goddamned bell!

D'Alessandro marched through the inner gate, made an "open it up" gesture over his head, and marched toward the outer gate, which swung inward as he approached.

He walked up to Charley, looked at him carefully for a moment, said, "You looked better with the beard. What the fuck are you doing here?"

Then he wrapped his arms around Castillo, which placed his face against Castillo's chest, and lifted him off the ground.

"Presumably, Mr. D'Alessandro, you know this officer?" Colonel Fortinot said.

"Goddamn right, Colonel," D'Alessandro said, dropping Castillo to the ground. "Charley and I go way back. Word I had was that he was in Washington trying to learn how to act like a lieutenant colonel."

"Something like that, Vic," Castillo said, chuckling.

"The major does not have authorization to be here," Fortinot said.

"He does now," D'Alessandro said and turned to Charley. "They made me retire when I came back from Afghanistan the last time, Charley. So I hired on as a fucking double-dipper. I'm director of security for the stockade. GS-fucking fifteen. I'm an *assimilated* full fucking bird colonel. Isn't that right, Colonel?"

Lieutenant Colonel Fortinot nodded.

"You came at a bad time, Charley—knowing you, no fucking surprise—we got a Gray Fox going," D'Alessandro said.

"That's why I'm here, Vic," Castillo said. "I came up with the intel that set that off."

"Again, knowing you, no fucking surprise. So what do you need?"

"Have you got a link to General McNab?"

"Data, imagery, voice. You wouldn't believe the gear your pal Casey has come up with."

"I'd like to talk to him," Castillo said.

"No problem. He's getting ready to go wheels-up in Morocco with the backup team. I think there's still an open link. Come on. We'll see." Then he had a second thought and pointed at Captain Brewster. "Who you be, Captain?"

"My name is Brewster . . ."

"Gonzalez's aide?"

"Yes, sir."

"You're on the Snoopy list," D'Alessandro said. Then he said, "D'Alessandro coming in with two. On my authority."

Castillo noticed for the first time that D'Alessandro had what looked like a flesh-colored hearing aid in his right ear and that a barely visible cord ran from it into the collar of his polo shirt. There was obviously a microphone under the shirt.

"Sir," Castillo said to Lieutenant Colonel Fortinot, "may I suggest you come with us?"

Lieutenant Colonel Fortinot nodded just perceptibly and then followed D'Alessandro, Castillo, and Brewster into the compound. First the outer gate, and then the inner gate, swung closed as they marched toward the single-story brick building that had once been the headquarters of the U.S. Army Stockade, Fort Bragg.

D'Alessandro led them down a corridor to a door guarded by a sergeant who had a CAR-4 cradled in his arm like a hunter's shotgun.

"They're with me," D'Alessandro said, and then added, to the microphone under his shirt, "Open the goddamned door!"

There was a sound of a deadbolt being released and then the door opened inward.

The room was square, about twenty-five feet to a side. In the center was a very large oblong table, with room for perhaps twenty people. There were six people sitting at it. There were paper maps on one wall and video monitors showing maps of various parts of the world—including the area around Abéché, Chad—on another. There was a row of twenty-four-inch video monitors showing areas in and around the compound. Charley could see the van in which they'd come.

There was a captain sitting at the far end of the table. D'Alessandro walked there and sat down next to him and gestured for the others to take chairs.

"This is Major Castillo," D'Alessandro said. "He's in on Snoopy. The captain is General Gonzalez's aide; he's on the Snoopy list. And you all know Colonel Fortinot. Major Castillo needs to talk to General McNab. We up?"

The captain nodded and said, "All green."

"Speakerphone all right with you, Charley?" D'Alessandro asked.

"How secure is this connection?" Charley asked. "This room?"

"Don't get no more secure."

"Speakerphone's fine," Charley said.

"Speakerphone green," the captain said.

"Old Fart for Snoopy-Six," D'Alessandro said.

Three seconds later, the surprisingly clear voice of Lieutenant General Bruce J. McNab came over loudspeakers Castillo could not see. "Now what, Vic?"

"Fellow here wants to talk to you," D'Alessandro said and gestured to Castillo.

"It's Charley, General," Castillo said.

Three seconds later, McNab asked, "As in Castillo, *that* Charley?"

"Yes, sir."

"You've always had a talent for showing up at the worst possible time. What's on your mind?"

"I know what you were looking for, sir, and that it's no longer there."

"Who the hell told you that?"

"It was my intel that set the wheels turning."

"Okay. So what?"

"My boss sent me here, sir, to both get your report . . ."

"I already gave my so-far report to your Uncle Allan. You're talking about Secretary Hall?"

"Yes, sir."

"Excuse me, sir," Captain Brewster said. "It was Dr. Cohen, the national security advisor, who telephoned General Gonzalez and said you were coming here at the personal order of the president."

The delay was just perceptibly a little longer before McNab's reply came.

"That sounded like Brewster. Is your boss there, too?"

"No, sir. He's in his quarters."

"That figures. He's got you babysitting Castillo?"

"Yes, sir."

"Okay, Charley, what do you want?"

"I think we may soon know where the airplane is, sir, and I'd like to discuss with you plans to deal with it."

"You're in on my schedule? Won't that wait until I'm back?"

"Yes, sir. Of course. But there's something else."

"Like what?"

"I need three radios like these and people to operate them."

"Jesus Christ, Charley, you of all people should know how scarce they are!"

"One for my boss, one for Dick Miller, who's in Philadelphia, and one for me."

"What's Miller—I thought he was in Angola or some other hellhole—doing in Philadelphia?"

"Sir, we think the intention is to crash that airplane into the Liberty Bell. Miller's been working with the cops to come up with a connection. A little while ago, he told me he had found connections. He couldn't tell me what over cellular phone. We need secure commo."

The delay before McNab replied now was conspicuous.

"Where the hell am I? In the twilight zone? The Liberty Bell?"

"Yes, sir. What I would like to do is take a radio to Miller—and to my boss—so they have them up by the time you get back here."

"You've got a plane to do that?"

"Yes, sir," Charley said. "Or I'm pretty sure I will have."

"Just 'pretty sure'?"

"Yes, sir."

"You want me to call Naylor and make sure you have an airplane?"

"I don't think that will be necessary, sir."

"Okay, Charley. I know how close you and the Old Fart are, so this probably isn't necessary, but I left a lieutenant colonel named Fortinot minding the store; you better find him and bring him up to speed on this."

"Yes, sir, I will."

"Okay. I'll be in touch. I have to get wheels-up now. Snoopy-Six out."

The captain said, "Secure voice gone to standby."

D'Alessandro asked, incredulously, "These rag-head bastards are going to try to crash this airplane into the Liberty Bell? What the fuck is that all about?"

"I don't know, Vic," Castillo admitted.

His cell phone tinkled and he pulled it from his pocket.

"Yeah?"

"My toy, against my better judgment, will be wheels-up in about ninety seconds," Fernando Lopez announced.

"Thank you."

"Maria's really pissed," Fernando said. "And I mean really pissed."

"I'm sorry," Castillo said.

The line went dead.

"I guess you missed the sign on your way in, Charley," D'Alessandro said.

"What?"

"The sign that says, 'THE USE, OR POSSESSION, OF PERSONAL CELLULAR TELE-PHONES ANYWHERE IN THE COMPOUND IS ABSOLUTELY FORBIDDEN.' "

"I can't do without it," Charley said. "That was word that my airplane is on the way. I've got to make—and expect—other calls."

"Sometimes, we just smash the phones," D'Alessandro said. "Other times, we castrate the offender."

"I have to have it, Vic," Castillo said.

D'Alessandro locked eyes with him for a moment, then finally shrugged.

"There's always an exception to every rule," he said, finally. "General Bruce J. McNab himself once told me that personally."

"It's about twelve hundred miles from San Antonio here," Castillo said. "That's about two hours and fifteen minutes flight time. That means we have that much time to find the radios, find three communicators, get them into civilian clothes, have them check out the radios, check me out on them, and get from here to Pope."

D'Alessandro looked at the captain.

"Can do?"

"I'm not only a green beanie, Vic, I'm a Delta Force guy in good standing. I can do fucking anything." He turned to Castillo. "It'll be cutting it close, sir, but it can be done."

[FOUR]
Pope Air Force Base, North Carolina
0025 10 June 2005

Sergeant Dwayne G. Lefler, USAF, who had sincerely believed the civilian who'd gotten off the Citation with no ID had been sent by Air Force counterintelligence to catch him with his security pants down, was still on duty at Pope Base Operations when Castillo led the three Delta Force communicators and Captain Brewster into the building.

Sergeant Lefler eyed with some suspicion Major C. G. Castillo, now attired in the Class A uniform prescribed for field-grade officers.

"Sorry about the confusion before, Sergeant," Castillo said, going to him and offering his Army ID card. "It couldn't be helped."

After examining the ID card, Sergeant Lefler said, "Yes, sir," handed it back, and then reached for his telephone and punched in a number.

"Major, I'm sorry to get you up again but I think you better come back down here."

Major Thomas F. Treward, USAF, appeared a minute or so later, took a good look at Castillo, and said, "Well, Major, back again?"

"This time we're looking for a civilian Lear that's supposed to be here right about now."

"The tower just cleared him to land," Treward said, gesturing toward the glass doors.

Castillo went outside and looked up at the sky.

There were a half-dozen flashing Grimes lights in the sky. After a moment, Castillo decided which of them were making an approach to the runway and followed them with his eyes. The first two aircraft in the pattern were USAF C-130s. The third was a glistening white Bombardier/Learjet 45XR.

Two minutes later, it rolled up to the tarmac before base operations and stopped. Castillo saw the copilot take off his headset and then get out of his seat. Castillo walked toward the plane. Before he got there, the door opened and the copilot got out, carrying a small bag.

He was a silver-haired man in his fifties whose zippered flight jacket was adored with the four-stripe shoulder boards of a captain. Castillo guessed that he was ex-military, maybe retired, who was on some sort of a list for people who needed a pilot for a light jet on short notice.

"You're Major Castillo?" the copilot asked, and, when Castillo nodded, went on: "Two questions for you. He wants to know how long the airplane will be on the ground? And what about transportation to Fayetteville?"

"I've arranged for a ride for you to Fayetteville, and made reservations for you in the Airport Motel, and on the Delta feeder flight to Atlanta leaving at eight forty-five in the morning. You'll connect in Atlanta to San Antonio. I'd like to get off the ground as soon as possible. What's the fuel aboard?"

"Enough for another nine hundred miles, maybe a thousand."

"There's an Army captain inside base operations. Name of Brewster. He'll take care of you from here on. If you'll ask him to send the others out, I'll talk to the pilot."

"Okay, thanks," the copilot said and walked toward the base operations building.

Castillo went in the airplane and walked to the cockpit.

"Wow, don't you look spiffy in your soldier suit!" Fernando Lopez said from the pilot's seat.

"Jesus, you didn't have to come, Fernando."

"Yeah, I did, Gringo. I seem to recall you saying it was important."

"I made reservations for two at the motel, plus two Delta tickets back to San Antonio."

Lopez shrugged. "So now it's reservations for one. Where do we go from here, Gringo? And when?"

Castillo stared at his cousin, considered the options, then nodded slightly. "Washington, Philadelphia, and then back here. Now."

"Just you and me?"

"Three guys—figure six hundred pounds—and another four hundred in gear."

"There's enough fuel remaining to make Washington—Ronald Reagan—I know those approaches and it's a good place to refuel. Okay?"

"Sounds fine."

"I don't suppose you remembered to check the weather and file a flight plan?"

"Weather's fine, and, yeah, they're holding our clearance to Washington with a fuel stop at Raleigh-Durham. I didn't know what your fuel remaining would be."

"We can change Raleigh-Durham once we're up," Fernando said.

"Did you remember to give the copilot some cash?"

"Indeed, I did. Which reminds me . . ."

He handed Castillo an envelope.

"What's this?"

"A thousand dollars."

"Thank you."

"Don't thank me. Thank Abuela."

"Abuela?" Castillo asked, surprised.

"Like she says, she's old but not brain-dead," Fernando said. "She's got a pretty good idea of what you do for a living. You wouldn't believe how long that money—and that's not all of it—has been in my bedside table waiting for you to need it. There's also a couple of pistols in my Jepp case."

"You didn't tell her about this, for Christ's sake?"

"Yeah. I promised her if anything ever happened I would tell her and I did. She said to tell you she's praying for the both of us."

"Jesus H. Christ!"

"Are you going to stand there blaspheming," Fernando lisped, "or are you going to see if our passengers are comfy, their seat belts fastened, and the NO SMOKING light is on?"

He pointed out the side window.

Castillo bent over and looked out.

The three Delta Force communicators, all dressed in sports jackets and slacks, were almost to the airplane, dragging enormous, wheeled, hard-sided civilian suitcases behind them.

"You told Abuela?" he repeated. "Jesus H. Christ!"

Then he turned and went into the cabin and helped the communicators load their enormous suitcases aboard.

"Raleigh area control," Castillo said into his microphone. "Lear Five-Oh-Seven-Five."

"Seven-Five, Raleigh."

"Lear Seven-Five passing through flight level twenty-five, on a course of twenty true, indicating five hundred knots."

"I have you on radar, Seven-Five."

"Request change in flight plan to skip fuel stop at Raleigh. Request permission Ronald Reagan direct at flight level three-zero."

"Raleigh area control accepts change of flight plan for Lear Five-Oh-Seven-Five. Proceed on present heading. Report to Washington approach control on reaching flight level thirty. Raleigh hands over Lear Five-Oh-Seven-Five to Washington approach control at this time."

"Understand maintain present course, report to Washington approach when at flight level thirty. Thank you, Raleigh."

Castillo turned to Fernando and gave him a thumbs-up. Then he looked at the altimeter and spoke into his microphone again.

"Washington approach control, Lear Five-Oh-Seven-Five."

"Seven-Five, Washington."

"Seven-Five is at flight level three-zero, on heading of twenty true, indicating 530 knots. Request approach to Reagan."

"I have you on radar, Seven-Five. Maintain present course and flight level. Report over Richmond."

"Seven-Five understands maintain present course and flight level, report over Richmond."

Castillo touched a small button on his headset which switched his microphone and earplug from TRANSMIT to INTERCOM.

"Okay, Fernando," he said. "Tell me about Abuela being old but not brain-dead."

"I wondered how long it was going to take you to get around to asking me about that," Fernando said, smiling at him.

"Come on," Castillo said, not pleasantly.

"It started right after we buried Grandpa . . ." Fernando began.

WINTER 1998

[FIVE]
Hacienda San Jorge
Near Uvalde, Texas
2130 15 November 1998

There were still almost a dozen cars packed in the drive of the Big House when Fernando returned from San Antonio and he remembered his grandfather saying that the only thing Spanish people liked better than a wedding or a christening was a funeral.

Well, he had a big one. A heart attack is a classy way to go and the funeral had been spectacular. They'd actually run out space to park airplanes at the strip, and even the Texas Rangers had sent an official delegation. Great-great-grandfather Fernando Castillo had been one of the original Texas Rangers.

There were lights on in his grandparents' bedroom, which meant Abuela was still awake, and he went there, through the kitchen, so he wouldn't have to deal with the hangers-on in the sitting room.

"How you doing, Abuela?" Fernando asked as he bent over his grandmother and kissed her forehead.

She was sitting in one of the two dark red leather-upholstered reclining armchairs facing a large television set.

"Holding up, I guess," she said, touching his cheek. "Carlos got off all right?"

"Yes, ma'am. I guess he really had to go; the minute we walked in base operations at Kelly and he gave his name, a pilot came up—a major—and said

his plane was on the tarmac. An Air Force Lear. Pretty spiffy for a lowly lieutenant, huh?"

"Carlos is a captain now," she corrected him. "And what he's doing is very
important."

That doesn't sound like just the doting opinion of a loving grandmother.

"Do you know something I don't?" Fernando asked.

"I heard you two talking last night," she said. "You know as much as I do.
So stop it. I don't want to spar with you, Fernando . . . your grandfather was
always saying that, 'I don't want to spar with you,' wasn't he?"

"Yes, ma'am, he was." He paused and then went on, "Abuela, the Grin . . .
Carlos had a couple of drinks last night. Maybe a couple too many."

"He had more than a couple too many," she said. "It's a family tradition,
Fernando. When Jorge was killed in Vietnam, your grandfather was drunk for
a week. And then, when we finally could bury Jorge, he was drunk for another
week."

"He loved Grandpa, Abuela."

"You don't have to tell me that," she said, then added, "Why don't you fix
yourself a drink and then sit in your grandfather's chair?" When she saw the
mingled surprise and confusion on his face, she further added, pointing to a
half-full brandy snifter on the table between the chairs, "I poured that when
you drove away. I've been waiting for you to come back to drink it."

"Anything you say, Abuela."

"We have to talk about Carlos," she said. "This is as good a time as any."

"Yes, ma'am. What is that, cognac?"

"Brandy," she said. "Argentine brandy. The difference is, the French call their
brandy 'cognac' and charge through the nose for it. I thought you knew that
story. "

"No, ma'am."

"We went to Argentina on our wedding trip, to the King Ranch. Your
grandfather was a classmate of Eddie King at A&M and he'd been down there
with Eddie several times before we were married. It was a fine place for a honeymoon. And when he found out that the Argentine brandy, which he liked better than the French, was just a couple of dollars a bottle, he was as happy with
that as he was with me. He loved a bargain and he hated the French."

"I know," Fernando said.

He went to a chest of drawers on which sat a tray with a bottle of brandy
and another snifter on it, poured the brandy and then went and sat in the reclining chair.

"I feel funny sitting in here," he said.

"You shouldn't," she said. "You're now head of the family. Your grandfather would approve."

She picked up her glass, raised it in toast, and said, "Here's to you, dear Fernando. Go easy on God, my darling. He's doing the best He knows how."

She took a healthy swallow of the brandy and then looked at her grandson.

"Let's talk about you, Carlos, and the family," she said.

"If you'd like."

"You will, of course, not immediately—but the sooner, the better—take over for your grandfather."

"What about Carlos? What about my mother, my aunts?"

"Your mother and your aunts have been provided for. Don't spar with me, Fernando, and pretend you didn't know that you and Carlos were going to get . . . what? . . . 'the business.' "

He shrugged his admission that he had known.

"And since Carlos is not going be around very much . . ."

"Abuela," he interrupted, "maybe . . . Grandpa's passing . . ."

"He didn't 'pass,' darling. He 'died.' "

"Maybe Carlos will get out of the Army now."

"That's very unlikely, I'm afraid," she said. "Take that as a given. Carlos will stay in the Army."

"Why are you so sure?"

"You're going to find out how important genetics are, my darling, as you get older. We really have no control over what we are. You have many of your father's genes. And your grandfather's, too. You have his temper, among other things. But your father is a businessman, as was your grandfather, and you have a businessman's genes."

"Carlos, on the other hand, has a soldier's genes?" he asked, almost sarcastically.

"His grandfather was a German officer. Way back on his mother's side there were Hungarian cavalrymen, including several generals. On his father's side, we go back to the Alamo. His great-grandfather fought, as a major, in the First World War. And his father, my darling Jorge, was a soldier who gave his life for his companions and was awarded the highest decoration the United States gives. I think it can be fairly said Carlos has a soldier's genes."

"I didn't mean to sound flippant," Fernando said.

"You did," she said, flatly.

"Then I'm sorry."

"I don't want an apology; I want you to pay attention."

"Yes, ma'am."

"Over the years, I've had many conversations with General Naylor about Carlos. Your grandfather and I did. Your grandfather, frankly, wanted Carlos to get out of the Army when he had completed his six-year obligation—that would have been in 1996—and come home, take his place in the business, get married, and produce a son to carry on the Castillo name."

"I understand."

"General Naylor, who is genuinely fond of Carlos, said he didn't think Carlos would be happy in the business not only because he's a very good soldier but because, with the exception of you, me, and your grandfather, he never really felt part of the family."

"Because we're Tex-Mex?"

"You're making it sound worse than it is," she said. "But yes. Because he's only half Tex-Mex. And for the same reason—he's only half German—he could not become a German, even though he speaks the language as his mother tongue and has considerable property there. General Naylor said, and your grandfather and I came to agree, that Carlos's family is the Army."

"Oh, Abuela! Jesus! Can I speak frankly?"

"Please do."

"I think Naylor's talking bull . . . through his hat. I was an officer. I knew a lot of people for whom the Army was home. But they weren't like Carlos."

"Why not?"

"For one thing, they didn't have people at home who loved them," Fernando said. "And for another, they had nothing else to do. And for another, they didn't have any money."

"Those were your grandfather's arguments, too. But he eventually came to see that General Naylor was right. Darling, there isn't always logic in these things."

Fernando threw his hands up in resignation.

"May I have some more of the Argentine *brandy?*" he asked.

"Of course."

He got out of his grandfather's chair, poured more brandy, raised the bottle to offer his grandmother more, which she declined, and then sat back down.

"Furthermore," he started off, "the Gringo's . . . sorry . . . *Carlos* is not really in the Army. He should be commanding a company at Fort Benning or someplace, playing golf, having dinner at the officers' club, worrying about his AWOL rate, the next inspector general's inspection, his next efficiency report, and living in quarters. That's the Army."

"He must be getting good efficiency reports. *Excellent* efficiency reports. According to General Naylor, he was promoted to captain on the five percent list, in other words, earlier than his peers, as an outstanding officer."

"Instead, he's living in an apartment in Washington and going to work in civilian clothing at the—do you know where?"

"At the Central Intelligence Agency," she said. "Where he is in charge of providing special security for CIA personnel in dangerous overseas areas."

" 'Special security' means he's running around Afghanistan protecting CIA agents 'who can't find their asses with both hands'—sorry, Abuela, that's the words he used last night—while they're looking for some Arab whose name I can't even remember. Or pronounce."

"Usama bin Laden," she furnished. "A very dangerous man. A Saudi Arabian who hates everything American. The CIA—and General Naylor—believe he's responsible for blowing up our embassies in Tanzania and Kenya last August. The State Department has placed a five-million-dollar bounty on his head."

"My God, Abuela, you and Naylor have been having some interesting chats, haven't you?"

"I'm getting a little tired, darling," she said. "Would you be willing to take as a given that Carlos will not be getting out of the Army anytime soon and go from there?"

"Yes, of course."

"I asked General Naylor if there was anything I could do to help and he said he thought it was unlikely that Carlos would come to me—or go to him—for any kind of help. But that he might go to you."

Fernando exhaled audibly and then said, "Yeah."

"What I want from you, Fernando, is this: Be there when Carlos needs you. Give him whatever he asks for. Your grandfather used to say that when people tell you they need a little help, they really mean money. The last thing Carlos will need is money—he has his own fortune and soon his share of 'the business'—but it is possible he could find himself in—how did your grandfather phrase it?—'a cash-flow problem,' 'a liquid asset shortage.' I think he would be uncomfortable if he had any idea I had any idea what's he doing. So don't tell him I know. If he does come to you, I want you to tell me. Will you do this for me?"

Fernando met his grandmother's eyes for a moment.

"Of course I will," he said, finally.

"One more thing," she said. "Just before God took your grandfather, he told me that he still had one faint hope: that Carlos would meet some suitable young woman, fall in love, and decide that what he really wanted out of life was a wife and family. He said he was praying for that. I have been praying every night. Would you pray for that, too?"

Fernando nodded. For some reason, he didn't trust his voice to speak.

XV

[ONE]
Ronald Reagan Washington National Airport
Arlington, Virginia
0125 10 June 2005

While the Lear was still slowing down on its landing roll at DCA, Castillo punched an autodial button on his cellular telephone.

The call was answered on the second ring.

"Three-zero-six," a man's voice said.

Those were the last three digits of the number Castillo's cellular phone had autodialed. It was the number of the supervisory Secret Service agent in charge of the secretary of homeland security's personal security detail.

If someone dialed the number by mistake—or even was "trolling" for interesting numbers—the three-zero-six answer didn't give much away.

"Mr. Isaacson, please," Castillo said.

"Welcome to our nation's capital, Don Juan," Isaacson himself replied.

"We just landed at Reagan, Joel. You sent someone to meet us, right?"

"Wrong."

"Why not?"

"I myself will greet you personally at Butler Aviation, to which ground control, I suspect, is directing you at this very moment."

The plug in Castillo's other ear was in fact at the moment carrying the order of Reagan ground control to take taxiway B left to Butler Aviation.

"To what do I owe the honor?" Castillo said.

"I was feeling generous," Isaacson said, then added: "Nice airplane, Don Juan."

If he can see the airplane, I should be able to see him.

Castillo looked out the window and saw Joel Isaacson leaning against the door of a black Yukon parked in front of the Butler Aviation fueling facility.

You're not supposed to have vehicles—except with flashing lights, etcetera—on the tarmac.

But I suppose if you are a very senior Secret Service guy, you can park just about anyplace you damned well please.

And all Joel heard was that I was bringing some special radio. He doesn't know how big or how heavy, and he wasn't about to help drag a big heavy radio from Butler to wherever he was supposed to park the Yukon.

"Joel, this is Master Sergeant Alex Dumbrowski," Castillo said as they all stood on the tarmac. "Sergeant, this is Mr. Isaacson of the Secret Service. He's in charge of Secretary Hall's security."

The two men nodded and shook hands but said nothing.

"Where's the radio?" Isaacson asked.

Sergeant Dumbrowski pointed at the enormous hard-sided suitcase.

"That's all of it?" Isaacson asked, dubiously.

Sergeant Dumbrowski nodded.

Ground service people walked up, dragging a fuel hose. Fernando Lopez climbed down from the Lear.

"Fernando!" Castillo called and Fernando walked over.

Castillo introduced him to Isaacson as his cousin.

Isaacson motioned one of the fuel handlers over and handed him a credit card.

"Put that fuel and the landing fees on that," he ordered.

"Thank you," Castillo said.

"What the hell, it's in government service—you can send us a bill for the charter, Mr. Lopez—and this way no one gets to see the bills."

"You have just made our lawyers very happy," Fernando said. "Thank you."

Isaacson didn't reply, turning instead to Master Sergeant Dumbrowski.

"All set up, how big is this thing?" he asked. "The antenna, I mean?"

Sergeant Dumbrowski wordlessly demonstrated with his hands the size of the expanded antenna.

"Jesus, that small?" Isaacson asked, rhetorically. "Still, Charley, if we set it up on the roof of the OEOB all kinds of questions will be asked. What about Nebraska Avenue?"

As OEOB meant "Old Executive Office Building"—almost everything in Washington seemed to be boiled down to acronymns—Nebraska Avenue was verbal shorthand for the "Nebraska Avenue Complex," off Ward Circle in Northwest Washington. Originally a Navy installation dating to World War II, there are thirty-two buildings on thirty-eight acres. It was now the home of the Department of Homeland Security. Secretary Hall had his official office there, although, as a practical matter, he most often used his office in the OEOB, which was right next to the White House.

Before Charley could reply, Isaacson asked another question, this time of Master Sergeant Dumbrowski.

"How far can you set up the antenna away from the working part?"

"About fifty feet," Dumbrowski replied. It was the first time he had opened his mouth.

"The boss's office is on the top floor," Isaacson said to Charley. "It's a lot less than fifty feet from it to the roof. And it has secure phones. And, no one will ask questions about one more antenna out there. Make sense?"

"Makes a lot of sense, Joel," Castillo said. "Sergeant Dumbrowski's also going to have to teach a couple of your people how to operate it—it's not that hard—so that it's covered all the time. Most important messages come in when the operator is on the john."

"You can start with me and my partner, Sergeant, okay?"

Dumbrowski nodded and then said, almost hesitantly, "Major?"

"Joel, the fewer people who know these radios exist, the fewer people are going to absolutely have to have them," Castillo said. "Okay?"

"For the moment, Charley, fine. But if this equipment is as good as you told the boss it is, I'll want to talk about getting some permanently."

"We can talk about that later," Charley said. "But this one goes back to Bragg with Dumbrowski when this is over. Agreed?"

"Agreed."

"Sergeant Dumbrowski is going to need a place to stay. Close to the radio."

"There's a bedroom off the boss's office. So far as I know, he's used it twice. I'll put the sergeant in there, and if the boss asks I'll tell him you said to do it. Okay?"

"You are devious," Castillo said.

"Talking about devious, two guys who work for an unnamed federal agency and who we haven't seen in years looked Tom McGuire and me up—purely for auld lang syne, of course—and then asked if we happened to know where they could find your friend Kennedy. Not together. They took four shots at us. First

Tom, and then me, and then two hours later another guy did the same thing. I guess they had a real hard time believing us when we said we didn't know anything about Kennedy's whereabouts and didn't think you did, either."

"Thanks," Castillo said.

"You want me to take this radio and the sergeant to Philadelphia with us?"

"Who's going to Philadelphia?"

"The boss is, I guess to try to keep the mayor from going ballistic when the commissioner tells him about the plans for the Liberty Bell. You mean, you didn't know?"

Castillo shook his head. "When?"

"First thing in the morning." Isaacson looked at his watch. "In six hours. He wants to be there early."

"Leave the radio where it is. I'm taking one to Philadelphia to give to Miller. And you'll have secure communications anyway, right?"

Isaacson nodded.

"Well, if that's it, Don Juan, I'll take the sergeant over to Nebraska Avenue."

"I wish you'd knock off with the Don Juan."

"I know," Isaacson said, smiling.

Charley looked at the Lear. They were almost finished fueling it and Fernando was doing the walk-around.

Charley got in the airplane and went into the cockpit.

[TWO]
Philadelphia International Airport
Philadelphia, Pennsylvania
0205 10 June 2005

Philadelphia ground control had directed them to the Lease-Aire hangar, so Castillo wasn't surprised to see, as they taxied up, two Ford Crown Victorias, with all the police regalia, and a third, unmarked Victoria.

Is that Betty's unmarked car?

As the Lear parked, Sergeant Schneider and Major H. Richard Miller, Jr., got out of the unmarked car. Miller was still wearing the ragged clothing from his father's garage that Betty had suggested he wear while meeting the undercover cops.

That triggered an uncomfortable thought: *Jesus, I've been telling these people I'm Secret Service and/or Hall's executive assistant and here I am in my Class A's.*

Three cops got out of the police cars. All were wearing the leather jackets of the Highway Patrol. One of them was a burly man with a lieutenant's bars on his jacket epaulets.

Ah, the brother who's going to break both my legs. I told him—or at least let him think—I'm in the DEA.

Shit!

As Fernando was shutting down the Lear, Castillo took off his headset, put on his beret, and went into the cabin. He found the Delta team arranging their gear and said, "You guys made up your mind which of you will stay here and which will go wherever the ever-changing winds of fate are going to take me?"

Sergeant First Class Seymour Krantz, who wasn't much over the height and weight minimums for the Army, smiled at him.

"I was with Major Miller in Afghanistan, sir, so if it's all right with you . . ."

"You'll go anywhere he's not, right?"

Krantz chuckled.

"Major Miller and I get along pretty good, sir."

"Okay. What I'm going to do is try to get a cop to sit on the airplane and then take Sergeant Sherman with us to help you get the radio set up."

They nodded and said, "Yes, sir," almost in unison.

Castillo opened the door and stepped down from the Lear.

"Where the hell did you get the airplane?" Miller asked by way of greeting.

"It belongs to my cousin Fernando," Castillo said. "Good morning, Sergeant Schneider."

"Good morning," she said, avoiding looking at him, and formally—and more than a little awkwardly—shaking his hand. "This is my brother, Lieutenant Frank Schneider, of the Highway Patrol."

Lieutenant Schneider was standing with his arms folded, looking the opposite of friendly. The other two Highway Patrolmen, both of them large and mean looking, stood behind him. One of them was the sergeant who'd driven him to the airport earlier.

And I wonder how long it took for you to tell Ol' Break My Legs that the Secret Service calls me Don Juan?

"Good morning," Castillo said. "Or, good middle of the night."

Lieutenant Schneider neither smiled nor offered his hand.

"You told me you was DEA," he accused.

"And you told me you were going to break both my legs," Castillo said. "One good lie deserves another, right?"

"What did he say to you?" Betty asked, aghast. "Frank, damn you!"

Castillo saw Sergeant Krantz, all five-feet-four and 130 pounds of him, struggling to get his huge hard-sided suitcase down from the Lear.

"Not to worry, Sergeant," Castillo said, pointing at Krantz, "I brought a highly skilled Special Forces assassin along to protect me."

The Highway sergeant chuckled.

At Ol' Break My Legs, not at me.

Miller recognized Sergeant Krantz.

"Let me give you a hand with that, Seymour," he said and went quickly to help him.

Castillo turned to meet Lieutenant Schneider's eyes.

She said, "Commissioner Kellogg told Highway that, until further notice, supporting Counterterrorism with whatever they want is the job. Chief Inspector Kramer ordered me to meet you and ask what you want."

"How much else did anyone else tell you?" Castillo asked.

"I know about the Liberty Bell, if that's what you mean."

"And who else was told?"

"The Highway commander and these officers," Schneider said.

"Keep it that way, Lieutenant, please," Castillo said.

Schneider nodded.

"So what do you need?"

"We've got a special radio. We'll need some place to set it up. And I need someone to sit on the airplane while we're here. And I'd like to talk to the undercover guy . . ."

"He's at the Homicide Bureau in the Roundhouse," Betty Schneider said. "But tell me about the radio, what does it need?"

"Someplace preferably out of the rain," Sergeant Krantz answered for him. "And someplace—a flat roof would be nice—not far from the controls, where the antenna will have a clear shot at the sky, the satellite."

"How big's the antenna?" Betty asked.

Krantz demonstrated with his hands and arms.

"There's a sort of porch on Building 110," she said, looking at Castillo. "You saw it. Would that do?"

He called Building 110 to his memory.

"Yeah, I think so."

Fernando and Sergeant Sherman walked up.

"This is Fernando Lopez," Castillo said. "And Sergeant Sherman, who's going to help Sergeant Krantz set up the radio. Fernando and I are cousins. This is Sergeant Betty Schneider, her brother Frankie . . ."

"*Frank*," Schneider quickly and firmly corrected him.

But I got another smile from the sergeant.

". . . *Lieutenant* Schneider of the Highway Patrol."

Schneider shook hands with Fernando. Betty smiled at him, looked a little confused, and said, "And that's Dick Miller."

"Dick and I go back a ways," Fernando said.

"You want to top the tanks off and get the weather and file a flight plan back to Bragg?"

"I'd rather go with you," Fernando said. "You have a problem with that?"

Castillo thought it over a moment before answering, "No. Why not?"

"Good," Fernando said.

"Okay, so what we have to do now is get the sergeants and the radio to the arsenal," Castillo said. "And me, Fernando, and Dick to the Roundhouse. You said the Homicide Bureau? What's the undercover officer doing there?"

"I'll take you and Major Miller and Mr. Lopez . . ." Lieutenant Schneider said.

"No," Betty said, flatly, cutting him off. "The sergeants and the radio go to the arsenal in Highway cars. I'll take Major Castillo, Major Miller, and Mr. Lopez to the Roundhouse."

"Thanks just the same, Sergeant Schneider, but I'm not really afraid of him," Castillo said.

"You better be, you sonofabitch!" Lieutenant Schneider said.

Betty was not amused. She was, instead, all business.

"What Lieutenant Schneider is going to do is stay here until we have a couple of uniforms sitting on your airplane," she said. "He can do that better than anybody else. And then he's going to catch up with us at Homicide. The other Highway car will take the sergeants and the radio to the arsenal. I'll call ahead and set it up for them. And that car will stay there to provide whatever transport we need. If you have any problems with that, Frank, call Chief Kramer. He's at Homicide."

Lieutenant Schneider looked for a moment as if he was going to say something, but, in the end, he turned wordlessly and walked toward his car.

Which almost certainly means that Chief Inspector Kramer has told him that Betty's running this operation and that he takes his orders from her.

Betty gestured for the others to get in the unmarked Crown Victoria.

Castillo got in beside her.

Their eyes met—momentarily—for the first time as she backed away from the hangar.

"Why the uniform?" Betty asked.

"It made sense at Fort Bragg," he said, and then, "You don't seem surprised."

"I picked up on that—that you're an Army officer, as well as a Secret Service agent, and the executive assistant to the secretary of homeland security—at Dick's house."

"Yeah."

"How do you know who you are at any given moment?"

"Sometimes it's difficult."

"And, I forgot, the head of catering for . . . what was it you said? . . . Rig Service?"

"Rig Service," he confirmed. "Sometimes I say I fly helicopters for them."

"And is there such a company?"

"Yeah, there is," Fernando said from the backseat. "And among other things I do for the Gringo whenever somebody calls up to check on him is say that he really is what he told somebody he is."

"'The Gringo'?" she repeated.

"Just a nickname," Fernando explained, and even though the car interior was darkened Betty knew he said it with a smile. "You're welcome to use it, too," he added.

"Thanks. But how do you know what he's told them?"

"Sometimes that's very difficult," Fernando said, chuckling.

He started to say something else but saw that she had her cellular telephone out and had punched an autodial button.

"Sergeant Schneider, sir," she said a moment later. "I just picked up Mr. Castillo at the airport and we're headed for the Roundhouse. I sent one of the Highway cars out to the arsenal. Mr. Castillo brought some kind of special radio—and a guy to set it up and work it—with him. The antenna has to go someplace where it can be aimed at a satellite. The porch roof of Building 110 will work. Is that okay with you?"

"Whatever he wants, Schneider," Chief Inspector Dutch Kramer could be heard, faintly but clearly. "You want me to call out there and set it up?"

"That would probably be a good idea, sir."

"Okay, done. I'll see you in a couple of minutes."

A security guard waved them through the airport gate.

Betty reached to the dashboard and turned on the flashing lights under the grille and the siren, stepped heavily on the accelerator, then turned her head.

"You were saying, Mr. Lopez?"

"Call me Fernando, please," he replied. "I was wondering why your brother wants to break the Gringo's legs."

"Jesus Christ!" Castillo exclaimed.

There was another momentary meeting of Betty's and Charley's eyes and she shook her head.

Charley said to Dick: "What *I'm* wondering is what you found out from the undercover cop. Can we get to that, please, Dick?"

"Charley, not only because I also wonder what you've done to annoy Betty's brother, I think you'd better wait and get it straight from the undercover cop. It's pretty weird."

"Give me what you think I can understand," Charley ordered.

"Okay. None of this is confirmed. But I think there's a good chance the guys who stole the airplane have been here in Philadelphia, as mullahs, visiting from Somalia."

"You mean the guys who actually stole the airplane or the guys behind the idea?"

"Maybe both. According to Britton . . ."

"Britton is the undercover cop?" Castillo interrupted.

"Right. When these characters showed up at Britton's mosque, he reported it. Chief Inspector Kramer took it to the FBI. The names these two guys gave at the mosque didn't mean anything to the FBI, so Kramer got photos of them at the mosque. The FBI got a match and said they were legitimate, they were pilots for Air Yemen and in this country for flight training . . . some place in Oklahoma."

"Probably my alma mater," Castillo said.

"What?"

"On my graduation leave—remember, Fernando?—for reasons that now seem pretty foolish, I went to Spartan—the Spartan School of Aeronautics; it's been around forever—and got my Airline Transport rating. They train pilots from all over the world; from small airlines that don't have their own facilities. It's in Tulsa."

"Okay," Miller said. "That fits. And according to Britton, it's all over the AAL community that the Liberty Bell's going to be taken out."

"AAL, Dick?" Fernando asked.

"Cop shorthand for 'African American Lunatics,' " Miller said. "And defined as African American—and some white guys, believe it or not—quote, Muslims, end quote, who are not part of the bona fide Islamic community and who happen to be black."

"I don't think I understand," Fernando confessed.

"I know I don't," Miller said. "That's why I want Charley to hear all this from Britton. I don't want to say something, imply something, that may not be the case."

"But we have the names—and photographs, you said—of these people?" Castillo asked.

"Photos, probably," Betty Schneider said. "We tend to hang on to photos. I didn't think to ask. But we don't have names."

"Why not?"

"The FBI didn't give them to Chief Kramer, and—when this came up just now—he said if he called down there he was probably going to get the duty officer, who would stall him until the SAC came to work in the morning, so we decided to wait for you."

"Jesus Christ!" Castillo exclaimed. "You said the undercover cop, Britton, is in Homicide. What's that all about, Betty?"

"Why don't we go back to 'Sergeant Schneider'?" she said.

"You mean until this is over?"

"No, that's not what I mean," she said. "The reason Detective Britton is in Homicide is because we picked him—Ali Abd Ar-Raziq—up for questioning in a homicide."

"You're talking about the undercover cop?" Fernando asked.

"Yeah. The AALs like to know where every other AAL is all the time and what they're doing. So when we really have to talk to them—more often when they really have to talk to us—we pick them up, with other unsavory characters."

"Jesus Christ! I wouldn't mind taking on the FBI duty officer as a Secret Service agent, but I can't walk into an FBI office in my uniform! They'd lock me up until—"

He banged his fist on the dashboard.

"We need those damned names!" Castillo said, clearly frustrated.

No one said anything.

"And I don't have any dates or anything," he said after a moment. "Betty, when was this?"

"I'll have to look it up, Mr. Castillo," she said. "And I can't do that until we get to Homicide or out to the arsenal."

"'Mr. Castillo'?" he parroted.

"Yeah. You're 'Mr. Castillo,' and I'm 'Sergeant Schneider.' Okay?"

"Whatever you say, Sergeant Schneider."

"We'll be at the Roundhouse in just a couple of minutes, Mr. Castillo," she said. "We'll deal with it then."

[THREE]
Homicide Bureau
Police Administration Building
8th and Race Streets
Philadelphia, Pennsylvania
0225 10 June 2005

Chief Inspector Dutch Kramer was almost visibly of two minds when he saw Major C. G. Castillo in his Class A uniform.

"What's with the uniform?" he asked.

"I never really got out of the stockade, Chief," Castillo said. "They sort of paroled me to the Secret Service."

"So why are you wearing it now?"

"I just came from the stockade," Castillo said. "Most of the guys in there think the Secret Service is a bunch of candy asses."

"And they're right. They're not as bad as the fing FBI, but they also think their sh—"

Kramer remembered gentlemen don't say things like "their shit don't stink" in the presence of ladies, and Betty Schneider was both one hell of a cop and a lady.

"Schneider tell you about what Britton came up with?" he asked, changing the subject.

"I think this is good stuff, Chief," Castillo said. "We'll have to check it out, but if these two at Britton's mosque went to flight school in Oklahoma they probably went to Spartan, in Tulsa. And I know they teach the 727 at Spartan."

"How do you know that?"

"I went there," Castillo said. "But we can't check it out until I get the names. What about their photos? Do you still have them?"

"I had one of my guys go through the files. He brought them over here."

"But no names?"

For an answer, Kramer shook his head and slid a manila folder across his desk—actually, that of the captain commanding the Homicide Bureau—to Castillo. It was labeled, using what looked like a broad-tipped Magic Marker, UNKNOWN MULLAHS 1 & 2.

There were perhaps twenty eight-by-ten-inch color photographs in the folder. Some showed the men, wearing robes and loose black hats—the sort of floppy berets favored by mullahs—but with creased trousers and wingtip shoes peeking out the bottoms of the robes, entering and coming out of a building Castillo presumed was the mosque where Britton was working undercover.

They had intelligent faces, and in several photographs—some of those in the folder were blowups of their faces—they were smiling.

Are these the guys?

How the hell can anybody calmly plan to fly an airplane into the ground?

He looked at Chief Inspector Kramer.

"We need their names," he said.

"Well, the FBI must have them. I call down there, the duty officer'll stall me, and we can't tell him why we want them. Or can we?"

"Can I have the number?" Castillo said. "I'll give it a shot. If that doesn't work, I'll think of something else."

"FBI."

"Are you the duty officer?"

"Who is this, please?"

"My name is Castillo. I'm with the Secret Service. Are you the duty officer?"

"I'll need more than that, Mr. Castillo."

"Okay. Write it down. Castillo, I spell: Charley-Alpha-Sierra-Tango-India, Lima-Lima-Oscar. Initials: Charley-Golf. Supervisory Special Agent. Assignment, Secret Service, Washington. Verification telephone number . . ."

As he gave the number, he sensed Betty's eyes on him and when he met her eyes she looked away.

". . . I'll hold while you verify," Charley finished.

That took four minutes, during which time Sergeant Betty Schneider looked at everything in the room but C. G. Castillo.

"How may I help you, Agent Castillo?"

"On or about twelve December 2004, Chief Inspector Kramer of the Philadelphia PD Counterterrorism Bureau gave you some surveillance photographs he had made of two Muslim mullahs he considered suspicious. You ran them, identified the men, and told Chief Kramer they were okay. Somehow, Chief Kramer didn't get the names you came up with when you made these people. He and I need them, and right now."

"That would come under 'Counterterrorism,' I suppose. If we ran these people, I'm sure their names are in the file."

"Can you get them for me, please?"

"What I'll do is make a record of this telecon and I'll put it on the chief of Counterterrorism's desk so he'll see it first thing when he comes in in the morning."

"I need these names now, not in the morning. If you can't get into the files, how about calling this guy up and having him come in?"

"Well, I suppose I could do that, but I'm not sure if he'd be willing . . ."

"Call him," Castillo interrupted. "Please. I'll hold."

"Agent Castillo? You still there?"

"I'm still here."

"I've got Special Agent Lutherberg on the line. He wants to know what this is all about."

"It's about the Secret Service needing the names of two men you ran and identified."

"That's not really telling us very much, is it?"

"That's all I'm going to tell you."

"Hold one."

"Agent Castillo?"

"I'm still here."

"Special Agent Lutherberg said to tell you he'll be happy to discuss this with you first thing in the morning if you want to come into the office."

"In other words, he's not going to get me the information I need now?"

"He'll be happy to talk to you about it in his office in the morning."

"I'd like to leave a message for him—one that applies to you, too—if that would be possible."

"Certainly."

"Fuck you, you candy-ass bureaucratic sonofabitch. I'm going to do whatever I can to burn your ass, his ass, and the ass of the special agent in charge over this. You would be wise to deliver the message *and* dig out the information that I need, because someone who *can* get you people off your candy asses will be calling shortly."

He slammed the phone down in its cradle.

"They do try one's patience on occasion, don't they?" Chief Kramer asked, innocently.

Charley took out his cellular telephone and punched an autodial key.

It was answered on the second ring.

"Three-zero-six."

"Charley Castillo. I need to speak with Joel Isaacson right now."

"Hold one."

That took three minutes.

"Isaacson."

"Charley, Joel."

"I knew I wasn't going to get any sleep. What's up, Don Juan?"

"I think there's a very good chance we have an ID on the guys who stole the 727," Charley began, explained why, and related the details of his telephone conversation with the duty officer of the Philadelphia office of the Federal Bureau of Investigation.

"My, we do use some really naughty words when we're peeved, don't we?" Isaacson said.

"Peeved is the fucking understatement of the year, the fucking decade. Can you do anything about those bastards, Joel?"

"I think so, yes. Where are you?"

"I'm in the Homicide Bureau of the Philadelphia Police Department. But call me on the cellular."

"Have they got a fax machine where you are?"

Charley looked at Sergeant Betty Schneider.

"I need a fax machine number," he said.

She left the office and returned in less than a minute with the number written on a sheet of notebook paper. He gave it to Isaacson.

"It was sent to you at the Mayflower," Isaacson said, "marked 'Please Deliver Immediately.' They did, and my guy sitting on your apartment sent it out to Nebraska Avenue, thinking I was still there. My guy there read it to me over the phone. So I'll call out there and have them fax it to you."

"What the hell is it?"

"I don't know; I don't want to know. It's probably a mistake."

"Jesus Christ, Joel!"

What he's saying, of course, is that he thinks it's from Kennedy. I wonder what the hell it is?

"As soon as I do what I can about the FBI, I'll let you know," Isaacson said. "Good job, Don Juan."

He hung up.

"Your boss?" Chief Inspector Kramer asked.

"A heavy-duty Secret Service guy. Good guy."

"You think he'll be able to do something?"

"If anybody can, Isaacson can. But fighting the FBI is like punching a pillow."

"Uh-huh," Kramer agreed.

"Can I talk to your undercover guy now?"

Kramer rose from behind the desk and motioned for Castillo to follow him.

They'd barely had time to introduce themselves when Betty Schneider came into the interview.

"Your fax came in, Mr. Castillo," she said and handed it to him. "It's addressed to somebody named Gossinger, but I have a hunch it's intended for you."

Castillo took the fax from her and read it.

Α Φαξ. . . . . <<

Φρομ: Ροβερτο Βονδιεμο
        Ρεσιδεντ Γ:.<<ενεραλ Μαναγερ
        Γρανδε Χοζυμελ Βεαχη & Γολφ Ρεσορτ
        Χοζυμελ, Μεξιχο

Βοσσ

Βοσσσσσ

Φορ: SEÑOR KARL W. GOSSINGER
     THE MAYFLOWER HOTEL
     WASHINGTON, D.C., USA

PLEASE DELIVER IMMEDIATELY ON RECEIPT!

MY DEAR MR. GOSSINGER:

   THIS IS TO CONFIRM YOUR RESERVATION FOR OUR FOUR DAY
ALL INCLUSIVE GOLF AND SNORKELING PACKAGE (FOR TWO)
COMMENCING JUNE 10, 2005.

   WE LOOK FORWARD TO HAVING YOU AND YOUR GUEST IN THE
GRANDE COZUMEL BEACH AND GOLF RESORT, WHERE WE ARE SURE

YOU WILL FIND EVERYTHING YOU ARE LOOKING FOR, AND THANK
YOU FOR CHOOSING US.

    UNFORTUNATELY, THERE SEEMS TO BE A SMALL PROBLEM
WITH YOUR AMERICAN EXPRESS CREDIT CARD. THE DATE HAS
EXPIRED AND WE REQUIRE AN UPDATE. I MUST ASK YOU TO
CALL ME AT YOUR EARLIEST CONVENIENCE TO HELP STRAIGHTEN
THE MATTER OUT. MY PRIVATE NUMBER IS 52-00-01 456-777.

    I HOPE TO HEAR FROM YOU VERY SHORTLY.

    WITH ALL BEST WISHES,

Roberto Dondiemo
ROBERTO DONDIEMO

Roberto Dondiemo, my ass!

"It's for me. Thank you very much, Sergeant Schneider," Castillo said.

"Sometime, when you can find time, you can tell me about Mr. Gossinger."

"I'd love to. I'll make time," Castillo said and then turned to Detective Britton. "I'll be right back, Detective Britton. I have to deal with this."

"Sure," Britton said.

He went to Fernando, who was talking—in Spanish—to a Homicide Bureau detective, handed him the fax, and said—in Spanish: "I sure hope you brought your Cozumel International approach charts with you."

"What the hell is this?" Fernando asked, in English, as Castillo punched numbers into his cellular.

"You said you wanted to go snorkeling in Cozumel," Castillo said.

"What?"

The call went through much quicker than Castillo thought it would.

"Roberto Dondiemo."

"Gee, you sure don't have much of an accent when you speak English, Señor Dondiemo."

"Thank you. I could say the same thing about you, Herr Gossinger. There's hardly any trace of German."

"Dare I hope you've straightened out the problem with my American Express card by now?"

"Indeed I have. Absolutely. It was . . . what's the English phrase? . . . a *glitch* of some kind. Can I take it that we'll soon have the pleasure of your company in the resort?"

"If I was sure I could find what I'm looking for, I would certainly come."

"I have a good idea where you can find what you're looking for, Mr. Gossinger. I could say I'm almost positive I can locate it for you."

"You wouldn't want to tell me now, I suppose?"

"I really think you should come down here, Mr. Gossinger. All work and no play, as they say."

"I probably will. But if I do, my party will be a little larger than originally planned."

"Why does that worry me?"

"It shouldn't. One of the people will be my cousin and the other two will be soldiers, taking sort of a busman's holiday."

"None of whom, I hope, have ever heard of me?"

"None of them have ever heard of you."

"I don't know why the hell I trust you, Mr. Gossinger. Maybe it's that boyishly honest face you have."

"But you do, right?"

"Against my better judgment."

"Tell me, does the Grande Cozumel Beach and Golf Resort have a flat roof?"

"Now that you mention it, yes, it does. Is that important, somehow?"

"And the rooms you've reserved for me, are they on the top floor?"

"No. As a matter of fact, you can walk directly from your accommodations onto the beach. We've put you into the Jack Nicklaus Suite. Will that be satisfactory?"

"That's very kind, but we'd much prefer to be on the top floor, which would give us a good view of the beach and where we could watch the waves go up and down. Will that be a problem?"

"Not at all. You'll be among friends here, one of whom happens to own the hotel. Your every wish will be our command."

Jesus, is he telling me Pevsner's there?

"How nice!"

"I was about to suggest that the best way to get here, probably, is through Miami."

"I have a plane."

"What kind of a plane?"

"A Lear 45X. Getting there will be no problem. But I always worry about getting delayed at customs."

"Put your mind at rest about customs. When may we expect the pleasure of your company?"

"I'll call again when I know."

"I'll be expecting your call, Mr. Gossinger."

When he put his cellular telephone back in his pocket, he saw that Betty Schneider and Fernando were looking at him. She had a telephone in her hand, her palm covering the mouthpiece.

"This one's for Supervisory Special Agent Castillo of the Secret Service," she said. "Wouldn't give his name."

He nodded and took the telephone from her.

"Castillo."

"Something wrong with your cellular, Charley?" the secretary of the Department of Homeland Security said.

"Sir, I was talking to . . . my new friend from Vienna."

"What did he have to say?"

"He wants me to come to Cozumel."

"He's in Cozumel?"

And doesn't want the FBI—for that matter, anybody, but especially the FBI—to know.

But Hall has every right to know.

"Yes, sir. And he says he's almost positive he knows where what we're looking for can be found."

"But he wouldn't tell you where? And he wants you to go to Cozumel?"

"No, sir, he wouldn't tell me. And, yes, sir, he wants me to go to Cozumel."

"He didn't say why?"

"No, sir, he didn't. I think I'd better go, sir."

"And what about General McNab?"

"After I see General McNab, sir, and presuming nothing turns up there that would shoot down Cozumel."

"That's a pretty bad choice of words, Charley."

"Sorry, sir."

Castillo thought he heard Secretary Hall exhale.

"Charley," Hall said, "when I said I wanted you to keep me in the loop I meant it."

"Yes, sir. I understand. I will, sir."

"You didn't tell me about your run-in with the FBI," Hall said, flatly. "I had to hear that from Joel."

"I thought I'd see what Joel could do first, sir. I didn't want to bother you."

"Bother me? Jesus Christ, Charley, we're running out of time!"

"I understand, sir."

"I'm not sure you do. Tomorrow morning—*this* morning, when I meet with the mayor at half past nine, I'm going to have to tell him."

"Sir, I thought we had until four something in the afternoon."

"The president said I'm to inform the mayor this morning. He said the mayor has the right to know. Which means I have to ask—more accurately, beg—the mayor for a little time before he pushes the panic button. And I'd like to be able to tell him something more than we're looking for the airplane and hope to find it."

"Jesus!"

"Like I said, we're running out of time," Hall said. "But the reason I called: When Joel came to me with your yarn about the FBI's intransigent stupidity, taking you at your word, I got Mark Schmidt out of bed. Taking me at mine, Schmidt seems as angry as you were. He told me that he would deal with it personally. You should be hearing from the special agent in charge of their Philadelphia office any minute. If you don't hear from him in the next fifteen minutes, call me."

"Yes, sir."

"Call me in fifteen minutes, whether or not you hear from them."

"Yes, sir."

[FOUR]

For the next fifteen minutes, Castillo sat in the interviewee chair in interview room 3. Sergeant Betty Schneider sat on the table beside Detective Jack Britton. Chief Inspector Dutch Kramer and Dick Miller leaned against the wall as all three—but mostly Castillo—tried to pull from Britton any bit of information that would fill in the blanks. Britton understood what was being asked of him, and why, and pulled all sorts of esoteric information about the mosque and its mullahs from his memory. None of it seemed useful, although Castillo found what Britton told him fascinating.

Castillo had kept looking at his watch and when fifteen minutes had passed he decided to wait one more minute before calling Secretary Hall and telling him there had been no contact from the FBI.

He was actually watching the sweep second hand on his wristwatch waiting for it to go back to twelve when the interview room door opened.

"Chief," one of the Homicide Bureau detectives said, "there's a guy from the FBI out here looking for a Secret Service Agent Castillo."

Kramer looked at Castillo, who made a wry face, and then gestured to the detective to bring him in.

A moment later a middle-aged, somewhat portly man with a plastic badge with FBI in large letters on it hanging from the breast pocket of his suit came into the room. He was neatly dressed, but he needed a shave.

He looked around the small room, taking a close look at everybody.

"Hello, Chief Inspector," he said, smiling at Kramer.

Kramer nodded at him.

"I'm looking, Chief, for a Secret Service man, Supervisory Special Agent Castillo. I was told he was in here."

Kramer pointed at Castillo.

"You're Castillo?" the man said. He obviously did not expect to see a supervisory Secret Service agent in an Army officer's uniform.

"Yes, I am," Castillo said. "Who are you?"

"I'm Alexander Stuart, the Philadelphia FBI SAC."

"Be right with you, Mr. Stuart," Castillo said as he took out his cellular and pushed an autodial key.

"Castillo, Mr. Secretary. The Philadelphia FBI SAC just walked into the room—

"I haven't had a chance to talk to him, Mr. Secretary—

"Yes, Mr. Secretary, I'll get back to you just as soon as I've had a chance to talk to him."

He put the telephone back in his pocket and looked at SAC Stuart.

"It would seem, Mr. Castillo, that there's been some sort of a misunderstanding," Stuart said.

"No misunderstanding. I needed some information and I needed it right then. Your duty officer wouldn't—or couldn't—give it to me and your counterterrorism man told me he'd talk to me when he came in in the morning. I couldn't wait that long so I called Washington."

"Apparently, it wasn't made clear to either of my agents how important this matter actually is," Stuart said. "What's it all about?"

"What this is all about is that I asked for some information and your people wouldn't give it to me. I need those names, Mr. Stuart, and I need them now."

"Special Agent Lutherberg, who heads my counterterrorism section, is on his way to the office. If he's not there already. I'll have those names for you very shortly."

Castillo grunted.

"I need some additional cooperation from the FBI," Castillo said.

"Which is?"

"As soon as we have the names, and the photographs, I want to run them—right now—past the Spartan School of Aeronautics in Tulsa, Oklahoma. I need to know (a) if they were students there about the time Chief Inspector Kramer gave you the surveillance photos he had made of them and (b) if they were students at Spartan, what sort of training they had; specifically, if they received training in Boeing 727 aircraft."

"Oh, so that's what this is about! That airliner that went missing in Africa."

Castillo ignored the remark.

"Now, can you get in touch with your Tulsa office directly, send them the photos and the names over your net, and have them go out to Spartan or am I going to have to do that through Washington?"

"I can contact them directly, of course," Stuart said.

"Would I offend you if I suggested you call your duty officer and get that started right now?"

Stuart met his eyes.

"That doesn't offend me, Mr. Castillo," he said. "But the language you used to my duty officer offends me. Offends me very much, frankly. Are you aware that we record all incoming calls after duty hours?"

"I didn't think that was legal unless the calling party is advised that his call will be recorded," Castillo said. "But if you've got a tape of my conversation with your duty officer, why don't you send it—*the entire conversation, not just my intemperate language*—to Director Schmidt?"

Stuart tried and failed to stare Castillo down, then looked away, to Chief Inspector Kramer. "Chief, is there a telephone I can use?"

"Schneider," Chief Kramer said.

Sergeant Betty Schneider, with a wholly unintended display of her upper thighs, slid off the table.

"Right this way, Mr. Stuart," she said.

When the door had closed after them, Detective Jack Britton pointed to Castillo, looked at Miller, and said, admiringly, "Hey, bro, your white boy pal is a real hard-ass, ain't he?"

[FIVE]
Office of the Commissioner
Police Administration Building
8th and Race Streets
Philadelphia, Pennsylvania
0345 10 June 2005

Police Commissioner Ralph J. Kellogg walked into his outer office, said good morning to Chief Inspector Kramer, Majors Castillo and Miller, Detective Jack Britton, and Sergeant Betty Schneider, who were sitting in chairs waiting for him, and waved them into his office.

Captain Jack Hanrahan, Kellogg's executive officer, waited until everybody was inside, then pulled the door closed.

Both Kellogg and Hanrahan were shaven, wearing suits and stiffly starched white shirts, and were obviously fully awake, although it was less than twenty minutes since Chief Inspector Kramer had called the commissioner at his home and suggested they needed to talk.

"Okay, Dutch," Kellogg said, "where are we?"

"Between Britton and Castillo, Commissioner, and with the somewhat reluctant cooperation of the FBI, we've IDed the people we think stole the airplane. They were here, at Britton's mosque."

"Is that going to help you find the airplane?" Kellogg asked Castillo, but then, before Castillo could reply, asked: "What's with the uniform? First step in declaring martial law?"

"I've been at Fort Bragg, Commissioner—and I'm about to go back there—to explain the uniform. And I have reason to believe we have located the airplane."

"You either have or you haven't. Which?"

"A source which has previously been right on the money has told me he's almost certainly located it. What I'll be doing at Fort Bragg is helping to set up the operation to neutralize it."

"What source?"

I was afraid you were going to ask that.

"Not to go farther than this room, Commissioner?"

Kellogg considered that.

"No. That's over. As I understand the plan, Matt Hall will be here at eight o'clock. Shortly after that, as soon as we've compared notes we're going to see the mayor. I want to be in a position to lay everything on the table in front of him. I now think promising to hold off telling until four this afternoon was a mistake. From now on, starting when Hall gets here, I'm going to tell the mayor everything I know. You understand? Now, what is the source of your information that the airplane has almost certainly been located?"

"Sir, you're going to have to get that from Secretary Hall. I can't give it to you."

"Great!" Kellogg said, visibly angry.

"Commissioner," Chief Inspector Kramer said, "Britton also tells us that there's a lot of talk at his mosque about something going to happen to the Liberty Bell and Constitution Hall."

"You mean the lunatics know?"

"Commissioner, there have been no details," Detective Britton said. "Just nonspecific talk."

"They must know something," Kellogg said. "Which means they know more than I do and a hell of a lot more than the mayor does." He paused and then went on, "Were you able to come up with a connection between Britton's mosque and the people who cleaned airplanes at Lease-Aire?"

"No, sir," Sergeant Betty Schneider said. "We haven't been able to find a direct connection. None of the names connected. So what they're working on now is relatives and known associates."

"Most of the people at the mosque, Commissioner," Britton explained, "have rap sheets for drugs and/or theft. Which would keep them from getting airport work permits. But if they wanted to snoop around this airplane company . . ."

"Lease-Aire," Castillo furnished.

". . . they could send a brother or sister, or the guy next door, who is clean and could get an airport work permit . . ."

Commissioner Kellogg held up his hand to cut him off.

"I get it," he said. "And checking that out takes time, right?"

"Yes, sir," Betty and Britton said, almost together.

"We don't have any time," Kellogg said. He looked at Britton. "If you went back to the mosque, what do you think you could find out?"

"Not much, sir. I can't ask too many questions."

"Who at the mosque would know?"

"The mullahs."

"And if we hauled them in, what would we learn?"

"Not much. They know all about the Fifth Amendment; they claim it if we ask if it's raining."

"How many mullahs?"

"There's one head man," Britton said. "Abdul Khatami, formerly Clyde Matthews, and then . . ."

"Has this guy got a sheet?" Commissioner Kellogg interrupted.

Britton answered first with his hands, mimicking the unrolling of a long scroll.

"Before he converted, Clyde was a very bad boy," Britton said. "He was in and out of the slam from the time he was fifteen. A lot of drugs, but some heavy stuff, too, armed robbery, attempted murder, etcetera. He was doing five-to-ten in the federal slam—for cashing Social Security checks he 'found'—when he converted. So far as I know, he's been clean since; he sends the faithful out to raise money for the cause."

"How many more mullahs would be likely to know something about the Liberty Bell?"

"Three, maybe four—no more than four."

"You have their names and where we can find them?"

"Yes, sir. But . . ."

"Send Highway to pick them all up, one at a time. Lots of sirens, lots of noise. I want it known that we've picked them up. Keep them moving between districts, no more than an hour in each district. Dutch, you work out the details."

"What are we charging them with?" Chief Inspector Kramer asked.

Commissioner Kellogg ignored the question.

"Your people will interrogate them, Dutch. With Britton and Major Miller watching through a one-way glass. Northeast Detectives is probably as good a place as any to do that."

Chief Inspector Kramer nodded.

"Sir," Britton said. "If I'm held much later than eight in the morning and this is going to take longer than that . . ."

"You're not going back undercover, period," the commissioner said.

"Sir, I'm the best chance we have to learn anything at the mosque," Britton argued.

"What's the other guy's name who's in there with you?"

"Parker, sir. He's a good man, but he hasn't been under long enough for them to trust him."

"Maybe they will start to trust him, once they figure out you've been in there," Kellogg said. "And this way, you get to stay alive. I want you available until this thing goes down."

"But, sir . . ."

"That's it, Detective Britton," Kellogg said, flatly. "That's what's going to happen."

"Yes, sir."

"And this way, when Hall and I go see the mayor and he turns to me and asks what I'm doing about this I can truthfully tell him we think we know who the guys who stole that airplane are, that we've rounded up the mullahs and pulled you out to interrogate them. Okay?"

"Yes, sir," Britton said.

"And we might as well start on getting a judge to authorize wiretaps on the mosque and every phone that looks promising. That'll take some time, but we should do it."

"Commissioner, we—Homeland Security and the Secret Service—have blanket authority to tap in a terrorist situation like this. All we have to do is report it to a federal judge later."

"I didn't know that," Kellogg said, surprised. "You can authorize that?"

"As a supervisory special agent, sure."

"If you were to ask for the help of the Philadelphia Department to help you put in your taps, I'd be happy to oblige."

"Thank you, sir."

Kellogg studied Castillo. "So you're a Green Beret major."

"Yes, sir, I am."

"And a supervisory special agent of the Secret Service? You told me you had the credentials, but . . ."

"It's on the up-and-up," Castillo said. "I was sworn in."

"How do you keep who you really are straight?"

"With difficulty, sir," Castillo said and glanced at Betty Schneider.

She shook her head.

"When I talked to Matt Hall earlier, Castillo," Commissioner Kellogg said, "he said he was going to come as quietly as he can. What did he mean by that?"

"Usually, Commissioner, when he goes to a city where the Secret Service has an office they'll send people—usually four to six, in a couple of GMC Yukon XLs—to back up his personal security detail. That attracts a lot of attention. If he said he's coming quietly, he doesn't want that attention. I don't know this, but what I think is that they called the Philadelphia office and told them to send a car—not a Yukon—to meet the plane. They may not have told—probably didn't tell—Philadelphia that the secretary is coming."

"What's his personal detail?"

"Two Secret Service guys. This morning, I know it will be Joel Isaacson—

who is more than a bodyguard and who is usually with the secretary. And almost certainly his partner, Tom McGuire, who is also more than a bodyguard."

"Are you going to the airport to meet him? With Sergeant Schneider?"

"No, sir. I'm just about through here. I'm going to Fort Bragg. As I said before, Secretary Hall wants me to be in on the planning to neutralize the airplane."

"Miller, where are you going to connect with Secretary Hall?"

"I don't know, sir," Miller said and looked at Castillo for guidance.

"I think you should meet him at the airport," Castillo said. "Even better would be you and Sergeant Schneider."

"Nobody's had much sleep. Will you be okay with that, Schneider?" Kellogg asked.

"Yes, sir. I'll be all right."

"Okay, then, that's done," Commissioner Kellogg said. "Miller and Schneider can bring him up to speed on the way in from the airport. You're going to the airport right now, Castillo?"

"Just as soon as my sergeant gets here from the arsenal. He may already be here."

"Okay, let's get started on hauling in these lunatics and putting in the taps. We may get lucky, despite what Britton thinks. I sure as hell hope so."

[SIX]

In the unmarked car on the way to the airport, Castillo called Secretary Hall again.

"Sir, I regret the hour but you said I should keep you in the loop."

"What's going on, Charley?"

"The commo gear here has been set up and linked with the one in your office and Bragg, so you'll have it when you get here. Dick Miller and Sergeant Schneider, who know what's going on here, will meet your plane and be available while you're here. There's nothing else I can do here, so I'm headed back for Bragg to meet General McNab. I'm on my way to the airport now."

"How are you doing with the FBI?"

"The FBI here has sent the photographs and the names of the two Somalians who were here over their net to the FBI office in Tulsa. The SAC tells me they will run them past the people at Spartan right away. They—Tulsa—told him they know the Spartan director of security; he's retired FBI. So it shouldn't take much time to confirm these are the guys we're looking for. It may already have been done. I'll bet my last two bucks that it's our guys."

"We're betting a lot more than your last two bucks," Hall said.

"The commissioner decided to bring in the mullahs from the temple to see if we can learn something," Charley said to change the subject. "He also wanted to tap their phones and was going to start getting the necessary warrants from a judge. I told him we had blanket authority to tap without a warrant. Do we?"

"Christ, you told him that and didn't know?"

"Joel told me the Secret Service did. Or I got that impression. I wasn't paying as much attention as I should have been. I'll take the heat, sir. I thought the taps—as soon as they can be installed—were important."

"We have a ten-day authority, starting when we tell a federal judge. But we're required to tell a federal judge first. If we can justify the tap—reasonable cause to believe—to the judge within the ten days, we can keep the tap. Otherwise, we can't use anything we intercept. You might want to write that down, Charley."

"Yes, sir. I'm sorry, sir."

"Joel's on his way over here now. I'll have him call a judge."

"Yes, sir. Thank you."

"What the hell were you thinking, Charley?"

"That we're running out of time, sir."

"Well, I can't argue with that. Call me as soon as you've talked with General McNab."

"Yes, sir."

As Betty drove the unmarked Crown Victoria up to the Lear, Castillo said, "You guys get on the plane." He looked at Miller. "And you take a walk, Dick. I need a private word with Sergeant Schneider."

When Charley and Betty were alone in the car, she looked at him and then away.

"You wanted to know about Karl Gossinger," he said.

"It's not important," she said.

"I was born in Germany. My mother's name was Gossinger. My father was an American officer who was killed in Vietnam. They weren't married, he never knew about me, and I never knew about him until my mother was about to die. When they heard about me, my father's family brought me to this country and I took his name. Not even Dick knows that story. Fernando does, but hardly anybody else. But I'm considered a German by the Germans and got a passport, etcetera. It's useful in my line of work."

"Why are you telling me this?"

"Because I don't want to go back to Sergeant Schneider and Major Castillo."

"Charley, I don't even remember the last time I had any sleep. I can't deal with this now. And I probably won't be able to—won't want to—deal with it when all this is over. You're just too much for me. You don't know who you are, how am I supposed to? Get on the airplane."

"Do I get kissed again?"

"No, you don't!"

"Okay. I had to give it a shot," Charley said. "I won't bother you again."

He got out of the Crown Victoria and was halfway to the Lear when she called, "Charley!"

He turned.

"You forgot your phone."

"Shit," he said and trotted toward the car.

I must have missed my goddamned pocket when I put it away.

He patted his shirt pocket. The phone was in it.

Betty hadn't gotten out of the Crown Victoria but she had pushed the passenger door open.

He slid onto the seat.

She touched his face with her hand and then kissed him as she had the first time. Not passionately, not coldly: tenderly.

Then she put her hand on his chest and pushed.

"Now get on the goddamned airplane," she said, "and, for Christ's sake, be careful!"

Miller was standing by the door of the Lear.

"Can I go back to the car now? Your private tête-à-tête with the lady over?"

"Not one more fucking word, Dick!" Castillo said and then went up the steps of the Lear.

XVI

"Richmond area control," Castillo said into his microphone, the glow from the instrument panel gently lighting him in the early morning light, "Lear Five-Zero-Seven-Five at flight level twenty-nine, on a heading of two-zero-niner true, airspeed five hundred."

"Roger, Lear Seven-Five."

"Request permission to change destination from Fayetteville to Pope Air Force Base. We have approach and landing clearance."

"Richmond area approves change of destination for Lear Seven-Five. Maintain present heading and flight level. Richmond turns Lear Seven-Five over to Pope area control at this time."

"Roger, Richmond. Thank you.—

"Pope area control. Lear Five-Zero-Seven-Five at flight level twenty-nine, on a heading of two-zero-niner true, airspeed five hundred. Estimate Pope in three-zero minutes. Pope special approach and landing permission, USAF six, this date. Request approach and landing."

"Lear Seven-Five, Pope. I don't have you on radar. Is your transponder operating?"

"Oh, fuck!" Castillo said and turned to Fernando. "Where do they hide the transponder indicator in this thing?"

Fernando pointed to the lower right of Castillo's control panel as he pressed his microphone button.

"Pope, Lear Seven-Five, our transponder is operating."

"Oh, there you are. Okay. Pope clears Lear Seven-Five to approach. Begin descent to flight level ten at this time. Report over Goldsboro."

"Lear Seven-Five understands begin descent to ten thousand at this time, commencing descent, will report over Goldsboro."

"That is correct, Seven-Five."

"Pope, please contact Captain Brewster at Eighteenth Airborne Corps, advise him of our ETA, and inform him we will require ground transportation."

"Sure thing, Seven-Five."

"Thank you, Pope."

"So tell me about you and the lady cop, Gringo," Fernando said. "Very nice!"

There was no response.

"Hey, Gringo, I thought you were going to tell me everything."

He looked over at Castillo. In the glow of the panel lights, he could see Castillo's head was slumped forward. Charley was sound asleep.

Fernando reached toward him to shake his shoulder, but changed his mind.

[TWO]
Pope Air Force Base, North Carolina
0455 10 June 2005

Fernando Lopez reached over in the cockpit and pushed Charley's shoulder.

"Hey, Sleeping Beauty! Wake up!"

Castillo almost snapped his head back, then looked out the windshield. They were moving down a taxiway, past a long line of Air Force C-130s.

"We're down," Castillo said, sounding surprised.

"With no help from you."

"Sorry, Fernando."

"Come on, Gringo, when was the last time you had any sleep?"

"I dunno," Castillo said after a moment. Then, "Where we going?"

"Ground control said take this until a FOLLOW ME meets us," Fernando said.

Castillo looked out the window again.

There was no FOLLOW ME vehicle in sight, but there was a ground handler waving his wands in the "keep coming" signal. As Castillo watched, the ground handler—now walking backward toward the opening doors of a hangar—made a "turn right" signal with his wands. When Fernando turned the Lear toward the hangar, he immediately got the "stop" and "shut down" signals.

"This is probably where Delta keeps its 727," Castillo said.

Confirmation of that came almost immediately. A tug backed out of the hangar. Two soldiers, wearing green berets and slinging their sidearms in shoulder holsters, hooked up the Lear to the tug, which then pulled it into the hangar. The doors immediately began to close.

Castillo saw Captain Harry Brewster and Vic D'Alessandro standing by the door of an interior office in the hangar.

"I'm impressed with your airplane, Charley," D'Alessandro said, greeting him with a handshake and a pat on the shoulder. "Where the hell did you get it?"

"Alamo Rent-A-Plane," Castillo responded. "Why are we in the hangar?"

"We got an en route call from General McNab, Charley—he's somewhere over the Atlantic, about three hours out—saying he wants to see you ASAP when he gets here. I figured it would be quicker here than to go to the stockade. The Globemaster will come here as soon as it lands to off-load the backup guys."

"He say why?"

D'Alessandro shook his head.

Fernando and Sergeant Sherman got out of the Lear and walked up to them.

"This is my cousin, Fernando Lopez," Castillo said.

"He's driving the airplane?" D'Alessandro asked.

"It's his airplane."

"How much did you have to tell him?"

"Just about everything."

"Pity," D'Alessandro said, straight-faced. "Now I'll have to kill him."

Then he smiled and put out his hand.

"Charley and I go back a long way," D'Alessandro said.

"I know," Fernando said. "He told me if you even looked as if you might give me trouble, I was to shoot you—twice—in the nuts."

D'Alessandro smiled, broadly.

"I like him, Charley," he said. "But I'll probably kill him anyway."

"You have anything else for me, Vic?" Castillo asked.

D'Alessandro shook his head. Captain Brewster said, "No, sir."

"I need some sack time," Castillo said. "I passed out in the airplane. And I have to change out of the uniform. Any problem taking Fernando to the VIP quarters?"

"No, sir," Brewster said.

"You live on the post, Sergeant Sherman?" Castillo asked.

"Yes, sir."

"I don't see any problem with you going home for a couple of hours. Give me your quarters number, and be prepared to be back here on thirty minutes' notice. Leave the radio on the airplane."

"Sir, if it's all right with you—you know how the wives are—I'd rather go out to the stockade with Mr. D'Alessandro."

"Your call, Sergeant," Castillo said.

"Okay," D'Alessandro said, "Brewster will take you to your quarters. I'll take Sherman to the stockade. And when I get a good—say, forty-five-minute—ETA on McNab, I'll call Brewster and he'll bring you out here. Okay with everybody?"

Everybody nodded. Captain Brewster and Sergeant Sherman said, "Yes, sir."

In Brewster's van, on the way to the VIP quarters, Fernando said, "That was sad, what the sergeant said."

"What?" Charley asked.

"He said he didn't want to go home because of his wife," Fernando said. "He's going off, God knows where, on something like this and he's having a scrap with his wife."

"That's not what he said, Fernando," Castillo explained. "What happened was that he went home earlier—when D'Alessandro picked him as one of the communicators. He told his wife he was going operational. She knew what that meant. He's going somewhere to do something he can't tell her about. He's Delta Force, so she knows that means he's going someplace probably unpleasant and he doesn't know when—or if—he'll be coming back. Special ops wives learn to deal with that. It's not easy, but they deal with it. He didn't want to go home, wake her up, get her all excited that he was back, and then have to put her—and himself—through the same thing again a couple of hours later."

"Jesus Christ!" Fernando said, softly.

"I don't remember the last time I had something to eat," Castillo said.

"Sir," Brewster replied, "there's probably ham and Swiss cheese in the 'frig in your quarters. And bread. But I don't know where else you'll be able to find something to eat tonight. Unless you want to go home with me."

"Thanks but no thanks. What I was thinking was breakfast. Can you get that sergeant to come by, say, at quarter to seven, with stuff to make breakfast? I'd go find a mess hall but I'll be in civvies, and we've got Fernando."

"Done. He'll be there."

When they went into the VIP quarters bedroom, Charley went to his luggage, took out clean linen, a tweed jacket, light brown trousers, a knit shirt, and loafers and laid everything carefully on the floor next to one of the beds.

"What the hell are you doing, Gringo?" Fernando asked.

"I would have liked to use the other bed for my nice clothes, but I took pity on a homeless wetback and told him he could use it. I don't want to waste any time when we get the call in the morning."

"It's already morning," Fernando said.

"With all possible tenderness and affection, Fernando, go fuck yourself. I can tell the big hand from the little hand."

Fernando chuckled, smiled, and went to his suitcase and started to lay out clean clothes on the floor next to his bed.

Charley took off his uniform and, trying to ignore the body odor that the miracle fabric now gave off, folded it and put it in his luggage. His feet and legs felt strangely light when he walked into the kitchen without his jump boots.

He made ham and Swiss cheese sandwiches. There was neither butter for the bread nor mustard for the ham and cheese. He carried one to Fernando in the bedroom. Fernando wolfed it down, commented, "That's a really lousy sandwich," and then asked if there was any more.

Charley made two more sandwiches and gave one to Fernando. As he ate the other, he stripped and put his T-shirt and shorts in one of the suitcases. He took his toilet kit into the bathroom, showered, shaved, and then crawled naked into bed.

He saw that Fernando was already in the other bed, lying on his side and probably asleep.

Charley turned off the lamp on the bedside table, rolled onto his side, and went to sleep remembering the touch of Betty's hand on his face and the soft warmth of her lips.

[THREE]
Pope Air Force Base, North Carolina
0735 10 June 2005

Major General H. V. Gonzalez was at the wheel of the Dodge Caravan outside the VIP guest quarters when Charley Castillo and Fernando Lopez walked out of the building. Captain Brewster had called ten minutes before—as Charley and Fernando were finishing their breakfast—to tell Castillo he had a firm 0745 ETA on General McNab's C-17 III Globemaster.

"Good morning, General," Charley said after he had loaded their luggage and gotten inside. "This is my cousin, Fernando Lopez."

Gonzalez put his hand over the back of the front seat and said, *"Bienvenida a Fort Bragg, Señor Lopez."*

"Thank you, sir," Fernando replied, in Spanish.

"I assume, Castillo," General Gonzalez said, switching to English, "that you have considered the question of giving Mr. Lopez access to classified material."

Well, fuck you, General!

"I have the authority, General," Castillo said, coldly, "to tell my cousin, or anyone else, what I think they have to know about this situation."

He spoke not only in Spanish but in the Tex-Mex patois peculiar to the San Antonio area.

Fernando picked up on his tone of voice, gave Charley a surprised look, and said to Gonzalez, in Spanish, "I don't know if this is pertinent or not, sir, but I'm a captain in the reserve and hold a top secret clearance."

Gonzalez grunted but did not reply.

When they got to the hangar at the airfield, Vic D'Alessandro was there, and so was another general officer, a major general, and his aide-de-camp, a captain. Both wore desert pattern BDUs and green berets.

"You're Castillo, I presume?" the two-star said, offering his hand to Fernando. "I'm General Chancey. I command the Special Warfare Center."

"No, sir," Fernando said and pointed at Charley. "He is."

"Sorry," General Chancey said, now offering his hand to Castillo.

"That's Fernando Lopez, General," Castillo said. "He's working with me on this."

General Chancey nodded and came up with a very faint smile.

Not another word was exchanged until D'Alessandro, after answering a wall-mounted telephone, announced, "The Globemaster's on the ground."

As Castillo watched from inside the hangar, the huge C-17 rolled slowly down the taxiway. The driver of the tug sitting just inside the hangar door started his engine.

The ground handler on the taxiway waved his wands for the aircraft to stop and cut its engines. The airplane stopped, but the two engines the pilot had not turned off continued to run. A door in the side of the fuselage opened and two men got out.

One was Lieutenant General Bruce J. McNab, wearing a desert camouflage battle dress uniform—and a green beret, Castillo noticed. The second man was wearing an Air Force flight suit. He went to the ground handler with the wands and spoke briefly to him. The man with the wands tucked them under his arm and gestured to the driver of the tug, who revved his engine and drove out of the hangar.

When the tug reached the ground handler, the ground handler climbed onto the tug, sat down on the back of it—facing the Globemaster—took out his wands, and made the prescribed "come ahead" gesture with them. The tug started to move down the taxiway, with the enormous Globemaster following it.

The Air Force officer trotted after General McNab and caught up with him just as he reached the hangar.

Castillo saluted. McNab returned it.

"Forgive me for mentioning this," McNab said, "but you're not supposed to do that, you know. I've just finished telling Colonel Torine how honored we are to have such a high-ranking *civilian*, the personal representative of the president, here to guide us in the accomplishment of our assigned tasks."

Castillo felt like a fool for saluting—it had been a Pavlovian reaction—but, on the other hand, sensed there was something in McNab's tone of voice that gave meaning—other than sarcasm—to what he'd said.

"Welcome home, sir," Castillo said.

"Goddamn, *two* senior *civilians* here to meet us," McNab said, spotting Vic D'Alessandro. "I didn't know you got out of bed this early these days, *Mister* D'Alessandro."

"Good morning, General."

"You got a secure place for us, Vic?" McNab asked.

D'Alessandro pointed to the door of the hangar's interior office.

"Last swept half an hour ago, General."

"Okay, let's go swap war stories," McNab said. "D'Alessandro, Torine, the generals, and, of course, Mr. Castillo."

Fernando looked at Charley, wordlessly.

Fernando gets left out here with the aides? No fucking way!

"Unless there's some reason he shouldn't, I'd like Mr. Lopez with me," Charley said.

"Yes, sir, of course," McNab said, putting out his hand. "My name is McNab, Mr. Lopez."

"Yes, sir"? What the hell is that all about?

"How do you do, sir?" Fernando said.

"I may have to kill him, General," D'Alessandro said as they walked across the hangar. "Charley's told him everything."

"Hold off on that until we don't need him anymore," McNab said.

The Air Force officer—the leather patch on his flight suit was silver-stamped with command pilot wings and the legend COL J.D. TORINE, USAF—smiled and shook his head.

When they were inside the office, McNab sat down at a desk as D'Alessandro closed the door.

"For the benefit of Mr. Castillo and Mr. Lopez," McNab began, "Colonel Torine commands the Seventeenth Airlift Squadron at Charleston Air Force Base, South Carolina. Before the Air Force—scraping the bottom of the barrel—promoted him, he was in charge of our C-22 here. When General Naylor laid this requirement on the 117th, Torine couldn't find enough sober Air Force types to drive the C-17 and had to do it himself."

Torine put out his hand to Castillo. "Were you really the worst aide-de-camp in the Army?" he said with a smile.

"If General McNab said so, it must be true, sir," Castillo said.

Torine and Fernando shook hands.

"I like your airplane, Mr. Lopez," he said.

"Thank you," Fernando said.

"If you would, Mr. Castillo," McNab said, "fill us in. General Naylor being General Naylor, we're all still pretty much in the dark."

What's with the "Mr. Castillo"? Everybody knows I'm a major.

"The airplane you were looking for in Abéché, sir, was—we're pretty sure—stolen by a Somalian terrorist group called the 'Holy Legion of Muhammad . . .'"

"The name doesn't ring a bell," McNab interjected. He looked at the others, all of whom shook their heads.

". . . who plan on crashing it into the Liberty Bell."

"Where'd you get this, Mr. Castillo?" McNab asked.

"From a Russian, an arms dealer. One of the names he uses is Aleksandr Pevsner. Another is Vasily Respin."

"I know the gentleman by both names. He's a genuine rascal," McNab said. "This sounds like a CIA fantasy. You said you got it? Where?"

"From Pevsner. In Vienna."

"What's in it for him? Don't tell me altruism."

"He wants attention diverted from some of his business activities."

McNab grunted.

"Anyway," Castillo went on, "the last word we had was that the airplane—now repainted with the registration numbers of Air Suriname—was last seen in N'Djamena, Chad, after a flight from Khartoum. Khartoum has no record of Air Suriname 1101 in Khartoum in the last six months."

"That could happen," Colonel Torine said and made a gesture with his fingers suggesting a bribe.

Castillo didn't respond, instead going on: "The airplane took on fuel, and filed a flight plan to Murtala Muhammad International, in Lagos, Nigeria. And never got there."

"Where do you think it is?" Colonel Torine asked.

"Kennedy thinks it's in South America," Castillo said, "by way of Yundum International . . ."

"Kennedy, who's Kennedy?" General McNab interrupted. "And where is Yundum International?"

"In Gambia, a hundred miles south of Dakar," Colonel Torine answered. "Another place where the more generous you are, the fewer questions are asked about where you really came from, or are really going."

"Who's Kennedy?" McNab pursued.

"Pevsner's guy. American. He's ex-FBI," Castillo said.

"First name Howard?" McNab asked.

Castillo nodded.

"He's *renegade* FBI, if it's the same guy I think it is," McNab went on. "A guy from the FBI was here, asking that if we ran across him anywhere to please let them know right away."

"That's a whole other story, sir, but I've seen his dossier. He hasn't been charged with anything."

"And I'm sure he gets a nice recommendation from Pevsner, right?" McNab said.

Castillo didn't reply.

"Where in South America?" McNab asked.

"I'm not sure it could make it across the drink to anywhere in South America from Yundum," Colonel Torine said. "Or from anywhere else on the West Coast of Africa. How is it configured?"

"It came out of passenger service with Continental Airlines," Castillo said. "All economy class, 189 seats."

"That probably means the short-haul configuration," Colonel Torine said as he took a pocket-sized computer from the pocket on the upper left sleeve of his flight suit. He started tapping keys with a stylus. "Typically, that would mean a max of about 8,000—there it is, 8,150 gallons. Giving it a nominal range of 2,170 nautical miles. That's without a reserve, of course."

He rapidly tapped more keys on the computer with the stylus.

"Suriname isn't in here," he announced. "But Georgetown, Guyana, is. That's right up the coast—no more than two hundred miles from Paramaribo, the only airport I know of in Suriname that'll take a 727. It's 2,455 nautical miles from Dakar to Georgetown. A standard configuration just couldn't make it."

"The fuel bladders," Castillo said.

"Okay, let's factor that in," Colonel Torine said, rapidly tapping the stylus. "A standard U.S. Army fuel bladder—that's another assumption we'll have to go with, that the bladders are Army bladders—holds five hundred gallons . . ."

"How did the 727 get to Africa in the first place if it doesn't have the range to cross the Atlantic?" McNab asked, and then, as the answer quickly came to him, added, "Sorry, dumb question."

Torine answered it anyway.

"More than likely via Gander, Newfoundland, to Shannon, Ireland. That's the longest leg—about seventeen hundred nautical miles, well within the range of a short-haul 727. Then down across France to North Africa, and so on."

Castillo had several unkind thoughts, one after the other. The first was that General McNab's question was, in fact, dumb. McNab rarely asked dumb questions.

Well, Jesus, he's just flown back and forth to North Africa and run a Gray Fox operation that went down perfectly. He's tired. I know how that is.

And while I'm still impressed with Torine's pocket computer, and with his dexterity in punching the keys with that cute little stylus, this is a little late in the game to start figuring how far the 727 can fly.

As if he had read Castillo's mind, Colonel Torine looked at him and said, "I guess I should have done this earlier, but, frankly, I've been working on the assumption that the 727 was headed for Mecca."

What did he say? Mecca? What the hell is that all about?

"Excuse me, sir?" Castillo said.

Torine's face showed *I have just let my mouth run* and he looked with some embarrassment at McNab.

"Tell him," McNab said, and then before Torine could open his mouth, went on: "General Naylor, probably because he thought I didn't have the need to know, did not elect to share with me why we were looking for the 727 in Chad, but . . ."

He gestured with his hand for Torine to pick up the story.

Torine looked at Castillo.

"You know who General McFadden is?"

"General Naylor's deputy commander at MacDill?" Castillo replied.

"Right," Torine said. "We go back a long way. When General McFadden called me to lay on the support of the C-17 for the McNab mission, he told me, out of school, that despite the current wisdom at CentCom that the 727 was going to fly to Philadelphia and crash into the Liberty Bell he thought that there was a good chance it was going to be flown to Mecca and be crashed into the *ka'ba*, thereby really enraging the Muslim world. It's an American airplane; they would probably find the body of the American pilot . . ."

"Jesus!" Castillo said.

"Which made a lot more sense to both of us than the Liberty Bell," McNab said. "And still does."

"General, I really think Philadelphia is the target," Castillo said.

"Far be it from me to question the judgment of the president's personal representative," McNab said. "Tell us about the fuel bladders, Torine."

God knows I am an expert on McNabian sarcasm, and, again, there's more to that crack than what it sounds like. What the hell is he hinting at?

"Okay, where was I?" Torine asked, consulting his computer again. "Okay. A bladder holds five hundred gallons. We don't know how many bladders were loaded aboard in Abéché . . ."

"I can find out, probably, when I get to Cozumel," Castillo said.

". . . but more than one. So let's go with what we know. Two bladders, 1,000 gallons," Torine went on, stabbing at his pocket computer with his stylus. "Figuring .226 nautical miles per gallon, that's . . . an additional 226 miles of range—2,170 plus 226 is 2,396. They'd run out of fuel 59 miles out of Georgetown."

"Factor in another couple of bladders," McNab ordered. "Tell me how many bladders it would take to give them the fuel they need. For that matter, tell me how many bladders they can get on that airplane."

"Okay," Torine said. "Two more bladders would give them another 226 miles. That'd get them across the drink with 160-odd miles to spare. Six would get them there with almost 400 miles to spare."

"We better figure they had eight," McNab said. "What about the weight?"

"I don't think it would be a problem," Torine said. "Let me check."

There was a knock at the door. D'Alessandro went to it and opened it.

A Special Forces master sergeant was standing there.

"You're wanted on the secure line, Mr. D'Alessandro," he said.

D'Alessandro opened the drawer of a desk and took out a telephone. He spoke briefly into it and then extended it to Castillo.

"Castillo."

"Dick, Charley," Major H. Richard Miller, Jr., said. "We have confirmation that the two guys who were at Britton's mosque were also at Spartan. Where they were certified in the 727."

"Great. That pretty much settles it, wouldn't you say?"

"It looks that way," Miller said. "There's something else, Charley."

"Okay. Go ahead."

"Betty Schneider said to give you a message."

"Equally great. What is it?"

"She said to give this to you verbatim, Charley," Miller said, uncomfortably.

"Well, let's have it."

"She said, 'Don Juan: I should have known better. Signature, Sergeant B. Schneider.' "

"Oh, shit!"

"What the hell did you do to her, Don Juan?"

"Is that all, Dick?"

"Yeah."

"I'll be in touch," Castillo said and handed the telephone to D'Alessandro.

I guess that Highway sergeant finally got around to telling Frankie Break-My-Legs, "Ha-ha, you know what the Secret Service calls Castillo, Lieutenant? 'Don Juan.' "

Goddammit to hell!

Castillo sensed McNab's eyes on him.

"That was Miller, sir," Castillo said. "We have confirmation that the two Somalis who were in Philadelphia were at Spartan—the Spartan School of Aeronautics—in Tulsa and are qualified in 727s."

"Well, then I guess the *ka'ba's* safe from these lunatics," McNab said. "Is that good or bad?"

"I crunched the numbers for *ten* 500-gallon bladders, 5,000 gallons," Colonel Torine said. "At 7 pounds a gallon, that would be 35,000 pounds. That would add 1,130 nautical miles of range—a total of 3,305—and still leave it 22,295 pounds under max gross takeoff weight."

"So they can fly just about any place they damn well please," McNab said. "What about direct to Philadelphia?"

"No," Torine said. "That's about 3,500 nautical miles. But let's be sure." He stabbed at the computer with the stylus. "3,361 nautical miles. Too far. Not even

factoring in a reserve, that's 65 miles short. And even factoring in more bladders, why would they want to arrive in Philadelphia with nearly empty tanks?"

"Good point," McNab said. "Presuming they learned from 9/11, they want
to arrive with as much fuel, as an explosive, as possible. Or possibly—always
look on the dark side—with as much trinitrotoluene as they can carry."

Torine started stabbing with the stylus again.

"Hold off on that," McNab ordered, touching his arm. "Okay, let's go with
the assumption the airplane is somewhere in the upper east quarter of the South
American continent, maybe even in Suriname. I'm presuming the CIA has
been told what your friend the ex–FBI agent told you, Mr. Castillo?"

"They haven't been told where it came from."

"Okay, they already have egg on their face about this, so I think we can assume there's been satellites all over that part of the globe, just as soon as they
could be redirected. They were probably spinning their wheels during the night,
but at daylight I think we can assume they're going to find it."

"Kennedy says he knows where it is and will tell me when I go down there."

"Go down where?" McNab asked.

"Cozumel, off the Yucatán Peninsula."

"I know where it is," McNab said. "Why won't he tell you on the telephone?"

"I don't know," Castillo replied. "But we have to play under his rules."

"When are you going down there?" McNab asked.

"As soon as we finish here," Castillo said, "and I report to Secretary Hall how
you plan to neutralize the 727."

McNab looked thoughtful for a moment and then said, "Gentlemen, will
you give Mr. Castillo and me a moment alone?"

Not looking very happy about it, everybody filed out of the room. McNab
closed the door and turned to Castillo.

"The problem is not how to neutralize it, Charley," he said, "but how
quickly we can do so."

We're back to "Charley"?

"I'm not sure I follow you, sir."

"What did you do, forget everything you learned in the stockade?" McNab
asked, not very pleasantly.

"Okay," McNab went on and looked at his watch. "It's oh-seven-fifty-five.
Let's assume that at this very moment analysts at Langley and Fort Meade are
going over the first of the daytime imagery downloads. It would be nice if they
came up with a nice clear photo of this airplane sitting on an airfield in Suri-

name, but I don't think we better count on that. Realistically, what they're going to come up with is half a dozen images which might be—even probably are—of our 727. But they're not going to pass that on to the DCI, much less the president, until they're sure. They'll direct the satellites for better pictures, and if they have assets on the ground—do you think there's much of a CIA operation in Suriname, for instance? I don't—they'll send him word to make a visual. How long is that going to take?"

"Hours," Charley said.

"How long is it going to take you to fly to Cozumel in that pretty little airplane of yours?"

"It's 930 nautical miles. A little under two hours. Maybe a little less; when Fernando checked the weather a half hour ago, there were some favorable winds aloft."

"So what we're saying, Charley, is that you will get a location on the 727 from his guy *before* the NSA and the CIA finish making sure they've found it. Presuming they do find it."

Castillo nodded.

"You trust your guy, Charley?"

Castillo nodded again and said, "Yes, sir."

"During those two hours, Gray Fox will be standing around with its thumb up its ass," McNab said.

"I'm not sure I know where you're going with this, General," Castillo said.

"I'm a little disappointed this hasn't occurred to you," McNab said. "But let's take it from the top. We can assume that when we get a firm fix on the 727, we'll be ordered to neutralize it."

"Yes, sir."

"How would you do that?"

Jesus Christ, why lay this on me? You're the guy who runs Gray Fox.

"What I thought you would do, sir, would be send a Gray Fox team—with Little Birds*—to wherever it is and neutralize it. Knock out the gear, maybe, or blow it up."

---

*There are two models of AH/MH-6 "Little Bird" helicopters. Both are equipped with GPS/inertial navigation systems and forward-looking infrared (FLIR) sensors.

The AH-6 is armed, most often with two seven-tube 2.75-inch rocket launchers and two 7.62mm M134 "miniguns." They can also be armed with .50 caliber machine guns, MK19 40mm grenade machine guns, Hellfire missiles, and Air-to-Air Stinger (ATAS) missiles.

The MH-6H assault helicopter is nearly identical to the AH-6, except that it is designed to carry troops and is not armed. Two or three troops can be carried internally and up to six externally on folddown platforms that resemble benches on either side of the fuselage.

"And when would I do that?"

"As soon as you got the word, sir."

"And what's the sequence of events? You should have thought about this, Charley. You're about to be Lieutenant Colonel Castillo. You're supposed to think ahead. Give me the sequence."

"I confirm the location, notify Secretary Hall—and you, to give you a heads-up—Hall tells the president and/or the secretary of defense, who tell CentCom to lay on the operation. And they give you the order."

"And then," McNab picked it up, "conferring with his staff to make sure everybody agrees on what should be done, General Naylor orders the 160th Special Operations Aviation Regiment at Fort Campbell to prepare half a dozen Little Birds, say, four MH-6Hs and two AH-6Js—we're not going to have to fight our way onto the airfield, but it never hurts to have some airborne weaponry available. And then CentCom orders the Seventeenth Airlift Squadron to send a Globemaster to Fort Campbell to pick up the Little Birds and bring them here so we can load the Gray Fox people . . ."

Now I know where you're going. And you're right, I should have thought about this.

"All of which is going to take time," Castillo offered.

"Yes, it will, Charley. You and I have been down that road together too many times before."

McNab let that sink in.

"Apropos of nothing whatever, Mr. Castillo, simply to place the facts before you, there are AH-6Js and MH-6Hs at the Special Warfare Center, for training purposes. There are thirty-odd special operators—most of them Gray Fox—eating their breakfast off trays inside the Globemaster that just brought them home from Morocco. By now, the C-17 III should be refueled . . ."

"You think I should ask General Naylor," Castillo said.

"Charley, I know you love him and I do, too, but Allan Naylor is not a special operator. He likes to—I guess has to—do things by the book."

"What are you thinking? Mount them up and send them to Hurlburt?"

Hurlburt Field, in the Florida panhandle near the Gulf Coast beach resort of Destin, is the home of the USAF Special Operations Command.

McNab nodded.

"You can get to anywhere in South or Central America from Hurlburt a lot faster than you can from here. Or Fort Campbell."

"Without asking General Naylor?"

"Without asking anybody," McNab said. "If the special assistant to the secretary of homeland security—sent here, according to National Security Advisor Dr. Cohen, at the personal order of the president—were to suggest to me that prepositioning a Gray Fox team at Hurlburt—from which it could easily be stood down—was a good idea, I think I'd have to go along."

Castillo didn't say anything for a long moment.

"That's a hell of a decision for a major to make," he said, finally. "When he finds out—and he will—Naylor is going to be furious."

"Yeah, he will," McNab agreed. "With both of us." He paused and then went on: "What separates really good officers from all the others, Charley, is their willingness to order done what they know should be done and fuck the consequences. Your call, Charley."

After a moment's pause, Castillo said, "Do it."

McNab nodded.

"Anything else you need here?"

"I'd like a C-22 pilot to come with me. I need an expert."

McNab nodded again, went to the door, opened it, and called, "Colonel Torine, will you come in here, please?"

Torine came into the office and closed the door.

"I think it would be a good idea if you went to sunny Cozumel with Charley. He needs a C-22 expert."

"From the look on his face, I don't think he thinks that's such a good idea," Torine said.

"Sir, with all respect, you're a colonel . . ."

"Who's an old Air Commando, which will be handy when you're dealing with the friendly folks at Hurlburt," McNab said.

". . . and I'm a major," Castillo finished.

"An old special operator," McNab said, evenly, "knows the guy in charge is the guy in charge."

"I don't see rank as a problem," Colonel Torine agreed. "You're the guy in charge."

"You've got civvies in your bag, right?" McNab asked. Torine nodded. "You better send somebody for it. The sooner you get on your way to Cozumel, the better."

"I already sent for it; from what you told me about the worst aide-de-camp in the Army, I didn't think I'd be going back to Charleston anytime soon."

"Okay, that's it," McNab said. "You two remember to duck." He walked to the office door. "Will you come in now, please, gentlemen?"

———

As they walked up to the Lear, Fernando asked, "Would you like to ride in the right seat, Colonel?"

"I was hoping you'd ask," Colonel Torine said.

Four minutes later:

"Pope clears Lear Five-Oh-Seven-Five direct Cozumel. Climb to flight level three-zero on course two-zero-niner. Report over Columbia. You are number one to go after the One-Thirty departing."

"Understand number one after the One-Thirty," Colonel Torine replied. "Understand flight level thirty, course two-niner-zero, report over Columbia."

Fernando turned around in the pilot's seat and looked into the cabin to make sure nobody was wandering around.

Sergeant Sherman was strapped into his seat, holding a can of Coke, looking out the window.

Charley was also securely strapped into one of the seats. He had reclined it to nearly horizontal and was sound asleep.

"Takeoff power," Fernando ordered. Colonel Torine carefully moved the throttles fully forward.

"Pope, Oh-Seven-Five rolling," Torine said into his microphone.

[FOUR]
Office of the Director
The Central Intelligence Agency
Langley, Virginia
0810 10 June 2005

Mrs. Mary Leonard, the statuesque, gray-haired executive assistant to the director of Central Intelligence, went into the DCI's office and closed the door.

John Powell looked up from his desk.

"Mr. Jartmann is here, boss," Mrs. Leonard said.

"Bring him in, Mary, please," he said to the female who probably knew more of the nation's most closely guarded secrets than any other female except Dr. Natalie Cohen.

"And," Mrs. Leonard added, raising her eyebrows, "Mrs. Wilson walked in on his heels. I think she went to the beauty parlor just for you; I must say she looks stunning this morning."

"I told her quarter to eight," the DCI said. "Have her wait, please, and curb your legendary charming hospitality. No coffee. Not even a goddamned glass of water."

"Yes, sir," Mrs. Leonard said.

"I'll deal with Mrs. Patricia Davies Wilson just as soon as I've seen what Harry Jartmann has for me."

"You're about to make a mistake there," Mrs. Leonard said. "A great big mistake."

"I am? How do you know that?"

"When you said her name just now, spittle flew. It's burning holes in the carpet."

He looked at her, shook his head, and smiled but said nothing.

"Let me handle her, between us girls," Mrs. Leonard said.

"You really think that's the way to go, Mary?"

"It's the only way to go. You want to get rid of the problem or exacerbate it?"

"You being a lady, I can't tell you how I'd like to get rid of the problem," Powell said. He waited for her to smile and then went on, "So what do I do?"

"Depending on what Jartmann's got for you—and I think he's got something—when you're finished go out the back door with him. Go to Photo Analysis. I'll transfer important calls to you there, and I'll let you know when I'm through with her."

"Jesus!" Powell said and then, "Okay, Mary. I again defer to your wise judgment. Bring Harry on."

Mrs. Leonard went to the office door, opened it, and announced, "The DCI will see you now, Mr. Jartmann."

When Harry Jartmann, a tall, tweedy, thin man with unruly hair, came into the office, she closed the door from the inside and leaned against it, watching and listening.

"Good morning, Mr. Director," Jartmann said.

"Good morning, Harry. What have you got for me?"

Jartmann held up a manila folder and wordlessly asked if he could lay it on the director's desk. Powell gestured for him to do so. Jartmann unwound the cord holding the folder closed, took out a sheaf of photographs, and spread them on the desk.

"What am I looking at?" Powell asked.

"These are fresh from Fort Meade. That's satellite imagery of the airfield at

Zandery, Suriname," Jartmann said, "at oh-seven-oh-five this morning. That's probably the 727 we're looking for."

"Probably won't cut it, Harry," Powell said.

"There was early morning fog," Jartmann said. "These have been enhanced, but, obviously, they're not what we'd like to have."

"Have to have, Harry," Powell clarified. "What makes you think this is the airplane?"

"Well, it's a 727, for one thing. We're sure of that. And while we can't read the registration numbers, we made out enough of the paint scheme to compare it with the known paint scheme of Air Suriname."

He paused as Mrs. Leonard walked across the room to the director's desk, picked up a telephone, and punched one of its buttons.

"Mary Leonard," she said, softly. "The DCI would like to see you right now. Come in the back door."

"And?" Powell said to Jartmann.

"Eighty percent probability that it's the same."

"If we don't have the registration numbers, all that proves is that an Air Suriname 727 is on an airfield in Suriname," Powell said, very softly.

He looked at Mary Leonard.

"He's on his way," she said.

Ten seconds later, the private door to the DCI's office opened and a man who could have been Jartmann's younger brother came in. He was J. Stanley Waters, the CIA's deputy director for operations.

"What's up?" Waters asked.

"Tell me about our assets in Suriname," Powell said.

"Off the top of my head, not very much," Waters said. "If memory serves, we have a guy just out of the Farm there, under cover as a vice-consul. Sort of first assignment, on-the-job training. What do we need?"

"There's a 727 sitting on the airfield at . . . where, Harry?"

"Zandery," Jartmann furnished. "Zandery, Suriname."

"*That* 727?" Waters asked.

"That's what we're trying to determine," Jartmann replied. "There was a ground fog this morning . . ."

"Through which we can't see the registration numbers," Waters said.

"Right."

"How long before we can get another satellite over *Zandery, Suriname*?" Waters asked, pronouncing each syllable.

"Reprogramming has begun," Jartmann said. "Probably an hour, hour and a half. Figure another thirty minutes to get the downloads here."

"Can we get our man out there and get the numbers sooner than that?" Powell asked.

"How much will be compromised if I get on the telephone?"

"Just tell him to get out to the airport and get us the registration numbers of any 727 on the field. We don't have to tell him why."

Waters picked up one of the telephones on Powell's desk.

"Get me the American embassy in . . . Jesus, what the hell's the capital of Suriname?"

"Paramaribo," Powell furnished in a quiet voice, suggesting to Mrs. Leonard that he was about to lose his temper.

"Paramaribo," Waters told the operator. "Put the call in to the ambassador—

"All right, the consul general. But I'll talk to anybody. I'll hold."

He looked at Powell.

"No embassy. Consulate general."

Powell nodded but said nothing.

Thirty seconds later, Waters ended the call with a stab of his finger to the switch hook and quoted, furiously, " 'Good morning, this is the consulate general of the United States. Our office hours are, . . .' *Goddammit!*"

He slammed the handset into its cradle and picked up another and punched several keys.

"This is Waters," he said. "We have a man in Paramaribo, Suriname. I don't know his name. I need his home phone number. And while you're at it, get me the home phone of the consul general—I don't know his name, either. I'll hold. But I'm in the DCI's office if we get cut off."

Mrs. Leonard looked at DCI Powell. He was looking at the satellite imagery.

"Ground fog!" he said, very softly. "Fucking *ground fog!*"

"Mr. Peterson," Waters said, two minutes and thirty seconds later. "My name is J. Stanley Waters. You know who I am?—

"If I told you I was calling from Langley, Virginia, would that give you a clue?—

"Yeah, that J. Stanley Waters. Now listen carefully. Just as soon as you hang up the phone, I want you to get out to Zandery airfield and get me the numbers, the registration numbers, of any Boeing 727 you see sitting out there—

"It's an airliner, three engines, one of them in the vertical stabilizer—the big fin in the back. I'm sure you've seen one of them. Now, don't take pictures, just get the numbers, write them down, go back to the consulate general—do you have satburst capability?—

"Then get on the telephone and call Langley. Ask for me or Mrs. Mary Leonard. The switchboard will be expecting your call. Got it?—

"Good. Now, how long do you think that's going to take you?—

"Why the hell should it take two hours?—

"Then break the goddamned speed limit! You've got diplomatic immunity! Jesus H. Christ! Get your ass out to the airport and get those goddamned numbers and get them now!"

He slammed the handset in its cradle.

"The airport is thirty-five miles from Paramaribo," Waters said. "And there's a strictly enforced thirty-five-mile-per-hour speed limit."

"Mr. Director," Mrs. Mary Leonard said. "Why don't you go with Mr. Jartmann and see if they can't do something to further enhance the photos we have? Or maybe there will be some others they can work on."

The DCI looked at her and said, very softly, "I think that's probably a very good idea, Mrs. Leonard."

He stood up and walked deliberately to the private door of his office and went through it. Jartmann followed him.

"I'll deal with the switchboard," Mrs. Leonard said to Mr. Waters.

"What that dumb sonofabitch is likely to do is take his camera with him—just to be sure—and get himself arrested for photographing a Suriname military installation. I'm sure they're concerned with terrorists in Suriname."

"He'll get you the registration numbers, Stan," Mrs. Leonard said with a conviction she didn't at all feel.

Waters walked to the outer office door. Mrs. Leonard walked behind him. He continued to the corridor, which he took back to his office.

Mrs. Leonard smiled at Mrs. Patricia Davies Wilson and said, "I'll be with you in just a minute, Mrs. Wilson."

Then she closed the door and called the chief switchboard operator and told her there would be a call, probably within the next two hours, from a Mr. Peterson in Suriname. It was to be routed to Mr. Waters's private line first and then to hers, but under no circumstances to the DCI. "He's got too much on his plate this morning to be bothered with this," she explained.

Then she went and opened the door to the outer office.

"Would you come in, please, Mrs. Wilson?"

Mrs. Wilson put on a dazzling smile and walked into the office. When she saw that Director Powell was nowhere in sight, she looked at Mrs. Leonard, curiously.

"Why don't you have a seat, please, Mrs. Wilson?" Mrs. Leonard said, waving at one of the armchairs. She walked to the DCI's desk and leaned against it.

"The DCI has been called away," Mrs. Leonard said. "Sorry. He asked me to deal with this for him. Perhaps if you had been able to get here at seven forty-five . . ."

"The traffic was unbelievable!" Mrs. Wilson said. "Perhaps it would be better if I came back when the DCI has time for me."

"That won't be necessary," Mary Leonard said. "This won't take any time at all and I know the DCI wants to get it behind him."

"What is it?"

"You've been reassigned," Mrs. Leonard said. "You're going back to Analysis. I don't know where they'll put you to work, but somewhere, I'm sure, where you'll be able to make a genuine contribution to the agency."

"But I like what I'm doing! I don't want to go back to Analysis."

"I'm sorry to hear that," Mary Leonard said. "But the decision has been made."

"I want to hear this from the DCI himself."

"I'm afraid that's out of the question."

"I'm being relieved of my duties, which, to the best of my knowledge, I have carried out to everyone's complete satisfaction."

"That's not exactly the case, I'm afraid. But I don't think we want to get into that, do we?"

"I demand an explanation!"

"Can I say you've demonstrated a lack of ability to deal with the problems you've encountered in the field and let it go at that? I really don't think you want to open that Pandora's box, Mrs. Wilson."

"Well, you think wrong," Mrs. Wilson said, flatly. "I have the right to appeal any adverse personnel action and I certainly will appeal this one."

Mary Leonard didn't say anything.

"This has something to do with what happened in Angola, doesn't it?" Mrs. Wilson asked.

"Yes, it does."

"Well, I may have made an error of judgment, but certainly not of a magnitude to justify . . ."

"Your major error in judgment . . . May I speak frankly?"

"Please do."

"Was in thinking you could lie to the DCI and get away with it."

"I never lied to the DCI. How dare you!"

"Didn't you tell the DCI that when you were in Luanda the assistant military attaché, a Major Miller—who was also the station chief—made inappropriate advances to you?"

"And he did. Of course he would deny it."

"At the time you said you were having dinner with him, during which you said he made inappropriate advances, you were actually otherwise occupied, weren't you?"

"I don't know what you're talking about."

"For the sake of argument, if you weren't having dinner with Major Miller when you said you were that would be dishonest, wouldn't you say? A lie?"

"You're going to take the word of an incompetent Army officer who never should have been given an assignment like that in the first place over mine? Well, let's see what the appeals board has to say about that!"

She got out of the armchair and started for the door.

"Before you start the appeals process, Mrs. Wilson, I think you'd better take a look at something I have."

Patricia Wilson stopped and turned.

"What is it?"

Mrs. Leonard walked behind the DCI's desk, opened a drawer, and came out with a manila folder. She took an eight-by-ten-inch photograph from the folder and held it out to Patricia Wilson.

"You ever see this man before?" Mary Leonard asked.

"Yes, I have," she said.

"And who is he?"

"He's a German journalist. His name is Grossinger, Gossinger, something like that. He works for a small newspaper in Germany. Or so he said. I ordered Major Miller to check him out."

"Was that before or after you went to bed with him? With this man?"

"What did you say?"

"I said, did you tell Major Miller to check him out before or after you went to bed with this man?"

"I don't believe this," Patricia Wilson said. "I just don't believe it. This man actually said I went to bed with him? And you believe him?"

Mary Leonard nodded. "Yes, he did. And I believe him. So does the DCI."

"Why—not admitting it for a minute, of course—would he say something like that?"

"Well, he probably decided that taking foreign journalists to bed after the most brief of associations was dangerous behavior for a regional director of the CIA—a married woman—and that the agency ought to know about it."

Patricia Wilson glowered at Mary Leonard.

"Your friend is not a German journalist, Mrs. Wilson," Mary Leonard said.

"He's an American, an intelligence officer working directly under the president to find flaws in the intel community. And he found one."

She locked eyes with her and let that sink in.

"I think this conversation is over, Mrs. Wilson, don't you?" Mary Leonard asked.

Patricia Wilson stalked angrily out of the DCI's office.

XVII

[ONE]
Aboard Learjet 45X N5075L
23.01 degrees North Latitude
88.01 degrees West Longitude
Over the Gulf of Mexico
0930 10 June 2005

"I think from here on in, I better stop calling you colonel," Fernando said to Colonel J. D. Torine, USAF, "and you start playing the role of pilot-for-hire. Okay with you?"

"Yeah, sure. Call me 'Jake.' "

"And when we're dealing with Mexican customs and immigration, I think it would best if you called me 'Mr. Lopez' and Charley 'Mr. Castillo.' "

"Sure," Torine said and smiled. "You seem to have a feeling for this line of work, Mr. Lopez."

"The way it is, Jake, is that Five-Oh-Seven-Five has unlimited, frequent, unscheduled permission to enter Mexican airspace. Usually, our destination is Mexico City, Oaxaca, or Bahias de Huatulco, but I don't think alarm bells are going to go off when somebody reads our flight plan to Cozumel."

He saw the look of curiosity on Torine's face and responded to it. "The family has a ranch near Bahias de Huatulco. Used to be cattle, but now it's mostly grapefruit."

"I didn't think Americans could own property in Mexico," Torine said, and then quickly added, "I don't mean to pry."

"You goddamned yankees *can't* own land down here," Fernando explained. "Which is why my mother *happened* to be in Mexico when I was born. That made me a Mexican by birth."

"Dual citizenship?"

Fernando nodded and said, "So was our grandmother south of the border when Charley's father came along. Charley screwed up the system when he got himself born in Germany, but two of my kids are also bona fide *Mexicanos*. We won't tell them that until we have to."

Torine shook his head, smiling in wonder. "Why not?"

"It causes identity problems," Fernando said, chuckling. "And, sometimes, official ones. The Counterintelligence Corps shit a brick when they found out that Lieutenant F. Lopez of the 1st Armored Division held Mexican citizenship. For a couple of days, it looked like they were going to send me home from Desert One in handcuffs."

"What happened?"

"Our senator told the secretary of the Army whose side the Lopezes were on at the Alamo," Fernando said, chuckling. "And that Cousin Charley was a West Pointer, and his father—my uncle Jorge—had won the Medal of Honor in Vietnam, and that he didn't see any problems about wondering where our loyalties lay."

"General McNab told me about Charley's father," Torine said.

"He bought the farm before Charley and I were born," Fernando said, "but he was always a big presence around the family. Our grandfather hung his picture—and the medal, in a shadow box—in his office. It's still there. We knew all about him. He was right up there with Manuel Lopez and Guillermo de Castillo."

"Who were?"

"They bought the farm at the Alamo," Fernando said, and then went on, "Jake, why don't you go back in the cabin and get out of the flight suit? And wake up Sleeping Beauty? I want to get our little act for Mexican customs and immigration straight with him."

Torine unfastened his harness and started to get out of the copilot's seat.

"Merida area control," Fernando said into his microphone, "this is Lear Five-Zero-Seven-Five. I'm at flight level three-zero, indicating five hundred knots on a heading of two-zero-niner. International, direct Cozumel. Estimating Cozumel in ten minutes. Request approach and landing to Cozumel. We will require customs and immigration service on landing."

"The only problem we have is if customs wants a look at Sergeant Sherman's suitcase," Charley said. "How do we explain the radio?"

"They might not want to," Fernando said. "They have the flight plan; they'll know we came from the States. People usually don't try to smuggle things *into* Mexico. And if they seem to be getting curious, you have that envelope I gave you?"

"Envelope?" Torine asked.

"The cash-stuffed envelope, Jake. It usually makes Mexican customs officers very trusting," Fernando said.

[TWO]
Office of the Commanding General
United States Central Command
MacDill Air Force Base
Tampa, Florida
0935 10 June 2005

When Sergeant Major Wes Suggins had gone into the office of the CentCom commander, General Allan Naylor, USA, to tell him that Frederick K. Beiderman, the secretary of defense, was on the secure line, Naylor, as he walked quickly to the phone booth, had signaled for Suggins to stay, which Suggins correctly interpreted to mean he was supposed to listen to as much of the conversation as he could overhear.

Suggins complied by leaning on the doorjamb of the phone booth while Naylor was on the horn, and Naylor held the handset as far from his ear as he could and still hear the secretary.

"Yes, Mr. Secretary, I'm sure we can handle this, and I will get back to you with how it's going," Naylor said, ending the conversation and thoughtfully replacing the handset in its cradle.

He looked at Suggins.

"I'm surprised that it took them this long to find it," Sergeant Major Suggins said, "not that it took this long after they did decide to tell us to neutralize it."

Naylor grunted.

"Is everybody here, Wes?"

"Yes, sir. I even mentioned to General McFadden, after we got the 'We found it' message, that you would probably want to see him shortly. He was on his way to the golf course."

"A sound mind in a healthy body, Sergeant Major," Naylor said. "Round 'em up."

"Yes, sir."

Just under five minutes later, what Suggins thought of as the "Heavy Brass" (General Albert McFadden, USAF, the CentCom deputy commander; Vice-Admiral Louis J. Warley, USN, the CentCom intelligence officer; and Lieutenant General George H. Potter, USA, the J-5 special operations officer) and the "Heavy Civilians" (Mr. Lawrence P. Fremont of the CIA and Mr. Brian Willis of the FBI) were all sitting around the conference table in Naylor's office.

The civilians, Suggins thought privately, weren't really needed. The CIA and the FBI had done their job. The stolen 727 had been located, even if that had taken a hell of a lot longer than it should have. But if they had not been summoned, Suggins knew, they would have felt left out, and Suggins knew how important it was to Naylor that the civilians felt they were part of the team.

General McFadden was even in uniform. Usually at this time of the morning, he was dressed for the links. It was his practice to come to his office early, read the overnight intel and messages, and then commence his physical training regimen. General officers were permitted to select their own method of physical exercise; McFadden had a permanently reserved 0845 tee time. Rank Hath Its Privileges.

"I've just spoken with Secretary Beiderman," General Naylor began. "CentCom has been tasked with neutralizing the stolen 727, which, as you all know, has been located at an airfield, Zandery, in Suriname. Secretary Beiderman made it clear that he wants this done as quietly as possible."

He looked around the conference table and had a sudden tangential thought.

I'll be damned. Here's my chance to zing McFadden. And I almost blew it.

"Let's see," Naylor asked, innocently, "who's junior?"

"I guess I am, General," Brian Willis of the FBI said. "But I'd really like to defer to someone in uniform."

"I associate myself totally with my learned colleague," Lawrence Fremont of the CIA said.

There were chuckles. General Potter said, "Cowards!"

"I guess you're next up on the totem pole, right, Lou?" Naylor asked.

"Only because the Navy refuses to appropriately acknowledge my talents," Admiral Warley said.

"Okay, Lou. How do we handle this?"

"The first thing that occurs to me is putting an umbrella over the coast of Suriname, and, if this plane tries to go anywhere, we force it to return to Suriname."

"And if it refuses to return to Suriname?" Naylor asked.

"Take it out, General," Admiral Warley said.

"Anything else?"

"The umbrella is Step One. Step Two, in my judgment, would be to send McNab's people in as backup in case the CIA is unable to quietly neutralize the airplane on the ground. I'm presuming you're already working on that, right Larry?"

"I don't want to give the wrong impression when I say, 'Sure we are,' " Lawrence Fremont of the CIA said. "We are, but I understand we have a one-man station there—he's the guy who made the visual confirmation—and there's not much he can do by himself. I'm sure help is on the way. No telling, frankly, how long that will take."

"Thank you, Larry," Naylor said. "And now we will hear from the next-senior officer, General Potter. Is there any doubt in anyone's mind that he will not suggest sending in the Peace Corps to reason with these people?"

There were chuckles.

"I agree with Admiral Warley that we send in McNab's people . . ."

"Why am I not surprised?" Naylor asked.

"But not with his priorities. I think McNab—Gray Fox—has the experience to deal with this sort of situation. If you order it done quietly, that's what you'll get."

"That's it?" Naylor asked.

"Yes, sir," General Potter said. "It looks like a no-brainer to me."

"And General McFadden?" Naylor asked.

"I really have nothing to add, General," General McFadden said.

Is he saying that because he's miffed at me? Or because there's really nothing to say beyond what's already been said? Potter's right, this is a no-brainer.

"Okay," Naylor said. "Everyone seems agreed that we should send General McNab's people—we're talking about Gray Fox to neutralize the airplane—and as soon as possible put fighter aircraft in the area—not entering Suriname airspace, of course, but over the Atlantic outside Suriname territory in case the airplane takes off. Whereupon, they will intercept it and order it to return to Zandery. If they fail to comply, they will shoot it down. That about it?"

He looked around the table. When his eyes met those of Admiral Warley, Warley said, "The Rules of Engagement, General? Are we going to give the pilots the authority to take the airplane down or do you want them to ask for permission? And from whom?"

General Naylor looked at General McFadden.

"Al?"

"When I heard the CIA had found the 727," General McFadden said, "I ordered an E-3* down there. The nearest one was refueling at Guantanamo. They said it would take thirty minutes to get it in the air. That was about thirty minutes ago. So it's probably wheels-up. It's about eighteen hundred miles from Gitmo down there. At a little better than five hundred knots, figure three hours twenty minutes. I also ordered up two KC-135s out of Barksdale.† Both are wheels-up, one headed down there and the other to Gitmo, where it will be on a ten-minute runway alert. I also have a four-plane flight of F-15s on a ten-minute runway alert at Eglin.‡

"Worst possible scenario: The 727 takes off in the next few minutes, whereupon we scramble the F-15s at Eglin to intercept. The intercept point would be about 150 miles south of Miami, a little south of Cuba. They could either order it to land at Gitmo or shoot it down.

"The decision to do either would be in the hands of the pilot. For obvious reasons that's risky. But there's no other way to go until we get the E-3 there and up and running.

"I admit this isn't an ideal situation, but the truth is, we just weren't set up to deal with an airplane sitting on a field in Zandery, Suriname."

"And the best possible scenario, Al?" Naylor asked.

Naylor was impressed with the action McFadden had taken and felt a little guilty for having staged "the junior speaks first" business.

"That would mean the airplane doesn't try to go anywhere soon—in other words, before we can get the E-3 down there, which will give us both a more

---

*The E-3 "Sentry" is an Airborne Warning and Control System (AWACS) mounted on a highly modified Boeing 707 airframe. Its radar dome, thirty feet in diameter and mounted fourteen feet above the fuselage, provides surveillance over a range of 250 miles from the earth's surface up into the stratosphere, over land or water. Additionally, the E-3 is equipped with a vast array of communications equipment, permitting communication with aircraft in its area, and, via satellite, with superior headquarters anywhere in the world.

†The KC-135, also based on the Boeing 707, is an in-flight refueling aircraft capable of dispensing 200,000 pounds of fuel through a probe mounted in the rear of the fuselage. Barksdale Air Force Base is located in northwest Louisiana.

‡The F-15 "Eagle" is an all-weather fighter whose maximum speed is more than twice the speed of sound (Mach 2.5). Eglin Air Force Base is on the Gulf Coast of Florida near Pensacola.

positive means of identification and communications here—in other words, take the shoot-it-down-or-not decision off the pilot's shoulders and hand it to you. Then we get McNab's people down there and they neutralize the air-plane—quietly, very quietly—before it gets in the air. That's possible, even if we shouldn't count on it. By the time McNab can get a C-17, Little Birds, etcetera, to Hurlburt—which, obviously, won't be in the next hour or two—I should have heard from the CIA where he can set the C-17 down in Suri-name."

"You've asked for that intel from the CIA?" Naylor asked.

"I'm told, General," Lawrence Fremont of the CIA said, "that it will take another couple of hours to get our man out to—and back from—an area about forty miles from the field that we show will take a C-17. But the data's a cou-ple of months old and we don't want McNab to get there and find the field is either under water or filled with lumber or scrap metal."

"I must tell the both of you I'm impressed with all you've done," General Naylor said. "Now, let's hear what General McNab has to say. Get him on the secure line and put it on the speakerphone, please, Wes."

"Yes, sir," Sergeant Major Suggins said and went into the Phone Booth, coming out in less than a minute. "You're up, sir," he said.

"General McNab, please," Naylor said.

"Speaking, sir."

"You've been made aware the 727 has been found in Suriname?"

"Yes, sir."

"Well, here's where we stand. The secretary of defense has tasked CentCom to neutralize the airplane. Everyone here is agreed that Gray Fox is the way to do it. Backed up by Air Force fighters which will intercept the plane should it take off before you can get your people there and either force it to land in Suri-name or shoot it down."

"In other words, sir, what you're hoping is that a Gray Fox operation to keep the airplane on the ground could be put into play as soon as possible?"

"Yes. You want to tell me how you would proceed?"

"Actually, sir, it probably will be less difficult than it seems. We're not going to have to land on a hostile airfield, for one thing, and I can't imagine that they are going to have any meaningful forces defending the airplane. So what has to be done is to put a half-dozen Little Birds—two gunships, four troop carriers—in a C-17 with thirty men, wait until I know where I could sit down the C-17—I've asked DIA about possible landing areas; I haven't heard back yet—and then go do it. 'It' is defined as anything from grabbing the airplane to blowing it up."

"You think you could take over the airplane, Scotty?"

"I think that's possible, sir. And that would be the best thing to do."

"This operation has to be done quietly, Scotty, you understand?"

"Yes, sir, I do."

"Staging out of where?" General McFadden said. "Hurlburt?"

"Yes, sir. Was that General McFadden?"

"Yes, it is."

"Sir, I'd appreciate any help you could provide about someplace to sit down the C-17."

"I'm working on it, Scotty. The CIA has someone—as we speak—confirming that a field about fifty miles from Zandery is usable. Between the CIA and the DIA, we should have confirmation shortly."

"Thank you, sir," General McNab said.

"Scotty, how long would it take you to get an adequate team of your people and the Little Birds to Hurlburt?"

"Not long at all, sir."

"How much is 'Not long at all' in hours and minutes, Scotty?" Naylor asked. There was a tone of impatience in his voice.

"As a matter of fact, sir, as we speak I'm in the shade of a C-17's wing, watching the Gulf of Mexico lap on the sandy beaches of Hurlburt."

"Do I understand you to say, General," Naylor asked, icily, "that you are at Hurlburt Field?"

"Yes, sir. With six Little Birds and thirty stalwart special operators, waiting for your order to go."

"Who authorized you to go to Hurlburt, General?" Naylor asked, coldly furious.

"Mr. Castillo suggested that if I organized the team and brought it to Hurlburt, it would save a good deal of time, sir. I could not fault his reasoning, sir, and acted accordingly."

"You are referring to Major Castillo, General?"

"In a way, sir. But I have been calling him 'Mister.' That seemed appropriate, inasmuch as he was at Fort Bragg as the personal representative of the president, sir. And in civilian clothing."

"You're a goddamned lieutenant general, Scotty!" Naylor exploded. "And you don't take goddamned 'suggestions' from a goddamned major! And you goddamn well know it!"

"With all respect, sir, he's not functioning as a major. The national security advisor made it quite clear on the telephone that he was coming to Bragg as the personal representative of the commander in chief, sir, and, as I said, sir, I have acted accordingly."

Naylor threw his hands up in outrage and disgust and looked around the room. The officers and civilians at the conference table were looking anywhere but at him. Sergeant Major Suggins was standing just inside the Phone Booth making signs with his hands, moving them between a gesture of prayer and a gesture meaning cool off.

Naylor tried to collect himself, thinking, *When you are angry, you make bad decisions in direct proportion to the level of your anger.*

You cannot afford to make a decision now you will regret later.

That sonofabitch! I'll nail his and Charley's balls to the wall when this is over!

"General McNab," General Naylor ordered. "Maintain your readiness to place this operation in action on my order. And only on my order."

"Yes, sir."

"And when this is over, you, Major Castillo, and I have a good deal to talk over."

"Yes, sir."

Naylor looked around the table.

"Does anyone else have anything for General McNab?" Naylor asked.

"General McNab," General McFadden asked. "Is Colonel Torine readily available?"

"No, sir, he's not."

"He went back to Charleston?"

"No, sir."

"Do you know where he is?"

"Yes, sir."

"And are you going to tell me?"

"Yes, sir. He should be in Cozumel about now."

"Cozumel? The island off the Yucatán Peninsula?"

"Yes, sir."

"You don't happen to know what he's doing on a Caribbean island, do you?"

"He went there with Mr. Castillo, sir. Mr. Castillo said he needed an expert in 727 series aircraft and Colonel Torine volunteered to go with him."

"I'll be a sonofabitch!" General McFadden said. "Thank you, General McNab."

"Yes, sir."

"We'll be in touch, General McNab," General Naylor said. "Is there any part of my orders, which you are to stand ready to implement this operation at my orders and only at my orders, that you don't completely understand?"

"No, sir."

"Naylor out," General Naylor said.

"When you have your talk with General McNab and this Castillo fellow, General, I'd like to be there," General McFadden said. "What the hell did he take Torine to Cozumel for? Why the hell did Torine go?"

Naylor threw up his hands in a sign of frustration. "There is a strong element of lunacy in special operators, General, and it's highly contagious," Naylor offered, resignedly. He looked at Lieutenant General Potter, who was his J-5 (Special Operations) officer.

"I was about to say, 'No offense,' " Naylor said. "But, goddammit, George, why should I apologize for stating the obvious?"

"No offense was taken, General," General Potter said.

[THREE]
Cozumel International Airport
Cozumel, Mexico
0940 10 June 2005

The preparations to get through Mexican customs without having to explain Sherman's radio and their small arms turned out to be unnecessary. As the Lear trailed a FOLLOW ME jeep down a taxiway at the small but grandly named Cozumel International Airport, Castillo saw an off-brown Mexican customs Ford F-150 pickup truck and three white Yukon XLs—with heavily tinted windows—parked where they were apparently being directed. A tall, dark-haired man wearing powder blue slacks and a yellow short-sleeved shirt—dressed for the golf course—was sitting on the hood of one of the Yukons.

Aleksandr Pevsner had come to the field himself to meet them. Castillo didn't see Howard Kennedy or any of Pevsner's bodyguards anywhere.

But they're almost certainly in the Yukons.

"That's Pevsner," Charley said. "But the odds are, he's not calling himself that now. Play along with me."

Two Mexican customs officers, armed with chrome-plated .45 ACP semi-automatic pistols, approached the Lear as the engines wound down and Charley opened the door.

"Welcome to Cozumel," one of them said in Spanish. "May we come aboard?"

"Of course," Charley said in Spanish.

Customs and Immigration lasted no longer than it took for the customs officers to rubber-stamp Fernando's certificate of permission for unlimited, frequent, unscheduled entry into Mexican airspace. They didn't even look very closely at anyone in the cabin.

Castillo waited until they had driven off in the pickup before getting out of the airplane.

Pevsner, smiling, waved at him.

"Welcome to Cozumel," he called in Spanish.

"Thank you, señor," Charley replied in Spanish as he walked to the Yukon and Pevsner slid nimbly off the hood. They shook hands.

"I'm afraid I've forgotten your name, señor," Charley said.

"Why not call me Dondiemo, Alex Dondiemo?" Pevsner said. "What's in a name?"

"Roberto's cousin, perhaps?"

Pevsner smiled at him. "Something like that," he said, and asked, "And who are you, today?"

"An American golfer named Charley Castillo, Señor Dondiemo."

"Funny, I would have thought a snorkler," Pevsner said, switching to English. "Snorklers are usually busy looking for something. Anyway, Charley, it's good to see you again. And who did you bring with you?"

"My cousin, Fernando Lopez, a copilot for the airplane, and a . . . I guess you could call him a super cellular telephone technician."

"And that's all?"

Charley nodded.

"And who are they really?"

"Fernando is really my cousin. The pilot is an Air Force colonel, an expert in 727 aircraft, and the technician is really a Special Forces sergeant."

"And no old associates of Howard's, excuse me, Roberto?"

"Not a one."

"He was so worried about that that he just couldn't bring himself to come out here to greet you himself," Pevsner said.

"He had no cause for worry," Castillo said.

"I tried to tell him that," Pevsner said. "But Howard is a worrier."

He gestured—a casual wave—in the direction of the two Yukons behind his. Doors on both immediately opened and half a dozen men got quickly out. They were all holding Uzi submachine pistols.

Charley recognized two of them from Vienna. One of them was the large East European who had pulled his jacket down, skillfully immobilizing him when he had been meeting nature's call in the men's room of the Hotel Sacher.

"You can put those away," Pevsner ordered in Russian. "And help our guests with their luggage." He turned to Charley and, still in Russian, said, "Why don't you ask your friends to join us, Charley?"

"What language are we going to speak?"

"Good point, Charley," Pevsner said in Russian and then switched to English. "How about English? A good hotelier like Alex Dondiemo would speak pretty good English, wouldn't you think?"

Charley smiled at him and asked, "And is it *Señor* Dondiemo?"

"Alex, of course, Charley. We're friends, right?"

"I hope so," Charley said and waved at the airplane. Fernando got off first, followed by Colonel Torine and Sergeant Sherman.

"Welcome to Cozumel," Pevsner said, offering his hand. "I'm Alex Dondiemo, your innkeeper. Charley and I are old friends."

"Fernando Lopez," Fernando said.

"Jack Sherman," Sergeant Sherman said.

"Jake Torine, Mr. Dondiemo."

"The bellmen will take care of your luggage," Pevsner said. "And it's hot out here in the sun. Why don't we go to the hotel? A little breakfast is probably in order."

He gestured toward the Yukon and then walked around the front of it. When Charley got in, he saw that there were two more "bellmen" sitting in the rear seat of the Yukon.

What did he expect, that an FBI SWAT team was going to erupt from the airplane, slap cuffs on him, and haul him off to the States?

He didn't think that was likely to happen, but it could have, and Pevsner stays ahead of his game by expecting—being thoroughly prepared for—the unexpected.

When Pevsner started up the Yukon and began to move, the Yukon parked behind him got in front of him and stayed there on the three-mile drive along a wide white beach to the Grande Cozumel Beach and Golf Resort.

When Pevsner cheerfully volunteered, "We like to think our beach is much nicer that Miami. Much nicer than any I know in Europe. The only one I know as nice is in the Florida Panhandle, around Pensacola," Charley understood that Pevsner was not going to talk about the airplane while they were in the Yukon.

He thinks we might be wired. Keep that in mind, Charley, he doesn't trust you.

[FOUR]

The Grande Cozumel Beach and Golf Resort was larger than Charley expected. The main building—there were cottages as well—was a sprawling, four-storey white building right on the beach. There was a very verdant golf course. As Charley watched, a long-legged blonde whose white shorts failed to conceal much of the cheeks of her derriere missed a long putt.

The main building had an underground garage, access to which was guarded by a muscular Mexican in a police-type uniform standing by a barrier that looked like it could stop anything up to an Abrams tank.

They had just gotten out of the Yukon when the third one, with the "bell-men" carrying their luggage, pulled into the garage.

They didn't have time to get into Sherman's suitcase.

Or did they?

Take nothing for granted, Charley.

There was a bank of elevators, guarded by another man in a police-type uniform.

Do they guard the elevators all the time or only when Pevsner's here?

They got in the elevator and Pevsner put a key in the control panel, then pushed a button marked PENTHOUSE B.

When the elevator started to move, Pevsner took the key from the control panel and handed it to Castillo.

"There will be more keys upstairs," he said.

When the elevator door opened, Castillo saw they were in a small lobby. There was only one exit from it: Open double doors showed a large living room overlooking the water.

As they walked through the lobby, there was an electronic buzz.

"Usually," Pevsner said, "that goes off only when a departing guest has souvenirs in his clothing. People just can't seem to bear to part with one—sometimes, more than one—of our silver bowls when they leave us."

Somewhat sheepishly, Fernando reached under his shirt and came out with the .45 ACP semiautomatic pistol he had been carrying in the small of his back.

"Well, while I admit there are people here who regard visiting North Americans as an easy source of income," Pevsner said, "you're really not going to need that."

"Fascinating detector," Castillo said. "I guess it would detect anything—say, a wire—right?"

"It's a very good detector, Charley," Pevsner said.

"Well, now that you know we're not trying to steal your silver," Castillo said, "can we get to the business at hand?"

"Absolutely," Pevsner said. "But first, come in and say hello to another old friend of yours."

He gestured for them to pass through the double doors. Charley went first, and, as he entered the room, Howard Kennedy walked up to him, smiling, and put out his hand.

"Mr. Dondiemo," Castillo said.

"Mr. Castillo," Kennedy said. "How good to see you." He looked at Pevsner. "Did I hear a buzzer just now?"

"This is Mr. Lopez," Pevsner said. "Charley's cousin. He has a .45."

"And that's all, Howard, we're not wired," Charley said.

Kennedy ignored the remark.

"You said something about needing a flat roof?" he said and motioned for Charley to follow him onto an unusually wide balcony, furnished with upholstered cast-aluminum deck furniture. Kennedy pushed a button on the wall as he went through open sliding-glass doors. There was an electric hum and the awning shading the balcony began to retract.

"Will that do?" Kennedy asked, pointing to the roof.

"Sherman?" Castillo called and Sergeant Sherman came out on the balcony.

Castillo pointed to the roof.

Sherman looked and then nodded.

"I'll probably even have room to put it far enough from the edge so it won't attract attention from the ground," Sherman said.

"Do you think you could find a bellman to show Mr. Sherman how to get to the roof? And help him with his luggage?" Castillo asked.

"As I told you on the phone, Charley, your wish is our command," Kennedy said.

"How long is that going to take you, Sherman?" Castillo asked.

"Not long," Sherman said.

He went to his enormous hard-sided suitcase, removed the control panel and its laptop-sized computer, and put them on a small desk beside the windows leading to the balcony and then closed the suitcase. When he started to pick it up, Pevsner snapped his fingers and two of the bellmen went quickly to him to take it from him.

Sherman looked at Castillo, smiled, and shrugged, as if to say, "What the hell, why not," and then started after the men with the suitcase.

Sherman touched the small of his back, as if adjusting a pistol in his waistband.

Sure, he's got a pistol. Delta Force, like Mr. Pevsner, tries to be prepared for anything.

I wonder why the detector didn't pick it up?

Or probably it did. It picked up both pistols at the same time but only Fernando fessed up.

Alex, my friend, your security isn't as hole-proof as you think.

As Sherman went out of the apartment, two white-jacketed waiters came in, each pushing a serving cart before him.

"I thought you might need a little something to eat after your flight," Pevsner said. "But before we do that, has everyone met my cousin, Roberto, sometimes called 'Howard'?"

Everyone shook hands with Howard Kennedy.

The waiters began laying out an elaborate breakfast buffet. When one of the chrome domes over a large plate was removed, Castillo saw eggs Benedict.

When they had finished setting up the buffet, both waiters took up positions behind the tables—much like "Parade rest," with their arms folded on the smalls of their backs—and waited to make themselves useful.

Pevsner snapped his fingers again, said, *"Gracias,"* and pointed toward the door. The waiters quickly scurried out.

"Now that we're alone, Alex," Castillo said, "are you going to tell us where the 727 is?"

"Have some eggs Benedict, Charley. There's plenty of time."

"No, there is not plenty of time," Castillo snapped. "Where's the goddamned airplane?"

The look on Howard Kennedy's face made it clear that Pevsner was not used to being addressed in that tone of voice and that he wasn't at all sure how Pevsner would react.

A cold look flashed across Pevsner's face, quickly replaced by a smile.

"If you eat your eggs Benedict, my friend, I will tell you where it is not," Pevsner said.

There was a sharp whistle, and, a moment later, Sergeant Sherman called, "Coming down!"

Everybody looked at the balcony.

An electric extension cord began to come down from the roof, followed immediately by a heavy, flat, tan rubber–covered cable.

Fernando said, "I'll get them," and walked quickly onto the balcony and caught the extension cord and cable.

"Plug the electric cord into the wall," Sergeant Sherman said. "It doesn't matter if it's 110 or not. We have a built-in converter. I'll plug the cable in."

"Got it," Fernando called back.

"We have 110-volt current," Pevsner said.

"Alex, where is it not?" Castillo asked, coldly.

"It's not at El Vigia," Pevsner said. "It was, but it's gone."

"Where's El Vigia?" Castillo asked, visibly surprised.

"About fifty miles south of Lake Maracaibo in Venezuela," Pevsner said.

"What about Zandery, Suriname? You're telling me it's not in Suriname?"

"Where'd you get that?" Pevsner asked in surprise. "As far as I know, it's never been in Suriname. Howard, did you tell him anything about Suriname?"

"Only that it wasn't going there . . . Oh, that's right. The ten-dollar-a-minute phone in the plane cut us off before I could tell you that, Charley, didn't it?"

"Jesus Christ!" Castillo said. "We've been working on the premise that it went from Gambia to Suriname. Why the hell did they paint Suriname numbers on it?"

"Possibly, they're trying to confuse you," Pevsner said, dryly, adding flatly, "The 727 went from Gambia to El Vigia."

"How many fuel bladders were aboard?" Torine asked.

"Thirteen were trucked into Abéché," Howard Kennedy answered.

"What was it doing in El Vigia? What's in El Vigia?" Castillo asked.

"There's a pretty good field there," Kennedy said. "Originally built as a private field by Shell to service their oil fields in Lake Maracaibo. Nobody could use it without Shell's permission. After the Venezuelans nationalized the oil industry, it occurred to the powers that be that having a private airfield—a no-questions-asked airfield; one that could handle large jets—could sometimes be useful. So it's still a 'private landing strip.' "

"So what's the 727 doing there?"

Pevsner and Kennedy looked at each other.

"I'd rather not tell you until I'm sure," Pevsner said.

"Why not?"

Kennedy looked at Pevsner for guidance. Pevsner gave it with a wave of his hand.

"Well, when it comes to payback time for our cooperation in your investigation," Kennedy said, "I don't want somebody—my former colleagues are very good at this—saying, 'Well, yeah, he did tell Castillo that the plane was in Chad, *but* we'd have heard about that anyway, and he did tell Castillo that the 727 was going to South America, *but* where else could it have gone? *And* when he told Castillo that the airplane was in El Vigia, having thus and so done to it, that was absolutely untrue. Pevsner gave Castillo nothing we couldn't have gotten ourselves, and, therefore, we owe him nothing."

"Tell me about 'thus and so,' Howard," Castillo said.

Kennedy put up both hands, palms outward, signaling, *Not from me, Charley.*

"Tell me, Charley," Pevsner asked, "do you think the government of Venezuela would admit to any knowledge of a stolen airplane, possibly in the hands of terrorists, having flown to a private landing strip near Lake Maracaibo?"

Castillo met his eyes but didn't say anything.

"Or," Pevsner went on, "that while it was there, it took on new registration numbers—a fresh identity—and a great deal of fuel, much of it loaded into fuel bladders, and then took off again?"

"Took off for where?" Castillo asked, softly.

"I've got a good idea but I don't want to tell you until I'm sure," Pevsner said.

"I have to know what you think," Castillo said.

"Let me run an off-the-wall scenario past you," Kennedy said. "With the understanding that you know that this is not what Mr. Dondiemo and I are telling you is likely to happen. Just for the sake of conversation, all right?"

"Okay."

Charley saw Fernando walk over to inspect the breakfast buffet. Then he found himself a chair, carried it to the table the waiters had set up, and then began to help himself to the food.

Colonel Torine was apparently inspired by Fernando's hunger. He got a chair and pulled it up to the table and then started filling a plate from the buffet.

"The eggs Benedict here are really quite nice, Charley," Pevsner said. "Why don't you join them?"

"Maybe because I would feel I was chewing while Rome burns?" Charley replied.

Pevsner chuckled.

Oh, to hell with it. I am hungry.

He found a chair and put it beside Fernando's and then went to the buffet.

Kennedy picked up another chair, wordlessly offered it to Pevsner, who smiled and shook his head. Kennedy then put the chair beside that of Colonel Torine and went to the buffet table and poured himself a cup of coffee.

Charley, on tasting the eggs Benedict, smiled.

"I'm pleased that you are pleased, Charley," Pevsner said. "They are to your satisfaction, no?"

"They're fine," Charley said. "Okay, Howard, shoot."

"This scenario needs to take certain things as given," Kennedy began. "One of them is that the people who have this airplane are considerably more skilled than those who flew the 767s into the World Trade Center. These guys are pilots, skilled enough to fly—navigate—a 727 across the Atlantic . . ."

"Supposition granted," Castillo said. "They're graduates of the Spartan School of Aeronautics in Tulsa. What else?"

"You know who these people are?" Pevsner asked, surprised.

Castillo nodded. "We even have their names and photographs."

"How do you know?" Kennedy asked, almost openly suspicious.

Well, what the hell, he used to be an FBI agent; good cops check.

"I'll admit it's circumstantial. Two guys from Somalia, mullahs, were in Philadelphia at a Muslim temple. The Philadelphia cops—their counterterrorism people—took their pictures and gave them to the FBI to run. The FBI ran them and hit. They were legally in the States to go to flight school. We have confirmation from Spartan."

"So there is a Philadelphia connection," Pevsner said.

"Circumstantial or not, that sounds solid," Kennedy said. "The one thing the bureau is good at is making IDs. They can do that with a computer; no original thought required." He paused as if gathering his thoughts and then went on, "And, knowing this, it would be reasonable to assume several more things. They may not know how close we are to them, but they know we're looking for the airplane. So how would intelligent pilots get a 727 to Philadelphia?"

"It's your off-the-wall scenario, Howard. You tell me."

Kennedy had just opened his mouth to speak when there was a faint musical rendition of the opening bars of Strauss's *Weiner Blut.* Pevsner took a cellular telephone from his trousers pocket. He spoke in Russian.

"Yes?—

"TI? That's all he got—

"Call him back and make sure that's all he got."

He punched the HANG UP key and put the telephone back in his pocket and looked between Castillo and Kennedy.

"I'm making up my mind whether I should tell you what that was," Pevsner said. "I'm concerned that Charley might act impulsively."

Everyone waited while he made up his mind. It took no longer than thirty seconds, but it seemed longer.

"The pilot of an aircraft that had to make an unscheduled stop—a warning light on the instrument panel suggested a hydraulic pressure problem—at El Vigia," Pevsner said, finally, "reports that while the problem was being attended to he happened to see a 727 aircraft in a hangar. Registration numbers and other painting were going on. Unfortunately, all he could see was the TI prefix. He said it was still dark."

"Damn!" Charley said. "What's 'TI' mean?"

"And that they were pulling masking tape from freshly painted red, white, and blue stripes on the vertical stabilizer," Pevsner added.

"When was this?" Charley asked.

"About four hours ago," Pevsner said. "He had to wait until he got to Bolivia—La Paz—before he could call."

"TI is the Costa Rican registration suffix," Colonel Torine said. "This pilot, Mr. Dondiemo . . ."

"If you call me 'Mister,' " Pevsner said with a smile, "I'll think you're suggesting I call you 'Colonel.' "

"Not at all, sir. *Alex.* How reliable is this pilot? Does he work for you?"

"He flies for an air cargo company with which I have a certain relationship. All of their pilots are reliable. As a matter of fact, now that I think about it, this one's an American."

"So they're painting red, white, and blue stripes on the vertical stabilizer of a Costa Rican 727, so what?" Charley said.

"El Vigra is not a maintenance facility, Charley," Kennedy said. "But if you want to change an airplane's identity without anybody seeing you or asking questions . . ."

"Okay," Castillo said, looking out the window at the ocean view then turning to the others, "Let's go with our 727 now flying Costa Rican colors. How does that fit in with your off-the-wall scenario?"

"I think it fits in very nicely, now that I've a moment to think," Kennedy said. "Okay, let's pick up the scenario . . ."

He stopped when Sergeant Sherman, trailed by the large East European Charley thought of as *the guy who suckered me in the men's room* came into the apartment.

"Pretty soon, Major," Sherman said as he sat down at the table where he'd put the control box and the special laptop computer. He plugged in the tan cable.

"One possibility, Charley," Kennedy went on, "that you might wish to consider is that these people are going to substitute the airplane they've stolen for an airplane that can approach Philadelphia without causing suspicion; an airplane that routinely goes to Philadelphia."

"Jesus," Charley said.

"For the sake of argument, let's say a 727 belonging to a Costa Rican airliner. All that they would have to do would be make sure that the bona fide Costa Rican airplane wasn't in United States airspace at the same time."

"How would they do that?" Castillo asked, and the answer, *Sabotage the clean airplane, quietly sabotage the clean airplane,* came to him as he spoke.

"How do you think a mechanic in, say, San José, Costa Rica," Pevsner asked, slowly, "would react to an offer of ten thousand dollars to do something to an aircraft that would take it out of service for twenty-four hours? Not blow it up, nothing that would cause suspicion, just take it temporarily out of service for a day?"

"What was Marlon Brando's line in *The Godfather,* 'Make him an offer he can't refuse'?" Kennedy asked. "In this case, he would probably have the choice between taking the ten thousand, doing what he was asked to, or having his wife and children disemboweled."

Castillo looked over at Sergeant Sherman, who sat wearing a small headset in front of the control device.

"Sherman, how we doing?" Castillo asked.

Sherman held his left hand above his head, the fingers extended.

One by one, he folded them.

"All green, sir," Sherman said.

Castillo walked to him and picked up a small telephone handset.

"Are we into Philadelphia?" he asked.

"Major Miller's at City Hall," Sherman said. "He's on a secure line to the arsenal base."

"Get him on," Castillo ordered.

Sherman pushed several buttons. "Line's green, encryption green," he said.

"Sergeant Schneider," Betty's voice came very clearly down from the satellite.

"Castillo here. Can you get Miller on here?"

"Hold one, Major," Sergeant Schneider said.

"Charley?" Miller asked a moment later.

"Right."

"Did you get the word they've located the 727 in Suriname?"

"No, they haven't. It's not in Suriname and never has been."

"What?" Miller asked, incredulously. "Charley, just before Secretary Hall and the commissioner went in to see the mayor—that's where we are, City Hall—he had a call from the CIA—from the DCI himself—that the airplane's at a field called 'Zandery' in Suriname. That's what he's telling the mayor."

"Well, the CIA is wrong again."

"McNab has been ordered to neutralize it," Miller said. "He's already at Hurlburt, about to go wheels-up."

"Listen carefully, Dick. This is what I need from you. Go out to the airport and find out what airplanes regularly land—I don't mean on schedule, just all the time—from Costa Rica and get back to me. Find out what Costa Rican airline regularly goes to Philadelphia."

"Were you listening, Charley? Did you hear what I said? The CIA has found the airplane. Confirmed. They even have a visual."

"That's not the one we're looking for. Now, goddammit, do what you're told! Now!"

He touched Sergeant Sherman's shoulder.

"Get General McNab on here."

[FIVE]

Major H. Richard Miller, Jr., looked around the small room off the outer office of the mayor of the City of Philadelphia. There were three other people in it. Sergeant Betty Schneider of the Philadelphia Police Department and Supervisory Special Agents Joel Isaacson and Thomas McGuire of the United States Secret Service.

"Interesting question," Isaacson said, dryly. "Who do you believe? The director of Central Intelligence or Don Juan?"

"I'll go with Don Juan," Agent McGuire said.

"He sounded very sure of himself," Sergeant Schneider said.

"Don Juan is always very sure of himself," Isaacson said. "Which is not the same thing as saying he's always right."

"I don't have the faintest idea where to get that information at the airport. Or that they'll give it to me without a lot of hassle."

"I'll go out there with you, Sergeant," Tom McGuire said. "Maybe my badge, plus my Irish charm, will be useful."

"You think I should barge in the mayor's office and tell Secretary Hall?" Miller asked.

"Not without more to go on than what Don Juan told you, I don't," Isaacson said. "But I think you should do what Don Juan wants done."

"Anytime you're ready, Sergeant," Tom McGuire said.

"I just had a wild hair," Sergeant Schneider said, thoughtfully.

She took out her cellular, scrolled through the names and numbers displayed on it, and pushed the CALL button when she had found it.

"Mr. Halloran, this is Sergeant Schneider, Betty Schneider. Remember me?—

"This is a strange question, Mr. Halloran, but please bear with me. Off the top of your head, do you know of any airline from Costa Rica that comes to Philadelphia frequently? I don't mean a passenger service, especially—

"Oh, you do know one? Could you tell me about it, please?"

Less than sixty seconds later, she covered the microphone with her hand and said, "Bingo! I think you'd better get Castillo back, Dick."

And thirty seconds after that, Miller reported, "The channel's in use."

"Keep trying," Sergeant Schneider ordered.

[SIX]

"Before you say anything, Charley," Lieutenant General Bruce J. McNab said, "let me tell you the latest words of General Allan Naylor vis-à-vis you and me. 'You're a goddamned lieutenant general. You don't take goddamned "suggestions" from a goddamned major! And you goddamn well know it!' "

"He found out you're at Hurlburt?" Castillo asked, but it was a statement, not a question.

"Yes, he did. And apparently he's not nearly as impressed with your status as the personal representative of the president as I hoped he would be."

"Well, I'll take the heat, sir. I still think it was a good idea to pre-position at Hurlburt."

"That's very noble of you, Charley, but he's right. Lieutenant generals should not take suggestions from majors, and, if they do, they should expect to feel the heat. What's up?"

"The airplane is somewhere in Costa Rica; it's been rerenumbered and rerepainted."

"Jesus, are you sure? The only reason we're not on our way to Suriname right now is because they haven't been able to find us someplace where we can sit the C-17 down."

"It's not in Suriname," Castillo said.

"You got that from your friend the Russian arms dealer, right?"

"Right."

"My God, Charley! Fort Meade has photographs of the airplane at Zandery. The CIA guy in Suriname made a visual and you're telling me they have the wrong airplane?"

"Yes, sir. They probably have a photograph of an Air Suriname 727 with the right numbers, because it's an Air Suriname 727. The airplane the Holy Legion of Muhammad has is probably in Costa Rica."

"Where in Costa Rica?"

"I don't know that yet."

"Have you told anybody else this?"

"No, sir. What I've done is send Miller out to the airport in Philadelphia to see what airplanes from Costa Rica routinely land there. What they're obviously trying to do is get into the Philadelphia area without ringing alarm bells."

"How are they going to do that?" McNab asked, dubiously.

He thinks I've lost my mind.

Have I?

"By immobilizing a bona fide Costa Rican 727 for twenty-four hours and sending the one they have in its place."

"You're going to have a tough time selling that to Naylor. He already thinks you're drunk out of your mind with authority you don't have."

"What if I'm right, General?" Castillo said. "And I'm not going to try to sell General Naylor anything. I'm going to tell Secretary Hall. I work for him, not General Naylor."

"Charley," McNab said, softly. "You're an Army officer assigned to Cent-Com J-5."

Castillo didn't reply for a moment, then he said: "General, until I'm told otherwise I will continue to obey the last orders I have—which are from the president—to coordinate with you the neutralizing of the 727. In that capacity, I am recommending to you that you prepare to neutralize the 727 in Costa Rica."

It took McNab ten seconds to reply.

"What the hell, Mr. Castillo, in for a penny, in for a pound."

"I'm now going to report to Secretary Hall what I've learned," Castillo said. "I'll let you know what he says."

"Do that," McNab said. "McNab out."

Charley touched Sergeant Sherman's shoulder.

"Get me Philadelphia again, please."

"Coming up," Sherman said, and, a moment later, "All green, encryption, green."

"Miller?"

"Sergeant Schneider, Major."

"Put Miller on, please."

"I think you better hear this first," Betty Schneider said. "Costa Rican Air Transport makes frequent flights into Philadelphia using its 727 aircraft at least once a week, sometimes two or three times."

"Jesus, that was quick!" Castillo said. "Are you sure?"

"Halloran—Lease-Aire—sold them the airplane. He services it when it's here. Flowers into Philadelphia and household goods into San José."

"Flowers and household goods?"

"Fresh flowers. They grow them in Costa Rica and fly them here to sell in supermarkets. And the household goods are for Americans who retire down there. They can bring their household stuff into Costa Rica without paying any duty on it."

"Jesus Christ, there's the connection," Castillo said.

"There's more," Betty Schneider said. "On the way up here, they stop at Tampa, go through customs there, drop off some flowers, and then come here."

"As a domestic flight," Castillo said. "Not an international flight."

"Right."

"And, obviously, there would be no questions asked when they topped off their tanks," Castillo said. "Where's Secretary Hall?"

"In the mayor's office with the commissioner."

"Get him on here, Betty."

"I don't think he or the mayor's going to like being interrupted."

"Go get him," Castillo said.

XVIII

[ONE]
Office of the Mayor
City Hall
Broad and Market Streets
Philadelphia, Pennsylvania
1015 10 June 2005

"What is it that's so important, Charley?" the secretary of homeland security said impatiently into the secure telephone, leaving unspoken the rest of the question: *that you decided you should interrupt my meeting with the mayor?*

Castillo knew what had not been said.

"The 727 is not in Suriname, Mr. Secretary," Castillo said.

"You mean it's taken off?"

"No, sir. What I mean is that the 727 stolen in Angola was never in Suriname."

"The DCI obviously has information, including satellite imagery and a visual by his station chief, that you're apparently not aware of."

"The Air Suriname 727 at Zandery, sir, is a legitimate Air Suriname 727. The one we're looking for, with a new identity, is somewhere in Costa Rica."

"You have this from your friend the arms dealer, right?" Matthew Hall asked, half sarcastically, half sadly.

"Yes, sir," Castillo said. "But Sergeant Schneider has just made the Philadelphia connection, which confirms what I'm telling you."

"What did she do?"

"What Pevsner suggested—he's in the process of finding out more—was that the Holy Legion of Muhammad plans to get through our security by substituting the airplane they have for an airplane that routinely comes to Philadelphia. Schneider found there is an airplane, owned by Costa Rican Air Transport, that flies fresh flowers to Philadelphia at least once a week. Lease-Aire sold them the airplane, and they service it when it's in Philadelphia. This ties in with what Pevsner told me that our airplane was at a private strip in Venezuela getting repainted as a Costa Rican Air Transport plane."

Secretary Hall looked across the small room at Sergeant Betty Schneider, who was leaning against the wall. He was aware that Joel Isaacson, Tom McGuire, and Major H. Richard Miller, Jr., were looking at him, waiting for his reaction.

That means they know about this Philadelphia connection, and, if they let Miller burst into the mayor's office, they believe it.

I would expect Miller to go with Castillo. They're like brothers.

But Joel and Tom, too?

Jesus Christ! I just finished convincing the mayor that the National Security Agency's satellites found the airplane in Suriname, that the CIA verified on the ground that it's the airplane we've been looking for, and the president has ordered "all necessary steps be taken" to neutralize it, that that operation is already under way and the situation is under control and there's no reason for further concern.

And now I'm supposed to go back in there and tell him, "Sorry, a little problem has come up"?

The first thing he's going to do is order an evacuation of Center City and go on television to tell the people there is a genuine threat of an airliner crashing into the Liberty Bell.

"Sir, are you still there?" Castillo asked.

"Hang on a minute, Charley, while I think," Secretary Hall said.

He looked at Sergeant Betty Schneider again.

"You believe this Philadelphia connection, Sergeant?"

"Yes, sir. It seems to fit."

"I'm going back in the mayor's office and tell him and Commissioner Kellogg that I have to go back to Washington immediately," Hall said, carefully. "To the White House."

She nodded.

"Tom, have them get the airplane ready," Hall ordered.

McGuire turned his back and spoke softly into a microphone in the lapel of his jacket.

"Inasmuch as I still believe the situation is under control, that we will be able to neutralize the airplane, I am not going to tell the mayor of this development," Hall said. He let that sink in a moment. "Sergeant, I would like an escort to the airport. I have to get there as quickly as possible."

"I'll be happy to give you an escort, Mr. Secretary," Betty Schneider said.

"If on the way to the airport, Sergeant, I told you I thought it would be helpful if you went to Washington with me, what would your reaction be? Please take a moment to think over your answer."

Betty Schneider pursed her lips and exhaled audibly.

"You understand, I think, what I'm asking, and why," Hall added.

She nodded.

"Major Castillo does have a way of upsetting the apple cart, doesn't he?" she asked, softly. "Just when you think things are under control, up he pops."

Joel Isaacson chuckled.

"Mr. Secretary," Sergeant Schneider said. "My orders from Chief Inspector Kramer are to provide you with any support you asked for. If you asked me to go with you to Washington, I'm sure I would go."

"Thank you," Secretary Hall said.

He put the secure telephone to his ear again.

"Charley?"

"Yes, sir?"

"You don't know where in Costa Rica?"

"No, sir. But according to Colonel Torine there are only two airports in the country that'll take a 727 . . . hold one, sir."

"Now what?" Hall snapped, impatiently.

"Sir, Mr. . . . my friend tells me that he is working on a positive location and should have it shortly. He said to tell you he's doing the very best he can."

"Tell him thank you," Hall said, and then went on: "Charley, I'm on my way to the White House. Stay close by the phone. I strongly suspect that our boss is going to want to talk to you."

"Sir, I was about to head for Costa Rica."

"And while you're doing that, you'll be out of touch?"

"It's about seven hundred miles from here. Figure an hour and a half in the air and thirty minutes to shut down the radio here and get to the airport. I'll be out of touch for a little over two hours, sir."

"You really think you have to go there yourself? Can't we get the CIA or Meade to find the airplane for us?"

"I think it would be best if I went myself, sir."

Yeah, and so do I. When the CIA learns that based on flawed information from them, Gray Fox is about to violate the sacred territory of Suriname and neutralize—probably blow up—a perfectly legitimate airplane, Langley's first re-action is going to be denial, and, way down the pike, taking action—maybe—to fix the problem.

"Get back in touch as soon as you can."

"Yes, sir. Of course."

Secretary Hall put the handset back in its cradle.

"Miller, I want you to come with us," he ordered.

"Yes, sir."

Hall started for the door to the mayor's office.

"I won't be long," he said.

[TWO]
Penthouse "B"
The Grande Cozumel Beach and Golf Resort
Cozumel, Mexico
1022 10 June 2005

"Okay, Sherman, get General McNab again," Castillo ordered.

Five seconds later, Sherman reported, "The link is down, Major."

"Oh, shit!" Castillo said. "Get Bragg and see if they know why."

"Already working on it, sir," Sherman said, and almost immediately, "I'm getting some green LEDs on General McNab, Major . . . Okay, sir, we're all up."

"General McNab, please," Castillo said into the headset.

"And now what, Major Castillo?" McNab himself answered.

"General, we have confirmation of what I told you before. It's now almost certain that the stolen airplane has been repainted with the color scheme of Costa Rican Air Transport, which regularly flies into Philadelphia with flowers from Costa Rica, and they intend to . . ."

"You did say," McNab interrupted, "did you not, Major, 'flies into Philadelphia with flowers from Costa Rica'?"

"Yes, sir, that's what I said. Flowers grown in Costa Rica and sold in supermarkets in the States. They go through customs in Tampa . . ."

"How convenient for General Naylor and CentCom. They can just hop in a couple of Humvees, drive over to Tampa International, and neutralize it there."

"Please, sir, let me finish."

"Why not?"

"Where they can top off the tanks and then file a flight plan—a domestic flight plan—to Philadelphia."

"And how are they going to explain to the customs people in Tampa why they are carrying so much fuel in U.S. Army fuel bladders?"

"I don't know, sir," Castillo confessed.

"What was Secretary Hall's reaction to this fascinating scenario? You did tell him?"

"Yes, sir. He told me he's on his way to Washington. To the White House."

"And?"

"That's all, sir."

"You probably won't have a security clearance much longer so I probably shouldn't be telling you this, but, for auld lang syne, with warm memories of happier times, I will. I have received further orders from General Naylor. I am immediately to proceed to a field near Kwakoegron, Suriname, there to hold myself in readiness to neutralize an Air Suriname 727 when ordered to do so. In compliance with these orders, I am presently, I would estimate, about forty or fifty miles south of Hurlburt Field, over the Gulf of Mexico."

"Yes, sir."

"Keep in touch, Charley. McNab out."

"It would appear, Charley," Alex Pevsner said as Castillo laid the headset on the table, "that no one seems willing to call off the plan to neutralize the wrong airplane in Suriname."

"Once something like that is started, it's hard to call it off," Castillo said. "The only one who can overrule General Naylor is the secretary of defense. He's not going to take what I think over the CIA . . ."

"Especially since the source of your information is an infamous Russian criminal?" Pevsner asked.

"Secretary Hall doesn't feel that way," Castillo said. "You heard what he said. And he's going to see the president . . ."

"And you think the president, looking at NSA photographs of an Air Suriname 727 on the field at Zandery, and with confirmation from a CIA man on the ground, is liable to decide that—how did that general describe you earlier?—'an Army officer assigned to Special Operations at Central Command'—is right and they're wrong? Especially since he knows I'm the source of your information?"

"When I get on the radio and say, 'I'm in Zippity Do Dah, Costa Rica'—or wherever the hell it is—'looking at the airplane,' they're going to have to pay attention." He touched Sergeant Sherman's shoulder. "Pack it up, Sergeant. We're going to Costa Rica."

"Hold it a minute, Castillo," Colonel Torine said. "Before you shut down the link. What if I got on there to General McFadden and tell him I think—I'm sure—you're right?" He paused, and added, "We go back a long way."

Castillo met his eyes.

"The most probable thing that would happen if we contacted anybody at MacDill would be that you would be ordered to place me under arrest and bring me to MacDill. I don't want to put you in that spot. But thank you, sir." He paused, and added, "Colonel, I think the best thing for you to do is escape from this drunk-out-of-his-mind-with-authority-he-doesn't-have lunatic, go to the airport, and hop on a commercial flight to Tampa."

"Well, you're right about authority you don't have, Castillo. You're a major, as General McNab pointed out. You can't give a colonel orders," Colonel Torine said. "And General McNab said two other things. He ordered me to go with you, saying you needed a 727 expert."

"As I recall, sir, you volunteered," Castillo said.

"That was my last order, which I intend to obey," Torine said. "And the second thing General McNab said that struck me as appropriate was, 'In for a penny, in for a pound.' " He met Castillo's eyes for a moment, then turned to Sergeant Sherman. "Is there any way I can help you tear that thing down, Sergeant?"

"I've got it pretty much under control, sir," Sherman said. "Major, do you want me to sign out of the net?"

"Just turn it off, Sergeant," Castillo said. "Before it occurs to General Naylor to get on there and order us all to the States."

Sergeant Sherman leaned slightly forward, pulled the power cord from the wall, and reported, "The link is down, sir."

Aleksandr Pevsner picked up the hotel telephone.

"Have the vehicles prepared to go immediately to the airport," he ordered, in Spanish. "We will be in the garage immediately."

"Thank you," Castillo said. "Thank you for everything, Alex."

"On the contrary, my friend," Pevsner said. "It is I who is grateful to you. You have made every effort to live up to your side of our arrangement. It's not your fault that emperors, czars, and high-ranking generals have the tendency to want to kill the messenger bearing news they don't want to hear."

"And somewhere down the road, Charley," Howard Kennedy said, "no matter what happens, someone—possibly even one of my former colleagues—is going to say, 'That's what Pevsner was trying to tell us.' And it's even possible this will be said with the right people listening."

He offered his hand and Charley shook it, and then shook hands with Pevsner, and, as he did, thought it would be a long time before he saw Pevsner again. If he ever saw either of them again.

He was surprised when Pevsner went to the basement garage with them and even more surprised when Pevsner got behind the wheel of one of the Yukons, obviously intending to drive to the airport.

As they were driving down the beach road to the airport, Pevsner turned to Howard Kennedy, who was riding in the second seat beside Fernando, and ordered, "Write down the San José numbers—all three of them—and give them to Charley, Howard."

"Yes, sir," Kennedy said.

"What San José numbers?" Castillo asked.

"There are three," Pevsner said. "I really hope you don't have occasion to use any of them. The one with the 533 prefix almost always knows how to get in touch with me quickly. The other two are those who will have what information I can come up with about where in Costa Rica you will find the plane. I hope to get that information to you as an in-flight advisory, but, if that doesn't work, call either of the other two numbers, ask for yourself . . ."

"Excuse me?"

"Ask for Charley Castillo. Better yet, ask for Karl Gossinger . . . you getting this, Howard?"

"Yes, sir."

"Ask for Karl Gossinger and they'll give you what information they have. If I'm unsuccessful, they will not know who Herr Gossinger is and say so."

"Thank you," Castillo said.

"Please don't call any of them unless it proves necessary. And if the first two have no information for you, that means I haven't been able to do as much as I would really like to have done," Pevsner said. "In other words, there would be no point in your trying to call me."

"I understand," Charley said.

Castillo felt a hand on his shoulder and turned his head. Howard Kennedy was extending a sheet of notebook paper to him. He took it.

"Try not to lose that, Charley," Kennedy said. "And when the time passes and you know you're not going to use any of them, why don't you burn that? I'd really hate to have those numbers fall into the wrong hands."

"You think your former associates would be interested in them, do you?"

"Oh, would they ever," Kennedy said.

Ten minutes later, Aleksandr Pevsner and Howard Kennedy stood by the hood of one of the white Yukons and watched as the Learjet took off.

[THREE]
Aboard USAF C-17 036788
25.418 degrees North Latitude
86.136 degrees West Longitude
Above the Gulf of Mexico
1115 10 June 2005

"Miami area control, Air Force Sixty-Seven-Eighty-Eight," Major Ellwood C. Tanner, USAF, said into his microphone.

"Go ahead, Eighty-Eight."

"Reporting my position. I'm at flight level thirty-three, estimating six hundred knots, on a course of one-two-five true."

"I have you on radar, Eighty-Eight. Be advised, any eastward deviation from your present course may put you in Cuban airspace."

"Acknowledge advisory. Air Force Eighty-Eight clear," Major Tanner said and made a note of the conversation on a knee notepad.

"Got a chart I can look at, Major?" a voice asked, and Tanner turned to see Lieutenant General Bruce J. McNab standing in the cockpit between the pilot and copilot positions.

"Yes, sir, of course," Tanner said. "We're a hundred miles off the Florida coast, about even with Miami."

"I saw that," McNab said, gesturing in the vague direction of a cathode-ray tube that showed the C-17's position and then holding his hand out for the chart.

Tanner handed it to him and McNab studied it for a moment, then held it out to Tanner.

"See where I'm pointing?" McNab asked.

Tanner looked.

"Yes, sir. Costa Rica."

"Specifically, Juan Santamaria International Airport in Costa Rica," General McNab said.

"Yes, sir."

"Now, what you are going to do, Major, as soon as you think Cuban radar has lost interest in us, is get on the horn and make an announcement that to avoid turbulence you would like to change your course to about one-seventy-two degrees."

"Which will put us on a course to Juan Santamaria, sir?"

"If there are any questions about why you're changing course, I don't want Juan Santamaria to enter the conversation, understood?"

"Yes, sir."

"If I told you that we're probably going to experience mechanical problems when Juan Santamaria is the closest alternate, then you would think I was prescient, wouldn't you?"

"Yes, sir, I guess I would."

"Good. It is valuable for junior officers to believe their seniors have mysterious abilities and know things they don't."

Major Tanner smiled at Lieutenant General McNab. This was not the first Gray Fox mission he had flown for Special Operations, but it was the first one he'd flown on which McNab was being carried. Knowing this, Colonel Jake Torine had briefed Major Tanner and two other pilots on what they might expect from the legendary Special Forces officer. The two cogent points of the briefing were to expect the unexpected and don't ask any questions or express an opinion unless asked to do so.

Major Tanner elected to violate one of the teachings of the briefing.

"Sir, is that where the 727 we missed in Chad is?"

McNab looked at him coldly.

"There is an old saying in the Army, Major, that lieutenants should not marry, captains may marry, and majors should be very careful about being prescient. It probably has an application for the Air Force."

"Yes, sir," Tanner said. "We usually stop getting pinged by Cuban radar about here." He pointed at the chart. "And I wouldn't be surprised if we started to encounter some upper-level turbulence a few miles south of that point."

"You've been warned about premature prescience, Major," McNab said and smiled at him.

General McNab then climbed down from the cockpit and went into the cargo bay. Despite the size of the enormous aircraft, it was crowded. Six Little Birds, their rotors folded, took up much of the space. There were four five-hundred-gallon fuel bladders lashed to the floor. There were crates of ammunition and rockets and rations and perhaps thirty plastic coolers that bore the bright red legend:

BASE EXCHANGE

HURLBURT FIELD

HOME OF AIR FORCE SPECIAL OPERATIONS

Scattered throughout the cargo bay, sitting on whatever they could find to sit on except the uncomfortable aluminum-pipe-and-nylon-sheeting standard seats, were thirty Gray Fox special operators—six officers, twelve senior enlisted men, and the twelve Little Bird pilots. One of the pilots was a captain, one a lieutenant, and the others chief warrant officers, two of whom were CWO-5s whose pay was only slightly less than that of a lieutenant colonel. All the pilots, in addition to being carefully selected and highly trained Army aviators with a minimum of a thousand hours in the air as pilot in command, were also fully trained and qualified as Special Forces soldiers. Their mission, once they had delivered the Gray Fox team to the ground, was to switch roles from helicopter pilots to what everybody called "shooters."

There were also a half-dozen mechanics whose primary function was the folding of Little Bird rotor blades, loading the Little Birds onto the C-17, and then unloading them, unfolding the rotor blades, and making sure they were safe to fly when the C-17 touched down. There were also two avionics technicians to make sure everything electronic on the Little Birds was functioning properly and two armorers to handle the weaponry. The technicians, too, were all fully qualified Special Forces soldiers, and when the Little Birds had taken off they, too, would switch to being shooters and establish a perimeter guard around the Globemaster.

Just about everybody was drinking a Coke or a 7UP or munching on an ice-cream bar on a stick or wolfing down a hot dog heated in one of two microwave ovens that were carried along routinely even if they didn't appear on any list of equipment.

The base exchange at Hurlburt had had a good day. General McNab would not have been at all surprised if some of the plastic coolers from the exchange held six, maybe eight, cases of beer on ice. He hadn't asked or looked, nor was he worried. His people were pros; they wouldn't take a sip until the job was done.

And three-quarters of the way down the cargo bay, on the only upholstered chair in the bay, a Gray Fox special operator sat before a fold-down shelf that held one of onetime sergeant Aloysius Francis Casey's latest communications devices.

He had just stuffed perhaps a third of a chili-and-onion dog in his mouth when he saw General McNab walking toward him. He started to chew furiously as he started to stand up.

McNab signaled for him to keep his seat and waited for him to finish chewing.

"I understand we're having a little communications problem, Sergeant Kensington," General McNab said.

"Yes, sir?" Kensington replied, momentarily confused at first, then following.

"Everything but imagery is down, I understand?"

Sergeant Kensington turned to the control panel and flipped switches. Green LEDs went out as he did so.

"Yes, sir, nothing's green but imagery."

"Well, you never can really predict when these things are going to work and when they're not, can you?"

"No, sir, you never really can."

McNab touched his shoulder, smiled at him, and walked forward in the cargo bay. He caught the eye of one of the CWO-5s, a massive—well over six feet and two hundred pounds—black man named Shine, whose bald skull reflected light and was thus logically known to his peers as "Shiny Shine," and motioned him over.

"A no-bullshit-the-general answer, Shine," McNab said. "Once I give you the coordinates, how long will it take you to program the computers?"

"Sir, that's done. We can be in the air in no more than ten minutes after the door opens."

"You never listen to me, Shine. That's probably why you're not a general."

"We're not going to Suriname, General?"

"I didn't say that, Shine."

"Come on, boss, I have to know. I've got a bag full of CDs of approaches to South American airfields. Maybe one of them's what you need. If so, all I'll need is fifteen minutes to reprogram. Otherwise it'll take me an hour, maybe a little more."

"You got anything in your bag for Costa Rica, by chance?"

"I don't know, boss. I'll have to check."

"Why don't you do that? And let me know."

"Yes, sir."

"Keep it as quiet as you can."

"When they see me going in the bag, they'll know something is up."

"Let them worry; it'll keep them on their toes."

"You're a badass, General," Mr. Shine said, smiling. "With all possible respect, sir."

McNab walked farther forward in the cargo bay, opened one of the white plastic coolers, took out a hot dog, a roll, put the hot dog in the roll, spread it heavily with chili and chopped onions, and put it into one of the microwave ovens.

[FOUR]
The Oval Office
The White House
1600 Pennsylvania Avenue NW
Washington, D.C.
1120 10 June 2005

"His plate is pretty full," the chief of staff to the president of the United States said to the secretary of homeland security. "Is this going to take long?"

Matthew Hall gave the appearance of someone who was annoyed, had been about to say something unpleasant, but had changed his mind and instead said something else.

"Is Natalie Cohen in there?" he asked. "If she's not, send for her."

He then opened the door to the Oval Office and went in, denying the chief of staff his privilege of going in first to announce him.

The president was sitting in one of two upholstered chairs facing a coffee table. Secretary of Defense Frederick K. Beiderman was sitting on the couch on the other side of the coffee table. The president looked up from pouring coffee.

"Speak of the devil," the president said. "How did things go in Philadelphia? Do we have one highly pissed off mayor on our hands?"

"We're probably going to have one, Mr. President," Hall said.

"You couldn't convince him that the problem is under control?"

"With some difficulty, sir, I think I did. The problem is . . . the problem is that the problem is not under control."

"There's been a problem neutralizing the airplane in Suriname? I didn't think they'd even had time to get there."

"The airplane in Suriname is not the 727 the terrorists have, Mr. President," Hall said.

"What?" the president asked, incredulously.

"Tell that to the DCI," Beiderman said. "He even has a visual from a CIA agent down there."

"I intend to tell the DCI, Fred," Hall said, pointedly. "But I thought the president should hear it first."

"Where are you getting your information, Matt? From the Russian?"

"From the Russian, yes, sir. Via Major Castillo. But there's more, sir."

"What more?"

"We've made . . . I don't know why I said 'we.' I had nothing to do with it. When I heard this first from Castillo, frankly I was as dubious as you, Mr. President, but, then, when I heard everything I became a convert."

"What 'everything'?" the president asked, impatiently.

"The Philadelphia police—with the at first somewhat reluctant help of the FBI—have identified the people who stole the airplane. Pevsner said they were Somalians and they are. They were in Philadelphia as mullahs and the counterterrorism people there took their pictures and made a positive ID . . ."

"Made a positive ID of who?" Dr. Natalie Cohen asked, entering the room. "I presume I'm invited to this meeting?"

"You're invited but you're probably not going to like it," the president said.

"Mr. President," Hall continued, "I've got Major Miller and a Philadelphia police counterterrorism officer, Sergeant Schneider, with me. I think maybe if you heard all this from them, it would be better than . . ."

"Bring them on," the president ordered, impatiently, then asked, "The same Major Miller?"

"Yes, sir. He's been in Philadelphia . . ."

The president gestured impatiently for Hall to bring them in.

Hall went to the door.

"Mr. President," the chief of staff said the moment it opened, "you've got the Speaker in ten minutes."

"Stall him," the president ordered.

"Will you come in, please?" Hall called.

First, Sergeant Betty Schneider and then Major H. Richard Miller, Jr., who was in civilian clothing, entered the Oval Office. Both were visibly nervous.

"Good morning," Dr. Cohen said, approaching them with her right hand extended. "My name is Natalie Cohen. Thank you for coming. I expect you recognize the president. The gentleman with him is Secretary of Defense Beiderman."

The president, who had risen from his chair when Cohen came into the office, walked to Betty Schneider and put out his hand.

"We're all anxious to hear what you have to tell us," he said with a warm smile, and added, as he gave his hand to Miller, "what the both of you have to tell us. And I've been anxious to meet you, Major."

Both said, "Yes, sir."

"You take it, Betty," Miller ordered. "I'll fill in."

"I'm very sorry but I have to go to the restroom," Betty Schneider said. "Right now."

"Just come with me, dear," Dr. Cohen said and led her through a door.

In under a minute, the national security advisor was back.

"Nobody thinks that's funny, right?" she challenged. "Good. Okay, Major, you're up."

Miller exhaled audibly. "I'll take it from the top," he began. "From the beginning, we thought there might be a Philadelphia connection. It came together one piece at a time, starting with the fact that the 727 is owned by Lease-Aire in Philadelphia. And then Castillo's Russian told him in Vienna . . ."

"Castillo's Russian?" the president chuckled.

"Yes, sir. I regret the choice of words."

"I shouldn't have interrupted you," the president said. "Please go on."

"The Russian national sometimes known as Aleksandr Pevsner," Miller began again, this time more formally, "who made contact with Major Castillo in Vienna told Major Castillo he believed there was a Philadelphia connection, although he gave no reason.

"But as one item of intel after another Castillo got from Pevsner—that the airplane was in Chad, for example, that it had been repainted with Suriname registry numbers—proved to be accurate, Castillo began to place more credence in the Philadelphia connection theory.

"It was there, but at first we didn't know where to look for it . . ."

"You're saying, Major, that the information this man Pevsner has provided has been both accurate and valuable?" Beiderman interrupted.

"Yes, sir. Everything he's told us so far has been right on the money. There is just no reason not to believe the latest intel he's given us."

"Which is?" Natalie Cohen asked, softly.

"That's right, you came in after the movie started, didn't you?" the president said. "The last tidbit from Castillo's Russian is that we are about to violate the sovereign territory and airspace of Suriname and neutralize the wrong airplane."

"My God!" Cohen said. "Where's the one we're looking for, if it's not in Suriname?"

"Somewhere in Costa Rica, ma'am," Miller said. "With a new identity."

"Wow!" Dr. Cohen said.

Sergeant Betty Schneider came into the room.

"I'm very sorry," she said. "And more than a little embarrassed."

"Don't be silly," the president said. "That happens all the time to Matt Hall. Every time he suspects that I'm displeased with him . . ."

"Jesus!" Hall said.

Dr. Cohen looked at the president in disbelief, shook her head, then smiled, and finally giggled.

Betty Schneider looked at her and then the president with enormous relief.

"The major was about to tell us . . . all right if I call you 'Betty'?" Cohen asked.

"Yes, ma'am."

"Betty, the major was about to tell us what you think these people are going to do with the airplane and exactly how they plan to do it," Cohen said. "Why don't you give it a shot?"

Betty gathered her thoughts—not as completely as she thought she had—and began, "Well, when Charley called from Mexico . . ."

" 'Charley' being Major Castillo?" the president interrupted.

"Yes, sir."

"And what's he doing in Mexico?" the president asked, almost rhetorically.

"He was in Cozumel, Mr. President," Hall said. "At the moment, he's on his way to Costa Rica. Same purpose: Finding and neutralizing the airplane."

"Dumb question," the president said.

"How's he moving around?" Cohen asked. "I'm concerned about airspace, territorial violations."

"His family has an airplane, a Lear 45XR," Hall said. "He borrowed that."

"His family has a 45XR? No wonder he can afford to live in the Mayflower," Dr. Cohen said.

"It also probably has something to do with his Secret Service code name," the president said.

"Excuse me?" Dr. Cohen asked.

"Don Juan," the president said, obviously pleased with himself. Then he saw Dr. Cohen's face and that she was obviously not amused and looked at Sergeant Schneider and went on, "What about when he called from Mexico, Betty?"

"When Castillo told Major Miller and I to go to the airport and find out what airlines regularly flew into Philly from Costa Rica," Betty replied, "I played a hunch and got lucky and called Terrence Halloran, who owns Lease-Aire, who owns the missing 727, and asked him what he knew about Costa Rican airlines flying into Philly. He knew of one right away. He'd sold a 727 to an outfit called Costa Rican Air Transport. They fly wholesale flowers, grown down there, into Philly at least once a week. They sell them in supermarkets."

"The Somalians are going to substitute the stolen airplane for a legitimate Costa Rican airplane?" Dr. Cohen asked.

"Right, Natalie," Hall said. "Castillo told me the Russian told him that the airplane was flown from Africa to a private field in Venezuela, near Lake Maracaibo, and given new numbers—Costa Rican numbers—there."

"Castillo's Russian is a virtual cornucopia of useful, reliable information, isn't he?" the president said, not at all pleasantly. "How nice if we could say the same about the CIA."

No one said anything for a moment

Miller finally broke the silence. "There's more, Mr. President. They pass through customs at Tampa on their way to Philadelphia, which means when they move on to Philadelphia they're a domestic flight, not an international flight. And they'll have clearance to approach the Philadelphia airport."

"It's what we cops call circumstantial, Mr. President," Betty said, now having lost her nervousness. "No positive, concrete, take-it-to-the-bank proof, but everything fits . . ."

The president raised his hand in a signal to stop.

"Fred," the president ordered, "call off the invasion of Suriname."

"Call it off, Mr. President?" Secretary of Defense Beiderman asked. "A complete stand-down?"

"I don't want those F-15s shooting down a Surinamese airplane. I don't care what you call it, just see that it's done."

"Yes, Mr. President," Beiderman said and walked toward a credenza that held two telephones.

"Or the CIA blowing one up on the ground," the president went on as if to himself. He picked up a telephone handset from the coffee table, said, "Get me the DCI. I'll hold."

It took less than twenty seconds to get the director of Central Intelligence on the line.

"This is the president, John. Now, listen carefully, as I have time neither to repeat myself nor explain nor debate it. I want no action of any kind taken in Suriname. None. Period. I'll get back with you shortly and explain this, but, right now, I want you to call off whatever you may have planned. Thank you."

He hung up.

He exhaled, looked around the room, smiled at Sergeant Schneider and Major Miller, and then had another thought, which caused the smile to fade.

"And how did the mayor of Philadelphia react on being informed that we still have a little problem with the Liberty Bell?" he asked.

"I didn't tell him, Mr. President," Matt Hall said. "He would have immediately gone on TV and ordered the evacuation of Center City Philadelphia."

"Jesus!" the president said. "Well, he's going to find out sooner or later. How do we deal with that?"

"There's no reason he ever has to find out, Mr. President," Hall said.

The president's eyebrows rose in surprise and it was a moment before he asked, "Presuming we can neutralize the real airplane, right?"

"Yes, sir."

"Worst-case scenario, the airplane leaves Costa Rica and makes it to Tampa, where we grab it on the ground," Hall said.

"That presumes they won't have a change of mind en route and fly it into a cruise ship parked in Miami Harbor, Disney World, or some other target that makes about as much sense. We have to do better than that, Matt," the president said.

"Shoot it down the minute it leaves Costa Rica," Beiderman said. "Over international waters."

"What we are going to try to do," the president said, "is quietly neutralize it on the ground in Costa Rica. I emphasize the word *quietly*. Is there any reason Gray Fox can't be trusted to do that?"

"Presuming we can find the airplane in Costa Rica, no, sir."

"Gray Fox is presently airborne on its way to Suriname, Mr. President," Secretary Beiderman said.

"I called the invasion of Suriname off," the president said, and now there was a very nasty tone in his voice. "Weren't you here when I gave that order, Fred?"

"Sir, normally we have instantaneous communication with a Gray Fox transport. But, at the moment, there's a glitch. It happens, sir. Sunspots . . . other things."

"You mean we are not in contact with Gray Fox?"

"For the moment, no, sir."

"How far is it away from Suriname?" the president asked.

"Several hours, sir."

"Between now and the time it gets to Suriname, Mr. Secretary of Defense, I want you to get word to General McNab that he is to divert to Costa Rica, there to await further orders in connection with his original mission. Jesus Christ, Fred, send F-15s after him and force him to turn around if that becomes necessary."

"Yes, sir. Where in Costa Rica, Mr. President?"

"General McNab is a resourceful fellow. Why don't we let him decide that?"

The door to the Oval Office opened.

"Mr. President, the Speaker is here," the chief of staff said.

"Well, for the moment we're finished here," the president said. "But I'd like everybody to keep themselves available."

"Why don't we all go to my office," Natalie Cohen said, "and have a cup of coffee and a Danish?"

[FIVE]
Office of the National Security Advisor
The White House
1600 Pennsylvania Avenue NW
Washington, D.C.
1150 10 June 2005

"I'm going to the situation room," Secretary of Defense Fred Beiderman announced. "I feel like a schoolboy in here, waiting to be called back to the principal's office. Maybe they've managed to reestablish contact with McNab. Anyone want to go with me?"

"I will," Secretary of Homeland Security Matthew Hall said.

"I thought I would take Betty and Major Miller to the executive mess for lunch," National Security Advisor Dr. Natalie Cohen said.

"Good idea," Hall said. "We'll meet you there."

"Secretary Hall," Major H. Richard Miller, Jr., said. "May I have a minute, sir?"

"Shoot," Hall said.

"Alone, sir. If you would, please, sir."

"You want to wait, Fred, or should I catch up with you?" Hall asked.

"Catch up with me," Beiderman said. "I'll walk slow."

He went through the door.

"I'll take Betty and leave you two alone," Dr. Cohen said.

"You can hear this, ma'am," Miller said. "I just didn't want Secretary Beiderman to hear it. I just realized he will anyway, so it doesn't make any sense . . ."

"Neither are you making any sense, Major," Hall said.

"It's about getting through to General McNab, sir. I don't think all the communication is down."

"I don't understand," Hall said.

"Sir, I've been on missions like this one. When it gets close to doing something . . . there's often a link that goes down."

"I don't understand," Hall said.

"I think I do," Natalie Cohen said. "There is a point in time after which, thank you just the same, General McNab doesn't want anyone looking over his shoulder offering friendly advice? He wants to get on with the job?"

"Yes, ma'am."

"Now, you know why he didn't want Fred to hear this," Cohen said and turned back Miller. "You know how to get through to him?"

"Usually, he leaves the imagery link open," Miller said.

"I don't know what that means," Hall said.

"It means he's still able to receive an image. Some people know that," Miller said. "If it's important, they'll send him one."

"An image? A picture?" Hall asked.

"Yes, sir."

"Of what?" Hall asked.

"Of a message. Right, Major?" Dr. Cohen asked.

"Yes, ma'am."

"You're saying you can get through to him with an image of a message?" Hall asked. When Miller nodded, Hall added, "Well, we're going to have to tell Beiderman that, of course."

"Maybe not," Natalie Cohen said. "Would he take a message from you, Major?"

"Yes, ma'am, I think he would."

"How would that work?"

"I'd write the message here, fax it out to the Nebraska Avenue place, and tell the operator to send it," Miller said.

"Nebraska Avenue?"

"Castillo set up a Gray Fox radio out there," Hall said.

Dr. Cohen pulled open a drawer of her desk, took out a sheet of paper, and handed it and a ballpoint pen to Miller.

"Go," she said.

"Ma'am, have you got a felt-tip, a Magic Marker? I need something big."

"Coming up," she said and went back to her desk drawer.

"Thank you," Miller said. "Mr. Secretary, I'm going to need the numbers, fax and phone, out there."

Hall went into the outer office, where Isaacson and McGuire were waiting.

"I need the numbers, phone and fax, for Nebraska Avenue," he said.

By the time Isaacson had retrieved the numbers from his handheld computer, written them down, given them to Hall, and Hall went back into Cohen's office, Miller had already fed the sheet of paper into the fax machine on the credenza behind Cohen's desk.

He gave them to Miller, who immediately punched them into the fax machine. The machine began to feed itself the paper.

"Did you see that?" Hall asked Cohen.

She shook her head. "No need to," she said.

Miller punched the numbers of the Nebraska Avenue office into his cellular.

"This is Major Miller. I just sent you a fax. Image it to General McNab— now. I'll hold for confirmation of receipt."

The fax machine finished expelling the sheet of paper. Natalie Cohen took it, read it, and handed it Hall.

"Let Betty read that—she's entitled—and then burn it," Natalie Cohen said.

"Burn it?" Hall asked as he handed the sheet of paper to Betty Schneider.

"There's no reason Fred has to know about this," Natalie Cohen said.

Betty finished reading the message and handed it back to Hall, who read it again.

THE WHITE HOUSE

WASHINGTON, D.C.

DR. NATALIE COHEN
NATIONAL SECURITY ADVISOR

Go all green now.

The president is trying to order Gen McNab to divert to Costa Rica

H. R Miller, Jr.
Maj, SpF

"You don't think Beiderman is entitled to know about this?" Hall asked.

"Entitled, maybe," Natalie Cohen said. "Like the mayor of Philadelphia was entitled to know the CIA hasn't really found the airplane. Did you tell him, Matt?"

He raised his eyebrows and shrugged his shoulders, a confession that he hadn't.

"Both of these young people had to make a tough choice between two correct loyalties," Dr. Cohen said. "Betty, to come here with you without telling her superiors in the cops what she knew about the not-found airplane, which some people would consider disloyal; and Miller had to tell you about General McNab's 'selective' communications setup. Which made him feel disloyal to McNab. Both made the right choice. There is not panic in the streets in Philadelphia, and I wouldn't be surprised if Beiderman shortly can communicate with General McNab. So leave it there, Matt, please."

She put out her hand.

"Anybody got a match?"

Secretary Hall laid a somewhat battered Zippo in Dr. Cohen's palm.

[SIX]
Aboard USAF C-17 036788
17.210 degrees North Latitude
82.680 degrees West Longitude
Above the Atlantic Ocean
1158 10 June 2005

"How very interesting," Lieutenant General Bruce J. McNab said and handed the message back to the Sergeant Kensington, who was manning the control panel. "I think you better put this in there."

He pointed to the burn bag tied to Kensington's shelf, which was actually a small canvas bag holding three thermite grenades—two for the radio, one for messages—in case it became necessary to destroy either or both to keep them from falling into the wrong hands.

Kensington did so, then looked at McNab, who made a "push 'em up" gesture with this fingers. Kensington turned to the control panel and started flipping switches.

"Coming up . . . all green, sir," Kensington said.

"I wonder where Miller got that stationery?" McNab asked.

"Knowing the major, sir, no telling," Sergeant Kensington said.

"We did not get any images, right?"

"No, sir, we didn't. The image link must have been down, too."

"See if you can get General Naylor on here for me, will you, please?" McNab asked.

"McNab, sir. We had a little communications problem so I thought I had better check in with you, sir."

"Where are you, General?"

"We just came out of the Gulf into the Atlantic, sir. The pilot estimates we have about four hours to go. That would put us . . ."

"There's been a change of orders, General."

"Yes, sir?"

"The president directs that you divert to Costa Rica."

"Costa Rica?"

"Either to Tomas Guardia International, on the west coast, or Juan Santamaria, which serves San José—your choice—there to prepare to neutralize the airplane we're looking for."

"I thought it was in Suriname, sir."

"That was apparently faulty intel, General."

"Yes, sir."

"Do you see where this is going to pose any problems, General?"

"No, sir. I can probably be on the ground at either field in, say, a little over an hour."

"Let me know when you get close to the coast," Naylor ordered. "We're trying to get you permission to enter their airspace. If that doesn't come through, you'll have to practice some sort of deception."

"Yes, sir. I understand. I'll think of something."

"Your further orders, again from the president, General, are to neutralize this airplane as quietly as possible."

"Yes, sir, I understand. Neutralize as quietly as possible."

"We'll be in touch."

"Sir, are you in a position to tell me where the airplane we're looking for in Costa Rica is? Specifically, I mean?"

"Not at this time. When I have that information, you'll get it. The CIA is working on it and they are in the process of moving satellites."

"Yes, sir. Well, if the CIA's working on it, then we'll certainly know for sure where the airplane is, won't we, sir?"

"Naylor out."

[SEVEN]
Office of the Commanding General
United States Central Command
MacDill Air Force Base
Tampa, Florida
1215 10 June 2005

General Albert McFadden, USAF, walked without knocking into the office of General Allan Naylor, USA, and stood before his desk for twenty seconds before Naylor sensed—or chose to acknowledge—his presence.

" 'The best-laid plans of mice and men'—you ever hear that, Allan?" McFadden asked.

"What went wrong now?" Naylor asked.

"I was just talking with Larry Fremont," McFadden said. "He's been on the phone to the CIA guy in San José, Costa Rica . . ."

"And?"

"The CIA guy says the way the Costa Rican Foreign Ministry is going to handle our ambassador's request for permission to enter their airspace is to stall for at least a couple of days."

"We expected something like that," Naylor said. "So we land without, do what has to be done, and let the State Department pick up the pieces."

"So I would interpret that to mean you believe the CIA?"

"That's a loaded question, Al."

"You want to shoot crap, Allan? How about taking *another* chance on the CIA?"

"What are you talking about? You sound like you know something."

McFadden laid a small map on Naylor's desk.

"What am I looking at?"

"That's the Golfo de Nicoya."

"Okay. There's nothing on the map but dirt roads and water."

"Larry's guy says there is a sandy beach about forty miles from Tomas Guardia International, and maybe fifty from Juan Santamaria, that'll take the C-17, and there's nothing around it for miles except fishing villages."

"That's too good to be true," Naylor said. "How does Larry's guy know?"

"Larry's guy says he heard that they were moving drugs through the area, went there 'while sportfishing,' checked it out, measured it, did compression tests, found some aircraft tire tracks—he doesn't know what kind of aircraft but not large ones—and thinks it'll take a C-17, based on what he read in an Air Force Manual about C-17 tire loadings."

"How much credence does he place in his guy?"

"That's a little problem. This guy is like the one in Suriname."

"What does that mean?"

"Think of him as a second lieutenant with the varnish still on his gold bars. What the agency does with their graduates is send them someplace where nothing is happening, where they get to practice being a spy and working under diplomatic cover."

"Oh, Christ!"

"Larry said to tell you this guy sounds like an eager beaver."

"As in, 'There's nothing faster than a second lieutenant rushing to officer's call'?"

"I think Larry was being complimentary," McFadden said. "I think he liked what he heard on the phone."

"Where is Larry?"

"He's trying to see if Langley has anything on this beach. He said I should tell you I have everything he knows, and he thought his time would be better spent seeing what else he could come up with."

"The admiral called the DIA and they had nothing on suitable landing areas in Costa Rica," Naylor said.

"Do we tell McNab or not?"

Naylor put his hands together so quickly that there was a loud pop.

"General McNab is not at the moment one of my favorite people," Naylor said. "And when I say, 'Yeah, we have to tell him,' I have that in mind. The decision to use, or not use, this beach has to be his. If it won't take the C-17, there will be a lot of dead people, and the 727 doesn't get neutralized."

Naylor stood up and walked across his office toward the Phone Booth.

[EIGHT]
Tomas Guardia International Airport
Liberia, Costa Rica
1310 10 June 2005

"I'll be a sonofabitch, there it is!" Castillo said as the Learjet taxied down a taxiway at another small but grandly named airfield.

There was a Boeing 727 aircraft, connected to both a tug and a generator,

sitting on the tarmac in front of a concrete-block building with a sign on it reading, in Spanish: CENTRAL AMERICAN AERIAL FREIGHT FORWARDING.

There were red, white, and blue stripes on the vertical stabilizer and along
the fuselage that looked to be freshly painted.

"There is *a* 727 with the right paint scheme and registration numbers. We
won't know if it's ours until we have a look inside," Colonel Torine said.

"You're right," Castillo agreed. "But I think we should tell MacDill this
one's here."

"You're calling the shots," Colonel Torine said.

"Tell the tower you want to box the compass, Fernando," Castillo ordered.

"I'd rather stay."

"We've been all over that," Castillo said.

There had been no in-flight advisories on their way from Cozumel to Juan Santamaria International Airport in San José advising them where the 727 could
be found in Costa Rica, and when Castillo had called the two numbers Pevsner had given him both of the people answering said that he must have the
wrong number, they knew of no Karl Gossinger.

"What are you going to do, Charley?" Colonel Torine had asked.

"If it's not here, it has to be at the other airport, Tomas Guardia."

"Or it's not here at all. You're still betting on Pevsner? He obviously doesn't
know where it is or we'd have gotten the in-flight advisory or one of those
numbers you called would have paid off."

"Or something happened. Maybe his people here couldn't find it here and
he couldn't get anybody to the other airport to see if it was there. Or he did
and there's a communications problem. But he was pretty sure the 727 is in
Costa Rica and I think we have to go on that. And if it's not here, then it has
to be at Tomas Guardia."

"How are you going to handle it?" Colonel Torine asked.

"We go to Tomas Guardia. Fernando gets permission to box his compass,
we go to the threshold of a runway, and Sherman and I get out with the radio,
go hide in the grass, and hope nobody sees us. You take the Lear to the nearest
airport in Nicaragua, where you can call MacDill and tell them where we are
in case Sherman can't get the radio up. And then we see what happens. We may
get lucky—and, God knows, I'm not counting on that—and actually find the
sonofabitch. If it's there and it looks as if it's going to take off, Sherman and I
can probably disable it."

"Why don't we just park the Lear and all of us get out?" Fernando said. "That would give us four people on the ground."

"Because somehow we have to get word to MacDill, and the only way to do that—we can't count on Sherman's radio—is for you to go to Nicaragua."

"Now that they're this close, they probably have some pretty good perimeter defense around the airplane," Fernando argued. "And Special Forces hotshots or not, you and Sherman adds up to two people."

"What I think we should do is split the difference," Colonel Torine said. "I get out of the airplane with you." He looked at Fernando and smiled. "That would make it two Green Beanie hotshots and one Air Commando hotshot. The bad guys won't have a chance."

"I don't like this, Gringo."

"Colonel, Sergeant Sherman and I can handle this," Castillo said. "It doesn't take much skill to shoot holes in airplane tires, but I suspect it's really going to piss off the local authorities. Why don't you go with Fernando? You'll be better at getting through to MacDill than he will."

"I don't know about that," Torine replied. "For one thing, he speaks much better Spanish than I do; he's going to have a lot of talking to Nicaraguan authorities to do. And, for another, this is more fun than I've had in years. I've always wanted to shoot holes in an airplane tire."

Fernando looked between them, shrugged, and then spoke to his microphone.

"Tomas Guardia ground control. Lear Five-Oh-Seven-Five. I've got a compass I don't trust. Request permission to go to the threshold of two-eight and box my compass."

The problem was how to get from the Lear where it sat on the threshold of the runway to a point two hundred yards north of the threshold, where the built-up area leading to the threshold and the runway suddenly dropped off precipitously.

There was waist-high grass on either side of the threshold. The area leading up to the threshold was paved with macadam for about a hundred yards. It would be easier, and faster, to run down the macadam and enter the grass where it ended. On the other hand, they would almost certainly be seen if they ran down the macadam.

They would probably be seen if they ran through the grass—they couldn't run bent over far enough to get beneath the top of the grass—but if they crawled through it so they would be concealed by the grass, crawling through it would crush the grass, leaving a visible path. Running through the grass, if they were lucky, would push the grass aside only momentarily and it would spring back in place, leaving little evidence that someone or something had passed through it.

"I think we better go through the grass," Castillo said. Colonel Torine nodded. Sergeant Sherman gave Castillo a thumbs-up.

"Fernando, turn it so the door is away from the tower," Castillo ordered. "As soon as you stop, we'll open the door and go. You'll have to come back here and close it."

"Now?" Fernando asked.

"Now, please."

"God be with all of you," Fernando announced as the Lear started to turn.

The grass was thicker than it looked and harder to push aside. The ground was very damp, not quite mud but slippery.

There was a handle on the bottom of Sergeant Sherman's hard-sided suitcase—Castillo idly wondered whether it had come that way or if the bottom handle was a Gray Fox modification—which permitted Sherman and Castillo to carry it between them.

But it was a heavy sonofabitch even without the weight of the two CAR-4 rifles and the bandolier of magazines Sherman had taken out of it and hung around Colonel Torine's shoulders.

The midday tropical heat did not help. Charley felt sweat break out before he was ten yards into the grass and he and Sherman were soon breathing very heavily. They had to stop four times and quickly swap sides as the strength of their hands on the handles gave out. The last time, when Charley scurried to get to the other side of the suitcase, his foot slipped, he fell flat onto his face through the grass onto the ground, where his knee encountered what was probably the only rock within five hundred yards.

Castillo was beginning to plan for what to do when, inevitably, the knee and/or his breath gave out and he would not be able to hold up his end of the suitcase anymore when the ground beneath his feet suddenly disappeared, he lost his footing, and started to slide downward.

There was about a fifty-foot difference between the ground—the original terrain—and the airport buildup. Castillo, Sherman and the hard-sided suitcase were about halfway down it before they could stop their slide. They had just done so, and exchanged glances, when Colonel Torine burst through the thick grass on his way down the steep incline. He was moving headfirst on his stomach, wildly flailing his arms in an attempt to stop himself.

Sherman started to giggle, and then both he and Castillo were laughing, although, as out of breath as they were, the laughing was quite painful.

Still smiling and chuckling, they pushed the hard-sided suitcase the rest of the way down the steep incline until they reached level ground.

"Fuck it, far enough," Castillo said, stopped pushing, rolled onto his back, and put his arm over his eyes against the bright sunlight.

A moment later, as he was still taking breaths in deep heaves, he felt a nudge against his side. From under his arm, without moving, he saw an old, battered military-looking boot.

Oh, shit! If Torine or Sherman wanted my attention, they wouldn't nudge me with a boot. They aren't even wearing boots.

He took his arm off his eyes.

There was a man standing over him, his face covered with green, brown, and black grease stripes.

"I understand that old Air Force fart wheezing like a rode-hard racehorse," Lieutenant General Bruce J. McNab said, "but you and Sherman? By God, what are people going to think?"

Castillo didn't reply. He forced himself into a sitting position. His arm was nudged, and, when he looked, McNab was holding out a plastic quart bottle of 7UP to him.

Castillo took it wordlessly, opened it, and drank from it.

"For your general information, the Air Force survived his crash landing," McNab said. "His dignity, unfortunately, took a beating."

"How long have you been here?" Castillo asked, finally getting his breath.

"Long enough, were I a wagering man, to lay heavy odds the 727 is here. I got a guy out there now taking a real close look."

"I'm pretty sure it's the one we're looking for," Charley said. "We taxied past it. It's got freshly painted registration numbers, and the red, white, and blue stripes on the vertical stabilizer Pevsner's guy saw on it in Venezuela."

Colonel Torine and Sergeant Sherman walked up.

"You all right, Jake? Nothing broken?"

"I'm fine."

"You okay, Charley?" Torine asked.

Castillo nodded.

"How is it that you're here, sir?" Torine asked McNab.

"McFadden and Naylor got me on the radio and said they'd found a sandy beach not far from here. Some CIA guy had done compression tests and, theoretically, it would take a C-17. With the fingers of both hands crossed, I decided to give it a shot."

"Obviously, it took the 17."

"More or less. We got down all right. But stopped for more than a couple of minutes, the Globemaster starts to sink in the sand. It was a hell of a job getting the Little Birds off; we had to keep the airplane moving all the time we were unloading. It looked like a Chinese fire drill."

"But you're unloaded."

"There's two gunships and four troop carriers about five miles away. Did I mention that the C-17 is taxiing up and down the beach, back and forth, back and forth? I don't know how long that's going to work. Nor do I know whether or not we can get it back in the air."

"Empty, you probably can," Torine said. "There's an awesome amount of thrust on a 17."

"Empty? What am I supposed to do with the Little Birds? Torch them?"

A tall, blond sergeant first class, dressed as was General McNab in a jungle camouflage uniform, came up. He had a CAR-4 hanging from his shoulder and was carrying what looked like a laptop computer in his hands like a tray. It was open.

"Stedder's in place, General," he said and started to hand the laptop to McNab.

"Will you hold it, please, Sergeant Orson?" McNab said.

Castillo got quickly up.

"Careful with that 7UP, Charley," McNab said. "This is the only one of these we have."

"Stedder reports the Lear has taken off, sir," Sergeant Orson said.

"Where's he going, Charley?" McNab asked.

"Nicaragua, to report where we are and that we think we've found the 727."

McNab grunted and looked at the laptop computer. It displayed an image of the 727 from the side.

Whoever's taking these must be on the roof of that building, CENTRAL AMERI-CAN FREIGHT FORWARDING, *whatever.*

The image also showed some movement. There were a half-dozen security guards in military-looking uniforms on the tarmac. When they moved, it was as if they did so in slow motion.

"Can he give us a close-up of the front door?" Castillo asked.

McNab typed rapidly on the laptop's keyboard.

The screen went dark, then lit up with an out-of-focus view of the forward part of the aircraft, which then came into focus.

All that could be seen was the top of the movable stairway. The open door was clearly visible but nothing was visible inside the aircraft.

"I don't suppose we'd see a hell of a lot more up the rear stairway," Castillo said.

"Probably less, Major," Sergeant Orson said. "The angles there are a bear."

"Don't call him 'Major,' Orson," McNab said. "We don't want anybody to know that he's one of us. Didn't you did see him skiing down the hill?"

Orson chuckled.

"Let's have another look at the whole airplane," Torine said.

McNab typed on the keyboard again and a few moments later an image of the 727 from the side appeared. And this shot showed other movement. An open-bodied Ford ton-and-a-half truck, loaded high with thin cardboard boxes, moved in jerking movements toward the airplane and two men moved jerkily toward the 727, obviously intending to open the cargo doors.

"Well, there's your flowers, Charley," McNab said.

"Which means they're getting ready to go," Castillo said.

"And what would you suggest we do about that?" McNab asked. "Keeping in mind the president wants this done quietly, which would seem to rule out telling one of the gunships to put a couple of rockets in it."

"Why don't we steal it back?" Colonel Torine asked.

"How would you propose that we do that?" McNab asked. "Can you fly that thing by yourself, Jake?"

"With Charley in the right seat, I can," Torine said and looked at Castillo.

"How can we do that quietly?" Castillo asked.

"Quietly is a relative term," McNab said. "Not very quietly would be to put a couple of rockets in it, which would leave a burned-out airplane for the television cameras of the world to see proof of our arrogant invasion of friendly Costa Rica. A little less quietly would be having the Air Force take it out after it gets in the air. A lot of airplanes—and who knows who else—are going to hear our pilot order the airplane to return here or get shot down. How the hell are we going to be able to deny that if he has to shoot it down?"

Torine grunted.

McNab added, "There's a flight of F-15s on their way from Eglin, by the way. Hell, they may even be here, out over the Pacific."

"They've probably built some sort of framework over the fuel bladders," Castillo said.

"What?" McNab asked.

"There's thirteen fuel bladders in the passenger compartment," Castillo said. "They'll have to be hidden from the customs guys at Tampa. So they will cover them with flowers. Hence, a framework."

"Okay, so?" McNab said.

"Which means they will have to be placed on that framework by the guys who stole the airplane, not by ground handlers, who would want to know what's up with the fuel bladders."

"Major," Sergeant Orson said, "when Sergeant Stedder was getting into position he said it looked to him as if there was a crew of four."

"They must have brought two guys to help carry the flowers up the back stairs," Torine said. "And protect the airplane."

"Making a total of four we have to take out if we're going to take over the airplane. Figure it's going to take them forty minutes to load all those flowers, six boxes at a time, up the front and back stairways."

"So that's how much time we have," McNab agreed.

"We don't know all they have is two more guys," Castillo said. "The sergeant said he saw four. There could be more."

"And they all have to be taken out, right?" Torine asked.

McNab grunted. "Odds are, we can't have a little chat with them and explain the futility of their position. We have to take them out quickly and then get that airplane off the ground quickly."

"How is Gray Fox equipped for snipers, sir?" Castillo asked.

"Well, there's one really good one, Major Castillo," Sergeant Orson said. "If I do have to say so myself. And Sergeant Stedder thought it would be a good idea if he took his rifle along when he went out to climb on the roof. How many do you think you're going to need?"

"What I'm thinking . . ." Castillo said and stopped when he saw the look on McNab's face.

"Go on, Charley," McNab said. "Let's see how much you remember of all that you learned with me as your all-wise mentor."

"What I was thinking, sir, is that I don't think the other two are pilots. Which means if we can take out the two pilots, the airplane couldn't be flown."

"And how do we get the pilots—or any of these people—to obligingly line themselves up for the attention of Sergeants Orson and Stedder?"

"A diversion," Castillo began, thoughtfully.

Tomas Guardia International Airport
Liberia, Costa Rica
1415 10 June 2005

Major C. G. Castillo, now wearing a black flight suit with subdued insignia that included the wings of a master Army aviator and identified him as CWO-5 B.D. SHINE, lay beside a small concrete-block building hoping he was further concealed by a fifty-five-gallon drum full of aromatic waste. His face was streaked with brown, black, and green grease. He had binoculars to his eyes and wore a headset, putting a small receiver in his right ear and a microphone at his lips. A CAR-4 lay on the ground beside him.

Immediately to his left, the other side of the reeking garbage drum, was Sergeant First Class Paul T. Orson, who was armed with a dull black bolt-action rifle based on the Remington Model 700 .308 Winchester caliber hunting rifle. About the only things that hadn't been changed were the caliber—known in the Army as "7.62×55mm NATO"—and the action. It now had a carefully chosen and tested barrel and, in place of glossy walnut, a matt black stock made up of fiberglass, Kevlar, and graphite. A dull black 10×42 Leupold Ultra optical sight was mounted on top.

Immediately behind them—literally, behind the garbage drum—and also armed with a CAR-4, was Colonel Jake Torine, USAF, now wearing a black flight suit whose subdued insignia identified him as CWO-3 P.J. LEFKOWITZ, a senior Army aviator.

A good deal was about to happen—Sergeant Orson thought of this as *all hell was about to break loose*—but there was no indication of this on the tarmac in front of them.

Another open-bodied Ford one-and-a-half-ton truck was pulled up close to the 727. A man on the truck handed down, four at a time, long, thin cardboard boxes to two men on the ground. They carried the boxes to the movable stairs rolled up to the front door and to the lowered rear stairway of the airplane. There they were passed to men wearing short-sleeved white shirts with captain's and first officer's shoulder boards and quickly carried up the stairs into the airplane.

Castillo had recognized the face of one of the aircrew as the guy had run up and down the stairs. He had seen his photographs in Philadelphia. He had not seen the second Philadelphia mullah nor had he recognized the two men who had also carried flowers into the aircraft up the rear stairs. But they had intelligent faces and he wondered if he had been wrong, that everybody was a pilot.

How the hell can you calmly load an airplane—with flowers, for Christ's sake—knowing you're going to die in it?

"Five . . . four . . . three . . . two . . . one," General McNab's voice said in Castillo's earpiece. "Showtime!"

"Heads up," Castillo said softly and, a moment later, realized it was entirely unnecessary. Sergeant Orson had his eye to the Leupold scope and the rifle was trained on the rear stairs of the 727.

The first thing to disturb the peace and tranquillity of Tomas Guardia International Airport was that of artillery simulators detonated near a small concrete-block building, painted in a red-and-white-checkerboard pattern, to one side of the runway. The simulators were intended to sound exactly like that of a 105mm howitzer shell coming through the air and detonating on contact. And they did.

At precisely that moment, two Little Birds popped up past the end of the runway where Castillo, Sherman, and Torine had fallen down the hill. Rocket fire exploded from the left Little Bird and a stream of 40mm grenades from the other. The rockets struck a fuel truck parked out of line of sight of the 727, causing an immediate explosion, and the grenades exploded in a line parallel to, and a few feet the other side of, the runway.

The face of the man near the bottom of the rear stairway was familiar to Castillo through his binoculars.

"Take him," he ordered.

There was an immediate crack as the sniper rifle fired.

There was no question in Castillo's mind that Orson would hit his target.

I have just killed that guy as surely as if I had pulled the trigger myself.

This philosophical observation was immediately challenged when the man in his binocular view, though obviously disturbed and surprised by what was happening—he was now looking up the stairs—was obviously still very much alive.

I'll be a sonofabitch, he missed!

Castillo looked over at Sergeant Orson just as the rifle fired again.

Castillo hastily put the binoculars to his eyes again.

The man on the rear stairway was now sliding, facedown, down the stairs.

"There was another one, farther up on the stairs," Sergeant Orson said. "I figured I'd take him first."

Four unarmed Little Birds now suddenly appeared, from four different directions, and rapidly approached the 727. There were six Gray Fox soldiers on the outside platforms of each, all dressed in black outfits topped with black balaclavas.

The Little Birds had made a "fly the needles" approach to the 727. Their onboard computer directed navigation systems, knowing within six feet both their position and that of the 727, had provided the pilots with indicators—"the needles"—on the control panel. So long as the pilots kept the needles where they were supposed be—increasing or decreasing airspeed, changing direction or altitude caused the needles to move—all four of the Little Birds were able to arrive, from four different directions, at a little better than seventy-five miles per hour, within seconds of one another.

The Gray Fox soldiers dropped nimbly from the benches before the skids of the Little Birds actually touched down. Some of them fired close to—not at—the security personnel, which caused the defending force to immediately raise their hands, fall to their knees, or both.

One special operator dashed to the flower truck, somewhat rudely removed the driver from behind the wheel, got behind the wheel, started the truck, drove toward the Central American Aerial Freight Forwarding building, and then jumped out, leaving the truck on a collision course with a Peugeot sedan parked in front of the building, which, in fact, occurred some thirty seconds later.

During those thirty seconds:

Two four-man teams of Gray Fox men rushed to the forward stairs. One man ran halfway up the stairs, from where he threw a Whiz Bang grenade through the open door. A Whiz Bang goes off with a great deal of noise and a blinding flash but does not produce shrapnel. Those in close proximity to a detonated Whiz Bang, however, usually have trouble hearing and seeing and generally appear confused.

As soon as the Whiz Bang went off, the man who had thrown it rushed the rest of the way up the stairs, closely followed by the three other members of what General McNab had dubbed the "Front Door Team." To get into the aircraft, it was necessary for the Front Door Team to step over the bodies of two men on the stairs.

Fifteen seconds after they entered the fuselage, two of the Gray Fox men came back out the door, went to the fallen men, and unceremoniously dragged them into the airplane.

As soon as they had cleared the door, the "Moving Stairs Team" of four Gray Fox soldiers started to push the stairs away from the aircraft.

Meanwhile, four Gray Fox soldiers—the "Tug and Chocks Team"—had approached the tug. One of them climbed aboard while the other three detached the tug's link to the front wheel of the aircraft and removed the wooden blocks from the aircraft's wheels. As soon as that was done, the tug started to move off. The Gray Fox driver set it on a collision course with the Peugeot and jumped off.

At the same time, the "Ground Auxiliary Power Team" went to that generator. One of them fired it up while a second made sure the cord was properly plugged into the aircraft. The other two made a hasty examination of the aircraft to make sure it was not connected in any unexpected other way with the ground. It was not.

And, simultaneously, the "Rear Stair Door Team" rushed to the rear stair doors. One of them, stepping over one body, climbed as far as he could—he encountered another body—and threw a Whiz Bang into the passenger compartment. It went off within two seconds of the one thrown through the front door.

The grenadier, closely followed by his team members, then went into the aircraft and twenty seconds later came out again.

He spoke to his microphone.

"Clear. No apparent damage. This fucking thing is full of flowers. What the hell is that all about?"

The team who had entered the aircraft through the front door began to descend the rear stairs. Master Sergeant Charles Stevens, who was in overall charge of both the Front Door and Rear Stair Door teams and had accompanied the latter, suggested to them that assisting in taking the bodies on the stairs aboard would be a nice thing for them to do.

He didn't use those words but they took his point.

As Castillo and Torine ran toward the aircraft, they saw a half-dozen brilliant yellow vehicles of the Tomas Guardia International Airport fire department racing across the field toward the blazing fuel truck.

So far, no one seemed to be paying much attention to what was happening near the 727, not even to the four Little Birds sitting there with their rotors slowly turning.

"APU's up and running, sir," Master Sergeant Stevens said to Colonel Torine. "We'll stick around until you get it moving."

"You stick around until I get one engine running," Colonel Torine said. "Then disconnect the APU and get out of here. There's nothing more that you can do."

"Yes, sir. Good luck, Colonel. You, too, Major."

He saluted as Castillo and Torine went up the stairs, which were slick with blood.

Colonel Torine got in the pilot's seat, adjusted it to accommodate his long legs, strapped himself in, and then looked around for something he finally found on the shelf over the instrument panel. He handed it to Castillo.

"Checklist, Charley," he said as he reached for the master buss switch.

"One, gear lever and lights," Castillo read.

"Down and check," Torine responded.

"Two, brakes," Castillo read.

"Parked."

"Three, battery."

"On."

"Starting number two," Torine said, which was not the next step on the checklist. Castillo looked over at Torine.

There was a whining sound as the Pratt & Whitney JT8D-9 turbofan in the vertical stabilizer came to life.

"You're going to have to go back and close the stair door, Charley," Torine said. "That's supposed to be done before you start the checklist."

"Yes, sir."

"The control's on the left bulkhead."

"Yes, sir," Castillo said and hurriedly got out of his harness and went through the cabin. He had to step over all four bodies again to reach the stair door control panel; his foot slipped in a pool of blood. When he looked down—he had not intended to—the sightless eyes of the man whose death he had ordered looked back at him.

He opened the control panel door, found the RAISE STAIR switch, threw it, and waited until a green light came on. He felt the vibration as Torine started the other two engines.

He started back to the cockpit and found himself looking again at the sightless eyes.

He took another step forward, then stopped. The Whiz Bangs had displaced four or five flower boxes; one of them was ripped open. Castillo scooped out its contents, turned, and laid them, not very gently, on the dead man's face. Then he went as quickly as he could back to the flight deck.

"Pick the checklist up at 'taxi,' Charley," Torine ordered.

"Yes, sir."

The 727 was moving. Charley wondered if you were supposed to move before you started the taxi portion of the checklist.

"One, flaps and runway," he read.

"Flaps, check," Colonel Torine responded. "Runway? That one." He pointed out the window.

Castillo saw a wind cone indicating that Torine was headed in the right direction to make a right turn onto the runway into the prevailing wind.

He also saw the Tomas Guardia International Airport fire department fighting, without any apparent success, the fire on the blazing fuel truck.

And he saw a Little Bird, six Gray Fox operators hanging on to it, fly right on the deck over the runway threshold and then drop out of sight. He looked around and saw no others.

"Two," he read from the checklist, "Takeoff data."

"In a manner of speaking," Torine said, "I already did the max takeoff gross weight figuring on this"—he motioned to his pocket computer and Charley remembered him furiously tapping its keys with his stylus in the hangar at Pope Air Force Base, figuring how far the stolen aircraft could fly—"so all we have to do is line it up with the runway and go."

"Yes, sir."

The 727 reached the threshold. His hand on the throttles and his feet never touching the brakes, Torine lined the 727 up with the centerline of the runway with a steady roll.

"Call out our airspeed, please," Torine said as he moved the throttles forward.

"Seventy," Castillo called when the airspeed indicator came to life.

"Eighty, ninety, one hundred, one twenty, one thir . . ."

"Rotating," Torine said.

The 727 put its nose into the air. A moment later, the rumbling of the landing gear on the runway died.

"Gear up," Torine ordered.

Charley found the switch and worked it.

"Gear up and locked," he reported.

"Okay," Torine said. "While I try to recall what all these switches and other stuff are for, why don't you see if you can turn on the Radio Direction Finder and whatever other navigation equipment you find? I'm going to head for the Atlantic."

[TWO]
Aboard Costa Rican Air Transport 407
11.374 degrees North Latitude
81.699 degrees West Longitude
Above the Atlantic Ocean
1505 10 June 2005

"Ah," Torine said. "I wondered how long that would take."

He pointed out his side window.

A USAF F-15 was on their wingtip. A moment later, a second appeared directly ahead and two hundred feet over them. And then a third F-15 appeared on their right wingtip.

"What do you want to bet there's one on our tail, too?" Torine asked.

The pilot of the F-15 on their left held up a hand-lettered sign. It read: "119.9."

"Tune the radio, please," Torine said.

Charley tuned one radio transceiver to 119.9 megahertz.

The voice of the fighter pilot came immediately into their headsets: "Costa Rican Air Transport Four-Oh-Seven, this is United States Air Force Six-Two-Two. Do you speak English?"

"Reasonably well," Torine replied after switching to TRANSMIT.

"You are directed to immediately commence a 180-degree two-minute turn and begin a descent to flight level ten. Do you understand?"

"Before I do that, son," Colonel Torine said, "what I want you to do is get on your Abort Mission frequency and relay the following to Central Command: 'Attention, General McFadden. I am in command of Costa Rican Air Transport Four-Oh-Seven. Regards. Jake.' "

"I repeat," the F-15 pilot said, "you are directed to immediately comm—"

"I'm not going to tell you again, son," Torine interrupted. "Get on the horn to CentCom now. Change the signature block to: 'Jake Torine, Colonel, USAF.' You read me?"

The F-15 pilot didn't respond for nearly two minutes. Then he said: "Sir, what is your wife's maiden name?"

"McNulty," Torine said. "Mary Margaret McNulty."

"Hold one, sir—

"Sir, CentCom directs that I accompany you to your destination. What is that, sir?"

Switching to INTERCOM, Torine looked at Castillo. "We never thought that far, did we, Charley? Where do you think we should go?"

"MacDill," Castillo said.

"You're anxious to face the wrath of General Naylor? I was going to suggest we go to Gitmo and give McNab and McFadden a chance to tell Naylor what heroes we are before we go home."

"What would we do with four bodies at Gitmo?" Castillo replied. "I'm open to any suggestion, but it looks like MacDill is the answer."

"What are you going to do with the bodies at MacDill?"

"You don't want to know, Colonel. What I would like is a 160th Black Hawk, with two muscular crew chiefs, to meet us there with a couple of stretchers."

"Air Force Six-Two-Two," Torine said after switching back to TRANSMIT. "Our destination is MacDill, repeat, MacDill. Advise MacDill that we will require a Special Forces Black Hawk and a stretcher-bearing team immediately on arrival. Acknowledge, please."

[THREE]
The Oval Office
The White House
1600 Pennsylvania Avenue NW
Washington, D.C.
1520 10 June 2005

"Mr. President," Secretary of Defense Frederick K. Beiderman said, "there's some good news from General McFadden at CentCom."

"That's good, for a change."

"It's fragmentary, sir, but . . ."

" 'Fragmentary' means you have only a part of it, right? Why does that worry me, Fred?"

"Sir, F-15s intercepted the missing 727 over the Atlantic . . ."

"Oh, shit, McNab couldn't neutralize it? That's . . ."

"Sir, Colonel Torine, who went to Mexico with Castillo?"

The president nodded.

"Sir, he's flying it. That's confirmed. The F-15s are escorting it to MacDill, in Tampa."

"I know where MacDill is," the president said. "Do we know—really know—that Colonel Whatsisname is flying it?"

"Yes, sir. That's been confirmed. They should be in MacDill in about two hours."

"Keep me posted," the president said and then changed his mind and picked up a telephone.

"In exactly fifteen minutes, get me General Naylor at CentCom," he ordered, hung up, and turned to Beiderman. "Maybe in fifteen minutes there will be more than fragmentary information. Have you told Natalie or Matt?"

"That's next, sir. Them and the DCI."

"Why don't we let Matt Hall tell the DCI?" the president said. "Tell Matt to tell him after I hear from Naylor."

"Yes, sir."

"Christ, I wonder how much of Costa Rica is left after McNab pulled this off? That's probably why we only have 'fragmentary' information."

"I asked General McFadden about that, sir. He doesn't know about collateral damage. He's not in contact with Colonel Torine or General McNab. General McNab's having communication problems again."

"I almost wish you'd have waited until you knew more," the president said. "But, of course, if you had, I would be all over you for not telling me earlier. Thanks, Fred."

"Sir, if we have the airplane, it's not going to crash into the Liberty Bell."

"I was just thinking the same thing. What about Major Castillo?"

"Nothing on him yet, sir."

"Yeah, I know. Our information is fragmentary. Tell Matt and Natalie, please, Fred, and then stay available."

"Yes, Mr. President."

[FOUR]
MacDill Air Force Base
Tampa, Florida
1710 10 June 2005

"Costa Rican Four-Oh-Seven, you are cleared for a straight-in approach to runway two-seven. The altimeter is two-nine-niner, the winds are negligible. Be advised there are a number of ground vehicles on either side of the runway. You are directed to stop on the runway at the end of your landing roll and to shut down your engines at that time. You will receive additional instructions at that time. Acknowledge."

"Fuck you," Colonel Torine said to a dead microphone and then pushed the TRANSMIT switch. "Oh-seven, I have the runway in sight."

He pushed the INTERCOM switch.

"I did remember, didn't I, Mr. Copilot, to put the wheels down?"

"Gear is down and locked, sir," Castillo reported.

"Well, then, let's see if we can't get this tired old bird on the ground without too many pieces falling off."

Ninety seconds later, Colonel Torine said, "Well, the thrust reversers seem to work. Now, let's see if the brakes do."

The second half of the runway was lined with vehicles, bright yellow fire-fighting vehicles, ambulances, wreckers, bulldozers, and Humvees—a large number of Humvees—all equipped with .50 caliber machine guns, all of which were trained on Costa Rican 407.

"I expect this is the modern version of the tumultuous welcome Roman legionnaires got when they returned to Rome after having vanquished the savages in far-off places," Torine said as the 727 began to slow very suddenly.

Torine threw the master buss switch.

"I wonder if it will ever fly again?" he asked. "The last flight of an airplane is always a little sad."

"Why won't it fly again?" Castillo asked, then, "Do you think we should try to get this crap off our face before we go out there and wave to the fans?"

"Jesus, I forgot all about it. Hell no, leave it on. It'll give them something to talk about."

He unstrapped himself and stood up and then gestured to Castillo to precede him from the cockpit.

When Castillo opened the door, now waving Torine ahead of him, movable stairs had been rolled up to the front door. When he stepped onto the platform at the top, he saw that their reception committee consisted of three high-ranking dignitaries: the secretary of homeland security, the Honorable Matthew

Hall; General Allan Naylor, USA, the commanding general of Central Command; and his deputy commander, General Albert McFadden, USAF.

Behind them was about a platoon of Air Police, half of them mounted in Humvees.

Colonel Torine saluted as he went down the stairs. Naylor and McFadden returned it.

"Jake, is that thing liable to blow up anytime soon?" General McFadden called.

"It may collapse of old age, sir," Torine replied, "but blow up? No, sir, I don't think so."

Castillo followed him down the stairs. As soon as his feet touched the runway, one of the Air Police, a major, headed for the stairs.

"I don't think you want to go in the airplane just yet, Major," Castillo said and stepped into his path.

The Air Police major gave him a withering look, examined Castillo's flight suit, and snapped, "Please step to one side, Mr. Shine."

Charley remembered that in addition to the grease on his face, he was wearing Shine's flight suit.

Since I was, before this happened, a major (promotable), I probably outrank you, you pompous shit. But fuck it.

He made an *After you, Gaston* bow to the major and stepped out of his way. The Air Police major ran up the stairs.

Castillo saluted Generals Naylor and McFadden. They returned it.

"I can't tell you how delighted I am that you pulled this off," Matt Hall said. "Welcome home, Charley. Colonel Torine."

"The president has asked me to convey his congratulations to you both," General Naylor said. "He is also concerned with collateral damage to the airport. I therefore think we should go somewhere where you can make a preliminary after-action report and then see about getting you cleaned up."

"A fuel truck, sir, burned at the airport," Colonel Torine said. "That's about the sum of it."

"There were no casualties?" Naylor asked, surprised.

"None on our side, sir," Castillo said. "And none on the bad guys' that we left at the airport."

"I don't understand," Naylor said.

The Air Force major came down the stairs, looking a little pale. He walked quickly to Generals Naylor and McFadden and softly told them, "There are four bodies on the airplane!"

"Sir," Castillo said, "may I respectfully suggest that you get Colonel Torine's after-action report first? I don't believe I will have anything to add to that, sir, and I really need thirty or forty minutes in the Black Hawk right now."

"What for, Charley?" Matt Hall asked.

"I don't think you want to know, sir," Castillo said.

"Yes, I do," Hall said.

"There's a few details I have to clean up, sir . . ."

"Those bodies?" Hall asked.

"Matt, I don't think you want that question answered," General Naylor said. "Colonel Torine, if you'll come with us, Major Castillo will join us just as soon as he can."

He gestured toward an Air Force Dodge Caravan.

"Major," General McFadden said to the Air Police officer, "I'm sure you were mistaken when you thought you saw bodies on the aircraft."

"Hey, Charley," the pilot of the 160th Special Operations Aviation Regiment Black Hawk said after the helo was loaded and its wheels left the ground, "where we going?"

"Sightseeing, Tom," Castillo said. "How about someplace along Alligator Alley where I could see some really hungry gators? The more, the better."

"I know just the place," the pilot said and banked the bird southeast toward the Everglades.

[FIVE]
Room 14B
Transient Field Grade Officers' Quarters
MacDill Air Force Base
Tampa, Florida
2005 10 June 2005

"Hello," Fernando Lopez said when he picked up the telephone.

"Major Carlos Castillo, please, the president is calling."

"He's in the shower."

"Did you understand what I said before? The president is calling."

"That won't get him out of the shower anytime soon."

"I will call again in five minutes. Please have Major Castillo prepared to speak to the president."

"I'll see what I can do."

"Thank you very much."

Charley came out of the bathroom two minutes later with a towel wrapped around his waist.

"Anything happen? What was on the phone?"

"The first was Elaine Naylor. We were expected for dinner five minutes ago. All is apparently forgiven by Uncle Allan. So get dressed."

"And the second?"

"That was Isaacson, to tell us he's on his way here to pick us up."

"That's all?"

"There was one more," Fernando said. "Let me think. Oh yeah. It was the president. I said you were in the shower."

"Oh, fuck you. I say that with all possible respect and affection."

"You mean you don't believe me?" Fernando asked, innocently.

Charley gave him the finger and started to get dressed.

The telephone rang again.

"Major Castillo," Charley said somewhat abruptly.

The startled voice at the other end replied, "One moment, please, Major."

"Charley? I understand you were in the shower," the president of the United States said a moment later.

"Yes, sir, Mr. President, I was."

"You'll have to wait until he gets off the phone," Fernando said five minutes later to Supervisory Special Agent Joel Isaacson. "He's talking to the president."

"Okay," Isaacson said. He seemed neither surprised nor impressed, but when Charley came out of the bedroom two minutes later he immediately asked, "So what did the president have to say?"

"None of your fucking business, Joel."

"Okay. If you're going to be a hard-ass, I won't tell you what I know."

"That the world isn't really flat?"

"A new addition to the Secret Service."

"Who?"

"While you two were flitting around the Caribbean, soaking up the sun, the boss sent me to Philadelphia. He was concerned that Betty 'Nice Boobs' Schneider was really going to have her ass in a crack for coming to Washington with us and wanted me to see what I could do."

"Which was?"

"I went to Chief Inspector Kramer—one cop to another—and asked him.

He said he didn't think she would have any problems, the mayor was never going to find that out, but he was worried about Ali Abd Ar-Raziq, aka Detective Jack Britton."

"Oh, yeah," Charley said.

"He said there was a very good chance the AALs would try to whack him—and that was before you stole the airplane back, which is really going to piss those people off. Whack him or his family. And could I offer him a job somewhere—anywhere—out of Philadelphia?"

"And you did?"

"I actually had to sell him on the Secret Service, but yeah. And I put a couple of guys in the Philadelphia office on the AALs until we get him and his family out of town. I wonder if he'll spot them?"

"Probably. That guy is one hell of a cop. I'm really glad to hear that, Joel. Thank you."

"He'll earn his keep," Isaacson said.

"I'm sure he will."

"And I figured what the hell, since I was already there, and I know the boss was really impressed with her, I asked Sergeant Schneider if she was interested in moving up in the world of law enforcement."

"And was she?" Charley asked.

His heart jumped.

"Yeah, sure. Once I told her how much a special agent makes. You know how little the cops get paid?"

"That's very interesting," Charley said. "I'm sure she'll be an asset."

"Who the hell do you think you're kidding, Gringo?" Fernando Lopez asked, laughing. "Your nostrils are flaring."

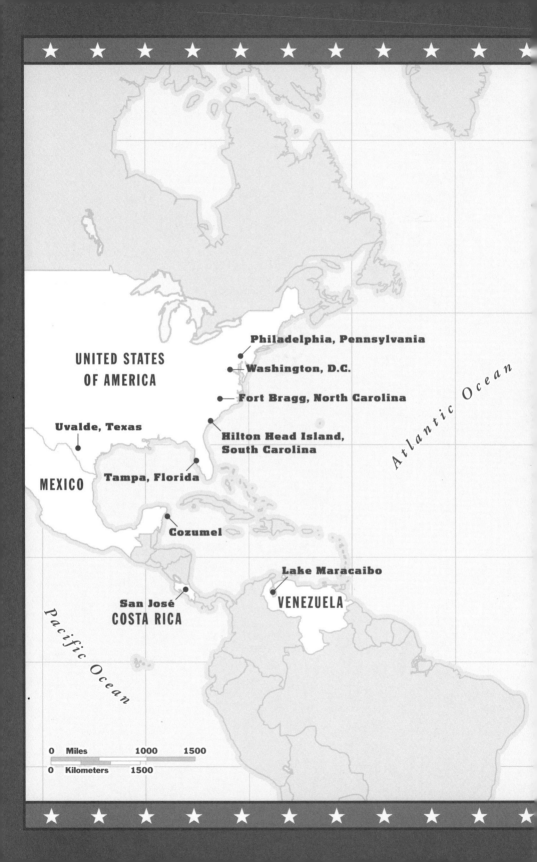

UNITED STATES
OF AMERICA

Philadelphia, Pennsylvania

Washington, D.C.

Fort Bragg, North Carolina

Hilton Head Island,
South Carolina

Uvalde, Texas

Tampa, Florida

MEXICO

Cozumel

Atlantic Ocean

Lake Maracaibo

San José
COSTA RICA

VENEZUELA

Pacific Ocean

| 0 | Miles | 1000 | 1500 |
| 0 | Kilometers | 1500 | |